THE TRAITOR

Book Three of
The Covenant of Steel

ANTHONY RYAN

orbitbooks.net

Cover design by Lauren Panepinto
Cover illustration by Jaime Jones

Maps by Anthony Ryan
Author photograph by Ellie Grace Photography

Orbit
Hachette Book Group
1290 Avenue of the Americas
New York, NY 10104
orbitbooks.net

First Edition: July 2023
Simultaneously published in Great Britain by Orbit

Orbit is an imprint of Hachette Book Group.
The Orbit name and logo are trademarks of Little, Brown Book Group Limited.

Library of Congress Control Number: 2023934089

ISBNs: 9780316430838 (trade paperback), 9780316430821 (ebook)

Printed in the United States of America

LSC-C

Printing 1, 2023

Dedicated to the memory of the late David Gemmell from whom I learned the lesson that the hero's journey is always more tragedy than triumph.

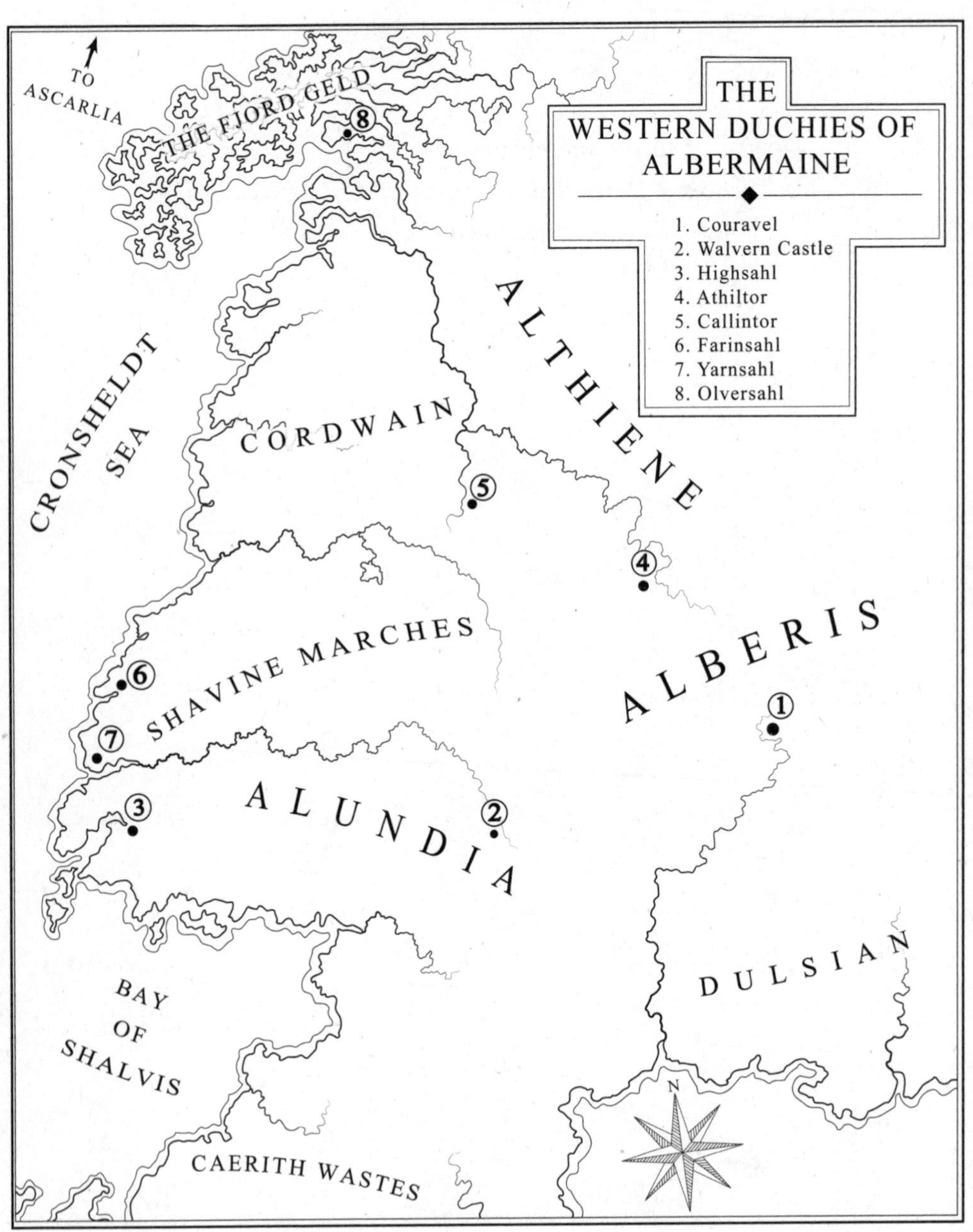
THE WESTERN DUCHIES OF ALBERMAINE
1. Couravel
2. Walvern Castle
3. Highsahl
4. Athiltor
5. Callintor
6. Farinsahl
7. Yarnsahl
8. Olversahl
TO ASCARLIA
THE FJORD GELD
CRONSHELDT SEA
CORDWAIN
ALTHIENE
SHAVINE MARCHES
ALBERIS
ALUNDIA
DULSIAN
BAY OF SHALVIS
CAERITH WASTES
N

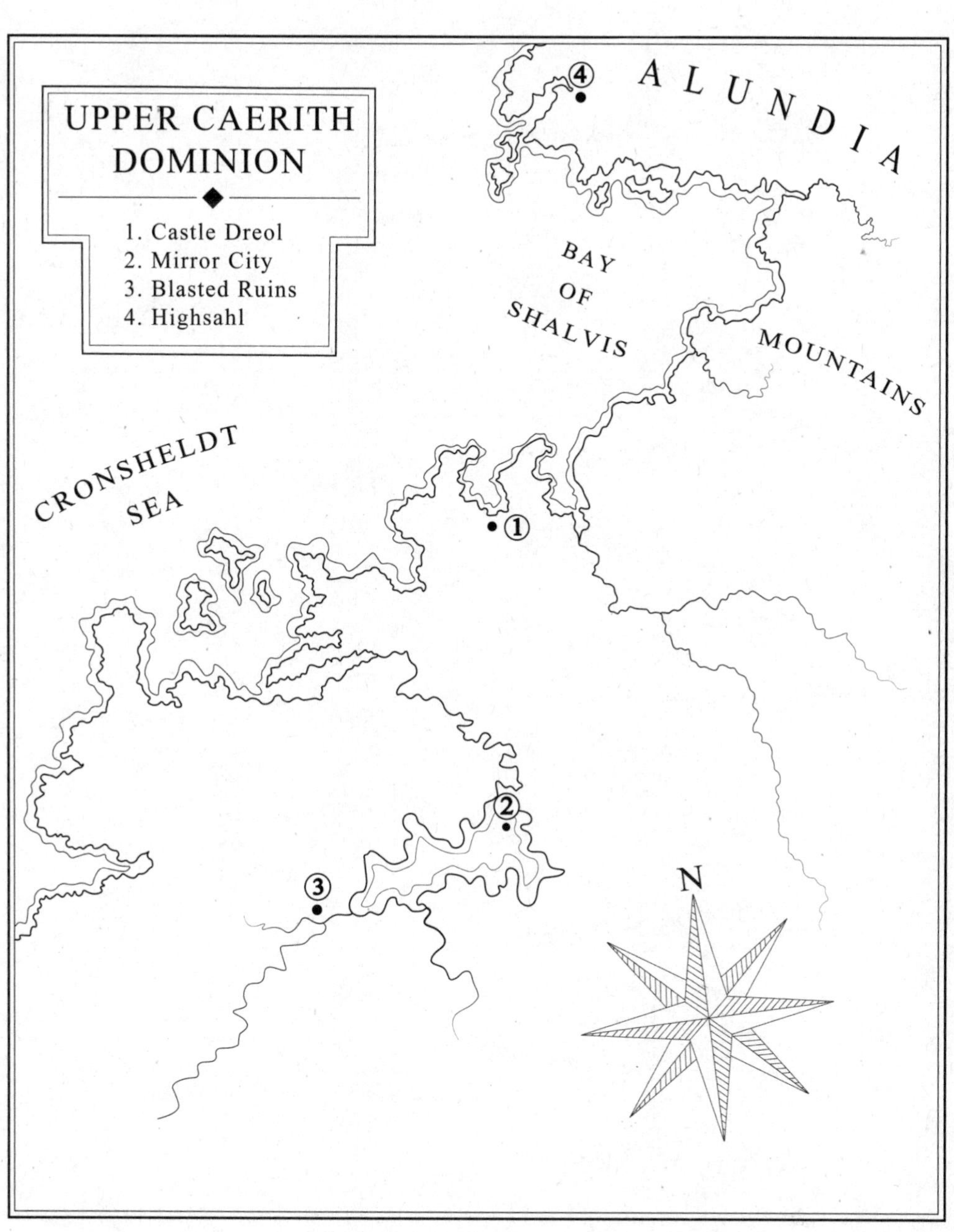
UPPER CAERITH DOMINION
1. Castle Dreol
2. Mirror City
3. Blasted Ruins
4. Highsahl
ALUNDIA
BAY OF SHALVIS
MOUNTAINS
CRONSHELDT SEA
N

Dramatis Personae

Alwyn Scribe – Outlaw, scribe and later Supplicant Blade in the Covenant Company

Evadine Courlain – Risen Martyr and Anointed Lady to the Covenant of Martyrs

Roulgarth Cohlsair – Former Knight Warden of Alundia, younger brother to Duke Oberharth

Ducinda Cohlsair – Daughter to the late Duke Oberharth and Duchess Celynne of Alundia

Merick Albrisend – Baron of Lumenstor, nephew by marriage to Oberharth Cohlsair

Lohrent Lambertain – Duke of the Cordwain

Gilferd Lambertain – Son and heir to Duke Lohrent

Viruhlis Guhlmaine – Duke of Rhianvel, possessed of ardent Covenant beliefs

Lermin Aspard – Duke of Dulsian, possessed of avid mercantile interests

Therin Gasalle – Dulsian ambassador to the Court of King Arthin

Jacquel Ebrin – Rhianvelan ambassador to the Court of King Arthin

Harldin Behrmain – Rhianvelan Cleric in service to the Anointed Lady, Co-Captain of the Lady's Shield, twin brother to Ildette

Ildette Behrmain – Rhianvelan Cleric in service to the Anointed Lady, Co-Captain of the Lady's Shield, twin sister to Harldin

Erchel – Slain outlaw of vile inclinations

Shilva Sahken – outlaw leader of the Shavine Marches

King Arthin Algathinet – Boy-King of Albermaine, formerly named Alfric Keville, son to Princess Leannor

Princess Leannor Algathinet-Keville – Sister to the late King Tomas, mother and Princess Regent to King Arthin

Ehlbert Bauldry – knight of famed martial abilities, champion to King Arthin

Altheric Courlain – veteran knight of high standing, father to Evadine, Knight Marshal of the King's Host

Luminant Durehl Vearist – Principal Cleric of the Luminants' Council, governing body of the Covenant of Martyrs

Luminant Daryhla Ahlpern – Member of the Luminants' Council, leader of the Orthodox Faction

Ascendant Arnabus – Senior Cleric in the Covenant of Martyrs, later leader of the Reformed Orthodox Covenant

Magnis Lochlain – Pretender to the Throne of Albermaine, also known as the "True King"

Lorine Blousset – (formerly Lorine D'Ambrille) Duchess of the Shavine Marches, former lover of Deckin Scarl the Outlaw King and associate of Alwyn

Dervan Pressman – Captain of Duchess Lorine's Chosen Company

Albyrn Swain – Supplicant and Lord Captain of the Covenant Host

Ofihla Barrow – Supplicant Captain to the Covenant Host

Delric Cleymount – Supplicant and senior healer to the Covenant Host

The Sack Witch – Caerith spell worker and healer, said to be of hideous appearance beneath the sackcloth mask she wears. Also known as the *Doenlisch* in the Caerith tongue

Wilhum Dornmahl – Disgraced turncoat knight formerly in service to the Pretender. Childhood friend to Evadine and commander of the Mounted Company of the Covenant Host

Eamond Astier – Former novice Supplicant and volunteer member of the Scout Company of the Covenant Host

Ayin – Soldier in the Covenant Host and page to Lady Evadine Courlain

Juhlina (known also as the Widow) – Former adherent to the Most Favoured pilgrimage sect, soldier in the Scout Company of the Covenant Host

Tiler – Former outlaw and soldier in the Scout Company of the Covenant Host

Lilat – Caerith huntress, friend to Alwyn

The Eithlisch – Caerith of arcane power and importance

Estrik – Soldier in the Covenant Host. Castellan of the Lady's Reach

Desmena Lehville – Rebel knight once in service to the Pretender Magnis Lochlain

Quintrell D'Elffir – Minstrel and spy in service to the Duchess Lorine Blousset

Adlar Spinner – Former juggler and soldier in the Scout Company of the Covenant Host

Archel Shelvane – Caretaker Governor of the Duchy of Althiene

Supplicant Hilbert Forswith – Former Senior Cleric of the Shrine to Martyr Callin in the Sanctuary Town of Callintor

Morieth – Caerith warrior of the *Paelith* horse clans

Corieth – Caerith elder of the *Paelith* horse clans

Turlia – Caerith elder of the *toalisch* warrior caste

Deracsh – Caerith elder and scholar

Shaelisch – Caerith elder of extensive years

What Has Gone Before . . .

Missive to the Luminants Council of the Eastern Reformed Covenant of Martyrs – Archivist's note: fragment only. Date and author unknown but believed to have been set down several years after the previously discovered fragment.

In my prior missives I was given to addressing you as the Blessed Brethren of the Council – this I shall do no more. It is clear to me now that you are not blessed, but cursed. This is the truth I have learned in my study of the Testament of Alwyn Scribe. The truth for which you sent assassins to kill me. Now, I find myself a homeless, wandering pauper, rich only in unwanted truth. Since this is the only weapon left to me, wield it I shall.

Previously, I related how Alwyn Scribe had risen from whorehouse orphan to trusted lieutenant of the Risen Martyr Evadine Courlain. It was a long road marked by betrayal, violence and the accumulation of secrets – two being greatest import: firstly, King Tomas Algathinet was the bastard son of his Champion Sir Ehlbret Bauldry and therefore an illegitimate occupant of the throne of Albermaine. Secondly, the supposedly divine resurrection of Evadine Courlain was not, in fact, the work of the Seraphile but achieved through the arcane agency of a Caerith mystic known as the Sack Witch. I further detailed how the Risen Martyr had been kidnapped and subjected to a farce trial by an alliance of Covenant clerics and Albermaine nobility. It was the intervention of Alwyn Scribe and his duel with Sir Althus Levalle that freed her, together with the assault launched by her loyal soldiers of the Covenant Company and a mass of devotional churls. And so, to the Shavine Forest they fled, carrying a grievously injured Alwyn.

Alwyn's recovery was slow. His principal injury suffered at the hands of Sir Althus leaving him at the mercy of recurrent, agonising headaches. His slumber was also tormented by dreams of his perverted and justly murdered associate Erchel, a phantom given to speaking curiously accurate visions of future travails.

This brief period of woodland skulking was interrupted by the arrival of Evadine's father, Lord Altheric Courlain, bearing an invitation to parley from King Tomas. Despite misgivings, Alwyn advised her to agree, and the Covenant Company set out for the cathedral city of Athiltor. The sojourn was marked by an accumulation of devotional souls adding greatly to the number who had flocked to Evadine's banner during her interlude in the forest. The outcome of the parley at Athiltor is well documented and therefore requires only a brief summation: Evadine received formal recognition as a Risen Martyr after swearing fealty to King Tomas.

Now bound by her oath to the crown, Evadine was obliged to accept King Tomas's commission to travel to the troubled duchy of Alundia. Once there, she would occupy the ruin of Walvern Castle as a means of demonstrating the authority of both king and Covenant. Before setting off, Alwyn sought knowledge of Alundia at the Covenant Library, where he was reacquainted with Ascendant Arnabus, the cleric who had overseen the farce trial of the Risen Martyr. Finding his suspicions stirred by the cleric's cryptic allusions to the Sack Witch, Alwyn attempted to force more information from him, only to be interrupted by Princess Leannor, sister to King Tomas. During this meeting, Alwyn divined that the princess was chiefly responsible for keeping her brother on the throne via a network of spies.

During the journey to Alundia, Alwyn's dreams continued to be troubled by visitations from the odious Erchel. Roused by the pestilent ghost's warning, Alwyn woke in time to save himself and Evadine from an attack by hired assassins, although the identity of their employer remained a mystery. Arriving at the Alundian border, Evadine and Alwyn endured a tense meeting with Duchess Celynne

Cohlsair, wife of Duke Oberharth, and Lord Roulgarth Cohlsair, the duke's brother and commander of his host. It is clear they were not welcome in this land.

Undaunted, Evadine led the Covenant Company on to Walvern Castle, finding it in a parlous state of repair. Nevertheless, Evadine ordered reconstruction of the stronghold and began patrolling the surrounding country. Awlyn and Wilhum Dornmahl, former lord and childhood friend of Evadine's, now commander of her mounted guard, discovered a burnt-out shrine and several pilgrims slaughtered by fanatical Alundian heretics. Hunting down the miscreants, they captured some and killed the others, freeing the lone survivor of the pilgrim massacre, one Mistress Juhlina, referred to by Alwyn subsequently as simply the Widow.

Shortly after, Lord Roulgarth arrived with a sizeable host demanding the captives be turned over to his custody. Alwyn is clear that the Risen Martyr's subsequent actions were driven by a desire to bring the smouldering crisis in Alundia to a head: she allowed the vengeful Widow to execute the captives, hanging them from the castle walls, and leaving Lord Roulgarth no option but to lay siege or cede to the authority of the Crown.

Alwyn depicts the subsequent contest for mastery of Walvern Castle as a gruelling and drawn-out affair, endured in the expectation that King Tomas would fulfil his promise to come to the Risen Martyr's aid should she be imperilled. It was only after the arrival of Duke Oberharth himself, together with the full strength of his mustered duchy, that the Crown Host deigned to appear, personally led by Princess Leannor. Evadine struck down the duke in the ensuing melee and the Alundian forces, exhausted by the siege, were swiftly routed.

All Alundia now lay at the mercy of the Algathinet throne, save for the port city of Highsahl, where Duchess Celynne still held sway. Grief-stricken and reputedly mad, the duchess refused all offers of parley, thereby forcing Leannor to order an assault. Alwyn describes how he further enhanced his martial reputation by orchestrating the main attack through the breach. Leading a small advance party to the ducal keep, he found to his horror that Celynne and her entire household had taken poison rather than allow themselves to be captured. The only survivor was the infant Lady Ducinda Cohlsair, saved by Alwyn rushing her to the Covenant Company Healer, Supplicant Delric.

In the aftermath of Highsahl's fall, Lady Ducinda was conveyed to the court of King Tomas, there to be betrothed to Princess Leannor's son Alfric. Princess Leannor ordered Alwyn and Sir Ehlbert Bauldry to hunt down Lord Roulgarth, now leading a dwindling band of Alundian rebels. Calling on his outlaw skills, Alwyn tracked down a former rebel, a guilt-ridden wretch who nevertheless agreed on the promise of riches to lead them to Roulgarth. Guided by the turncoat, they pursued Roulgarth and his nephew Merick Albrisend into the mountains bordering the Caerith dominion.

Alwyn recounts his confrontation with a defiant Roulgarth, however, before a blow could be struck, the turncoat, apparently maddened by his own treachery, gave voice to a shout of such volume that it dislodged a vast slab of snow and ice from the mountain above. Alwyn found himself carried off by the avalanche, fetching up battered but miraculously alive in Caerith territory.

As he lay insensate beneath a pile of snow, Alwyn received another visitation from the dream-haunting ghost of Erchel. This time the leering spectre offered a vision of the impending death of King Tomas.

Rescued by a reluctant group of Caerith, Alwyn relates how he was saved from immediate execution by virtue of his prior association with the Sack Witch. Known to the Cearith by the name *Doenlisch*, she was clearly a person of considerable importance who appeared to arouse unquestioning respect. The Caerith also captured Roulgarth and Merick, who were spared on the weight of Alwyn's word. During his time among the Caerith, Alwyn befriended a hunter name Lilat who showed him the ancient ruins of a once mighty civilisation now brought to ruin. After a beating at the hands of a dispirited and vengeful Roulgarth, Alwyn prevailed upon the exiled lord to teach him the sword, mainly by pointing out that it provided an opportunity for the man to beat him every day.

Alwyn's time with the Caerith came to an end with the arrival of a mystic known as the *Eithlisch*, a physically imposing figure who appeared to command only marginally less awe than the *Doenlisch*. The *Eithlisch* compelled Alwyn to follow him into the heart of a nearby mountain, a cavernous space piled with ancient bones. Here, Alwyn's narrative presents the most difficulty for the devout scholar, for he describes an event that can only be termed as both arcane and unnatural.

Alwyn claims that, upon touching a finger to the ancient skull of a crow, his mind was somehow transported to a bygone age. He found himself in the tower shown to him by Lilat, overlooking the nearby city, whole, not ruined, and conversed with a man who called himself a historian. It was apparent to Alwyn that they had met before, although he had no memory of it. He came to understand that it was his future self that previously spoke to the historian, revealed now as the author of the Caerith book once entrusted to Alwyn by the Sack Witch. Before this arcane visitation ends, Alwyn witnessed the destruction of the city below by its own inhabitants, recognising it as the beginnings of an event we call the Scourge.

Upon waking, Alwyn found himself alone with Lilat in the mountains. She informs him he has been sent back to his own people, and she had been dispatched to find the *Doenlisch*. Roulgarth and Merick have been permitted to stay among the Caerith, the Alundian lord now named as *Vahlisch*, or Swordmaster, by the *Eithlisch*.

Together, Alwyn and Lilat made their way to Walvern Castle, traversing a land ravaged by a war that had worsened in his absence, despoiled by atrocities committed in the name of the Risen Martyr. Elevated to command Evadine's Scout Company, Alwyn effectively became the Risen Martyr's spymaster, a role to which he was eminently suited.

Soon after the arrival of a royal messenger brought news of a resurgence of the Pretender's Revolt. Magnis Lochlain, false claimant to the throne of Albermaine, had re-emerged, forming an alliance with the Duke of Althienne. As father to the fallen Duchess Celynne, Duke Guhlton Pendroke had foresworn his allegiance to the Algathinet dynasty, determined upon revenge and the recovery of his granddaughter.

Holding true to her oath to King Tomas, Evadine rejected Alwyn's advice that she allow this current crisis to play out and make peace with the victor. The Covenant Company marched for the capital, gathering recruits along the way. The subsequent journey is well known to those who studied the career of the Risen Martyr, the episode earning the name of 'the Sacrifice March' due to the number of commoners who expired from exhaustion or privation. Undaunted by such losses, the great mass of devotional churls rendezvoused with the Crown Host under the command of Princess Leannor.

At this juncture, the Pretender sent a messenger, Lady Desmena Lehville, stating that King Tomas had been captured in a skirmish, a claim Alwyn knew to be false thanks to Erchel's nightmare visitation. Knowing that Evadine's future security lay in a swift conclusion to this crisis, Alwyn suggested Princess Leannor parley with the Pretender. This would be done on the artifice of hearing his terms but would, in fact, provide a venue for Alwyn to employ his gift for hearing lies.

The two hosts came together at a shallow valley north of the capital city of Couravel. To Alwyn's surprise, the subsequent parley revealed that King Tomas was slain not by the Pretender's hand but by Duke Guhlton. Enraged by this revelation, Princess Leannor drew a dagger and struck the duke dead, whereupon battle erupted. Thanks to Alwyn's careful positioning of the Covenant Company, the Pretender was captured in the ensuring struggle and his horde finally defeated after much slaughter. The Battle of the Vale marked the ultimate end of the Pretender's War.

In the aftermath of victory, the captive Pretender requested that Alwyn take down his testament prior to his execution. During their time together, Alwyn learned that Magnis Lochlain was in fact the bastard son of King Tomas's brother Arthin, who died before ascending the throne. After witnessing Lochlain's gruesome end, Alwyn described a brief interval of embittered drunken indulgence interrupted by news from his spies intimating that the Luminants Council was gathering its own Covenant Company and plotting against the Risen Martyr.

Evadine reluctantly granted Alwyn permission to investigate the suspect location of the Dire Keep in the Shavine Forest. However, upon arrival, Alwyn is immediately captured along with the Widow, Woodsman, and Tiler. While held captive in the partially ruined keep, Alwyn was reacquainted with one Danick Thessil, an outlaw leader he thought slaughtered at the Moss Mill Massacre, now commander of the Luminant Council's growing army. The enigmatic Ascendant Arnabus also reappeared at this juncture, together with Luminant Durehl Vearist. Together they attempted to force Alwyn to confess the true story of the Risen Martyr's resurrection.

After his first bout of torture, Arnabus came alone to Alwyn's cell and revealed himself as an ancient, arcane soul and former associate of the Sack Witch. For many years, he had been trying to win back her lost favour. Left to contemplate his fate, Alwyn was freed from his bonds by Lilat. He had sent her away before the Battle of the Vale but she tracked his footsteps to the Dire Keep, using her uncanny gift for finding a way in to ancient places to free him. Together, they rescued the Widow and the others before attempting to flee the keep.

Finding themselves cornered, Alwyn's companions hurled themselves into the fray, Woodsman falling slain in the ensuing fight. They were saved by the arrival of Evadine and Wilhum leading the Mounted Company, who swiftly put the Council soldiers to flight. Alwyn takes off into the woods in pursuit of Arnabus, but instead finds Luminant Durehl. With difficulty, he quelled his vengeful rage and stilled his hand. Evadine, however, was not so restrained.

Herein lies what you, Cursed Brethren, would term the ultimate blasphemy. In short, Alwyn Scribe states that, in contradiction to Reformed Covenant Doctrine, Luminant Durehl did not die by his own hand. No, he was murdered, and it was the Risen Martyr's hand that wielded the knife. Furthermore, Alwyn compounds his own damnation by describing how he and Evadine Courlain lay in lustful union while still bathed in the blood of a slain cleric. As even the laziest student of history knows, all that came next can be said to have arisen from this sinful event.

I do, naturally, have more to tell, more truths to cast at your false Covenant. It is my fervent hope that these truths will be the means of your downfall, Cursed Brethren, for you have surely earned it in ways it will now be my pleasure to relate in full . . .

THE TRAITOR

PART ONE

Sister Queens you call yourselves, but it is a hollow title. For it is revealed to me by the Seraphile themselves that your power arises from deceit. Your savage misrule is founded upon naught but the empty legends you term gods and sustained through base oppression.

Liars, I call you.

Thieves, I call you.

Murderers, I call you.

False queens you are while I, through the divine agency of the blessed Covenant of Martyrs, stand as the only true monarch in a world of tyrants. You sought my answer, cursed sisters. Now you have it.

Extract from *Martyr Evadine's Epistle to the Sister Queens of Ascarlia*

Chapter One

What do you know of the Malecite, Alwyn?

Words drifting to me through a fog of post-carnal confusion. My chest, sticky with sweat and the detritus of the forest floor, rose and fell in concert with Evadine's naked form, equally besmirched. She groaned a little as I stirred, her dark tresses sliding over my blinking eyes as they took in the surrounding scene with mounting alarm. A dozen paces away, the corpse of Luminant Durehl Vearist lay amid the roots of an aged oak. His half-lidded eyes were dull and unseeing, the blood no longer flowing from the deep slash across his throat. *Evadine's cut*, I remembered. *The Risen Martyr's murder . . . Or, the first just execution by the self-crowned Ascendant Queen.*

What do you know of the Malecite, Alwyn? the question intruded once more, spoken in the voice Sihlda used years ago, employing that searching tone designed to impart rather than summon knowledge. I could recall the day she had asked me this for it came early during my tenure in the Pit Mines. Her lessons hadn't yet taken hold then, my attempts to copy the letters she demonstrated were a clumsy embarrassment and her many questions revealed the shameful ignorance of a youth who had imagined himself worldly. She had captured me, however. The promise of what she offered was too tempting and so when she enquired about the Malecite I responded with diligent promptness.

They are the wellspring of evil in the world, I said, a truth known to all those raised within or, in my case, on the fringes of Covenant belief. *They are the bad and the Seraphile are the good.*

So the scrolls tell us. Sihlda inclined her head in agreement but, as ever, her lesson would never end with just one question and one answer. *But have you ever seen the Malecite? Or heard their voice?*

Of course I hadn't. No one had. Even deranged, fanatical Hostler, most devout of outlaws, claimed no personal experience of the Malecite, although he ranted about their perfidy with irksome constancy. *They don't work like that,* I replied. *They don't appear to folk, they . . .* My still barely educated younger self fumbled for the right words. *They influence, get into people's souls somehow.*

Get into? Sihlda had asked, the small quirk of her mouth and upraised brows telling me we had reached the point of her lesson. *Or are they invited in?*

Evadine groaned again, the sound now possessed of a questioning note. She jerked and stiffened against me, eyes widening in surprise as they found mine. For a second it seemed there was an accusation there, a creasing of her brow and tightening of the mouth that might even signify reproach. But it was gone quickly, replaced by a languid smile before she rested her cheek upon my chest. The feel of her skin, warm, soft and wonderful, brought a fresh stirring of lust, as did her lean, muscled flesh, speckled by leaves and dirt. How long had we coiled together on the ground?

Attempting to parse details from the event, I found that it had passed in a dreamlike whirlwind of released desire and confusion. I would like to ascribe the act of rutting like a beast within sight of a murdered senior cleric, his blood still beading my skin no less, to some form of arcane influence or temporary madness. However, by now you will, most honoured reader, know that I will never assail you with base lies. The ugly, unvarnished truth is that the Risen Martyr Evadine Courlain and I came together in willing, if gore-spattered, union and I will not shirk the weight of all that came next by pretending otherwise.

"We should . . . get dressed," I said, even though I didn't want to, the feel of her was more potent than any drug.

"Yes," she agreed, shifting to lay her head at a more comfortable angle, reaching up to play her fingers over my face. "We should . . ."

The Malecite, another voice posing another question, this time unspoken. A voice I had recoiled from, told myself it held a vile and obvious lie. I recalled how I had laughed at him at first, then sobered when I saw the seriousness of his expression. I had just concluded the narrative he craved, recounting the events of my life up until the moment of our arcane meeting, ending it by avowing the fervent desire to return to Evadine's side.

Despite it all? he asked me, face drawn in both judgement and confusion. *Despite what you know her to be?*

Her mission is a winding and complex path, it's true, I began only for him to shake his head in impatience.

Not that. He leaned towards me, eyes widening in realisation as he scrutinised my features. *You don't know yet*, he murmured. *Of course.*

Don't know what? I demanded. The tumult of rage and madness from outside was growing closer, making it clear our time was short.

What you told me, he said, then sighed, closing his eyes. *What you will tell me, regarding Evadine and her true nature.*

I stared at him, baffled but also fearful, refusing to prompt him further, but he told me anyway. *Evadine*, he said, *serves the Malecite.*

It was the sound of horns that caused her finally to rouse, grunting in annoyance at the distant but unmistakable keening. *A hunting horn*, I realised. *But who hunts for who?*

"Where did Ulstan get to, I wonder," Evadine sighed, sitting up and casting about for her warhorse. Spying him nuzzling a juniper bush a dozen paces off, she got to her feet, brushing leaves and soil from her naked flanks. The sight of her flesh, pale but red in places, birthed another resurgence of unwise lust and I forced my gaze away. Unfortunately, I immediately found it ensnared by the bleached, sagging emptiness of Luminant Durehl's face.

Foremost cleric of the realm, I knew. *Loudest voice on the Luminants' Council, murdered by a Risen Martyr with a legend built on a lie . . .*

"Alwyn." I looked up to find Evadine regarding me with an expression of muted exasperation. "Get dressed," she added, pulling her black cotton shirt over her head.

The hunting horn pealed out again, closer now, and I spent the next few moments in a frantic scramble to clothe myself. Fortunately, the task was swiftly done as my recent captivity and escape from the Dire Keep left me with only trews, shirt and boots, plus a sword belt and sundry stolen weapons. Evadine had chosen to come here in full armour and required my help in getting it buckled on in some semblance of order before the sound of approaching horses echoed through the woods. Fixing the last greave into place, I wondered at the fact that stripping it all away had seemed to take no time at all.

I drew my purloined falchion upon glimpsing the first flicker of horse and rider through the trees, there had been seventy or more Council Host soldiers at the keep and it stood to reason a few had escaped Evadine's charge. However, the familiar glimmer of blue enamelled armour caused me to lower the weapon.

"Wil!" Evadine called out, raising her hand in greeting. In response, the captain of the Covenant Mounted Company spurred his mount to a trot, six riders at his back. As they closed upon us, my gaze once again slipped to the murdered Luminant.

"A breaker of laws," Evadine said and I turned to find her regarding me with grave assurance. "Laws set down by both Covenant and Crown. Death was his due."

"I know," I replied, voice quiet as Wilhum reined in and dismounted a short way off. "But still, I beg you, allow your scribe to spin this tale. The truth will not help us."

A frown of annoyance passed across her brow, the expression of one secure in her convictions yet compelled to deceit. It was a small moment, gone in an instant, but I tend to think of it as Evadine Courlain's last true concession to reason. Soon, the Ascendant Queen would have no truck with the cowardice of concealing her crimes, for to her, they were not crimes at all.

"Very well," she murmured. "Spin away, my love."

"Evie." Wilhum dragged his helm from his head, breath steaming and concerned eyes tracking over Evadine's begrimed face and armour. "Are you hurt?"

"Nary a scratch," she assured him.

"I'm fine too," I told him. "Got plenty of scratches, though."

Wilhum gave an amused grimace as he looked me over, shaking his head. "I told her you could be counted on to slip any snare without our help." His humour evaporated upon catching sight of the Luminant's body. Despite his time at Evadine's side, he had never been a particularly devout soul, but even he paled at what he beheld. "Is that . . . ?"

"It is," I finished. "Luminant Durehl and I were captives together at the Dire Keep. He had been lured there by Ascendant Arnabus, that vile creature who oversaw the trial at Castle Ambris. Apparently, Arnabus has been plotting to seize control of the Covenant for many years." I let out a regretful sigh and moved to crouch at Durehl's side. "He told me how Arnabus had whispered in his ear about the danger posed by the Risen Martyr, persuaded the council to recruit their own host. It was only after his capture this poor old bastard realised his mistake. When we escaped, I told him to flee into the woods, telling him I'd find him later. It seems Arnabus or Danick Thessil found him first."

"Danick Thessil?" Evadine asked.

"The commander of the Council Host. A soldier turned outlaw I had thought slain at Moss Mill, though I daresay he goes by a different name these days."

"An outlaw will know many places to hide in these woods," Wilhum pointed out.

"He won't be hiding," I said. "He and Arnabus will be making all haste to Athiltor, hoping to muster what forces they can. We should expect some form of Council edict condemning the Anointed Lady as a heretic." I rose, offering Evadine an apologetic frown. "I know you wanted to avoid this, but the Covenant of Martyrs will fracture. A schism of the faithful is upon us."

"The Anointed Lady enjoys the love and devotion of the commons and the faithful," Wilhum said.

"Not all. The Covenant has stood in its present form for centuries. Folk have spent generations comforted by its permanency. That won't just vanish overnight." I shifted my gaze to Evadine, speaking with complete honesty now. "Make no mistake, my lady. We have another war to fight."

* * *

"Ow! Ffff—!" Tiler clenched his teeth as Ayin worked a needle through the lips of his deepest cut. The narrow-faced spy shuddered with the combined effort of bearing his pain and biting down on profane curses. Ayin's reputation was well known among the Covenant veterans and most were smart enough to curb their tongue in her presence.

"Stop squealing, piglet," she chided, drawing the thread through the wound with practised smoothness.

"You were lucky," I informed Tiler, peering at his injury, a slanting, four-inch slash from jaw to neck. "A little lower and you'd be joining them."

I inclined my head at the piled dead, mostly Council Host soldiers with only three exceptions: two of Wilhum's riders lost in the melee and one bulkier but unarmoured form. The Widow crouched at the corpse's side, having taken it upon herself to prepare Liahm Woodsman for the grave, washing his face and hands before resting them on his chest. I hadn't thought of them as friends, in fact I could recall her exchanging only a few words with the former woodcutter. But she was ever a strange woman and her actions not always easily understood.

"The dead can care for the dead," Tiler said, a familiar saying among outlaws. I looked down to see him settling a hungry gaze on the corralled prisoners. There was a score of them, made small by their absence of armour or weapons, twitching under the glare of their guards.

"You promised me, my lord," Tiler said in a manner that reminded me why I disliked him so much.

"I promised you Danick Thessil," I told him. "So you'll have to wait, at least until Athiltor." I turned to Ayin, watching her put a knot in the neat row of stitches. "When you're done, you two scour this place for documents. The bodies too. I want every scrap of paper, inscribed or no."

I found Lilat perched on a ruined column that had formed part of the keep's smaller west-facing gate. Her brow creased in a bemused frown as she watched a troop of Covenant soldiers dig a grave pit nearby. "You put them in the earth," she said, speaking in Caerith as was our habit when alone. "Is this done to seed the soil?"

"It's . . ." I began then fell silent, the reason why we customarily buried our dead never having occurred to me before. The Caerith, I knew, simply carried their expired loved ones into the forest and left them to rot. *Apart from the chosen few they put beneath the mountain*, I reminded myself, the memory of all those piled bones bringing an unwelcome shiver. "It's just how things are done here," I said, searching for the right word before adding, "*Jurihm*." It meant both habit or tradition depending on the inflection.

"*Jurihm*," she repeated with a vague nod. The huntress stiffened a little as she shifted her gaze to where Evadine stood in what had been the central courtyard of this keep. One of the prisoners knelt before her, hands bound behind his back, head bowed and trembling under the weight of the Anointed Lady's stare. She asked him questions I couldn't hear, though her face held none of the calm solicitation I remembered from her prior encounters with captives. I knew her attitude towards our foes had changed during our time apart, the months when she thought me dead and the Alundian rebellion still raged. The Covenant Company was rich in quietly spoken tales of her angry condemnation of captured Alundian rebels, more than a few of whom had danced at the end of a noose when they refused to recant their heresy.

"You lay with her," Lilat said, a simple, uninflected statement of fact delivered in a tongue that no one within earshot could understand. Nevertheless, I couldn't contain an instinctive start at her bald honesty. "I smell her on you," she added by way of explanation, continuing to regard me without expression save for a raised eyebrow.

Looking into her steady gaze, I was unable to divine any emotion attached to this statement. I pondered the notion that she might be jealous, but found it unlikely. Perhaps she was angered by my lack of caution, for even she knew the danger inherent in what had happened in the woods. However, my gift for parsing meaning from face and posture remained strong. A moment of additional scrutiny revealed an incremental narrowing of her brows that told of something I found more troubling than jealousy or anger: disappointment.

Beset by the rarest of sensations, to wit: finding I had nothing to say, I could only dumbly return her regard until she consented to direct her scrutiny at Evadine once again. "*Morkleth*," Lilat said. "You remember this word?"

I did, but resented the implication. "She is not cursed," I said.

"It has other meanings. The man you called the Chainsman, he was *morkleth*. Not only cursed but outcast. He committed no act that your people would term a crime, but still the *Eithlisch* decreed he be shunned and driven away. It is the role of the *Eithlisch* to seek out those that will one day bring danger to the Caerith." She nodded at Evadine, who had taken a step closer to the cowering captive, questions emerging from her lips in a hard, demanding snap. "He would not have suffered her to live among us. I wonder why your people do."

Evadine serves the Malecite . . . I pulled my looted cloak about my shoulders to conceal a shudder, moving away with a parting mutter. "You do not understand her, or us. This is not your land."

"*Morkleth* has the same scent," she replied as I walked away, voice soft but I heard it. "Wherever it may be found."

By the time I reached the courtyard the prisoner had slumped on to all fours, his face pressed into the ancient, cracked flagstones as he sobbed under the weight of Evadine's enquiry. "How many are at Athiltor?" she grated, leaning down to shout the question into his ear. "How many, you unbelieving cur?!"

"J-just . . ." the fellow gabbled through snot and tears. "Just a . . . simple soldier, m-my lady. Only joined cos they paid a full silver for the first week . . ." I could see no signs of torture on him so this state of compliance had been achieved through terror alone.

"Silver?" Evadine's scowl deepened into a glower. "You sell your very soul for a disc of metal?"

"G-got . . . children, m'lady," he gabbled back. "Their ma died last winter so had to leave 'em with their grandmother. Gotta feed 'em . . ."

This allusion to soon-to-be-orphaned infants, real or the imaginary product of mortal fear, made scant purchase on Evadine's resolve. "A father should set an example for his children," she stated, her hand going to her dagger. "Even though it may cost him his life."

"May I crave a moment with this man, my lady?" I said, stepping closer. My interruption drew a brief glare of anger before she mastered herself, hand slipping from the dagger's hilt. I smiled and gave a meaningful inclination of my head to the snivelling man on the ground. Nodding, she stepped back, allowing me to crouch at the prisoner's side.

"Let's get you up, shall we?" I said, grasping his shoulders, gently easing him into a sitting position. The face he revealed as he straightened was that of a man somewhere close to his thirtieth year. He had several scars, old and new, a soldier's face if ever there was one, with an accent that marked him as hailing from Alberis.

"You're a fair long way from home, eh?" I asked, removing the stopper from a canteen and holding it to his lips. "How long since you took the first coin?"

"Years, my lord," he replied after taking several hearty gulps, eyes continually tracking Evadine's tall form pacing back and forth across the courtyard.

"Kingsman, were you?" I asked, never one to stint on flattery. "Got that look to you."

"Just the ducal levies. Tried for the Crown Company once but the sergeant said I was too slow with the halberd. Truth was he wanted a bribe to let me in and I'd no coin for him."

"Sergeants." I shook my head in sympathy. "Bastards all. What's your name, soldier?"

"Turner, my lord. Abell Turner."

"Very well, Abell Turner. As one soldier to another, I'll make you a fair offer. Your life and your liberty in return for truth. How's that sound?"

His eyes darted towards Evadine once more as her boots scuffed the flagstones. Turner risked a glance at her hard, impatient face before his focus snapped back to me, face filled with the desperation of a drowning man flailing for the most tattered rope. Still, he managed to surprise me with his next words. "My men, my lord. They're just poor fellows like me. Some I served with before, joined only because I did . . ."

He fell silent at another, louder, scuff from Evadine's boots, bowing his head with a shudder of fearful expectation. This was the first time I had seen how the Anointed Lady's rage could be as potent a force as her love.

"Life and liberty for them too," I promised, ignoring the harsh sigh this provoked from Evadine. "But they, and you, will have to swear fealty to the Risen Martyr and an oath never again to take up arms against her." I looked deeper into his eyes, stripping all solicitation from my voice as I added, "For to do so will cost you far more than blood."

His throat constricted and I realised he was fighting the urge to vomit. "Swear it I shall, my lord. My fellows too, on my soul."

I nodded, putting a tight smile on my lips. "Now then. The man who leads you, not the cleric, the one who commands the Council Host, what name does he go by?"

"Captain Sorkin, my lord. Truth be told, I can't recall hearing his first name."

"And what do you know of this Captain Sorkin?"

"A man who knows his business when it comes to soldiering, that's for sure. Had far worse captains in my time, though few who were so quick with the whip. Doesn't stint with the flogging, does the Divine Captain."

"Divine?" Evadine said, the hardness of her tone causing Abell Turner to cower yet lower to the ground.

"It's what they called him, my lady," he said, tone heavy with abject contrition. "The Ascendant and other clerics. His rank in the Covenant Host."

"You were garrisoned at Athiltor?" I asked, keen to recapture the man's attention.

He bobbed his head. "Aye, my lord. Six or seven weeks of drill before we were ordered here."

"You recall the Anointed Lady asked how many are at Athiltor. She and I would like an answer."

"I spoke truth when I said I didn't know. There were recruits arriving all the time, and what with all the works going on it was hard to gauge a true count."

"Guess," Evadine instructed.

"Five thousand, six at most. At least that was when we marched out. More kept coming, like I said, and . . ." He hesitated and I saw a decision in his face, the look of a man deciding which way to throw his lot. "And there was talk of others, hired swords from the east and across the south seas. There were already a few dozen of those savage archers there when we left, don't rightly know how to say the name of their homeland."

"Vergundians," I said, glancing at Evadine to share a moment of grim remembrance of their deadly skills during the siege of Walvern Castle.

"Aye." Turner bobbed his head again. "That's it, my lord. Ragged and grimy looking lot they were, cut-throats the lot of 'em. Seemed strange the Covenant would spend coin on such folk."

"You spoke of works," I said. "Describe them."

"Digging mostly, trenches and breastworks. Some walls but they weren't solid like a castle, not much stone to be had at Athiltor."

I questioned him for close on an hour, probing for more details. The revealed picture indicated that Danick Thessil, in his new guise as the Divine Captain Sorkin, had managed to gather a reasonably disciplined force at the Covenant's holiest city. It would also soon be expanded by a good many mercenaries and protected by freshly constructed fortifications. Evadine made a few forceful interjections, her questions pointed in their inference:

"What of your captain's dealings with the Crown?" she demanded. "What bargains did Ascendant Arnabus strike with the Algathinets?"

In response, Turner could only shrink under her baleful glare and stutter out denials. "N-never saw a Crown agent the whole time I was there, m'lady. As for the Ascendant, saw him talking to the D— the captain a good deal, but never spoke to him myself."

"Come the morning," I said once satisfied I had wrung all pertinent knowledge from him, "you and your fellows will swear your oaths and depart this place." I leaned closer, fixing his gaze. "If you know who I am, you know I can hear a lie clear as any bell. If I catch even the smallest whisper of falsehood on the morrow . . ."

"You won't, my lord." He pressed his forehead to the flagstones. "And . . . I thank you. The renowned mercy of the Scribe and the Anointed Lady is surely no lie."

"Seven thousand trained troops," Wilhum sighed, holding his hands out to the fire. The hour was late and Evadine had summoned him to discuss our sudden wealth of intelligence, the palaver held out of earshot of the rest of the company. A veteran of more battles than either Evadine or I, Wilhum found little encouragement in our news. "Behind trenches and breastworks. Plus a bundle of Vergundian archers and Martyrs know how many more foreign bastards waiting for us." He offered Evadine an apologetic wince. "It's not a good prospect, Evie. My counsel: send Alwyn and I to Athiltor for a proper reconnaissance and take yourself back to Couravel to remind the Princess Regent of the value of your current alliance and have Lord Swain marshal the Covenant Host to march on Athiltor. We can, at least, be certain of their loyalty to you regardless of what the Luminants might proclaim. If joined with the Crown Company, we'll have sufficient numbers to end this matter, though I'd rather not mount a campaign with winter on the way."

"I cannot treat with the Princess Regent," Evadine stated. "For there is no such person. There is merely a woman who happens to be the sister of an unworthy bastard. The Algathinet family has maintained its hold on the throne through guile, murder and deception. I've little doubt they also had a hand in the villainy that took place here, well hidden though it may be. It's time, Wil. Time to complete my mission."

Wilhum's expression assumed a rigid blankness, regarding her in silence before looking to me, face still stiff but alarm writ large in his gaze.

"Alwyn and I are of like mind in this," Evadine told him. "There being no other course available to us." She took a deep breath, releasing it with grave slowness. "To save all I must risk all. I must be queen, the Ascendant Queen. In me, Crown, commons and Covenant will be unified and the Second Scourge averted. Only then can this realm know peace."

Wilhum's eyes lingered on me and I knew he hoped for words of restraint, words I couldn't offer, not then. I was now as much Evadine's captive as Turner and his comrades. I knew the grave import of her words. I knew what it portended, but I met Wilhum's searching eyes with an expression of sombre agreement.

He turned back to Evadine, voice faint and barely audible above the crackle of the campfire. "You know I will follow you in this as I have followed your every step since the Traitor's Field. For loyalty is what I owe you, Evie." He paused, drawing breath to add, "But you must know that this course invites war with Crown and Covenant both. I have no surety we have the strength for either."

"Fighting both at the same time is folly, to be sure," I said, addressing my words to Evadine. "We deal with the Covenant first. Victory is the best fuel for rebellion, and that is what we are about, make no mistake. We triumph at Athiltor before making any mention of the Ascendant Queen's rise."

"You speak as if we have an easy battle ahead of us," Wilhum said. "Time is as much our enemy as this Divine Captain and his heretic host. Time to glean further intelligence. Time to gather forces we will surely need to storm the holy city."

"I'll send my keenest scouts to Athiltor in the morning. And Eamond will ride with all haste to Couravel to summon the Covenant Host. I'll also pen a letter to Princess Leannor relating what happened here, making it clear that resolving this crisis is Covenant business. I doubt she'll wish to embroil the Crown in such a schism of the faithful. In fact, she'll probably relish the chance to play peacemaker if it proves a protracted struggle, which it won't."

"The Covenant Host won't be enough," Wilhum insisted. "Even if they can march here in time."

"The commons of the Shavine Marches and Alberis have answered the Anointed Lady's call before. They'll do so again."

"A mass of untrained churls is no match for real soldiers."

"No, but their numbers may turn the tide if need be. As for our own want of seasoned troops, I've a notion of where to find more." I offered Evadine a regretful shrug. "Though I warn you, my queen, the price is likely to be steep."

Chapter Two

The walls of Castle Ambris had a cleaner look than I remembered. The streaks of soot and mingled effluent that once marred the castle's flanks were gone now, presumably scrubbed away with assiduous regularity by order of the duchess. Even during her years in the forest, Lorine had managed to impose a sense of orderliness on her surroundings. Deckin commanded the band but Lorine held dominion over the camp and woe betide anyone who besmirched it. I recalled how she had birched Erchel's boyhood arse bloody when he decided to take a shit within smelling distance of our roasting pit.

The adjoining village of Ambriside had also grown in both size and cleanliness; whitewashed walls in place of grey wattle and the thatching lacked the usual scorched patchiness. The field where Evadine had once stood atop a scaffold awaiting unlawful execution was now a stretch of well-maintained grass where gaggles of children played and a company of ducal soldiers paced through their drills. The impression of orderliness was further enhanced when these soldiers, spying a large group of armed riders following the road to the gate, quickly formed ranks and marched to bar our path.

"The Anointed Lady and Risen Martyr Evadine Courlain requests an audience with Duchess Lorine," I told the youthful captain standing at the head of the hastily assembled cordon. He stood in the middle of the road, eyeing us with a careful shrewdness that did much to diminish his boyish appearance. I saw no scars on his face but the way he appraised our number bespoke one well attuned to martial matters.

"Captain Scribe, is it not?" he enquired, surveying the Mounted Company without particular hostility, but also a creditable pitch of caution. As was customary, his attention had lingered most on Evadine, albeit with none of the typical awe or lust. "I saw you fight the Pretender at the Vale," he added. "Quite a scrap that was." His accent was distinct in its common origins. A lad from the fields, or perhaps the forest? Lorine always did have a sharp eye for talent wherever it might be found.

"Between you and me, he was an average swordsman at best," I replied, without rancour despite my tendency towards a darkened mood at mention of the Pretender. "And it's Sir Alwyn Scribe these days, but why stand on ceremony?" I nodded to the banner flying above the battlements, the silver hawk seeming to flap its wings as the red pennant snapped in the wind. "She is in, I take it?"

"She is, my lord." He gave a short bow and stood aside, barking out an order for his men to form column. I took note of the way they changed formation, almost the equal of the Crown Company in their speed and precision. "It will be my honour to escort you to the duchess's presence," the young captain added, bowing again.

"Did you train this lot?" I enquired as I guided Blackfoot along the road to the gate. Like much else here, this showed signs of recent improvement. Once a rutted track prone to foot-sucking muddiness in the rain, it was now protected by a covering of flagstones. "They seem a good deal livelier of foot than I recall."

"I did, my lord," the captain confirmed with a note of pride. "These are the Chosen Company, the duchess's personal guard."

"Meaning she chose you too." I saw him stiffen at that and he volunteered no more words until we entered the courtyard.

"If the Anointed Lady would be kind enough to wait," he said, bowing once more, "I shall announce her arrival to the duchess. Please help yourselves to fodder and water for your horses."

"So," Evadine said as we led our mounts to the trough. "This is the woman who raised you, is it not?" She spoke in a quiet tone but there was a tension to her bearing I didn't like, her features stiff with the effort of keeping a disapproving scowl at bay. I had given her a short but unvarnished account of my upbringing in Deckin's band, complete with thievery and murder as well as isolated moments of humour or kindness, most of which featured Lorine.

"In a way," I said. "Though you'll find her of far less matronly appearance than you might expect."

"I've heard some tales. The Fox of the Forest, some call her. Other names are not so kind."

Hearing the sharpening edge to her voice, I leaned closer. "It would be best if you allowed me to handle this negotiation. Lorine may be of mostly mercenary inclinations, but she does have her pride. Nor is she swayed by faith or reputation."

"Do I hear a command, my lord?" There was a taunt in Evadine's eye as she arched an eyebrow at me, also a promise, one that stirred a fierce desire to go in search of a conveniently private corner of this castle. Our tryst in the forest remained a vague swirl of memory, but, like the first taste of any drug, left a growing thirst for more.

I coughed, mastering the urge to reach for her. "Please," I said. "Just let me talk to her without interruption and I'll secure the Ascendant Queen her army. And when it comes time to agree the price—"

"The price doesn't matter," Evadine cut in. "Promise her whatever is needed, but don't expect me to pretend to like it. If this fox-mother of yours has any wit about her at all, she'd know it for a lie in any case."

Lorine Blousset, Duchess of the Shavine Marches, chose to receive her esteemed guest in a small chamber in the tower forming the join between the castle's east and north facing walls. Despite its less than grand dimensions, the tower room was rich in furnishings and carpeted with a large bearskin rug. It was upon said rug that Evadine and I found the duchess when entering the chamber. Lorine was dressed in a modest gown of grey-blue cotton, her copper hair flailing as she wrestled with a small, giggling child. Various toys were strewn about, spinning wheels and bright painted blocks, but the child held a miniature wooden sword. He laughed as he assailed Lorine with a series of swipes. Undaunted, she chased him across the furry battleground, growling like some manner of monster, hands raised in clawlike threat.

"Duchess Lorine," the young captain said, boots stamping the flagstones. "I have the honour to present . . ."

"Alwyn!" Lorine greeted me with a broad smile then grimaced as the boy turned to slap his wooden blade against her arm. Growling again, she scooped him into her arms and got to her feet, the boy's excited laughter subsiding into frowning curiosity as she brought him to me. "Bryndon," she said, holding the child out to me. "Say hello to your uncle."

I accepted the burden of this still frowning child with an uncertain smile, one that faltered when he tapped his wooden sword to my nose. "It's all right," Lorine assured me. "He only hits people he likes."

Looking into the boy's serious gaze I saw the unmistakable glint of his mother's green eyes and the reddish sheen to his mop of curls. I could see little of his father in his small features, but that, of course, didn't mean anything. Of his two parents, I wasn't surprised at all to find that his mother had the strongest blood.

"Duchess," I said, making to hand the child back but he confounded me by dropping his sword and curling up into my arms. Resting his head against my chest, he promptly closed his eyes, small thumb working its way into his mouth.

"Best hold on to him for now," Lorine advised. "He wails something fierce if you interrupt his naps."

"As you wish." I shifted, cradling the child and turning to Evadine. "May I introduce . . ."

"The Anointed Lady herself." Lorine stepped back and sank into a deep bow. "The Risen Martyr honours my home with her presence. The Blousset family is famed for its faithfulness." Straightening, she turned to address the young captain. "Dervan, be so good as to inform Master Dubbings we have guests. He is to prepare a feast and entertainment for tonight. Those jugglers from last week are still loitering about the place, I believe. It would be nice if they earned their board. Find suitable lodgings for Lady Evadine and Lord Alwyn, and I'm sure we can make room in the barracks for their soldiers."

Captain Dervan hesitated. "You wish to be alone then, my lady?" he asked, casting a pointed glance at the unguarded door.

Lorine raised her eyebrows and pursed her lips in apparent puzzlement. "If I did not I would have made it clear, would I not?"

"Of course." Dervan delivered his lowest bow yet before departing the room with stiff-backed alacrity.

"And close the bloody door!" Lorine called out when his boots echoed on the stairwell outside. "A dutiful young man but lacking many graces," she said when the latch snicked into place.

"He certainly doesn't have a noble's voice," I observed which brought a smile to Lorine's lips.

"Isn't he just so observant, my lady?" she enquired of Evadine. "Always the way with Alwyn. Sees it all, even when you don't want him to."

"My captain has many gifts," Evadine returned. "And I thank the Seraphile for each and every one."

"Yes." Lorine's humour faded, her scrutiny lingering on Evadine before slipping back to me. I caught the glimmer of understanding in her eyes as they tracked over my face, rich in recently acquired bruises. "I'm sure he's been very useful to you. What was it this time?" She raised a hand, touching her fingertips to the graze on my chin, a trophy from the beating delivered by an enraged Arnabus. "Heretics or traitors? I must confess, my lady, I never expected to encounter a woman who could accrue more enemies than myself, although most of mine have long since departed this world."

"Heretics and traitors both," I said, keen to limit this conversation to the most pressing concerns. "And the reason for our visit."

"Ahh. War again so soon, is it?" Lorine sighed and turned away, moving to a dressing table atop which an array of small glass bottles had been set. There was a score or more, all varying in colour and size. She plucked one from the collection and held it up to the light streaming through the room's only window. The glass had a faintly pinkish tinge that cast an interesting abstract shadow on the rough hewn wall. "Perfumes are my only real vice these days," Lorine said, removing the bottle's small crystal stopper and wafting it about. I caught the aroma from several feet away, a pleasing melange of floral notes with a faint tang of citrus.

"This one comes from beyond the southern sea," Lorine continued, her tone and bearing becoming markedly less amenable as she spoke on. Also, her attention was now mostly directed at Evadine. "I'm reliably informed that its varied ingredients must be caravanned across many miles of desert, having been harvested from distant lands unknown to our most worldly scholars. When the last round of slaughter raged, I found it near impossible to increase my collection, or purchase enough grain to prevent the poorest of my churls starving, since all the hands that would have reaped the harvest had been dragged off to battle. By my reckoning at least one in ten didn't make the return journey from our famous victory at the Vale. And you know, Alwyn, I was ever a dab hand with numbers."

She paused, sharing a moment of silent regard with Evadine. "But then," Lorine added, smiling once again as she returned the stopper to the bottle, "that's the way with war. Always bad for commerce, unless your trade is in weapons. Mine is not."

"I am sure," I began, choosing my words with considerable care, "my Lady Duchess knows that when war comes to your door the option of not answering the knock is rarely indulged. I would never presume to tell a duchess her business, being but a lowly scribe, albeit with a lordly title, but you must be aware that while war can bring interruptions to trade, it also brings opportunity. I recall a man of my prior acquaintance once saying that war is the wolf, and wise are the crows that grow fat on its prey."

Something dark flickered across Lorine's features before she looked away, setting the perfume bottle down. I had known employing one of Deckin's favourite sayings would have an effect, but hadn't expected anger. There was little doubt in my mind that her love for the fallen Outlaw King hadn't faded, or her grief. Lorine continued to stand in wordless regard of her collection for long enough to try Evadine's patience.

"In truth, we come here with the gravest news, my lady," she said, forgetting my enjoinder to leave the talking to me. "Luminant Durehl

Vearist lies dead at the hands of one of his own clerics. A vile, wretched heretic named Arnabus who seeks to exert dominance over the Covenant of Martyrs. This creature also saw fit to abduct and torture the man who stands before you now, a soul I know we both cherish. As Alwyn's oldest friend and a true daughter of the Covenant, would you not wish to aid us in crushing this heresy and bringing the criminal Arnabus to justice?"

"Daughter of the Covenant, eh?" Lorine let out a faint laugh. "I am daughter to a man and woman who cut throats and poisoned folk for coin, and be assured they enjoyed their work, given they were so good at it. If either of them made it through the Divine Portals I would confess myself astonished. As for Alwyn and our long-standing friendship—" a wry but fond smile played over her lips as she spared me a short glance "—that, I'll grant you, warrants further consideration."

She clapped her hands together, causing the child in my arms to whimper in annoyance before his mother took him back. "But that can wait," Lorine said, carrying a now restless Bryndon to the door with a brisk step. "I must see to your welcoming feast and this lordling needs his midday feed."

"Time is against us . . ." Evadine began but Lorine had already hauled the door wide and exited the room.

"Delay your war for but one night, my lady," Lorine's voice echoed in response as she descended the tower steps. "I'm sure your soldiers will thank you for it."

The jugglers provided an amusing evening's entertainment, albeit through accident rather than intention. They consisted of a trio I assumed to be mother, father and son, and it was the latter who provided most of the merriment. His parents tossed their various balls and batons about with a lithe grace and skill that told of a lifetime's practice while the equally trim and athletic son clearly needed a few more years seasoning. Several times he dropped the batons hurled his way by his father, much to the hilarity of the audience of Covenant soldiery and local notables. On one occasion the lad took a leather ball full in the face when his mother cast it at him while balanced atop her husband's shoulders. Still, this clumsy youth reacted well to his own mistakes, responding to the jeers of the crowd with florid bows and grins that showed only affable good humour rather than the glowers of embarrassment frequently exhibited by his parents.

Evadine and I had been afforded the honour of sitting with Lorine at the long table. It was positioned atop a raised dais to provide the best view of the entertainment while also emphasising the duchess's status. The Anointed Lady enjoyed pride of place at Lorine's right while I sat to her left, eating but little of the many courses conveyed by a continual procession of servants. I found the peacock the most tasty, the unfamiliar meat rich and gamey, enhanced by a honey and rosemary glaze. However, the lingering effects of my captivity in the bowels of the Dire Keep made my appetite small, as did the tension instilled by Evadine's rigidly inexpressive demeanour throughout.

"You could have come to me, you know," Lorine commented after I related a carefully edited account of what had happened at the keep. "If the object was merely to discover what might be occurring at that old haunted ruin. I have my own . . . discreet resources."

"The value of a secret erodes with every ear that hears it," I replied. "Besides, I wasn't sure how Shilva Sahken would have reacted if I were to make free with intelligence meant only for me."

"Shilva." Lorine gave a rueful chuckle. "A woman I respected almost as much as I detested, and I detested her a great deal."

"Deckin always trusted her."

Once again her face darkened at mention of her departed lover, but this time she consented to offer a reply. "We both know he trusted a good many more people than he should have." She started a little as one of the juggler's batons landed on our table, shattering a crystal goblet and spattering us both with wine. Silence descended quickly, save for a few chuckles from the Covenant soldiers, these fading amid the abruptly thickened air. The clumsy youth stood in the centre of the feasting chamber, frozen in the act of catching an invisible baton. The lad's winning smile from moments before had a twitchy curve to it now, his parents flanking him in blank-faced trepidation.

"You missed," Lorine said, picking up the baton and tossing it back to the young juggler. Laughter erupted with the loudness that arises from relief, making me wonder if the Duchess of the Shavine Marches was always so lenient with cloddish hirelings.

"I think you've entertained us long enough for one night," Lorine went on, clapping her hands. "Master Dubbings, my guests require music!"

The juggling trio bowed and departed with a wise measure of haste while Dubbings, the grey-haired, stiff-backed master of ducal household business, clicked fingers and waved his arms about to summon a mandolin-bearing minstrel to the floor.

"You'll have to forgive the lack of choral accompaniment, my lady," Lorine said, inclining her head to Evadine. "Quintrell plays with an exquisite hand but even he admits his voice is somewhat frog-like." She turned to the waiting minstrel. "'The Mists Over the Water', if you would, Master Quintrell."

A few bars from the mandolin proved Lorine no liar. This man played with a deft but commanding touch, the notes pure and resonating with all the heart-tugging tragedy required of this particular song. As the melancholic tune filled the chamber my attention wandered to Ayin, for she always did love music. She sat at the end of the long table and those who didn't know her would have seen a winsome maid staring at the minstrel in mixed fascination and sadness. I saw small beads glimmer in her eyes, the music stirring her to a pitch of emotion that couldn't be roused by the sight of violent death. When the last few notes of the 'Mists Over the Water' faded away to loud applause, Ayin didn't clap, merely lowering her head, eyes closed and slim shoulders betraying a restrained shudder.

"Going somewhere, my lord?" Lorine asked as I rose from my chair.

"You provided us with fine entertainment this night, Duchess," I said. "It's only proper that I return the favour."

I knew better than to touch a hand to Ayin's shoulder, instead securing her attention with a faint rap of my knuckles to the table. "Plays well, doesn't he?" I asked, nodding to the minstrel who had begun strumming a lively tune.

"He overstressed the final note of the first verse," Ayin said, smooth brow creasing as she worked the heel of her hand into her eyes. "Otherwise, not bad, I s'pose."

"Duchess Lorine tells me he's a poor singer. It would seem a shame for the feast to pass without at least one song, don't you think?"

Ayin's eyes widened in alarm, shifting to survey the chamber and the many people at feast. "I . . . can't," she said.

"You've sung in front of folk before," I pointed out. "Hardly a night goes by in camp when you're not singing something."

"That's different." She lowered her head again, squirming a little as I thought how strange it was that she should be frightened of anything, not least the prospect of doing what she did best in front of an audience.

I leaned a little closer, speaking softly. "Your captain requires a distraction, and you will provide it, soldier."

A resentful scowl added another crease to her forehead causing me to take note of the meat fork sitting close to her hand. However, Ayin was ever a dutiful soul and, clenching her fists, got to her feet, chair scraping loudly on the wooden boards.

"My Lady Duchess," I said, voice raised as Ayin made her way from platform to floor. "It is my pleasure to present Trooper Ayin of the Covenant Company. She has consented to provide us with a song of her own creation."

"This little bird is a soldier?" Lorine asked, pursing her lips as she afforded Ayin a modicum of scrutiny.

"Yes she is," Evadine stated with glacial precision. "As fine and loyal a soldier as I have ever known." Her tone softened as she gave Ayin a warm smile. "With perhaps the purest voice in all Albermaine."

"Quite a boast." Lorine shrugged and raised her goblet to Ayin. "As you will, little bird. Quintrell is at your disposal."

Ayin bobbed her head in a jerky approximation of a bow and turned to the minstrel, speaking in hushed tones. At first, he regarded her with amused indulgence, but I saw his interest pique when she began to hum a tune. Even quiet and wordless, Ayin's voice had a power to command notice, especially from those steeped in music. Within a few moments, Quintrell began to reproduce her tune with his mandolin, the soft, lilting melody I recognised as the opening bars of "Who Will Sing for Me?", Ayin's eulogy for those lost on the Sacrifice March.

Clasping her hands together, she moved to the centre of the floor, allowing the mandolin to play for a short while before she began to sing. "*Who will sing for me, my dear? Who will sing for me? When the field is cleared and the harvest done, Who will sing for me?*"

The words and the tune were simple, easily picked up and unchallenging to even the coarsest voice, but when carried by Ayin it became something else, something far more complex that couldn't fail to find purchase on the heart. All other sound in the chamber fell away, eyes and ears rapt by the slender young woman with a voice that reached effortlessly to the lofty beams above.

"*I toiled all day with scythe and plough, Who will sing for me? With ne're a coin for the seed I sow, Who will sing for me?*"

I moved to Lorine's side, finding her as snared by Ayin as all others. She only consented to look my way when I touched her arm. I said nothing, merely inclining my head at a side door towards the rear of the chamber, one I knew led to a stretch of broad battlement known as the Duke's Perch. Lorine gave a rueful arch of her brows and got to her feet. It said much for the command of Ayin's voice that only a few of the Shavine nobles at the top table rose to mark their duchess's departure with a bow.

"That girl is quite remarkable," Lorine said, leading me through the door as the guard stationed there hastened to drag it open. "Where did you find her?"

The air greeting us on the Duke's Perch had the edge of late autumn wind to it, making me wrap my cloak about my shoulders. A few sentries lined the battlement but they all strode swiftly out of earshot in response to the duchess's dismissive wave. I followed her to the bulky, weathered crenelations, looking down at the sprawl of Ambriside and the forest beyond, the thick blanket of treetops dappled in silver by a full moon.

"Cutting Erchel's balls off in Callintor," I replied, seeing little point in concealing the truth.

"So, it truly wasn't you after all." A faint grin played over Lorine's lips as she spared me a sidelong glance. "I remember when I heard about Erchel's fate. Seemed a little extravagant for our Alwyn. 'The lad's a killer but only when he needs to be,' Deckin used to say. 'Need to temper him a good deal if he's to lead this band one day.' I reasoned that years in the Pit Mines had done more tempering than he ever could."

"That they did, but they didn't temper a liking for torment, even for Erchel, though the vicious little weasel surely deserved the end she gave him. As with many in the Covenant Company, Ayin is more than she appears."

"Mad singing girls, disgraced turncoat nobles, outlaw scribes." Lorine laughed shortly. "Your Risen Martyr shows a fondness for those with scant place in the world." All humour slipped away as she stood a little closer, eyes narrowing. When she spoke next, I heard an unwelcome judgement in her voice, one rich in maternal disapproval. "You're fucking her, aren't you?"

I said nothing, stiffening in annoyed discomfort. I couldn't decide if I was irked more by her insight or her censorious tone.

"At least you didn't insult me with a denial," Lorine muttered, resting her arms on the stone and shaking her head. "You and women, Alwyn. It was never a good mix. Gerthe, Martyrs preserve her soul, used to laugh about the ease of robbing you blind. Now you choose to sully the precious flesh of the Anointed Lady herself, Risen Martyr and divine servant of the Seraphile. A most base and carnal sin, committed by a notorious outlaw, no less."

"I'm a lord now," I muttered back, which earned me a waspish, snorting laugh.

"Let me tell you something, oh my wayward cub." Her voice became an urgent hiss as she leaned closer. "The sum of what I've learned about lords, ladies, and all others who claim nobility in this realm: it's all shit, and they know it. Titles mean nothing. Blood and kinship mean nothing. There are three things that matter in this realm: coin, land, and the ability to summon soldiers to fight those who would seek to take the first two from you. Everything else is a farce played by folk born into their role or come late to the stage, like me and you. Your divinely ordained bitch may have the most complex role of all. But it's still just that, Alwyn, an act, even if she doesn't know she's playing."

"I've seen things," I said, for some reason finding it hard to meet her eye. "Travelled far and witnessed much that shouldn't be, but is. In the Fjord Geld and the Caerith Wastes I saw enough to convince me that what she says is true. The Scourge actually happened, and when she tells me another is coming, I believe her, for her insight is real, divine or not."

I risked a glance at her features, finding a yet greater depth of disparagement in her glare. "Do I need to tell you who you sound like?" she asked.

"Hostler was mad. I am not."

"But *she* is. And don't pretend you don't see it. Madness in those we love can be a snare, one that can bind you just as much as it does them." She paused, features softening into sorrowful introspection. "I once told you I knew of Deckin's madness, but I followed him for the sake of the love we shared. And you know how that ended. What end will you follow your mad love to, I wonder?"

"The throne," I stated in bald honesty, knowing carefully phrased allusion would avail me nothing. "Before the year is out Evadine Courlain will be crowned the Ascendant Queen of Albermaine. When that happens, and harbour no doubt that it will, she will forget neither friend nor enemy."

"That woman has no friends, only those she'll use to serve her deluded mission, and that includes you. A woman like that doesn't love, she possesses. Willing or not, you've made yourself her slave and the only rewards a slave can expect for his labour are torment and death."

The flat certainty with which she spoke heralded an angry silence as I clenched my jaw to cage unwise words. At the time I told myself this rage came from Lorine's pig-headed, prejudiced folly. Now I know it to be the natural response of a fool hearing unwanted truth.

"If you want no part of her cause," I managed to grate out after a prolonged pause, "why bother receiving us at all?"

A gust of wind blew a tangle of copper curls into Lorine's eyes as she gazed out at the view, looking deep into the forest. "Last week I received a missive from our dear princess regent. It was a fine letter, neatly inscribed and carefully phrased. Princess Leannor thanked me for my loyal service at the Battle of the Vale and promised funds to succour the families of those who had lost folk in the fighting. She also avowed particular concern for my son and the need to ensure his proper schooling, given he will one day be duke of these Marches. The princess feels that the royal court would be the best place for such schooling, an education she expects to last several years."

"It's the Algathinet way," I said. "Build allegiance through a mix of kindness and threat. They'll seek to make Bryndon one of them, probably betroth him to a cousin of suitable age and station. All the while he remains in their clutches thereby ensuring his mother's continued loyalty. Rest assured, Duchess, the Ascendant Queen would never sunder a child from his mother so cruelly."

Lorine turned to face me, face pale save for the scattering of freckles across her nose and cheeks. Even after all these years the combination gave her a girlish appearance, although when she spoke her voice was that of an outlaw hardened by grim experience. "If you win," she said, "I had no hand in it, but I'll bend the knee to your mad Martyr all the same. If you lose, I had no hand in it and I'll cheer along with the mob when they hang her. I trust this is understood."

I inclined my head. "Of course, my lady."

She gave the smallest of nods. "You can have Captain Dervan and his Chosen Company for your war against the heretics in Athiltor. Any churls within the Shavine Marches who wish to march under the Anointed Lady's banner are also free to depart their lands, not that I'd be able to stop them in any case."

"And after that?"

"If war with the Algathinets ensues, it's your war, Alwyn. Until such time as I can gauge the winner, that is, whereupon you may well find yourself facing Dervan as an enemy rather than an ally. Don't look at me like that. You know how this game must be played. Still, if you're right, it won't come to that, will it? Which brings us to another matter."

So here it was, the culmination of this dark bargain. I remained silent, merely inclining my head in invitation. Stating a price for goods you've yet to purchase is never a good tactic.

"By my reckoning," Lorine said, "close to one-third of all farmland in the Shavine Marches is owned by the Covenant. Perhaps your Anointed Lady, in her wisdom, will share my belief that such a state of affairs is in need of rectification."

"That depends on how much rectification would be required."

"All of it. Plus the rents for the last two years. I've little doubt the Covenant's coffers are deep enough to cover it."

Promise her whatever is needed, Evadine had said but I held off on stating my agreement. Lorine would suspect a trap if I agreed without haggling. Besides, doing so chafed my outlaw's instincts. "One year of rents," I said. "And half the land."

"Two-thirds," she countered. Smiling, she extended her hand for me to kiss. "And I'll throw in the minstrel, since he accompanies your little bird so very well."

Chapter Three

Quintrell was Lorine's spy, of that I had no doubt at all. A minstrel who couldn't sing most likely had to supplement his income by means beyond music. Besides, he had the mostly silent manner and careful eyes of a soul for whom observing while remaining unobserved was second nature. I didn't blame Lorine for placing an agent in our midst, she had an investment to protect after all. Nor did I doubt the minstrel knew I divined his true role within moments of him reporting to me the following morning. Even my relatively short tenure as Evadine's spymaster had taught me that a surprisingly large portion of this strange game is played out in the open.

"Minstrels are often widely travelled, are they not?" I asked him. He had presented himself at the stables where the Mounted and Scout companies were preparing to march out. He wore plain garb today rather than the motley silks of the previous night, his mandolin consigned to a waxed bundle and slung over his shoulder. I saw no weapon on his belt but felt there must surely be at least one hidden knife somewhere about his person.

"That they are, my lord," he agreed, an affable smile on his lips. He was not a particularly handsome specimen, but well groomed, his beard and moustache trimmed short and oiled into spear points. He also had an accent I couldn't place, mixing inflections from all duchies while being too rough for a noble and too refined for a commoner. "I've played from one end of the realm to the other, although never had a warmer welcome than in Duchess Lorine's house."

"Ever venture further? Across the sea, or the southern mountains? I've use for folk who can converse in other tongues."

"Sadly, our own tongue is the only one I know." He was a good liar, but I saw it in the fractional hesitation before he gilded the untruth with another bow. "Though I've memorised a few Ascarlian phrases thanks to my time in the Fjord Geld."

I grunted and heaved my saddle on to Blackfoot's back. "Do you know letters?"

This time he chose not to lie, perhaps warned by Lorine that too much falsehood would surely gain my notice. "I do, my lord. A fair hand, so I'm told, though not as fair as yours, I'm sure."

"So am I." I turned to Ayin who stood regarding the conversation with an unusual tension, arms crossed and head half lowered. "What do you think, Trooper Ayin?" I asked her. "Happy to teach this one your songs?"

"Only if he teaches me to play," she said, the words a rapid tumble, and I saw how she darted a glance at the mandolin on the minstrel's back. It occurred to me that she rarely expressed a desire for anything and found the act of doing so uncomfortable. I guessed it to be yet another legacy of her dread mother; Ayin had learned at an early age that asking for things brought only punishment.

"How about it, Master Quintrell?" I asked the minstrel. "Ever take a student?"

"A few." He inclined his head at Ayin who, I saw with a spasm of astonishment, actually blushed. "Though none with so fine a voice. It shall be my pleasure to teach you the ways of the mandolin, my dear."

"Very well," I said, reaching for the saddle's straps. "Mount up, I assume the duchess was kind enough to provide you a horse. We ride within the hour."

"I shall, my lord." Quintrell bowed again then gave a hesitant glance over his shoulder. "But, if I may first crave another indulgence." He beckoned to a figure standing in the shadowed lee of the doorway. The youth who stepped into the light did so at such a crouch I at first thought him the victim of some deformity. As he came closer, still huddled, I recognised the clumsy juggler from the feast. Unlike Quintrell, this one was almost jarringly handsome, although the pleasing, square-jawed arrangement of his features was marred by the livid bruise on his cheek.

"I present Adlar Spinner, my lord," the minstrel said. "With your permission, he should like to accompany us."

"As your servant?"

"As a soldier," the juggler said, raising his head for the first time. He spoke with a forceful note but blanched and lowered his face once again upon meeting my eye. "If it please your lordship."

Another spy? I immediately discounted the thought upon noting the youth's evident fear, something punctuated by the nervous squeal of his guts. Such things were very hard to fake.

"Straighten up," I snapped. Adlar Spinner gave another shudder then complied, losing his crouch to stand a few inches shorter than I. His frame had a sturdy, honed look to it that told of constant exercise but, save for the bruise on his cheek, no evidence he had known a day's violence in his life.

"Your father give you that?" I asked, pointing to the bruise.

"I fell, my lord."

"Balls you did. Here's a word of advice for you, lad: don't lie to a man when you're seeking his favour, you've no skill for it. So, was it your father?"

The juggler blinked and fidgeted, shooting a glance at Ayin before answering. "My mother, my lord," he said then forced a smile. "Gets a temper on her when our performances don't go so well."

I had expected a shamefaced confession as to his father's violent, possibly drunken ways. It would have given me the opportunity to ask Adlar if he had returned the blow in kind then dismiss him when he said no. *Come back when you lay the bastard out, boy. No use for milksops in this company.* Taking a punch from his mother put a different complexion on things.

"Can you ride?" I asked him, staring into his eyes to ensure he remembered my injunction against lying.

"In truth, no, my lord."

"Know how to wield a halberd?"

Swallowing, he shook his head.

"Sword? Bow?"

Another shake of his head.

"War's coming fast upon us." I turned away to finish saddling Blackfoot. "And I've no time to play the tutor to a clumsy jackanapes. If you're so keen on marching under the Lady's banner, pick up a pitchfork and fall in step with the churls."

"Adlar," Quintrell said. "Show Lord Alwyn what you can do."

The quiet assurance in the minstrel's tone caused me to look again at Adlar, finding the lad had resumed his fidgeting.

"If you've a skill to sell," I said, "let's see it."

"I'll need a knife," he said. "Mother sold all of mine back in Farinsahl."

"Here," Ayin said, plucking one of her blades from its sheath at the small of her back. Twirling it, she stepped forward to offer it to Adlar.

"And," the juggler coughed, "a playing card, or piece of parchment, if it please you."

"The Anointed Lady doesn't allow games of chance in her company," I said.

"Not to worry." Quintrell gave Adlar a reassuring wink and produced a deck from the satchel at his side. "These are a mite tattered, but will serve, I think." He plucked one of the cards from the deck, holding it up. "The Green Lady? She's always been lucky for me."

Adlar adjusted his grip on the knife then nodded to the minstrel. Quintrell flicked his hand and the card spun into the air for the smallest fraction of a second before Adlar's arm blurred and Ayin's knife flashed, too fast to see. However, I did hear the thud of it striking the stable's timber wall, my eyes snapping to the sight of the handle shuddering, the blade skewered precisely through the Green Lady's head.

"A pleasing trick," I said, recalling an outlaw from Deckin's band who could perform a similar feat. A Cordwainer fleeing the rope in his homeland, the fellow had too wayward a tongue to last long enough to demonstrate the practical use of his skill. Myself and the other cubs had tried to emulate the man's ability only to earn a cuffing from Lorine when we lost a knife attempting to sink it into a broad oak from ten paces.

"But just a trick," I added. "Can you do anything else?"

The youth lowered his head again, fumbling for words so Quintrell spoke for him. "You said you had a use for those who speak other tongues, my lord. Adlar speaks four."

"Really?" I kept my gaze on the juggler, receiving a nod in response. "What are they?"

"Ascarlian, my lord. Also, Etriskan, as spoken beyond the southern seas, Ishtan, the most common language of the east, and Vergundian, at least the dialect spoken in the central plains."

This gave me pause. What little I had heard of the plainsmen's tongue was a meaningless babble and they were notorious for their insularity, meaning few outsiders could speak their language. "How do you come to know Vergundian?"

"My mother is half-Vergundian, my lord. She taught me."

That explains the temper. "Say something, then," I told him. "Something in the savages' tongue."

This was a calculated barb, intended to nudge him to anger, but he merely blinked and spoke a short phrase. "*Trekash iret mekrova.* 'Arrows are truth.' The creed of my mother's clan." He fell silent, looking at me in expectation. "Did I . . . say it correctly, my lord?"

"How the fuck should I know? There are Vergundian mercenaries at Athiltor, perhaps some are even your kin. Think you can sink a knife into them if need be?"

He forced some additional straightness into his spine, meeting my eye. "I'll do what's required of a soldier in the Lady's service, my lord."

"You'd better. Death by flogging is an unpleasant fate." I turned to Ayin. "Give him Woodsman's horse and enter his name in the ledger, Scout Company. Half pay until he's trained. And," I added, glancing at her knife still pinning the Green Lady to the wall, "find him some knives."

It is my experience that those who gain a taste of war soon lose their appetite for more. When steel clashes and the bolts and arrows fly it's not long before would-be heroes and braggarts discover unforeseen depths of cowardice. Similarly, ardent believers, finding themselves faced with unvarnished evidence of mortality, will often transform into philosophising doubters keen to find a quiet, peaceful corner to continue their meditations.

So I will confess a measure of surprise at the willingness of the common folk of the Shavine Marches to once again flock to the Anointed Lady's banner. I glimpsed a few familiar faces among the gathering throng as we began the march to Athiltor, the fervent devotees who had followed Evadine's first progress to the holy city. Denied battle then, it was apparent they hungered for one now. I saw features hardened with determination, some bearing the scars of their previous service. Others were the guileless, wide-eyed, open-mouthed sheep swept up in the fervour and excitement of an encounter with history. These, I knew, were the most likely to melt away at the first clash, but their numbers remained impressive.

Bitter experience won on the Sacrifice March had made me glean all the supplies I could from Lorine, something that required an additional promise of payment beyond our already struck bargain. I also insisted Evadine appoint veterans of previous crusades to lead companies of adherents, making sure they carried sufficient gear and food to at least form camp and feed themselves come evening. Furthermore, the number of miles to be covered per day was restricted to no more than ten, easy for trained soldiers but not a mob of churls. As with the grim trek to the Vale, lack of proper weapons was the starkest deficiency in our growing host. Those who had answered the Lady's call before knew to bring an axe or billhook but most had neglected to arm themselves at all. On this point, Lorine proved intractable, mostly for want of stocks rather than thrifty obstinacy.

"My storehouses are filled with grain, not blades, Alwyn," she told me on the third day out from Castle Ambris. The duchess had decided to ride with her Chosen Company at least part of the way, a sign of ducal approval for the Anointed Lady's cause. "I said I'd let my churls march with your Martyr. I didn't promise to arm them."

Unwilling to lead a mostly weaponless host to Athiltor, Evadine agreed to my suggestion that seven-foot pikes be cut from the forest. The work required three days, stretched to five by the continual arrival of more recruits. The pikes were crude things, just stripped branches with one end whittled to a point, but they were far better than nothing. Although clearly impatient, Evadine acceded to another four-day interruption to the march while Wilhum and I did our best to instil some semblance of discipline upon this ragged host. As expected, the strictures of military life sent many scurrying back to their farms and villages, but most stayed and suffered through the daily bouts of drill. When we resumed the march, it was an untidy but mostly cohesive column that snaked along the eastward road, resembling a monstrous centipede in the way it bristled from end to end with pikes.

The swelling of our ranks began to drop away when we approached the border with Alberis. They still came, but in their dozens rather than hundreds, bringing tales of others who had opted to flock to Athiltor rather than the Lady. Listening to these accounts, it became clear to me that Evadine's rise had never been as universally lauded among the faithful as I thought. Many were so steeped in Covenant orthodoxy as to doubt her Martyrdom, although had wisely kept such sentiments concealed until this moment of crisis. Even more surprising was the depth and scope of this divide in doctrinal adherence.

"Lost it to my own brother, my lord," one surprisingly cheery soul informed me when I enquired after the bloody patch over his right eye. "Spoke against the Lady, he did. Called her . . ." He faltered, casting nervous glances at the pike-bearing recruits filing past. "Names best unspoken," the one-eyed man continued with a cough. "Couldn't abide that so we got to fighting. I lost an eye. He lost his life and I'd call it a fair bargain. Least now I'll get to plough his fields with a steady hand. He was a terrible drunkard as well as a heretic, see?"

Others told of long-standing neighbours transformed into bitter enemies, families sundered as sons warred with fathers or sisters with brothers, all for the sake of the Risen Martyr. Since the start of the march I had been industrious in spreading the story of Luminant Durehl's murder and the council's supposed seizure by the devious schemer Arnabus. I retain a perverse pride in these acid-toned missives in which I imbued Arnabus and the dread Captain Sorkin with all manner of unnatural malignancy.

"*Know that this false cleric and his captain serve not the Seraphile but the Malecite,*" one of my more strident passages intoned. "*Know that they practise the most vile rituals. Know that children have fallen into their clutches and their blood spilled in arcane rites to slake the Malecite thirst for blood.*"

I was, of course, no stranger to deceit, but even I consider these pamphlets to represent an apogee of the liar's art. Arnabus did certainly possess unnatural abilities and I harboured no small measure of malice towards him as a result. His intrusion into my dreams in the guise of Erchel's ghost left me with an abiding sense of violation for which I intended to extract fulsome redress. But, despite the cleric's evident malevolence, I had no real sense that his actions arose from any adherence to the Malecite, not that it prevented me from pretending otherwise.

The fact that my disingenuous pamphlets found so many ardent believers is something I look upon now with as much shame as professional satisfaction. Ayin and the few other scribes in our number were industrious in producing copies. These were in turn handed to scouts and any recruit with a horse who would carry them to towns and villages within two days' ride. My artful dishonesty was then proclaimed to all who would listen and the pamphlets pressed into the hands of the literate. I was confident the stories would grow with the telling, acquiring more lurid details than I could conjure, and so it proved. By the time we neared the Siltern River, there were those among our ranks willing to swear to the Martyrs that servants of the Heretic Ascendant had sacrificed their son or daughter to the Malecite before their very eyes. Disturbingly, most appeared to believe this had happened despite cautious enquiry of those who knew these folk revealed them to be mostly childless.

"No such thing as a bad lie," Lorine quipped one morning, another pearl of Deckin's wisdom. "As long as it's useful." We had just watched Evadine suffer through one particularly gruesome account sobbed out by a kneeling man in ragged garb, his feet dark with the mud of several days' travel.

"They cut her from chin to belly, my lady!" the fellow wailed before casting himself at the Anointed Lady's feet. "Drank her blood and laughed and danced, they did! Oh my poor dear sweet Illsah . . ."

"He said her name was Elmah when he started," Lorine observed, turning away and not bothering to keep the disgust from her face. "What strange magic you weave, my lord Scribe."

"Words have power," I agreed with a shrug. "Especially when you write them down. As for lies, I learned long ago that you can only really sell them to a willingly gulled audience."

"Do you think she knows that?" Lorine cast a pointed glance at Evadine, now resting a comforting hand on the weeping father's head. "Or have lies and truth all become a jumble for her?"

She spoke with an incautious volume that brought a warning scowl on my brow. "Truth always wins out in the end, my lady Duchess," I said. "Once this is all settled, I'm confident it will once again ascend to a place of reverence in this realm. Under the rule of the Ascendant Queen, the Testament of Martyr Sihlda Doisselle will predominate in Covenant lore, and there was never a better guide to both truth and justice."

The disgust on Lorine's face shifted into squinting doubt for a moment, then, as she moved closer to me, hardened into grim realisation. "So," she sighed, "that mad bitch really has captured you." A sad, shallow curve formed on her lips and she raised her hand to stroke my cheek, a gesture I knew to signal a farewell. "I find I much preferred you a cynic, Alwyn."

"Anyone can be a cynic," I said. "Cynicism is not wisdom, merely an excuse to watch the world burn when you should be helping to quench the flames."

Lorine arched her brows. "But are you quenching, or stoking?" Her hand dropped to her side and she stepped back, not allowing me the chance to reply. "I believe, my lord, it is time for me to return to my duties. The work of a duchess is far more burdensome than I ever imagined. Besides, I believe I've had my fill of witnessing battles, and I'm sure your Martyr will be glad to see the back of me."

I bowed low. "Your diligence is rightly famed, Duchess. I shall convey your gracious parting words to the Anointed Lady."

"My thanks, my lord." As I straightened, Lorine came close, arms enfolding me in an embrace of surprising warmth. "For the first time, I'm not entirely sure we'll ever meet again," she murmured into my ear. "But I do hope so, Alwyn. You and Bryndon are the only true family I have left." As she drew back, she clasped my hands and I felt something small and hard against my palm. "Parting gift," she said, voice much softer now. "One of my mother's favourites. The ingredients are very expensive and difficult to mix in just the right proportions. It's so potent it doesn't even need to be drunk. A single drop to the skin is enough and it barely leaves a mark. The effects are akin to a seizure of the heart, the kind that took my dear husband from me not so long ago."

She gripped my hand tight, pressing the bottle into my flesh, gaze steady with unmistakable meaning.

"I know my scrolls too, Alwyn," she said. "And, at heart every Martyr's tale is a tragedy, one that holds no room for love. Mad or not, she surely knows that." Releasing my hand, Duchess Lorine Blousset turned and strode away, shouting for her servants to fetch her horse.

"Does it look the same?" Evadine asked as we reined to a halt atop a rise a quarter-mile south of our objective. Coming here had been my idea, one I wasn't sure she would agree to. In fact, she seized upon it with a bright-eyed enthusiasm I felt stemmed from a desire to be away from the main body of her growing host for a day or two.

She sermonised less these days, the nightly invective that had once been a feature of life in the Covenant Company was a thing of the past now. She still led supplications once a week but her sermons were shorter and more prone to utilise passages from the Martyr Scrolls, where before she relied on unrehearsed words arising from nowhere but her heart. I had yet to ask her why, but saw a new reticence in the way she spoke to the common folk, a closed stiffness where before she had greeted them with warm tactility. I ascribed this shift, something in truth I had begun to notice after my return from Caerith lands, to the ever increasing burden of her responsibilities. Soon she would be a queen, not just a Martyr, and while a queen should serve her people, she cannot be of the people.

These, at least, were the comforting tales with which I salved my swelling disquiet. For, to be in love, I know now, is to be a fool.

Below us the vast, spiral-tiered crater of the Pit Mines lay in its grim, grey-sided majesty. "Yes," I told her. "Much the same." By my estimation, the famed royal prison was mostly unchanged save for the sparseness of its inmates, just a few dozen standing about in small, fearful clusters. The bodies littering the ramp were more numerous.

"No sign of guards," the Widow said, bringing her mount to a halt nearby. She had taken a troop of scouts to the keep overlooking the mines, bearing word of the Anointed Lady's arrival and demanding the lord in residence, whoever he might be these days, open the gates and depart this place immediately. "Keep's empty too," Juhlina added, "save for a few servants. They said the lord and his men did some killing when they caught word of our approach but took to their heels this morning." She inclined her head at the inmates below. "It seems strange this lot didn't run off too."

"No," I replied, kicking my heels to urge Blackfoot to a walk. "Not everyone forsakes their home so easily."

The chain on the gate took a few blows with a pickaxe before it consented to shatter. For many years the great oaken doors had rarely been fully opened and ancient hinges groaned and squealed as they swung aside. The few inmates nearby instantly fled at the sight of us, moving in a slow shuffle that told of weakened muscles and a parlous diet. One stumbled to her knees when she tried to run, attempted a feeble rise then gave up with a hopeless sigh. As had often been the case when I dwelt within these walls, I couldn't place the age of this inmate. She stared up at me with tired, resigned eyes set in features besmirched by soot, dirt and the creases that come with hardship rather than passage of time.

"How long since they fed you?" I asked, crouching at her side, the sunken hollows of her face stark with shadows.

"Days," she rasped, the grating croak of her voice causing me to reach for my canteen. "Punishment, his lordship said," she went on after a weak gulp or two. "He did that, sometimes. And—" her weary eyes slipped to a nearby corpse, dusted in gravel, dried blood discolouring the sackcloth garb "—this, when he got angry. Got terrible angry last day or so. Guessed you'd be the reason, eh?"

She bared yellowed teeth in a smile then coughed up something that stained her lips dark red. "The name of this lord?" I enquired, taking hold of her shoulders to stop her collapsing into the dirt, feeling the bones beneath her threadbare garb.

"Never . . ." she smiled again ". . . thought to ask." Her eyes dimmed and she sagged, though I felt the faint thrum of a pulse when I put a hand to her chest.

"See to this woman!" I snapped, summoning soldiers to my side. "Get her to the keep. Water but only a little food for now. Gather up these others too. Make it known that they are freed by the word of the Anointed Lady."

Questioning of the surviving inmates revealed the recently fled Lord Warden of the King's Mines to be a knight named Aurent Vellinde. A man of far more industry and cruelty than the late Eldurm Gulatte, it was apparent Sir Aurent had accrued a long list of crimes during his tenure, the worst of which being his hasty massacre of prisoners when word of the Anointed Lady's approach reached him. Astute as well as sadistic, the lord warden clearly had a gift for gauging a changing wind. Apparently, he had also heard my story and decided not to risk a visit with so uncertain an outcome. I sent the Widow and my best trackers in pursuit but knew their quarry had too great a start to be caught. However, I did make careful note of Vellinde's name and the documents found in his chambers were useful in providing clues to his future whereabouts.

"Death by hanging," Evadine promised me that night. "One of the first decrees of the Ascendant Queen the moment she sits on the throne. Unless my lord chamberlain would like something more elaborate."

We lay together in the lord warden's bed, entwined atop a mattress where, it occurred to me, poor lovelorn Eldurm had once lain, his mind no doubt beset by dreams of the woman I held in my arms. I had seen enough to concede the possibility that ghosts may have substance in this world and couldn't suppress a shudder at the thought of the dead knight's spectre standing over us, his grey, rotted face set in miserable, depthless envy.

"Lord chamberlain?" I asked. Despite our unquiet recent exertions, I felt a need to keep my voice low. This chamber was three storeys above the main hall where the rest of the Scout Company bedded down. I knew most would never even entertain the notion that Evadine and I were engaged in anything other than planning the coming campaign, but maintaining some measure of circumspection seemed wise.

"You'll require a suitably grand title if you're to be my consort." She nuzzled at my ear. "Or do you find it not grand enough, I wonder."

Consort. The word rang with hollow absurdity in my head, but so did all the alternatives. *Husband. Prince . . . king?* I was and would never be any of those things. A Risen Martyr had no need of a spouse, or any form of base human love, not when she was filled with the grace of the Seraphile.

The feel of her lips on my neck was enticing, but I shifted away from her, swinging my legs off the mattress to sit up. The lord warden's chamber was dark save for a faint glimmer from the embers smoking in the fireplace. Still, I remembered this room well. Sir Aurent had seen fit to adorn the walls with various weaponry and shields, presumably trophies or loot from his battles and tourneys. Such vanity had never troubled Eldurm, for all his faults. It made me hate Aurent more while deepening my fear of his predecessor's ghost.

"What's wrong?" Evadine asked, stroking a hand down my back.

"I wrote you many letters here," I said, my eyes drifting to the shadowed bulk of the desk near the window. "Or rather, I wrote letters for Lord Eldurm to sign. I always wondered how many of my words you actually troubled yourself to read."

"For a time I read all his letters in full. I felt I owed him that much. I knew how badly he had fallen, you see?" The mattress bounced as she sat up, arms enfolding me, chin resting on my shoulder. "Poor old Eldurm was a victim of a spell I never cast, not knowingly. I stopped reading his letters in any detail when I noticed how much his wordsmithing had improved. The penmanship was too accomplished, the contents too poetic. His words had ever been clumsy, but they were his words, and they were true. Your words were plainly written by a soul who had no love for me at all." She put her lips close to my ear, voice soft and breath hot. "What letters would you write to me now, my lord?"

Lust stirred with fierce inevitability, but still I didn't reach for her. Eldurm was not the only ghost in this place and I was preoccupied by the tour I had taken of the Pit's deepest shafts. There I found a small nook in the tunnel wall where once a foolish, arrogant youth had begun his second education under a woman now proclaimed a Martyr. *Also a murderer*, a treacherous voice from the darker corners of my mind reminded me with sibilant cruelty. *She collapsed the tunnel, remember? She killed them all. All those faithful idiots . . .*

Evadine's embrace tightened as another shudder ran through me. "Why did we come here, Alwyn?" she asked me. "What did you hope to find?"

A pertinent question for which I had no answer. There had been a faint hope that I might discover one of Sihlda's congregation here. Carver perhaps, somehow miraculously spared Sihlda's final judgement on the damned souls who followed her. Mayhap he had continued to live out his days revering the woman who had killed his brothers and sisters in faith. But Carver was dead. They all were, nothing but rot and bones made part of the substance of this dreadful place. More than the false hope of survivors was the basic need to see it again, walk the same tunnels where I had transformed from thief to scribe, look upon that mean nook and feel Sihlda's presence once more. But, if she were among the ghosts littering this crater of horrors, like Eldurm, she refused to make herself known.

"If my queen would be so gracious as to grant me a boon," I said. "I want the Pit Mines destroyed. The shafts all collapsed and the crater filled in. What was done here was never justice, merely slavery born of greed. I submit that the Ascendant Queen's reign should be free of such things."

She clasped my chin with gentle fingers, guiding my lips to hers, voice grave with a sincere promise. "Granted, my lord. With all my heart."

Chapter Four

We spent another three days at the Pit Mines while I oversaw the caravanning of the iron ore recently hewn from the seams. All the heaving carts would be transported to Duchess Lorine in lieu of payment for the supplies provided to the Covenant Host. The shafts would remain unworked until the time came for their destruction, but I saw little point in forgoing easy profit.

Most of the former inmates, those capable of movement, chose to join the Anointed Lady's cause and march in our wake as we returned to the main body of the crusade. During our stay, Evadine had resumed her compassionate ways in tending to these unfortunates, winning them over with her usual effortless combination of kindness and carefully phrased solicitation. In truth, thanks to the murderous efforts of Sir Aurent Vellinde, the freed miners made a meagre contribution to our numbers, the strength of which began to worry me when the host forded the Siltern to tread upon the soil of Alberis.

"We were gaining ten to twenty a day the last few weeks," Ayin reported that evening as the Anointed Lady's Crusade made camp. Evadine had retired to her tent, once again without providing a sermon, leaving me to review our current dispositions and the state of our gathered intelligence. My status as de facto marshal of this host remained unspoken but also uncontested. Strictly speaking, Wilhum and I held equal rank but he exhibited no resentment at Evadine ceding command to me, apparently content with leading the Anointed Lady's cavalry. As my keenest eye for numbers, Ayin had fallen into the role of both adjutant and quartermaster. Tonight she came armed with her ledgers and tallies that told a disquieting story. "Today we had a grand total of five, and one of them had a bad wound to the buttocks. A crossbow bolt loosed by his own father when he ran off."

"Folk are certainly of a different stripe here," the Widow confirmed. With my attentions focused on the entire host, leadership of the Scout Company fell to her and she had been diligent in her duties, sending patrols far and wide. "Today we happened upon a village where they'd hung their Supplicant from the spire of his own shrine for speaking in support of the Lady. Also found one of our proclaimers lying in a ditch with his throat cut and pamphlets stuffed in his mouth."

"Our total strength?" I asked Ayin.

"Eight thousand, one hundred and thirty-two," she replied with customary promptness. "Though, Supplicant Delric says at least one of those that followed you from the Pit Mines is unlikely to see the dawn. Also, he said to tell you that the rest will be capable of no more than tossing a few stones at the heretics."

"Put them on the carts," I said. "They'll serve as drovers until they get their strength back." Turning to the Widow, I continued, "There'll be no more pamphlets. The proclaimers will stay with the host from now on. Scouts are to patrol in groups of five at least. Send that minstrel and his knife-juggling friend to the villages ahead of us. They'll make out they're paupered players fleeing the oncoming war and gauge the allegiance of the locals. We'll send recruiters wherever they find folk in favour of the Lady's Crusade and skirt those likely to be troublesome."

"All of northern Alberis is likely to be troublesome," Wilhum said. "There's nowhere in the whole of Albermaine more wedded to Covenant orthodoxy."

"We don't have to take the land," I replied. "Or the people. Just the holy city. With that, we have the Covenant."

"Eight thousand is a decent number. But even with the duchess's soldiers, we've at best a thousand trained troops among this mob."

"Eamond must have reached Couravel by now. Swain and Ofihla will have their companies on the march. Three thousand veterans, foot and horse. Once we join with them, this war is won." I paused, grimacing. "Save the actual fighting."

"Assuming Leannor allows us the leisure to settle this matter. Or that Arnabus and his outlaw captain remain content to sit and await our approach."

"Much of war is conducted in ignorance of the enemy's intentions." I couldn't recall where I'd read this rejoinder, and may even have come up with it myself. Either way, it seemed appropriate. "This one is no different. Lord Wilhum, henceforth you will keep the Mounted Company within sword reach of the Anointed Lady at all times. If Arnabus and Thessil do choose to venture out and contest our advance, she will surely be their principal target."

The royal messenger found us ten days later, announced by the fluttering Algathinet banner cresting a hilltop to the south as the hour tipped past noon. The herald rode at the head of a twelve-strong band of mounted kingsmen, none of them knights as far as I could tell. I had wondered if Leannor would send Sir Ehlbert, the word of the King's Champion being so much harder to ignore than this court functionary. The fact that she hadn't could indicate unspoken approval for our course, the Princess Regent having no more love for the Luminants' Council than did Evadine. The contents of her missive to the Risen Martyr, however, tended to exhibit the opposite sentiment, albeit in suitably floral language.

"We are aware of the grievous harm and insult done to the Anointed Lady by the actions of the rogue cleric Arnabus," the messenger read from an unfurled scroll while perched atop a fine black mare. I assumed the beast had been bred for its placidity for it continued to chew its bit and remain still throughout the recitation. Rather than receive the royal missive in camp, Evadine had ridden out to meet him with myself, Wilhum and the full Mounted Company. The fact that Covenant soldiery outnumbered those of the crown by a considerable margin was not missed by the kingsmen. Unlike the messenger's mare, they fidgeted in constant agitation, worried eyes roving the unwelcoming faces of the riders flanking the Risen Martyr.

"That these are crimes under law of both Crown and Covenant is not disputed," the messenger went on in his carefully modulated tones, stripped of accusation or approval, "and, as such, they require an accounting before the appropriate courts. Therefore, in furtherance of the peace I know to be the cherished desire of both the king and the Anointed Lady," the messenger paused, just for a second, his throat working to banish a catch, "all those currently following the Lady's banner are commanded to return to their homes and allotted lands forthwith. Lady Evadine's presence is formally requested at court where the Princess Regent will receive her full account of this matter and take all necessary steps to ensure justice is served."

The messenger, marked as no fool by the way he smothered a nervous cough, walked his mare towards Evadine, arm outstretched to proffer the scroll. When she made no move to accept it, the cough succeeded in escaping the messenger's throat. "I . . ." He swallowed. "I am instructed to remind Lady Evadine of the oath she gave on bended knee to Good King Tomas not so long ago. Said oath binds your service to King Tomas's heirs, as I'm sure my lady recalls."

Evadine said nothing, merely turning to me with a raised eyebrow.

"Your message has been noted, good sir," I told him with bland courtesy.

His eyes flicked between myself and Evadine. Behind him the agitation of the kingsmen grew a notch, warhorses tossing their heads as they sensed the thickening tension. "Then," the messenger ventured, "you have no reply for the Princess Regent?"

"Princess Regent," Evadine repeated, voice soft and a puzzled crease to her brow. "I know this person not. I do know Leannor Algathinet currently calls herself by various titles, but I will not sully my soul with the deceit of acknowledging falsehood. If, good sir, you are minded to tell her anything, tell her that. Now, I bid you good day and safe travels."

One of the kingsmen bridled at this, hand slipping towards his sword. He was forestalled by the commanding bark of his sergeant, but not before Wilhum and the Mounted Company had begun drawing their own steel.

"Sheath your blades!" Evadine snapped. "These men come to me in peace and will depart so. Spilling blood at a parley is something I leave to others."

The messenger blinked, disconcerted by the pointed reference to Leannor's actions at the Vale. However, his outrage didn't prevent him walking his mare back to his own line. Once again, the man's lack of foolishness made itself plain in the short bow he offered Evadine before wordlessly riding off, the kingsmen close behind.

I watched them disappear over the hilltops to the south then glanced at Evadine, broaching a careful murmur. "Open defiance might not be wise at this juncture. Not with one war yet unfought."

Evadine merely smiled and patted a hand to Ulstan's neck before tugging his reins and turning him about. "We have stepped beyond mortal laws now, Alwyn. Henceforth, only the Seraphile may command me."

I sent the Widow off to shadow the royal messenger's party to ensure they hadn't been accompanied by a larger body of troops. Juhlina returned after three days reporting the country south of our line of march clear of all forces, though she had seen a good many people heading to and from Athiltor.

"Those moving south seemed a good deal more ragged than those going north," the Widow said. "We managed to question a few of both, made out like we were free swords deciding which side to throw in with. Those going south were all from Athiltor. From what they told us, life in the holy city isn't especially pleasant just now. Lot of folk being flogged or even hanged for heresy. There's Vergundians and various other ne'er-do-wells hanging about and helping themselves to whatever they fancy. Every able body has been conscripted into the Council Company, but desertion is a constant problem. Plenty of orthodox-ites came flocking in when word of the Lady's Crusade started to spread, but many left soon after. The Divine Captain is too fond of the lash and too spare with the coin."

"Arnabus?" I asked. "The council?"

"Talk is one of the Luminants is now dangling upside down from the cathedral spire. Seems Arnabus ordered him hung by his ankles until he died. Before hanging him, they stripped him naked and carved the words 'Traitor to the Covenant' into his belly. Arnabus himself is rarely seen outside the cathedral, though the Divine Captain is said to be everywhere at once, overseeing work on the defences or sniffing out fresh necks for the noose."

"Did you hear any word of Swain?" For the past two days I had expected to receive news of the Covenant Company proper. It was my intention to merge our forces amid the open country south-west of the holy city, there to engage in some much needed reorganisation and training before advancing north.

"Neither word nor sign," the Widow said. "But if they'd come to grief we would have heard tell of a battle by now."

"Rest the scouts tonight. Come the morn, divide them into parties of three and have them range across all points south for ten miles. Any who happen upon Captain Swain are to tell him to bring his host directly to Athiltor with all haste. We'll endeavour to rendezvous at the crossroads where the eastern and northern King's Roads meet."

"And if we don't find them?" Juhlina directed a pointed glance at the surrounding encampment, untidy by most military standards, and the ragged clusters of pike-bearing churls blundering through their nightly drill. Her doubtful tone and disparaging scowl invited a rebuke I didn't voice. The Widow's demeanour since the Dire Keep had been even more taciturn than usual, but also exhibited a good deal of unspoken knowledge, especially whenever her gaze drifted towards Evadine. Still, I valued her candour and the insight of one untroubled by blind devotion to the Risen Martyr.

"Then," I said, "we'll soon find out if this lot are as devoted as they claim."

Since my encounter with Danick Thessil at the Dire Keep I had known he would prove a canny opponent. A veteran soldier's experience married to outlaw instincts made him a man not to be underestimated. Yet, when it came, his first gambit in this war still succeeded in taking me by surprise, shamed as I am to admit it.

The Lady's Crusade took three more days to approach within striking distance of the holy city. The crossroads where I had hoped to find Swain's troops stood barren, the small hamlet surrounding it silent and abandoned. The carts that would normally have busied this meeting of trade routes were notably absent. So were those who sold wares and drink to drovers and traders. I knew by now that people wishing no part of imminent battle had an uncanny knack of disappearing when the hour was at hand, vanishing to whatever refuge they could find amid hills or forest. Years of war had made this a habitual migration for many, as much an aspect of life as the harvest or stocking up for the winter. I drew some comfort from this, reasoning that if there was ever a land in need of peace, it was Albermaine. When Evadine rose to don the crown, who but the mad would wish to contend her? Such, dearest reader, are the delusions of those lost in the maze of love.

With the Scout Company off in search of Swain I was obliged to press Wilhum's riders into patrol duty, dispatching him with two-thirds of his strength to scout the approaches to Athiltor. I was also scrupulous in organising the camp, making sure its irregular sprawl didn't extend too far and setting out a tight picket line. Evadine took up residence in the hamlet's largest building, an inn that doubled as a brothel and therefore benefited from some comfortable beds. Now back among the ranks of the crusade, there was no prospect of sharing such comfort with her that night, much to our mutual frustration.

"None?" she demanded of Ayin with an untypical snap to her tone. "No new recruits at all?"

Ayin clutched her ledgers tighter and lowered her gaze. She had been called to the inn to provide an accounting of our numbers, a task performed with her usual guileless honesty. "No, my lady," she said, her voice suddenly small. "There haven't been any for several days now." Darting a worried look at me she added in yet quieter tones, "Also, others have been . . . leaving. Our strength is five hundred and eighty-three less than it was last week."

"How?" Evadine's voice acquired an edge. "Where did they go?"

"They deserted," I cut in as Ayin squirmed under the Anointed Lady's gaze. "As with any army when battle draws near, those who thought themselves brave and faithful often find they are neither. As for the lack of recruits, we should remember that this land hasn't known a season without war for a long time. Folk are wearied of constant strife, my lady."

This brought a softening to her brow, and a glance of apology at Ayin. "My thanks, trooper," Evadine told her with a forced smile. "Your diligence does you credit as always. Go now and rest."

"We can't wait here," I said when Ayin had departed, leaving us alone in the low-ceilinged room that served as the inn's drinking den. "There's little chance of increasing our numbers and every day that passes saps our strength further. I would have preferred to join with Swain and Ofihla's companies, but by the time they arrive, if they ever do, we may have no army left to speak of."

"Then we press on to Athiltor," Evadine stated. "Demand Arnabus surrender and take the city by storm when he refuses."

"Storming prepared trenches with barely trained soldiers invites disaster. Thessil may be a cruel commander but he's far from foolish."

Evadine shook her head. "Cruel or foolish, it matters not." She paused, meeting my eye with a familiar certainty. "I have seen it, Alwyn. This crusade will take the holy city."

"A vision?" I asked receiving a nod in response.

"It came to me last night. It will be a bloody day to be sure, but take it we will. And there on the steps of Martyr Athil's sacred cathedral, the Ascendant Queen will proclaim her rise."

If the prospect of impending monarchy pleased her, it failed to show in the preoccupied cast to her face as she slumped into one of the rickety chairs. "The visions," she whispered, putting a hand to her brow. "Such a burden sometimes."

"A burden we share," I promised, moving to grasp her shoulder. "I'm here. I always will be. Know that above all else."

She looked up at me, reaching to clasp my fingers, then withdrawing her touch when the clump of boots outside told of guards taking up station for the night. "I'd best see to the pickets," I said, squeezing her hand before bowing and making for the door.

* * *

"Not a chance he can do six," Ayin said, the disbelief in her voice a contrast to the rapt fascination on her face as she watched Adlar Spinner demonstrate his skills. His performances had become a nightly ritual on the march, folk gathering round the tent he shared with Quintrell to witness the spectacle of various items cast into the air in a dancing arc. Curiously, the clumsiness he had exhibited in Lorine's hall had vanished, his remarkably dextrous hands achieving feats some might ascribe to arcane influence, so impossible did they seem. One of his favourite tricks was to garner random objects from the crowd, pendants, weapons or sundry trinkets, and juggle them with much the same skill he displayed with balls or clubs. Tonight, he spun a glittering circle of knives, starting with three then snatching another from his belt every few turns to increase the number.

"A wager I'll take, my dear," Quintrell said, smoke blossoming from his mouth as he raised his pipe to Ayin.

"Lady says not to gamble," Ayin replied with a scowl that proved short-lived, so enraptured was she by the spinner's antics. I was surprised, in truth near shocked, to read in her expression something more than mere delight at a novel spectacle. It was an interest of a kind I had thought beyond her and found its abrupt appearance discomfiting.

"All the girls love Adlar," Quintrell muttered, leaning towards me on his camp stool. At first I thought there may be some barb in his comment but his features were soft with shared confidence. "But they're always disappointed. Not so the boys. Have no worry for your pet, my lord."

"She no one's pet," I replied, but relief kept my tone mellow. "At least I won't have to warn him about the dangers of straying hands." A cheer went up as Adlar plucked yet another knife from his belt and added it to the expanding circle of dancing blades, Ayin clapping in excitement. "For a fellow who took a punch from his own mother on account of his clumsiness," I observed to Quintrell, "he seems to have acquired a remarkable confidence."

"The duchess cautioned me as to your suspicious nature." Quintrell puffed more pipe smoke and leaned a little closer. "You imagine him an agent of hers, one I contrived to slip into your company by virtue of clever mummery." He bit his pipe stem to let out a wry chuckle. "Such a novelty to meet a man with a mind even more prone to artifice than my own. Although, I daresay the Lady Lorine beats us both on that score, eh?"

My attention slipped back to Adlar who was now turning in a slow pirouette, the knives arcing to yet greater heights. "So, if he's not her spy, what is he?"

"A lad I'm fond of who needed to escape a bad place, to wit: his family. His mother is a spiteful creature of endless criticism and his father her craven slave. I encountered them many times over the years. We players form a loosely aligned nation of our own in many ways, so frequently do we cross paths at the fairs and castles of this land. I've known Adlar all his life, off and on, and every time I saw him he appeared yet more miserable, and clumsy. Constant harping, and beatings, will sap the surety from any hand, even those as skilled as his. He needed to leave. It's the way of things, all children must eventually venture beyond their family's embrace, sometimes for fear that it might crush them."

"I daresay this loose nation of players must be a fruitful source of gossip. Folk who constantly tour the grand houses of the realm entire will surely have interesting stories to share."

Quintrell puffed and said nothing, though a half-grin lingered on his lips.

"I wonder," I persisted, narrowing my eyes to ensure he saw the hard, purposeful glint, "if your travels ever took you to the Algathinet court?"

"Duchess Lorine pays me." The grin lingered on his lips, though the flintiness of his gaze was a match for mine. "You do not, my lord."

"You're here at your lady's behest, in service to our shared cause. If you have intelligence that might aid us . . ."

What gems of knowledge this minstrel might possess, however, would not be unearthed that night, for it was then that a distant shout echoed from the darkness beyond the picket line. Most of those present paid it no heed, still captured by the juggler's tricks, but I had ears well attuned to the pitch of loudly voiced alarm. Evidently, so did Quintrell for we rose in unison, searching the blackness untouched by the picket's torches.

"Quiet!" I barked as the spectators began to cheer again. Adlar's glittering arc slowed then collapsed in the thickened silence, soon broken by another shout from the gloom, this one accompanied by the drum of galloping hooves.

"Beware!" a voice echoed from the shadows. "Rouse . . . the Lady!"

I pushed my way through the throng to the picket line, finding a line of pike-bearing guards exchanging puzzled glances. "Are we attacked, my lord?" a wide-eyed youth enquired. "Should we sound the horns?"

"Shut up!" I snapped, ears straining for more of the unseen herald, whoever they might be.

"Look to the Lady!" The source of the shout finally came into view, horse and rider resolving out of the dark fifty yards to my left. I ran towards him, barking out orders for the archers among the pickets to lower their weapons. Seeing me, the rider changed course, whipping his plainly exhausted mount to a final burst of speed.

"The Lady, my lord!" I recognised Tiler's sharp, pale features as he dragged his horse to a halt a few paces off. "They're here!"

"Who?"

"Vergundians, hired blades."

"Which direction?"

He shook his head, sagging in the saddle to drag fresh air into his lungs before blurting an answer. "No. They're already here. Thessil sent them ahead of us. The inn. They're under the inn!"

I shouted as I ran, rousing every soldier I saw while leaping campfires and skirting tents. My words were barely intelligible, but the flash of the longsword in my hand and the furious intent on my face were unmistakable. By the time the inn came into view, I had at least fifty armed crusaders at my back. My speed increased at the sight of the guards lying still at the door to the inn, then flared to an unreasoning sprint at the tumult of combat from within. The doors slammed open as I barrelled through, immediately stumbling over the bloodied corpse of a Vergundian. I expended a precious second regarding his slack-mouthed features framed by silk-adorned braids, skin flecked crimson from an opened throat, then kicked his body aside and charged on.

I spared scant time in surveying the scene, it was mostly a chaos of struggling figures clustered at the far end of the room. Splintered floorboards lay everywhere among streaked and pooled blood. Short, curve-bladed knives flashed and screams of challenge and pain abounded. Through the crush I caught the merest glimpse of Evadine backed into a corner, face set in grim resolve, her longsword slicing and cutting with tireless efficiency.

I recall a feral shout escaping my lips before I plunged headlong into the melee. Only the first one I cut down remains clear in my memory, a stocky hired blade wielding a hatchet, his hair cropped short as is custom for those often given to wearing helms. He turned in time to take the point of my sword full in the face, the thrust delivered with enough force to drive the blade clean through the skull. I maintained my charge, putting my shoulder into his chest and propelling his twitching form into the press of bodies. A red fountain erupted as I dragged the longsword from his head, hacking left and right, only dimly aware of the Covenant soldiers rushing forward on my flanks. The rest is a blur of frenzied violence I consider myself fortunate not to remember. I know I lost my sword in the chaos of it all, for when reason descended, I found myself strangling a Vergundian, spitting a torrent of obscenities as I thrust his already charred, smoking head into the burning coals of the fireplace.

"Burn, you fuck!" I grunted in a final outburst of ferocity, letting his head loll into the flames as I drew my hands back from his throat. They came away red to the wrist, scraps of flesh dangling from my fingertips. I staggered upright, desperately scanning the ruination for Evadine. She stood in the centre of the room, longsword dripping blood at her side. Bodies littered the cramped mess of the drinking den, blood on every surface. Some of the Covenant soldiers were finishing off the wounded assassins while others just stood, chests heaving, faces blank with the befuddlement that dawns in the aftermath of first battle. The urge to rush to Evadine was strong, pull her close and press my lips to hers. I quelled it with difficulty, but the glance we shared sufficed to reassure me she had suffered no injury. Her black cotton garb was torn in places, revealing a few scratches but no cuts of note.

A flicker of a smile passed over her lips before she looked away. A frown creased her brow as she smoothed a trembling hand over her hip, then her belly, a gesture to which I should have afforded much more notice. However, the sudden growl behind her banished all other concerns. The Vergundian was huge, a raging, wild-eyed bull of a man who must have concealed himself beneath the floorboards with great difficulty. He surged from a pile of bodies, curved knives in both hands, too close to Evadine, too fast for me or her to cut him down.

The knife flicked past Evadine's ear in a silvery arc, missing her by a fraction before burying itself in the Vergundian's eye. He staggered about for a time, his own knives dangling from limp fingers as he performed a dance that might well have been amusing at another time. It ended when Ayin, face streaked red and hair matted with gore not her own, stepped up behind him and slit his throat from ear to ear.

I turned towards the front of the inn, finding Adlar Spinner framed in the doorway, still crouched in the aftermath of his throw. The bleached stillness of his features made it plain that this was the first time he had used his skills to end a life.

"This bastard's not dead." The gruff voice of a soldier provided another distraction. He stooped over the body of a Vergundian, hand fisted in the ribboned braids to drag his head from the boards. The plainsman's features were slack, but his half-opened eyes betrayed a glimmer of animation.

"Stop," I said as the soldier put a dagger to the Vergundian's throat. "Leave him be."

The soldier was clearly a veteran of previous crusades and probably a few wars. His swarthy, scarred face, still flushed with the fury of recent combat, bunched in puzzlement as I came closer. "A dead man's tongue doesn't wag," I explained before turning to the juggler still frozen in the doorway. "How about it, Master Spinner? Care to earn your coin for a second time?"

Chapter Five

The Vergundian didn't wake until midday, by which time most of the camp had broken up and the crusade begun its march towards Athiltor. Keeping my prisoner alive in the intervening hours had been a taxing business, the mob of vengeful followers that gathered at the inn assuaged only by a brief sermon from the Anointed Lady herself.

"Do you imagine me a murderer?" she demanded. "Moreover, do you imagine me a fool? This man has my protection, for he is but another victim of heresy. Through him, we will learn the disposition of our enemy. Through mercy will victory be achieved."

Possibly due to the fact that these were the most words they had heard from their Risen Martyr in many days, they sufficed to keep the Vergundian alive until dawn. While the host shambled into its ragged marching order, I and the most trusted of my scouts remained behind, as did Adlar Spinner. The bodies had been dragged from the inn and heaped outside without ceremony, although there had been something ritualistic in the way crusaders came to cast spit or piss upon the pile. I made sure our captive could see the corpse mound through the ruined doors, but the sight of the fly-shrouded horror appeared to concern him hardly at all.

"*Uttrach!*" he hissed at me after I banished his confusion with a bucket of ditch water. "*Triack lemil, ja vorca kir-ech!*"

"*Uttrach* means coward, my lord," Adlar Spinner supplied in response to my questioning glance.

"And the rest?"

The juggler shifted in discomfort; his complexion still largely devoid of colour. The stain of killing will linger on some souls longer than others, and I had a fancy that the events of the previous nights had dispelled any idealised notions this youth may have harboured towards the trade of soldiering. His fear and distaste for the task set him were plain in the glances he darted at the inn's other occupants. Ayin sat in a corner, quill poised over an open ledger. She had washed her face but her hair retained a matted spikiness. The Widow rested herself against the counter nursing a cup of brandy. I couldn't tell if her lack of expression came from boredom or anticipation. Lilat stood at the furthest remove, huddled against the wall with her hood drawn over her features. I knew she would leave if this encounter degenerated into torment, and found I was grateful for it. Tiler was the most animated, pacing back and forth on the only patch of unsplintered floorboards.

I had gotten most of his story last night. The outlaw related how he had, over the course of several days, managed to ingratiate himself with a party of hired blades heading for Athiltor. His description of the holy city matched what the Widow had gleaned from those fleeing along the King's Road: hangings and floggings, thieving mercenaries and a fearful population. It was a full week before a drunken crossbowman from the Divine Captain's inner circle had let slip his commander's cunning stratagem of secreting assassins in the Malecite Whore's most likely resting place on the road to Athiltor. Realising the imminent danger, Tiler garrotted the loose-tongued crossbowman, stole a horse and made all haste for the crossroads. The thought of what might have happened had he been only a moment slower put a tremble to my hand as I toyed with one of the curved knives of which these Vergundians seemed so fond. This example had been found in the captive's hand, and I saw a distinct glimmer of outrage in his gaze as he watched me fiddle with it.

"He said," Adlar paused to swallow, "'Kill me, if you've the balls.'"

"Oh, we've got the balls, you goat-shagger!" Tiler snarled, advancing towards the captive. "But you won't when we're done! We'll give you to her." He stabbed a finger at Ayin. "She knows how to treat your kind."

I met his eye, shaking my head. Tiler bit down on another snarl and resumed his pacing.

"This is an interesting weapon," I said, twirling the blade I held. "What's it called?" The knife was, in truth, a novel design I hadn't seen before. Blade and handle had been fashioned from the same piece of steel, a seven-inch, double-edged sickle attached to a twisted grip with a ring in place of a pommel. I had seen how the Vergundians would fix the ring over their forefinger when they wielded it, the double edge enabling them to slash as well as stab while the ring prevented it falling from their grasp.

"They call it a '*trakiesh*', my lord," Adlar said.

"*Trakiesh*," I repeated, keeping my focus on the Vergundian, bruised features twitching in anger. "Does this word have meaning beyond just a knife?"

"My mother had one," Adlar said. "She called it her 'soul-blade'. Vergundians are given a *trakiesh* by their clan chief when they come of age, but only if they are judged to have a soul. They don't think about such things the way we do, my lord. A soul is something that can be lost, or even stolen from the weak or the cowardly. Those judged as soulless are cast out. They believe their *trakiesh* can take in the souls of others, which will add to their power in the spirit lands when Mother Death comes to claim them."

"Savage superstition," Tiler muttered.

"Ah," I mused, tapping the knife's tip to my lips and enjoying the sight of the Vergundian's glare. I assumed a Covenanter would exhibit much the same rage if a plainsman pissed on a Martyr Shrine altar. "So," I went on, "I assume he would greatly desire the return of this thing."

Adlar shot a wary glance at the prisoner. "I suppose so. In truth, my lord, I don't know."

"Then ask him."

The juggler nodded and spoke to the Vergundian, the question short and flat but provoking a far longer, spittle-flecked diatribe in response. The plainsman lunged forward in his bonds, teeth bared and eyes blazing, issuing forth a gabble of invective from which I could parse no individual words.

"That was a no, I take it?" I enquired when the Vergundian fell silent.

"From what I can gather, *trakiesh* can only be won in battle and cannot be bargained for. The very notion of buying or selling them is offensive."

"But selling yourself is not? Is he not, in any way that matters, a whore? For he sold his body for coin."

Adlar remained silent and I turned to see him offering an apologetic wince. "There is no Vergundian word for whore, my lord. They look upon such things in . . . very pragmatic terms. Even if he understood the question, I doubt he'd find it an insult. If that was your intention."

"I see. Then, since his kind are so fond of pragmatism, let us be equally so. Ask him if he truly wants to die, or would he prefer to be given a horse and leave to ride from here without further injury?"

Tiler's pacing came to an abrupt halt, but another glance from me kept the unwise exclamation from his lips. I expected another angry eruption from the Vergundian in response to Adlar's translation, but this time his reaction was one of squinting suspicion. Watching him settle into a sitting position, I realised that under the red-brown grime and grazes, his face was that of a man somewhere north of thirty years. This was a veteran mercenary and not some easily gulled youth. A man such as this might not fear death, but neither would he relish death with the eagerness he pretended. Also, I doubted he would be so ignorant of his paymaster's tongue.

"Were you at Walvern Castle?" I asked, looking closely at his face. "We killed many Vergundians there. As I recall, they screeched like stuck pigs, did they not, Trooper Tiler?" I added, casting the question over my shoulder.

"Like cats fucking, more like," he supplied. "Begged for mercy when we finished them off, too."

The plainsman tried to hide it, but the fractional crease to his brow and resentful hardening of his lips told the tale. "Enough," I said, holding up a hand when Adlar began to translate. Offering a bland smile, I rose and dragged two chairs from the thicket of disarrayed furniture. Sinking into one, I gestured for the Vergundian to take the other.

"Just sit," I snapped when he continued to lie on his side, face set in a suspicious scowl. "And we'll talk like men with a deal to strike rather than angry children. Or—" I gave his knife a meaningful twirl "—I can end this now."

The Vergundian grunted and levered himself to his knees, then his feet, standing in tall and prideful defiance before consenting to take the chair. "A stolen *trakiesh* brings only bad luck," he said in thickly accented Albermaine-ish. "You should know that, *ahlen-trahck*."

Since he seemed disinclined to explain this obvious insult, I raised an eyebrow at Adlar. "*Ahlen-trahck* means 'slave to a woman', my lord," the juggler said. "Among the clans, only men lead. Those who show affection or regard for women are scorned."

Slave to a woman, I thought, finding enough truth in it to bring a grin to my lips. Ayin and the Widow, however, were less amused. "Slaves are we?" the Widow asked, stepping away from the counter and hefting her short-staved war hammer. Worrisome as this was, I found myself more concerned by the sight of Ayin setting down her quill, a familiar blankness of purpose stealing over her features.

Gifted with a lifetime's experience in sensing a situation about to descend into violence, I barked out a command. "Everyone out!"

Lilat was the first to leave, Adlar not far behind, not bothering to keep the relief from his face. I was obliged to direct some hard stares at Tiler and the Widow before they consented to follow, while Ayin continued to sit in expressionless regard of the Vergundian.

"He's a bad man," she stated in response to my weighty glare. "I can tell."

Her definition of a bad man was narrow but I didn't doubt her perception. Fearless warrior or not, the man before me remained a brutal wretch. His list of crimes would be long, including several that would earn him the same fate as Erchel. Still, I had a war to win and, as Tiler repeatedly demonstrated, even wretches have their uses.

"I know," I told her. "But the Lady has need of him."

Despite his disparaging attitudes to women, the Vergundian had the wit to avoid Ayin's gaze as she proceeded to the door, speaking only when she had departed the inn. "Do you really allow her to geld men?" Apparently, there was at least one thing these plainsmen feared more than death.

"You imply that I could stop her if I wanted to," I said.

The Vergundian whispered something, head lowered and bound, hands shifting in what I took as a ritual. *All I need do is threaten to cut his balls off, after all*, I concluded before nudging the man's feet with my boot. "I think we've danced long enough," I said. "You're a hireling. All hireling's have a price. I assume the one the Divine Captain offered for the Anointed Lady's head was large indeed. You do know he sent you and your brothers to certain death?"

"The price was equal to the risk," he replied. "The priest, the only one left in that devil city of yours. He showed us a chest of gold. All the riches of your Covenant. He made solemn promise it would be sent to our clans when word arrived of the . . ." He stumbled over whatever unflattering title he had been about to speak, eyes slipping to the door through which Ayin could be seen idly tossing stones at the piled dead. "Your woman-chief's death. Such riches would make my clan great."

"This is why you come west to sell your skills? To enrich your clans?"

This appeared to cause him some genuine puzzlement. "Why else? The clan is all."

"Even if the priest didn't lie, there will be no gold for your clans now. But—" I leaned forward, making sure he saw the intent in my face "—there can still be. Double the priest's offer, in fact. Enough gold for you to return to the plains and be hailed for the riches you bring."

"You wish knowledge. Where the captain puts the fools he calls warriors. How deep he digs his pointless ditches."

"No. My weasel-faced friend has told me all that. From you, I require something else."

Night had the effect of transforming the great spire of Martyr Athil's cathedral into an ominous black spike, its jagged, buttressed flanks catching a scattering of abstract, flickering shadows from the many campfires littering the city below. "At least there's no chance we'll lose sight of our objective," I said, turning to the armoured form crouched at my side. "Eh, Captain?"

Dervan's youthfully handsome features bunched beneath a covering of soot, the stuff also smeared on his armour and that of his men. They lay amid the long grass fringing the southern bank of the Fletway river, a shallow but lengthy tributary of the Siltern that provided the holy city with its water. We were joined by the full Scout Company and a hundred or so carefully chosen volunteers from the main body of the crusade with proven battle experience. Close to four hundred in all, a scant number to assault an entrenched city, at least in typical circumstances. Fortunately, if my turncoat Vergundian did his expensively purchased part, it should prove more than adequate.

The crusade had come within striking distance of Athiltor that afternoon, immediately sprawling into a camp that stretched in a broad semicircle to east and west. In accordance with instructions, they gave every appearance of an army preparing for siege. Trees were felled from the nearby wood and emplacements dug, all accompanied by a cacophonous hammering to signify the construction of engines. Come the first onset of dusk, I led Dervan's men-at-arms and my augmented company in a wide, arcing march around the city's western fringe. Upon reaching the river, we dropped into the long grass and crawled the few hundred yards that took us within sight of the earthen mounds forming the defences abutting the bank. I knew from both Tiler and the turncoat that the Divine Captain had positioned the bulk of his mercenaries here, the flat ground offering the most likely avenue of attack but also the best killing field for archers.

Assaulting an enemy's strongest point went against all the military logic I had read or accrued. Far better to lay siege and starve the Council Host into submission. However, with the crusade bleeding strength by the day and winter not far off, this matter had to be settled quickly. I was risking much this night on the promise of a treacherous hireling, as Wilhum had been keen to point out.

"Fail and all is lost," he said during a brief conference with Evadine before I set off. "This man Thessil will surely know that we've spent our best coin on a bad bet. He won't be long in launching a sortie to finish us off."

"There will be no failure here, Wil," Evadine stated with a placid smile. "Alwyn's plan is sound and has my full confidence. Ready your riders and sound the horns to gather the faithful. I have words for them."

I caught only part of her sermon as we slipped away, her voice once again imbued with that strange ability to make every listener feel as if she spoke only to them. The assembled crusaders were a rapt, adoring multitude as she blessed them with her words. Had I been less subsumed in my own form of devotion to this woman, I might have perceived in their staring, open-mouthed faces a resemblance to a drunk presented with a sudden surplus of long denied liquor. For many, this sermon would be their only reward for all the miles they had marched in her name. Yet, I knew most, if not all, would count themselves wealthy beyond measure for having heard the Anointed Lady speak at this most auspicious of moments.

"I did not ask for this," she began, "nor did I wish for it. No true servant of the Covenant would ever desire such a circumstance. To bring war to this place above all others shames me to the point of agony. But it is a torment I shall bear, as I'll bear any burden in service to the Martyrs' example and the Seraphiles' grace. Now I must ask what burden are you willing to bear . . ."

The rest was lost to me as I led my Fools Hope on their possibly suicidal march, but the cheers that erupted shortly after made it clear that the Anointed Lady had once again demonstrated an effortless gift for rousing her flock to a pitch of willing sacrifice.

"Remember," I cautioned Dervan as we awaited the signal from the silent mounds ahead, "not every soldier in the Council Host is a hired blade. Some are ardent orthodox-ites and will gladly die for their cause. If you find yourself opposed, don't spare. A fanatic who drops his sword is likely to pick it up again once your back is turned."

The young captain's face bunched to a yet deeper degree and I sensed a certain distaste in the curl of his blackened lip. "Would you have me ignore the customs of war, my lord?"

"Customs of war." I smothered a laugh and shook my head. "The Lady Duchess gave me to believe you had seen your share of battle, sir. If so, you should have learned by now that custom is best saved for courts and dances."

"Not to me," Dervan insisted. "What honour I possess will not be stained by murder, nor will my men."

I squinted at him, unable to contain a question born of bafflement. "Where did she find you exactly?"

The captain stiffened. "Duchess Lorine, in her grace and condescension, was good enough to recognise my dutiful service at the Traitors' Field."

"A place where I recall your former duke happily passing sentence of death upon captives. Do any head lopping yourself that day, Captain?"

He bared his teeth, his answer emerging in a slow grate that told of rapidly expiring patience: "No, I did not."

I might have taunted him further, but the appearance of a blazing torch atop the earthworks put paid to such amusements. "Well," I said, raising myself to a crouch. "You're about to get plenty of opportunities to test your principles. Form your company into a wedge as soon as we clear the trenches, make for the south-facing defences."

"I know the plan," he snapped before adding a scorn-laden honorific, "my lord."

"Then fucking do it."

I moved forward, touching hands to the shoulders of the scouts and veteran volunteers before pausing at Lilat's side. I had tried to insist she take no part in the night's work but this time she wouldn't be dissuaded.

"You understand your task?" I asked her in Caerith.

"Find the building with the books," she said, hefting her bow. "Keep it safe."

"And?" I added, nodding to the dozen archers at her back. They were a mingling of poachers and hunters drawn from the crusade's ranks, all skilled with the bows they carried, though none so much as her.

"Stay with these *Ishlichen*," Lilat replied with a sullen shrug. She didn't like the prospect of straying far from my side in time of danger.

"The books are important," I told her. "I wouldn't trust this task to anyone else."

She consented to afford me a doubtful grin before I moved away to take up station at the head of the Covenant contingent. The Widow fell in on my right, Tiler on my left and Adlar Spinner to my rear. The juggler seemed ill at ease in his cast-off brigandine, constantly squirming and tugging the collar away from his chafed neck. He professed ignorance of the sword so I had armed him with a sturdy hatchet and given unambiguous instruction regarding his role this night. "Your only task is to keep me alive. Do not stray more than a yard from my side. Use those knives of yours to keep foes at bay, the hatchet is only for when you run out."

He gave a queasy smile of agreement and succeeded in surprising me by not throwing up during the march or the wait. The rest of my command had assumed a loose arrowhead formation. Our usual light but hardy garb had been forsaken for the mismatched collection of armour, plate and thick leather, worn for battle. Like Dervan, my own armour was smeared with soot and the various straps greased to prevent betraying noise. Still, a few let out a faint squeal as I started forward.

The run to the earthworks covered a distance of no more than two hundred paces, but it felt far longer. Despite all the confidence I had exhibited for this plan, I will confess that I took every step in partial expectation that a hail of arrows and bolts would arc up from the defences at any moment. Then, as we neared the mounds, this fear was replaced by a suspicion that I would crest the earthwork only to find Danick Thessil and his full strength waiting.

Fortunately, my appraisal of the Vergundian proved sound for I found his greedy self standing atop the mound with a dozen fellow plainsmen. He greeted me with a curt nod as I ascended the steep slope, taking in the sight of a score of Council soldiers lying dead amid the trenches on the far side. Some lay with their throats sliced open and gaping, a few still leaking steam into the night air. Others were feathered by arrows. The work of the few seconds before the turncoat waved his torch. There were others here besides the Vergundians, hired blades and a few Council men standing in tense uncertainty.

"Not all wanted to join us," the turncoat explained, flicking a hand at the bodies.

"How many guarding the cathedral?" I asked, glancing back to see Dervan's company nearing the base of the earthwork.

"Fifty, maybe. The Divine Captain gathered up the rest and took them to the southern works. Your woman-chief's caterwauling made him nervous."

"The priest?"

"At the cathedral." The Vergundian shrugged. "As far as I know."

"Get this lot in some sort of order and follow me. I'll need you to feather the guards on the cathedral steps."

"Our deal was to let you in. Not to fight."

"And if you want payment you'll help take the cathedral. Unless you'd rather trust to chance it won't be looted when this place falls."

I watched Captain Dervan lead his company over the mound and form up on the ground beyond. A cluster of inquisitive Council men appeared to gawp at the sudden appearance of ducal soldiery in their midst. After the Vergundians put arrows into some the others promptly fled. I took satisfaction from the fact that they chose to climb the earthworks and pelt away into the darkness rather than carry the alarm into the city. If the rest of Thessil's recruits shared a similar pitch of loyalty this would be over far sooner than I hoped.

Dervan led his well-ordered formation off at a rapid march without further preamble, heading towards the south-facing defences while maintaining a decent remove from the outer barrier of earthworks. From beyond the city proper I heard a muted but growing tumult that indicated the enthused mass of the Anointed Lady's Crusade was now hurling itself upon Thessil's trench lines. I knew many would fall at the first clash and forced down the resultant images of piled dead or maimed bodies. *A necessary distraction*, I told myself, the thought bringing a bitter taste to my mouth.

"Form up!" I shouted, descending the slope and hurdling the corpse-filled trenches. The Scout Company resumed their arrowhead formation and we set off towards the cathedral at a steady run. Considering this was a city now under fierce assault, our progress was remarkably unimpeded. Many Council men or hired blades who witnessed our passing did so in dumbfounded silence, often wisely choosing to take to their heels. A few more dutiful souls called out alarms as they ran and, inevitably, those possessed of foolish courage or unreasoning devotion tried to fight us.

"You daft old bastard," Tiler grunted, cutting down a spindly, grey-haired fellow in a loose-fitting mail shirt who attempted to bar our path, swinging a halberd with neither skill nor strength. The fanatic elder screamed as Tiler's falchion sliced his unprotected legs, his shouts becoming rasping recitations of the Martyr scrolls as we ran on and left him clutching his wounds. A few yards on, a crossbow bolt came whistling out of the gloom to strike sparks from the helm of one of the crusader veterans. The soldier stumbled but didn't fall and the Vergundians running on our flanks let fly with a salvo in response, their efforts rewarded by a scream as the unseen assailant received their reward.

Predictably, resistance stiffened as we neared the cathedral. One scout was lost to a volley of bolts and arrows and we were obliged to cut our way through a hastily drawn up line of Council men about twenty strong. They took the charge head on without faltering, but the fierceness of the subsequent melee sent most running, leaving a half-dozen on the ground twitching or still.

"Time to earn your pay!" I called to the Vergundian turncoat upon catching sight of the cathedral steps. Here waited two lines of halberdiers, all markedly better armoured than those faced so far. The first rank stood at the base of the steps and the second at the top, a few crossbowmen among them. They numbered perhaps fifty in all and arrayed themselves with the neat, immobile discipline of true soldiers. These, I felt certain, were Danick's best.

I held my company in place as the Vergundians began their work, drawing and loosing their strongbows with unhurried accuracy. To their credit, the Council soldiers on the steps bore the first few volleys without moving, even as five of their number slumped down with shafts jutting from the gaps in their armour. The countering salvo from their crossbows cut down two of mine before the plainsmen's next volley claimed another brace of Council men. A subsequent salvo felled most of the crossbowmen as they laboured to recharge their weapons, a stark demonstration of the advantage of bows over crossbows at close range. At this point whoever had charge of the defenders realised the folly of maintaining an unmoving line. A shout went up whereupon the soldiers in the lower rank levelled their halberds and charged.

"For the Lady!" I cried out, longsword held high, the scouts and crusaders at my back responding in kind with fervent volume, following as I charged. There is a point in every battle where all attempts at maintaining order become redundant and a chaotic scrum is the only viable tactic.

My longsword met the blade of the halberdier who barred my path, sweeping it aside before I whirled and hacked at his neck. I had aimed for the gap between his helm and breastplate, but caught the rear of his head instead, colliding metal ringing with a curious, bell-like purity. The blow succeeded in stunning the halberdier long enough for the Widow to smash his unarmoured chin into pulp with her warhammer. Another Council man came at me with his weapon raised level with his shoulders, driving the spiked point at my face. I dodged it by inches and felt the rush of a fast-moving object flick past my ear. The thrusting halberdier staggered back, gurgling with one of Adlar Spinner's knives buried in his throat.

Slashing to either side, I forced my way through the few remaining opponents and on to the cathedral steps. The second rank descended at a run to confront us, several falling dead as the Vergundians loosed another volley. With the ranks of our enemies so thinned, the subsequent melee was brief if bloody. This small elite of Thessil's Council Host was nothing if not determined, each cutting down at least one of mine before our blades pinned them to the steps. A few continued to fight regardless of severe wounds, a stocky man thumping away with a broken haft of his halberd while blood spurted from the slit in his neck.

"Servants of the Malecite Whore . . ." he gasped out in a red spray when a blow from Tiler's falchion finally sent him toppling.

"Shut it, you heretic fuck!" Tiler snarled, thrusting the point of his blade into the dying man's mouth. "It's you!" He glared into the Council man's wide eyes as he bore him down, driving the blade deeper. "You serve the Malecite, not us! You hear me?"

It was here that Adlar lost his struggle to contain his gorge, spilling the contents of his guts on to the body of the man he had slain. "Tiler," I called to the outlaw as he tugged his falchion free of the corpse. "Take half our number. Scour the gardens and the sleeping quarters. If you find any Luminants or senior clerics, make sure they remain alive and unmolested to greet the dawn."

I turned to the Vergundians, finding my former captive eyeing me with a mix of eagerness and tense suspicion. "Stay away from the chapel," I said, gesturing to the cathedral. "Any relics or holy objects are not yours to take. Otherwise, help yourself."

They were already swarming up the steps before I finished speaking. I had little doubt that, come the dawn, we would discover more than a few supposedly divine Covenant treasures missing and found I couldn't care less. *Faith resides neither in gold nor in craft*, Sihlda had always said. *But in the heart and the soul, neither of which can be stolen or falsified.*

"Master Spinner!" I said, turning to see the juggler still staring at the vomit-spattered corpse at his feet. He looked up at me with the expression of a child caught in the aftermath of a terrible transgression. "Follow close, if you please." I started up the steps. "And don't forget your knife."

Chapter Six

The interior of the cathedral was all gloom and angular, multi-hued shadows cast by the numerous stained glass windows. Torches sat unlit in stanchions, and not even a candle flickered in the alcoves and sconces. Our boots echoed loud as we made our way from the great arched entrance to the high vaulted chamber of the main chapel. There, a single figure knelt before the altar, its marble slab laden with a dense array of gold caskets of varying dimensions.

Striding along an aisle flanked by empty pews, my pace increased as I discerned the identity of this supplicating personage. I had expected his capture to require many hours of searching the hidden corners of this vast building, should we find him here at all. But there he knelt, head bowed and unmoving in apparently serene acceptance of his fate.

I stopped a dozen paces short of him, holding up a hand to halt the others. "Check the vestry and the crypt for any hiders," I instructed, gesturing for the Widow and Adlar to remain where they were as the rest of the Covenant soldiers hurried off.

My sword dripped blood across ancient, intricate mosaics as I took the last few paces to the altar. The kneeling figure didn't turn at my approach, which I found stoked my anger to a fiercer heat. He wore just plain clerical garb and I stared at his exposed neck, memories of the Dire Keep rising. When he slowly raised his head and began to speak, his voice was thick and laboured, as if in pain, but lacking the fear I expected, and wanted.

"Tell me, my lord Scribe," Arnabus said, nodding to the altar, "have you ever before beheld the relics of Martyr Athil?"

I said nothing, but I couldn't resist shifting my eyes from his inviting neck to the shiny reliquaries arrayed on the marble platform before us. Each stood with its doors opened, their sacred contents lost to the shadows that dominated this unlit space. There were more than I thought existed, stirring a blasphemous notion that there might be enough body parts here to fashion at least two Martyr Athils.

"The most holy objects in all Covenant-dom," Arnabus continued in his aggravatingly untroubled tones. "As a servant of the Martyrs' example, do you not feel compelled to kneel before them as I do? There—" he raised a hand, finger quivering to point at a tall, narrow casket at the edge of the altar "—Martyr Athil's thigh bone. Next to it—" his finger shifted to a less impressive box "—the small toe from his left foot. Wars have been fought to possess these treasures and yet you show no reverence. Why is that?"

I said nothing, instead focusing my scrutiny on Arnabus, seeing how he clutched one hand to the knotted jumble of the robe covering his belly. Below his knees the tiles were dark with a spreading pool of viscous liquid.

"A disagreement with my esteemed captain," Arnabus explained. He smiled, but I saw the pain in his narrow, pale features. "Not a fellow to take criticism lightly, it transpires."

The anger leached from me then, the old, familiar urge towards retribution that had fuelled much of my life fading to a small itch. I detested this man a great deal, but confronted with the stricken, broken creature he had become, the need for blood abated.

"Finish the bastard," the Widow stated. "Or let me do it. Woodsman is owed a reckoning, and so are all the folk we lost this night."

"Why would I kill him when he still has so much to tell me?" I replied. "There's bound to be a healer among the clerics Tiler's turfed out of this place. Find one."

"Sadly, brother . . ." Arnabus rasped. "I doubt I have the . . . time for further conversation." He slumped forward, setting his head on the edge of the altar's dais as if it were a pillow.

I crouched at his side, myriad questions buzzing my head but finding I could articulate only one. "Why? Allying yourself with a half-mad rebel outlaw, hiring mercenaries you must have known could never be trusted. This was always a hopeless prospect. So why?"

Arnabus's voice was a whisper, shot through with a familiar taunting lilt. "You know why . . . Scribe. So did . . . our elder sister. Perhaps now, she'll . . ." He paused to convulse, spitting a glob of blood from his mouth then drawing a ragged breath to speak on. "She'll remember me . . . with a fonder heart."

"You did all this to win the Sack Witch's favour? Torture, murder, war. She would have no part of this."

A sound that was a mingling of a groan and a sigh came from his lips. "I forgot . . . how young you still are. Still so . . . innocent." He gave a feeble flap of his hand, beckoning me closer. His features hardened as I leaned towards him, voice the forced rasp of a man determined to imbue his final words with significance. "You know what Evadine Courlain is, Scribe. Even though you won't admit it to yourself. Not yet. My sister once told me it would be this way . . . that we must await your . . ." Arnabus's lips twisted into a smile ". . . epiphany. As ever, I didn't listen. I thought if I could stop it . . . she would love me again."

The smile faded and he looked into my eyes, gaze unblinking. "The Isidorian Codex . . . Scribe. Look there for . . ." a pulse of his old sardonic wit passed across his face ". . . illumination."

I thought he would die then, but it had ever been the role of this man to frustrate me. So, instead of peacefully slipping into the death he had earned, Ascendant Arnabus dragged a final parcel of air into his lungs and craned his neck to address my companions. "Now," he told them in a loud, agonised grunt, "I think . . . I should illuminate your friends in the true story of Martyr Evadine's resurrection. You see . . . my children . . . it was not the work of the Seraphile at all . . ."

My sword descended with enough force to not only cleave both his neck but also chip a decent-sized chunk from the dais beneath. Apparently, this vandalism has never been repaired and you can still see it today. Arnabus's blood seeped into the very fabric of the stone and his end is forever marked by a dark, triangular notch in otherwise pristine marble.

I stooped to gather up a portion of Arnabus's robes, using them to wipe clean my longsword. "You two stay here," I told the Widow and Adlar. "Ensure the plainsmen don't take any of the relics. I'll be back shortly."

I started along the aisle but halted at the Widow's strident question. "What did he mean?" Glancing back at her, I found her features set in a demanding scowl. "What he said about the Anointed Lady. What she is, and her resurrection."

My gaze slid briefly to the juggler who, fortunately for him, seemed more interested in gaping in horrified fascination at both Arnabus's disembodied head and the collection of relics. "The maddened ramblings of a dying man," I told the Widow. I made sure to meet her eyes before adding with careful emphasis, "Best forgotten and never spoken of again."

Not one to be cowed, in truth I had doubts she was even capable of fear at this juncture, Juhlina returned my stare in full measure. She did, however, say nothing more as I strode from the chapel.

By dint of sheer violence and force of will, Danick Thessil managed to survive the night, an example of martial courage and ferocity those under his command signally failed to match. After Ayin had completed a full accounting of losses, it became clear that the Divine Captain's host had been a mostly hollow contrivance. The bulk of the hired blades disappeared the moment Evadine led the crusade into the trenches. Many of the Council soldiers, unwilling conscripts from the city or surrounding villages, were equally quick to throw down their arms and beg mercy. Despite this, Thessil had succeeded in holding up the advance for a time. Clustering his most ardent fanatics together at the crest of the central earthwork, he beat back two assaults and might have defeated a third if Dervan's Chosen Company hadn't appeared to strike at his rear. With the last of his soldiers slain, Thessil remained atop the mound, hacking away with a sword in one hand while holding aloft a banner in the other. It bore a cup and flame and, I would learn later, stood as the sigil of what had been termed the Reformed Orthodox Covenant. I would guess it stands as one of the most short-lived factions in Covenant history. Evadine forbade her archers from taking Thessil down, instead insisting this worst of heretics be clubbed to the ground, there to be roped and hobbled like an unbroken horse.

By dawn the city entire was in our hands, what survived of it at least. In the Fjord Geld and Alundia I had witnessed the fate of cities fallen to storm and, even though this havoc was born of Covenant devotion, Athiltor proved no exception. Fire tore through the rows of houses where the layfolk dwelt, consuming all within, including a good number of townspeople who had taken to their cellars for shelter. Others, those either foolish enough to venture forth or driven from their homes by the conflagration, were slaughtered in the streets by the Anointed Lady's Crusade. When presented by inarguable evidence of her divine favour, all semblance of the military order I and Wilhum had tried to instil on the march abruptly vanished and they became a mob.

Upon leaving the cathedral I had been forced to intervene to stop a cluster of crusaders tearing the robes from a group of captured female Supplicants. The intent of their tormentors was plain in the wild-eyed, desperate cast of their faces, besmirched by battle and the urge towards domination of the vanquished that arises in victory. My authority proved sufficient to forestall their impending crime, even dispelling their madness to a certain degree. I ordered the half-stripped clerics be taken to the cathedral and the crusaders to stand guard on the steps, promising the worst of punishments should I discover they had failed to comply.

Other horrors confronted me as I went in search of Evadine. Some I prevented, others I could not. The larger the group, the more likely they were to turn on anyone who sought to interrupt their amusements. I saw several minor shrines consumed by flames, though took some relief from the sight of the Covenant Library standing still intact and guarded by Lilat and her small cluster of archers. This night, at least, would not bring a repeat of the crime against history that had occurred when Olversahl fell to the Ascarlians.

I found Evadine atop the mound where Thessil had made his stand. She stood with her back to the flames, head cocked at a curious angle as she looked upon the Divine Captain. Bound hand and foot, he thrashed on the ground, all the while unleashing a torrent of defiant abuse that caused me to wonder why she hadn't seen fit to have him gagged.

"Cowardly bitch!" Thessil's teeth shone white in a face blackened by soot and congealed blood, eyes bright as he voiced his challenge. "Loose these bonds and fight me, whore! We'll see who has divine favour! Let all know your claims are false!"

"Filthy cur!" a crusader sergeant grunted, face dark as he emerged from the cordon of onlookers, bloodied halberd raised.

"No, good soldier," Evadine said, smiling and waving the fellow back. "Tarnish your steel no further this night, I beg you. Especially not with the blood of one so wicked as this."

"Tarnish, is it?" Thessil let out a shrill laugh. "She tarnishes you all, you fucking fools! Can't you see her for what she is? This is no Martyr! She damns you all with her lies!" His fevered gaze fixed upon me as I climbed the slope and, to my surprise, calmed a little. "Scribe," he grunted, sagging in his bonds, "if you still harbour any regard for all Deckin taught you, you'll cut this bitch down where she stands."

"He once showed me how to sever a man's tongue so that he won't choke to death on blood," I replied. "So I'd advise you to curb yours, Captain." I turned to Evadine and bowed. "The cathedral is in our hands, my lady. All relics are secured. Also, the library is intact and under guard."

She nodded in vague approval then raised a quizzical eyebrow. "Arnabus?"

"Dead." I inclined my head at Thessil. "By this one's hand, apparently." A lie, to be sure, but not completely.

Thessil jerked on the ground, growling a sullen interjection. "That faithless dog deserved worse. Wanted me to sully my honour with craven flight."

I ignored him and extended a hand to the city. The flames were rising high now, spreading from the lay-folk's quarter to the artisans' district. "I'll need Davern's and Wilhum's companies to put a stop to this."

This brought a crease to Evadine's brow and she spared the growing inferno a short glance, as if noticing it for the first time. In the past the sight of wanton destruction would cause her distress. Not so now. I saw a narrowing of her gaze and a twist to her mouth, the light of the flames dancing in her eyes, and was that beginnings of a smile? In truth, it was just a flicker of expression, quickly vanished, but I had seen it and, of all terrible things I witnessed that night, I felt this to be the worst.

"Indeed, my lord," she told me with grave conviction. "I will not have the first day of my reign marked by the destruction of the holiest of cities."

"Reign, is it?" Thessil cried out from the ground, twisting to cast his words at the surrounding crusaders. "You hear that, you servile dogs? She intends to make herself queen! This is not a crusade. It's a rebellion, for which you'll all hang . . ."

His words became a discordant jumble as Evadine delivered a hard kick to his back, sending his bound form tumbling down the flank of the earthwork and into the midst of the crusade. I heard Thessil scream out some additional furious denunciations even as the first blows were struck. But soon, as more blades rained down, defiance turned to brief, shrieking agony, then silence.

"A trial would have suited us better," I advised Evadine. "A demonstration that the Ascendant Queen will be the upholder of laws in this land, not a tyrant."

"A fair point, Alwyn." She inclined her head in faint contrition. "But he tried to kill you, and that will be the worst crime in my realm. Come—" she started down the slope towards the burning city, beckoning for me to follow "—and let us calm this tempest."

In all, five Luminants were found alive in the aftermath of Athiltor's fall. Only one had been executed during Arnabus's brief tenure. The unfortunate fellow continued to hang inverted and rotting from the cathedral spire until I had him cut down and consigned to the crypt. Others had fled when Arnabus first made his play for ultimate power over the Covenant, leaving this lot behind. I suspected because all but one was too old and infirm to mount an escape. Despite their age, the Luminants displayed swift efficiency in reasserting their authority. By noon they had assumed their seats in the council chamber and set about reassembling the coterie of Ascendants and lesser clerics that once saw to the administration of the holy city.

Evadine and I found them busily sorting documents and assigning tasks amid a gaggle of functionaries, though they deigned to afford the Anointed Lady a warm welcome.

"Your swift action and undaunted courage will never be forgotten, Ascendant Evadine," a tall Luminant with steel-grey hair assured her when Evadine strode to the centre of the chamber.

"My thanks, Luminant Daryhla." Evadine bowed with gracious humility "And I have little doubt your own actions in the face of this outrage will stand as an equal example of faith and fortitude."

To this the Luminant responded with only a distracted nod before returning her attention to the ledger before her. Although the youngest of the surviving council, she was Evadine's senior by at least two decades and, I assumed, a cleric of considerable experience. However, I saw little real intelligence in her countenance. Instead, there was only the stiff presumption of one accustomed to power. To her and the other clerics present, Arnabus's heresy had been merely a bizarre if frightening interruption in the flow of normality. None had yet to realise that he had been but a minor obstruction and the true harbinger of change had just walked into their chamber.

Had Sihlda ever taken her rightful place upon this council, I felt certain she would have paid far more heed to the Mounted Company soldiers filing in to line the walls. It was only at the echo of their boots as they stamped to attention that Luminant Daryhla and her aged colleagues consented to afford the Anointed Lady their full notice.

"My thanks, Ascendant," Daryhla said, using her quill to gesture at the soldiers, "but with the Great Heretic and his vile captain slain, I feel such protection is not warranted." She smiled. "We thank you once more for your service and command that you garrison your soldiers within the cathedral precincts to await further orders."

"Orders?" Evadine repeated. "From whom?"

"The council, of course." A certain irritation crept into the Luminant's voice then, but her gaze also showed a burgeoning alarm as it traversed Evadine's soldiers.

"What council?" Evadine spoke with soft deliberation, but these two words succeeded in heralding an abrupt silence in the chamber. All eyes turned to her, the various clerics straightening from their ledgers and documents, some in grim awareness, others in blank mystification.

"We may be reduced in number," Daryhla said and I felt a twinge of respect for the steadiness of her tone, "but it behoves all true servants of the Covenant to lend their strength to rebuilding . . ."

"Rebuilding what?" Evadine cut in. "A nest of venal liars intent on nothing but their own comfort and enrichment? You imagine I spilled blood and led good and honest people to battle and death to succour your long corrupted rule? No, your day is done and you are Luminant no longer, for that very name is an abomination to the Martyrs' example. They had no need of grand titles, nor the vast wealth in which you cloak yourselves. Nor, from this day forth, shall the Covenant."

Daryhla's courage proved a deep well, for she stood with stern resolution, regarding Evadine with hard-eyed defiance. "What is your intent?" she demanded. "Make yourself as great a heretic as the creature we just deposed? Like him, will you do bloody murder in this most sacred place?"

"You deposed no one," Evadine reminded her. "And it was the greed and indolence of this council that allowed one such as him to rise. As for bloody murder." She paused, a kindly smile on her lips. "Why would I kill you? As of this moment, you are a person of no consequence whatsoever. Of course—" she opened her arms, tracking her gaze across the scared or resentful faces of the lesser clerics "—all true servants of the Covenant are invited to stay and glory in this new dawn. Their labour and knowledge are welcome. But none shall henceforth call themselves anything but a Supplicant and any who act in service to self rather than Covenant shall be named heretics."

Evadine settled her focus on Daryhla once more. "You are welcome too, Supplicant Daryhla, if you think yourself equal to the task of mere humility. If not—" she inclined her head at the door "—get you hence and sully this holy place no longer."

There was dissent, of course. The vaulted halls of the cathedral rang with shouts of rage and despair as a small army of clerics found itself evicted from a place it had called home for centuries. When it became apparent that this scouring of the holiest of shrines would not be accompanied by violence, beyond some hard shoving and an occasional punch, the shouts became yet louder.

Captain Dervan, not troubling to conceal his disgust at the general disorder, blankly refused to lend his troops to quelling it. His company had suffered a half-dozen dead and the same number wounded in their assault of Thessils's rear flank. Paltry losses in comparison to some of the fights I'd seen, however the commoner captain plainly felt them keenly.

"Duchess Lorine sent us here to fight a battle," he stated, pointedly failing to address me by noble rank. "It is won, in no small part due to our efforts. Therefore, I shall be marching my company back to Castle Ambris forthwith."

Having no avenue for argument, beyond offering a bribe which I knew would likely rouse this dutiful fellow to violence, I countered his discourtesy with gracious thanks for his company's service. He didn't bother bowing or commenting further before stomping off to marshal his soldiers for the road.

Daryhla and the other defrocked Luminants proved an exception to the prevailing chaos, departing the cathedral with a dignity and rectitude I couldn't help but admire. True to her word, Evadine ensured they enjoyed safe passage to the cart waiting at the foot of the cathedral steps. However, I felt that the scale of humiliation suffered under the eyes of the onlooking mass of crusaders was tantamount to violence. The oldest of the Luminants, a small, wizened ancient with misted eyes and scant grasp on events, began to weep uncontrollably as he slumped on to the cart.

"Save your tears, brother," Daryhla said, resting a hand on the spotted dome of the ancient's head. "This is but a passing moment." She directed a glare at Evadine standing at the summit of the steps, shouting loud enough for the crowd to hear. "When we return, it will be at the head of a royal host and all shall be as it was."

For once, eloquence seemed beyond Evadine. She had maintained a mostly serene demeanour throughout this task, but the former Luminant's bold resistance seemed to weary her. "Oh," she said, not bothering to raise her voice and waving a dismissive hand, "just go away, you stupid old cow."

Silence reigned as the cart trundled towards the King's Road, trailed by a ragged column of loyal clerics. There were far more of these than I liked, dozens of the scribes, healers and scholars that formed the administrative glue not only for this city but the Covenant entire. I had tentatively raised the possibility of forcibly detaining the more learned and capable, but Evadine wouldn't hear of it.

She waited until the cart had faded beyond the more distant ranks of the crusade before commencing her speech, calling the mass of eager adherents and more fearful townsfolk closer. The latter, understandably, kept to the fringes of the gathering. I had been efficient in having the bodies of those claimed by the madness of the previous night cleared away. However, I remained starkly aware that many of those now assembled to hear the Anointed Lady's word had lost friends and loved ones in the battle to secure her rise.

"There will be no more death here," Evadine stated, her voice carrying to all ears with its usual effortless command. "All who bore arms against me in this place are hereby pardoned, for they were deceived. Know that through me the Seraphile have decreed an end to councils. Nor will there be differing ranks among the clergy, for these breed the pestilent twins of ambition and greed, both of which are barriers to the Seraphiles' grace. Henceforth there will only be Supplicants, humble in their service to the Risen Martyr who is in turn most humble in her service to the Seraphile. Let this day be the birth of the Covenant Resurgent."

Evadine paused to allow the cheers and brandished weapons to rise and fall. It had been her intention to proclaim not just her ascendancy over the Covenant this day, but also her status as queen. Thankfully, on this occasion at least, she was content to defer to my counsel that such an unambiguous challenge to the Crown should wait. We had an army on hand, that was true, but the storming of Athiltor had not been without cost. With winter coming on, I had little hope of swelling our ranks and my scouts still reported no sign of the Covenant Host. The dismissal of Leannor's messenger would surely have alarmed the Princess Regent, but hopefully not to the point of war, especially when the royal coffers remained denuded by the Alundian Crusade and the Pretender's War. We stood at the dawn of a fresh struggle, of that I had not the slightest doubt, but stalemate suited us best at this juncture.

"Know that I have only love for you in my heart," Evadine went on as the cheers faded. "Know that the blood you shed and the friends you lost in this holiest of causes, painful though they be, are not in vain. You have done more than I could ever ask of even the most devout souls. And so, any who wish to return to their homes may do so now without fear of disfavour. Go, and bear my love and gratitude with you for all your days. But, for those who wish to stay at my side, I bid you welcome. For I will need you. The Covenant Resurgent will need you. The enemies we vanquished in this place are but one trial and rest assured we face many others. I have never promised you an easy path. I have never promised you anything but blood and sacrifice, for that is the reward of those who truly wish to serve this Covenant that we cherish. So, I ask you, my brothers and sisters, in this most divinely blessed place, will you hold to me?"

The sound that greeted her was more a roar than a cheer, delivered with unreasoning force. Remarkably, I saw many of the townsfolk joining in. In the space of one short address Evadine had won the hearts of people who had suffered her wrath only hours before. Often I had witnessed her capacity for wielding power through mere oratory, but the ardency she aroused that day was of a different order, so much so that it became another facet of her legend. The Risen Martyr's address to the faithful from the steps of Athiltor Cathedral is a frequent subject of both paintings and poems. Although, as is generally the case with the laggards and wine soaks that comprise the artistic clique, most fail to include me in their renderings. To be fair, I kept mostly to the shadows during her speech. Being seen too often at Evadine's side might invite unwelcome scrutiny and rumour. We had been discreet, but I found the threat of exposure a constant worry. The Risen Martyr must be pure, her soul and body unstained by base carnality.

"A few more speeches like that," Wilhum told Evadine as we returned to the vaulted corridor leading to the chapel, the crowd's adulation still raging outside, "and we'll have an army ten times our current size."

"For now, I'd settle for just Swain and Ofihla's companies," I said.

Wilhum and I fell in alongside Evadine as she strode back to the council chamber. The crowd's acclaim continued to echo loud enough to smother our footsteps, but, far from displaying any exultation at the effects of her speech, her face was set in a preoccupied frown.

"I've sent heralds to every shrine, village and town within reach," I ventured when she failed to speak. "Proclaiming the birth of the Covenant Resurgent under the sole authority of the Risen Martyr. We'll also need to send some form of address to Leannor, carefully worded, of course. Letters to the duchies too. Duchess Lorine is an ally, of sorts, but we'll need others . . ."

"No." Evadine came to a halt, turning to face me. Her expression was stern but guarded, a combination I had rarely seen in her.

"No allies?" I asked.

She shook her head. "No letters. Words on parchment won't suffice. You must go yourself, as my ambassador. Measure the devotion of the dukes and their attachment to the Algathinets. When you return, I'll decide what alliances we forge, if any."

"We'll need support, Evie," Wilhum said, stepping closer and lowering his voice. "The Algathinets will have some notion by now of what you're planning. Without allies . . ."

"The Seraphile are the only ally I need."

Wilhum stiffened at the edge colouring her words, and I saw a small twitch of regret pass across Evadine's brow before she added in a softened tone, "Still, with more soldiers the price we'll pay in blood should be lessened, that's true. Hence, my loyal ambassador's mission." She turned to me with a brisk smile. "One I would prefer you undertake without delay."

"If I'm to be your chamberlain, I'll need to organise things here," I said. "The Covenant accounts alone will take weeks to scrutinise . . ."

"I'll see to that myself. Besides, since you allowed those plains savages to make off with the bulk of our gold, the accounts would appear to have lost most of their importance."

The Vergundians and sundry hired blades had disappeared before dawn, piling all the riches they had scraped from the cathedral on to a caravan of stolen carts and making haste along the eastern road. Their looting had been swift but efficient, draining all the easily opened coin stores and thieving various treasures from the Luminants' quarters. However, they had been good to their word and left the Covenant relics untouched. A full count of the Covenant's remaining coin was yet to be made but, even though it would complicate matters, I wasn't overly perturbed by the loss. The Covenant's true wealth, as Sihlda had always been at pains to point out, lay not in coin but land. Even with the loss of lands ceded to Lorine, a season's worth of rents would restore a good portion of what had been lost. Beyond that, a decent harvest come the following summer would afford the Covenant Resurgent riches far beyond anything even Deckin had dreamed of in his maddest moments.

"Payment was promised in your name." A growing heat coloured my own words now, stoked by the clear disparagement in her manner. *And when had she ever called anyone a savage before?* "Would you have had me break your word? Perhaps do murder to preserve the gold, slaughter those who opened the door to this city?"

"Of course not!"

I clenched my jaw and straightened as she rounded on me, her words fading into the undaunted cheers from outside. Her fierce, reproachful glare was brief but sent a jolt of pain through my heart.

Never before had she directed such a pitch of anger in my direction. Looking away, she drew in a slow breath. “My word is given, lord Scribe,” she said. “Depart for the northern duchies tomorrow and leave the governance of this Covenant to me.”

Chapter Seven

I took Ayin and the Widow with me, along with a dozen of my most trusted scouts. Tiler I left in Athiltor in charge of the Scout Company with orders to keep scouring the country for any sign of Swain or Ofihla. Also joining my mission of diplomacy were Quintrell and Adlar Spinner. A minstrel and a juggler would, at the very least, provide some measure of amusement to nobles I suspected might not offer the warmest of welcomes. Lilat came too, of course, an unbidden but inevitable presence wherever I went. She had a tendency to disappear during the day's march, apparently finding the wooded hills through which we passed an irresistible playground.

"Slow and fat," she said the third night out from the holy city, dumping a brace of rabbits beside the campfire. "How do your people manage to go hungry in a land like this?"

I offered only a vague grunt in response, distracted by reading the volume I had procured from the Covenant Library: *From Banditry to Lordship – A History of the Pendroke Family, Wardens of Althiene.* Calling at the library that morning I had been disappointed to find Aspirant Viera gone, the senior librarian presumably having chosen to trail in the deposed Luminants' wake rather than submit to the Anointed Lady's heretical rule. Most of the other librarians had followed her lead, leaving behind a trio of youthful but keen custodians.

"The Isidorian Codex?" a doe-eyed young woman in a noviciate's robe repeated when I stated the object of my visit. She blinked her large eyes, mouth set in a small circle of surprise.

"You have it?" I asked.

"We did, my lord." Another blink. "Aspirant Viera kept it locked up along with certain other volumes. I'm afraid she took them all with her when she . . ." The novice trailed off, grimacing in nervous regret.

"I see," I said, forcing a smile. "What can you tell me about the codex?"

Much of her trepidation slipped away then, her posture putting me in mind of her absconded superior in its stiff, scholarly surety. "Martyr Isidor was said to be the only prophetess of the early Covenant," she told me. "Slain in the most foul manner by unenlightened kings in far distant lands. They took exception to her predictions regarding the disaster that would befall their realms should they continue to shun the Seraphiles' love. So dangerous were these prophecies that her followers took to recording them in a cypher, the key to which was lost. Some scholars have attempted to decode them with only partial success. Consequently, her scroll is short compared to many of the first Martyrs and her name not widely known even among the faithful."

A book of cyphered predictions, I mused. *But not so cyphered as to prevent Arnabus reading them.* "Do you know if the Great Heretic ever came here asking for the codex?"

Her fortitude wavered a little at this but, after a hard swallow, she managed to provide a mostly quaverless reply. "No, my lord. Such things are far above my station."

Viera would be on the road to Couravel, I knew, presumably riding a cart bearing a chest of forbidden books. Intercepting her was well within my means, but also a clear signal of my interest, one she would surely share with the deposed Luminants and, most likely, Leannor's agents. Keeping the secret would be a simple matter, if I was prepared to murder Viera and any travelling with her, which I was not.

"Do you have any notion where I might find another copy?" I asked the novice.

"Sadly, copies of the codex are exceedingly rare, my lord, reserved only for the most respected archives. There is most likely one to be found in the cathedral in Couravel. It's also possible Ascendant Hilbert has one in his personal archive in Callintor. He and Aspirant Viera kept up a lively correspondence regarding the more obscure texts in Covenant lore."

Hilbert. A name I recalled well, but not with any fondness. "Thank you, Supplicant," I said. "You have been very helpful."

"Just a novice, my lord." She bowed her head, adding in a reverent whisper, "But greatly honoured to serve the Anointed Lady."

"I'm glad to hear it. Your name?"

More blinking of overlarge eyes, this time accompanied by a startled frown. "C-Corlina, my lord, noviciate custodian."

"Well, you were yesterday. Today you're Supplicant Corlina, senior librarian of the Covenant Library." I ignored her stuttered thanks and nodded to the stacks. "Your first task is to provide me with concise but detailed histories of the ducal houses of Albermaine. Your second is to compile a full list of every volume Aspirant Viera stole and places where replacements might be found. I'll collect it when I return in a few weeks."

The history of the Pendroke family she had provided was long on lurid detail regarding their origins as one of many bandit clans inhabiting the famously inhospitable hill country of northern Althiene. For generations the Pendrokes had enriched themselves through a combination of base thievery and hiring themselves out as mercenaries to those they termed "southron weaklings". All that changed with the rise of King Mathis, First of the Algathinets, who promised more than mere coin in return for loyal service. The Pendrokes' alliance with the Algathinets had, after several decades of strife, brought them overlordship of all Althiene and all the wealth that entailed. Over the long years of Algathinet dominance, this alliance had proven to be a mutually beneficial arrangement, until Duke Guhlton's much loved daughter chose to take her own life when Highsahl fell. Now the Pendrokes were a broken dynasty, their sole claim to power resting in the small personage of Lady Ducinda, Duchess Celynne's daughter. With Ducinda betrothed to the boy King Arthin and most of her immediate relatives slain at the Vale, actual governance of Althiene now lay in the hands of Duke Guhlton's second cousin, Lord Archel Shelvane. It said much for the authority of the Pendroke family throughout Althiene that Leannor had been obliged to place a blood relative in charge of the duchy. It also told me something of Shelvane's character. What manner of man serves the woman who broke the compact of parley to slay the head of his own family?

The sound of Ayin's voice drew my attention from the book. The soft and perfect sound drifted from the larger fire where the rest of the party sat. Quintrell's mandolin added a harmonious underpinning to the song that followed, one of Ayin's nonsense compositions that usually aroused appreciative laughter. Tonight, however, the concoction of rhyming doggerel heralded a sombre mood. The words themselves were the usual meaningless mishmash, but the tune told another story. Looking across at the oval of her face, rendered yellow in the campfire's glow, I perceived a sadness I hadn't before. I had always suspected there might be an unseen depth of feeling beneath Ayin's guileless exterior and now saw it revealed in stark detail.

Witnessed one battle too many? I wondered. *Cut one too many throats?*

I looked away when the plaintive call of her next verse sent an uncomfortable lurch through my chest. The list of horrors witnessed by this young woman had been long and not limited to battle. The Sacrifice March loomed largest, but I knew she had also seen grimness aplenty during my absence from the company when Evadine and the Crown Host completed the subjugation of Alundia. *And it's far from over*, I knew, watching her complete the song with a modest inclination of her head for the applause she received. I couldn't see her blush when Adlar pressed a kiss to her cheek, but was sure she did.

No more, I decided with sudden conviction. *No more war for her. When we return she'll spend her days at the cathedral and sing all the songs she likes.* The thought was accompanied by a pang of guilt-tinged envy. I could spare her what came next, but I couldn't spare myself.

There are some who claim that noble blood carries with it the essence of greatness. Those born with this remarkable stuff coursing through their veins are, it is asserted, imbued with gifts of intellect and fortitude to which the lower orders can never aspire. It should come as scant surprise, cherished reader, that I have never held to such notions. Yet, if I had, they would most certainly have been dispelled by my first glimpse of Lord Archel Shelvane. The banner of House Shelvane that hung behind his chair was emblazoned with a boar of unfeasibly long tusks. But I fancied this was not the reason this caretaker of the Dukedom of Althiene was known as the Pig of the North. Personally, I feel this name to be an insult to pigs, an animal of which I have always been fond.

"No council?" Lord Archel enquired amid a sputter of wine and half-chewed pie. His fleshy face formed what I took to be a squint, although it was hard to tell under the mingled grease and sweat that covered his wobbling jowls. "What d'you mean, man? How can there not be a Luminants' Council?"

"It has been dissolved, my lord. The Anointed Lady Evadine Courlain, Risen Martyr and First Among the Faithful, has ordained it so." I maintained an even tone as I spoke, one stripped of doubt, presenting myself as a messenger bearing plain and inarguable facts. Although I saw little of intelligence in Lord Archel's small eyes, I did note a measure of cunning in the way they glinted in the light of the many candles adorning his table. I had been offered neither a seat nor a share of the copious feast arrayed before him.

He held court in the hall where once his slain cousin had sat, a spacious chamber dominating the ground floor of Castle Pendroke. Unlike other ducal seats, this holdfast was not located in the heart of a city or attached to an adjoining town. Constructed three centuries before, this grim fortification of tall granite walls and high watchtowers sat amid the southernmost cliffs and crags of the Althiene mountains. Getting here had entailed an unpleasant journey of inconstant weather and perilous tracks. I knew from my research that Castle Pendroke had never been successfully stormed, and only infrequently besieged. One look at its location made it plain as to why. It also caused me to wonder why the late Duke Guhlton hadn't simply fortified his position here when he broke with the Algathinets. If he had, I harboured little doubt it would be to his far more astute ear I would now be relating my news.

"Dissolved, is it?" Lord Archel said, displaying a habitual tendency to repeat the last words to make purchase on his mind. He burped, long and loud, then reached for a wine goblet. We were alone in his chamber apart from a single servant and a brace of guards. Another choice that made me judge this man not a complete fool. "Can I assume," he continued, after several gulps sent crimson rivulets across his jowls, "this was done with the full approval of the Princess Regent?"

"Covenant matters lie outside the province of the Crown, my lord," I replied. "As I'm sure you are aware."

"So, no." His goblet made a loud thunk as it connected with the table, falling over to spill its contents. Lord Archel barely seemed to notice, reaching for another slice of pie while his servant quickly recovered and refilled the fallen vessel. *This bugger has never wiped his own arse*, I decided, watching Archel chew, small eyes aglitter.

"Why come all this way to tell me, Scribe?" he asked after much mastication.

"The Anointed Lady wishes to present her compliments, my lord." I summoned a faint smile, ignoring the obvious barb in his failure to address me by my title. "And invite you to attend supplications at the Holy City at your earliest convenience, where she shall be honoured to afford your rule of this duchy her blessing."

"Blessing, is it?" His lips, small stripes of shiny pinkness in a sweaty blanket, parted to reveal unswallowed food as he laughed. "Pray tell, what use is a blessing, Scribe? Can it pay my servants, my soldiers? Can it get all those dirt grubbers and coin-hoarding merchants to pay their fucking tithes?"

"The blessing of the Anointed Lady will do much to win the hearts of the faithful in your duchy, my lord. And, as word of her ascension spreads, so will the weight of her word increase. She is aware of your difficulties in this land, of course. Word has reached her of those who still swear fealty to a fallen, traitorous duke and infest the hill country, plotting rebellion."

"They do more than plot," Archel huffed, pushing his plate aside and reaching again for his goblet. "Murdered my nephew last week, they did. He was an awful wastrel, to be frank, but his mother never tires of pestering me about it. Strung up a dozen clansmen for the crime, but that's not enough for her. Wants the hill country burned and left barren. Vicious bitch." He gulped more wine. "Just like our mother."

"My condolences." I formed my face into something suitably grave and sympathetic. "While I'm sure you wouldn't stoop to such extremes, and neither would the Anointed Lady, she has never stinted in bringing her strength to bear on those who engage in unjust rebellion. I have little doubt she would do so while Althiene stands imperilled, especially since you appear to be in want of reinforcement from the Crown."

"The Crown, eh?" A facility for concealing his thoughts was not among the negligible gifts enjoyed by this man, for the calculations churning within his skull were plain in his squinting gaze, the small eyes near disappearing amid the bunching of cheek and brow. "Princess Leannor promised me five hundred men-at-arms to garrison this draughty pile come the summer."

Whether this was true or not mattered little. Here we had arrived at the crux of whatever bargain might be struck betwixt this cunning glutton and the Covenant Resurgent. "The summer is many months away," I pointed out. "While I need but send a galloper to Athiltor and you will have five hundred Covenant soldiers garrisoned here by winter's dawn."

Somewhere beneath the flesh of Archel's face, his tongue worked to move something about his mouth. His jaw snapped and a piece of bone appeared clamped between his teeth, a scrap of gristle dangling from the protruding end. I had thought the many battlefields I had seen to be rich in the most disgusting spectacles I could ever wish to behold. This came close to outdoing them all. "Soldiers who'll follow my orders?" he enquired, lips squirming around the bone.

"Of course. As long as such orders do not conflict with Covenant lore."

He snorted and the bone vanished into his maw, his nostrils flaring in a grunt of apparent satisfaction. "Tell your Risen Martyr I'll be glad to receive her blessing, once her soldiers have assisted me in securing this duchy. 'Course . . ." he paused to belch again ". . . I'll need to pay my own levies too. The rents for all the Covenant lands held within the borders of Althiene should suffice."

I could have argued more, bargained him down as I had Lorine, but my desire to rid myself of his presence was too strong. Besides, once the Ascendant Queen sat on the throne this particular agreement could be renegotiated and if this fool didn't like it, I had already compiled a list of other Pendroke relatives likely to prove more amenable.

"The people of Althiene are fortunate in their governance, my lord." I complemented this, one of the most outrageous lies I have ever uttered, with a bow of obsequious depth. By way of a reply Lord Archel Shelvane contrived to both burp and fart in unison.

Upon being conveyed to the presence of Lord Lohrent Lambertain, Duke of the Cordwain, I wondered if his reception might be a deliberate attempt to provide a contrast to his ill-mannered neighbour. His keep, Castle Norwind, was a sprawling holdfast occupying the high ground above the Cordwain port city of Leavinsahl. When I presented myself at the castle gate, the guard captain greeted me with a curt civility and lack of surprise that made it clear my visit was expected. This impression was cemented by the fact that, instead of meeting me alone save for servants and soldiers, the duke treated me to an audience with both himself and his eldest son, Lord Gilferd. He sat to his father's right, a young man a few years my junior, his face a youthful mirror of the duke's austere, high-cheekboned countenance.

"We bid you welcome, Lord Scribe." The duke addressed me in a gravelly voice that told his age better than his appearance. I knew from my recent reading that this man was near seventy and his heir the fruit of his third marriage, the others producing only daughters. His smile was tight and far from warm, while Lord Gilferd had no smile for me at all. Seated behind the two lords was a dozen-strong party I took to be the duke's chief retainers and principal advisers. They were a mismatched lot of grizzled knights and skull-capped scholars, none of whom appeared any happier to see me than their liege lord. The most significant personage among them was a tall, ashen-haired woman in the grey robe of an Ascendant. Of them all, only her demeanour was, predictably, openly hostile.

"I am both honoured and humbled to stand before you, my lord." Sensing that the blatant flattery I had shown to Lord Archel would find scant welcome here, I gave a bow of strictly appropriate depth. "And, if I may speak as a soldier, also grateful."

The duke arched an eyebrow. "How so, my lord?"

"Why, in every battle I've fought, it has been my fortune to have brave Cordwainers at my side."

"It is the point of honour for the Lambertain family that we never shirk our duties." Despite his words, I detected no pride in Lord Lohrent's tone. "The king calls for soldiers and we answer. Such is the way with dukes and kings."

"Your loyalty is to be cherished by any monarch." I bowed again before speaking on with brisk formality. "I come before you bearing the word of the Risen Martyr and Anointed Lady—"

"And heretic!" The interruption came in the form of a shrill exclamation from the Ascendant. The woman rose to her feet, features quivering with genuine outrage. "The vilest of heretics, in truth! A desecrator of the Covenant. I beseech you, my lord—" she swung her fierce gaze upon Duke Lohrent "—cast this known murderer and liar from your keep . . ."

"Ascendant Hielma!" When raised to a commanding bark, it transpired that the duke's voice held no gravel at all. Falling abruptly silent, the cleric sank back into her seat, posture stiff and jaw clenching.

"My apologies, Lord Scribe." Lohrent afforded me another tight smile, even thinner than the first. "I abhor all manner of rudeness to my guests. It has long been the custom of the Cordwain that those who present themselves in peace are received in kind."

"I suffer no offence, my lord." Inclining my head, I shot a pointed glance at the Ascendant. "Change is ever a painful thing to the rigid of mind, especially one steeped in unearned privilege."

I turned away from Ascendant Heilma's reddening visage, addressing my next words solely to the duke. "The Risen Martyr wishes it known that she blesses your house and your duchy. She would be both honoured and delighted to formalise this blessing should you attend her at Athiltor."

"An invitation I thank her for." Lohrent followed this response with what I knew to be a deliberately prolonged pause. It was a ploy I had used when questioning prisoners. The desire of the needy to fill a silence will often provoke ill-chosen words, or even the spillage of secrets. I bore it with a bland patience, my eyebrows raised in only slight expectation. I saw a faint pulse of amusement pass across the duke's face before he spoke again.

"I understand you were kind enough to bring players to my keep," he said.

"I did, my lord. A trio, in fact. A juggler, a minstrel, and a singer possessed of the purest voice and finest verses in all Albermaine."

"An impressive boast."

"I am not given to boasting, my lord. If you would care to hear her sing you will know me no liar." Another barb in the Ascendant's direction, one that provoked a caustic laugh.

"Hear her I shall." The duke put his hands on the arms of his chair and pushed himself upright. His household all followed suit while I sank to one knee. "Tonight," Lohrent added. "What kind of host would I be if I failed to honour such a singular guest with a feast? We shall talk more when I've heard your songbird. But I caution you, to win your desired reward, her song need be special indeed."

Ayin, as ever when it came to music, didn't disappoint. Her performance came after Adlar had captured the audience's attention with a dazzling display. After an impressive opening with the usual clubs and balls, he provided a parting spectacle by asking the crowd to volunteer various objects for him to juggle. One of the duke's knights had given over his longsword, presumably in the expectation that

Adlar would surely drop it as he cast the sundry items, eight in all, into the air. He didn't. The sword he flung high while working the collection of pots, bottles and goblets into a rapid circle. When the sword descended, he cast the smaller items high, caught and flung the weapon again before catching the other items and repeating the process.

Quintrell eschewed a solo performance in favour of acting as Ayin's accompanist. At my urging, she began by delighting the feasting lords, ladies and court functionaries with renditions of popular favourites. The tunes were jolly at first, the kind that usually invited the audience to join in, but not tonight. They all stared in growing fascination at this slender girl with a voice and face that many might fancy to be a Seraphile made flesh. As I hoped, fascination turned to moist-eyed rapture when she sang her own compositions. "Who Will Sing for Me?" engendered a great deal of eye wiping followed by riotous applause, but it was "The Warrior's Lament" that provided the crowning glory of Ayin's night.

"*The days of this war, they grow ever longer. The deeds of this war, do darken my soul . . .*"

As she sang, I took careful note of Lord Lohrent's reaction, finding his face set in serene appreciation rather than the wonder I hoped to see. His son, however, was a different matter. Lord Gilferd stared at Ayin with the unblinking but nervous agitation of a young man finding himself lost in his first amorous obsession. I found this gratifying and worrisome in equal measure. A smitten heir to the Cordwain duchy may prove useful, but a spoilt lordling intent on pursuing a low-born soldier in the Covenant Host was a potential complication. No doubt, he looked upon Ayin and saw an enchanting waif with a voice that could pierce the heart. Finding her to be something else entirely would assuredly bring resentful disappointment.

Lord Gilferd's father apparently had a similar gift for observation to my own. "Stop squirming, boy," I heard him mutter in sharp rebuke when he noticed his son's increasing loss of composure. The youth barely seemed to notice, his excitement only mounting as Ayin approached her final verse.

"For I'll face my fate a man of great sorrow, I'll face my fate deserving I know."

As the last note drifted into the beams of the chamber there came a short moment of unbroken silence, then the crowd erupted in applause, all save the duke rising to their feet to hail the songstress with claps and cheers, none louder or more enthusiastic than Lord Gilferd.

Inevitably, Ayin and Quintrell were compelled to provide several encores by an audience unwilling to let them go. Ayin was clearly bemused by the acclaim but the far more seasoned minstrel asked them to call out their favourite tunes, to be sung only if they filled his hat with coin. This brought about a good deal of shouted disagreement as Quintrell roved the room, hat outstretched and coins clinking as differing factions vied to hear their songs sung. The ongoing noise enabled me to lean closer to the duke and murmur a question.

"Special enough for you, my lord?"

"A remarkable talent, to be sure, Lord Scribe." He inclined his head. "Especially in one so young."

"Then come to Athiltor and hear her again." I nodded at his son, now staring at Ayin with what can only be called stupefaction. "Bring Lord Gilferd, if it please you."

A spasm of irritation passed over the duke's face as he turned to his heir. "Sit straighter," he snapped. "Dukes-to-be don't slouch at table." Father and son exchanged a glare of mutual resentment before the youth consented to lower his gaze and stiffen his back into a marginally more regal pose.

"I'm curious," Lohrent said, turning to me, "did Lord Archel consent to receive the Anointed Lady's blessing when you called upon him?"

That he knew of my visit to his eastern neighbour was no surprise. This man exuded the assured confidence of one who had successfully navigated the often lethal currents of Albermaine politics all his life. Such a man would not be wanting for intelligence.

"He did," I said. "Despite the many difficulties that beset his duchy. Difficulties the Anointed Lady will be pleased to assist in addressing."

"Really? With coin or soldiers?" He grunted a laugh and waved a hand to spare me the chore of phrasing a suitably evasive reply. "You imagine I have need of the Anointed Lady's aid? There are no rebels within my borders."

"And yet, the Algathinets starve your duchy. Since the fall of the Fjord Geld, Cordwain ports are forbidden trade with the Ascarlians. Lady Evadine feels the time for enmity with our northern neighbours has passed, that perhaps a more pragmatic and profitable course is needed."

The duke's humour faded as he leaned closer to me, voice lowered. "I see you are a clever man, my lord, so let us speak plainly. My acceptance of your lady's blessing would signal to all that I recognise her authority over the Covenant. It would also make it clear that I approve of her dissolution of the Luminants' Council. My own sympathies aside, a fellow as insightful as yourself will also know that my recognition means nothing. It is the Crown's favour you require. Without that, the Risen Martyr is merely a heretic occupying a stolen cathedral."

"Your frankness is refreshing." I bowed in appreciation. "And, in truth, I do pretend to some measure of insight. Such things arise from a close study of history, which is rich in examples of those who were called heretics only later to be hailed as Martyrs, or even kings."

Lohrent's brow furrowed and his features slipped into an aspect of careful scrutiny. He said nothing for a time while Ayin began a rendition of "The Braggart's Folly", a lively old ditty about a comedically lovelorn knight. This time the audience chose to join in, clapping in rhythmic accompaniment and singing along at a thankfully loud volume.

"When first you came before me," Lohrent said, the song ensuring his voice was lost to all but me, "I thought you an older man. I see now you are, in fact, little more than a boy. Tempered by hardship and battle, to be sure, but still just a boy. And your Risen Martyr is naught but a deluded girl beset by imaginings she mistakes for visions. You are dangerous children at play, lighting a fire you can't hope to control."

He shifted, directing a nod at Ascendant Heilma seated towards the end of the high table. She hadn't joined her voice to the rest of the room, instead focusing all her attention on myself and the duke's unheard conversation.

"That woman has been ministering to my household for over twenty years," Lohrent told me. "She was there when the blood fever took my first wife and she was there when childbirth took my second. She is all kindness, all goodness, all wisdom. She desires no war, in fact always counsels against it. When she speaks of the Martyrs' example I hear truth in her words. When you speak of your Anointed Lady, I hear only blind devotion unencumbered by any truth at all. I know what you came for, Lord Scribe, and you will leave empty-handed. I will not throw off a lifetime of faith to bargain for scraps from a madwoman's table. Now—" he gave me one of his tight, thin smiles, inclining his head at Quintrell and Ayin "—I thank you for the entertainment you provided this night. In the morning you will take yourself from this keep and never cast your shadow upon my door again."

Chapter Eight

In some ways, former Ascendant Hilbert had changed a great deal since our prior acquaintance. His Ascendant's garb was gone, replaced by the plain grey Supplicant's robe expected of clergy in service to the Covenant Resurgent. Also, despite the fact that my departure from Callintor was only nigh two years ago, his face appeared to have acquired an additional matrix of creases about the eyes and forehead. In most other respects, however, the man remained the same self-important, overly ambitious prig I remembered.

"The Risen Martyr's chamberlain is always welcome here," he said, starting to hunch his shoulders in a bow then stopping when I held up a hand.

"We are all of equal rank now," I told him, putting a version of Duke Lohrent's empty smile on my lips before adding, "brother."

He greeted me in the nave of the Shrine to Martyr Callin, a far less well-kept space than I recalled. Dust was piled in the corners, and I spied more than a few clusters of rat droppings. The sanctuary city itself was also much quieter these days, the streets mostly bare of seekers bustling about their tasks. Similarly, I counted only a handful of custodians, most of whom melted into the shadows when my party rode through an unguarded gate. I knew without asking what had occurred here and it could be summarised in one word: schism. News of Athiltor's fall to the Anointed Lady had forced a choosing of sides. Those of orthodox sympathies, the majority judging by the barren streets, took to their heels while those cleaving to the Risen Martyr remained. That Hilbert counted himself among the latter came as a surprise, though I harboured considerable doubts that it stemmed from any devotional leanings.

Contrary to my ever vindictive character, I found watching him squirm provided all the satisfaction I needed. It was true that this man had once attempted to cast me out of this city and to face Lord Eldurm's vengeance. But the sight of Hilbert struggling to contain his disgust and disdain for this inescapable meeting sufficed to balance the scales. This was a petty man, so a petty revenge suited him well.

"Of course," he said. I saw him try and fail to summon a smile of his own, something I found amusing yet didn't fault him for; it was simply beyond him to pretend regard for one so low-born as I. "I have prepared a full list of those currently residing in Callintor. Supplicants, custodians and seekers. I was intending to take it to Athiltor to present to the Anointed Lady myself—"

"No need," I cut in. "I'll take it to her. I also require access to your personal archive. You do have one, I assume?"

The urge to lie was writ large on his face, but, though prideful, he was never stupid and it didn't persist for long. "I do." His shoulders sagged a little in defeat. "Though I have had little leisure for my personal passions of late."

"The Isidorian Codex. That is among your passions, is it not?"

A wariness supplanted the resignation on his face and he clasped his hands together, I assumed, to banish a nervous twitch. "Yes, I . . . have been attempting to translate it for some time now."

"Translate?" I frowned. "You mean decipher."

A flicker of his old superiority showed in the twist of his mouth, but he was wise enough to quell it. "The original text was cyphered, yes. But once decoded, it was revealed to have been written in Urhmaic, the language of the first Martyrs. It's a notoriously difficult script to parse into Albermaine-ish. I'm afraid my progress has been meagre . . ."

"Show me."

I hoped Hilbert had been lying, but one look at the texts he placed before me in the shrine's small library told a different tale. The original book provided by the Covenant Library, itself a copy of a far older tome, was a densely inscribed scrawl on rough brown parchment. Hilbert's deciphered text consisted of a stack of loose pages in his ever untidy hand. A scholar he was, but a scribe he was not.

"This is all?" I asked, leafing through the few dozen sheets that comprised his translation of the Urhmaic text.

"As I said, time has been short of late."

A brief review of the translated pages revealed mostly rambling and cryptic monologue rich in allusions to names I didn't recognise and pre-Covenant beliefs which meant little to me. One passage did catch my eye due to the multiple revisions that marred the text. One word in particular had been underlined several times, the parchment surrounding it filled with others, all crossed out.

"This word seems to have presented some difficulty," I said, pointing out the mess of scribblings.

"Yes." Hilbert grimaced in scholarly annoyance. "*Metreveus*. It has multiple meanings in Urhmaic. All negative in connotation, but an exact parallel is hard to come by."

"What's the closest?"

He pursed his lips in consideration before responding. "'Tyrant', probably. But also, it can be rendered as a conjoining of both 'great' and 'persecutor.'"

"Persecutor of who?"

"If I may?" Hilbert held out his hand and I passed the pages to him. "Here," he said, pointing to another passage a few pages on. "It's a dense verse in the original, so the translation may not be exact. The closest literal translation reads as 'And the *Metreveus* shall cleanse the land beyond the mountains with such fury that not a life will be spared. It shall be scourged once again. Know ye all that ash and ruin shall be the legacy of the *Metreveus*.'"

The land beyond the mountains . . . Scourged once again. Was this what Arnabus had wanted me to see? Did he imagine Evadine to be this *Metreveus*? If so, I required no further clues to deduce the identity of the land beyond the mountains.

"Was she right about anything?" I asked Hilbert. "Martyr Isidor. Did any of her prophecies come to pass?"

"Supposedly, she was the most accurate prophet known to history. However, the events she is said to have foreseen took place in antiquity, in the shadowed age between the rise of the First Martyrs and the blossoming of the Covenant. Contemporary accounts from those days are scant, but some do accord with her recorded statements, particularly those that pertain to plague or disaster."

"Arnabus." I settled a steady eye upon Hilbert's face. "The Great Heretic, did he ever come here and view this work?"

Hilbert stiffened, the wariness stealing over him again. I saw him debate the lie, then, wisely, decide against it. "Yes," he said after an uncomfortable cough. "He did. Curiously, he read the deciphered text without recourse to the translation, displaying no difficulty in doing so. I thought he might be play-acting at the time. Even then, I could tell a duplicitous soul when I saw one."

I returned my attention to the documents, debating whether to take them with me. I assumed Senior Librarian Corlina would set herself to the task of completing the translation with earnest energy, but doubted one so young possessed the required knowledge. "The Anointed Lady wishes you to continue your work on this," I said, returning the pages to Hilbert. "It will be your principal task from now on. When it's complete, have the translation copied by a neater hand and sent to me at Athiltor. Also . . ." I paused to engage in a pointed survey of the room. Like the rest of the building's interior, it was rich in piled dust and possessed a musty odour. "This shrine is a disgrace. Have it swept and scrubbed as soon as possible."

"The seekers who did such work all left," Hilbert protested. "And those that remain are needed to tend the fields."

"Then do it yourself. A broom is not a complicated device, brother. Now, before I depart, I require one more document from you."

To my considerable relief, Master Arnild was not among those who had chosen to flee the sanctuary city. I found him and a half-dozen colleagues at work in the scriptorium. Their stooped backs and gnarled fingers led me to the perhaps uncharitable conclusion that their decision to stay had more to do with infirmity than devotion.

"The Scroll of Martyr Ihlander," Arnild said, stepping back to allow me a view of his latest work. The mighty-thewed Ihlander, first Covenanter King of Albermaine, rose with axe in hand above a tide of heretics, his crown blazing like the sun thanks to the gold Arnild had embossed into it.

"Exquisite work as ever, master," I told him with an appreciative bow. "So fine it grieves me to tell you to put it aside." I handed him the bound sheaf of parchment I had obtained from Hilbert.

"'The Testament of Ascendant Sihlda Doisselle,'" he read, unfurling the bundle.

"'The Scroll of Martyr Sihlda,'" I corrected gently. "It's an incomplete text but I've added the necessary additions and amendments."

Arnild's wrinkled brow creased as he read the first few passages. "Some of this is familiar from Ascendant – I mean to say – Supplicant Hilbert's sermons."

"Yes, it would be. I require copies, Master Arnild. One in your full finery, the rest to be produced as fast as your fellow scribes are able."

"How many?"

"As many as parchment and ink allow. I'll leave coin to buy more. As soon as copies are complete they are to be sent to a shrine along with this letter from the Anointed Lady." I handed him another document, one I had penned that morning and signed in Evadine's name. It instructed the recipient to make Martyr Sihlda's scroll the principal source of inspiration for future sermons until further notice. This wasn't the first missive I had issued bearing my reasonable facsimile of Evadine's signature, something she was content for me to do since she found dealing with correspondence tedious.

"You will continue this task until every shrine in Albermaine has received 'The Scroll of Martyr Sihlda,'" I told Arnild. "Also, this scriptorium is now under your sole charge. Supplicant Hilbert will be busy with other matters."

"Pretty isn't it?" Ayin asked, holding the brooch up to the midday sun as it poked out from behind a bank of ominous clouds. We rode together at the head of the party, following the King's Road to Athiltor. The brooch was an arrangement of oak leaves fashioned from what my outlaw's eyes judged to be real gold. Shining bright in the centre of the leaves was either a genuine ruby or one of the best forgeries I had seen.

"That it is," I agreed. "Where did you get it?"

She pouted at the suspicious edge in my voice. "It was a gift, I'll have you know. The duke's son was very appreciative of my singing. In fact, he wanted me to stay and be the keep's singer in residence. I didn't know that was a thing."

"It isn't." I chose not to espouse my belief that young Lord Gilferd had additional duties in mind for his would-be singer in residence. "He must have been very disappointed when you said no."

"I suppose." She angled her head, studying the way the light caught the ruby. "He did say I was always welcome back, though. Gave me this, a token of his good intentions, he said." She smiled and consigned the brooch to the purse at her belt. "A sweet lad, didn't you think? So few of them about."

"Sweeter than his father." The thought occurred that, with Lord Lohrent so blatantly setting himself against Evadine's cause, Ayin and her lordly suitor might find themselves facing each other across a battlefield before long. It further cemented my determination to spare her the coming tribulation, a conviction challenged immediately by her next words.

"Quintrell wants me to come away with him." Ayin related this news with a typically bright, distracted air. As was often the case when riding, her face was raised to the sky, better to track the birds flittering between the trees.

"Does he, now?" I turned in the saddle, looking back at Quintrell. Apparently unperturbed by my hard glare, he inclined his head and grinned.

"Yes," Ayin said. She tilted her head to an imperious angle, preening a little. "He thinks my talent is wasted in this company. He promises great riches if I join him in a tour of the eastern lands."

I resisted the urge to look at Quintrell again, Ayin's words leading me to a grim conclusion. *Meaning he wants to forsake his obligation to Lorine and get far from these duchies while there's still time.* The spying minstrel's desire to take Ayin along was surprising, but then her voice was undoubtedly valuable and he didn't know her well enough to recognise the danger she represented.

"What did you tell him?" I asked.

"That I serve the Anointed Lady, of course." She smirked. "Thank you for looking so worried, though."

It was now plain that the notion of keeping her cloistered at Athiltor presented an increasing list of difficulties. She grew bored so easily. This, combined with resentment at being left behind, could stir up dormant tendencies. Also, Quintrell might be faithless to his paymistress, but he wasn't wrong.

"You should consider it, at least," I said, stripping the reluctance from my voice. I said goodbye to Toria for sound reasons. Now perhaps it was time to say goodbye to Ayin. "Wouldn't you like to be rich?"

She squinted in surprise. "You'd let me go?"

"Could I really stop you?"

Ayin shifted, her pony tossing its head as it sensed her rider's distress. "I am sworn to the Lady's service," she told me with a sullenness I hadn't seen for a while.

"Then go but remain in her service. Folk in the east are still largely ignorant of the Risen Martyr's tale. You could spread the story far and wide, with song if you like."

She shook her head, small features hardening. "My place is here, with her and you. We've still so much to do. I'd like to see it all, the day she becomes queen, the day she marries you. Will you be a king then?"

The shock on my face must have been stark for she let out a taunting laugh. "Thought I didn't know, eh? Ayin's just a simple songbird who sees nothing." She stuck out her tongue. "Well, I see a lot, Alwyn Scribe. And you weren't even all that careful, were you?"

I averted my gaze, saying nothing as Blackfoot plodded along the frost-hardened ruts of the road. Once again, I suppressed the urge to cast a worried glance at Quintrell, though I was confident we were sufficiently ahead of the column for him not to have heard.

"It's all right," Ayin said, amusement still colouring her tone. "Love is of the Seraphile, so it makes sense she would share it. It's all rather lovely, actually. Perhaps I'll write a song about it; 'The Lady and the Outlaw.'"

Finally, after much churning of panicked thought, I managed to rasp out a question. "Who else knows?"

"Wilhum, at least I think so. The Widow too. She's awful jealous by the way."

"She told you this?"

"No." She sighed in exasperation. "I told you, I *see* things. Because it's me seeing them people think I don't."

More silent plodding as I whirled through myriad calculations. *What to tell her? What to do with her? Why would the Widow be jealous?* It all stopped when Ayin revealed a yet deeper well of insight when she said, "Some secrets can't be kept. They're just too big."

I slumped in the saddle, the storm in my head subsiding into a bitter weariness. "I know," I muttered. "Still, I'll ask you to keep this one. For now, at least."

"I will. But—" she wagged a finger at me "—no more talk of sending me away."

I smiled, knowing I should feel guilty, but didn't. To face what lay ahead I would need all my friends. The guilt came later, and the weight of it still brings me low so many years on.

We met Wilhum and the Mounted Company half a day's ride from Athiltor. He greeted me cheerily enough, but there was a guarded aspect to his eyes that put me on edge. Guile was never one of Wilhum's gifts and I never experienced the slightest difficulty in gauging truth or falsehood in his words.

"Patrol or something more serious?" I asked, nodding to the column of riders at his back, all girded for war.

"It appears your old comrades are determined upon a resurgence." He forced himself to meet my eye as he spoke, one of the most obvious tells on a liar's face. "Every day since you left, churls have been turning up with petitions. A few walked all the way from the Shavine Forest to bring word of outlaws. Much pillaging has been done, murder too."

"Duchess Lorine is more than capable of dealing with it," I said, keeping careful watch on his features.

Wilhum shook his head. "Our Lady wants the commons to know that the Covenant is their protector. We'll ride around conspicuously for a few days, lay an ambush or two."

I was certain that, whatever his true mission, it had nothing to do with outlaws. These days, outlawry in the Shavine duchy fell under the sway of Shilva Sahken, and Tiler had assured me she and Lorine had a mutually beneficial arrangement when it came to keeping the forest clean of miscreants. Wherever he was going, it wasn't to the Shavine Forest. I also knew that the entire Mounted Company would not ride forth unless under Evadine's express order. If Wilhum wouldn't tell me his purpose, she would.

"Well, happy hunting," I said, tugging Blackfoot's reins. "Be sure to hand over any captives to the duchess. She won't take kindly to arbitrary hangings in her domain."

"Swain's finally turned up, by the way," Wilhum said as I started forward. Glancing back, I saw his face set in a forbidding grimace. "Unfortunately, he has a very good excuse for his tardiness."

Arriving in Athiltor, I found Swain was busy mustering the Covenant Host upon the broad expanse of cobbles leading to the cathedral steps. One glance at the ranks sufficed to tell the tale: recently stitched cuts, dented breastplates, an eyepatch or two. I didn't have Ayin's facility for numbers, but my soldier's eye gauged the full strength of the host at perhaps three-quarters of what it had been.

"I assume the Princess Regent wasn't content for you to simply march out from Couravel," I observed, dismounting from Blackfoot. I searched the ranks for faces I knew, letting out a relieved sigh at the sight of Ofihla sternly rebuking a halberdier for a loose belt buckle. She seemed hale as ever but sported a fading bruise on her jaw and a new scar across her nose.

"Orthodox rioters," Swain said. "At least that was the claim. When Trooper Eamond arrived with the Lady's summons, we mustered that very day. It seems the princess has spies either in our camp or close to it. By the time we set off, every street surrounding the barracks was blocked with a barricade. We had no option but to fight our way out of the city, harried at every turn. Archers on the rooftops, orthodox-ites darting out from alleyways to cut throats. They were a surprisingly disciplined lot for rioters, I must say."

"Captives?" I asked.

"We only took a few, and they weren't talking. We caught an archer I recognised as a kingsman, but he claimed he was acting only in the name of the True Covenant. I cut the fingers from his right hand and let him go."

"Getting soft, Captain?"

Swain shrugged. "Never felt right to execute a soldier for merely following orders."

"How long did it take to fight your way clear?"

"Two days, all told. And it didn't end when we cleared the city walls. We were ambushed and obstructed near enough every day on the road. Also, many of the bridges betwixt Couravel and Athiltor had suspiciously caught fire and burned down to the stumps." Swain's features took on a dark cast, self-reproach writ large in his eyes. "And so, we were not here to assist in the Lady's greatest triumph."

"There'll be other triumphs, I'm sure." I inclined my head at the neat rows of soldiers. "What's this in aid of?"

"The Lady has an address to make. Some kind of edict, she said." He gave me a sidelong glance. "She told me of your mission to the north. Any luck?"

"Lord Shelvane can be bought. Duke Lohrent cannot, nor is he sympathetic. I think his son might be in love with Trooper Ayin, though. So that's something."

"War on two fronts, then." Swain grimaced. "Not a pleasant prospect, my lord."

"No, my lord. It isn't."

We shared a muted grin at the absurdity of addressing each other with titles bestowed by a dynasty with which we were now tacitly at war.

"Stand to!" Ofihla's familiar bark echoed across the plaza. "All will pay heed to the Anointed Lady!"

Evadine appeared at the top of the cathedral steps in full armour, black enamelled plate still contriving to gleam despite a mostly overcast sky. Spots of rain began to fall as she started to speak, an ill-omened beginning to what I recognise now as the dawn of the whole bloody mess that ensued. Then, however, I stood and listened in expectation that the woman I loved was about to stir her audience to yet greater heights of adulation.

"I see before me soldiers of the Covenant Resurgent," she stated, voice strident with unconcealed anger as it echoed across the Covenant Host and the thickening crowd of crusaders and townsfolk at the fringes of the plaza. "And I see their wounds. I see the absence of those I called friend and comrade, brave souls who fought at my side from the Traitors' Field to the Vale. Where are they? I ask. Murdered, is my captain's answer. Murdered by base deceit and betrayal. Not slain in honest and honourable battle, but fallen to daggers and arrows wielded by curs in the pay of a family I now fear may be corrupted beyond all hope of redemption."

Evadine paused, lowering her head as a wave of grief passed through her. *Is this the time?* I wondered. *Is this the moment she proclaims herself the Ascendant Queen?* Had I been here, I would have counselled against it, even now. We still lacked the strength for open war. However, it transpired that the Anointed Lady had something else to proclaim that day.

"And from where does this corruption arise?" she asked, raising a pale but furious visage to survey her audience with a demanding glare. "This is the question that plagues me. I will confess failure, friends. I will submit to your harsh judgement for I have been weak these past days. I have allowed myself to wallow in the seduction of hope. Hope that the struggle before us can be avoided. Hope that the Algathinets and their venal servants can be saved, turned away from the path they have been lured to. That weakness ends now. Now I see the source of their corruption. I see the wellspring of evil in this realm and will tolerate it no longer. The Malecite, friends. They have corrupted our Crown. With their whispered promises and arcane perversions, they have used the wounds of strife to infect the body of this land, and I know now the agents of their vileness. For decades have they walked among us, untroubled, welcomed even. Charm workers, we call them. Soothsayers, some will claim. Healers even. I tell you they are none of these things. The Caerith and their pestilent rites have brought us to this pass. Now is the time we say no more."

The growl of affirmation from the crowd made it clear that, once again, the Anointed Lady's words had found their mark. I have learned in subsequent years that it is far easier to rouse people to hate than it is to love, a lesson I think Evadine learned at a far earlier age.

"Henceforth, under Covenant law all Caerith are excluded from the Realm of Albermaine," Evadine continued, brandishing an unfurled scroll which presumably listed this new edict in detail. "All Supplicants are commanded to instruct their parishioners to shun the Caerith in all things. None shall be given shelter by the faithful. None shall be fed by the faithful. The faithful shall not trade with or consort with the Caerith in any way. Covenant soldiery will also take necessary steps to seek out all such heathens within our borders and convey them back to their own domain, by force if needs must. This land must be cleansed, friends. Scoured clean of the arcane vileness that has laid it low. But this is only the first cleansing. To truly cure ourselves of the sickness that pollutes all, be they of the commons, the Covenant, or the nobility, must receive the blessing of my hand, for only in my hand resides the favour of the Seraphile. Therefore, I summon the boy named as King Arthin Algathinet to Athiltor to receive my blessing. Should he refuse, I will go to Couravel and insist upon it. Will you march with me when I do?"

The cheers were perhaps the loudest I ever heard her receive, making it clear that the numbers of adherents in the city had swollen in my absence. Even so, I barely heard it, my attention being solely focused on Evadine still brandishing her edict, calling out her demand over and over again. The crowd roaring ever louder each time.

"Will you march with me?! Will you march with me?!"

The chant began then, the discordant chaos of adulation shifting into a familiar refrain, one I had hoped left behind when the Sacrifice March met its bloody terminus at the Battle of the Vale: "We live for the Lady! We fight for the Lady! We die for the Lady!"

Chapter Nine

The door to Evadine's chambers was closed and guarded by two armed Supplicants I didn't know, a man and a woman so similar in stature and feature they must have been siblings, perhaps twins.

"The Lady is in communion, my lord . . ." the male Supplicant began, his angular face registering a peevish shock at my snarling response as I shoved him aside and pounded on the door.

"Get the fuck out of the way!" Hinges rattled and timbers shook under my fist. "Evadine!"

"The lady," the Supplicant said, grasping my arm, "is in communion."

I rounded on him, staring into a stern, unyielding face. It was the kind of face I had encountered many times, one not easily cowed and exuding an implacable sense of duty. Whoever these two were, Evadine had chosen her guards well.

"Step back, my lord," he instructed me. The tightening of his grip on my arm had me taking the required backward step, but only in order to draw my sword.

Blood would certainly have been spilled in that hallway if Evadine hadn't chosen to open the door. I expected to find her defiant. Instead, the face that appeared in the gap was chastened, fearful even. It lingered for just an instant before retreating into the gloomy recess of her chambers. "Lord Alwyn may enter," I heard her say in a thin voice.

"Put your hand on me again," I told the male guard as I pushed into the room, "and you'll find out what it's like to endure life without it."

Slamming the door behind me, I forced a few calming breaths into my lungs before turning to confront Evadine. She had removed her armour and stood clad in a woollen shawl covering her plain cotton trews and shirt. A fire blazed in the hearth but I saw her shiver, eyes averted from mine.

"An Edict of Exclusion?" I asked. Although I tried to quell my anger, my voice still shook as I spoke. Thanks to Sihlda's history lessons, I knew such a thing was not unprecedented. King Mathis III had issued one against a particularly bothersome clan of Vergundians. The Luminants' Council had attempted a similar tactic a century before when an irksomely popular sect arose to threaten a schism. Never before had one been issued against the Caerith, however.

"I had to," Evadine said, her voice little more than a tremulous mutter.

"That's where Wilhum's gone, isn't it?" I advanced towards her. "He's not scouring the woods for outlaws. You sent him to round up all the Caerith he can find and drag them to the border."

"I had to," she repeated, backing away. Unusually, her long hair hung free today, veiling eyes that darted scared glances at my face.

"The Caerith." Reaching her, I felt an urge to clamp my arms to her shoulders, shake answers free of her lips. Instead, I forced myself to a halt, glaring at her downcast visage behind a curtain of dark tresses. "The people who saved me, healed me, sent me back to you. One of them rides and fights at my side. Do you intend to have me cast her out?"

"She can stay." I saw a glimmer of solicitation behind the veil. "An exception granted for her loyal service. My boon to you . . ."

"I don't want your fucking boon!"

Once again, the urge rose to grab her. Rage and, absurdly, a welling of lust causing my hands to shake. Even with my anger boiling, my mind chose to summon images of our past intimacy, provoking a compulsion to strip her naked, lay her down. She wouldn't stop me. Some lustful instinct told me so. The way her eyes brightened behind their covering, the way her arms slipped to her sides, opening in invitation. Passion, it seemed, can be stirred as easily by enmity as affection.

Metreveus. It seemed is if I heard this word spoken rather than in my head, and the voice that spoke it was not my own. It was the voice I remembered from all those lessons imparted down in the dark, the voice that stood alone in the story of my life for only ever speaking truth. *Metreveus*, it said again and I felt the desire seep from me. *Tyrant. Persecutor.* A lesson Sihlda had never in fact taught me, but surely would have.

"How many battles for us?" I asked, turning away from her, finding the intense heat of the fire preferable to her regard. "How many lives lost and taken? All on your word, Evadine. This is not what I fought for."

"You know I do not have agency over the visions afforded me," she said, a steadiness creeping into her tone now. "The Seraphile grant me knowledge and I must act upon it."

For the first time I was forced to confront a question I had, through a good deal of sophistry and distraction, avoided: *What, in truth, are her visions?* Until now, I had veered between a nebulous conviction that she was in fact receiving messages from beyond the Divine Portals, and the thought that she might possess a form of the arcane power the Caerith called *vaerith*. Her visions were too accurate to deny. Too consistent in the outcomes they wrought to be merely the product of a disturbed mind. Of course, such pondering soon revived the historian's words, though I pushed them away with firm resolve. *Evadine serves the Malecite.*

She has done too much good, I insisted to myself. *We have done too much together for it all to be in service to the malign.*

"The Seraphile told you to harry and hunt the Caerith?" I asked her, my anger diminished now, but still it put a quaver in my voice. "It hardly seems like an act born of eternal grace?"

"They showed me, Alwyn." She moved closer, her hand clasping mine. "They gifted me a vision of the world's fate if we do not do this. I know your affection for these people, but even you can see the danger they pose. The power they possess threatens us. I have known this all my life, from the day my father set a Caerith charm worker to banish the visions from my mind. Then I thought him a capering fraud with his gabbled cants and rattling charms. But also I recall the fear in that man's eyes. For years I thought it the fear of a practised liar finding himself confronted with inarguable truth. Now, I see that he feared the truth I would one day expose: the dark mission he and his kind pursue in our lands. That was why he concocted that foul physic for me to drink. He told my father it would purge me of what he called the twistings in my mind. I didn't want to drink it, but my father insisted and I was ever a dutiful daughter. Three days of suffering followed, suffering surely intended to kill me. I writhed in a world of agony, sustained only by the knowledge that the Seraphile would surely preserve one chosen to convey their message. And preserve me they did. When I woke from my torment, the charm worker was gone, vanished in the night without even waiting for his payment."

Her grip tightened on my hand. "Your anger pains me, Alwyn. The fact that we have to hide what we share pains me. But pain must be borne, by me and by you. Our mission is greater than us."

I turned to her, finding her hair parted as she moved closer still, that perfect face pressing a cheek to mine, smooth warmth meeting roughened, scarred flesh. The thrill of it remained as intoxicating as ever. I recall deciding not to reach for her, then doing so, pressing her against me. I recall deciding not to kiss her, then putting my lips to hers. The kiss was long and I felt a spasm of frustrated agony when she broke it.

"Pain must be borne," she said in a breathless whisper, casting a glance at the door.

I dragged air into my lungs and stepped back. "I'll not be party to a purge. I've seen enough massacres in this life."

"And I would not command you so. Wilhum will oversee this edict and you know his kindness. He has orders to spill no blood in this commission. The Caerith will be exiled. That is all."

And so are paths chosen in life when we confront a crossroads. Ever, it is the easier road we tread, the one that promises familiarity, continuance, love. Many times have I cursed myself for not taking the harsher road in that moment, for it would surely have been the less treacherous. But, even now, I know that there in that room, choice was an illusion. She could have commanded me to bring fire and slaughter to all Albermaine and, despite much protestation, I would still have chosen it as the easy path, because it was her path.

I jerked my head at the door. "I don't like your new guards."

A relieved smile played over her lips and she pulled her shawl tight, straightening her back, once again the Anointed Lady. "Supplicants Harldin and Ildette came all the way from the Duchy of Rhianvel to swear their allegiance to our cause. There was a good deal of antipathy between the Luminants' Council and the Covenant in Rhianvel long before Arnabus seized Athiltor. Harldin and Ildette arrived at the head of fifty armed Supplicants. They call themselves the Lady's Shield, something I'm minded to indulge since they seem so keen upon it. They also delivered a letter signed by all the senior clerics in the duchy, recognising my authority and requesting my blessing. Isn't that nice?"

"It'll certainly be useful. But the clerics are not the duke. I don't suppose they brought a letter from him?"

"No, but they did bring a message. Duke Viruhlis is ardent in his faith and fully supportive of my actions. Rhianvel was never as troublesome as Alundia for the Algathinets, but their rule has long been a source of resentment among many of the nobility, not least the ducal family."

"I'd feel more secure if he'd sent a thousand men-at-arms under his own banner rather than a few Supplicants bearing a letter he hasn't signed."

"Apparently, the duke is keen to engage in negotiations before openly stating his support. Accordingly, his ambassador to the Court of King Arthin awaits you in Couravel. I trust you'll arrange a suitably discreet meeting."

"Couravel? You want me to go to the capital? Now?"

"Of course. Who else could I trust to deliver my summons to the king?"

"To which I suspect Leannor will respond by sending you my head in a sack."

"She will not." Evadine smiled, shaking her head. "Still, you don't fully understand the nobility, Alwyn. She will receive you, hear your message, dismiss it, and send you on your way. Anything else would be improper."

"She didn't seem to care about propriety when she stuck her dagger in Duke Guhlton's neck, during a parley no less."

"Deeds performed on a battlefield are different, parley or no. The business of court demands the observance of strictures, if she still wishes to attach the trappings of legitimacy to her son's rule. Besides, there is more work for you in the capital than suffering Leannor's company. You will pay a visit to the Dulsian ambassador too. I've a suspicion his duke may be the most persuadable to our cause, if properly compensated.

Also, I wish to take advantage of your insight into the common folk. Rumours abound of how hard life in the towns has become these days, what with the princess regent piling ever more excise on liquor and other comforts. Or, at least, I hear she plans to, and will flog any who dare raise their voice in objection. I am told her spies are busy compiling lists of names, those deemed troublesome or disloyal. Her brother's fate seems to have birthed in her a great and terrible suspicion, one that may even have unbalanced an already disturbed mind. Such altered thinking in one with utmost power breeds fear, a fear that could be stoked to useful heights."

I arched a quizzical eyebrow. "Already disturbed?"

"Since we're on the subject, I recall a few rumours flitting about in the days following the death of Leannor's husband. Lord Keville was old, certainly, but hardly infirm, despite his years. Not a man to succumb easily to illness."

"Leannor is a madwoman who once murdered her husband. That's the tale you intend to spin?"

The smile Evadine put on her lips was apologetic, but an air of command coloured her next words. "I am not the storyteller here, Alwyn. That I leave to you. And I'm confident you will find all the grist you require in Couravel."

She never asked me to lie before. The thought dogged me for much of the following day, and would continue to do so during the trek to

Couravel. I had, of course, lied on Evadine's behalf many times, but often without her knowledge and never with her express approval. Yet I set about my preparations with all my customary diligence.

"Make all haste," I told Tiler, handing him a brick-sized box. It was a sturdy contrivance edged in iron with a strong lock, as befitted its contents: every gold sovereign that could be garnered from those corners of the cathedral the Vergundians hadn't managed to rummage. The sum value of the box was impressive but not immense, but as a signal of good intentions, gold in all its untarnished shininess is hard to surpass. It was a measure of the trust Tiler had won from me, albeit uncoloured by any affection, that I felt confident in placing this treasure in his hands. Although, I had felt obliged to send two of my most trustworthy scouts along as escorts.

"I shall, my lord." Tiler knuckled his forehead and secured the box amid the saddlebags of his mount.

"She'll ask the reason for your request," I advised as he climbed into the saddle. "Tell her we need intelligence on the mood of the capital's commons."

He settled on to his horse's back, narrow features forming a cautious frown. "And the real reason?"

"If you don't know, she can't wring it out of you."

"Shilva Sahken's more one for cutting than wringing." Tiler grimaced. "Still, nice box of coin should cool her temper."

"When she gives you what you need, get yourself to Couravel, quick as you can. Keep to the shadows and find me when you've made the necessary introductions."

Tiler knuckled his forehead again and kicked his heels, he and his pair of escorts galloping off along the westward road.

I spent the evening going over the histories of the Keville family provided by Senior Librarian Corlina. To my annoyance, there was nothing of particular interest, the only marked anomaly being the untimely death of Lord Alferd Keville, father to our current boy king.

Sihlda said you deserved a better bride, my lord, I thought, tapping a finger to Lord Alferd's name. What little I had gleaned about

Leannor's betrothal and subsequent marriage to a man over twenty years her senior made it plain it hadn't been a love match. *The nobility,* Sihlda once told me, *marry almost exclusively for advantage. Love is ever a petty concern to them.*

I saw from the text below Leannor's entry that she had been only fifteen when married to Lord Alferd. *Little more than a child forced into the bed of a man who must have appeared ancient.* Leannor had never struck me as lacking in either wilfulness or spite, and this particular arrangement seemed fertile ground for both. My eye tracked to Lord Alferd's name once again and the date of his death inscribed beneath it. *Old but still hale, so they said. An untimely end, unless someone helped him on his way.*

I decided to risk taking the whole Scout Company along, at least part of the way, reasoning I may well have use of them should a hasty retreat from Couravel prove necessary. Eamond rode with us once again, recently returned from his mission to summon the Covenant Host. The former novice, now formally named a Supplicant by Evadine, sported a few grazes from his adventures in Couravel and the subsequent journey north. Moreover, I saw less of the keen, idealistic youth I had trained the previous spring in this battle-hardened soldier. His ardency in Evadine's cause remained, but there was a new caution to his gaze that bespoke a soul repeatedly exposed to violence. After some shameful wrangling of conscience, I also asked Ayin to join us. Athiltor no longer struck me as the safe refuge for her I had imagined it to be. Lilat once again followed wherever I went, despite my urgings that she go home.

"The *Eithlisch* gave me a task," she said, shrugging. "It's not yet done."

"Your task was to find the *Doenlisch*," I reminded her. "Yet all you do is traipse around after me." My tone held a forced harshness, designed to stir enough pique for her to forsake whatever alliance she felt existed between us. Instead, it only served to amuse her.

"Your woman said very bad things about my people," she said, mouth quirking in a restrained smile. "That must have made you angry."

Lilat tended to refer to Evadine as "your woman", or sometimes "the woman who speaks a lot". Mostly, she regarded the Anointed Lady with a vague sense of bemusement, an expression that deepened when surveying the crowds of people who came to hear the sermons of the Risen Martyr. "She doesn't do anything," Lilat said when I asked her about this apparent mystification. "She only talks. Words are just air." This she said in Caerith, phrased in a manner that made me conclude it must be an oft-repeated saying among her people.

"The Caerith are wise in many ways," I said. "But in this, they are utterly wrong."

I pondered the wisdom of leaving Quintrell and Adlar behind. The minstrel and his wayward allegiances were a complication I could well do without. Also, despite the man's objections, I still didn't fully trust his juggling companion, sworn soldier to the Covenant Host though he was. In the event, they made the decision for me by simply saddling up and falling in with the others come the morning of our departure. Quintrell met my enquiring glance with a customary grin while Adlar exchanged a joke with Ayin.

"You know Couravel well, Master Quintrell?" I asked, climbing on to Blackfoot's back.

"Better than I'd like, my lord. It's the worst maze of shit-stinking rat runs I've ever encountered, and I've travelled far, as you know."

"Ever play for the royal court?"

"Can't say I've had the honour."

"Then let's see if we can rectify that." I touched my heels to Blackfoot's flanks, nudging him to a walk and guiding him towards the southward road. "Though I warn you, the princess regent is likely to be parsimonious in her applause."

Chapter Ten

Ayin and Eamond made a surprisingly convincing couple. Quintrell took on the job of concocting their disguise, deftly altering their garb and appearance to create the picture of dispossessed newly-weds forced from their homes by the storms of war. They were shorn of all accoutrements that might signal membership of the Covenant Host, or sympathy for the Anointed Lady, their weapons limited to well-concealed daggers.

"You understand your task?" I asked, after surveying their appearance to my satisfaction.

"Ascertain the mood of the commons in Couravel," Eamond responded promptly. "Seek out pockets of discontent and identify the leaders."

"I'll make a list, shall I?" Ayin suggested with helpful earnestness.

"No lists," I told her. "As far as anyone will know, you can neither read nor figure numbers. Keep any names in your head."

"Couravel is a city beset by the foulest poverty, my lord," Eamond said. "A mass of folk ripe for the Lady's message . . ."

"No preaching either." I swallowed a sigh of exasperation. These two were not the best choice for this, but my most skilled spy was off on his mission to the Shavine Marches. I doubted Quintrell would have had any difficulty slipping into the required role, yet resisted making the request. Outlaw instinct told me it would be best to keep that one well within my sight.

"Feel free to appear as devoted as you like," I told Eamond. "But make no mention of the Lady. If the subject comes up, act confused, ask questions. It's important we know how they feel about the Risen Martyr. But—" I raised a finger for emphasis "—no preaching. Understood?"

Receiving a firm nod from Eamond and a shrug of agreement from Ayin, I surveyed the crossroads where we had encamped the night before, finding it gratifyingly empty. The hour was early and the ground covered in a fine mist, late autumn making our breath steam. The Scout Company was secluded in the forest, far enough away from the road that their fires wouldn't be noticed. The crossroads lay ten miles west of Couravel, a meeting of minor cart tracks rather than the busier junctions of the King's Road.

"You'll go on ahead," I told them. "We'll meet back here in seven days. If any of us don't return by the dawn of the eleventh day, make all haste to Athiltor and convey your tidings to Lady Evadine."

"Why wouldn't you be here?" Ayin asked, a concerned frown creasing her brow. "You're just going to talk to the princess, aren't you?"

After which she may well decide to hang me, I didn't say, vexed as I was by visions of Magnis Lochlain's demise. *Or worse*. "I have other business that may delay me," I told her. Fixing each of them with an intent eye, I went on, "Remember, listen more than you talk. Watch but don't act. If you're threatened, play the craven and run away. Kill only if your mission is discovered. And—" I focused my attention on Ayin "—bad men are to be shunned in all respects. I don't care how bad they are."

She responded with a weary roll of her eyes. "I don't do that any more."

"Good. Keep it that way." I nodded to the westward track. "Time to go."

Lilat required no disguise for her mission, given that it involved staying out of the city completely. I sensed a forced air to her protestations, the obligation to stay at my side competing with her detestation of towns and cities. Even from this distance she complained of a foul stench and her mood had darkened with every mile we drew closer to Couravel.

"When we leave," I told her, "I'll try to do so by the northern gate, but that may not be possible. If so, you'll have to track us."

This earned me a puzzled look and a shrug. "So I shall."

"Stay hidden. Take no more game than you need, keep a careful watch on the roads. Should a large body of warriors appear from any direction, I must have word of it. Meaning you'll have to find us in the city. Do you think you can do that?"

No shrug this time. Instead, her face twitched in disgust and she gave a resigned nod. "Why not? I've crawled through stink and shit to save you before."

The banner hung over the great edifice of the cathedral of Couravael in a shimmering blaze of white and black. An impressive, and assuredly expensive, assemblage of silk panels arranged into a rectangle at least fifty feet long. The symbology was a modified version of that emblazoned on the banner Danick Thessil had wielded during his final stand in Athiltor: a cup surrounded by a circle of fire. The motif was archaic in origin but still familiar to anyone with more than a passing knowledge of Covenant lore. The cup symbolised Martyr Stevanos, the first Martyr, a humble potter by trade. The flames represented the form of his martyrdom, burned to death for the crime of preaching love in a time of hate. My scholar's memory told me the design had been popular during the foundation of the Covenant, but these days such things tended to be viewed as frippery. Apparently, this had been one of the core tenets of the Most Favoured pilgrimage sect the Widow had spent much of her prior life following.

Regarding the silken assemblage with muted curiosity rather than outrage, Juhlina felt moved to offer an apposite quotation: "*Those who are true in their Devotion require no trappings, nor baubles, nor anything save a soul open to the Martyrs' example.*"

"Martyr Ahlianna?" I asked, finding the passage unfamiliar.

"Melliah," she said, arching an eyebrow at me. "My lord's scriptural knowledge is lacking."

"There are a lot of scrolls."

We viewed the cathedral from across the central plaza that

dominated this most favoured quarter of the city. The towering, much-buttressed structure sat directly opposite the royal palace. The cathedral's spire rose higher than any portion of the monarch's domain by a considerable measure. Further contrast came in the fact that the palace was surrounded by tall and sturdy walls, while the cathedral was ever open to receive the faithful. I had pondered before if this place had been constructed to emphasise the eternal paradox of antipathy and alliance that characterised the relationship between Crown and Covenant. If so, the fact that the banner's presence had been tolerated thus far told me that the attitude of the palace's occupants now tended more towards concordance than conflict. A shared enemy will often forge strong bonds.

"Can I assume," Quintrell ventured, "that we will not find a resting place within the cathedral precincts this evening?"

"Not unless you're keen to wake up with your throat cut." I tugged Blackfoot's reins, turning his head towards the palace.

Gaining access to royal personages is ever a tedious and protracted business, made more so when one presents oneself as the ambassador of a woman apparently intent on defying or usurping Crown authority at every turn. All the functionaries who greeted us, from the guards at the palace gate to the various courtiers encountered during the subsequent prolonged journey, showed expressions of either outright disdain or glowering suspicion. Added to this were the clerics, for the palace seemed far busier with them than during my infrequent prior visits. Supplicants, Aspirants and a few Ascendants witnessed our passage through multiple corridors and halls with expressions set in naked hostility. I was quick to notice that all wore a robe bearing the cup and flame symbol on their breast.

Eventually, we were conveyed to a tall, narrow chamber with a chequerboard marble floor, bare of any seating, with windows too high to offer an easy escape. "You will wait here, my lord," the stern-faced courtier escorting us said with a barely perceptible bow before exiting the room. Our escort of a dozen kingsmen placed themselves outside the doors at each end of the chamber. They closed with a loud, booming echo followed by the clatter of keys turning in locks.

"They might've left us somewhere with a fireplace, at least," Quintrell griped, pulling his cloak about his shoulders. His absence of awe at his surroundings made me doubt his earlier claim that he had never been here before. By contrast, Adlar was all bright-eyed wonder. During the journey through the palace, he had stared at the passing finery and opulence with unabashed fascination, which he now focused upon the wooden relief carvings decorating the panelled walls of this chamber.

"Such artistry," he whispered, pointing to a particular scene. It showed a hunting party, a king on horseback, presumably one of the early Mathises or Arthins, long spear held aloft as he pursued a boar through the woods. "Have you ever seen the like, Master Quin? The detail is extraordinary."

Quintrell sniffed. "There are marble reliefs in the eastern Free Ports that make this look like the whittlings of a blind dull-wit." I saw a previously unsuspected nervousness in the way his hand fidgeted on his mandolin, something he covered by strumming a few notes. "Judging by our welcome," he said, "I don't suppose I'll get to play for the court after all, eh, my lord?"

"I wouldn't be too sure," I said. "I'm sure you must know a few mourning dirges."

"They didn't take our weapons," the Widow pointed out, hefting her warhammer. "That's hopeful." The rarely seen grin on her lips faded in the face of my inexpressive glance. "What do I do if they take you?" she asked.

"Let them."

I saw her hands tighten on the warhammer's haft. "I won't be a captive again."

"You will, because I order it."

Her glare of resentful defiance might well have led to raised voices if the lock in the far doors hadn't rattled afresh. They swung open to reveal a large man in a doublet bearing the Algathinet crest, a long-sword at his belt. He stood there for a moment, grim, bearded features regarding me in silence with no regard for my companions.

"Scribe," he said, voice little more than a gruff mutter.

"Lord Ehlbert," I responded, offering a bow of appropriate depth. Quintrell and Adlar both immediately sank to one knee while the Widow adopted a combative stance, raising her weapon and setting her feet. It was an outrageous breach of etiquette and a brazen challenge, one Sir Ehlbert barely seemed to notice.

His gaze flicked to the Widow for the briefest second before fixing upon me once again. "Come with me," he said. "These others are to wait here."

"With some comfort and refreshment, I trust," I said as he turned away. "Or has all civility vanished from this palace?"

"Civility?" Ehlbert's beard, thicker and less well kept than I remembered, bunched in amusement. "Bring chairs," he told the guards posted at the door. "And some wine for our honoured guests."

Standing aside, he gestured to the long corridor beyond. "Your audience has been granted, Lord Scribe. I advise you not to waste any more time."

Before coming here, I had wondered if Leannor would receive the Anointed Lady's ambassador in full view of her assembled court, the better to disparage and dismiss his message. Instead, I took solace from the fact that she chose to meet me alone, save for Sir Ehlbert. He led me through yet another set of doors to an ascending stairwell, presumably located within one of the palace's many towers. Leannor waited in the small, shadowed chamber at the top of the steps.

The narrow windows were shuttered and most of the light came from the blaze in the hearth and a few oil lanterns. She sat in a high-backed chair with a kitten in her lap. Next to her was a table upon which sat a mass of papers. I noted how the various scrolls and stacked documents were neatly arranged at the far end of the table, but this orderliness dissipated the closer the papers were to Leannor. The fine rug beneath her chair was littered with scraps of paper which provided amusement for the two other kittens at play there. I also saw that the stones surrounding the fireplace were stained dark with the ash that results from burnt parchment.

"Your Majesty," I said, taking the knee before her, head lowered in the customary position of a knight greeting one of the highest station. "I bring tidings from the Anointed Lady and Risen Martyr . . ."

"I know why you're here, Scribe." Leannor's voice was only marginally less of a mutter than Lord Ehlbert's. "Get up."

Standing, I spared a glance at Ehlbert who had positioned himself with his back to a window. The shadows made it impossible to read his face. They also might offer an advantage should he choose to draw his sword. The fact that I had been permitted to keep mine offered no consolation at all.

"I like cats," Leannor said, recapturing my attention. She lifted the kitten from her lap, holding it close to her face, smiling as its small paws batted her chin. "They're straightforward creatures, you see. Despite a reputation for cunning, they are in fact completely trustworthy and affectionate. All you need do is feed them, play with them, scratch them in the right places . . ." she paused to tickle the kitten's belly, provoking an appreciative purr ". . . and they love you. Until you die, that is. Then they'll probably eat your corpse before going off to find someone else to provide food and scratches. Cats, I find, are both loyal and uncomplicated."

She stooped to place the cat at her feet, sparing a moment to smile as the trio instantly entangled themselves in a stumbling play-fight. "Three cats at war," she said, looking up at me. "A fitting metaphor for this realm at present, eh, Scribe?"

"I have learned that war is never an inevitability, Your Majesty. In the end, it is a choice."

"One you and the Anointed Lady appear to be enraptured by. Unless I mistake your recent actions."

"The Covenant of Martyrs was seized by the despotic heretic Arnabus, a man with whom we were both familiar. I find it hard to credit that Your Majesty regrets his passing."

"I do not. In fact, I should greatly have liked to see it. You killed him yourself, did you not?"

The clang of the sword on the marble dais. The dark gush that painted the altar. The Widow asking, "What did he mean . . . ?" "Justice was done by my hand," I said, unable to keep the defensive stiffness from my voice. Leannor, of course, failed to miss it.

"Swiftly too." She raised her eyebrows in apparent consternation. "So swiftly, much has been lost to history as regards the Great Heretic's motivations. Surely there was a good deal he could have told us."

"A regrettable loss to scholarship, but there could only ever be one end for so corrupted a soul."

We fell into a silence broken only by the mewling of her kittens until I attempted a change of tack. "I should like to enquire as to the well-being of Lady Ducinda."

"She's as happy and healthy as a girl her age should be," Leannor told me. "And a great comfort to my heart these trying days. I did always wish for a daughter. She and Arthin play together a good deal, as they should. A bond forged in childhood will serve them well when the rule of all Albermaine falls upon their shoulders."

"I should greatly like to see Lady Ducinda, Your Majesty. If you would grant me the boon."

"Why? Do you imagine I lie? That, in truth, her ladyship spends her days confined to a cold dungeon and fed scraps?"

"Of course not." I didn't elaborate but Leannor's insight was keen today.

"So, you feel a rescuer's obligation, Lord Scribe." She let out a faint laugh and shook her head. "Such a mass of contradictions you are. A cut-throat outlaw of savage reputation who can wield a quill as well as he can a blade. A man of great knowledge matched only by his facility for deceit. He has done the foulest deeds in service to a woman who's as mad as the most rabid bitch, yet he harbours concern for a little girl he once saved."

Her humour evaporated quickly and she turned to pluck one of the scrolls massed on the table at her side. "Here," she said, holding it out to me. "I should appreciate your peerless acumen as regards this missive, my lord."

The scroll was a letter, inscribed in a hand so clumsy that I felt scant surprise when reading the signature: "*Your humble and most loyal servant, Lord Archel Shelvane, Governor of Althiene*". The contents were a poorly phrased but, I must admit, mostly accurate account of my conversation with Archel. His memory played him false in the number of Covenant soldiers promised to his garrison, a thousand instead of five hundred, but this may have been an unsubtle attempt to gild his tattling.

"I met with Lord Shelvane," I said. "The meeting was no secret. Lady Evadine is keen to offer her blessing to all who will accept it."

Leannor's gaze was unwavering. "On the promise of soldiers, apparently."

"Lord Shelvane was fulsome in describing his current difficulties. It is the role of the Covenant Resurgent to succour the faithful in their hour of need."

"I understand you also paid a call on Duke Lohrent in the Cordwain. No letter from him yet, but I expect it soon. Care to share what he told you?"

"We engaged in a lively discussion regarding our differing views on the correct form of Covenant belief, Your Majesty."

"Told you piss right off, you mean. It seems your lady's ledger is somewhat bare when it comes to allies, Scribe."

"The Seraphile are the only allies my lady requires. However," I went on to forestall her rejoinder, bowing again, "you must know that she greatly cherishes the regard and favour of your house above all. Accordingly, I come bearing an invitation. Your Majesty, I enjoin you to make a grand procession to Athiltor. All will be joy and celebration when the princess regent and the king tread upon the steps of the holiest shrine in Covenant-dom, there to receive the Anointed Lady's blessing."

Despite her guile, Leannor had never been especially gifted in masking her emotions. Now, however, her face took on the most impassive aspect I could recall. She stared at me in unblinking, apparently passionless scrutiny. It was an expression that made me distinctly nervous, for I had seen it before: the face worn by very dangerous folk when they're deciding if they're going to kill you. While the princess regent continued to stare, I resisted the impulse to let my gaze stray to Ehlbert, though my ears were alive to the smallest sound that might indicate the scrape of steel on scabbard.

"Tell me, Lord Alwyn," Leannor said finally, "are you as mad as she is, or is this all some grand design of yours I've yet to properly divine?"

Nervous as I was, I couldn't help bristling. "My lady is not mad."

Leannor shifted then, eyes narrowing, a fox catching the rabbit's scent. She allowed her scrutiny to linger for a second before letting out a soft hiss. "So that's it," she said. "Whatever your love for her, it's meaningless. You think because she soils herself with your churl's cock it means anything? You pitiable, idiotic fool. A woman such as her has no need of love. I have known Evadine Courlain since childhood and never have I encountered a soul more dangerous, more lost in manipulation. It's set so deep in her bones she doesn't even know she's doing it."

I let the rage boil, saying nothing as it steamed then simmered, resisting the urge to spill forth all manner of caustic observations on her own character. In retrospect, the fact that a personage as aware of her own failings as Leannor felt justified in passing judgement on another should have told me something. There were questions I should have asked. Questions about her childhood encounters with Evadine, about her knowledge of the Courlain family. Yet I didn't. I just stood and suffered through the rage that only the blindest form of devotion can stir.

Eventually, after much grinding of teeth, I managed to grate out a reply, "The chance for peace stands before you, Your Majesty. Do you truly imagine this realm can withstand another war without fracturing from end to end?"

As far as my best research can establish, there is but one painting depicting this meeting. It is clearly the work of a skilled hand, but, as ever seems to be the case, one biased by Algathinet sympathies. It captures the chamber in all its gloominess with an uncanny accuracy not shown to its principal subjects. In this rendering, I am but a squint-eyed conniver leering in patent duplicity and lust at a poised and resolute princess regent, her features stricken by inner turmoil. In fact, her expression at that most critical moment was one of grim but reluctant necessity. For once, my gift for reading faces deserted me, for I saw regret in the cast of Leannor's eyes, when I should have seen decision.

"Your message has been received, Lord Scribe," she said, reaching down to pick up one of the kittens when it began to nibble at her slippers. "And we will think upon it. I have much to ponder and many advisers to consult. If you would be good enough to await my response, I shall provide it within the week. We shall be happy to provide lodgings for your party, if you so desire."

"Most generous, Your Majesty." I bowed, still angry but stripping my tone bare of anything but bland gratitude. "But I shall make my own arrangements."

"Best steer clear of the cathedral." Leannor didn't look up from the kitten in her lap, smiling as she tickled it between the ears. "And, while I will, of course, publicly state that you enjoy our protection, I am unable to furnish guards or guarantee your safety in this city."

This brought a surprising laugh to my lips, and I felt my anger dissipate. "My safety has never been guaranteed anywhere, Your Majesty. Why should Couravel be any different?"

Quintrell guided us to an inn of his acquaintance which, he promised, was suitably appointed to provide both protection and discretion. I deduced from the warm welcome the minstrel received from the generously proportioned proprietress that he was no stranger to this small but comfortable repose. It sat at the apex of a bend in the river, overlooking a bridge that connected this mostly residential quarter to the workshops that dominated the south-eastern parts of the city. The building sported three storeys, so stood a good deal higher than the surrounding maze of rooftop and chimney. At Quintrell's urging, we took the two rooms on the upper floor. I had misgivings about occupying so high a place, since it would likely complicate matters should a swift escape prove necessary. However, the minstrel argued that the benefits of a decent vantage point outweighed the risks. Besides, it transpired he had made provision for this very circumstance.

"Good and strong," he said, lifting one of the floorboards beneath the window of the larger room. The revealed coil of rope was thick, one end secured to a sturdy oak beam. "Placed here with Mistress

Radget's permission many moons ago. It'll reach all the way to the street, though I usually find it's best to abscond via the rooftops, don't you, my lord?"

"Never thieved nor spied in a city before," I said. "So I bow to your greater knowledge, Master Quintrell."

He slotted the board back in place and gestured for me to join him at the window. "See there?" Quintrell pointed to a dim shape rising from the perennial cloud of woodsmoke towards the city's eastern edge. Some squinting revealed it as a chimney, taller than most others. "The stack of Couravel's busiest farriers," the minstrel explained. "The one point in the city entire that remains visible from roof height regardless of the hour, since the forge master keeps his furnace blazing at all times. Every alley betwixt here and there is narrow enough to leap and the farrier's workshop is just a stone's throw from the east-facing wall."

"A wall which will surely be patrolled," I pointed out.

"There's a way through." Quintrell gave one his grins and I divined he had just ensured his own survival should this mission have a dire outcome: I wouldn't leave him behind if he knew the only avenue of escape.

I grunted and turned to the Widow and Adlar. "I've a sense the princess regent is affording our Lady's invite more consideration than I expected. We're obliged to wait here for her reply."

"You think she'll actually do it?" Juhlina asked. "Go to Athiltor and humble herself to the Lady?"

"No. But Leannor is accustomed to negotiation. I suspect she'll counter with some form of compromise. A meeting away from Athiltor, something suitably ceremonial that avoids any suggestion the king or his mother have abased themselves. Leannor will paint herself as the peacemaker, attempting to heal the rift in the Covenant."

"You think the Lady will accept such a compromise?" The Widow's question had a weight to it I didn't like, her tone almost accusatory.

"I'll find out when I relate the princess regent's response," I said, glancing over my shoulder at the close-packed streets below. "In any event, we must be wary. The court has proclaimed our protected status, but I'd lay odds there are a dozen or more orthodox fanatics currently sharpening their knives. We'll keep watch through the night. Spinner, you first, then Master Quintrell, then Trooper Juhlina. I'll take the early shift."

Chapter Eleven

I slept poorly, beset by dreams distressing enough to jar me awake long before my shift on watch. I blinked at the darkened room, the dregs of the nightmare fading too quickly to catch any details. Despite the sweat beading my skin and the thump of my heart, I felt a modicum of relief that Erchel hadn't been a feature of this night-time visitation. Him, I always remembered. But, since Arnabus was no longer alive to invade my slumber, the wretch had been absent for some time now.

"Unpleasant dreams?"

Sitting up on my bed, I wiped grit from my eyes and made out Juhlina standing at the window. Her profile was outlined in the dim glow from beyond the half-open shutters. It had never struck me before how regular her features were, how well proportioned. Viewed from this angle she appeared a comely woman of nigh thirty years, the shadows concealing the nicks and scars that marred all of us who marched under the Lady's banner.

"I don't remember," I said, reaching for the water jug sitting beside the bed and downing a hefty gulp. The innkeeper had offered wine along with our evening meal, but I declined, keen to keep a clear head. It hadn't saved me from bad dreams or an aggravating headache. The *Eithlisch*'s arcane healing of my damaged skull made them a rare occurrence, and all the more taxing for their rarity.

"No decapitated Great Heretics then?" the Widow persisted. Her profile dipped, voice softening. "Wish I could say the same."

"You have nightmares?" I knew it a foolish question the instant it escaped my lips. *She watched a bunch of fanatics slit her little girl's throat. Of course she has nightmares.* Still, the notion of her dreaming about Arnabus troubled me.

"Sometimes," she said. "I dream of Lysotte, but less so now, for which I'm grateful. She is never happy in dreams, only in my waking memory. The Great Heretic is a new addition. It's always in the cathedral, after you left to find the Lady. His body starts to move. It sits up and reaches for its head, blood still pumping from the stump. Strangely, I do nothing. I don't scream or run. I just stand and watch as a dead man tries to fix his head back atop his shoulders. I know he has something to tell me, something I need to hear. But he never quite manages to make the head fit. Still it talks, that head, all dribbled blood and mumbling, but I can never make out what it's saying. It wears a terribly earnest expression; desperate you might say."

Shadows shifted on her face as she turned from the window, regarding me with steady eyes. "Any notion of what he's so keen for me to know, my lord?"

"Feel at leave to just call me Alwyn," I said. "At least when we're alone."

I set the water jug down and got to my feet, hands rubbing the small of my back to banish the ache. The innkeeper's mattress needed a few more bushels of straw for my liking. Joining her at the window, I ignored her expectant gaze and looked out at the gloomy rooftops below. The persistent pall of woodsmoke thinned at night but didn't fully dissipate, creating a drifting fog that obscured much. True to Quintrell's word, the glow of the farrier's chimney flickered like a beacon through the haze.

"He was about to say something," Juhlina persisted. "Something about the Lady. You killed him for it."

"I killed him because he was a vile murderer and intriguer, one who orchestrated the kidnap and torture of you and your comrades, if you recall. Not to mention the fact that he drove a schism into the Covenant that claimed hundreds of lives."

"I don't mourn him. I just want to know what he was going to say."

"Why?"

"I have done much at your side, under *her* banner. I told you once I did it for vengeance, at first. After that, because it seemed the only place I fit in this world. The Covenant Host is different from all other armies that march across this realm. It fights but it doesn't massacre, doesn't loot or pillage or lay waste. Some part of me felt we were doing something good, building something better."

"We are."

"Are we? Because all I see is yet more war."

"War that will end with the Lady's ascendancy. Ultimately, she promises peace where all others who claim power promise nothing but the fruits of their own greed. Hold to that, if nothing else."

"I still need to know." Her tone was quiet but insistent, flat in its refusal to be diverted. "You killed him for a reason. What was it?"

I looked at the door to the adjoining room where Adlar and Quintrell slept. Neither of them were given to snoring, but I heard no indication that either was awake.

"The reason we were taken," I said, lowering my voice. "What happened at the Dire Keep. Arnabus and Luminant Durehl wanted to wring something from me, a tale they imagined would bring down the Risen Martyr."

"Were they right?"

"Possibly, if it were true." I paused, assailed by an urge to tell her, confess it all. For one who lives much of his life juggling varying forms of deceit, there is a terrible temptation in confidence, for the unburdening of secrets brings relief. But, a burden shared is still a burden, and I had no wish to endanger this woman with the unvarnished falsity of Evadine's resurrection.

"Apparently," I went on, "they had convinced themselves there was something arcane in the Lady's healing at Farinsahl. Arnabus was ever a gifted spinner of lies, so concocted a lurid story of unnatural Caerith rites. That's what they wanted from me, testimony that she wasn't a Risen Martyr at all but some creature of malevolence. Come the morn, Arnabus was going to set his torturer on you and make me watch. If Lilat hadn't crawled out of the stonework when she did . . ." I trailed off into a sigh. "That's why I killed him."

I perceived a measure of mollification in Juhlina's bearing, perhaps even a mite of disappointment. Sometimes the secrets you seek amount to little. "You were there, though," she said. "When the Lady woke."

"I was. Though I didn't see the moment of her restoration. She'd been dying for days, then one morning she was well again. I can't account for it. All I can do is accept her word. As she drifted towards death one of the Seraphile came to her. And so was she risen."

I sensed there was more this woman had to say, her lips tight and jaw clenched in the manner of one caging words.

"Speak your mind," I said. "There are few whose word I can trust."

"You . . ." she began, then hesitated, avoiding my gaze before speaking on. "You're too close to her."

She's awful jealous, Ayin had said, and I saw a portion of that in the nervous wince that passed across the Widow's face. But mostly I saw concern. She feared for me.

"I'll say no more," she said as I fumbled for a response. She lowered her face before turning back to the window. "It's hours until dawn. You should sleep more."

"I think I've had my fill," I said. "I'll take the rest of the watch."

She didn't argue, moving wordlessly to her bed. I averted my gaze when she started to strip, something she did with the unabashed habit of soldiers. Strangely, for the first time the glimpses of her well-muscled flesh before she slipped under the blankets lingered longer in my mind than I wanted them to.

Idiot, I chided myself, turning my scrutiny to the streets. As the hours wore on, I found myself wishing that a band of orthodox assassins would appear out of the gloom. At least it would give me something else to think about.

My meeting with the Dulsian ambassador to the court of King Arthin proved to be a terse affair. Lord Therin Gasalle allowed me into his house, a modest but comfortable domicile that sat under the shadow of the palace walls, with a haste that left scant room for the usual niceties. I had requested the meeting the previous day via the conventional route of sending a servant, in this case Adlar, with an introductory letter. He returned with a verbal invitation to present myself the following morning, and to come alone. The ambassador was a tall man of scant muscle, which I felt made him resemble a stork or other wading bird. The impression was enhanced by the way he dipped his head out of his doorway, jerking it about as he surveyed the street for watchful eyes.

"You're the Scribe?" he said, closing the door. I expected to be led to a study or other discreet room, but we continued to stand in his narrow hallway.

"Lord Alwyn Scribe." I bowed. "Lord Therin, I assume? I expected to be greeted a by a servant . . ."

"A servant?" He rasped out a caustic laugh. "By the Martyrs, man, are you mad? I sent all the servants away last night. We are alone." A faint noise from outside caused him to start. It was just a cat's distant mewing, but still it put him on edge. "Were you followed?" he demanded.

I expect so. The princess regent has spies aplenty. Deciding it best to leave the thought unsaid, I replied in a tone of quiet confidence, "No, my lord. I assure you I was very careful."

"Good." He ran a hand through the wispy hair crowning his scalp, then wiped sweat on his robe. It left dark stains in the expensive red velvet. "Now then." He straightened, sweaty hands clutching the hem of his robe. "I believe you have a message for Duke Lermin."

"I do. It's a brief thing, really. Merely the greetings and best wishes of the Risen Martyr and Anointed Lady Evadine Courlain, Ascendant of the Covenant Resurgent. She wishes Duke Lermin to know of the high regard in which she holds both him and his family. Accordingly, she extends an invitation for the duke to attend Athiltor where it will be her pleasure to bestow her blessing upon him."

"That is . . ." I watched the apple of Lord Therin's throat bob as he swallowed ". . . all, then?"

"What else would there be, my lord?"

"I received correspondence from Duke Lermin only a few days ago. Once word reached him of the . . . changes in Covenant hierarchy, he expressed his confidence that a representative from the Anointed

Lady would call upon me. When they did so, he instructed me to make fulsome use of all profitable opportunities."

I had heard folk ask for a bribe many times, usually with considerably more artistry and markedly fewer words. As yet, I had done only scant research regarding Dulsian, there being so much else to occupy my attention. I knew Duke Lermin had a reputation for avarice, but that hardly set him apart among the gaggle of venal graspers that comprise the nobility of Albermaine. Still, such stark evidence of the man's greed was welcome. Honest bribery always made things less complicated.

"The Lady's sermons hold no injunctions against profit," I said. "However, to aid our mutual understanding, perhaps my lord would be kind enough to provide an example."

His stork's neck bulged again before he spoke on. "As I'm sure you know, Duke Lermin has been in dispute with the Covenant for quite some time over the disposition of grants and rights as they pertain to the fishing villages on our southern coast. More than half of these villages are either owned outright or in part by the Covenant. Furthermore, smaller trading vessels often choose to unload their cargoes through these minor ports, since the Covenant demands less in the way of excise than does the duke or the Crown."

"Of course," I said, a bald lie because I knew none of this. "It strikes me as a singularly unfair state of affairs, my lord. One the Crown should have resolved many moons ago."

"Indeed they should. If, erm . . ." He coughed, as well he might for our conversation was on the cusp of slipping into outright treason. "If the Anointed Lady were to . . ." He stuttered to a halt, eyebrows raised in an expectant prompt. I indulged in some small sadism by putting a puzzled frown on my brow and staying silent.

"Oh," I said finally in apparent comprehension, causing him to sag in relief. "I'm sure something could be arranged," I continued. "An accommodation that would benefit all parties. The Lady shall be glad to discuss the matter in detail when Duke Lermin presents himself at Athiltor."

Lord Therin frowned at this. Although, after some internal debate, all played out on his gaunt, moistened face in stark clarity, he consented to nod. "I shall, with all discretion, convey your message to the duke, my lord."

"Excellent." We stood in silence until I gestured to the door, which he duly opened, once again dipping his head out to check our surroundings.

"All seems clear . . ." he whispered.

"Glad to hear it, my lord!" I said, voice echoing along the street. I clapped him on the shoulder as I exited the house. "My heartfelt thanks for such an agreeable meeting!" I bowed with florid appreciation, then looked up to regard a slamming door.

Walking away, I wondered if my theatrics might have scuppered this tacit agreement and found I didn't much care. If Duke Lermin's representative to the royal court was a man of such unimpressive character, it didn't speak well of his master.

Lord Jacquel Ebrin was a half-foot shorter than his Dulsian counterpart but made a far more noteworthy impression. A stocky man with a copious beard of dense copper curls, the Rhianvelan ambassador to the court of King Arthin greeted me with a raised tankard the moment I entered the tavern. The place had been of his choosing, no fearful, clumsy bargaining in a hallway for him. Instead, Lord Jacquel felt no compunction in calling out my name and clapping a hand to my shoulder in full view of the establishment's rowdy clientele.

"The Scribe himself, by the Martyrs' many arses!" He gripped my shoulder in fierce comradeship before turning to address the tavern entire, ale spilling from his tankard as he raised it high. "Behold, you sodden curs, a true hero of the Pretender's War! Drink to his health, or may the Malecite damn your souls!"

The man was evidently well known here, the crowd responding with a hearty cheer and raised vessels, although I detected a few ribald insults and boos among the general din. Lord Jacquel himself let out a hearty cry before downing the remaining ale in his tankard with a few hefty gulps.

"More, good lass," he said, handing the empty receptacle to a serving maid. "And one for Lord Alwyn. Also—" he winked, leaning closer to her "—a cup of brandy to go with 'em, eh? All on my slate, mind. This man pays for nothing under this roof."

After the girl scurried off he turned to me, both hands gripping my shoulders now, eyes tracking me from feet to face. "Scribe doesn't suit you, m'boy," he told me, squinting in appraisal. "I was expecting a pinch-faced bundle of sticks. Should've known better, I s'pose. No mere scribbler could've humbled the Pretender. Come." He pushed his way through the throng, jerking his head for me to follow. "Let's play some dice. Hope you brought coin, m'boy. I'll stand for your drinks but not your wagers."

I followed him to a quiet alcove with a table and chairs. Despite the liveliness of the place, it was noteworthy that this comfortable and relatively quiet spot remained unoccupied. A set of dice and a cup sat atop the table, swiftly scooped up by Lord Jacquel as he took his seat.

"Cat's Claw," he said, rattling the dice. "I trust you know how to play?"

"I do, my lord." I sat and nodded my thanks to the serving maid who had been swift in bringing our drinks. "Though I've never been one for games of chance."

"Really?" Jacquel raised a thick eyebrow in surprise. "Thought all outlaws loved a wager." He slammed the cup down on the table and held it there, looking at me in expectation.

"Two," I said.

"Four," he countered before raising the cup. The upper faces of the revealed dice, six in all, showed three cats, one mouse and two foxes, making our opening gambits a tie.

"Dealer's privilege," I said, adding, "Outlaws who gamble are also the most likely to fight among themselves. The band I ran with had very strict rules about such things."

"Deckin's lot, wasn't it?" Jacquel left the cats where they were and scooped the remaining dice into the cup. "Heard of him. Outlaw King of the Shavine Woods, or some such."

"Some called him that, including himself."

"There's a rumour he was your father." Jacquel rattled the dice and slammed the cup down again before placing two sheks alongside it. A smart bet given the modest odds. "That true?"

"No. Though I'm told he was fond of the whorehouse where I was born. Hence the rumours." I matched his bet with two sheks of my own, then added a third.

"Trying to buy the pot, eh?" Jacquel's beard parted in a smile. If he matched my counter bet, he would raise the cup and the game would be decided on the value of the revealed dice. If he didn't, he would forfeit and the coins were mine.

"Play the dice as they fall." I smiled back. "Not as you want them to fall."

"Deckin teach you that?"

"No. That I learned for myself after they cut his head off."

The Rhianvelan grunted and added a shek to the pot before lifting the cup with a flourish. To win, all the dice on the table needed to show four or more cats. He had five.

"Should've bet a full tiel," Jacquel grumbled, sweeping the coins into his purse. "Another game?"

"Certainly, my lord."

We played a dozen games all told, during which time Lord Jacquel consumed two tankards of ale and three cups of brandy. I didn't bother trying to match him, divining quickly that this was that rare breed of man whose wits don't dull when drunk. It was a trick I had never acquired. Evidence of his apparent immunity to the effects of liquor was demonstrated by the time we completed our twelfth game, whereupon my purse was notably lighter and his heavier. I suspected weighted dice, but when I held them I felt no lean to the cubes of carved and polished bone. This fellow was both lucky and careful in his wagers.

"My lord duke never gambles, y'know," Jacquel commented, wiping froth from his beard. He had requested the maid bring a bowl of dates and popped them into his mouth between gulps. "His piety won't allow it. Not like his father. There was a man who would happily play cards, dice, and all manner of games from dawn till dusk, when he wasn't sticking his ducal member into anything of woman born. Useless, daft old reprobate. I miss him terribly." He let out a nostalgic sigh and sipped from his brandy cup. "By the time Lord Viruhlis inherited the duchy, much of it was owed to others. All Rhianvel damn near impoverished by the vice of its own duke. I wasn't much older than you then, m'boy. It's been a long road back for us, what with all the wars and such. But, thanks to our pious duke and his peerless head for finance, we're about as rich as we're ever going to get."

As he dropped the dice into the cup and passed it to me, I saw the humour on his face supplanted by a certain gravitas. It seemed we were about to get to the point.

"So, there's little the Anointed Lady can offer," I said, rattling the dice and upending the cup. "Two."

Jacquel's expression didn't change, regarding me with unblinking focus as he teased fingers through his ale-sodden beard. "Three."

The raised cup revealed two cats, my first stroke of real luck in this entire game. "The Anointed Lady's blessing is not nothing," I went on, leaving the cats in place and returning the other four dice to the cup. "As those ardently devoted Rhianvelan Supplicants who turned up in Athiltor recently were keen to attest." I set the cup down and placed five sheks alongside it. "Or does your duke's piety not match theirs?"

"I'd match his piety against anyone who calls themselves a devotee of the Covenant, except perhaps your Lady." He reached into his purse and extracted a full tiel, placing it alongside my sheks, then adding another. "That is not the subject of this evening's conversation, m'boy."

"Then what is?"

Jacquel reclined in his chair, tankard in hand, but, for once, he didn't drink from it. Instead, he spent a prolonged interval shifting his gaze from me to the cup and coins on the table. "An utterly foolish bet, wouldn't you say?" he asked me eventually. "The odds stand squarely in your favour. And yet, here I am, risking a goodly portion of my purse's contents on the unlikely outcome that there will be no more than one cat revealed when we lift up this cup. It's the kind of bet Lord Viruhlis's father made all the time. Now your Lady asks my lord to make another, with no less than his life and entire duchy as the stakes."

"She merely offers a blessing. The blessing of a Risen Martyr who has actually felt the touch of the Seraphile. What faithful soul could ever refuse such a thing?"

"A blessing can become a curse quickly enough, lad." He jerked his head at the cup and coins. "Are you going to match my bet?"

"I will." I opened my purse and extracted the required funds, setting them down. "I'll also sweeten the pot. It's my understanding that, some twenty-three years ago, King Mathis ruled in favour of Duke Guhlton of Althiene regarding a longstanding border dispute with Rhianvel. Something to do with a silver mine in a particular valley, I believe."

Once again, Jacquel's expression didn't change. "My lord is well informed."

"Thank you. I'm no scholar of law, but even a cursory reading of the petitions and judgement make it clear the matter had assuredly not been decided in accordance with Crown statute or accepted precedent."

"Guhlton was always the Algathinets' most loyal dog." Jacquel consented to smile. "Until the day he wasn't."

"Favouritism and base corruption are not the Lady's way. I should like Duke Viruhlis to know that, if this matter ever falls to Lady Evadine's judgement, it will be decided purely on its merits."

Jacquel finally drank from his tankard, draining it dry with practised swiftness. Setting the vessel down, he rested his elbows on the table, leaning forward. "A silver mine is a rich addition to any pot," he said. "But merely a trinket compared to the price my duchy would end up paying should your Lady find herself evicted from Athiltor. The Covenant now exists as a broken thing, but even the shards of a shattered vessel can cut."

He fell silent and nodded to the upturned cup. Lifting it, I beheld two foxes, an owl and a mouse. No more cats.

"My thanks for a very enjoyable evening, my lord," Jacquel said, sweeping the winnings into his purse and getting to his feet.

"An evening without apparent resolution," I pointed out.

"Oh, I wouldn't say that. I'm resolved to tell the duke that you are a very poor dice player. All other resolutions will have to wait upon his word." He pulled his cloak over his shoulders, buckling it at the neck before pausing to favour me with a grin of surprising warmth. "Don't worry overmuch, m'boy. He's his own man and doesn't put the same stock in my advice as his father did. Besides, he's besotted with your Risen Martyr, even though he's never met her."

Lord Jacquel Ebrin afforded me a respectful bow, then turned and began pushing his way through the crowd. Left alone in the alcove, I pondered the dice and my mostly empty purse, unable to decide if I had been robbed or favoured this night.

Chapter Twelve

By now, cherished reader, you will know me as a soul with old and unpleasant memories of whoremasters. Therefore, when greeting the man Tiler led me to on the fourth night of our stay in Couravel, forcing myself to adopt civil manners was no easy thing.

"Knew Deckin, did ya?" the fellow demanded, leering close enough to let me catch his stink of unwashed skin, liquor staining both breath and garb, and the wit-addling brand of pipe smoke. Even if Tiler hadn't made me aware of this man's profession, I would have known it instantly. To be a master of whores is to be the worst of bullies, employing habits no doubt learned in childhood, but refined and magnified to the point where they become profitable. Surveying his blunt, mutton-chopped features, besmirched and near-ragged leather jerkin cladding a meaty form, more fat than muscle but plenty of both, I felt a familiar itch in the hand closest to my dagger.

"That I did," I said, crediting myself with the flatness of my tone.

"Me too." The fellow straightened a little. "Ran with him for a full season when I was a lad."

I knew this instantly as a boastful lie, but not one I was willing to gainsay, at least not yet. "Is she inside?" I asked, nodding to the door behind him. Tiler had led me to this cramped street in the city's south-eastern quarter shortly after finding me at the inn. His swiftness in seeking me out was no surprise, since such things were ingrained in the outlaw's soul. Here, the smoke sat thicker over the rooftops, allowing for meagre light even during the day. At night, it was a gloom-shrouded maze, the thick shadows broken only by the occasional glimmer from between closed shutters. Even the drinking dens were quiet, havens for those for whom liquor rather than merriment was their principal aim. By now I had seen enough of cities to know that they all have places such as this, a street or a whole quarter given over to those the more fortunate like to pretend do not exist.

"She's waiting." The whoremaster's eyes shifted between Tiler and I. "Her time's precious, even if it's just talking you're after. That's what Shilva's man here said. You just want what she knows about . . ." He fell silent, glancing about in a manner that told me he was just bright enough to recognise the danger of secrets as well as their value. "Her late customer," he finished with a grin of self-congratulation for his own clever circumspection.

"That's right," I said. *Could just knife him*, I thought as I took the silver sovereign from my pocket. But, according to Tiler, this fellow was affiliated with Shilva in certain criminal matters. Leaving him dead on the steps of his own brothel would therefore not bode well for my future dealings with a woman who had become what Deckin never could, a true monarch of outlaws.

The whoremaster turned the sovereign over in his fingers before consigning it to his own pocket, hunching as he did so, as if fearing an attempt to take it back. "Another when you're done, right?"

"Right," I replied, voice clipped by thinning patience.

He bristled a little at the unspoken challenge, but wisely shuffled aside, jerking his head at the door. "The room at the top. Can give you one turn of the glass only. She's gotta earn her keep like all the rest."

This was so reminiscent of the whoremaster who had so dominated my boyhood that I found my hand halt as it touched the latch, letting it fall to my dagger. Tiler, attuned to the shifts in mood that indicate impending violence, quickly stepped to my side.

"I'll watch the street, my lord," he said, smiling tightly but with a warning glint to his eye. This was not our place, after all, and who knew what friends this brutish stinker had lurking in the surrounding shadows.

"Come and get me if there's trouble," I told him, pushing the door open and stepping inside.

The woman who greeted me in the room at the top of the house was surprising in many ways. Her smile more cheerful and lacking in artifice than I expected. Her face was painted but in artful enhancement rather than concealment. Her hair was a cascade of blonde curls and ringlets contrasting well with the black silken gown that clad her fleshy but undeniably enticing form.

"My lord Scribe, is it not?" she enquired in an accent possessing only a faint echo of an Alundian burr.

"At your service, good mistress," I said, bowing before stepping into the room and closing the door behind me. I found the place neatly arranged with various small ornamentations and perfume bottles clustering on the dresser and shelves. My practised eye picked out some items of genuine value among the bric-a-brac, something the whoremaster had either missed or didn't care about.

"You'll service me, will you?" Her cleavage jiggled as she laughed, reclining on the large bed that was the room's principal feature. "Usually the other way around for poor Nuala."

"Is that your real name?"

"Martyrs no." She laughed again. "I learned early in my career that people would pay more to fuck Nuala than they would plain old Magrid, daughter of the vineyard washerwoman. Strange isn't it, the importance we attach to names?"

"I've often thought so." I gestured to a comfortable-looking chair padded in velvet. "May I sit?"

"You're paying, my lord. Do as you please."

I shifted my sword belt to a more comfortable angle and sat, regarding a woman who returned my scrutiny with a complete absence of trepidation or uncertainty. "What name did King Tomas know you by?" I asked her.

I hoped for some measure of shock, but she merely let out a languid sigh, her robe slipping from a pale thigh as she raised it to rest an arm on her knee. "I thought as much. To know a king's secrets, seek out his whore. That's your intent, is it not?"

"It is my understanding that King Tomas visited you regularly, back when you lived in a far nicer house in a far nicer street. If you are privy to certain information of use to me, I will pay you well to share it. A business arrangement of mutual benefit."

"I think I like you, my lord. Your directness is refreshing." Nuala sat up, adjusting her robe into a semblance of modesty. Rising from the bed, she went to a dresser and plucked the glass stopper from a decanter of wine. "Care to join me?" she asked, pouring a generous measure into a crystal goblet. "It's good stuff, all the way from home. Harder to get these days since your armies ravaged the place."

"I was absent for the ravaging," I told her. "And I'll forgo the wine, thank you."

"To business then." Nuala took a sip of wine and perched on the edge of her bed. "My profession has provided me the gift of divining others' intentions, especially men. You are harder to read than most, but not impossibly so. It is my deduction that you used your outlaw connections to seek out anyone who might know a hidden tale or two about the Algathinets. I expect you hoped to find a maid or other servant with a grievance, some outcast from the royal household willing to sell the gossip they accrued. Instead, your search led you to me, King Tomas's only whore. At least, so he told me and I've no reason to doubt him. For a king, I must say he was a terrible liar. But a kind man, in his way, who was always good to me." She paused to take another sip of wine. "Do I miscalculate, my lord?"

"No." I knew then this was a hopeless enterprise. This woman might have secrets aplenty in her clever head, but she had no intention of sharing them, not with me in any case. "This—" I flicked a hand at the room "—hardly seems a fitting abode for one who once enjoyed royal favour. Doesn't that strike you as unfair?"

"Tomas paid me what I asked for, no more, no less. It is how I like things, my lord. Good business is done on the basis of a simple compact, an understanding that what passes between both parties is private. I have no secrets for you, regardless of the price."

"The price would be enough to get you out of this house, away from that filth downstairs."

She smiled and shook her head. "I don't work for that filth downstairs. He works for me, although he's paid to pretend it's the other way around. Keeps the gangs away. However, this house is mine. Admittedly, I've had more lucrative periods in the past, but my earnings are sufficient for my immediate needs and a comfortable retirement. Also, I've long since cured myself of the disease of ambition. My apologies for your wasted journey, Lord Scribe."

She saluted me with her goblet and drained it before returning to the dresser for a refill.

"In which case," I said, "I request only a question. A question I will pay one silver sovereign for you to listen to. You are not obliged to answer."

She paused in the act of pouring more wine. "Fancy you can read the answer in my face, eh?" She shrugged. "Very well. I'll play your game." Turning to me, she crossed her arms. "Ask away."

"Did Princess Leannor murder her husband?"

Even in the best of liars, there is always hesitation. A barely perceptible pause before expression shifts their features, the briefest delay in the denial escaping their lips. I saw none of it now. Nuala's caustic, disparaging laugh erupted instantly, her mirth allowing me a generous view of her quivering flesh as the robe parted.

"I'm told his marriage to Princess Leannor was far from happy," I persisted as her mirth faded. "And, despite reputedly fine health, he expired rather quickly."

"Obligated or not," she said, returning herself to the bed with a playful bounce, "that one I'll happily answer. Tomas did like to talk. In truth, I think he preferred talking to fucking. It's common among my more important customers. Wealth and influence make a man lonely, I find. So, yes. I knew all about his sister and her dreadful marriage to that old dullard. From what I could gather, Lord Keville wasn't cruel, exactly, just disinterested in his bride. As for her, Tomas said she found the old goat more boring than a sack of turnips. Once they'd done their duty and the royal sprog was whelped, I doubt they spent more than a day in each other's company. Curious then, that I recall Tomas telling me how awfully upset Leannor was when Keville popped off. He was the one with all the smarts, y'see. Knew all the secrets and tricks that keep this realm intact. 'She's afraid,' he told me. 'Afraid of what this means for her boy.' Doesn't sound like a woman who'd just done her husband in, does it?" Nuala laughed again, shaking her head. "Sorry, luv. Your dog's barking at the wrong rathole."

She relaxed into her pillows, smoothing out her robe. "Now, my lord. Unless you have other requests to make of my person, I'll bid you good night."

I didn't bother with further bargaining or cajoling, nor with threats. Some folk can be swayed by such things, but not all, and certainly not this woman of peerless self-possession. Rising, I went to her side table and placed a silver sovereign there before bowing and moving to the door.

"By the way," she said as I lifted the latch, "Tomas called me Magrid. He's the only one I ever let do that." She twiddled her fingers in farewell and dismissal. "So nice to meet an interesting and distinguished man. But please don't ever come back."

Out on the street, Tiler greeted me with a questioning glance that fell into a frown when I shook my head. "Sorry, my lord," he said. "She's all I could find. Searched high and low for former servants, too. Turned up a valet who was so aged he barely remembered his days at the palace."

"It was always a long bet," I told him. "Here." I tossed another sovereign to the whoremaster, or rather the brute Nuala paid to play the role. The sight of him angered me less now I knew who really held power in this house. "Guard her well," I added, "she deserves it."

He replied with a cautious nod and stepped towards the door to resume his place. Just one single step, but it saved my life. The crossbow bolt pierced his head at a sharp angle, allowing me to gauge the elevated point from which it had been launched. I caught a brief flicker of shadow at the edge of the rooftop before the stricken brute staggered into my line of sight. His eyes rolled back in his skull and drool spilled from his lips. I expended a precious moment in frozen fascination of his sagging, gibbering features, the face of a dead man who didn't yet know he was dead. My second salvation came in the form of Tiler slamming his wiry self into my side, sending us both into collision with the alley wall.

From above, I heard the multiple snap of loosed crossbows. Sparks flew and cobbles exploded, stinging my face with grit as I huddled against the brickwork. A final bolt shattered mortar an inch from my nose, causing me to reel away, still entangled with Tiler. Falling, I dragged myself clear of the outlaw's grip and scrambled upright, scanning the rooftops for more assailants. Nothing.

"They get you?" I hissed at Tiler.

"Nicked my leg, the bastards," he hissed back, grunting in pain as he rose to a crouch, knives clutched in both hands.

"They'll be reloading." I drew my sword and started towards the shadowed recess of the alley. "Stay close."

I covered only a few feet before a man-sized shadow descended to bar my path. I dropped into a crouch, sword drawn back for a thrust, then saw that the shadow barring my way wasn't moving. A closer look revealed a man in dark cotton garb with a scarf tied about his features. Fortunately, he also had one of Adlar Spinner's throwing knives buried in the side of his neck.

A shout then a thud snapped my attention to the mouth of the alley where another body lay twisted upon the cobbles. The gash in its skull was the signature wound of the Widow's warhammer. Grunts and screams came from above, one more corpse falling to the ground with a crunch of breaking bone. It was followed by two others, both very much alive and clutching crossbows. They landed heavily and immediately began scouring the surrounding shadows for targets. I decided it would be best not to allow them the leisure to find us.

The nearest was a dozen paces off, allowing him time to turn and grip the lock on his crossbow, but not enough to aim it. The bolt went wide as my sword described a swift arc, cutting deep into his unprotected shoulder. His comrade was quicker, bringing his weapon to bear with a creditably calm swiftness. I embraced the man I had just maimed, wrapping an arm about his torso and drawing his twitching form close. The second assassin cursed and stepped back, angling his crossbow to aim at my legs. Tiler didn't let him loose the bolt, ducking low at the fellow's back to slash both knives across his hamstrings.

Hearing the thump of more boots on the cobbles, I dragged the dying man in my arms around to confront the fresh threat. Fortunately, I beheld only Juhlina and Adlar. "Got four," the Widow told me. "The rest ran off."

"Shut yer squealing!" Tiler snarled, driving a kick into the belly of the man he had hamstrung. The assassin, however, was too lost in his pains to heed the warning, continuing to scream and clutch at his bleeding legs. "D'you need him to speak, my lord?" Tiler enquired, pinning the man down with a boot on his chest, knife poised to deliver the killing blow.

"He-heretics!" the wounded man grunted, courage flaring in the face of impending death. He showed white teeth amid a soot-blackened face. "Slaves to the Malecite Whore!"

"Enough of that," Tiler advised, pressing his boot harder into the defiant fellow's chest. "Who sent you, squealer?"

"We know who sent him," I said. "I doubt a blade hired by the Algathinets would be so resolute. Also, they wouldn't have missed."

"Might be more," the Widow warned, scanning the rooftops.

"True enough." I gestured to Tiler to step back. "Let him go." Crouching at the faithful assassin's side, I looked into his blazing, uncowed eyes, feeling a mix of admiration and disgust. "You are a servile dog to unworthy masters," I told him. "If you ever open your heart to the truth of the Lady's word, come find us at Athiltor. She forgives all."

I straightened, sparing a glance for the dead whoremaster who had unwittingly saved my life. "Let's go," I said, gesturing for them to follow as I started off at a steady run. "We collect the horses, then we're gone from this city."

"The princess's answer?" Juhlina said, falling in at my side.

"I think she just gave it. She might not have had a hand in this, but she surely knew about it. Our welcome in this city has been worn through."

"So, it's war then."

I huffed out a laugh, uncoloured by any vestige of humour. "It was always going to be war."

Chapter Thirteen

We waited two full days for Eamond and Ayin to appear at the crossroads, but the junction remained conspicuously empty of all travellers. I hoped there might at least be some carts and passing traders willing to share gossip and rumour, but even this was denied me.

"It's likely the princess has closed the city," Quintrell said. "Your sudden absence would not have gone unnoticed, my lord."

I saw wisdom in his reasoning. Our departure via one of the minor southern gates in the city walls had barely raised the heads of its two bored-looking guards. Either Leannor had expected to receive news of my death or, in the event I survived, didn't think I would run just yet, her answer for the Anointed Lady being so important. It was a reminder that the princess regent was clever but also possessed an excess of confidence in her own machinations.

"They're young but they're smart," the Widow told me as we sat at the fire on the second night at the crossroads. "If there's a way out, they'll find it."

"I shouldn't have sent them," I said. Worries over Ayin's behaviour had dogged me since I sent her and Eamond on their mission. The more I dwelt upon it, and her past misdeeds, the more foolish an enterprise it seemed. *Send a fanatic and a mad girl to act as spies. Days and nights traipsing around the worst corners of Couravel, no doubt full of unkind words and grasping hands.* Could Ayin's repressed but, I suspected, dormant urges resist all such temptation?

"Time is our enemy, my lord," Quintrell said. He wore a grimace of sympathetic reluctance, but still managed to pique my anger. "The princess regent will be drawing her plans, summoning her retainers . . ."

"I know," I snapped, tone sufficiently harsh to silence the minstrel, the Widow and Adlar who up until now had been humming a tune and juggling his knives. Sighing, I tossed a twig into the fire. "One more day . . ."

As was her wont, Lilat appeared out of the darkness without any warning. Somehow, she had imbued her pony with the same stealthiness. She had led it through the Scout Company pickets unnoticed, hooves barely making a sound on the grass. The others all started, Adlar readying a knife for a throw and the Widow reaching for her warhammer. Quintrell, a fine spy but no warrior, dropped to all fours and scurried to the far side of the fire. Lilat ignored them and strode to my side, features grim. "Soldiers," she said. "Came from the east, met with more from the city, then headed north. A man we know led them."

"The big man? Lord Ehlbert?"

She shook her head. "The man we met on the death walk north. The one who looked like the woman who talks."

Altheric Courlain. Lord Marshal of the King's Host, and Evadine's father. I had always wondered if, when the time came, he would be willing to put duty before family. Now I had an answer. "How many?" I asked, getting to my feet.

Lilat replied with the sour frown that appeared whenever she was called upon to reckon large numbers. "Many," she repeated with an impatient shrug.

"It appears the princess already had a plan in mind." I moved to the horses, hefting Blackfoot's saddle. "Mount up. We ride for Athiltor."

"In the dark?" Quintrell said.

"Rest assured, Master Minstrel, if your horse stumbles and you end up breaking your neck, I shall mourn for you. Perhaps for as much as an hour. Maybe two."

We maintained a slow trot along the northern road until dawn, whereupon I ordered the company to a steady canter. I had to resist the temptation to spur to a full gallop, knowing it would leave us with exhausted mounts by nightfall and it was a long trek to Athiltor. I also opted for the most direct route to the holy city, even though it risked crossing the line of Sir Altheric's march. I entertained a faint hope that we might move fast enough to get ahead of the lord marshal, given the time Lilat had taken to find us, but knew it much more likely Altheric had at least a day's lead. However, this afforded the chance to properly gauge his numbers.

"I reckon it as a thousand horse," Tiler said. He crouched at the edge of the road, fingers exploring the many hoof and footprints marring the verge. Tiler did not possess the skills of the late and much missed Fletchman, lost on a mountainside to a treacherous cur the previous winter, but his tracking ability was still superior to mine. "The tracks don't tell you much as regards numbers, but all the dung they left behind does." His hand outlined a deep print in the earth. "Heavy cavalry, too. No sign of foot."

"A strong force," the Widow commented. "But not the entire strength of the Crown Host. And why march on Athiltor without infantry?"

"Unless they're not going to Athiltor," I said. "The road forks a dozen miles on. We'll find an answer there."

We reached the fork in the road the following morning after a much needed but frustrating overnight rest. The wealth of horse dung on the eastward fork told the tale clearly. I didn't need a tracker's eye to see that Lord Altheric had led his command away from Athiltor. Tiler also advised that they had increased their pace.

"The lord marshal has somewhere to be," I concluded. "Somewhere he has to reach by a certain day."

"This road has several branches," Quintrell pointed out. "They could be headed anywhere in northern Alberis."

"It's also the principal route to Althiene."

"Why would they be heading there?"

I recalled the letter Leannor had shown me in her tower room, the untidy, obsequious hand of the proxy governor of Althiene. *Your humble and loyal servant, Lord Archel Shelvane.* "Because they were invited." I kicked my heels, sending Blackfoot into a gallop and calling out to the whole company. "Our Lady is in danger! We ride hard from here on!"

We came to Stonebridge two days later. It was an obvious destination, being the only crossing point offering easy passage into Althiene for a large number of horsemen, the others consisting of ferries or rickety wooden bridges barely worthy of the name. Our ride had been hard on both riders and horses, even sturdy Blackfoot plodding with a lowered head, fatigued by another bout of galloping during the dwindling hours of daylight. The bridge and the village that surrounded it were concealed from view by a tall, wooded hill. Cresting it, I saw the bridge brightly lit, torches flickering along its granite span to illuminate the banner rising from its centre, the long-tusked boar of House Shelvane fluttering in the breeze. The torchlight cast a wavering glow over a full company of ducal cavalry arrayed on the far side of the bridge, the halberds of another two companies of infantry glittering to their left and right. Approaching the southern end of the bridge was a far smaller group of riders clad in the dark colours favoured by the Covenant Host. Evadine tended to eschew banners and other frippery, but I had little difficulty in picking out her tall form riding at the head of this party.

Answered a call to parley from the Pig of the North, I concluded amid a sudden welter of self-reproach. *Because I wasn't there to counsel against it, and I told her he could be bought.*

At first, I felt the plummeting gut that comes with arriving too late to avert catastrophe. But then my eyes discerned the shifting mass of shadows south of the village; Lord Altheric's host moving to close the trap, but doing so at a walk rather than a gallop. Had I been in the Lord Marshal's place I would have done two things he had not. Firstly, I would have placed a rearguard atop this hill. Secondly, I would have ordered a full-tilt charge to the village regardless of the dangers of galloping over ground in the dark. It seemed to me that, as a commander, Evadine's father was a curious mix of overconfidence and caution.

Or, I pondered, *he hopes to form a cordon around his daughter and beseech her to surrender without battle.* In any case, this lack of urgency at the critical moment gave me an opportunity I wasn't about to squander.

"Our Lady is in dire peril and needs warning!" I called out to the company. "Strike out to the west for a short way, then ride for the bridge with all haste. The kingsmen may try to stop us. Don't delay yourselves by fighting or helping fallen comrades. Warning the Lady is your sole object!"

I paused to stroke a regretful hand over Blackfoot's drooping neck. He tossed his head and cast a baleful eye over his shoulder. "Sorry, my snobbish friend," I said, before kicking my heels hard into his flanks.

Despite his tiredness, Blackfoot spurred down the slope and on to the field below with impressive speed. The Scout Company followed without hesitation, many hooves drumming the earth to a volume I knew Lord Altheric and his kingsmen wouldn't mistake for thunder. I guided Blackfoot towards the west for a count of twenty, then tugged the reins to point his head at the village and its brightly lit bridge. This manoeuvre created a gap betwixt ourselves and the Crown cavalry, but I doubted it would be wide enough to render us immune from attack. It couldn't be helped. With the trap about to be sprung, my prime concern had to be getting Evadine clear regardless of the cost.

We covered little over half the distance to the village when I heard the first sounds of combat, the clang and crunch of colliding armour and horseflesh to my rear. The tumult was soon followed by the melange of thuds and whinnies that told of a fallen horse and rider. I closed my ears to it and forced Blackfoot to a faster pace. Lord Altheric was now faced with the unpalatable choice of continuing his slow advance or ordering a pell-mell assault. I gambled that his love for his daughter, if such sentiment remained in his heart, would make him opt for the former, or at least expend some precious moments in anguished dithering.

The sounds of clashing horses faded as we reached Stonebridge village, a quick backward glance revealing most of the company still following. The confines of the village forced me to slow Blackfoot to a trot. I expected to force my way through a gaggle or two of gawping villagers, but the narrow streets and yards remained curiously empty. Perhaps the folk here had the good sense to seclude themselves when large numbers of soldiers appear out of the dark.

Emerging on to the broad thoroughfare leading to the bridge, I exhaled in relief at finding Evadine and her party paused. She hadn't yet started Ulstan along the shallow arch. Instead, she sat and regarded my approach with a curious frown rather than alarm. The twin Rhianvelan Supplicants were reined in on either side of her, their faces exhibiting poorly restrained resentment.

"Alwyn?" Evadine asked in bemusement as I brought Blackfoot to an untidy halt.

"My lady," I said, dragging in a series of ragged breaths before forcing the words out. "We must ride from this place!" I pointed to the darkened fields south of the village. "You are betrayed. Lord Altheric comes . . ."

"Leannor sent my father?" The puzzlement on Evadine's face shifted into anger and she muttered, "Spiteful bitch."

"We have no time!" I nudged Blackfoot closer and reached for Evadine's reins. "We must go . . ."

"Dear Alwyn." Evadine took hold of my hand, her own clad in a gauntlet. It occurred to me that she and the rest of her party were fully armoured, not the attire one would wear to a parley. "Worry not." She patted my hand and gently disentangled it from her reins. "Still, it warms my heart that you came so swiftly to my rescue."

"They're here, my lady," Harldin, said. The Rhianvelian Supplicant and his sister drew their swords in an uncanny display of synchronicity, placing their mounts between Evadine and the village. From the sudden tumult of thundering hooves, it seemed Lord Altheric had finally decided to abandon his caution. The mounted kingsmen soon appeared, their tall, heavy warhorses shattering fences and raising squawks and squeals from livestock.

"Guard our Lady!" I called to the Scout Company, drawing my

sword. They wheeled their horses about, forming a thin line, readying weapons to receive the charge. My scouts were lightly armoured and I doubted they could withstand a concentrated assault by knights and men-at-arms in full plate. We could only hope to delay them long enough for Evadine to get clear. Casting a desperate glance at her, I saw that she remained as free of alarm as before, watching the oncoming kingsmen with a brow drawn in sadness.

An eruption of challenging cries from the onrushing kingsmen drew my gaze back to the village. About half thronged the narrow streets with the remainder choking the thoroughfare to the bridge. Their numbers worked against them in such confines, slowing their charge to an untidy, cramped trot. It made them an easy target for the dozens of crossbowmen and archers now streaming from the surrounding cottages.

Bolts and arrows loosed at such close range are capable of piercing all but the best plate, while also tearing through the quilts that covered the flanks of the kingsmens' warhorses. Dozens of both fell screaming at the first volley, their already slowed advance immediately transforming into a chaotic shambles. The crossbowmen and archers hurried to climb on to the rooftops, better to aim their projectiles at the seething mass of horsemen. As they did so, yet more soldiers emerged from the cottages. I was quick to recognise them as veterans of the Covenant Host, moving with disciplined efficiency to form squads before hurling themselves at the Crown soldiers. Halberds stabbed and hacked in a controlled but lethal frenzy, sending even more kingsmen and their horses flailing to the ground.

Realisation dawned as I watched the unfolding carnage. A trap had been set here, to be sure. But not the one I had so cleverly divined.

"Poor Father," I heard Evadine say, voice small, as if voicing an entreaty to the Martyrs. Turning, I saw her staring at the struggle in the village with abject sorrow. "At least spare him the ignominy of capture."

"You had a vision," I said. "You knew Shelvane intended treachery. My mission to Couravel was just a blind, something to make Leannor think you vulnerable in my absence."

The sadness slipped from Evadine's features, replaced by a guarded look, one I found jarring for it verged on hostile. "Yes," she said, voice barely audible above the clamour. "I had a vision. But you were not part of it, Alwyn."

A fresh uproar from the north end of the bridge had me wheeling Blackfoot about in alarm. There was a second jaw to this trap, after all. However, I saw no Althiene levies streaming over the span to assault our rear. Instead, the meagre torchlight played over disarrayed ranks, halberds wavering as infantrymen milled about in confusion. A new sound came echoing across the river then, easily recognised as the signature note emitted by a great collision of armour. I knew enough of battle now to gauge the progress of this clash by ear alone. After the initial clamour came the cacophony of clang and thud arising from a fierce melee. It was a short affair, quickly giving way to the collective groan of dismay voiced by soldiers facing calamitous defeat. Sounds of combat became the screams of the maimed or the dying, interspersed with the plaintive yells of those pleading for mercy.

When the cries began to fade, a figure resolved out of the shadows at the north end of the bridge, a tall man in full armour atop an impressive grey charger. A party of knights rode at his back, one bearing a banner showing a rearing red horse framed by silver trees: the sigil of the Duke of Rhianvel.

Duke Viruhlis Guhlmaine was younger than I expected, the face revealed when he removed his helm that of a man only a few years my senior. He might also have been described as handsome, had not the pallid skin, hollow cheeks and dark-ringed eyes, tinged with red, distracted from any aesthetically pleasing impression. His hair was also shorn down to a scalp that showed numerous healed cuts, as if this shearing had been done with an unskilled hand. In truth, he resembled a victim of some form of illness, if not madness given his poorly shaved head and the tendency for his recessed, reddened eyes not to blink as he talked. However, his bearing and voice were strong, vital even.

Upon traversing the bridge, he promptly dismounted from his charger, removing his helm to stare fixedly at Evadine for what felt like an unseemly interval. When she bowed and began to voice a greeting, Duke Viruhlis forestalled her by sinking to one knee, head lowered. The banner men who escorted him all followed suit.

"Know that I am yours, my lady," the duke informed Evadine in a tone filled with grave assurance. "Know that my strength is yours. My soldiers are yours. All I have—" his head dipped a little lower "—is yours."

Besotted, I thought, recalling Lord Jacquel's parting words in Couravel. *Even though he's never met her.* Seeing the way this pale-faced noble trembled in anticipation of the Anointed Lady's word, I couldn't fault the old dice-player's judgement.

"Rise, my lord," Evadine told him, voice warm with welcome. "And know that, on behalf of the Seraphile, I accept your service. As I behold your actions this day, I see no greater embodiment of the Martyrs' example."

"You . . ." Viruhlis darted a glance at Evadine, then quickly lowered his face once more. "You honour me beyond words, my lady."

All this gracious exchanging of mutual admiration would have been more seemly if sounds of slaughter hadn't continued to echo from the north bank of the river. The village had quietened now, a quick survey revealing streets littered with the bodies of slain kingsmen, gleaming armour dotted here and there with the darker forms of our own fallen. However, the unabated chorus of screams to the north told of a massacre in progress.

"With the battle won, my lady," I said, regaining Evadine's notice, "perhaps it's time to end the bloodshed."

"The blood of those who would contest the Lady's word must be shed," Duke Viruhlis said. "Down to the last drop, if need be." There was no sign of trepidation in him now, his face appearing almost skull-like as he glared up at me, save for his eyes, which had a fiery look I had seen in many a true fanatic. "I have brought all the faithful of Rhianvel to her side this night. They know well the value of justice, soldier."

"I'm a lord," I replied, matching his stare and unable to keep the disgusted curl from my lips. "And the Lady is merciful in her forgiveness."

I saw a twitch in his face and a flex to his gauntleted hands that put an itch in mine. Rarely do I find myself detesting a man with such alacrity, but the Duke of Rhianvel had managed to win my hatred with just a scant few words. *Not only words*, I corrected myself, seeing the devotion blossoming in the duke's gaze when Evadine spoke. *What man does not hate his rival?*

"My lord Scribe speaks truth," she told Viruhlis, though without any note of admonition. "Please, my lord, there has been enough conflict this night. Calm your people, for I wish to speak to them."

"As my lady commands." Viruhlis bowed again and rose, turning to bark out a command to one of his banner men. "Sound the muster. Tell them that the Anointed Lady is safe. They will gather to hear her word."

"What of the captives, my lord?" the fellow asked, wheeling his horse about.

"Bind them to await the Lady's justice. But if that wretch Shelvane is among them, bring him to me."

Lord Shelvane, to my considerable surprise, had died fighting. Quite bravely too, by all accounts. When the Althiene line broke he spurred his horse into the gap, laying about with a mace until a Rhianvelan pikeman brought him down. The faithful mob that had followed their duke to the Lady's side hadn't stinted in mutilating Shelvane's body, hacking off his head and limbs, which were then hung from the bridge. A squint of displeasure from Evadine had sufficed for Duke Viruhlis to order the gory decorations removed.

The other foe to distinguish himself that night had been Lord Altheric Courlain, though not by dint of courage. Rather, it was the speed with which he had fled the field that aroused most comment, not least because he had left all but a handful of his soldiers dead or captive in his wake. While this led many in the Covenant Host to dub him the Craven Marshal, personally, I couldn't fault his choice. When a fight is lost, why loiter in acceptance of your own demise? Better to run and hatch a plan for revenge. There was a crumb of comfort to be had in the fact that Altheric's flight had spared his daughter the embarrassment of capturing her own father.

There were three discrete contingents to the crowd that gathered to hear the Anointed Lady's sermon that morning. The Covenant Host under Captain Swain were arranged in neat ranks to Evadine's right. On the left stood Duke Viruhlis and his five companies of Rhianvelan ducal levies, two of horse and three of foot. In the centre were a yet greater number of common folk, and a decidedly unappealing spectacle they made. These were the accumulated mass of devoted faithful drawn from all corners of Rhianvel and beyond, for the Covenant has many outposts in the wild lands to the east. As with the crusaders of the Sacrifice March and the advance on Athiltor, there was little uniformity in their appearance, their garb ranging from ragged to rich. What marked them as different from other common crusaders was their wealth in weaponry and armour. It was mismatched and ill-organised, pike-wielders standing alongside bill-men and those with bows or crossbows scattered among the throng rather than clustered into companies. However, there were none without arms and, judging by the stains and scars that proliferated throughout this crowd, all had put them to use the night before.

Before delivering perhaps her most famed address, Evadine rode Ulstan to the apex of the stone bridge's arch. I must say that this event is one the painters and illuminators tend to get right. The sun was bright that morning but partially hidden behind a blanket of cloud driven by the northern winds. The way the sunlight shafted across the landscape made for a dramatically arresting backdrop as the Anointed Lady's mount reared then settled. I heard a collective gasp from the crowd, flushed with anticipation. I fancy all present knew this moment to be the precipice. Here the final line would be crossed, and they did not fear it. Why would they, with the Risen Martyr, whose divine insight could not now be doubted, here to lead them to the ultimate glory of the Covenant?

As was typical, her voice carried when she began to speak, yet I feel there was a new timbre to it that morning. Her sermons had never lacked for conviction, but always she allowed for nuance, for an acknowledgement of human frailty. The Anointed Lady's words the morning after the Battle of Stonebridge held no such subtlety, nor would any of her subsequent proclamations.

"To those of you who have marched with me this far," she began, "I thank you. To those who have come to me now in this most dreaded hour, I thank you. But also, I must warn you. The path before us will be bloody. The task set to us by the Seraphile demands every ounce of strength we can muster, for our enemy is cunning, and vile in their cunning. Here, they tried to trap me, setting my own father as my captor. Measure their vileness in the way in which they set father against daughter, as they set brother against brother, for the soil of this land is seeded by the graves that are the harvest of the Algathinets' endless wars. But this is merely a minor facet of their evil."

She paused, stiffening in the saddle as if reluctant to impart ugly but necessary truths. "Know that it has been revealed to me that the one who terms herself princess regent has been a servant of the Malecite since childhood. She it was who steered her father into tyranny. She it was who whispered poison into the ear of her own brother so that he might sink this realm into the mire of war. She it was who murdered her own husband with poison. Yes, friends, it is true. The one who would govern this land is a murderous servant of the Malecite and her blighted blood also runs in the veins of the child she would set upon the throne. Henceforth, as Risen Martyr and the voice of the Covenant Resurgent, I decree that we have no king. The Algathinet dynasty has been judged by the Seraphile as unfit to rule."

She paused, closing her eyes as if to gather strength, a woman compelled to accept the most burdensome task. When she spoke again, her voice held the faintest catch, but all still heard this signal of profound sorrow. From this moment, all who followed her would understand that the Anointed Lady's subsequent actions were not her fault. Every death that marked the line of our march from now on could be laid at the Algathinets' door alone, for they had driven the Risen Martyr to these inevitable, inescapable extremes.

"Friends," she said, opening her eyes to let the love she held for her adherents shine forth, "I have been commanded to bear a weight I never asked for. I have never wanted power. I have never wanted to rule, but the Seraphile have seen fit to place this task upon my shoulders and I'll not shirk it. Let this day mark the dawn of a new age, for I stand before you not just the Risen Martyr, but also the Ascendant Queen!"

The crowd's roar was unnerving in its immediacy. Every soul, with the exception of myself, the Widow, and Lilat, let out a wordless shout of affirmation. Weapons rose in a waving forest of blades. The faces of the common crusaders radiated a pitch of manic adulation that even Evadine's most captive audiences hadn't yet matched.

She let the roar continue for only a short time before raising her hand for silence. Usually, it would take a moment or two for the shouts to dwindle, but now the hush descended with the swiftness of an axe blade. I have pinpointed several contenders for the precise genesis of what I term the wrenching; the shift of sentiment and thought that would cause my path to veer in so wild a course. Now I come to write these words, I believe it truly began that morning. It wasn't just that I heard her lie where before she spoke truth, albeit her version of truth. It wasn't just this new certainty that seemed to exude from her every pore. No, it was the people. The way they fell so absolutely silent at this woman's mere gesture. All of them, from the Covenant Host to the Rhianvelan levies and the mass of common faithful, wore the same tense, expectant, hungry expression. Evadine's facility for compelling others to her will had disturbed me before. Now I found it stirred what I can only call terror. It was a deep, pulse-pounding, sweat-inducing realisation that no soul should ever wield such power. I still loved her, of course. I still rushed to cloak my fear in comforting lies, but I know now this was the moment. I also know myself a coward for not walking away at that very instant.

"As your Ascendant Queen," Evadine continued, "I require that your service be consecrated by an oath made in the sight of the Seraphile. Will you kneel and swear yourselves to me now?"

They knelt as one. Duke Viruhlis and his levies, all the captains and soldiers of the Covenant Host and the great horde of adoring crusaders, dropped to one knee and lowered their heads in supplication. And I. I knelt too. As I did so, I saw both the Widow and Lilat failing to follow suit. Juhlina's face was set with hard suspicion while Lilat's expression was one of puzzled amusement at the whole bizarre episode.

"Kneel!" I hissed at them both, meeting the Widow's eye and jerking my head at the crowd. Any glimmer of heresy before the eyes of this worshipful mob might have fatal consequences. Brows heavy and jaw bunching, Juhlina consented to kneel and lower her head. Lilat followed her example, mouth quirking as she smothered a laugh.

"Will you swear," Evadine said, voice modulated to one of hard formality, "to serve me in both war and peace?"

Once again the response was instantaneous. The accumulation of voices spoke with such unity it was as if this had been rehearsed. "I so swear!"

"Will you swear to follow the Martyrs' example with your every deed and thought!"

"I so swear!"

"Will you swear to staunch no effort nor spare no strength in our cause? Will you swear to fight every foe and triumph over every host brought against us?"

"I so swear!"

It became a chant when Evadine raised her arms in an invitation for her adherents to rise, and rise they did. Feet stamping and weapons brandishing with each repeated shout, the sound of it echoing so loud I wondered if Leannor heard it all the way off in Couravel.

"I so swear! I so swear! I SO SWEAR!"

Chapter Fourteen

"Strike now, my queen. Strike with all we have."

In the scant few hours since first meeting him, Duke Viruhlis had, wittingly or not, endeavoured to provide me with yet more reasons to dislike him. Not least of which was the implacable, doubt-free manner in which he offered our new monarch advice. The fact that Evadine was so willing to listen irked me even more.

She frowned in attentive silence as the duke continued to set forth his stratagem. We had taken over the largest domicile in Stonebridge, a two-tiered house positioned near the bridge. The place was probably considered a mansion in this village, but felt like a cramped hovel with so many captains crammed inside to attend the Ascendant Queen's council of war. The house had been the home of a man known as the Tollmaster, a title that afforded him authority over the village and surrounding lands, as well as a generous share of the coin paid by those traversing the bridge. Whoever this functionary had been, he and most of his villagers had wisely taken to their heels when the Covenant Host appeared on the western horizon two mornings prior. Those few who remained consisted of stubborn or infirm old folk and their brave younger kin.

The assembled captains clustered around a large rosewood dining table. There were eight in all, including, somewhat to my irritation, the Rhianvelan twins who now rarely strayed more than a few feet from Evadine's side. Discussion inevitably centred on our next course of action, causing me to express some annoyance at the fact that no one had thought fit to bring a map from Athiltor.

"The Covenant Library is rich in all the charts we could ever need," I said, gaze lingering on Swain. Of all Evadine's captains, I credited him with the most sense. Duke Viruhlis, however, found our want of maps of no concern at all.

"Here is Couravel," he said, reaching across the dining table to place a bottle in its centre. "Here is Stonebridge," he added, setting a goblet down at the other end. "We must march from one to the other with all dispatch, defeating any enemy who seeks to bar our path. I know the way to Couravel well, Lord Scribe. Therefore, a map would seem unnecessary given the simplicity of our task."

"Marching immediately for Couravel has the benefit of surprise," I conceded, "but also invites battle. Leannor was foolish to gamble so much on this trap, but she can still muster substantial numbers."

"And a swift march will deny her the time to do so," the duke insisted, addressing his words to Evadine. "If numbers are a concern, I've little doubt the good folk of this realm will rise to the Ascendant Queen's cause. Have not thousands already done so?"

And much good it did them, I thought. "We gathered many to our banner on the road to Athiltor," I said. "But not so many as when we marched north from Alundia. The commons are weary of war and wish only to be left in peace. Our seat of power is in Athiltor, where the most ardent followers of the Risen Martyr continue to gather. My queen, I must counsel a delay while we build our host into something the Algathinets will have no hope of contesting."

"It won't be long before the autumn rains come," the duke persisted, unblinking gaze still locked on Evadine. "Spelling an end to campaigning until the winter frost, and that brings its own bundle of obstacles to moving an army. The chance to end this war with but one stroke lies before us, my queen. We must take it."

Evadine's eyes slipped from the bottle to the goblet and back again, her face showing only calm reflection. "My thanks for your counsel, my lords," she said. "The choice betwixt caution and risk is ever a fraught one." She favoured me with a smile. "Yet, we must remember that we act with the Seraphiles' blessing, something that negates all risk." She rapped her knuckles to the table and stood back. "We march for Couravel today. Captain Swain, you will return to Athiltor to muster all forces that may be found there. Once mustered, march south and join your strength to ours with all speed."

"As you command, my queen," Swain said, bowing.

Evadine turned to me, her manner one of a queen addressing a minor functionary. I understood the need for artifice, especially since our secret appeared to be so widely known. But still, it stung. "Lord Alwyn, you will take your company and scout the approaches to the capital. If the false princess is determined upon a battle, it would be best to discover where she intends to meet us, don't you think?"

I resisted the urge to glance at Viruhlis, knowing the triumph I saw on his face would transform my chafed pride into anger. Instead, I put a bland half-smile on my lips and bowed low. "Indeed so, my queen."

It irked me then, as it irks me now, to admit that Duke Viruhlis was right and I was wrong. For the commons did rise to the Risen Martyr's cause, not in their dozens as they had during the latter stages of our advance on Athiltor. But in their hundreds, and, as we drew nearer to Couravel, in their thousands.

I cannot fully account for it. But, by the time the spire of the Couravel cathedral jutted above the southern horizon, the ever-growing multitude had formed a vast, miles-long sprawl in the Ascendant Queen's wake. I knew some were stirred by old grievances against the Algathinets or their favourites. Others were the simpletons that will join any crowd and chant any creed, drawn by nothing more than the lure of belonging. A smaller number consisted of, I've no doubt, those hopeful of a share in the loot that would surely be plentiful in the aftermath of the capital's fall. But most came for Evadine. She spoke and they believed her. Her sermons were once again regular affairs, sometimes two or three times a day, and never did she fail to rouse them to the same repeated exhortation: "I so swear! I so swear! I so swear!"

"It's not just devotion, my lord," Quintrell opined as we watched another hundred or so villagers abandon their homes to join the thousands on the road. "Nor can it entirely be ascribed to the queen's oratory, impressive as it is."

"Then what is it?" I enquired, watching with dispirited impotence as a young woman with a babe in her arms hurried into the throng and disappeared from sight. She carried no provisions that I could see and her garb was scant protection against the weather. As with the Sacrifice March, many ill-prepared or elderly followers had fallen out of the march. The first bodies had appeared the day before, just a few, but I knew there would be a great deal more before this was over.

"Change," the minstrel said. "A great and profound shift in the order of this realm is at hand, and they know it. They sense it, even if they can't explain how or why. The scales of the world have tilted, and we have the good fortune to be on the weightier side."

I said nothing, knowing that the rewards many of these folk would receive amounted to hunger, sickness or, should they have the misfortune to face battle, death. Still, I took some comfort from Quintrell's judgement.

"You've no doubt as to our victory, then?"

"None at all. I've travelled far and witnessed the fall of kings before. It always starts like this. Kings, queens and emperors often make the mistake of seeing the nobility as the source of all threats. But it is among the commons that the true peril lies. Loyal or cowed nobles will not save them when they can no longer count upon the quietude of their people."

The minstrel's optimism was borne out by the absence of Crown patrols ahead of our line of march. The Scout Company ranged widely, finding only churls at work or hurrying to join the march. Of soldiers, they found none. Leannor must have had word of Altheric's failure by now. It had probably been delivered by the lord marshal himself, along with an abject apology, if he had any sense. It was my firm expectation that he, or, more likely, Sir Ehlbert, would muster all the forces at their disposal and advance to meet us. I considered the line of low hills ten miles north of the capital to be the most apt spot, as any astute commander will always seek to overlook their foe. But the

Ascendant Host, as it was now called, crested this ridge without incident.

A siege then, I reasoned. I halted Blackfoot atop the highest hill, peering at the distant grey haze that marked the capital. The prospect of investing such a place was daunting to say the least. We had no engines or any with the skills to build them. While in Couravel, I had made discreet enquiries as to the location of Master Aurent Vassier, the artisan who constructed the mighty contrivances that pierced the walls of Highsahl. It transpired that Aurent, always a clever fellow, had disappeared from the city along with his family months before. I hoped he had found some quiet corner of the world to settle in, untroubled by demands for yet more deadly devices.

Battering rams? I wondered, eyes straying to the stretch of woodland below the ridge. *And a great many ladders.* I judged that the sheer scale of the city might work to our advantage. It would take an army many times the likely size of Leannor's forces to cover every yard of the battlement. *Send the churls to attack in several different places*, I decided, a scheme starting to form in my mind, much as it had before the walls of Highsahl. *Force Leannor to divide her strength, then send our best troops at the weakest spot.* A smile played upon my lips as I realised Duke Viruhlis would be almost certain to beg the honour of leading the main assault. *With any luck, the corpse-faced bastard will get himself killed.*

However, within moments the Widow's call served to banish my mounting good humour. "They've gone."

"What?" I asked, watching her trot Parsal, her swift-footed hunting horse, to the crest of the hill.

"Gone. The lot of them." She gestured to the city. "The gates are all open. I didn't want to venture too close for fear of archers on the walls, but I spoke to some folk in that orchard down there. They said the king and his mother marched out two days ago, taking all their soldiers with them on the north-west road. Lot of talk that they're headed for the Cordwain. Rumour is Luminant Daryhla has barricaded herself in the cathedral, though, along with a great many orthodox loons determined to die rather than surrender it to the Heretic Whore." She smiled. "Their words, not mine."

"The Cordwain," I repeated. A surprising move, but not lacking in sound judgement. With her plan to eliminate Evadine ruined, Leannor would have been quick to take account of her allies. Rhianvel was plainly against her. Alundia was a war-ravaged waste inhabited by people who would gladly see her dead. The Shavine Marches under Duchess Lorine could hardly be counted upon for loyalty, and neither could the avaricious Duke of Dulsian. That left the nobility of Alberis, Sir Ehlbert and what remained of the Crown Company, and the staunchly loyal but distant Duke Lohrent of the Cordwain. When her scouts brought word of the size of Evadine's crusade, it would have taken a far stouter, and more foolish, heart than the princess regent's to stay and gamble on the whim of battle. Luminant Daryhla and her band of fanatics created an unwanted complication. Good sense dictated that we pursue Leannor with all speed, but Evadine would want to seize the cathedral in the name of the Covenant Resurgent. The king and his clever mother had slipped the noose, at least for now.

"Come," I said, preparing to turn Blackfoot. "We'd best share our glad tidings."

The Widow, however, failed to stir in the saddle. Her face held an expression I'd rarely seen in her: guilt tinged with apology. I knew what she was about to say, yet the words struck me with unexpected force. "This is where we take our leave, Alwyn Scribe."

Despite her evident regret, I also saw a resolve in her eyes that made me abandon the impulse to argue. "Finally had enough, eh?" I said instead, forcing a note of good humour.

"If I hadn't already, I surely would tomorrow." She glanced at Couravel. "We've seen a city fall before, and I've a sense this'll be worse. The Risen Martyr no longer commands an army, she leads a horde. You know what's going to happen when they get here. They came for blood, and they'll have it, battle or no. I'll take no part in it."

I nodded, unable to gainsay her reasoning. I could have pleaded with her, made a heartfelt declaration that we, the steadfast and true soldiers of the Covenant Host, would do what we could to protect the people of Couravel from the storm. But it was a big city, and the crusade was vast. She was right, I knew what was coming.

"Where will you go?" I asked her.

"The minstrel had plenty of stories about the eastern kingdoms. Or perhaps I'll head south, take a ship across the sea. They say there are lands beyond the red deserts filled with all manner of strange and fabulous beasts. War is all ugliness. I think I'd like to see some wonders." She smiled again, this time mixing both warmth and sadness. "You could come with me."

Surprised by the sudden catch in my throat, I coughed before speaking again. "You know I can't."

The smile slipped from her lips, but I saw no recrimination as she lowered her gaze. "I know *she* is going to destroy you. In soul if not in body. You've been a bad man in your time, Alwyn Scribe, as I've been a bad woman. But we've also done good where we could. From here on, all I see for you is more bad."

She turned Parsal about without further delay, trotting to the base of the slope whereupon she spurred to a gallop. I watched horse and rider fade into the woods, catching glimpses as she sped away. Strangely, I found the hope that I might see her again one day was of an equal pitch to the fervent desire that I would not. I felt a discomfiting certainty that, should the Widow and I ever meet again, she would look upon a man undeserving of her regard.

The blame for the fire that destroyed the ancient cathedral of Couravel has been a source of endless debate. Those who adhere to the creed of the Risen Martyr will avow with absolute conviction that it was started on the express orders of Luminant Daryhla. Faced with the hour of the Ascendant Queen's triumph, the last leader of the orthodox Covenant determined upon immolation of herself, her followers, and the cathedral along with all its sacred treasures. Algathinet sympathisers are equally fierce in their assertions that it was done either on the instruction of the Malecite Whore, or was just the most heinous act committed by the ravening mob of fanatics she unleashed. For myself, I have no light to shed upon this mystery.

All I know is that the cathedral burned that night and I watched it happen.

As the Widow predicted, there was no holding the crusaders when the news spread that Couravel stood undefended. Evadine had the Covenant companies form disciplined ranks in order to make a dignified entry into the city, but by midday the first fires were already burning. I have come to understand that there is a madness lurking in the hearts of most people, a beast waiting to be unleashed when presented with defenceless prey and the absence of consequences. The Rhianvelan contingent was the first to invade the outlying districts, wreaking random havoc and violence. I believe it was the thickening scent of smoke that drew the rest, triggering a primal urge to take part in a feeding frenzy before the chance faded. As the crusade poured in, the people poured out. Long columns of fleeing townsfolk appeared on the southern road as day slipped into evening and their city burned at their backs.

I watched disaster unfold from the safety of the ridge where Juhlina had taken her leave. I'll not pretend to have harboured even the slightest urge to lead the Scout Company into such chaos in the hope that they might defend the defenceless. Had I done so, I have no doubt there wouldn't have been a company to command by morning. All that awaited us in those fiery streets was death and madness. The youngest among my scouts were plainly resentful of being forced to miss the climax of the Ascendant Queen's march, but also wise enough to confine their complaints to a few hard glances in my direction. The veterans, by contrast, exhibited mostly relief.

"Worse than Highsahl, I reckon," Tiler commented in between gulps of brandy. He hadn't quite drunk himself into a stupor yet, but the loll of his head and increasingly slurred speech told of an impending collapse into oblivion. Still, guttered as he was, he remained content to sit in place. Even the lure of copious loot hadn't been enough to shift him. "Flames are . . ." He trailed off into momentary confusion, eyes dimming before abruptly snapping open. "Taller! Don't y'think, m'lord?"

"You're almost out," I observed, nodding to the dregs sloshing in his brandy bottle. Reaching into my pack, I extracted a flask of grog and tossed it to him. "Drink up, Sergeant."

"Martyrs bless ya', m'lord." He knuckled his forehead and did as he was bid, collapsing on to his back after a few gulps.

"Lord Alwyn." Quintrell's grave tone raised my gaze to the city once more in time to see a great blossoming of flame rise from its centre. A dull boom reached us a heartbeat later, the bright orange flower roiling briefly above the smoke before fading. The sight was jarring in its similarity to the vision of long ago I had been gifted in the hollow mountain. *The first Scourge. Evadine serves the Malecite . . .*

"What was that?" Adlar asked. He was the only one not seated, spending the passing hours pacing the hilltop as he stared at the spreading fires with fascinated horror. Unlike the other youngsters in the company, he exhibited no desire to partake of the unfolding calamity.

"The cathedral, I believe," I said. "My guess is that Luminant Daryhla had the place stocked with oil, perhaps to fend off an assault. Doesn't look like it worked."

The cathedral roof was visible through the haze now, resembling the blackened ribs of some beast consigned to a firepit as the flames licked away the flesh of tile and wood. Tiler was right, this was far worse than Highsahl. The building would be ash by morning and so would most of Couravel.

"I don't understand," Lilat said. She had sat close to me throughout the night, face set in a constant frown of grim bemusement. She spoke in Caerith, something she hadn't done for weeks as her command of Albermaine-ish increased. "That place was sacred to your people, was it not? Like the hollow mountain."

"It was," I agreed, eyes lingering on the fast disappearing roof of a structure that had endured for centuries.

"Then why burn it?"

I shrugged, resisting an impulse to relieve the unconscious Tiler of the flask I had given him. "Why does a spiteful child throw stones at a cat?"

This only served to deepen Lilat's confusion. "Your children throw stones at cats?"

A shout from the shadowed slope below had us all roused and reaching for weapons, save for the inebriated Tiler. We had heard the clamour of fighting an hour or so past, most likely the crusade colliding with orthodox diehards when they closed upon the cathedral. It wasn't impossible that some had escaped the city.

"Hold," I called out when the archers among us trained their bows on a pair of riders appearing out of the gloom. The perennially sour expression worn by the twin Rhianvelan Supplicants was fully in evidence as they reined in, making me regret my command. *Couldn't see them in the dark, my queen. An unfortunate accident of a kind all too frequent in war.*

"Lord Scribe," Harldin greeted me with a barely sketched bow. It occurred to me that I had never heard his sister speak once and wondered if she might be mute. Certainly, the way she glowered at me before turning an even more baleful eye upon Lilat spoke as loudly as any words. These two were fond of casting judgemental glances in my direction, but the sight of a Caerith transformed self-righteous pique into simmering rage.

"What?" I replied without rising. Basic civility felt beyond my grasp at this juncture, and I didn't bother swallowing a laugh when both of them bridled at the patent insult.

"The queen commands your presence," Harldin said, voice clipped with the effort of caging the words he actually wanted to speak. "She awaits you at the cathedral."

I considered pointing out that Couravel no longer possessed a cathedral, but saw little point in baiting them further. "Tell her I'll be along presently."

"We are to escort you," he said. "Alone."

The many years since have given me leisure to ponder the faint note of relish that coloured the Supplicant's tone in that moment. Things may have unfolded very differently if I had paid it more heed. But I was tired, sickened, and my mood darkened by the thought of having to suffer the stench and sights of Couravel's fate first hand.

So, I got wearily to my feet, shaking my head when Lilat rose with me.

"No. Stay here."

"You go, I go," she insisted, slipping her bow on to her shoulder.

"The queen said alone, my lord," Harldin interjected with an impatient snap to his voice. "Your Caerith whore will remain here and not offend the queen's sight."

An angry murmur rose from the Scout Company then, many getting to their feet, weapons in hand. Lilat's status had never been formally stated, but she had ridden with us long enough to be seen as a comrade. Also, the tale of her actions at the Dire Keep was something of a minor legend among the Covenant Host.

"Watch your mouth," young Adlar growled, spinning a knife and drawing an affirming growl from the rest.

"Leave it," I told him, casting a hard, commanding glare around the others to ensure they lowered their weapons. Instead of moving to saddle Blackfoot, I headed for the wide trunk of a nearby yew, provoking a tetchy outburst from Harldin.

"You would have the queen dally further, my lord?"

"Allow a man a moment to piss, won't you?" I replied, disappearing behind the yew. While I certainly didn't pay sufficient notice to the man's eagerness, it did stir enough caution in me to take a small precaution. I finished my uncomfortable business after a deliberately prolonged interval, then went to saddle Blackfoot. Mounting up, I gave Lilat a reassuring grin which did little to alleviate her agitation.

"They smell wrong," she told me, still speaking in Caerith and turning a suspicious eye upon the twin Supplicants. "Eager, like wolves closing upon a wounded stag."

"If they try anything, I'll kill them," I said simply. "Wait for me here. Whatever happens, don't go into the city. It's a bad place for you."

I kicked Blackfoot into motion and started down the slope, the Supplicants falling in behind. "One day soon," I informed Harldin, "you and I are going to have a very meaningful discussion about manners."

He replied with a glare that was neither as angry nor as fearful as I would have liked. Another warning I failed to notice on this night filled with folly.

Chapter Fifteen

Evadine awaited me in the main square amid a blizzard of swirling embers. The roar of the flames consuming the cathedral rose and waned in concert with a stiff wind sweeping across this benighted city, worsening the fires with every gust. My journey here had been oddly peaceful, albeit veiled in smoke billowing in thick roiling drifts lit by an orange glow, echoing with the crack and tumble of collapsing houses. Fortunately, my twin companions were no more interested in conversing with me than I them, and the largely empty streets instilled a curious sense of serenity. The fires had become so fierce even the crusaders had fled. I heard distant screams here and there, caught glimpses of loot-laden figures, but it was apparent that Couravel had been abandoned to its fate.

Upon entering the square, I discovered that the royal palace remained intact, untouched by the flames due to some miraculous chance. The contrast with the cathedral it faced had been stark before. Now it was appallingly comical. The towering walls of one of the Covenant's holiest shrines still stood, but as the blackened flanks of a raging inferno. The charred ribs of the roof had vanished, the building's innards eaten away entirely. I thought of all the gold-encased relics that had adorned the altar at King Arthin's coronation, now surely reduced to a pile of melted slag and ashen bone. Still, the sight of it was easier to look upon than the face of the woman I loved.

I had seen her angry before, but not like this. For Evadine, rage was a rare and brief storm, but the hard intensity of her expression as she watched me rein Blackfoot to a halt was starkly unfamiliar. Had I not known her so intimately, I might have thought she hated me.

Swain was there too, shoulders slumped, and head lowered, though I saw the shame that made a misery of his face. A cordon of Covenant soldiery lined the square, but too distant for any to hear what might be spoken above the roar of the flames. The twin Supplicants dismounted before I did, closer than I would have preferred. Even before Evadine spoke, I knew what this was about. Swain's shame said it all. *How could she know? After all this time.*

"Will you not kneel before your queen?" she asked me, curt and formal as I continued to sit in the saddle, the hard, rapid thump of my heart paining my chest.

"Your pardon, Your Majesty." I felt a very small pulse of pride for the steadiness of my voice, and the absence of a tremble when I climbed from Blackfoot's back and began to sink to one knee.

"Actually, don't," Evadine instructed. "Stand, my lord. I have questions for you, and should like a clear view of your face as I ask them."

I did as she said, remaining still, features as blandly impassive as I could make them. She came closer, halting just out of reach, and I saw that she held a sheaf of parchment in her hand, one I couldn't help but stare at. She clutched it tight, the pages crumpled in her fist.

"This?" she asked, raising the sheaf when she noticed my scrutiny. "Always so curious about words on paper, aren't you, Alwyn? Always so keen on your endless quest for more knowledge. Well—" she unfurled the sheets "—allow me to share this latest treasure, one you went to such lengths to procure." She shifted her gaze to the parchment. "'A Partial Translation of The Isidorian Codex, prepared by Supplicant Hilbert Forswith at the request of Lord Alwyn Scribe.'"

"An important but neglected part of Covenant lore," I said. "A fine addition to the Covenant Library—"

"BE!" Evadine's face quivered as she smothered my voice with her own, the light of the cathedral blaze bright in her unblinking eyes. "SILENT!"

She stared at me for what felt like an age and, much to my surprise, my fear slipped away under the weight of her gaze. I saw something her rage couldn't mask: she still loved me. It is the young man's folly to imagine such a thing offers protection when, in fact, it only ever increases danger.

"Supplicant Hilbert presented himself to me this very day," Evadine went on, brandishing the pages, voice hoarse but controlled. "Having travelled here with Lord Swain, who, I assume, had no inkling of the contents of the gift that the learned Supplicant wished to place in my hands. Evidently, he thought I might find it interesting. And I did, Alwyn. There's a great deal of babbling nonsense in this screed, to be sure, almost as if it consisted of nothing but the collected scribblings of a madwoman rather than a prophetess. But then, I have been called mad more times than I care to recall, so I kept reading."

She leafed through the pages, then resumed her recital. "'Be it known. That the one who will be called Risen will not rise. She will be healed. And her healing will be wrought not by the Endless Ones in whose service I struggle, but by those who cleave to heathen rites. The sackcloth witch will heal her but the false Risen will claim a blessing and, in so doing, a kingdom.'"

Evadine's hands shook as she lowered the parchment. I saw her anger dim then, brows drawing together, hopeful, beseeching. "Will you lie to me again, Alwyn?" she asked. "Will you tell me that this is falsehood and that you did not allow a Caerith witch to put her filthy hands upon me?"

I spared a short glance at Swain, seeing his features bunched in the agony of this moment. His loyalty to Evadine had always been absolute, something unbreakable and unimpeachable. I knew he had already answered this question, rendering any story I might concoct irrelevant, not that I could have conjured one equal to the task in any case.

"You were dying," I said, meeting Evadine's pleading eyes. "There was no other choice. If we hadn't . . ."

Evadine let out a wordless cry, more a scream than a roar. It was a sound I had never heard from a human throat, louder than anything a human throat could produce, possessing enough power to send a jolting shudder through me. She reeled away, once again gripping the pages tight in her fist, her other hand on her belly as if trying to ease a terrible ache.

"You . . ." She staggered, sagging, a sob colouring her voice. "You have made me an abomination before the Seraphile. I stand corrupted in both body and soul."

The sight of her distress stirred a desire to reach for her, embrace her now as I did in private, regardless of all the eyes watching us. But I didn't. Perhaps it was the sound she made, so ugly, so *wrong*. Perhaps it was the deep, but as yet unacknowledged, realisation that what existed between us was gone, shattered in this very instant. But, in truth, I feel it was more mundane than that. It was her anger, her condemnation, her self-interested revulsion. No gratitude. No appreciation for all I, Swain, Wilhum and so many others had risked to save her. The supposed soiling of her soul wiped it all away, for she was the Anointed Lady. She was the chosen of the Seraphile. A delusion forever broken, unforgivably so.

"No," I told her, my own voice raised with harsh, grating defiance. "We made you the Risen Martyr. We made you the Ascendant Queen. And look—" I raised my arms to the surrounding panorama of destruction, feeling the embers sting my skin "—look at what you did with it."

She froze, regarding me with features so twisted with animus I felt I looked upon a stranger. Then she came for me, her sword hissing from its sheath in a blur, her attack so swift and unexpected I barely got a hand to my own blade before she closed the distance.

"My lady!" Swain stepped between us, hands raised in placation. "My lady, I beg . . ."

His words ended in a choking gurgle when Evadine's sword slashed across his throat. The thick spatter of blood on her skin brought her to a halt, standing in shocked silence to watch Swain collapse to his knees, hands clutching his neck in a vain attempt to staunch the crimson flow. He rasped out another few words before he fell face down on to the cobbles, voice too riven with blood to make them out. I fancy he was still attempting to beg her pardon when his heart pushed the last drop from his wound.

"You," Evadine said, pale but once again human features regarding me in horrified accusation. "You forced me to this."

The past few seconds had seen me rooted to the spot, the sudden tumult of change too much to comprehend. But now I did. Now I saw what I had to do.

"Alwyn Scribe, you are hereby restrained by command of the Ascendant Queen." Harldin spoke with a prideful confidence, clearly enjoying the moment. He might have lived if he hadn't made the mistake of trying to clamp a hand to my shoulder. "Surrender your arms . . ."

The pommel of my sword caught his upper jaw as I drew it, shattering teeth before breaking his nose. He staggered back a foot or two, all the space I needed to reverse the blade and spear him from chin to nape. "Consider that your lesson in manners," I grunted, kicking his twitching body off the blade.

It transpired that his sister was not mute after all, for she hurled herself at me with an ear-paining screech. I sidestepped the wild, downward swing of her sword and replied with a slash at her legs. She was fast, however, steel ringing as she parried the stroke. Had she not been subsumed with the need for vengeance, she would have stepped back before mounting another attack. Instead, she pressed forward, raising her blade for a thrust and leaving herself open to a solid punch to the face. I drove my shoulder into her chest as she stumbled, stunned by the blow, casting her aside.

"How could you do this, Alwyn?" Evadine demanded, crouched over Swain's now immobile body. For some reason, she still clutched at her belly, whatever pain it caused her rendering her face into a mask of tear-streaked anguish. "How could you do this to us?"

Evadine serves the Malecite. Words spoken by a man I called a liar. Words I now knew as truth. Suddenly, it was all so starkly clear. The many, many dead of Alundia. The Sacrifice March. The irrational devotion of her crusaders. The cathedral dying in a bright blossom of flame lit by a maddened mob, just like that ancient Caerith city so long ago. The sickening absurdity of it almost brought a laugh to my lips.

"The Scourge," I said, voice soft, for I spoke more to myself than to her. "It was there at every turn. Always in your sermons. A promise, not a prophecy." I did laugh then, though it emerged as more a retching cough. "The Second Scourge, Evadine!" I levelled my sword at her, casting my free hand at the remnants of the blazing cathedral. "It's here! *This* is the Second Scourge, and we made it!"

She replied with another roar, this one more akin to a snarl, still as inhuman as before. Teeth bared, she crouched, sword gripped in both hands, preparing to meet my charge, a charge I would never make.

The sound of many boots pounding the cobbles saved me, provoking an instinctive ducking of the head to avoid the sweep of the halberd that would have sliced it from my shoulders. I killed the wielder with a practised jab of my sword point to the unarmoured gap betwixt his pauldron and breastplate. Before he fell, I took relieved notice of the colours he wore, black and green, marking him as one of Duke Viruhlis's men. It would have grieved me yet further to have cut down my own comrades this night.

More shouts from all around caused me to whirl, parrying a sword thrust, then sidestepping another. The duchy men formed a tight cordon around me now, an inward facing thicket of blades I couldn't hope to cut through. Yet, I tried. *Evadine serves the Malecite.* I could see her, still crouched over Swain's body less than a dozen yards away. I knew with utter certainty that she was the one living soul in this world who needed to die. All the havoc I had helped her wreak as a Risen Martyr would weigh upon me all my days. But what a harvest she could reap as the Ascendant Queen of Albermaine.

So I hacked and slashed at the soldiers between us, driving their weapons aside to slice at exposed faces in the hope of forcing a way through. My fury was such I barely felt the stabbing thrust of a halberd's spike into my upper leg, my sword cutting open the face of the man who wielded it, slicing through eyes and bone. I kicked him away and renewed my frenzied progress, ignoring the wetness streaming down my leg. The next blow caught me on the side of the head, a roundhouse swipe of a poleaxe haft which sent a blaze of sparks across my vision. But I was no stranger to a ringing skull and my sword's reply cut through the haft and the hand that held it. Just for a second the way to Evadine was clear, a few steps and it would be over. Had I not comprehended her true nature, the sight of her in that instant might have frozen me in place. She sat now, cradling Swain's head in her lap, weeping in abject grief and regret.

"Evadine serves the Malecite," I grunted the words out like a chant as I forced myself on, my leg now like ice, a thick trickle of blood streaming from the wound to my head. Evadine made no effort to rise, her sword lying at her side as she continued to weep over the face of the man she had murdered. She looked up as I loomed over her, my sword raised high for the killing stroke. I froze as our eyes met, her tearful, grief-wracked visage staying my hand better than any shield.

"Would you kill us, Alwyn?" she asked me, shifting her hand from Swain's flaccid features to rest it upon her belly. "Would you kill the child we made?"

I had only seconds to stand there gaping in shock before a flurry of blows brought me down. Stumbling to my knees, a gauntleted fist rebounded from the back of my head. I collapsed, spitting iron-tinged bile.

"Stand back!" Duke Viruhlis stood over me, his pale features for once suffused with colour, a dark red of fury and contempt. I felt my grip on consciousness slip away as he spoke on, barking orders to his men. "Bind this traitor!"

"You . . ." I sputtered, raising my hand to grasp at his greave. "You don't understand . . . You have to . . . stop her . . ."

"Get your filthy hands off me, traitor!" Viruhlis punctuated his instruction with a hard kick to my gut. He was a strong man and the force of it was enough to finally drag me into the dark.

PART TWO

Know this, oh king of many kingdoms – I am your enemy. This role I did not choose, for you have thrust it upon me. You name yourself Protector of all Faiths, and yet you sully mine at every turn. You harbour those who seek to destroy me. You sponsor liars and spies within my borders. Your court turns away my missionaries yet lends a willing ear to exiled traitors. But, above all my tainted brother, you are set against me by the evil that pollutes your soul: the malice of disbelief. Cloak yourself in all the lore and philosophy you wish, but a soul mired in the worship of nothing can be redeemed only through my blessing. Those who deny it, as you do, must accept destruction as their fate.

Extract from *Martyr Evadine's Epistle to Saluhtan Alkad IX of Ishtakar*

Chapter Sixteen

I suppose it was inevitable that Erchel would return during this, my lowest ever ebb. I have no notion of how long I lay in that cell somewhere in the bowels of the royal palace. I know I woke at times and, when I did so, I raved. I have dim memories of my plaintive entreaties echoing through indifferent halls, though what exactly I said forever eludes me. Mostly, however, I drifted in dream-filled delirium. I gabbled pleas at fallen friends and enemies, stumbling from one blank-eyed yet living corpse to another. I recall sinking to my knees before the cadaverous spectre of King Tomas. He seemed to find me amusing.

"She serves the Malecite, does she?" he asked, rotting features twisting into a grin. "I could have told you that, Scribe."

But it was mostly just a confused pandemonium interspersed with bouts of pain as my body suffered through its wounds in the waking world. It was only when Erchel found me that the chaos settled, the formless melange of memories solidifying into something recognisable, in form if not location. Pale fog drifted across narrow waterways fringed with reed-covered banks. It reminded me of the marshland I had travelled through on the back of the Chainsman's cart, but wilder with a harsh, chilly edge to the air.

"Martyrs' arses, Alwyn," Erchel commented, squinting as he surveyed my beaten person. "But you're a fucking mess, aren't you?"

"What are you doing here?" I groaned in response, hoping this particular vision would slip into misty confusion like all the others. Being lost in a swirl of nightmare was still preferable to the company of this long-dead pervert. "You were Arnabus's creature, something he stole from my memories. He's dead, so why haven't you joined him?"

"Can't do that," he replied cheerfully. "*She* won't let me. The curious thing about Arnabus's particular skill is that, in making use of your memory of me, he managed to entangle a portion of my soul. It was enough for the Sack Witch to seek out the rest of me. Pluck me from the path."

"Path?"

His humour shifted into discomfort and he looked away. "Y'know. The path that takes you . . . wherever you're going."

"And where were you going?"

"Dunno, exactly. It was a long path, though. Plodded along it for fuck knows how long before she came for me." He spoke on quickly, apparently keen to change the subject. "She's a little concerned, y'see? I get the feeling this wasn't supposed to happen. Not yet anyways."

"That's a shame," I mumbled, continuing to huddle, feeling soft earth beneath my back and half expecting it to sublime into nothing whereupon I would find escape from this misbegotten bog. It didn't. Groaning in angry resignation, I sat up, slapping Erchel's hand away when he attempted to prod the bleeding wound on the side of my head.

"What do you want?" I demanded. "What does *she* want?"

"To save your silly carcass, what else." Erchel gave me a pitying look and moved away to kick a loose stone into the still waters. "Shitty place, this. Any idea where it is?"

"Don't you?"

"No. Not a clue. It's like that, being her slave. Spend my time flitting from one curious spot to another. Although, I do get to meet all sorts of interesting people. Granted, most of them are dead or close to it. But even then, they usually have something to say that's worth hearing."

I frowned at him, climbing to my feet and blowing air into cupped hands. "So, it's not just me who gets to enjoy the dubious pleasure of your company."

In life, a jibe like this would have provoked Erchel to voice a few harsh but poorly phrased insults. In death, however, he merely huffed out a good-natured laugh. "It was just you at first, but not any longer. She tells me I have a talent for this. Seems it was one of the reasons she took me from the path."

I knew the Sack Witch's abilities to be impressive, but that she had somehow trapped Erchel's shade in this place of shifting dreams made it clear her reach was far longer and more powerful than I suspected.

"All right, then," I said. "Let's hear it. What cryptic, barely useful pile of horse shit do you have for me this time?"

"Just this." Erchel raised his hands, gesturing to our surroundings.

"A fog-bound bog. What of it?" I stared at him in expectation but received only a shrug by way of reply.

"I'm supposed to come here?" I pressed. "Find something here, perhaps?"

"I don't know. She just wants you to see it. Look around a bit. See if there's anything you recognise."

Sighing, I did as he bid, scanning the landscape with scant enthusiasm until my eye alighted on a regular shape in the haze. Moving closer, I saw it was a building, a shrine in fact judging by its spire. It was small by Covenant standards, little more than a shack surrounded by a cluster of sheds and a livestock pen. A shrine in the middle of a marsh. I knew of only one such place.

"Sihlda's shrine," I said. In fact, if I was right, this was the Shrine to Martyr Lemtuel in the heart of the Cordwain marshes. Sihlda had been sent here by jealous senior clerics in the hope she would wither into irrelevance. Instead, she built it into a revered place of healing and pilgrimage, until she gave shelter to a pair of knights and a pregnant noblewoman, the act that saw her consigned to the Pit Mines.

"I'm supposed to come here?" I asked Erchel.

"How the fuck should I know? Don't even know where this arsehole of a place is." Erchel gave another affable smile and started to walk off, the fog around us growing thicker with each step he took.

"She may not appreciate my situation," I called after him. "But I strongly suspect I'm currently locked in a cell awaiting a traitor's death. Quite badly wounded into the bargain."

"Sounds nasty," he called back. "Best of luck with it all."

"Erchel!" My voice echoed into a swirl of grey mist, the last vestiges of the marsh disintegrating around me in a smeared, meaningless spiral. "How do I get out?"

"You've always managed it before." His increasingly distant voice rang with taunting laughter. "Have faith, Alwyn. If the mad bitch didn't take that from you too."

It was Supplicant Delric's needle that woke me, Erchel's laughter and the dregs of the dream banished by rhythmic pulses of pain as the healer worked to stitch the cut in my upper leg. The icy air of the marshes was immediately replaced by the damp, musty chill of a cell. I gazed blearily at grey walls streaked with green until another jab of the needle had me jerking, a shout erupting from my mouth.

"Stay still," Delric snapped, glancing up from his work. "You certainly don't want my hand to slip just now." His face and voice possessed a hardness I hadn't seen before, leastways not directed at me. He resumed his task, saying nothing more, but his expression was that of a man compelled to a much resented chore. I forced myself to look at the wound, seeing a narrow cut an inch from my left hip. The surrounding skin was red from Delric pinching the lips closed, but I saw no sign of the deeper hues that told of corruption.

I lay back on what felt like a sackcloth mattress filled with thin straw, trying not to move and suffering through the pain. Usually, Delric would anoint the stricken flesh of his charges with some form of numbing balm before setting to work with the needle. In my case, it was plain he hadn't bothered. The cell was unremarkable save for its dimensions, bigger than most, with a high, barred window near the ceiling. I would have preferred bare walls since this portal offered no means of glimpsing the outside world while filling my prison with a constant draught of cold air.

"What did she tell you?" I enquired of Delric.

"That you tried to kill her," the healer replied, not looking up. "That

Albyrn Swain, a man I served alongside for years, lies dead at your hand, traitor."

"The first is true. The second is a lie." Breath hissed through my teeth as he tied off the final stitch. Clenching fists through a spasm of agony, I spoke on, striving to keep the desperation from my voice. "Still, I don't suppose it matters." I watched the healer apply a clean bandage to the wound, then set about gathering his things. "Haven't told her, have you?" I asked, bringing his movements to an abrupt halt. "About your part in her healing. You haven't told her that it was your idea for me to go in search of the Sack Witch."

He kept his face averted, but his eyes slid to meet mine, narrow and fearful.

"That's good." My fingers explored a scabbed bump on the side of my head. It ached when I prodded it, but not with the constant throb that had afflicted me after Althus Levalle cracked my skull. "Don't," I added, meeting Delric's gaze and hoping he perceived my honest intent. "She'll kill you, and anyone else she suspects had a part in it. Just like she killed Swain."

"There were many eyes there," he said, though his tone was far from that of an ardent believer. "Witnesses—"

"That there were," I cut in. "All Duke Viruhlis's men, I'd guess. None of our own people. Doesn't that tell you something, Supplicant?"

He looked away again, hands trembling as they hesitated over his accoutrements. "She ordered no harm done to you," he said. "Pending trial, though she has yet to state when that will take place."

"And the war?"

"Rumours fly thick and fast, it's hard to know what to believe. Scouts report that the False King leads his army north, however."

"Scouts? *My* scouts?" Visions of dire punishments visited upon Lilat, Tiler and the others came to mind. Ayin and Eamond were also potential victims of Evadine's fury, but the fate of Couravel spoke ill for their prospects in any case. I could only hope they had enough sense to get clear of the city and make themselves scarce.

Delric shook his head. "They've vanished. Most of them, that is. A handful came in, those whose loyalty to the Ascendant Queen outweighed that owed to a man now condemned a traitor." He paused, running a hand over his mostly bald scalp. "She will be crowned today . . ." He faltered and faced me squarely for the first time, voice lowered to a tremulous, rapid whisper. "At the coronation she will announce something, Scribe. A great and wondrous gift from the Seraphile, she calls it."

"The child, I know," I said, the words emerging in a flat mutter even though I found myself beset by the perverse desire to laugh. "A gift from the Seraphile. Her holy, blessed womanhood remains unsullied by base human lust." The mirth bubbled in my chest but swiftly died when the movement summoned another bout of pain. "She has to kill me now," I murmured when the flare abated. "I don't know why she hasn't already."

"Yes, you do." Delric gathered the rest of his things into a satchel and pulled the strap over his shoulder, rising to his feet. "I can do nothing more for you, Scribe. I'm sorry."

"Supplicant," I said as he moved to the cell door, making him pause in the act of raising his hand to knock for the guard. "You need to flee. Choose a quiet moment and get as far from her side as you can. But don't tarry. Otherwise, the knowledge you possess will be your doom."

Delric's hand hovered for another instant before he lowered it and reached into his satchel. "Went to some pains to hide this, didn't you?" he said, crouching at my side again. Opening his hand, he revealed a small cotton-wrapped bundle, somewhat stained by the hiding place I had consigned it to when pretending to piss. A clenching of my buttocks told me the healer had been assiduous in his inspection of my person.

"I won't ask what's in this," Delric added, the cotton falling away to reveal the small vial Lorine had given me in Castle Ambris. "But a traitor's death is an ugly thing, so I'll not begrudge you an escape."

I thought of telling him that I was far too great a coward ever to contemplate suicide, but didn't. I had another use for this vial. Better if Delric imagined this to be his last act of compassion for a former comrade. "My thanks," I said, taking the vial, adding in a smaller murmur, "Remember what I said. Fly far and fast."

He gave no sign of agreement, just a final glance of farewell before returning to the door and knocking loudly for the guard. It swung open almost immediately, making me suspect whoever stood on its other side had been straining to hear our conversation. I caught a glimpse of a hard, brutish and familiar face as the door lingered open to allow Delric to exit, then it slammed closed with an echoing boom.

I heard none of the Ascendant Queen's proclamation from the steps of what had been the Couravel cathedral. Even Evadine's gift for projection couldn't reach me here. I did hear the cheers, though. A vast outpouring of worshipful acclaim that went on for what felt like an age. I would learn the detail of her speech later, but the words rendered on a page surely fail to capture what must have been her most powerful oration. She condemned the Algathinets for the deceit and cowardice, pronounced sentences of death upon Arthin, his mother and any who still marched behind their banner. "Henceforth, friends, we can no longer allow ourselves the luxury of mercy." Her audience of soldiers and crusaders cheered all of this with happy abandon, but it was her final revelation that brought forth the great chorus of adulation.

"Know that on this very morn I was visited by the Seraphile," she told them. "And that from their blessed touch, I received the greatest of gifts. Long have I suffered the knowledge that service to the Covenant would rob me of the joy of motherhood. It is a burden I have borne gladly, albeit with pain. Now that pain is ended, for the Seraphile have ordained that this realm, now reclaimed for the Covenant Resurgent, cannot fall into the disunity and strife that arises from the uncertainties of succession. Know that in my womb there grows a child. A child given life by the Seraphile themselves. A child that will one day ascend these very steps and wear this crown. A child that will complete the great work we have begun. This child will lead your children and grandchildren to the greatest glory. This child will be no mere Ascendant monarch, but a Transcendent Emperor. Under this child's divine guidance, all the world will know the Seraphiles' love."

In truth, for all my scholarly passions, I remain glad to not have borne witness to this most momentous speech. I'll confess that this may be in part because she made no mention of me at all. Not a single word, even to condemn my treason or spin some lie regarding my mythical role in some insidious Algathinet plot. From here on, the tale of Alwyn Scribe, the redeemed outlaw who had fought for the Risen Martyr when she stood atop the scaffold, the lieutenant who had been so conspicuous at her side, would be stripped from her story.

"Trial," I said with a soft but bitter grunt as I listened to the ongoing cheers. There would be no trial for me. Delric was right. I retained my life for the simple reason that Evadine still harboured love for me. My brightest prospect would be to spend my remaining years in this cell. The darkest, that she would, sooner or later, find her affection dwindling to the point that my worrisome existence could no longer be tolerated. I found this by far the more likely outcome. Evadine was, whether she realised it or not, a being of malice. Such a creature, for that is how I now thought of her, would see me quietly disposed of before long.

My options were therefore limited. I could orchestrate an escape of a kind this very moment. If Lorine was to be believed, the vial I had once again consigned to its uncomfortable hiding place was so potent it would do the job with but a single drop. Terrifying as the thought of years' long incarceration or impending murder might be, I simply couldn't do it. I have acquired a certain humility these many years, but the scale of my self-regard has never dipped so low as to permit even the slightest consideration of suicide. Which left but one course.

Timing would be crucial. I needed to heal, but not so much that my captors thought me fully recovered. But, neither could I dither too long. I felt I could almost hear Evadine wrestling with her thoughts, veering from our shared delusion of love to the moment of my betrayal. Then there was the child. Our child. The more I pondered it, the more the notion of my son or daughter growing up under Evadine's care grew to sickening proportions. The very idea of fatherhood had always been beyond me, a weight of responsibility I had never wanted, even if my issue hadn't been ordained for tyrannical rule by an insane mother.

Didn't think about all this when you lay with her, I reminded myself, one of Lorine's occasional aphorisms coming to mind: *All men are as putty when they let their prick take charge of their brain.* The welling of guilt and self-recrimination made me wonder if this had been Evadine's scheme all along. To ensure her triumphant ascendancy, an heir was vital. An heir possessing both our gifts. What kind of monster would she make of such a child? I couldn't abide the thought of it. I have never been one for oaths and such, but, lying there in that damp, chilled stone box, I swore that I would wrest my child from Evadine if it cost me my life. Had I been of a more rational mind, I might have paused to consider how many other lives this would cost.

Two weeks of dull routine passed. Lacking something to scratch tally marks into the wall, I twisted the sparse straw littering the floor into loops to mark the passing days. Once a day the door opened and my brute-faced gaoler would provide a bowl of gruel and a cup of water before replacing the bucket containing my effluent. Having taken the bowl and cup from the day before, he would exit the cell and slam the door with not a word exchanged between us. I recognised the man as the amiable turn-screw who led me to Magnis Lochlain's cell to record his testament. Even so, I made no attempt to break his rigid silence. The flat, unyielding mask of his heavy-set face was discouragement enough. But I also didn't wish to form any bond with a man I would probably have to kill before long. I was careful to slump on to the mattress when he came, sparing him a miserable, listless glance while I shivered and shuddered. Better he thought me still lamed, even though Delric had done his work with typical excellence and my wound healed well, showing no sign of corruption.

I waited three days before testing my strength, and then only at night. At first, I could manage to totter from one wall to another, teeth gritted against the throbbing heat in my hip. I fell repeatedly, swallowing my shouts of pain, then forcing myself back to my feet and resuming the stumble. Within a week, I could walk without falling, albeit with a pronounced limp.

In addition to conditioning my body, I honed my mind. I was no stranger to imprisonment, or escape, but never purely on my own agency. Getting free of the Pit Mines had required years of combined labour by Sihlda's congregation, costing all but three of their lives in the end. My escape from the Dire Keep had in fact been a rescue, thanks to Lilat's gift for infiltrating ancient ruins. I could expect neither aid nor rescue here, though I worried that the huntress might get herself killed making an attempt. So, I sought inspiration not from personal experience, but from the stories I had heard from Deckin's band.

I never met an outlaw who didn't love a story, either the telling or the hearing. Some, like the enigmatic Raith, were taciturn by nature, but even he would spin a brief yarn or two from time to time. Given the nature of our occupation, tales of capture and escape were frequent at the fire, and it was to the treacherous Todman I looked for guidance. Todman, you see, was perhaps the most accomplished escaper I ever encountered, and his tales were not merely the boasts of an overly prideful bully. He knew all the knots and, more importantly, how to slip them. He knew locks and how to pick them. Most of all, he knew gaols, for he had been both a prisoner and a gaoler.

"Boredom is your friend and the turn-screw's enemy," he told a collection of us keen-eared cubs one night. Todman was a man of considerable faults, but his innate brutality was rarely visited upon children. I'll give him that. All the older outlaws would entertain us with their varied, often incredible tales, but Todman was always more in the vein of a teacher. His stories were lessons, and, though I'd already begun to detest him when still just a cub, even I could recognise their value.

"Gaolers do the same thing at the same hour day after day," he said. "Their lives are ruled by habit, and that's where you'll find your chance. They'll be more watchful when you're a new face, for the freshly caught are more likely to try to slip the snare. Make 'em get used to your face, your own habits. Every time they turn their eye on you, make sure you're in the same place doing the same thing. You need to be exactly where they expect you to be, until you need to be somewhere else. In that instant, that moment when you're not there, that's your chance, for they always hesitate. Just for a second." Todman snapped his fingers. "They'll be looking the wrong way, asking themselves, *Where's that fucker gone?* That's when you either kill them or lay them low. Killing's better because a dead man won't come to his senses and raise the alarm before you've managed to get his keys into the right lock."

Keys were the real treasure, of course, and my silent brute jangled them all the way to my door every day. I could gauge the length of the passage from the sound, also the squeal of the gate at the far end. Fortunately, I heard no muttered voices accompanying the squeal, meaning it lacked a guard. I had a decent knowledge of the upper reaches of this building thanks to my visits to Lochlain's cell. It was an old, unkempt structure but, as befits a prison, rich in iron gates and heavy doors. I knew my brute to be the master of this place, probably relieved to have kept both his job and his head after the Algathinets' flight and the Ascendant Queen's arrival. That kind of relief breeds loyalty, a keenness to prove one's worth. Therefore, the master gaoler had taken on the role of overseeing the Traitor Scribe himself, and every time he did so, the keys to every lock in this building dangled from his belt.

After another week, I had recovered to the point where my limp was greatly reduced, but the pain of movement remained fierce. Getting clear of this building was one thing. Slipping through a part-destroyed city infested with the Ascendant Queen's host would require all the stealth I could muster. I forced patience upon myself, spending the hours between bouts of exercise attempting verbatim recitals of the key scholarly works Sihlda had impressed into my mind in the Pit.

I was a few verses into the *Epic of Queen Liselle*, the only female monarch of the Algathinet dynasty, when the echo of footsteps from beyond the door brought a plummet to my heart. I could recognise the gaoler's footfalls by now, but my sudden despair came from the fact that his heavy clomp was accompanied by another, more purposeful and measured stride. I had left it too late.

Still, I got to my feet and moved from the mattress, pressed into the far corner of the cell with my vial of deadly poison in hand. If one drop could fell a man, a few more would see to the gaoler's companion. There would be more waiting, of course, an escort for the Traitor Scribe to his final meeting with death. Probably followed by an unmarked grave in some rarely visited forest. I had no choice but to risk it. If I could just escape the building and get to a horse, I might have a chance.

Calculation faded as the key rattled the lock. I plucked the stopper from the vial, holding the small glass vessel away from me in preparation for casting forth its contents. When the door swung open, the gaoler did all that was expected of him. Halting in baffled indecision at the sight of my vacant mattress, he let out a puzzled huff before beginning to turn his head. My arm tensed and I began to flick my wrist, then stopped when the gaoler's companion stepped into view.

"You look like a bundle of cold shit," Wilhum informed me, nostrils wrinkling in disgust. "And you smell worse."

I said nothing, panicked gaze flicking from his burgeoning grin to the vial in my hand. The gaoler had fully recovered his wits by now and his practised eye was quick to fix upon this previously unseen object.

"What's that?" he growled, taking hold of the cudgel dangling from his belt. "You been hiding trinkets? That's not nice."

"Now, now, my good fellow," Wilhum said, resting a hand on the gaoler's meaty shoulder. "I'm sure my lord Scribe has merely been concealing a small keepsake."

"He's not a fucking lord any more." The brute's features darkened and he shrugged off Wilhum's hand to advance upon me. "And your warrant's only for a visit. Till the queen says otherwise, this fucker's mine . . ."

The pommel of Wilhum's dagger produced a curious sound as it struck the rear of the gaoler's skull, almost bell-like in its hollow ring.

The blow sufficed to bring the brute to a halt, but didn't fell him. Instead, he stumbled forward, head lolling and mouth emitting a puzzled groan.

"More granite than bone," Wilhum grunted, bringing the dagger's pommel down once more. This time the gaoler went to his knees and it required an additional blow before he consented to collapse, already flattened nose flattening further as it broke on the flagstones.

"What is that?" Wilhum enquired, sheathing his dagger and nodding to the vial in my hand.

"Poison," I replied, carefully replacing the stopper. "Kills on contact with the skin, so I'm told."

"Oh. Keep it close. I've a fancy we'll need it before the night's out."

Chapter Seventeen

We exchanged no words as we made our way from the cell and along the passage to the gate. Unlocking it required sorting through the copious bundle of keys crowding the gaoler's ring. It was only when it squealed open, and I stepped through to find the stairwell beyond empty, that I permitted myself a question.

"I assume you're here on your own agency?" I asked Wilhum, voice soft as I peered at the shadowy upper reaches of the stairwell. In addition to his keys and purse, I had relieved the gaoler of his cudgel and stood ready to crack the skull of any unfortunate guard who might descend to bar our path.

"It seems I am once again shorn of a monarch to serve," Wilhum replied. His tone was light with forced humour but, glancing at his face, I saw features rendered grim with shame. Summoning a smile, he added, "Betraying self-crowned royalty is becoming something of a habit for me, it seems."

"One I'm grateful for," I said, voice lowered to a whisper as I started up the steps in a cautious crouch. "What made you do it?"

Wilhum gave no reply until we had reached the apex of the stairwell, finding ourselves confronted by a very solid and very closed door. "When I returned, when I came to this city of ashes . . ." he began then trailed off, eyes clouding. "It's not her, not now. The woman I looked upon, the woman I called friend since childhood, she's no longer there. And she's done . . . things."

"What things . . . ?" I began, then fell silent at the sound of conversation beyond the door. It was muted by heavy oak and iron, but I fancied I discerned at least three different voices. They sounded calm enough, their muffled words interspersed with short bursts of laughter.

"We've no time," Wilhum muttered. "They'll be on their way by now."

"They?"

"That Rhianvelan horror and her gaggle of lickspittles." Wilhum's handsome face bunched in a sympathetic wince. "Today our queen was heard to say that she wishes to be cleansed of all treachery. It's a new habit she's adopted, speaking in code that those who grovel around her compete to decipher. However, I feel this one was a trifle obvious."

"Is that how you got a warrant to visit me? Told her you were going to cut my throat."

"The warrant is as fine a forgery as I've ever encountered, her signature a true work of art." Wilhum drew his sword and hunched in readiness. "You are to be congratulated on your friends, my lord Scribe."

"You heard the man downstairs." I moved to the door and gently began testing the keys in the lock. "I'm no fucking lord."

It was the fifth key that turned the lock. I took comfort from the fact that the laughing guards on the other side would assume it was their master returning from the traitor's cell. I was less comforted by the knowledge that escaping this place probably entailed killing them all. I had concealed Lorine's vial in the gaoler's purse. Taking it out, I removed the stopper and put my shoulder to the door.

I had hoped to fling the barrier aside with enough speed to achieve surprise, instead the heavy lump of wood and metal swung open with an irksome absence of dramatic haste. Consequently, the five men crowding the guardroom beyond were revealed one at a time, each blinking in surprise as the expectant sight of their master failed to materialise. Instead, they were confronted by a barefoot man in ragged, besmirched shirt and trews clutching a cudgel in one hand and small bottle in the other. Thankfully, the failure to secure surprise worked in my favour, for, after comprehending the meaning of my appearance, they came for me as one. Consequently, it was an easy matter to douse their faces with one flick of the bottle.

The effect was shocking in its instancy. The five of them reeled back from the door, hands clutching at their faces. The screams that followed were mercifully short but dreadful enough, shrieks of purest agony that cut to the bone before a spasming rictus clamped their jaws shut. Terror blazed in their gaping eyes, red foam bubbling from their mouths as they writhed, boots drumming on the flagstones, the air thick with guttural choking then stained by the stink of voided bowels. Had I been provided a more copious diet in recent days, I would surely have vomited.

"Martyrs," Wilhum breathed, staring at the bodies, still now, save one that continued to twitch as a stream of crimson drool flowed from his lips. Swallowing his gorge, Wilhum directed a distasteful glare at the bottle in my hand. "Quite a brew you have there."

I saw that the vial retained a few drops of the pale unremarkable liquid and carefully replaced the stopper before consigning it to the gaoler's purse. Such a thing was too useful to be wasted.

Wilhum stepped carefully over the carpet of bodies to retrieve two cloaks hanging from pegs on the far wall. "Here," he said, tossing one to me. "Probably not the best idea for the Traitor Scribe to wander about with his face uncovered."

Getting clear of the building required some more unlocking of gates and doors, our path mostly unimpeded by guards. It transpired we had left all but two dead in our wake. The final pair were stationed at the main exit, a lanky youth and a bewhiskered veteran. The youngster dropped at the first kiss of the cudgel to the crown of his head, his older comrade stepping smartly aside and raising his empty hands when Wilhum advanced upon him with levelled sword.

"Sorry," I told the veteran before laying him out with the cudgel. The risk of him raising the alarm as soon as we departed was too great and we had no time to bind him. After a quick appraisal of the younger guard's feet, I relieved him of his boots and the belt holding his falchion before pulling the hood of my cloak over my head.

"We make for the eastern palace wall," Wilhum said, gently easing the main door open. "Best not to run—"

"I know," I cut in, annoyed that he would presume to teach me elementary lessons in not attracting unwanted notice. "I'm the outlaw, remember?" I added, offering a grin in response to his frown.

"No," he sighed, stepping out into the night. "We're both outlaws now."

The blocky, unadorned building that served as the palace prison stood apart from the main structure of the royal residence. It sat between the outer and inner walls, a neglected but necessary architectural embarrassment to this former seat of Algathinet power. As a consequence, the path between the walls was patrolled with less frequency and vigilance than the inner precincts, allowing Wilhum and I to maintain a sedate progress. My hip bothered me a good deal more now, and I had to resist the urge to limp lest it draw the eye of the sentries on the inner wall.

"So," I asked Wilhum in a strained mutter, keen for the distraction of conversation. "How did your Caerith hunting expedition go?"

"It was a farcical waste of time," he replied with no apparent regret. "The Caerith who abide in this realm have a remarkable facility for melting into the shadows when danger threatens. As you might expect there were informants aplenty. 'There's a bunch of 'em encamped in those hills, m'lord. I swears it. Practising all manner of dark rites they are, too. Give us a sovereign and I'll take you straight there.' Almost always nonsense, of course. Even when we did get a credible whisper of one, they'd gone by the time we arrived. After months of traipsing about, our only catch was a frail old man living in a hut in the southern Cordwain. Seemed doubtful he'd live out the winter, so I just let him be. Nice old duffer he was too, so far as I could tell. Couldn't speak a word of Albermaine-ish, if you can believe that."

"I can't. All the Caerith who come here speak our tongue. He was play-acting." *And*, I added inwardly, *probably much older than he appeared.*

"Cunning old sod." Wilhum's chuckle lacked rancour, though his humour vanished at the faint echo of shouting from the direction of the prison. "The horror appears to have found our leavings. Time to run."

Fresh agony flared in my hip as I struggled to match his sprint for the eastern wall. I came close to stumbling a few times but the fear of recapture by Harldin's vengeful sister kept me upright. I caught up with Wilhum at the base of the wall, finding him holding a thick knotted rope. Glancing up, I saw one end affixed to the top with a grapple.

"After you," I said, receiving an emphatic headshake in return.

"You are the object of this enterprise." He forced the rope into my hands. "No arguments. Now climb."

My hip felt like it was on fire when I began the ascent, and blossomed into a raging inferno by the time I crested the wall. This outer barrier to the palace grounds lacked a battlement, requiring me to lever myself on to uneven brickwork at the top. I expected to have to wait for Wilhum to climb to my side before throwing the rope over, but found another already fixed in place.

"Hurry, my lord!" an urgent voice hissed from below. Looking down, I beheld Tiler's upturned face. He sat astride his mount, clutching the reins of two other horses. I felt an unexpected surge of relief at the sight of Blackfoot's pale coat. Clearly, Wilhum had help in orchestrating tonight's events. Hearing a fresh tumult from the direction of the prison, I glanced down to ensure he was nearing the top, then took hold of the second rope and began my descent. I performed the feat with a distinct absence of grace, my attempts to brace my legs against the wall constantly frustrated by my wound. The strength in my left leg was almost spent by the time I reached the grassy verge at the base.

"Here, my lord." Tiler reached down to hand me Blackfoot's reins. The warhorse greeted me with a snort and a toss of his head, nickering in annoyance when I tried and failed to mount him. After three more attempts, each more painful than the last, I succeeded in the task, unable to contain a shout as I swung my leg over the saddle.

"Careful," Tiler warned. "Plenty of patrols about."

Studying his tense features, I was struck by the unexpected pleasure of finding him here. Of all the scouts, he had been the one I felt certain to desert for safer climes at the first opportunity. "My thanks," I said. "For coming."

He spared me a tight, wary grin before resuming his survey of the blackened, part-ruined streets to our right. "You came for me, my lord."

"You shouldn't feel obliged to call me that any longer. In fact, I think I'd prefer if you didn't."

"Then what do I call you?" I was surprised to see that the question seemed to genuinely baffle him.

"Scribe, if you like. Or just Alwyn. I believe I've grown weary of titles."

"Right," Wilhum said, striding across the verge to take the reins from Tiler before mounting his own charger. "We'd best be off."

"Can't go the way we came in," Tiler advised. "The eastward quarter's thick with patrols since it got dark. Reckon we should head for the western road. Fewer houses still standing there, so less reason for them to scout it. Also, the gatehouse is mostly tumbled down. Got caught in the fire, see."

"That'll mean passing through the square," Wilhum said, casting a cautious glance in my direction.

"Can't be helped, my lord."

"Wasting time," I said, kicking my heels to compel Blackfoot into a walk.

The wind and rain of the intervening days had scoured much of the ash from the ruins of Couravel, but a good deal of it lingered. The night breeze raised the pall of detritus in gritty, eye stinging gusts as we followed the line of the outer wall to the main square. As a result, I was denied a fulsome view of what awaited us there until a yet stronger wind swept the ugly cloud away to reveal the scaffold. The intervening distance was too great to make out the identity of the three bodies hanging from the crossbeam atop the platform, yet a sudden, grim certainty caused me to bring Blackfoot to a halt.

"Alwyn!" Wilhum said, voice hard with urgency. I ignored him, trotting Blackfoot towards the scaffold then stopping when the faces of the hanged came into view. A handful of Covenant soldiers were stationed around the platform and reacted to my appearance with baffled immobility, even though I was sure they must have recognised me. I barely heard their increasingly alarmed exchanges as they debated what to do, so fixated was I on the dead. *She has done . . . things.*

Former Ascendant Hilbert had been blindfolded before the drop, I assumed at his request. Even so, I recognised his curiously peaceful features, somehow retaining an air of superiority even in death. *Had to bring the translation to her personally, didn't you?* I asked him, silently. *Thinking it the key to your future importance in the Covenant Resurgent. I suppose I should have warned you, even were she not a creature of the Malecite, there was never any chance she would favour one such as you.*

A groan escaped me upon turning to regard the figure hanging alongside Hilbert. "I told you to fly far and fast," I murmured to Delric's unresponsive features which were a stark contrast to the cleric's. Hanging often has a way of rendering the face into a tensed, mottled bruise, sometimes freezing expressions at the moment of final agony. So it was with Delric, his lips still drawn back from his teeth, as if snarling. Although a man of gruff manners, this was the only time I had seen him express any sign of aggression.

Despite the already raging grief, it was the sight of the third figure that sent the coldest blade of ice through my chest.

"We told her not to try, my lord." Tiler's voice was heavy with shame, his distress enough to make him forget my injunction against use of titles. "Wouldn't listen. Just slipped away into the shadows the very night they took you. 'Course we looked but there's no tracking her."

The sergeant in charge of the Covenant soldiers had recovered enough wit to assert his authority now, hefting his halberd and striding towards me. "Lord Alwyn Scribe, you are named a traitor . . ."

Blackfoot responded to my touch on the reins with practised speed and precision, rearing to deliver a kick of his forehooves into the sergeant's face. The fellow sprawled back, face a bloodied ruin. The soldier to his right was little more than a boy, probably a new recruit to the host, fully aware of the tale of the Traitor Scribe but with no experience of Captain Alwyn. Had I been of less concentrated mind, I would probably have met his reckless charge with a blow that would have wounded or stunned him. Instead, I buried the edge of my stolen falchion in his forehead, kicked the body aside and dismounted Blackfoot. The other soldiers, all older and considerably wiser, stood aside as I climbed the steps of the scaffold.

Lilat's features were another contrast to Delric's, being so badly scarred and bruised. Like him, her death had been slow, the band of raw flesh around her neck testament to the fact that she had fought all the way to the end.

"Alwyn!" Wilhum called again, no longer attempting to quell his voice. Dimly, I heard raised voices from the direction of the main palace gate, soon followed by the grind of the great doorway being hauled open.

"Did you watch this?" I asked Wilhum, still unable to look away from Lilat's face. "Did you stand there and do nothing while the sentences were read out? Did you cheer along, perhaps?"

"I couldn't do anything to stop it!" The mingled anger and anguish in his voice caused me to turn, finding him stricken with desperate entreaty. "But I can save you." A loud clatter came from the direction of the palace, indicating the main gate was now fully open. "Please Alwyn!"

I used the falchion to cut the rope and gathered Lilat's limp form into my arms. My hip gave forth a fresh wave of agony as I laid the corpse over the saddle, then climbed up behind. I know I shouted with mingled pain and grief then, for I recall the soldiers retreating a few more paces, but our subsequent flight from the city is all just a vague, shadowy thing from thereon. I know there was a short but savage fight with the Rhianvelan guards on the eastern gate, but the details of it are forever lost. I also have no memory of pausing at the scaffold, but according to Tiler before riding away with Lilat's body, I turned and spoke to the soldiers thus: "She's not a queen. Nor is she a martyr. It's a lie, and we are all fools. Leave this city and go to whatever place you call home. If you do not, when next we meet, I'll kill you all."

I forced myself to look at Lilat's body in full after I set it down in the forest. I had no desire to see the marks of torture that marred her flesh, but wouldn't allow myself the cowardice of looking away. The least she deserved was a proper accounting of her suffering.

I found several burns and numerous unstitched cuts. There were also smaller marks I knew came from a long thin blade thrust deep into muscles to tweak nerves. I wondered what questions they asked of her, and knew they would have made little sense of any answers wrung from her lips. I wondered too if Evadine had been there, standing in stern witness to the torment inflicted on one of the Caerith she hated so much. I doubted it. I still knew her mind, or at least the portion of it that believed itself human. Like many a tyrant, Evadine considered herself the opposite. To her, such extremes were necessities, not cruelties. Also, while she was content for atrocities to be carried out on her behalf, she would feel no desire to partake herself. Such things are beneath a queen's dignity, after all.

"You leave your dead to the forest," I said, smoothing a hand over Lilat's brow. When it came to the treatment of their fallen, Caerith custom was pragmatic to the point of indifference. But I felt sure those who abandoned the shell of their loved ones to nature's mercy must practise some form of ritual, one I berated myself for not bothering to learn during my time among her people. Still, I felt compelled to offer a eulogy, even if it amounted to no more than clumsy words spoken by a guilty fool. I fought to summon the image of her face as it had been, but all I could see was this battered, ruined mask devoid of life.

"I used to think," I continued, pushing the words out through a choked throat, "that I didn't want you to follow me. I never asked you to, did I? But, when I woke on that mountainside to find you there, I was grateful. Grateful for your guidance, your knowledge. Grateful most of all for being my friend, for I have so few. And grateful for every step we shared. I'll swear no vengeance in your name. You wouldn't have wanted it, and we're beyond vengeance now. One last thing I'm grateful for is that you won't have to see what I'm going to do."

My fingers teased the curls of her hair, wondering why it had never occurred to me before that it was of a shade far darker than any other Caerith I had encountered. "Legacy of your Albermaine-ish ancestor?" I asked her, recalling the *Eithlisch's* story of Lilat's familial origins, how he had rescued her great-great-grandmother from a miserable existence in some minor noble's holdfast.

"Mayhap there's a castle somewhere in this benighted land you could've claimed by right of blood." I laughed but it emerged as a ragged sob, the first of many. There in that small clearing, I hunched over the corpse of a woman whose friendship I didn't deserve, and wept until the sky turned dark and I had no more tears to shed.

"We could've dug a grave for her," Tiler said when I returned to the camp. The hour was late but the fire small, lest it draw enquiring eyes. Thanks to some hard riding, we were at least thirty miles from the city, but our predicament warranted caution. Evadine would have every rider under her command scouring the country for the Traitor Scribe.

"Her people don't do that," I replied, slumping down beside the fire, then wincing at the pain it provoked in my hip. For a time, I lost myself in miserable contemplation of the fire's meagre flames, looking up when Tiler voiced a meaningful cough.

"They've been wondering," he said. "About where we're going next."

I glanced around at the twoscore soldiers encamped close by. They were all that remained of the Scout Company and Wilhum's riders who counted loyalty to their captains above faith in the Ascendant Queen. Quintrell and Adlar Spinner were among them, the minstrel's presence more a surprise than the juggler's. It was hardly an army, but I fancied I had a notion where to find one.

"North," I said. "The Cordwain. That's where the king's host marches, so we'd best join them."

"Leannor will have your head off your shoulders in a trice," Wilhum said.

"She can be vicious when the mood takes her," I conceded. "And not so clever as she imagines, but I reckon she's clever enough to recognise the value of my counsel. Who else knows better the mind of her enemy?"

Shifting my gaze to Tiler, I saw the grim countenance of a man considering a deeply uncertain future. "I ask no one to come with me," I told him. "You're no longer under my command and my task is perilous." I stood, raising my voice to address the camp. "You've done enough, all of you. I won't judge anyone who chooses their own path from here on. Go with my thanks, and best wishes for a more peaceful life. But, come the dawn, I ride north and my every act will be directed towards the fall of Evadine Courlain."

"North is not the wisest choice."

The voice came from the black wall of the treeline beyond the fire's glow. Startled soldiers reached for weapons, but I did not. This voice I knew.

"She's on the march," the Widow continued, her features revealed by the fire as she strode from the gloom, leading Parsal by the reins. Going to her haunches, she extended her hands to the flames. "Couravel's emptying out. At least, it was a few hours gone. The entirety of the Ascendant Host is heading north." There was a tension to her face I recognised from the aftermath of combat, also I saw bruises and scratches on those hands and a fresh scar tracing from her forehead into her hair.

"Did they catch you?" I asked.

"They tried, and paid for it." She glanced over her shoulder as another, smaller figure slipped from the shadows. "Luckily, I had some help."

As Ayin emerged into the light I found her appearance more alarming than Juhlina's, even though she lacked any sign of injury. She kept her eyes averted from mine, saying nothing as she sat close to the fire, arms crossed tightly about her midriff. I saw stains of a darkly familiar hue on her clothing.

"Eamond . . . ?" I began only to fall silent at a warning glare from Juhlina. Ayin lowered her head further, still unspeaking. A story to be gleaned at another time, and I was sure I wouldn't enjoy hearing it.

"I found her travelling with a group of townsfolk who'd fled the city," Juhlina said. "They were in the midst of being set upon by a bunch of crusader scum keen to spread the Ascendant Queen's message. Got a mite more than they bargained for with us two. We kept one alive, a helpful fellow with a lot to say." I appreciated the fact that the gaze she directed towards me then was devoid of smugness, mostly at least. "About captive traitor scribes and such."

Perhaps I don't know her mind so well, after all, I thought. I had been so sure Evadine would spend all her energies in pursuit of me and had only one explanation for her decision to march north instead. *She had a vision.*

"You saw her host?" I asked.

"Yesterday," Juhlina confirmed. "We were headed back to Couravel. I'm not altogether sure what we'd have done when we got there, but—" she shrugged "—we did. The hour was late but we caught wind of a fracas at the eastern gate, got there just in time to see you lot riding off into the night. Some Rhianvelan cavalry out looking for you nearly caught us, but we got away. Come the morn, the host marched out, following the northern road."

"So, how'd you find us?" Tiler enquired with a suspicious squint.

"Because we camped on this very spot when we were scouting the approaches to the capital." Juhlina plucked a twig from the ground and threw it at him. "Besides, you're not so hard to track. Idiot."

"The lure of wonders across the sea wasn't so great, then?" I said.

The Widow looked away with a shrug. "I was halfway to the coast when I realised I'd nowhere near enough coin to buy passage." A bald lie, since I knew her to be the most frugal member of this company. Still, it was not the time to press the matter.

"So," Wilhum mused, running a hand through his hair. "Heading north is out of the question."

"We need to catch up to Leannor's host," I said. "Allied with Duke

Lohrent, she'll at least have a chance. More so with my counsel." Turning to the onlooking circle, I sought out Quintrell. "If you would care to share your insight, master minstrel."

"Insight, my lord?" he said in bland puzzlement.

"Don't call me that, and no more artifice, if you please. The only route we can take to the Cordwain lies through the Shavine Marches. The question is, which way is your duchess likely to jump?"

He kept his features inexpressive, save for a slight hardening of the eyes. "I do not presume to speak for the duchess. I fancy you would know better than any that she is, very much, her own woman."

Indeed I did know this, as I knew that Lorine could be counted on to act in her self-interest. Having allied herself with Evadine before, she would be considered suspect by Leannor. Also, Lorine would take a typically pragmatic view of the odds in this grand game, judging Evadine the most likely winner. *Then I'll need to convince her that the price of victory is far too high*, I decided.

"Sleep well tonight," I told the camp. "If you're here come morning, we ride for the Shavine Marches. If you're not, accept my thanks and be sure to ride swiftly for distant lands. The Martyr we followed in our foolishness no longer has any truck with forgiveness."

Chapter Eighteen

They all stayed, which surprised me. This collection of erstwhile outlaws, fanatics, churls and disgraced former lords chose to wage war against one they had thought a Risen Martyr not so long ago. I had spent some time at the fire the night before relating what I knew of her true nature, a task that involved a full account of my days among the Caerith. Whether they believed it all, I couldn't say. But, as I owed Lilat the truth, so I owed them. Accordingly, though it pained me, I also forced out a confession of all that had passed between myself and Evadine. Inevitably, this led to a singular realisation, although only Juhlina felt able to voice it, and then not until we were on the road the next morning.

"So, do you hope for a boy or a girl?" she asked, riding alongside me. I saw a taunt to her expression, also a certain judgement, though it was not altogether unkind. However, my mind was still too full of Lilat's mauled, lifeless face to allow for the levity of banter.

"I don't need you to measure the scale of my stupidity," I said. "Rest assured, I know it full well."

"She has to kill you. I assume you know that too. You are living proof of her falsity. Not only is she no Martyr, risen or otherwise, the child in her belly is not a blessing of the Seraphile. I'm surprised she hasn't brought her full strength against us by now."

"She's guided by more than fear of discovery."

"Her visions, you mean?" Juhlina grunted in derision. Apparently, she hadn't been fully convinced by my campfire confession. "Surely just more mummery."

"Too many times I saw her perceive what was to come, with too much clarity for it to be a sham. Her visions are real, but they don't come from the Seraphile."

"Careful." She shifted in her saddle, a wary frown on her brow. "You're starting to sound like a man I used to follow from shrine to shrine. A man I've since come to realise was as mad and mean as a rabid weasel."

"Mad?" I sighed, shaking my head. "Perhaps I am. These last days I've seen enough to drive a man to madness. In a way, it's fitting, don't you think? A mad queen should be brought down by her mad lover."

I looked back over our short column, seeing Ayin riding at the rear, mounted on one of the spare horses Tiler had stolen from an unfortunate farmer. The perpetual cheerfulness I knew so well was gone now, her eyes distant and features grim. "Has she said anything?" I asked Juhlina. "About Eamond, or anything else?"

"Barely a word since I found her. Got awful upset when I asked about it, crying and such. It was a shock since she never does that. Still knows how to use that knife of hers, though."

I turned my gaze ahead, beset by yet another welling of guilt. "I should never have sent them off like that. Little more than children, and I had them play the spy."

"She's not a child," the Widow insisted. "However she appears. And you made your choices, we all did. We all marched behind a false Martyr's banner for many a mile. And we made her a queen. So it's up to us to bring her down." She hesitated, face tensing with the need to say something I wouldn't want to hear. "And you know what that might mean. For her, and for the babe she carries."

Of course I know! I kept the harsh retort from my lips, instead closing my mouth and spurring Blackfoot to a trot. "I'll scout the track for the next mile," I said, not turning. "Alone."

We skirted the southern walls of Couravel at a good distance, wary of encountering any troops Evadine may have left behind. The route was free of enemies, but not others. By noon, we had ridden past well over a thousand bedraggled, burdened people making their way back to the city they had called home only weeks before. Most were keen to get clear of our path, unsure of our loyalties and scared by the arms we bore. Some, however, were bolder. These were usually those with little or nothing to carry, impoverished, starved townsfolk driven to return to the only home they knew.

"You!" one old man called out, bony arm extended to stab a finger in my direction. "You're the scribe! I know your face, you bastard!"

I said nothing and kept Blackfoot plodding on, raising a hand to halt Tiler when he turned his horse towards the vocal pauper.

"Look at us!" the old man demanded, and I found myself unable to resist his command. He stood with his arms spread wide, gesturing to the stooped, wearied folk around him. At his side, a boy of perhaps seven years clutched the old man's trews, staring at me with wide, guileless eyes. *A grandchild, maybe? An orphan of the fire, Martyrs forbid? This old codger the only family he has left.* "Look what you did to us!" the boy's aged guardian railed. "You and your bitch Martyr! Look at what you did!"

I could have stopped, attempted to offer whatever words of contrition I might be able to muster. Perhaps shared some of our supplies. But our stocks were meagre and had to last us to the Marches. Also, I saw no use in words now. Words had brought us to this. My scribblings and Evadine's sermons, words that birthed flames and beggared thousands. So I didn't stop. I rode on until the old man's ranting faded away. For the rest of the journey, I pulled the hood of my cloak over my face whenever common folk came into view.

We reached the eastern fringe of the Shavine Forest ten days later, the cool air beneath the vast roof of branches bringing a sense of relief. Even away from Couravel, the country had been thick with dispossessed people, most fleeing south. Careful questioning by Tiler brought forth tales of dark deeds committed by the Ascendant Host as it marched towards its reckoning with the Algathinet army.

"One poor sod was a bit too slow in swearing his loyalty to the queen," Tiler reported. "So they strung him up. Lots of folk with backs striped by floggings too, mostly for talking back, but some for not knowing their scripture. Then there's the queen's taxes. The way they tell it, every chicken, goat, cow, or horse betwixt Alberis and the Cordwain border has been gathered up to feed the queen's army, along with all the coin they can scrape from the villages they pass through. Thought Alundia was bad, but this is another story altogether."

I knew this stretch of forest reasonably well, it being favoured by Deckin's band during the summer months when merchant trade between Alberis and the Marches was more plentiful. Some of the old, winding trails we used in those days were faded from lack of use, but remained passable. I chose to lead us along the most overgrown routes, reasoning that, despite the delay it caused, they would be the least patrolled. When Wilhum and Juhlina raised concerns regarding our seemingly wayward course, Tiler let out a caustic chuckle.

"We're outlaws now," he told them. "Folk like us don't move in straight lines. My old man used to say, 'A man who walks straight in the Shavine Forest marks the path to his own hanging.'"

Despite my caution, it was barely another day before I became aware of our progress being tracked. The signs were subtle and easily missed by those not raised amid these trees; a muting of birdcalls now and then, a sapling branch twitching without a hint of wind, the faint scent of human sweat on the breeze. Tiler sensed it too, a dark tension lowering his brow as he unhitched a crossbow from his saddle.

"Leave it," I said. "We're here to make friends, remember? Besides, they're just watching."

"For now," he replied, but consented to retie the crossbow's strap. "Last time I came here, the Yollands had sway of this patch. A right nasty bunch."

I didn't know the name. "Yollands?"

"A west Alberis clan. Moved in after Deckin's fall."

"They pay tribute to Shilva?"

"It's the Marches, Captain. Everyone pays tribute to Shilva."

"Then we have something in common."

The watchful Yollands didn't make themselves known for another two days, by which time we had entered the deep woods proper. A dozen or so ragged miscreants appeared at our picket line come nightfall, demanding a toll for safe passage. Looking over their emaciated faces, poorly patched garb and unimpressive weaponry, I deduced this was more an act of beggary than thievery.

"Pickings thin these days?" I asked the tallest, assuming him to be the leader. It transpired my judgement was off, for the fellow replied only with baffled hostility, snarling and brandishing a rusty cleaver. It was the stockier, considerably younger man at his side that spoke up.

"The new queen's got a fondness for the lash and the noose, right enough," he said with a sniff. Looking closer, I marked him as more boy than man, little more than fifteen years old, albeit with features bearing the hardiness and scars of a born outlaw. "Uncle Troff's dangling from a shrine spire a few miles north thanks to her. Him and a brace of my cousins, too." He scanned me with shrewd eyes that lingered longer on my face than my sword. "You who I think you are?"

"Who do you think I am?"

He quailed a little under the weight of my gaze, lowering his eyes to mutter. "The one they calls the Scribe. Deckin's son, so they say."

"They say wrong. But they call me the Scribe, right enough. Here." I emptied half the sheks from my purse and handed them to him. "Won't have it said I don't pay my toll when it's due. Now, piss off."

"Turned against her, din't ya?" the lad persisted. "That's the word on the wind, anyways. You're gonna fight her, right?"

I paused to survey the youth's band, most of whom were little older than him, a couple even younger. This, I realised, was the remnant of a once feared clan crushed by the Ascendant Queen's wrath. As I knew better than most, outlaws with a grudge could be useful.

"That's right," I said.

The lad exchanged glances with his fellows, receiving affirming nods in response. He swallowed and straightened, steeling himself to meet my eye. "Can we come?"

"Uncle Troff deserves a reckoning, does he?"

"He was a mean old bastard. Gave me this." The young outlaw

touched a hand to the scar on his chin. "But he was blood. Yollands always settle a blood debt."

I raised an eyebrow at Tiler, who shrugged. "They've got no horses."

"Doesn't make much difference in the forest." I turned back to the vengeful youth. "You know the ground between here and Ambriside?" He nodded. "Good, you can scout us a path, one that steers us clear of others who'll come looking for a toll. Can you do that?"

Another nod.

"What's your name?"

"Falko, m'lord." He attempted a salute of sorts, pressing a knuckle to his forehead in a clearly unfamiliar gesture. Those born to the outlaw life aren't taught churlish ways.

"Just 'Captain' will do." I tossed him the purse with my remaining sheks. "Your first pay as a trooper in the Free Company. Share it out, then come and eat."

"Free Company?" Tiler asked as we made our way back to the fire.

"Has a ring to it, don't you think?"

"Free Host sounds better. More impressive, like."

"Host, eh?" I quelled a bitter laugh. "Let's leave off changing it until we count our numbers after departing Ambriside."

I hadn't expected a warm welcome from Lorine, considering frosty refusal to be the most likely outcome to our meeting. However, it was jarring and shaming in equal measure to find that her principal reaction was one of pity.

"You fucking idiot, Alwyn." She regarded me with an expression rich in forlorn judgement, a parent confronted by a disappointing child who refuses to learn any lessons. "I gave you the means to end this months ago."

"I couldn't." I fought the urge to lower my gaze and shuffle my feet. "Not then."

I watched her bite back more words before letting out a thin sigh and crossing her arms as she surveyed the cluster of moss-covered ruins she chose for this meeting. Young Falko and his kin had been true to their word and guided us along a quiet and uninterrupted course until we came within a few miles of Ambriside. I decided not to risk simply presenting myself at the castle. These days were far too uncertain for such boldness. Instead, I had Tiler don churlish garb and go on ahead to deliver a surreptitious message to Captain Dervan. As Lorine's most trustworthy soldier, I reckoned him the most likely conduit to the duchess's notice. We were obliged to wait three days for a reply, one of the Chosen Company riders appearing with a terse note instructing me to come alone to a place both Lorine and I knew well.

"I thought another band might've moved in by now," she said, eyes tracking over the ancient stones. "Always made such a comfortable hideout."

"They think it's haunted," I explained, relating something Falko had told me upon receiving her message. "Deckin's ghost roams far in the Shavine Forest, so they say, but lingers nowhere so much as here."

"Ghost." Lorine let out a laugh, soft and sad. "You'd think he'd do me the courtesy of a visit once in a while."

"He'd be proud of you if he did."

Lorine turned back to me with a thin smile. "Flatter me all you want, Alwyn. It doesn't lessen the scale of your cock-up." She advanced on me, an angry glint in her eye, finger stabbing at my chest. "You were supposed to kill the mad bitch with that poison I gave you, or wasn't that clear?"

"Could you have killed Deckin?"

That brought her up short, her finger pausing in mid-poke as it pressed into my jerkin. For a moment I thought she might slap me, but, after a short bout of glowering, she lowered her arm. "Her divinely conceived child *is* yours, I assume? Or was she fucking the whole Covenant Host?"

I swallowed a flurry of profane retorts. Antagonising her further would avail me nothing. Besides, considering my many misjudgements, a modicum of chastisement was due. "Yes, the child's mine, and I intend to claim it."

"Folly upon folly." Lorine threw up her hands and began to pace the ground. "This is what you come to my door with?"

"I come to you in the hope that you'll see the danger she poses."

Lorine snorted a scathing laugh. "I believe I did. Long before you, in fact."

"I mean the true danger. You look at her and see an insane tyrant, but she is more than that. The power she holds comes from the darkest source. If she takes this realm, no soul will be safe from the storm she'll unleash. Not a churl, a knight, a duchess, or an infant lord."

Her face tightened, my barb striking home. She could abide many things, but not a threat to her child. "And how do you know this?" she asked, some of the anger leached from her tone.

"I travelled far and saw a great deal, as I told you." I hesitated. Being a pragmatist in all things, Lorine had never had much truck with matters ethereal or arcane. "In the Caerith lands there are . . . people, places with power. Places where the past can be seen . . ."

"Oh, you had a vision, did you?" Her expression, vaguely amused but mostly appalled, made it plain I was wasting my time. "Forgive me. For a moment I thought you were about to present me with some actual evidence. Little did I suspect you'd been granted some otherworldly insight by a bunch of savages. Did they ask you to drink something first, perhaps? Snort some mysterious powder?"

"They aren't savages." I gritted teeth to quell my ire. "They are a people of ancient lore and custom, and, unlike us, wisdom too. They remember what we have forgotten. What they showed me was real. As real as you and I in this moment . . ."

"It doesn't matter, Alwyn!" She rounded on me, eyes blazing. "I can't deal in visions, real or not. I must deal the cards as they fall, for my son's sake. For the sake of everyone in this duchy who looks to me for protection." She paused, drawing in a long, calming breath. "I'm sorry, but you don't have the winning hand. I'll keep my soldiers away from battle as long as I can, but I've already received a summons from both the Ascendant Queen and the princess regent." She forced a smile, sorrowful but also sympathetic. "You were right. Before the year's out, Evadine Courlain will be the unquestioned Queen of Albermaine."

She moved back to me, clutching my hands in hers. "If I thought you would, I'd beg you to flee. Get to a port and find the fastest ship you can. Don't come back, though it pains me to think I'll never see your idiot face again. But you won't, will you?" She came closer, head lowered to press against my chest. "The answer's no, by the way," she said, voice hoarse. Stepping back, she raised moistened eyes to meet mine. "I could never have killed Deckin, no matter how mad he got."

She reached to the belt of her riding coat and unhooked a hefty purse. "For your war chest," she said, handing it to me. Opening it, I blinked at the yellow gleam. Further inspection revealed a purse containing a dozen gold sovereigns, more wealth than I had ever held in my hands. "I called in some loans," Lorine added, palming the tears from her eyes.

"My thanks, Duchess," I said, pulling the purse's ties tight.

"For what? I never gave you anything. In fact, this meeting never took place."

"Yet still." I bowed with formal correctness. "I thank you."

She nodded, for a moment all poise deserted her and her features bunched, cheeks reddening and fresh tears brimming her eyes. But it was a flicker of weakness only, gone in a trice. Her parting words were brisk, matching her stride as she walked away. "I've no more poison for you. So, if she's takes you alive, you'll have to make your own arrangements."

Chapter Nineteen

The borderlands between the Shavine Marches and the Cordwain bore several names. The Scrapes was the most common term, but I had also heard them referred to as the Crags, the Cuts and the Scars. All fitting names for this dense maze of deep ravines, wide gorges and steep-sided tors, all overgrown with dwarf pines and wild, impassable hedges. I had seen the Scrapes from a distance but never traversed it. After only one day's experience of the place I fully understood the description I once heard from Deckin's lips: "Never did I see land that was more an arse ache to travel. A graveyard for outlaw band and army alike."

I knew from Sihlda's history lessons that the region had in fact seen several military campaigns descend into ruinous chaos. In the distant days before the Algathinet dynasty, successive Shavine warlords had sought to lay claim to the Cordwain with its wealthy ports and verdant farmland, only to find their ambitions thwarted thanks more to terrain than battlefield defeat. An army seeking to traverse such ground would find its march grinding to a crawl. I now understood why the Cordwain had remained an independent duchy despite its avaricious southern neighbour.

The Scrapes stretched across the north of the Shavine Marches for near eighty miles west to east, its oddly beautiful complexity broken only by the winding course of the Durrine River. This waterway presented a formidable barrier in its own right, deep and fast with few natural crossings created by the numerous rocks that constricted its flow into a constant churn.

"It's a smugglers' route, Captain," young Falko explained, having led us to what he promised was the most secluded crossing point. At first glance I saw no clear way to the northern bank, seeing only a frothing stretch of rapids interrupted by a few jutting boulders. "One of my cousin Relko's favourites."

"So you've crossed here yourself?" Wilhum asked him.

"Can't say as I have, m'lord. But I seen it done." Falko showed crooked teeth in what I assumed to be an attempt at an encouraging smile. "Safer than it looks. There's stones under the water that offer firm footing, y'see, for horse as well as folk. No use in a smugglers' trail that a pack horse can't ford."

"Firm footing, eh?" Wilhum studied the busy river with a deepening frown. "I think I'll watch you do it first, my young friend. If you don't mind."

Falko nodded and set off with a creditable absence of dithering, wading his way across a seemingly deadly flow a good thirty paces wide. I heard Tiler and some of the scouts exchange muttered wagers on whether the lad would be swept away, but at no point did his feet descend into the water further than his knees. Sloshing free of the river, he scaled the far bank before disappearing into dense foliage. I expected him to reappear shortly, waving a signal that the way was clear, but he didn't.

"Could be he's finally had enough of the soldier's life," Wilhum suggested.

I spared a glance for Falko's kin, seeing increasing agitation as they murmured among themselves. If their boyish clan leader had intended to desert our cause, he hadn't shared it with them. Besides, the few weeks I'd spent in his company left me in little doubt of his commitment to vengeance.

"I don't think so," I said, turning and beckoning Tiler forward. "Bring your crossbow."

"Better if I go," Wilhum said, stepping into my path when I started towards the river. "No way of knowing what's waiting over there. We can't risk our valiant captain."

"Every day is a risk now." I tried to push past but he remained firmly in place.

"This lot follow you," he said, dropping his voice and inclining his head at our minuscule army. "Not me. If I fall, it doesn't matter."

"He's right, Captain," Tiler said, stepping to Wilhum's side. Scanning the flat resolve on their faces, I let out a sigh.

"All right," I said. "But get back here sharpish if there's any trouble. We'll find another way across."

I called Juhlina and a dozen more to my side as Wilhum and Tiler made their way to the far bank. They paused at the treeline, Wilhum drawing his sword and Tiler priming the crossbow, then they slipped into the shadowy green wall. I saw and heard nothing for a long count, long enough to make me debate the wisdom of leading the rest of the company over in a rush. Then I heard it, the distinct and familiar echoing of ringing steel.

Cursing, I surged into the river with Juhlina and the rest following. The wiser course would have been to fade back into the forest, since we could soon find ourselves facing a whole company of Evadine's troops. But there was no hesitancy to this act; leaving them behind was simply unthinkable. Splashing through the flow at the run, not without a wince or two from my still aching hip, I scrambled on to the bank. The clang of clashing swords grew louder and more violent now, causing me to draw my own blade and charge into the bushes without waiting for my comrades to catch up.

I came upon Tiler first, standing in twitchy indecision with his crossbow half raised. Falko crouched beside him, unhurt as far as I could tell, though he held his long dagger clutched tight. Beyond them two figures fought in a whirl of swordplay, blades flashing with a fluent ferocity that only the knightly class could produce. The contest ranged across a patch of leafy ground bordered by the steep granite tors that were so common to the Scrapes. I saw a score of figures standing atop the tors, dark silhouettes broken by jutting sword hilts or spearpoints. A few held bows, though none were drawn.

"He told us to stay out of it, Captain," Tiler said, face dark with chagrin. "Said it was a private matter."

A yell drew my gaze back to the two contestants, seeing Wilhum sidestep a thrust to allow me a clear view of his opponent. Desmena

Lehville had lost her fine blue enamelled armour somewhere since our last meeting. The former herald to the Pretender was clad now in hardy but somewhat ragged leather and cotton garb. Her once bobbed honey blonde hair had grown, tied into a tight braid that whipped about as she continued her deadly dance with Wilhum. The comeliness that I noted in her features at our last meeting was gone too, her face rendered ugly by a snarl that mingled contempt with hatred. Wilhum's handsomeness was similarly dimmed by his own furious visage, set in a dark glower as he fended off a flurry of strokes and replied with a thrust to Desmena's midriff. She parried the stabbing blade and whirled, bringing her sword around in a swift arc, angled as to lop Wilhum's head from his shoulders. He ducked it with scant room to spare, losing a few hairs from the crown of his head in the process.

"Stop this!" I shouted, striding towards them. As is often the way with those lost to the frenzy of combat, they didn't hear me, or didn't care if they had.

Wilhum batted aside Desmena's next slash at his legs then lunged, attempting to drive his shoulder into her chest and send her sprawling. She was ready for him, however, twisting aside and trapping his sword arm under her own before delivering a headbutt to his nose. Wilhum shook off the pain and replied with a punch to Desmena's jaw, the impact enough to loosen her grip. Seizing his chance, Wilhum kicked her legs from under her, raising his sword for a killing stroke.

"Enough!" Steel rang as Wilhum's descending blade met mine. He rounded on me, his face that of a man lost to anger, eyes wild and blood streaming from his nose.

"Finish it," Desmena gasped from the ground, staring up at Wilhum with undimmed hatred. "You fucking coward!"

Eager to comply, Wilhum began to raise his sword again then shouted in frustration when I grabbed hold of his forearm. "I said enough," I said, pushing him back. He tensed, still primed for killing, and might well have turned his fury upon me if the ominous creak of drawn bow staves hadn't drawn our eyes to the figures above. The archers among them bore ash longbows, a common poacher's weapon in the Cordwain and notoriously difficult to master due to the strength required to bend the thick stave. From the unwavering stance of these archers, I deduced them all to be masters of their craft and therefore highly unlikely to miss at such range.

"Hold!" Desmena shouted, huffing as she got to her feet. She spared me a baleful glance before raising her head to call out another command. "This matter isn't settled, and I told you buggers not to interfere." Turning back to me, she levelled her sword at my face. "I know the service you did the True King in his final days, Scribe, so I've a mind to spare you. But this one—" her sword swung towards Wilhum "—deserves no mercy."

"Nor do I ask it," Wilhum spat back, his defiance rendered slightly comical by the nasal tone in which it was delivered.

Seeing them crouch in readiness for renewed violence, I placed myself between them, keeping my sword lowered. "Life on the run is hard, isn't it?" I asked Desmena, adopting an air of sombre conversation as I allowed my eye to rove her ragged garb. "And you've been at it longer than I. Wouldn't you rather rest a while?"

"I'll rest when this fucker's dead," she grunted, shifting to the side and forcing me to move to keep myself betwixt them.

"Hardly the language of a countess," I observed. "If you still lay claim to such a title."

Her brow furrowed as her focus fixed on me. "I claim all that was due to the True King. An oath we've all taken."

"And how does this fulfil your oath?" I jerked my head at Wilhum. "Petty vendetta was not Magnis Lochlain's way, and I fancy I knew him well before the end."

Desmena's features bunched in suppressed grief, a certain needful glint shining in her eyes. "You were there," she said. "You saw him die."

"I did. And you know it was I who took his testament. He had a great deal to say, some of it about you." I slid my sword into its scabbard, resting my hands on my belt. "Agree to a parley and I'll tell you all about it."

Desmena's band, a thirty-strong group comprising all that remained of the once mighty Pretender's Horde, had established a stronghold of sorts atop a large, steep-flanked tor a mile north of the river. In truth, it was more a miniature plateau, affording clear views of the approaches while its thick covering of pine and bush hid the rebels' stockade from prying eyes. They were a disparate group. Among those that gathered to encircle us I saw a handful of minor nobles rubbing shoulders with churls. There were also a few hired blades who had forsaken their mercenary inclinations. I knew well that Lochlain had enjoyed a facility for changing folk, steering those of base character to a higher calling, real or imagined. I also knew that Desmena's love for her fallen True King was matched only by her animus towards Wilhum.

She allowed only myself and Tiler into her stronghold. I briefly considered asking Ayin to join us, perhaps she could leaven the thickened atmosphere with song. But she remained as miserably silent as ever and I doubted our host would be receptive in any case.

"A cunning construction," I complimented Desmena, casting an eye over the wooden walls of her holdfast, each carefully arranged among the rocks and trees as to be nigh invisible from outside.

"There are those among us who depend on concealment for a living," she replied, I assumed in reference to the longbow-bearing poachers. "And skilled carpenters too."

"How long have you been here?"

Her brow creased with irritated impatience. It was clear the woman of affable charm I had met on the eve of battle was gone now. Life as a fugitive often has a hardening effect, day after day of constant threat tends to strip a soul down to its essentials. "Long enough, Scribe," she snapped. "And I didn't bring you here to win your approval or bandy gossip. You have a tale for me, and I'll hear it now."

I inclined my head to a stack of brandy barrels nearby. "In which case, I'll trouble you for some refreshment, for this tale is long."

I was permitted only one cup of brandy when I began my recitation of the Pretender's testament. But, as the story continued, more were provided as my audience settled into rapt and, I fancy, appreciative attentiveness. To be a scribe is to be a storyteller, as words written on a page should be as easy to follow as when they are spoken. I thought about making some modifications to Lochlain's story, omitting episodes that revealed him as the flawed human being he had been rather than the self-sacrificing hero these folk imagined. But I didn't. As far as my facility for detecting lies could tell, he had told me his story without recourse to falsity, laying bare memories that were painful as well as damning. He had committed base murder during his time as a hired blade in the eastern kingdoms. He had been a thief and a fraudster. He had married three times and abandoned each wife, in one case leaving a child behind.

"The child's name?" Desmena asked, so far her only interruption.

"He didn't say. In truth, I don't think he knew her name, having taken to his heels the night of her birth."

She lowered her gaze. The hour had grown late and the light of the fire we sat beside painted her bruises and swollen jaw in garish hues. "That is not the act of the man I knew." I heard no accusation in her voice, just a grim disappointment.

"Because the man you knew was not that man," I said. "As he grew older the more his past misdeeds pained him. 'There is much I wanted to atone for, Scribe,' he told me. 'When I took the throne, I would have sent for my child, if she could be found. I would have made her a princess.'" I drained my cup and held it out to be refilled by the dagger man who had charge of the barrel.

I paused to take a sip, savouring the burn on my tongue. This was good stuff. "Sometimes," I went on, "I think his rebellion was one grand act of atonement. An attempt to depart the world a better man. He told me the tale of when it all began, one miserable rainy day at a village in the eastern Rhianvel borderlands. Lochlain had come west with a small mercenary band, hoping to earn coin in the local dispute between Rhianvel and Althiene. At the village he found an old man being flogged to death by the local lord for failing to pay rents. Lochlain said it was the old man's cries that stirred him to act, for he didn't beg for his life, but the lives of his family. 'And that fat noble just laughed, Scribe,' he said. 'Just laughed and kept swinging the whip.' He killed the lord and freed the old man, but it was too late. He died in Lochlain's arms. Naturally, the lord's kin came in search of justice. The old man's village rose in support of the heroic warrior from the east and so began the first step on the road to the Pretender's Revolt."

I drained another two cups of brandy before the bulk of the tale was told, relating Lochlain's proclamation of his claim to the throne by right of blood. I noted Desmena's attempt to conceal her surprise that this claim had in fact possessed a nugget of truth. I went on to describe how disaffected churls from Rhianvel, Althiene, and later Alberis, flocked to the Pretender's banner, leading to his first battles proper with the Algathinets. The following years saw the tide of success ebb and flow with the seasons. A harsh winter saw his horde dwindle only to swell come the spring.

"But always," I said, setting my cup down for I would need unclouded wits for what came next, "victory eluded him and he realised that to win Albermaine his promise of a better future must be extended beyond the commons to the nobility. Which brings us to you, my lady, and your brother."

Desmena's face betrayed a small twitch of emotion, but she said nothing as I continued. "Lochlain said this of you both: 'Never was I blessed with two more faithful lieutenants. One all kindness and selfless generosity, but with the courage of a lion in battle. The other with the skills of the most fearsome knight, and the keenest mind hidden behind a mask of beauty. And they believed, Scribe. They believed in the rightness of our cause. Had I a hundred like them, it would be me ordering the gallows built this day.' It grieved him when your brother fell, for he sensed that this one loss had doomed him. 'A king rises or falls not on his own merits, but on the merits of those who swear him fealty. From that day on, the True King's Host knew only defeat.'"

Desmena's jaw bunched and I saw her throat constrict as she blinked, averting her eyes. "That . . ." She swallowed again. "That sounds like him, to be sure." Taking a deeper breath, she faced me. Although tears trickled down her face, her expression was hard now, implacable. "Did he tell you how my brother died?"

"I heard the tale from Wilhum . . ." A harsh, grating laugh cut my words short, Desmena leaning forward to hiss at me.

"An ambush in the Althiene mountains, yes? An unfortunate mischance in the chaos of war. That's what he told you? Did that faithless coward tell you he rode away and left my brother to die?"

"He told me Aldric broke his neck in a fall from his horse," I said, my voice flat for I sensed the outcome of this meeting was now finely balanced. "He told me Magnis Lochlain had to drag him clear of the fight else he would have joined him in death. Sometimes, I think he wishes he had."

"A tale he likes to tell, I'm sure. But I have more than one score to settle on his account. It was his family who strung my father up like a common outlaw."

"Is a child not innocent of his family's crimes?"

"Innocent? When it comes to my father's fate, I know he is not." Desmena fell silent, head lowered and features tensing with both memory and contained rage. I also saw a perturbed crease to her brow, one that made me wonder if she fully believed in the source of her own enmity. If so, she was unwilling to disclose it now.

I let her wallow in introspection for a moment before speaking on, keeping to the same neutral tone. "All I can say is that I have no doubt as to Wilhum's love for your brother. I know he gave up all claim to his family's lands and titles to follow the man he loved into the True King's service, and that he still grieves for what he lost. I also know he's my friend, one who has risked all to save my life and therefore I'll risk mine for him. Make no mistake, my lady, to get to Wilhum, you will have to kill me and all who follow me."

Desmena's expression tightened further and I felt it best not to allow her time to voice any counter-threats.

"But," I went on swiftly, "if you have an inkling of what has occurred beyond this refuge, you will know that the time for personal feuds is over, or it should be. We have far more grave matters to address."

"Your Risen Martyr crowned herself queen and you tried to kill her," Desmena said. "Yes, we heard. I assume your treachery was bought with Algathinet gold?"

"Your assumption is wrong."

The heat in my words caused a ripple of unease in the encircled audience, although Desmena reacted with a satisfied grin. "No, I thought it unlikely," she said. "It must have been hard, raising your sword against the woman you love. Tell me, is she truly pregnant with a child conceived through the Seraphiles' blessing?"

"It's true that she's pregnant."

Desmena let out a disgusted laugh, shaking her head. Thankfully, she didn't feel obligated to point out the obvious conclusion. "So, Scribe, you ask me to set aside just grievance for the sake of your own cause. A cause not our own."

"It is your cause. Justice was the True King's mission, was it not? He spent his life trying to bring an end to tyranny, and tyranny is the least of what the Ascendant Queen has to offer." I got to my feet, turning to address all of Desmena's band. "Do you think this is what the True King would have wanted? His best and most loyal soldiers skulking in the wilds like common outlaws?"

"You may have taken his testament, Scribe," Desmena said. "That doesn't mean you speak in his name."

"You're right, it doesn't. But then, who does? You hide here and do nothing while chaos and slaughter rule this land. Lochlain would not have hidden at a time like this. This I know."

An angry murmur rose from the band then, one I was glad to hear. Anger was good. Anger is a spur to action. Also, I saw more than a few shamed expressions among the circle of faces. My barbs had been well chosen.

"What would you have us do?" the dagger man demanded. "Sell ourselves to you? Your army is pitiful."

"Our numbers are small, yes," I conceded. "But will grow in concert with the Ascendant Queen's cruelty. And hers is not the only army in this realm. The King's Host will soon join with the Duke of the Cordwain. I know many of you will not abide an alliance with the Algathinets, but I ask you to set aside your hatred for the sake of a greater purpose, as the True King would have done."

Their reaction was not what I expected. I knew this lot would not be won over with a few words and allusions to the greatness of their fallen leader. In truth, the most I could hope for was to recruit one or two and negotiate safe passage without further violence. Yet, instead of argument I received puzzlement, the array of faces exchanged bemused glances, a couple even smirking.

"So," Desmena said. "You haven't heard."

"Heard what?"

"The combined forces of the Crown and the Cordwain met the Ascendant Queen's Host in battle four days ago. They were utterly defeated. Duke Lohrent was killed and his son has retreated to Castle Norwind. Rumours fly about the fate of the king and his mother, but it's widely held that they fled north, perhaps hoping to seek refuge in the Fjord Geld. In any case, your war is already over, Scribe. Evadine Courlain is now the uncontested monarch of this realm."

Chapter Twenty

The aftermath of a battle is never a pleasant sight, but usually, the ugliness lingers only for a day or two. The corpses of nobles or men-at-arms will be carried off by comrades or kin for burial. Common levies were typically interred in a mass grave while local churls could always be counted on to scour the field clear of weapons and the myriad detritus that proliferates in the wake of slaughter. Not so the site of the Ascendant Queen's triumph over the Algathinets. Here the dead lay where they fell, stripped of arms and valuables then left to rot. Consequently, the stink of the place reached us long before it came into view.

Reining Blackfoot to a halt atop a low rise, I was able to gauge the course of the struggle from the position of the bodies. About a hundred were spread out in a wavering line from west to east, where the number of dead swelled to create a ghastly mound. The general absence of crows or other scavengers indicated the easiest meat had already been picked clean. The bulk of the corpses were strewn or clumped together in a curving northward procession which ended near the summit of a tall hill known locally as the Crest. Accordingly, the name used most often by scholars when recording this event would be the Battle of the Crest.

"Met them in the base of the valley," Wilhum mused as he surveyed the scene with a grimace of professional disdain. "Didn't guard their left flank well enough. I'd guess Duke Viruhlis led the charge with his knights, smashed a way through. After that, the outcome was never in doubt." He nodded to the corpse-strewn hill to the north.

"They should've stayed up there, forced Evadine to advance up the slope. Whoever Leannor put in charge of this farce deserves to hang, if he's still alive."

"I'd wager she put herself in charge," I said. "She never was one for tactics."

"I'd have thought she'd put her host in Ehlbert's hands, or Lord Altheric."

"Ehlbert's a fighter, not a general. And Lord Altheric's cachet is most likely exhausted after his failure to capture his daughter. Leannor probably suspects his loyalties."

"Must be over a thousand dead," Juhlina commented, voice muted by the rag she held to her nose against the stench.

"Twelve hundred and fifty-six," Ayin said, drawing surprised glances from all present. Apart from a quiet mutter of negation whenever I tried to rouse her to speak, these were the first words we had heard from her lips since Couravel. "So far as I can see," she added.

I didn't push her, but resolved to elicit more when we camped that night. "A grievous toll," I said. "But not so great as to rob Leannor of her host."

"This isn't all of it," Desmena said. To my surprise, it had been easy to persuade her to lead us to this site, albeit at the cost of two golds from Lorine's purse and all the spare horses Tiler had stolen in Alberis. She accompanied us with her full company of diehards, maintaining a watchful silence throughout the journey. As a condition of handing over the gold, I had made her swear not to renew her duel with Wilhum. It was an obligation I also imposed on him, much to his annoyance.

"Don't be fooled by her supposed devotion to a dead pretender," he warned me. "She has always put her own ambitions above all."

The first heads we found were arrayed on stakes running along the crest of the hill. Over fifty in all, each one with the word 'heretic' carved into their foreheads. The brown flakes of dried skin covering each gaping, empty-eyed face made it plain this torment had been inflicted before decapitation.

"I know this one from Highsahl," Tiler said, peering at one of the heads. "A knight from the Crown Company."

"How can you tell?" Juhlina asked, grimacing at the ragged, crow-pecked flesh.

"This." Tiler prised the head's mouth open to pluck something shiny from the upper jaw. "He won't need it, will he?" he said, ignoring Juhlina's disapproving scowl as he consigned the gold tooth to his purse.

"It seems they got lazy after this," Wilhum observed, surveying the gently sloping flank of the hill's north side. I detected a small quaver beneath the forced humour of his tone. Good people will resort to flippancy when confronted with sights that should have sent them screaming.

Many more heads lay in a mound, the bodies in a less orderly pile close by. I was grateful for the days that had passed since this outrage, for the whole field would surely have been swarmed by flies when the meat was still fresh. The carnage became more chaotic further down the slope, decapitation giving way to swift murder, many of the slain lying face down, their throats cut and hands tied behind their backs. The sprawl of corpses continued for more than a mile, tracing over the undulating fields in a parade of massacre.

"Stop counting," I told Ayin, seeing her scanning the scene with a familiar frown of concentration on her brow. Her lack of shock or distress troubled me, looking upon this field of horrors with an expression that betrayed only vague interest. Besides, I didn't need a full accounting to know that the bulk of Leannor's forces had met their end in the rout after the battle. It was common for the victors to pursue the vanquished, slaking the bloodlust of combat in cutting down the fleeing foe. However, there was a clear method to these killings that told of something beyond a vengeful frenzy. Most of these soldiers had surrendered, casting their arms away to seek quarter. Evadine had forbidden the Covenant Company from partaking in the slaughter after the Traitors' Field. Now she had no further use for such scruples.

"Alwyn," Wilhum said, drawing my eye to a singular atrocity. This body had been affixed to a cartwheel suspended from a hastily constructed scaffold. It hung, naked, streaked in blood and ordure, head sagging on to a chest of greying, chilled flesh. Moving closer, I saw a few cuts and plentiful bruises on the corpse, but nothing that would have constituted a fatal wound. *Spared torture but hung up to bear witness to all this*, I surmised, staring up at the bleached face of Altheric Courlain.

"Can't say I ever liked you, my lord," I told him in a grim mutter. "But you deserved a better end than this."

I was unable to contain a startled gasp when the former knight marshal of the King's Host opened his eyes to regard me with a gaze as rich in judgement as it was pain. He tried to say something, but it emerged as a croak. Still, I was able to catch some intelligible words as we cut him down.

"Our fault . . . Scribe . . ." A foul stench gusted from his throat. "Yours and . . . mine . . . Our fault . . ."

Lord Altheric lasted through the night until the first glimmer of dawn. We bore him away from the battlefield, camping amid a patch of woodland a mile north. Wrapped in blankets, I had him propped against a tree and went about lighting a fire while he drifted in and out of sensibility. He managed to drink only a small portion of the water we poured into his mouth, his body convulsing in a manner that made it clear it was beyond saving. After seeing him suffer for an hour or more, I told Ayin to leave off holding the canteen to his lips.

"I will have private words with his lordship," I said. Alone at the fire, I watched Evadine's father slump into sleep, fully expecting to see the laboured rise and fall of his chest cease at any moment. But, once again he surprised me, jerking awake to spend a few moments gazing at his surroundings in bleary incomprehension. Then the memories flooded back and he shuddered, a plaintive sob escaping his lips.

"Are . . ." he began, voice a grating, faltering thing so different from the knight who had called out commands on so many battlefields. "Are . . . you proud of . . . what you've done, Scribe?"

"No, my lord," I said in flat, simple honesty. "I am not."

"Good . . . you shouldn't be. But then—" he raised his head, cracked lips drawing back from his teeth in a parody of a smile "—neither should . . . I, eh? It was us, after all. You . . . and me. We made her into . . ." He tensed, biting down a scream. "Into a woman who . . . would do this to her own father."

"I didn't make her a monster," I said. "I didn't set frauds and mystics to torment a child beset by visions not of her choosing."

"I'll accept . . . my burden of guilt, Scribe. But yours is greater . . . I did what I thought was right. It was a grave mistake. But it is not an easy thing . . . to hear your child speak things she shouldn't know. Things no soul should know. Had her mother lived . . ." His eyes dimmed in weary despair for a second then flared into sudden anger. "But still, your crime is worse. I sought to contain her visions. You fed them. You . . . made her a queen. Now see what she does . . . with her kingdom."

I forced my eyes not to stray from the fierce accusation in his gaze. It was the least of what I was due. Nor did I seek to deny his judgement. The battlefield and its stink, stinging the nostrils even at this distance, were testament to all my machinations on Evadine's behalf. I was and remain guilty of the most terrible crimes, and never will I be done with paying the toll.

"I need to know how it started," I said. "How her visions began."

Altheric's blanketed form shifted in a tremulous shrug. "Nightmares, or so I thought. She would . . . rave in her bed. Let out the most terrible screams, but also . . . words. Sometimes I knew them, sometimes . . . she spoke in languages she had never heard. But I had. My father . . . was King Arthin's ambassador to the court of the Saluhtan of Ishtakar . . . so I learned the eastern tongue at a young age. And one night . . . I heard my daughter speak in that tongue. She spoke of knives wielded in the dark . . . of sons murdered by a deranged father. She spoke of the great throne room in Ishtakar . . . drenched in the blood of its ruler's kin. I wanted to believe it just another . . . nightmare. Told myself she had overheard me speaking the eastern tongue . . . concocted her dream from stories I told of my youth. But . . . weeks later, word reached us that Saluhtan Alkad had purged his own family . . . all his sons slain by his order in a single night."

I knew this story well, both from Sihlda and, in more detail, from Lochlain, who had been a mercenary in Ishtakar shortly before the infamous palace massacre.

"You knew," I said when Altheric lapsed into silence, the light in his eyes dimming. "You knew her visions were real."

"Some things . . . cannot be borne, Scribe." He jerked; face contorted as he sought to force vehemence into his words. "My daughter . . . could not be a witch, or a seer, or . . . anything other than the kind, beautiful girl she was supposed to be. I owed her mother that! I owed Evadine that, even if she hated me for it!"

He subsided into huddled exhaustion, a shrunken remnant of a once renowned warrior awaiting the release of death. I should have pitied him, but found sentiment beyond me.

"Perhaps it would have been different," I said, speaking more to myself than to him. "Had she not been tormented. Perhaps the Malecite might not have claimed her. Or, she was theirs from the start and it made no difference. I doubt we'll ever know."

Altheric gave a weak cough and slumped to his side, the blanket falling away to reveal his weakly labouring chest with its many bruises. Rising, I helped him to sit up, pulling the blanket tighter about his torso. "She wept, you know," he murmured, voice small now, a whisper of acrid air from barely moving lips. I crouched at his side and leaned closer, straining to hear. "She wept . . . as they strung me up . . . as her mob slaughtered my soldiers. She wept."

A tremor ran through him and a final, glaring light shone in the gaze Lord Altheric Courlain turned upon me. "Swear, Scribe!" he demanded, voice filled with all the lordly authority he could muster. "Swear that you will rescue my grandchild from her clutches!" A hand darted from under the blanket to grip mine, his eyes both implacable and pleading. "Swear it!"

"I so swear, my lord." I returned his grip, staring into his eyes and seeing a small glimmer of gratitude before they rolled back into his skull and he collapsed into my arms. Come the dawn, we buried him in the forest beneath the branches of an old oak. I marked the trunk with a small x in case I should one day return and provide Sir Altheric with a more fitting grave.

"I'd say a few hundred horse." Tiler palmed soil from his hands as he rose from inspecting the tracks marking the ground a mile north of the battle site. "A smaller number of foot trailing behind. Heading north-west, so I'd guess this'll be the Cordwainers making all haste to Castle Norwind, what's left of 'em. Strange there's no sign of a pursuit, though."

"She needs to capture the king and his mother," I said. "Subduing the Cordwain can wait."

"Makes our choice easy, at least," Desmena said. "If it's a war you want, Scribe, the only vestige of an army to be had is at Castle Norwind. Might take weeks for the queen's host to hunt down the royal party. Months even. I saw the True King gather thousands to his banner in less time."

"*Our* choice?" Wilhum asked her with a pointed smirk, earning a baleful glower in response.

"We need the Algathinets," I said, causing Desmena to turn her darkened gaze upon me.

"For what?" she demanded. "That vile dynasty ended on a bloody field miles back."

"A kingdom needs a monarch, a royal banner to rally behind. Your True King knew that. How far do you imagine his rebellion would have gotten if he hadn't claimed royal blood? Algathinet blood at that."

"Saving what's left of the royal brood is not what my company followed you for."

"Then why did you? If it wasn't for two gold sovereigns and a string of horses, what was it?" We matched stares for an uncomfortable moment until Wilhum consented to break the tension.

"This all seems somewhat moot, in any case." He gestured to the surrounding country of rolling farmland. "They could have gone anywhere. Finding them is likely impossible."

I nodded to the north-east. "There. That's where we'll find them."

"That way lies the marshes," Desmena said. "Mile after mile of midge-swarmed bog, all the way to the coast."

"True. But also home to the Shrine to Martyr Lemtuel." I spurred Blackfoot to a trot, glancing back at Desmena when she failed to follow. "Come or don't, the choice is yours. But if you do, be prepared to fight to save Algathinet blood, for that is our cause now."

Despite my confidence in our destination, just a few hours traversing the marshland made it plain that finding the shrine would not be as easy as I'd hoped, dream-gifted vision or no. Fortunately, there was one among us who had been there before.

"The shrine sits atop an island of firm ground in the very middle of the marshes," Juhlina said. "But you have to work your way through a maze of causeways and smaller islets to get to it."

"You remember the route?" I enquired. Her response was not as swift as I would have liked, and tinged with uncertainty.

"I was little more than a child when the Most Favoured led us here," she said. "Of all the trials he put us through, plodding through this shite-hole was probably the worst. Although there was that time my cousin froze to death on an Althiene mountainside when we were trying to find the abandoned Shrine to Martyr Uhlbeck." Noting my impatient frown, she added, "If we can find the Knoll, I think I can guide us the rest of the way."

"The Knoll?"

"It's a trading post. The marsh folk go there to sell their eel catch and peat cuttings. Just a small settlement of a few dozen huts, but it's hard to miss once you catch sight of it." She looked around at the misted reeds and waterways before raising her gaze to the grey sky. "If we head west for a day or two, we should happen on one of the tracks that leads to the Knoll."

Two days turned into three, then four, our steps in daylight beset by swarms of voracious bugs and frequent stumbles into the green-tinged waters of the marsh. The ground, such as it was, had a tendency to deceive. Firm footing would transform into damp mush at the first touch of hoof or foot. Nights brought relief from the blood-hungry midges, but not the damp air of this place, which set many of us to coughing and made for poor sleep.

When we encamped on the fourth night, I sought out Ayin, finding her alone, as was usually the case these days. She greeted me with a tight, wary glance as I sat beside her, then turned away in apparent contemplation of a stagnant pool nearby.

"If you don't want to talk," I said, "I can't make you. But I will ask it. As your friend."

She kept her eyes averted, but I saw a shadow pass across her features before she replied in a low mutter, "Then ask."

"What happened to you in Couravel? Where is Eamond?"

Ayin said nothing at first, instead plucking a small stone from the ground and tossing it into the pool. One of the curious features of the marshes was a tendency towards cloudless skies at night, the light of the half-moon transforming into curved slivers on the pool's surface.

"We did as you said," she told me when the ripples began to fade. "Played the roles you set us, which was the easiest part of it all. There were many like us in Couravel then, the lost and beggared come to eke what living they could in the streets. Getting lost among so many was easy, but not so easy to avoid the eye of those who prey on the unfortunate. The sight of our knives dissuaded most, but not all. We hid the bodies best we could and moved on." A troubled crease appeared in her brow, her voice taking on an additional weight. "I knew Eamond had killed before, but I'd never seen him do it. You know . . ." she paused and swallowed ". . . you know what I've done. It might surprise you to hear I never enjoyed it. It was just something Mumma told me I had to do, and like all good children, I did what I was told. Eamond was different. He would get this look . . ."

Ayin trailed off and tossed another stone into the pool, this one birthing a tall splash. "I tried not to think on it," she went on. "Most of the time he was his old sweet self. And I kind've liked it. All the sneaking about, listening to other people's chatter, singing for supper come the evening. We found a tavern where they gave us room and board to have me sing each night. We got lucky there, for every few nights some folk would gather in the basement and whisper things they didn't want others to hear. We'd heard plenty of angry gossip, but this lot weren't just sharing their complaints about the king and his mother. They were plotting. They were wary of us at first, but seeing the same faces day after day wins trust and soon we found ourselves welcome at their plotting sessions."

She gave a slight, humourless laugh. "It was all silliness, their grand schemes. And they changed from day to day. At first, they were going to kidnap the boy king, somehow, get him away from his mother's evil clutches. Then they thought it would be best to kidnap Lady Ducinda instead, set her up as a queen. When they realised that wouldn't work, they decided the only thing to do would be to raise the whole city in rebellion. There were never more than two dozen people gathered in that basement, yet they convinced themselves all they had to do was daub a few slogans on walls, build a barricade and thousands would come flocking to their banner."

She fell silent again, eyes shifting from the rippling pool, her frown deepening. "There was one among them called Trench who did most of the talking. Shouted the loudest. Called for the most outlandish schemes. It only took me a day or two to make him out for what he was. Only a man with no real fear of capture would be so ardent. Eamond wasn't convinced. He liked Trench, you see. Trench was quick to quote Martyr scrolls and avowed a good deal of love for the Anointed Lady. But I knew a liar when I saw one. I think just to shut me up, Eamond agreed to follow Trench after one of the meetings. He was careful, a man who knew the streets well, but he wasn't used to being tracked by the likes of us. We followed him to another tavern, a place in the artisans' quarter where the liquor costs more, but the alleyways don't stink of shit so much. There he met another man, better dressed than most, but not so much as to draw notice. He had that look that tells you he's dangerous, even though I saw no weapon on him. They spoke only briefly, then went their separate ways. Instead of following Trench some more, we followed the well-dressed man and, sure enough, he took himself off to a small side gate in the palace walls."

"Trench was one of Leannor's spies," I said. "She has many, or used to."

Ayin nodded, her face clouding further. "I told Eamond we should just leave. Our time was getting short and we hadn't found anyone who might be of use to the Lady's cause. Those folk gathering in that basement were going to be dangling from a rope soon enough and we'd best be far gone by then. But Eamond . . . He was awful angry at Trench."

Her head dipped lower still, saying nothing until I prompted her. "Eamond killed him, didn't he?"

"Did more than that. He lured him to our room in the tavern when I wasn't there to stop him. I'd gone to the market to buy supplies for the road. When I got back . . ." She swallowed and looked up at me, face stricken. "After the Lady touched me, all the bad things I'd done seemed to fade away, like nightmares I could hardly remember. I never thought on it much, 'cause I didn't want to. When I opened the door and found Eamond with Trench, it all came back. I stood there, still as a statue, watching him cut away. I knew he looked just like I did when you kicked that shed door open back in Callintor." Her voice remained steady, but the tears streaming down her cheeks told of terrible inner pain. "I was mad, wasn't I, Alwyn? That's why you looked after me. Poor mad little girl with her oh-so sharp knife."

"I care for you because you deserve my care," I said. "Because that's what we do for those we love. Besides, there's far more blood on my pages than yours."

She squeezed her eyes shut, face bunching in misery. "I was mad, but I got better, at least I think I have. Looking at Eamond, I knew he was just as mad as I ever was. Maybe more. 'The spymaster's name?' he kept asking Trench as he cut, even though Trench was plainly dead by then. 'Tell me his name!' I told Eamond to stop, but he barely heard me. I shoved him to get his attention and he . . ." Ayin shuddered, hugging herself and slumping forward with a sob. I went to her, raising her up, holding her close.

"It's all right," I whispered. "You don't have to say any more."

She shook her head, sniffing and coughing to get the words out.

"He came for me, just like those others. The ones Mumma told me to hurt. He was raving, Alwyn. Said things I never suspected had even entered his head. Said I should be his. Said I'd been willing to whore myself to that duke's son up north. Said the Lady herself had warned him about me. Warned him that I wasn't true to the cause. That I would betray her. He hadn't wanted to believe it, but now he saw the truth."

She sagged in my arms, tears flowing freely now. I held her until the shuddering sobs faded into shallow gasps. "Why would she say that to him?" she asked me. "Why, Alwyn?"

"A vision," I sighed. "She had another fucking vision." The realisation stirred a plethora of uncomfortable questions. *How much has she seen? How far and how deep does her insight go?* I pulled Ayin closer, both for her comfort and mine, before turning her to face me. "Did you kill him?"

Ayin drew in a long breath and wiped her sleeve across her face, shaking her head. "I tried not to." She paused and winced. "I cut him, deep and bad across the face. Hoped it would be enough to get him off me. Tried to run, but he came for me again, screaming, raving, sure to draw notice. I needed to shut him up."

She subsided into weeping. To my surprise she pressed herself to me, resting her head on my chest, slender form pulsing as she sobbed. "It was clean," she whispered when her sorrow subsided. "Quick jab to the chest. I don't think he felt it much. I stood there staring at him for such a long time. My thoughts were all a jumble again, like they were before. I only remembered where I was when I smelt the smoke. Then I knew I had to run. By the time I got to the south gate, the fires were raging. I didn't really get my mind back until Juhlina found me a few days later."

I sifted through my memories of Eamond, finding mostly the earnest if occasionally incautious youth of sincere piety. But there had been moments of concern, instances where faith morphed into savagery at Walvern Castle and elsewhere. Had it all been a mask? Had he always been like Ayin used to be, keeping it hidden for months until the Ascendant Queen gave him licence to let it loose? It occurred to me that I had never asked Eamond about his time as a novice Supplicant, assuming him just one of dozens inspired by the Anointed Lady to forsake the old, venal Covenant. It was possible that he hadn't chosen to leave his shrine at all, but been cast out. It was equally possible that months of war and brutality had simply driven him mad. He certainly wouldn't be the first innocent soul twisted into monstrosity by terrible experience.

"Was it all lies, Alwyn?" Ayin asked me. She was calmer now, but her moist eyes glimmered with a forlorn entreaty. "What the Lady told us. She's not really a Martyr is she?"

"No," I said. "Quite the opposite."

"But she touched me . . ." Ayin bit down on another sob. "She made me better."

"She has a power, a way of capturing the hearts of those she meets. That's undeniable. We've seen her do good with it. I'll not deny that either. But I think it was all done to bring us to this. She wants all the world to fall to ruin. That is her object." I reached for Ayin's hands, clasping them tight. "And we have to stop her. We helped make her a queen, so it's only right we bring her down. If you're willing."

Ayin gave no answer, instead pressing a kiss to my hands before releasing her grip. Rising, she made her way to the larger fire where Quintrell sat. "Play," she said, stooping to retrieve his mandolin and pushing it into his hands. "I've a yen to sing tonight."

And sing she did. For the first time in what felt an age, I heard Ayin's song once again, one of her wordless tunes, more sorrowful but also more powerful than any she had sung before. The hum of muted conversation faded from our camp as her song drifted across the marsh. It hurts me to think of it now, for it was the one moment of unalloyed beauty I would know for quite some time.

Chapter Twenty-One

We found the Knoll the following day, guided not by to Juhlina's navigation but by the column of black smoke rising above the fog covering the northern horizon. The settlement was named for the monolithic mound of rock about which it had formed. Its smooth flanks were streaked in soot as we rode free of the mist, all the dwellings surrounding it ablaze and the ground littered with bodies. Although it seemed likely that whoever had done this was gone, I ordered the company to dismount and approach with caution, sending Desmena's band circling around to close the escape route. However, there was no one left alive in the Knoll to flee. The doors to the huts had been barred on the outside, the smoke streaming through the thatch thick with the stench of burnt meat. Those who had somehow escaped their fiery prisons had been hacked down, their blood still pooling amid mud rutted by hoof and boot.

"Every soul slaughtered," Juhlina said, casting spit on the ground. "Children too."

"Why?" Wilhum wondered, his gaze lingering on the sight of a charred body hanging half out of a window. "Punishment perhaps? A refusal to avow the Ascendant Queen's cause?"

"More base than that," I said. "Evadine can't afford witnesses to the Algathinets' end."

"These folk probably didn't even know where they are," Juhlina said.

"Even so. Whoever she sent to see to this business wasn't willing to take the risk." I strode to where Tiler was crouched in examination of the settlement's westward track.

"Forty," he told me. "Maybe more. Heading due west."

"In which case," Juhlina put in, "someone here gave them misleading directions." She nodded to the track snaking through the marsh to the north. "The shrine is that way."

"They've at least an hour's start on us, Captain," Tiler advised. "Won't be long before they realise their error."

"Then let's not tarry," I said, hurrying to mount Blackfoot.

Despite my urgency, attempting to move through marshland with any haste is a fruitless enterprise. Discomfited by the infirm ground, Blackfoot proved unwilling to rouse himself to more than a half-trot, and the other horses were even more cautious. It wasn't until late afternoon that the spire of Martyr Lemtuel's shrine resolved out of the thinning mist.

Knowing this as a place of considerable importance in the tale of Sihlda's life, I had expected more than a collection of mean, one-storey buildings with walls that hadn't seen a lick of whitewash in many seasons. The shrine itself was just a slope-roofed barn adjoining a spire that looked ready to topple over at any second. There were a few outbuildings, all fallen into disuse, and a livestock pen lacking most of its fence, not that there were any animals to keep it in. The place would have appeared absent of all life but for the thin pall of smoke wafting from the shrine's only chimney. I thought Leannor would have at least kept sufficient kingsmen around her to form a picket line, but there was nothing to bar our progress across the causeway of sunken logs.

The shrine's door opened when I reined Blackfoot to a halt on the firm ground beyond the causeway. Sir Ehlbert Bauldry had done me the courtesy of greeting us in full armour, the sheen of it indicating a good deal of recent polishing. His longsword gleamed brighter still as he twirled it before coming to a halt a dozen paces off. He said nothing, simply reversing his grip on his sword, setting the point on the earth and resting his hands on the pommel. He wore no helm and his bearded face was set in stern expectation rather than accusation.

The shuffling of feet drew my gaze to the shrine's doorway. Princess Leannor clutched the two children to her side with firm hands. Unlike Ehlbert, her expression was dark with righteous condemnation.

"I should have known she would send you, Scribe!" she called out. "Once a cut-throat, always a cut-throat!"

King Arthin, although still a boy, clearly possessed enough understanding of the circumstances to stand in regal defiance. Next to him, Lady Ducinda seemed guilelessly unperturbed, raising her small hand in a wave and smiling shyly. I returned the wave and climbed down from Blackfoot's back, provoking Lord Ehlbert to swing his sword to readiness.

"At least you've the guts to face me alone," the King's Champion grunted, settling into a fighting stance.

I ignored him and strode towards the shrine, unbuckling my sword as I did so. Ehlbert stood in perplexed indecision for a moment, then hurried to bar my path. "Hold there, villain," he said, sword point hovering just a few inches from my throat. The sound of creaking bows snapped his eyes to my rear, where I assumed Desmena's archers were training their arrows on him.

"Don't," I said, raising a hand. Fixing my gaze on Ehlbert's face, I saw to my amazement that he was genuinely afraid. I knew it wasn't on his own account, for I doubted such a thing was possible. After Tomas's death he had been reduced to a grieving shell of a man. Now, it appeared he had found others worthy of his protection.

"I would have words with the king, my lord," I said with a formal bow of my head. "If you would permit me."

Ehlbert's face continued to twitch as he stayed in place, sword as straight as a knight of his skill and strength could make it. Still, I saw a glimmer of understanding as his eyes met mine. "If you're not here for blood," he said, "why are you here?"

"To keep my word," I told him, stepping to the side before proceeding to the shrine. I knew I risked him cutting me down in mid-stride, and could have done nothing to prevent it. Yet, he didn't raise his blade against me, instead moving alongside until I came within a few feet of Princess Leannor and the children, sword poised all the while.

"Your Royal Majesty," I said, sinking to one knee and addressing my words to the boy king. "I come to honour my oath sworn before Crown and Covenant, and beg humbly that you will accept my service." That said, I raised my sheathed sword above my head in offering.

"What is this, Scribe?" Leannor demanded. "Do you play with us now? Are you so cruel?"

"Would that we had time for explanations, Majesty." I looked up, meeting her gaze, hoping she perceived the grave intent in mine. Her attire and bearing were no longer that of a princess, one who had held sway over an entire realm. She wore a plain dress of brown wool with a shawl wrapped about her bodice. Her hair was tousled, and I saw for the first time, streaked with grey. This was just a woman scared for her life and the lives of the children she pulled closer to her side.

"But we do not," I continued. "Suffice to say that my allegiance no longer resides with the false Martyr Evadine Courlain, and I've the scars to show for it. I offer myself and my company to the king's cause. I also bring warning that our enemies draw near and we must depart this place forthwith."

Leannor simply stared at me in baffled consternation while her son harboured no such reticence. "Your service is neither wanted nor requested, traitor," he told me, face tilted to an imperious angle. "I'll have no truck with turncoat churls . . ."

"Oh, shut up, Alfric!" This crisply spoken instruction came not from the boy king's mother, but from his betrothed. Lady Ducinda twisted free of Leannor's grip and skipped towards me. "He's a nice man," she said, pressing a kiss to my cheek. "He saved me, you know. You said so yourself, Auntie," she added with a defiant pout at Leannor.

"It gladdens my heart to see you, my lady," I told the girl, bringing a flush to her cheeks.

"Get away from him!" her guardian hissed, coming forward to take Ducinda's hand, dragging her back. Until now, I had thought Leannor's attitude to the girl mostly one of basic self-interest. But the way she crouched to clutch Ducinda to her breast bespoke a deep and genuine affection.

"Majesty . . ." I began, struggling to conjure the words that might overcome her justifiable prejudice, but an urgent shout from Tiler forestalled further persuasion.

"Captain!"

Turning, I found him pointing to the befogged reed banks beyond the causeway. I saw nothing, but soon heard the muted splashes and snorts that told of a mounted party making its way through the marsh.

"We've no time to flee," I said. Rising, I fastened my sword to my belt and glanced at Ehlbert. "No hope you've a company of kingsmen hidden about the place, I suppose?"

Ehlbert's eyes narrowed as they shifted from me to the as yet unseen enemy in the mist. "The last of my knights is buried over there," he said, jerking his head in the direction of the livestock pen. He hesitated, reluctant calculation furrowing his brow until I saw decision dawn and he lowered his sword.

"How many?" he asked.

"More than we have." I nodded to Leannor and the children. "Best if you stay with them."

I strode off without waiting for an answer, calling out to Desmena. "If you've a mind to flee," I told her, "now would be the time. If not, I have need of your archers."

I expected to see the scowling, vengeful personage of Supplicant Ildette emerging from the fog on the far side of the causeway. So, it was with a welling of disappointment and regret that I beheld the sight of Captain Ofihla Barrow.

"Scribe," she said, bringing her horse to a halt. She spoke with typical gruffness, heavy brows drawn in a manner that indicated she had no more love for this outcome than did I. Behind her, riders wearing the dark armour of the Ascendant Host reined in their mounts, which pained me yet further. I saw several faces I recognised among them, some I had fought beside, others who had ridden with Wilhum. He sat mounted alongside the rest of the Free Company, positioned a decent remove from the causeway. Seeing a brief spasm of anguish pass over his features as he beheld his former comrades, I hoped he could find the resolve to fight them. Desmena's band was nowhere in sight, making the disparity in our numbers even more stark. Still, I exhibited no lack of confidence as I returned Ofihla's greeting.

"Captain. I find I lack the words to fully convey how sorry I am to see you here."

"And yet you still use ten where one will do, eh?" A grudging smile appeared on her broad, weathered face. I didn't return it.

"I thought you above murder," I said. "The murder of children, in fact. It was you who burned the Knoll, I assume?"

Ofihla stiffened, jaw clenching. "I did the queen's bidding. As I am sworn to do. As are you, my lord."

"An oath does not bind me to murder, especially one given to a false Martyr. Where in the scrolls is it written that the slaughter of innocents can ever be sanctioned?"

The captain's visage darkened, an angry murmur rising from the soldiers at her back. Swords scraped from sheaths as they readied themselves. Any faint hope I harboured that prior comradeship would give them pause faded quickly in the face of their mounting rage. Evadine's hold on those who chose to stay in her service had evidently grown to the point where once good folk were now willing to massacre the defenceless in her name. The realisation stoked my own temper, Blackfoot nickering in anticipation as he sensed my mood.

"Did you cheer when she hanged Captain Swain?" I asked Ofihla. "Did you rejoice in the death of the man you followed for years?"

"Swain died begging pardon for his actions," she shot back, hefting a mace I recognised as belonging to the fallen captain. "I carry this in his honour."

I grated a harsh laugh, shaking my head. "You no longer have any honour. Can't you see that? All of you." I raised my voice to a shout, casting it at the soldiers under her command. "Evadine Courlain damned us. Our souls are forever sullied by service in her cause. Join me and at least try to cleanse yourselves before she sets you to yet more crimes."

It was a hopeless appeal, but heartfelt. If I, Ayin, Wilhum and the others could unshackle ourselves from Evadine's influence, why couldn't they?

"We live for the Lady!" they yelled back in enraged defiance, weapons stabbing the air with each phrase of this detestable chant. "We fight for the Lady! We die for the Lady!" I understood then that the Ascendant Host were all too far gone, too subsumed in what they imagined to be their queen's love to permit any hope of redemption.

"Enough talk, Scribe!" Ofihla brandished her stolen mace at me, teeth bared in a feral snarl. "Surrender the Algathinet brood and face justice for your crimes. In return, I'll promise you a swift end."

"Really?" I took a firmer hold on Blackfoot's reins, drawing my longsword and resting the blade on my shoulder. "I can't promise the same for you."

In all the time I had known her, Ofihla Barrow had been brave and skilful in battle, but never reckless. Whether it was simple rage that undid her, or the befuddling effects of such deep subservience to Evadine's influence, I couldn't say. But her charge across that causeway was the only truly foolish thing I ever saw her do. Kicking her heels hard into her charger's flanks, she came on at the gallop, marsh water rising in a white froth as horse and rider pounded across the half-sunken bridge of logs.

Letting out a whinny of challenge, Blackfoot reared, expecting me to spur us forward to meet the charge. Instead, I tugged hard on the reins, keeping us in place as Ofihla charged, her company following close behind. As instructed, Desmena's archers waited until she was halfway across before rising from their concealment amid the tall reeds fringing the banks to either side. When loosed at such close range, a shaft launched by a longbow will pierce unguarded flesh with ease, sometimes even puncture armour. Sadly, the broad-head hunting arrows used by Desmena's archers only glanced off Ofihla's plate as she closed on me. The archers did, however, manage to sink a trio of shafts deep into her charger's flanks.

The warhorse stumbled just as Ofihla was about to come within sword reach, bloody froth erupting from its mouth as it went down in a welter of crimson water. The captain rolled clear of the flailing beast before it could drag her down with it. Struggling to her feet, she let out a wordless shout of frustration and splashed towards me, then stiffened as a keen-eyed archer found the gap between her pauldron and gorget. I watched her collapse, thrashing, into the water, then turned my full attention to her oncoming comrades.

The first, a veteran I remembered from atop the walls of Walvern Castle, came at me with his mouth gaping to issue a rage-filled scream, longsword extended to thrust at my face. Fortunately, he was not so well armoured as his captain and a second volley from the longbows succeeded in felling both horse and rider before they cleared the causeway. Another stroke of luck came when this fellow's death spasms dragged on his mount's reins in such a way as to make them fall directly into the path of those charging behind. Soon the causeway became a chaos of struggling, rearing horses whipped by riders who appeared to have lost all reason. It was an irresistible target for the archers, their shafts taking a deadly toll that stained the marsh waters a yet deeper shade of red.

Despite such carnage, the bulk of Ofihla's subordinates remained unharmed on the far bank and many were not as devoid of sense as their captain. A dozen or more dismounted and started wading through the water on either side of the causeway. It was slow going and made them targets for the archers, but we had so few. Also, the crossbowmen among our foes soon recovered their wits and began to reply in kind. A shout drew my eye to the sight of a longbowman collapsing into the reeds with a bolt buried in his chest. More volleys followed, forcing our archers to take cover while the wading dismounts struggled on to firm ground.

I flinched from the angry buzz of a crossbow bolt passing within an inch of my head, then raised my sword high in the prearranged signal for our counter charge. A brief thunder of drumming hooves and Wilhum led half our number against the enemies to my left, Desmena leading the rest to the right. Swords and axes rose and fell in a frenzy, leaving a growing pile of bodies among the reed banks. Undeterred, the Covenant soldiers came on, forcing their way through the water in a dense throng. Our archers were forced back, scrambling clear of the reeds and retreating before turning to resume their barrage, taking a fearful toll before their shafts were exhausted.

At the causeway, the Covenant soldiers before me soon managed to shove the corpses of horses and comrades aside, then hurled themselves forward. I loosened my hold on Blackfoot's reins, the signal for him to rear, his hooves lashing our assailants with deadly effect. The first few were sent reeling with cracked skulls or crushed faces before Blackfoot lowered himself to trample another victim. A mounted Covenant rider saw his chance and came at me, axe raised to chop at my mount's head. I parried the descending weapon with a thrust of my longsword, then pushed deeper, angling the blade to stab into the axeman's neck. As the rider fell, dismounted soldiers mobbed me, stabbing blades like the steel teeth of a closing jaw. I hacked and slashed at every screaming face while Blackfoot reared again and again, hooves flailing.

Weight of numbers inevitably forced us back, Blackfoot suffering several cuts. None were deep enough to bring him down, but they did succeed in stoking his rage. Whirling, he began to lash out with his rear legs, succeeding in forcing our foes to retreat a few paces, but also dislodging me from the saddle. I landed hard, only just rolling clear when a soldier darted forward, slashing his falchion and receiving a hoof to the jaw as reward for his courage. Blackfoot's enraged frenzy caused him to whirl away from me, allowing me to regain my feet, but also giving my enemies a chance to renew their assault.

I drove aside a longsword thrust, elbowed its owner in the face, pivoted and hacked down a dagger man who leaped at my back. After that, much of this inglorious battle dims in my memory, becoming an ugly melange of merciless combat. I was aware of the surrounding struggle degenerating into a murderous brawl shorn of all order. I caught a glimpse of a dismounted Juhlina, her warhammer lost somewhere, repeatedly driving punches into the face of a soldier pinned beneath her knees. Another reared up behind her, hatchet raised, only to be brought down by Adlar. The juggler descending on the soldier with knives in both hands, stabbing with manic abandon.

After hacking the legs from under another enemy, I collided with a hard, unyielding figure. Snarling with the bestial animus unique to this kind of fight, I readied my longsword for a thrust and found myself face to face with Sir Ehlbert. His features were far more composed than mine, stern and purposeful, but lacking the mania of battle.

"Your pardon, Scribe," he grunted before stepping away from me, his sword blurring into a shimmering arc as he lopped the arm from a Covenant soldier. Striding on, he parried a thrust and hacked his blade deep into the attacker's shoulder, all in one fluid movement. I had seen Ehlbert in battle before, but never at such close quarters and the next few moments demonstrated in unambiguous terms how utterly foolish I had been ever to consider facing him in personal combat. The Covenant soldiers wilted around him like wheat before the scythe as he maintained a steady progress through their ranks, killing or maiming with each stroke of his longsword. Such controlled ferocity would have put many soldiers to flight, but Evadine's hold on this lot was not so easily undone. Time and again they threw themselves at Ehlbert, heedless of the doom he promised, and time and again he killed them.

Sensing a shift in the balance of this fight, I raised my sword high once more, calling out to those among our number still standing. "Rally to Sir Ehlbert!" I didn't wait to gauge the response, instead rushing to Ehlbert's side to slash down a blade that jabbed at him. Once again, sense of time and detail became lost in the red mist of combat, my awareness shrinking into a deadly focus. My longsword moved in reflexive instinct as I hacked down those I had commanded not so long ago.

It was the chill splash of water on my face that returned me to sensibility. Blinking, I found myself waist deep in the marsh, chest heaving and body beset by the ache of overworked muscles. Nearby a Covenant soldier, mercifully not one I knew, coughed out a thick torrent of blood and slipped below the surface. More bodies bobbed around me, some feathered with arrows, others hacked and leaking red blossoms into the water, some still twitching their way towards death. Not all were enemies: I spied the youthful, empty face of a Yolland floating beside a member of Desmena's band.

Guttural shouts drew my gaze to the bank where a wounded Covenant soldier crouched, encircled by Tiler and four Free Company riders. "Yield, you stupid fucker!" Tiler commanded, to which the soldier responded by lunging at him with a dagger. I turned away as a flurry of blades descended to silence the fellow's defiant cries. Ehlbert was striding back towards the shrine, sword sheathed, his work done.

Wading to the reed bank, I dragged myself free of the marsh, kneeling and trying to recover strength while I surveyed the cost of battle. I reckoned we had lost near half our number in the course of wiping out Ofihla's company. A few survivors lay on the ground, clutching wounds none among us had the skill to properly tend. I saw Falko Yolland and his kin moving from one fallen Ascendant soldier to another, looting the dead and finishing the wounded. On a different field I would have stopped them, but here I didn't. Saving those snared by Evadine's spell would avail us nothing. Henceforth, there could be no quarter given in this struggle.

Rising, I walked stiffly along the bank, taking relieved satisfaction from the sight of an unharmed Wilhum pressing a bandage to Adlar's arm. My relief deepened upon finding both Juhlina and Ayin alive. The Widow sported several livid bruises but seemed otherwise unhurt. At first I thought Ayin must have suffered a severe wound, both her arms being red from fingertip to elbow. Moving closer, I saw the besmirched dagger in her hand and realised the blood wasn't her own. Both of them were crouched at the side of a third, burlier figure in armour, the arrow jutting from a gap in her armour, jerking in concert with her diminishing breaths.

"Do it!" Ofihla grunted at Ayin, red spittle flying from her lips. "Finish it!"

"I can't." Ayin's words were a faltering whisper from a grief-choked throat. Seeing me, she blinked tears, shaking her head in apology. "I can't . . ."

"It's all right," I said, sinking down at Ofihla's side. Her broad, strong-jawed face had always been difficult to age, but, bleached to the point of marble whiteness and riven with pain, now appeared childlike.

"Do you have testament to make, Captain?" I asked her, resting a hand on her head.

"Foul me not, traitor." She jerked, but lacked the strength to escape my touch. A spasm ran through her, provoking a whimper from her lips. I watched fear vie with rage on her features, her skin growing colder with each passing second. Resilient as ever, she mastered herself with a few shallow breaths before meeting my eyes, words emerging with laboured precision now. "My testament . . . is a question . . . if you'll answer it."

"I will."

"Why?" A plaintive, needful light shone in her gaze. "Why . . . did you turn against her?"

"Why does a man cast water on a burning house? I had no choice, Captain."

"Liar . . ." She jerked again, pain overcoming strength at last. "You always . . . plotted . . . schemed. She told me. Told me . . . how her love . . . blinded her . . . Caerith witchcraft . . . she said . . ." Ofihla's words subsided into shivering agitation, her eyes dimming as the last few pulses of her heart drained the blood from her body. I saw her fight it, forcing animation into herself by sheer effort of will, although her eyes now saw nothing and the words emerged as a faint, sibilant rasp. "Toria . . . what ever became . . . of her?"

"Sailed far away to search for a famous treasure," I said. "I hope she found it."

"I would . . . have liked . . . to see her . . . again . . ."

For the next few moments I knelt and watched Captain Ofihla Barrow slip in and out of consciousness. She tried to speak again, but the words were a formless babble. Finally, all the light in her eyes gone and her features sagging, she breathed her last and lay still.

Chapter Twenty-Two

"Castle Norwind is a formidable stronghold," Ehlbert said. "But the Cordwainers suffered grievous losses at the Battle of the Crest. I doubt they have the strength to hold it against the False Queen's host, and she's sure to bring her full number to crush us once she learns we've gone there."

"Our options are few," I said. "Go north and you'll need to take a ship to the Fjord Geld to face an uncertain welcome from the Sister Queens of Ascarlia. South means many miles of territory under Evadine's control. East takes us into Rhianvel where her support is strongest. West to the Cordwain at least offers the chance of allies. Castle Norwind could also serve as a rallying point for those who oppose the Ascendant Queen's rule. Every day she spends on the throne stirs more discord, so we can expect our numbers to grow."

We convened this conference in the vestibule of the shrine, a small space that suited the diminutive size of our war council. Myself, Wilhum, and Juhlina stood while Leannor and Ehlbert sat beside the small fireplace. Our diminutive king had already made his intentions plain in a shrill tantrum before his mother packed him off to bed.

"I decree death to all traitors!" he stormed, straining in Leannor's grip as she dragged him to the room he shared with Ducinda. "I want their heads, Sir Ehlbert. You hear me? We will march immediately to Couravel and reclaim the palace. I command it!"

His exhortations ended with the slamming of the door. Leannor's brief but furious tirade was muted by the barrier, but when it opened again I caught a glimpse of the boy king huddling in chastened misery on his bed.

"For all we know," Leannor said, "the new duke of the Cordwain could already have negotiated an alliance with the False Queen. I had a sense the son was not so passionate in his antipathy towards her as his father."

"Evadine has no more use for negotiation," I said. "Should Gilferd attempt it, his most likely reward will be an invitation to kneel before the axeman."

"He didn't strike me as the wisest of men," Ehlbert said. "Fought well enough at the Crest, though, from what I saw, even after his father was cut down. The desire to avenge the old duke may work to our advantage."

"Vengeful or not, he still lacks numbers," Leannor pointed out. "As do we. You expect too much of the commons, Scribe, if you think they'll rise en masse to bring down a tyrant. Such things take years to fester, and with summer fading most will be more concerned with ensuring they've enough fuel and victuals. We can prolong this war, but winning it requires time. Much depends on whether young Duke Gilferd will even consent to open his castle to us."

I glanced at the door to the main chapel beyond which Ayin's sweet song echoed. "Oh, I think there's one among us he'll open it for."

Duke Gilferd Lambertain had aged considerably in the weeks since I had seen him last. The besotted youth who had been so fascinated by Ayin was now a tired young man of many worries. His eyes were red and sunken above high cheekbones, the hollows beneath enhancing his cadaverous aspect. He received us in the hall where his father had recently convened a feast in my honour. The retainers and lords who had attended my meeting with Duke Lohrent were mostly gone now, presumably rotting among the fallen at the Crest. All that remained were a trio of hard-faced knights, all sporting the scars of battle. I was dismayed to find the ashen-haired person of Ascendant Heilma also in attendance. Her pinched, glaring countenance was a picture of anger, save for a smug curving of the mouth. It has been my experience that the character of a fanatic is rarely enhanced by being proved right.

Our party consisted of myself, Leannor and Ayin, acting in the unlikely role of personal bodyguard to the princess regent. I took some gratification from the softening of the young duke's features upon seeing her. Also in the way his eyes lingered on the brooch I insisted she pin to her jacket.

"If he asks," I had told her when we approached the gate of Castle Norwind, "tell him you wear it every day."

This earned me a disparaging roll of her eyes. "He's not that stupid."

"My lord Duke," Leannor said now, extending her hand to Gilferd. "Please accept my thanks for your hospitality." She wore the only dress remaining to her that could lay claim to the word finery; a mourning gown of mostly black silk and cotton that suited the occasion.

Gilferd regarded her outstretched hand impassively, remaining seated for long enough to make me wonder if he would crown the insult by refusing to partake in the courtly ritual. Some vestige of propriety remained to him, however, for he consented to rise.

"My father was always very particular in such matters," he said, kneeling and pressing his lips to Leannor's hand. "Your Majesty."

"His loss grieves my heart more than I can say," she told him with grave solemnity. "Know that he will be honoured for all eternity by my family."

Gilferd gave no reply to this, instead, rising and crossing his arms, his focus shifting from Leannor to me. "So, Scribe," he said, "it seems you've come to sing a very different song this time."

"A traitor's song," Ascendant Heilma piped up, the curve of her lips twisting into outright cruelty. "The same song in fact. Just sung for a different master. One he'll betray in time, I've no doubt."

I let the subsequent silence linger for a heartbeat, knowing a heated retort would gain no purchase here. Nor would lies or empty promises. "My crimes have been many, my lord," I told Gilferd. "My misjudgements great and terrible in their consequence. When I came here before I was a man in love with a lie, lost in a dream of delusion. Now, I am awake."

"Heed not the word of this creature!" Heilma cried, her voice pitched just shy of a screech. "Your father was wise enough to send him away. Do the same."

Gilferd turned to her, eyes hard with resentment. "I am not your pupil any longer, Ascendant," he said, voice soft but precise. "And you are not my tutor. Keep your counsel until it's asked for."

Heilma's face was lacking in flesh, but still contrived to quiver at the rebuke. "Your father—"

"Is dead!" Gilferd cut in. "And so are all but a handful of his knights and soldiers. All committed to war upon your advice, as I recall. Hold your tongue or depart this chamber."

Turning to regard his visitors once more, his gaze inevitably lingered on Ayin. "How it gladdens my heart to see you again, my lady," he said, smiling for the first time. The somewhat awkward young man I had met before might have stuttered these words, but this man spoke with honest and unabashed fluency.

"Told you last time," Ayin said, returning his smile. "I'm not a lady—"

"In point of fact," Leannor cut in, "this most excellent young woman has just been appointed as my principal lady-in-waiting, a role which requires noble rank. The king was glad to bestow the honour this very morning." That the king had done no such thing was, of course, completely moot. In any case, I doubted Gilferd cared much either way.

"Lady Ayin." He bowed low. "Please accept my congratulations upon your elevation."

"Erm," Ayin said, eyes flicking to me for guidance. Upon receiving a small nod, she added, "Thanks very much." She hesitated, glancing about the chamber and shifting in discomfort. I saw Ascendant Heilma glaring in unconcealed fury, something Ayin noticed too. Taking a short, fortifying breath, she asked Gilferd, "Can we talk? Just you and me, I mean."

"A capital notion," Leannor said, inclining her head at Gilferd. "For I find I am quite wearied by our journey, which was long. Lord Alwyn and I shall withdraw. Perhaps we could talk further tonight, my lord?"

Gilferd's eyes barely shifted from Ayin. "I believe that would be best, Your Majesty. My chamberlain will see you to your quarters. Your escort may bed down in the barracks, where there is ample space."

I bowed to the duke as Leannor strode from the chamber. Retreating a step, I paused to speak quiet words of advice to Ayin, which she forestalled with a shake of her head. As Gilferd was no longer a boy, she was no longer a girl. Still, I didn't like it. "You don't have to promise anything . . ." I told her in a murmur, falling silent when she shook her head once more.

"Don't worry about me," she said with a tight smile. "I got better, remember?"

Ayin never told me all that transpired between her and Duke Gilferd behind the closed door to his feasting chamber. Yet, come the evening, he was willing to kneel before King Arthin IV and swear loyalty as long as he drew breath. Gilferd's oath was followed by a feast of sorts, a brief affair that featured no juggling or songs even though both Adlar and Quintrell offered to perform. Gilferd's mood was noticeably lighter, but this was still a place of mourning.

"What did you say to him?" I asked Ayin when the muted revels had come to an end. Keen to gain a better appreciation of the castle's defences, I requested she join me for a tour of the sparsely occupied battlements.

"The truth," she said with a shrug. "He'll do what you want," she added in exasperation when I prodded her for a more fulsome explanation. "That's all that matters, isn't it? Besides, I'm a lady-in-waiting now. I answer to the princess, not you."

She grinned in the face of my frowning mutter, "My apologies, my lady."

"I didn't make him any promises, if that's your worry." She hooked her arm through mine, resting her head on my shoulder. "Thanks for caring, though." She stepped away, surveying the winding battlements of Castle Norwind with a critical eye. Sometimes I forgot she had seen as many battles as I and possessed a soldier's judgement. "Too few," she said. "We had more at Walvern Castle and we barely held it."

"I know." I watched a pair of sentries trace a course along the south-facing wall, noting the wide gap between them and their neighbours. Even though this was just the night watch, things would only be slightly improved come the dawn. Ayin's facility for numbers left me in little doubt as to the state of the duke's forces. All our strength combined amounted to little over eight hundred men and women in arms. Matched against the might of Evadine's unnaturally inspired host, we could expect to hold this castle for no more than a few days.

"How long until she comes, do you think?" Ayin asked me.

"Weeks, most likely. Perhaps months, if fortune smiles."

"It won't. As soon as she learns you're here she'll come for you. You know that." Ayin put her back against the wall, wincing with regret at voicing an obvious but unwelcome conclusion. "We can't stay here. I think you know that too."

I looked to the south, mentally calculating distances and obstacles. "Always it seems the Shavine Forest lures me home."

"The princess won't like it," Ayin warned. "Skulking in the woods isn't very royal, is it?"

"Neither is skulking in a marsh. The forest is the only refuge we can seek now."

Come the morning, I advised Leannor and the duke of my plan. The princess was surprisingly amenable to my suggested course, Duke Gilferd less so since I was essentially asking him to abandon his duchy.

"Lands and castles can be recovered, my lord," Leannor told him. "But you must be alive to do so."

After much discussion, Gilferd agreed to march for the Shavine Forest, but insisted on a week's delay to allow for preparations and mustering of additional recruits. To this end, myself and Juhlina spent the intervening days roving the surrounding country in search of those fleeing the Ascendant Queen's fury. We found a few small groups of destitute people with tales of burnt villages and stolen food stocks. Some of the younger folk were willing to join us, but most were too sunken into miserable terror to even contemplate rebellion. Questioning them, it became clear to me that to them Evadine had become something more than a Risen Martyr or usurping queen.

"She sees all, m'lord," advised one old woman atop a cart being dragged along by her family. "My dearest husband spoke against her, far from any of her followers who might have heard. Whispered it too. Still, they came for him. Hanged him they did and set their torches to our homes. All for a mere whisper."

I felt the likelier story was of an informant scurrying off to the Covenant Host to earn a few sheks by tattling on his loose-lipped neighbour. However, the truth remained that Evadine's visions were a very real threat, more worrisome even than her advantage in numbers. I was sure a vision had prompted her to set Ofihla scouring the marshes for Leannor and the children. I also suspected they had played no small part in her victory at the Crest. Yet, it didn't render her infallible. She hadn't known the truth about her supposed resurrection until she heard it from Hilbert. Nor had it warned her of my escape from the palace in Couravel. I thought back to the fall of Olversahl, that terrible night where Evadine had suffered the wounds that should have killed her. *She expected to die that night, but she hadn't . . . because of me. An outcome she hadn't foreseen.*

"Something's churning in that head of yours again," Juhlina observed. I realised I had brought Blackfoot to a halt, my brow drawn in thought. The party of dispossessed churls had resumed their weary northward trudge, none having felt compelled to enlist in the king's cause.

"What is it?" Juhlina prompted when I continued my silent pondering.

"She doesn't see me," I said. "Evadine. Her visions. I'm not in them."

"How can you be sure? She sees so much."

"I can't, but I . . . feel it. Also, if her visions could guide her to me, would any of us still be alive?" There was something more, a suspicion I didn't feel comfortable voicing to Juhlina. Something Ofihla had said as she lay dying: *She told me how her love blinded her . . .*

"If it's true," Juhlina ventured, "it gives us an advantage, does it not? As long as you remain with the king, she can't find him." We both stiffened as the realisation sank home. We had ridden at least five miles from Castle Norwind this day, more the day before.

Cursing, I put my heels to Blackfoot's flanks and set him galloping north, calling out to the others to follow.

It required another intervention from Ayin to persuade Gilferd of the urgent need to march away from his ancestral seat. I suspect the deciding factor was the threat that, if he chose to stay, he would most likely never see her again. Thanks to our recruiting efforts, the host that filed out of Castle Norwind the following morning amounted to over a thousand foot and horse. I hoped to garner more along the way, but had no illusions that our ranks would rise to match our enemy for a very long time. Leannor had been right. Ahead lay months, perhaps years of attempting to prosecute a war from hiding. Years in which Evadine's cruelty would be sure to grow, swelling our numbers but wreaking havoc in the wider realm. These years would also see the birth of the child she carried, our child, the heir to a queen intent on malice. The knowledge led to days of troubled pondering and nights beset by vividly unpleasant dreams, although Erchel remained blessedly absent, for now.

At my suggestion, this nebulous Crown Host made for the coast roads rather than risk the more direct route to the Shavine border. I harboured no doubts that Evadine had already gathered her forces for a rapid march on the upper Cordwain. It would go very ill for us if we happened across one of her outlying patrols. Each day Gilferd would ride ahead with a small escort, often accompanied by Ayin, stopping at every village and town to call for volunteers. As duke of this land he could have made these commands instead of pleas, but I didn't fault him for his largesse. Even the most uneducated churl could gauge the chances of our success and any pressed into service were likely to desert at the first opportunity. Still, there were those who answered the call. Often these were those a little too old or too young for the muster that had carried so many of their kinfolk off to disaster. They tended to be those with an abiding sense of duty to the slain Duke Lohrent, for he had plainly been well thought of here. Also, as we neared the coast, we garnered a few dozen hired blades who had been making for the ports. I entertained few illusions regarding the longevity of their loyalty, but trained soldiers were hard to come by.

By the time we were on the coast road proper and heading south, Ayin reported our number at over fifteen hundred. I reckoned perhaps half could be counted on to acquit themselves well in the event of battle, a prospect I was keen to avoid. However, such hopes appeared to be dashed when Tiler came galloping up to me early on our third day on the coast road with news of an armed host arranged atop the hills a mile ahead.

"Didn't want to get too close," he said. "Since there were plenty of archers among them. Put their numbers at around four, maybe five hundred. Loose order, too. But they showed no signs of shifting."

"Any cavalry?" Sir Ehlbert asked.

"Only foot, so far as I saw, my lord. Could have their horse hidden on the lee of the hill, I s'pose."

"So." The knight stroked his ever thicker beard in contemplation. "Do we go through them or around them?"

"Hopefully neither," I said. The thought that my realisation about Evadine's visions might be wrong nagged at me. Had she divined we would take this road and sent a force to block our path? If so, why only a few hundred when she commanded thousands?

Turning to Duke Gilferd, I asked, "Would you, perchance, possess a truce pennant I could borrow, my lord?"

Gilferd and Leannor insisted on accompanying me, which meant Ehlbert came too. As our party rode under the truce banner towards the hill and the nature of our potential enemy became clear, I knew it would have been far better to have come alone. Still, I took some comfort from having had the foresight to have Tiler carry the banner. Oft times, it requires an outlaw to parley with another outlaw.

I raised a hand to halt our party at the base of the hill. Surveying the top, I saw an array of people in varied garb, their line lacking military precision, but remaining steady nonetheless. Those in the centre were the most well armed, all bearing swords or axes, some wearing armour. The sun was high overhead, and I had a clear view of their faces which were rich in runic tattoos. The tallest of them stood to the fore, a blonde woman with a longsword slung across her back. She stared down at us with her arms crossed and head tilted in careful appraisal for what I knew to be a deliberately prolonged interval. Given the circumstances, it might have been prudent for our party to climb the hill, but a member of the royal family could not be seen to humble herself in such a way. Commoners present themselves to royalty, not the other way around. I saw a very slight shift in the tall woman's posture, which I hoped signalled amusement rather than offence, before she unfolded her arms and started down the hill.

"I hope she still likes you," I muttered to Tiler, receiving a wary grimace in response.

"She never liked me," he said. "Last time we met she called me the Lady's Rat."

I watched the tall woman come to a halt a few paces away. She didn't bow or offer a greeting, indicating we had probably exhausted her concessions to courtesy.

"Princess," I said, turning to Leannor, "it is my honour to present to you Shilva Sahken. A woman of noted mercantile success in this region. Mistress Shilva—" I bowed to the outlaw queen "—Princess Leannor is honoured by your visit."

Studying Shilva's mostly impassive features, I was struck by how little she had aged. A few more lines creased her eyes and forehead, but otherwise she was the same woman I had watched Deckin embrace all those years ago. Seeing her brow furrow as she returned my scrutiny, I knew the same could not be said for me.

"Fuck me, young Alwyn," she said. "But you've gotten old. Damn sight bigger too. Not quite Deckin's stature, though. Seems he was wrong about his favourite bastard."

"He was wrong about many things."

"That's no word of a lie, to be sure." Shilva's narrowed gaze tracked from me to Tiler, where it narrowed further in evident disdain, before moving on to my noble companions. "Pardon my manners," she said. "Never sure how to act around you lot. Lords, knights, princesses and such. If you can still call yourselves that. Way I hear it, there's a new queen these days." She centred her focus on Leannor, a smile broadening her lips. "Awful keen to get her hands on you she is too, love. One hundred gold sovereigns for that dainty head, no less. Two hundred for him—" she jutted her chin in my direction "—but only if he's alive."

"Quite a sum," Leannor replied, her voice lacking the affront I expected. "Are you here to collect?"

Ehlbert nudged his horse forward, hand resting on the pommel of his longsword. He and Shilva matched stern, unyielding stares. I knew she remembered him from Moss Mill where she had come perilously close to capture and execution, leaving slain kinfolk behind in her escape. An old grudge perhaps, but for the queen of Shavine outlawry, I knew that didn't matter.

I began to formulate an attempt at humour, something to lighten the mood and shift Shilva's attention back to me, but Leannor spoke first. "You're not here to fight," she said, flicking a hand at the folk on the hill at Shilva's back. "Outlaws don't engage in open battle. And if earning a reward from the False Queen was your object, you could do so simply by running off and telling her where we are. Instead, you choose to bar our path and await a parley. So, Mistress Shilva, I ask, with all respect, what do you want?"

Shilva's lean, handsome features tensed, anger darkening her eyes. But I sensed no aggression in her. This anger was directed elsewhere. "Been many things in my time," she said, voice low at first but growing in volume as she spoke on. "Thief, pirate, smuggler, and, aye, I've done murder when the need arose. But I've never been a beggar, till now." She spared a glance in my direction, one rich in accusation. "But that's what this one's Risen Martyr has made of me."

"She's not my Martyr," I said. "Not any longer."

"It was her you sent your rat there to bargain for. Her you had me serve, not knowing I was cutting my own throat with the service."

It was faint, but I heard a catch in her voice, one that spoke of grief and pride scraped raw. Once again Leannor's insight had found the mark. Shilva hadn't come to fight. I looked again at the outlaws on the hill above, seeing how ragged they appeared. This was no army of cut-throats but yet another group of dispossessed fleeing the Ascendant Queen's wrath.

"She came to the Shavine Forest," I said to Shilva.

"Her soldiers found every hideout with ease," she confirmed. "Every store of loot. Every camp. Almost all my smuggling coves raided and the cargoes seized. Hundreds have dangled at her word, including my own kin. Clans that ranged the Shavine for generations are now extinct. How could she know such things, Alwyn?" Accusation gleamed in her gaze once more. "Who could possibly have told her?"

"She needs no informants," I said. "It's something else that guides her. And it'll guide her to you, unless you join us."

Shilva's jaw clenched. "How am I to trust your word? You were at her side for so long."

"Then trust mine," Leannor said. "As princess regent I vouch for this man. He has risked his life to save my children. This I have seen, as I see the depth of his guilt. As I see yours, Mistress Shilva. You desire a reckoning for all you have lost." Leannor leaned forward, extending her hand. "Pledge yourself to my son's cause, and I'll see you have it."

Shilva stayed where she was. Only a fool strikes a bargain after the first offer. "Service must be paid for," she said. "In consideration as well as coin."

"The king will be happy to proclaim a royal pardon for all crimes committed by yourself and your band," Leannor assured her. "As for coin." She turned to me with a raised eyebrow. "Lord Alwyn is the king's treasurer as well as his marshal."

Taking the hint, I reached for the purse Lorine had given me. I was careful to ensure Shilva caught sight of the contents as I opened it. Extracting a single gold sovereign, I tossed to her, saying, "Merely a token payment. In recognition of your willingness to parley."

Shilva turned the coin over, grunting in satisfaction at the sight and feel of real gold. "I'll want half that purse, if we're to join with you."

"A tenth," I countered, gesturing to the outlaws on the hill. "Unless you've an army to give the king."

"An army? No." Shilva moved to take Leannor's hand, pressing a kiss to it. "But I do have a fleet, which I fancy is of more use at this time."

Chapter Twenty-Three

The port of Tarisahl formed a crescent of close-packed houses around a horseshoe-shaped bay on the Cordwain coast. Upon ascending the bluffs south of the port, we found it currently home to several dozen ships of varying dimensions. Small barques lay anchored alongside three-masted merchantmen and long-hulled schooners built for traversing the deep ocean.

"I present the smugglers of Albermaine, Your Majesty," Shilva said, bowing to Leannor. "All that were willing to come here on my command, that is. A fair few decided they'd make for friendlier ports when the mad bitch set her dogs loose upon us."

"Impressive, Mistress Shilva," Leannor said, without much conviction. "But, ignorant as I am of such things, even I can tell this is no war fleet."

"They'll fight if need be," Shilva replied. "But their mission is to carry us away. There are a thousand places to hide in the Westward Isles. Once established, we will have the whole of the west-Albermaine coast to raid. Truth be told, it was my intention to take only my own band. We were on our way here when we happened upon you. Since I'm now sworn to your service, you may as well come too."

"You suggest we flee?" Ehlbert asked her. "The king cannot abandon his kingdom and still lay claim to the Crown."

"If he stays here for too long, he won't have a head to wear it." Shilva's scowling curtness made it plain that her grudge against the King's Champion hadn't abated, regardless of her new found royal allegiance. "You could try to follow the Scribe's plan," she went on.

"But scurry off to the Shavine Forest and you'll find the roads betwixt here and there are now thick with her soldiers." Shilva's expression softened as she looked again at Leannor. "I'm sorry, Your Majesty, but fleeing is your only choice now. And here—" she inclined her head at the ships in the bay "—I gift you the means of doing so."

We spent a further week in Tarisahl, allowing time for Gilferd to gather more recruits from the townsfolk and surrounding country. The local nobility were mostly willing to throw their lot in with the new duke, although a few discreetly absented themselves shortly after our arrival. The commons of the port and the churls from the nearby farms were less amenable to the notion of sailing off to an uncertain future. Our ranks grew by about a hundred, but no more. As this region had yet to feel the weight of the Ascendant Queen's reign, I couldn't fault these folk for their reluctance. Evadine's reaction upon coming here to find her quarry vanished stirred a good deal of guilt in my breast, but there was no time to waste convincing these people of their impending fate.

I spent the days drilling the newborn Crown Host with the assistance of the veterans in our company. Some of the recruits had marched under the Cordwain banner in various campaigns, but most had not. Hours of attempting to get them to stand in a disciplined line educated me in the difficulty of the drill master's task, provoking a sorrowful yearning for Swain and Ofihla. Under their harsh but expert tutelage, I had little doubt our nascent army would be marching in step in no time.

We drilled on the broad, cobbled wharf of Tarisahl, the only stretch of flat ground in the port. In organising the Crown Host, I followed the Covenant example, dividing them into three ranks according to size. The tallest and strongest in the first rank, all armed with pikes or whatever long arms we could gather. Behind them were the stocky or mid-sized with their axes, halberds and billhooks. To the rear were the dagger men and women. Such armour as we possessed was patchy and two-thirds of our number lacked a helm of any kind. I had visited all the merchants in this port, those who hadn't fled, in search of arms and armour, or at least sturdy clothing. The results had been mixed, but at least every soldier now sported a jacket, blanket and some form of weapon.

Come the end of the fourth day of drill, I finally managed to get them into formation and stumble through a semblance of an advance. It had required a good deal of shoving and shouting from myself and the veterans, but it did represent a modicum of progress. Not that all who witnessed it were impressed.

"That was fucking pathetic," a voice to my rear observed after I had dismissed the recruits for the day. The sun was low above the western horizon, obliging me to shield my eyes to view this critical spectator. I made out a slight figure with a mass of unruly dark hair only partially contained in a silk scarf. She wore seafarer garb, her broad belt featuring a dagger on either side.

"Sergeant Ofihla would've striped our backs for such a performance," the sailor added. "Where is she, by the way?"

"Dead," I replied, my voice suddenly thickened. We had never been given to overt displays of affection, but the impulse to pull her into an embrace was irresistible. Toria consented to return the hug, just for a moment, before extricating herself.

"It's only been a couple of years," she said, squinting up at me. "But you look like it's been ten."

I found I had to swallow to get the rejoinder out, the words emerging in a hoarse exhalation. "That's what happens when you fight the good fight."

"That's what you've been doing, is it, Alwyn?" Her tone was as caustic as ever, but her expression soft enough to tell me she hadn't come to judge, at least not too much. "I did tell you," she added when I couldn't summon an answer.

"And you were right," I managed with a strained, hollow laugh. "I truly am the worst of fools."

This brought a small grin to her lips as I took a more fulsome look at her garb. Her jacket and trews were finely tailored, if weathered by sea air, and each of her twin daggers bore a gemstone in their pommels, a ruby on the right and a sapphire on the left.

"So," I said. "You found it then? Lachlan's hoard."

"I found something." Toria jerked her head to the quay where a narrow-hulled vessel of dark timbers waited at anchor. The *Sea Crow*, I recalled. It appeared Toria had decided to make the smuggler's craft her new home.

"Come have some grog," she said. "And I'll tell you all about it. And you can tell me just how much of a fucking idiot you've been without me there to wipe your arse for you."

Upon climbing the gangway to the *Sea Crow*'s deck, we were met by a dark-skinned woman I remembered from the night I had seen Toria board this vessel for the first time. "Hope he's come to pay us, Captain," she said, casting a surly eye at me. "Been sitting in this shithole long enough, I reckon."

"You'll sit in all the shit I tell you to, Mahlia," Toria informed her, tone placid but eyes hard. "For as long as I will it."

The two women matched stares until Mahlia consented to lower her head in a fractional display of subservience. "Now," Toria told her, beckoning for me to follow as she strode across the deck, "fuck off and fetch me and this famous fellow some grog."

"Captain?" I asked, following Toria through a hatch in the quarterdeck. "What happened to Din Faud?"

"Sitting pretty on his home island in the middle of the southern seas. He practically owns the place these days, though not officially. He still sails hither and yon on the *Morning Star* when the mood takes him, but he's more a merchant than a sea captain now, accruing great profits too, thanks to me."

Toria led me to a door at the rear of the lower deck, opening it to reveal a spacious cabin rich in silk drapery and soft cushions. A ginger cat of villainous aspect rose from its bed amid the satin softness to bare its fangs at me with a hiss. "Looks like a whore's palace, doesn't it?" Toria said, shooing the cat away with a flick of her wrist. It gave a grating mewl of annoyance and scrambled up hull planking to perch on the overhead beams.

"Din Faud's taste," Toria went on, "but I can't be bothered to change it. Besides—" she unbuckled her dagger belt and set it down on a rosewood deck before sinking into the cushion-covered couch "—it's so comfy."

"You must be quite the sailor." I settled myself into the tall-backed chair at the captain's desk. "To rise so high so quickly."

"Not really. I can haul a rope and secure a sheet with the best of them, but I'm no expert at catching the wind. I leave all that to the first mate. The third mate sees to all that boring stuff with charts and stars and such. And the bosun beats the merry shit out of anyone who takes exception to my orders. It's a nice and neat arrangement, all told."

"So, if you didn't kill Din Faud to take his ship, how did you become captain?"

Toria grinned, reclining on the silken cushions. "He adopted me. There was this whole ritual on the foredeck with incense and burnt parchment, after which I became his daughter, in the eyes of his gods, at least. It seemed to be good enough for the crew, most of them anyways. The *Sea Crow* was his gift. She's just one of his ships, y'see. He had several when you met him, and now three times as many. I suppose I'll inherit the entire fleet one day."

"I take it these ships were bought with Lachlan's treasure. You really did lead him to it, didn't you?"

Toria's mouth quirked in the manner of one privy to an amusing secret, her reply forestalled by a sullen Mahlia arriving with a cask of grog and two goblets. "Crew's been talking," the woman said, casting a baleful look at me. "Having this one on board sits ill. They're saying he'll draw the Cursed Queen's eye upon us."

"Then they can piss off and find another berth," Toria replied with cheerful disdain. "While you can stand post outside. I don't want any visitors."

"Cursed Queen?" I asked when Mahlia closed the door with a pointed slam.

"It's what they're calling her across the southern seas," Toria said. "Ascarlians too. All manner of unlikely tales swirling as regards her supposed powers. I tried telling my lot she's just a madwoman with strange dreams, but sailors are ever mired in superstition."

"Would that you were right." I reached for the cask and poured a generous measure of grog into both goblets. "To Brewer," I said, handing one to her and raising the other. "And so many other good folk lost to a false cause."

A shadow passed across Toria's face. "Brewer's dead?"

"That very night in Farinsahl, slain by the duke's men sent to kidnap the Anointed Lady. Most of the others are gone too. Ofihla, Swain, Delric . . ." *Lilat, hanging on the scaffold . . .*

"Brewer wasn't such a good man, as I recall," Toria said. "But he was a friend, of sorts, so I'll drink to his memory. Swain and Ofihla too." She downed some grog, eyeing me carefully. "Did *she* kill them?"

"She killed Swain and Delric, for the crime of saving her life. Ofihla died trying to kill me."

"Quite a tale you have to tell me, Alwyn."

I smiled and drank. The grog was good, smooth on the tongue and slipping down the throat with far too much ease. I hadn't been drunk for a while and found I relished the prospect. "I'll have your tale first," I said after draining the goblet and reaching again for the cask. "And my share of the treasure, if you'd be so kind. I've an army in want of pay."

"Sadly, I've the story but not the gold. Unless you count knowledge as wealth, that is." Toria settled back into her cushions, cradling her goblet. "Once we put to sea, Din Faud proved true to his word and sailed directly for the Iron Maze. He had plenty of questions, as you might expect. But I had no answers for him save the map. It would have been an easy matter for him to steal it and have his crew pitch me overboard, but he didn't. A bargain sealed with coin means a great deal to his people. To them, breaking such a pact is like taking a shit on a shrine altar. Besides, I think he started to develop a fondness for me after I knocked out one of his sailors with a block and tackle when he got too free with his hands.

"It transpires the Iron Maze is well named. Hundreds of close packed rocky islands where the sea churns white in the channels and the tides can smash a ship to splinters if you venture near at the wrong hour. Din Faud knew his business, however. It took ten days of careful navigation, but eventually we reached the island circled on the map."

Toria paused to gulp more grog, lips forming a rueful smile. "It was just a great spur of rock rising from the roiling waves, one of so many others. At high tide it appeared there was no way to land a boat on it, but when the seas calmed a bit, you could make out a hollow in its base. Din Faud ordered a boat lowered, but not all the crew were enthusiastic about risking the journey. I've never seen him draw his sabre, but just the sight of him putting a hand to the hilt was enough to fire their courage. I never thought I'd be more scared than I was at the Traitors' Field, but getting inside that rock managed it. The boat heaved and slid all over the fucking place, but once in the shadow of the island's innards, the sea calmed. So dark it was we had to light torches. Further in, we found a flat stretch of rock near level with the water, and a cave beyond. Din Faud left a couple of sailors to watch the boat and led the rest of us inside the cave. There were those among us who whispered of ghosts and such, but I saw nothing more alarming than a spatter of shit from the birds nesting there. That is, until we found the cavern with the pool."

Toria's brow creased as she leaned forward on her couch, goblet clasped in both hands and forearms resting on her knees. "It was an ill place. As I said, I saw no ghosts, nor heard any spectral voices. But that cavern had a chill to it that went deeper than cold. I knew Din Faud felt it, his crew as well. One of them turned and fled, whimpering and cursing his way back to the boat. It may have been the sight of bones that did it. They were scattered about, a mess of ribs and spines save for the skulls. Two of them, black with age, lying in such a way it seemed they were staring at each other.

"But the pool was the strangest thing about that place, for it was utterly still save for a few ripples when water dripped from the ceiling. Otherwise, it was like a mirror. We scoured the cave and found a chest, just as ancient as the bones, the lock that secured it rusted so much it only took a few blows with a spade to crack it. Din Faud allowed me the honour of opening it, which I did with all due ceremony, feeling quite smug about it all. I flung back the lid, expecting to be dazzled by the gleam of piled riches. But there was no gleam, just a bunch of scrolls with not a single coin among them. It was a right fucking disappointment, I must say.

"I stormed about the cavern for a time, turning the air foul with curses. I kicked the bones in my anger, sending a few of them into the pool, and that's when I saw it. Deep, deep down, revealed by the broken mirror of the surface. There was my gleam. Just a very small glint from the light of our torches, but bright enough to draw me in. Tugging off my boots, I called to the crew to shine their torches closer and dived in, though Din Faud warned against it. The gleam was brighter under the water, like a candle flickering at the far end of a long tunnel. Fuck, it was cold, but the heat of my need kept me going. I kicked and flailed to get deeper, my lungs burning with the strain. Twice I was forced back up, gasping in all the air I could, then diving once more. That final attempt, I saw it. Just for an instant, but I saw it clearly. As great a mass of treasure you could ever dream of seeing, so far down at the bottom of that pool there's no hope of any human soul ever touching a finger to it."

Toria let out a sigh and drained her goblet. Rising, she moved to the cask for a refill. "Curiously, Din Faud didn't appear overly bothered by my report, being principally occupied with the contents of the chest. There were books among the scrolls, apparently, including a captain's log. Something about the tightness of the chest's lid must have preserved it, for its pages could still be turned without flaking. Even I could tell the script was ancient, but Din Faud is a man of considerable education. 'Be it known,' he said, reading from the final page, 'that I, Calim Dreol, called the Hound of the Sea by some, do make this testament of sound mind, if diminishing health. I swear by the Martyrs that all words set down here are true, and so do I beseech the Seraphile for forgiveness, though I know it will not be bestowed on so unworthy a soul as mine.'"

"The testament of the Hound of the Sea," I said, my scholarly interest piqued. "A treasure in itself."

"Din Faud still has it, if you'd care to make him an offer. Though the price will be steep. The Hound listed not only all his many crimes but also his voyages, in great detail. Din Faud was amazed by just how far the pirate had travelled, sailing seas barely known to sailors even now. Not only had he written it all down, he'd mapped it too. The scrolls in the chest were charts, so well preserved it was as if they'd been drawn yesterday. That was the real treasure, Alwyn. For in those charts were routes unknown to modern seafarers. Straits long thought unnavigable, but the Hound had sailed them. Passages that would take weeks off the sailing time for merchantmen. Others that would be a prize gift to any smuggler. Din Faud's hands shook as he unfurled one after the other. All that gold, so close but forever out of reach, yet he didn't care one turd for it. I had made him a very rich man, hence the whole making me his daughter and giving me his ship thing."

I grunted a laugh and drank some more, feeling the onset of liquor-induced bitterness, albeit tinged with a good deal of irony. "Of the pair of us, I reckon you got the better throw of the dice." My goblet tipped over as I set it down, spilling a few drops on to the fine rosewood desk. I mumbled an apology and wiped my sleeve over it before fumbling at the cask's spile for a refill.

"Let me," Toria said, holding the vessel under the tap. "Not to be critical, Alwyn, but you used to hold your drink a lot better."

"I used to do a lot of things better, like not getting my friends killed. Not as much, anyways." I took the goblet from her and drank down half the contents, uncaring of the ominous roil from my belly. "Tell me, did the Hound's testament make any mention of Lachlan at all? I mean, it was his treasure at the bottom of that pool, right?"

"It was. And the source of the hatred he harboured for himself. Lachlan and he were brothers, y'see. As boyhood thieves, one had forsaken the Shavine Forest for the sea, the other stayed. In later years, they found one another again and Lachlan beseeched his brother for a safe place to hide his loot. As is the way of things, the more gold and jewels Lachlan placed in the Hound's safekeeping, the more his pirate's mind got to plotting. Also, it was plain Lachlan was fully mad by the time the Hound struck him down in that cave. 'Had I not done it,' he said, 'I know he would have murdered me in time.' But he knew he was damned for this crime, and so cast the cursed treasure to the depths of the pool and waited for death to claim him. The last words in his testament were, 'For this is my due.'"

"Brothers," I slurred with a laugh. "That's a turn-up. Berrine would like to know that nugget, I'm sure. Not that I'll ever see her again. Also, she's got no books to write it in, any more. All burned down, just like Couravel. Strange how flames have a habit following me about." This miserable observation emerged in a muffled sputter, making me realise my head was resting on the damp surface of the desk. I pushed myself upright, finding Toria staring down at me with a concerned grimace.

"Should've gone with you, shouldn't I?" I said, head lolling. I wondered if the ship had put to sea since the cabin seemed to be heaving about. "But I couldn't. Not then. Had to stay . . . for her."

"Don't fret yourself too much." Toria patted my head with the awkwardness of one unused to expressing sympathy. "You're just an idiot, much like every man I ever met."

For reasons unknown, this struck me as extremely funny, though my subsequent mirth emerged as a series of sobs. "I'm more than that. I'm the fool who sired the future. The bastard who fathered another bastard who, I strongly suspect, is going to grow up to finish what his mother started." I frowned, struck by my certainty that Evadine's child would be a boy. How could I know that? I couldn't, and yet, I did.

"If you're waiting for me to tell you it's not your fault . . ." Toria trailed off with a helpless shrug. "But it's not *all* your fault, Alwyn. And now, at least, you've got me to help you put it right."

"No." I shook my head, growling in insistent denial. "Not you too." I stood up, which proved a singular mistake due to the fact that my legs no longer possessed the will to support me. Some chaotic lurching saw me colliding with the hull until I collapsed into a corner, wondering why Toria had dimmed the lamps so much.

"Not you . . ." I repeated as she hovered above me in a blurry mix of disapproval and commiseration. "I won't kill you too . . ."

Chapter Twenty-Four

I was roused from my drunken torpor by a gust of wind possessing the familiar sharpness of mountain air. Instead of the dry planking of the *Sea Crow*'s deck, my face was pressed against an irregular wall of unyielding granite. I blinked befogged eyes against a flurry of snow, not so thick as to conceal the tall peaks marking the boundary between Alundia and the Caerith dominion. Icy speckled cliffs loomed above to form a narrow channel between two mountains, a place where the wind was funnelled into a persistent gale. The walls of the channel came together a few dozen paces ahead, creating a dip between the neighbouring peaks. From the erosion of the rock, I assumed it must become a small waterfall in summer. Now, with the air so chill, the stream that fed it had frozen. My presence here was too impossible to be real, and too real to be a dream. So, when I heard her voice, it was with a lurch of excitement, but scant surprise.

"I'm sorry, Alwyn."

She stood a short distance away, blonde hair trailing in the wind, a few strands whipping about that overly perfect face of hers. Her expression was drawn in both sympathy and regret.

"For what?" I asked her, unable to keep the bitterness from my voice. "I mean to say," I went on, getting to my feet, "there is so much to apologise for. So much you could have warned me against." My bitterness blossomed into outrage as I advanced upon her. "So many good people slain that could still be drawing breath."

She gave no answer, meeting my anger with unflinching acceptance.

"You're the one with the book, remember?" I demanded, halting before her. "The book that surely details all of it. All the missteps I could have avoided."

"Is that what you think?" The compassion on her face shifted into shrewd, if affectionate, judgement. "Had you been able to chart the course of your life, would you really have changed so much? Or would you have found reasons, excuses, to deny it? Would her love have been so easy to refuse, Alwyn?"

"Yes!" Even though this denial emerged as a growl from between clenched teeth, I heard the hollowness of it. The Sack Witch, known as the *Doenlisch* to the Caerith, had an inerrant way of cutting through delusion to find the truth. Knowing that didn't make me any less angry.

I turned away from her, stomping my feet and hugging myself against the cold. "No Erchel this time?" I muttered.

"He has a task elsewhere, one more suited to his talents."

"When alive, his talents consisted mainly of cruelty and perversion. How can you sully yourself by making use of one such as him?"

"Death transforms us, Alwyn. Those mighty in life often become weak when their spirit slips from the cage of flesh. The weak can become strong. The cruel, compassionate."

"Having met him recently, I'm bound to say he's just as cruel as he ever was."

"Not all change is instant. Erchel will have many opportunities to shape himself anew. As many as he needs, for time moves differently in the plains beyond life. Your time, however, grows short."

"If you came to tell me I'm going to die soon, I fancy I already reckoned that out for myself." I turned back to her, finding a fond smile on her lips.

"I have missed you," she said, which only served to stoke my resentment.

"The *Eithlisch* has been looking for you," I said. "He sent a *veilisch* to find you. Her name was Lilat. She died a terrible death on my account. But, you know that, don't you?"

The smile faded, and she nodded. "Some things I can prevent. Others I can't."

"And my death? Which is that?"

"I don't know yet. I came not to offer words of death, but guidance in life." She raised her arms to encompass our surroundings. "My people call this place *Kain Laethil*."

A Caerith phrase, one I hadn't heard before, although I knew the words. The literal translation amounted to "narrow valley winter". "Not a valley," I murmured after some pondering. "A pass, in winter. The Winter Pass. That's what the Caerith call it?"

"They do. A passage through the mountains that divides your lands from ours, one that only forms in winter. Here lies the path back to the woman you love."

The woman you love. Words that stabbed deeper than expected. And was that judgement in her tone? Had I actually disappointed her?

"It's not possible to love a monster," I said, which brought a pitying frown to her brow.

"Oh, Alwyn," she said. "Of course it is."

She blinked, and the landscape changed, the chill mountain pass vanishing the instant she closed her eyes. When she opened them, we stood on a hillside of long grass swaying in a stiff breeze. Once again, she had brought me to an unfamiliar spot. Below us sat a broad crescent-shaped bay, the white sand of the beach assailed by tall waves sweeping in from a grey sea. Nearby stood a stone-walled stronghold, small in comparison to most. From the absence of a banner and the state of its walls, I deduced it had been out of use for a long time, though not yet fallen to ruin.

"Where are we now?" I asked the Sack Witch, half expecting a cryptic response, so the precision of her reply came as a surprise.

"The northern coast of the Caerith dominion. This bay was often visited by a man I once knew, a pirate by trade but an explorer at heart. You remind me of him in some ways, though he had a far more vicious temper, and a good deal more greed."

"The Hound," I said in realisation. "You knew the Hound of the Sea?"

"Calim hated that name, styling himself as the Overlord of

the Cronsheldt Sea. He had grand visions of achieving royal recognition one day. 'Steal enough of their gold,' he told me, 'and they'll give you anything to have it back.' It was thanks to me that my people allowed him to land here and trade for the shiny metals and stones your kind worship so. They even let him build a castle, of sorts." She nodded to the abandoned stronghold. "He named it Castle Dreol, intending it to be the seat of his family for generations to come. There's a well within its walls for fresh water and you'll find the sarcophagus in the crypt filled with all the gold and gems your army will require."

"You want me to come here?"

"I think you'll find there is nowhere else for you to go. Not unless you intend to flee to far-off lands and leave your son in his mother's clutches. I have had glimpses of what will happen if you do. They weren't pleasant."

"So you knew, centuries ago." My anger mounted once again, stoked by the sense of being controlled by another's will; a puppet forever dancing to her hand on the strings. "You knew all that would happen. You knew what Evadine would become."

"Not become. What she always was. As you were always going to turn against her. But, no. I didn't know all of it when I once stood in this same spot with a man who fancied himself a lord of the ocean. Ultimately, I control nothing, Alwyn. All I can do is guide."

More heated words rose to my lips, but I let them wither, suddenly wearied by it all. She was right. The paths of my life had always been my choice. I could have deserted before the Traitors' Field. I could have let Evadine perish after Olversahl. I could have stayed her hand when she sliced open Luminant Durehl's throat. But I hadn't.

"Does she know?" I asked the Sack Witch. "Does she know what she is?"

"No. The malignity that dominates her is sublimely deceitful. In her own mind, she is all you pretended her to be: a champion of the poor and oppressed. A bringer of justice and enlightened rule. A soul divinely blessed to undertake a great mission. This belief runs deep in her, so deep it may be impossible to shatter."

The Sack Witch came towards me then, features once again filled with tender remorse. "One more thing," she said, raising a hand to caress my cheek. "The *Eithlisch* is harsh in his manners and has no love for you or your people, but you can trust him. For he will know that your cause aligns with his. When you meet, tell him you must seek out the stone feather."

"And what is that?"

"The key that unlocks all lies." She stepped back from me, offering a final, sorrowful smile, and blinked.

I awoke in a hammock, jerking into awareness with a violence that tipped me from my canvas bed to connect painfully with the deck beneath. My head felt as if it had not one, but several hatchets buried in it, and my bladder and guts were bloated to the point of nearly bursting.

"See?" I heard Toria say, looking up to find her offering a grin to a far less amused Juhlina. "Told you he wasn't dead." Toria angled her head to survey my splayed form, mouth quirking to smother a laugh. One of my feet was still entangled in the hammock, and I flopped about in an unsuccessful attempt to dislodge it.

"The princess regent was expecting you at council," Juhlina said, moving to drag my foot clear of its canvas snare. "I've had the entire company scouring the city for your drunken arse."

After some grunting effort, I succeeded in raising myself to a kneeling position. "The charts," I said to Toria. "Did Din Faud give you any copies?"

"Here," I said a few hours later, tapping a finger to the chart splayed out on the table. Leannor had taken over the mansion of a merchant who had fled the city. It boasted a fine library with many maps, but I fancied none were so detailed as the one before us. Although a copy, the excellence of the cartography was still evident in every line and letter. I had only a partial knowledge of sea charts, but those I had seen before were rarely so comprehensive as this rendering of the lower reaches of the Cronsheldt Sea. Compass lines intersected at key points and finely inscribed numbers indicated the depth of the ocean at regular intervals. Calim Dreol may never have risen to be Overlord of the Cronsheldt, but I would be forever happy to dub him the King of Map Makers.

The bay under my finger had been easy to find due to its crescent shape and the fact that it was the only point on this map marked with a symbol indicating a fortress. "The Caerith Wastes," Leannor said with a doubtful frown. "That's where you want us to go?"

"I do, and thanks to Mistress Sahken, we have the means to transport our entire force there. It has a natural harbour, a castle, fresh water, and our enemies will have scant chance of striking at us there."

"As we will have scant chance of striking at them," Ehlbert pointed out.

"Nor do we now," I countered. "This will be our base. There we can train our host, send ships back to the realm to gather more recruits, and there will be more, have no doubt of that. When we're strong enough, we march on Albermaine."

"The Caerith are famously hostile to outsiders," Leannor said. "You imagine they will simply allow us to land a large body of soldiers on their coast?"

"I do." I hesitated, unwilling to risk the scorn that would surely arise if I explained the source of my certainty. "They know me. I enjoy the favour of the *Eithlisch*, their principal shaman." An exaggeration bordering on outrageous deceit, but a necessary one. "Besides, they are endangered too. Evadine hates their kind with a passion. A crusade against the Caerith has long been her ambition. All of which makes them a powerful potential ally."

I fell silent, stepping back from the table and watching the calculation on Leannor's face. I had already resolved to take the Free Company and abandon her here if she refused this course. I would bring Lady Ducinda too, a task involving a risky abduction under Sir Ehlbert's nose, but I was determined not to abandon her to Evadine's doubtful mercy. Not so her betrothed. I would happily leave the king in his mother's care, as his demanding manners and recurrent tantrums were becoming decidedly irksome.

Discerning a good deal of resistance in Leannor's bearing, I decided the proposal required some gilding. "Also," I said, "I'm reliably informed that the current state of the royal purse will be greatly improved by what we find in this stronghold."

"Pirate's treasure, is it, Scribe?" Ehlbert asked, brows knitted in sceptical amusement.

"In truth, yes," I replied, addressing my next words to Leannor. "You have my word on it, Majesty."

Leannor was gracious enough not to pass comment on the merits of this statement, instead looking to Shilva. "Mistress Sahken, have you counsel to share?"

"I'm all for sailing away as soon as is practical, Majesty," Shilva said, her shrewd gaze focused on the map. "There are various places in the Westward Isles that offer sanctuary, though none boast a castle and so sound an anchorage. Also, the isles are a good deal more distant from the realm. If the Scribe speaks true, and I've no reason to doubt him, this appears a better option. Yet, I too worry over the Caerith's response, shaman's favour or no."

"I can sail ahead to parley," I said. "Captain Toria possesses the swiftest ship in our fleet. She tells me she can reach this spot in six days with a decent wind. Once there, I will seek out the Caerith and send word if they welcome us."

"And if they don't?" Leannor asked.

"Then you will hear nothing from me and the Westward Isles will be your destination."

Leannor stood in silent regard of the map for a while longer before turning to Gilferd. "And your counsel, my lord Duke?"

The young lord's reluctance to abandon his duchy was plain in the hardness of his features, but they softened somewhat when he glanced at Ayin. Thanks to her status as the princess regent's only lady-in-waiting, she was rarely far from Leannor's side now. This had the fortunate outcome of ensuring she was present whenever Gilferd was called to council. I watched her give a barely perceptible nod, the duke letting out a heavy sigh before bowing to Leannor.

"I cannot give surety that all my soldiers will consent to sail off to distant lands while their homes stand imperilled," he said. "But I have sworn myself to the king's cause and am therefore bound to follow."

"Very well." Leannor straightened and turned to me. "Lord Scribe, I will furnish you with a letter for our soon-to-be allies, one I'm sure you can assist in phrasing. You will sail with the first tide."

I was surprised at the depth of my regret at having to leave Blackfoot behind. He responded to my farewell treat of a proffered apple by snatching it from my hand and shifting his head to an indifferent angle as he chomped away. "I'll miss you too," I said, stroking his neck, which he at least consented to acknowledge with a snort. I left him in the care of the stable master at Leannor's stolen mansion with instructions to set him loose should the Ascendant Queen's army hove into view. The thought of him being pressed into service in her host sat ill, since I might end up facing him in battle before long.

The *Sea Crow* sailed forth with the morning tide and the next few hours provided a stark reminder of why I detested ship life. "I had hoped I would never have to do this again," Wilhum groaned, echoing my thoughts as we leaned over the starboard rail. Most of the Free Company were in a similar state, save for Quintrell and Juhlina. The minstrel's career had seen him sail far and wide while Juhlina's prior life of endless pilgrimage had involved more than a few sea crossings to distant Covenant outposts.

"There's many a shrine in the Westward Isles," she told me, her face lacking the pale grey tinge afflicting myself and the others. "The Most Favoured had us spend the better part of a year sailing from one to the other."

It transpired that Toria was more active in her role as captain than she let on, striding about the deck and calling out orders to the sailors in the rigging. "It's mostly for appearances' sake," she confided come the evening. "Captains are supposed to shout a lot, y'see. The crew expects it."

The sea retained a grey choppiness for the first two days before the sky cleared to allow for calmer waters. More sails were hauled aloft and the *Sea Crow* took on a speed that matched Toria's boasts. "This is nothing," she said with an air of pride. "Should see her when she catches the south-easterlies on the southern seas. It's like she's flying."

We encountered no other vessels for the entirety of the remaining voyage, something I ascribed to the reluctance of captains to venture into waters beset by war. Also, Shilva Sahken had made it known that any ship or merchant who traded with the Ascendant Queen would no longer enjoy her protection. In either case, I was grateful for the empty seas and absence of eyes to witness our course, although I didn't know how long it would be before Evadine received a vision of the king's current whereabouts. The frequency of her arcane insights had always been mysterious. But, given her efficient suppression of potential enemies recently, I suspected she now experienced visions on a regular basis, causing me to wonder: *What will that do to an already disturbed mind?*

I pushed such questions away, knowing I had no choice but to concentrate on the task at hand. Besides, the more I thought of her, the more I dwelt upon what we had shared, memories that were as enticing as they were painful. And the child, of course. The son yet to be born. *My son.* It all made for poor sleep and long days suffering the twin miseries of seasickness and anxious brooding.

So it was with considerable relief that, near noon on the fifth day at sea, I heard the lookout's cry from the crow's nest: "Land to southward!"

Toria's third mate was plainly a skilled navigator, for the bay hove into view shortly thereafter. The northern coast of the Caerith dominion was dominated by cliffs and rocky inlets inhospitable to ships seeking anchorage. Yet, here in this one spot, there sat a curving beach of white sand fringed by grassy bluffs, all overlooked by a small stronghold atop a nearby hill.

"No one's come to greet us," Toria reported after scanning the bluffs with a spyglass.

"They'll be along soon enough," I said. "It would be best if we claimed the castle for the king before they do."

"I thought they liked you," Wilhum said. "You lived among them for months, learned their language and such."

"The Caerith here are not those I know." I judged it best not to share my concerns over the reception I was likely to receive from the *Eithlisch*, should he deign to appear. "A little caution seems prudent."

Castle Dreol resembled a large house rather than a stronghold, albeit one built with scant concession to comfort. Its walls stood about fifteen feet high, enclosing a narrow tower only fractionally taller. Fitting an entire company into such a space was impossible, so I ordered tents pitched outside the walls. The gate that once filled the arched entrance was long vanished to either thievery or the elements. A survey of the surrounding country revealed a stretch of woodland to the south, but I refused Wilhum's suggestion he lead a party there to gather timber for a replacement.

"The Caerith are protective of their forests," I said, eyeing the distant trees with an increasing sense of foreboding. This land appeared empty of people, but I had no doubt our arrival had been observed, one way or another. "Come." I turned away, stepping through the vacant gateway. "We have a treasure to find."

The tower, if it could truly be called worthy of such a name, was solidly built, but its interior lacked any feature save a solid set of stone steps leading to the roof. I set Adlar to climb up and take station as a sentry while the rest of us embarked upon a search for the crypt. It was young Falko who found it, his thief's eyes best attuned to seeking out a hiding place.

"Here, Captain," he said, crouching to run the tip of his dagger along the mortar surrounding a particularly large flagstone. "Sits a little lower than the others, and the mortar slips down beneath the stone when you scrape it."

Toria and I drew our own daggers and joined him in scraping at the mortar until most of it had flaked way to leave a gap. It required a good deal of levering and heaving to get the stone raised, hauling it aside to reveal a set of rough-hewn steps disappearing into darkness.

"Three torches," I said. "Just me, Lord Wilhum and Captain Toria. The rest of you, keep guard." I didn't doubt the commitment of those who had followed me this far, but the sight of riches can inflame even the most resolute to nefarious action.

The air inside the crypt was all musty dampness, since it appeared the Hound of the Sea hadn't bothered to line its walls with stone. Loose earth hissed and subsided as we descended, displaced by the inrush of fresh air. The space was small and cramped, most of it taken up with the sarcophagus. It was much like those to be found beneath castles throughout Albermaine, its sides decorated with relief carvings and lid fashioned into the stone image of a recumbent man with a sword resting on his chest.

"Thought a lot of himself, this Hound," Toria commented. The light of her torch revealed a handsome, bearded face rendered in stone with masterly craftsmanship. The decoration on the sides of the sarcophagus were a catalogue of ships in full sail and various seafaring motifs, all displaying much the same impressive skill with the chisel. Calim Dreol had stinted in constructing his crypt, but not, apparently, in the fashioning of his coffin, even though he was destined never to occupy it.

"Ready?" I asked Toria, resting my hands on the edge of the lid. We shared a smile then, wry with the strangeness of arriving at a moment we had striven for but never truly expected to arrive: the discovery of a real, true treasure.

"This better not be another fucking bundle of charts," she grunted, setting her weight against the marble slab.

The lid consented to shift only after all three of us strained at it for long enough to make our arms ache. A short, grinding movement, then another shove, and it slid clear of the coffin. I felt a pang of relief when the effigy tumbled off the sarcophagus but failed to shatter on the soft earth of the crypt. Testament to vanity or not, it was too finely made a thing to deserve such casual vandalism.

Toria let out a sigh as she lowered her torch to illuminate the coffin's interior, raising the gleam of untarnished gold and glitter of gems. Ancient coinage and jewellery covered the bottom of the stone box, the pile broken here and there by small statues of bronze and jade draped in pearls.

"All this," Wilhum said, casting a puzzled glance at Toria, "and you never came to claim it until now?"

She shifted in discomfort, shooting a wary eye in my direction. I had told Leannor's council that the location of this treasure had been discovered among the Hound's papers, thinking it a more plausible explanation than being guided to it in a dream conjured by a Caerith witch.

"The Hound wrote much of his journal in code," I explained. "One that defied decipherment until I came along."

Wilhum gave a placid nod in response, but I could tell he wasn't convinced. Fortunately, he consented to refrain from further questions. "A full appraisal of the wealth here would require a more expert eye than mine," he said, reaching into the coffin to raise a handful of chunky gold coins. "But I've little doubt we now possess riches enough to fund three armies, never mind one."

"And an awful temptation," Toria added. "'Specially when your company is a bunch of outlaws."

"Former outlaws," I corrected, though I saw her point. "We'll pack up a quarter of it, which you'll carry back to Tarisahl and present to the princess regent with my compliments. Tell her also to take ship and bring the host here forthwith."

"We haven't parleyed with the Caerith yet," she pointed out. "Don't you want to wait for them?"

"They've already given us leave to stay," I said, turning away to mount the steps.

"How do you know?" Wilhum asked.

"They know we're here and haven't killed us." I started up the steps, then paused to add, "Yet."

Chapter Twenty-Five

The *Sea Crow* departed with the next tide under darkened skies, portending a storm. It duly arrived come dusk, hard, lacerating gales sweeping in from the sea driving thick curtains of rain against the shore. The Free Company huddled in their tents until the wind tore them from the pegs, forcing a retreat to the shelter of Castle Dreol. To alleviate their damp, confined misery, and also soothe any larcenous inclinations, I handed each of them a gold coin from the Hound's trove. Reactions were surprisingly varied. Falko and the other Yollands were wide-eyed with gratitude, Adlar and Juhlina only mildly interested, and Tiler puzzled by his own absence of greed.

"Was a time I'd've slit every throat here just for this," he muttered, brows furrowed as he repeatedly flipped the coin. "Now, I can't think of a single thing to spend it on."

"Consider it a pension," I advised. "No war lasts forever."

Tiler gave a half-amused grunt and consigned the coin to his pocket.

Quintrell's reaction was the most noteworthy, mainly for his curious inability to mask it. I saw it clearly as he beheld the coin I handed him, as pure an expression of naked avarice as I had ever seen. Catching my eye, he immediately strove to conceal it, forcing an offhand laugh and avowing a desire to keep the token for all his years as a souvenir of his days fighting the evil queen. I hadn't thought him an overly greedy soul before now. Duplicitous and barely trustworthy, certainly, but this was my first true glimpse of the mercenary lurking under all that charm. It made me wonder why I had allowed him to stay with us. With Lorine refusing to take up arms against Evadine, continuing to harbour her self-confessed spy seemed foolish. But, although no fighter, the minstrel had become a fixture of our company. The others appreciated his music and gift for finding humour even in the worst of times, something I realised now to be yet more artifice. Quintrell navigated the world from behind a facade of ingratiation, as befitted a spy. But, while I could tolerate a spy, a professional liar subsumed in greed was another matter.

I gave a good-natured laugh and, still smiling, leaned closer to whisper in his ear: "Go near the crypt and I'll kill you."

As the night wore on and gales lashed the castle walls, the company made itself as comfortable as it could and tried to sleep. They spread out across the floor in their blankets and bedrolls, lying cheek by jowl. The veterans among them managed to sleep, as did the Yollands, for whom this could hardly be called hardship. Others remained awake in restless agitation, casting worried glances at the surrounding walls of aged stone buffeted by the raging storm outside.

For myself, I made no attempt to sleep, taking up position on the stairwell. I couldn't divine the source of my certainty that any slumber I attempted would soon be interrupted, but didn't question it. Nor did I feel any great surprise when the sound of a very loud voice cut through the blustering howl of the wind.

"ALWYN SCRIBE!" it boomed, rousing much of the company who began reaching for their weapons as the voice continued in Caerith. "Get your *Ishlichen* carcass out here!"

"Stand easy," I told Tiler and the other soldiers who had begun arming themselves. I rose and descended the stairs, steeling myself for the confrontation to come. Pausing next to Juhlina, I lowered my voice to impart what might well be my final order: "Stay here. Keep them all inside."

The Widow was plainly unconvinced. "I'll come with you," she said, hefting her warhammer.

"No!" I gripped the haft of her weapon, forcing it down. "Whatever happens, don't attempt to fight them. If they cut my head off and make sport with my innards, you will do nothing. You hear me?"

She bridled at the harshness of my tone, but consented to reply with a stiff nod.

We had sealed the tower's doorway with tent canvas, which took a while to undo before I emerged to find my vision immediately swamped by sheeting rain. Sputtering, I pulled my cloak over my head, making out the sight of a very large figure standing in the castle gateway. The *Eithlisch* wore no covering tonight and stood revealed in all his bare-chested monstrosity, flesh blazing white with each flare of lightning. I fought a panicked urge to retreat, call the company to arms and secrete myself at the top of the tower while they faced his wrath. A shameful notion, but I'll not deny I considered it for a heartbeat longer than is seemly. However, there are some confrontations even the worst coward cannot evade. I had something to answer for, and I knew there was no shirking the punishment.

Labouring towards him through the swirling gale, I saw that the *Eithlisch*'s fists were clenched, water streaming down the knotted trunks of his arms to cascade from ball-sized knuckles. His impossibly broad chest swelled as I drew nearer, a flash of lightning revealing the wall of his teeth. They weren't bared in a smile.

I halted within reach of his arms, feeling it would be pointless not to. I remained silent, instead squinting up at his grimacing, rage-filled visage in grim expectation. I could claim to have awaited my impending fate with serene acceptance, but, cherished reader, you know me better than that. I trembled under the weight of his stare, my guts roiling so badly I thought I might dirty my trews at any second. But I'll always take some pride in the fact that I didn't run, not even when the monster moved closer, towering over me, his face now quivering with fury. Still, he said nothing, but he didn't need to.

"Yes," I told him, shouting above the wind and forcing myself to meet his baleful eye. "Yes, she died. Yes, I got her killed." I took a long deep breath, savouring it, for I knew it might be my last. "But so did you, when you sent her away. You knew the *Doenlisch* wouldn't be found unless she wanted to be. You also knew Lilat wouldn't willingly leave my side . . ."

The roar that came from the *Eithlisch*'s mouth was the equal of the storm's thunder. I closed my eyes, waiting for the first blow to fall, but instead of the sound of my skull crushing under the weight of his mighty fist, I heard the dull crump of shattered stone. Opening my eyes, I saw the *Eithlisch* on his knees, driving punches into the flagstones of the castle courtyard. I saw no blood on his knuckles, no sign that this caused him any injury at all, save for anguish, for he continued to roar, shards of granite fountaining around him. I had known him to be a being steeped in whatever arcane power the Caerith shared, but watching him vent his rage, I beheld something elemental, something beyond human.

He stopped after much of the courtyard had been transformed into grit, hunching over, a rebounding curtain of rain outlining his heaving torso. From some deep hidden recess of courage, I found the fortitude to speak again. "If you're done, we have much to discuss. I'm told you can lead me to the stone feather. It's important, apparently."

It transpired that the *Eithlisch* hadn't come alone, not that his companion appeared any happier to see me.

The *Eithlisch* responded to my words with a stone-faced glance before stomping off into the night, whereupon the tall, lean form of Lord Roulgarth Cohlsair emerged out of the pelting rain. His garb was a strange melange of knightly armour and Caerith accoutrements. A longsword hung at his belt, but the spear-like weapon, the *tahlik*, was slung across his back. The former Knight Warden of Alundia said nothing by way of greeting, instead pointing to the distant treeline before disappearing into the swirling gloom.

Come daybreak, I gathered Wilhum and Juhlina before leading them to the forest. We were met at the edge of the woods by a dozen *toalisch*, different from the other Caerith warriors I had seen in that they all wore swords or carried halberds in addition to their *tahliks* and flat bows. Some were also partially clad in ring mail rather than the usual hardened leather. The *toalisch* escorted us into their camp of conical shelters where every eye regarded us in glowering suspicion. It was hard to gauge their number accurately, for the camp was clearly extensive. The swift appearance of the *Eithlisch* last night made it plain we were expected, so I assumed they had established themselves here before our arrival.

We found Roulgarth in a small clearing tutoring a group of warriors in the use of the halberd, calling out instruction in accented but serviceable Caerith. His pupils wielded the weapons well enough, but without any semblance of order to their line.

"Scribe," Roulgarth said, looking me up and down with an expression that held ample judgement but scant welcome. "Not dead then?"

I ignored Roulgarth's jibe and nodded to the *toalisch*. "They'll need to learn some proper drill if they're to stand a chance against the Ascendant Queen's Host."

"So you made her a queen, did you? How proud you must be." Roulgarth afforded me a thin smile, reminding me that, while the skills I had learned from this man had surely saved my life, the dislike between us was entirely mutual. The moment of tension lengthened, growing taut enough that it might well have escalated if another voice hadn't intervened.

"Is that Wilhum Dornmahl I see?" a young *toalisch* asked, separating himself from the practising warriors to approach us. He spoke Albermaine-ish with a slight Alundian burr, but in all other respects he appeared so fully Caerith that it took me a second to recognise Merick Albrisend, Roulgarth's nephew.

"The most defeated knight of every tourney he entered, as I recall," Merick continued, offering Wilhum an overly florid bow.

"A tourney isn't a battle," Wilhum replied, though I detected no particular rancour as he returned Merick's bow.

"True enough," Merick conceded before turning to me, his humour fading, though he did consent to offer a nod. "Scribe. I couldn't quite believe it when the *Eithlisch* told us you were coming, intending to make war on your bitch-martyr no less. Yet here you are."

"As are you," I replied. "Hope you can fight better than when I knocked you on your arse at Walvern Castle."

A barb like this would once have brought at least a peeved scowl to Merick's brow, but now he merely laughed. "That I can, thanks to my uncle and these folk I'm proud to call brother and sister." He gestured to the *toalisch*, most of whom had left off their practice to spectate upon this exchange. Scanning them, I recognised one of the warriors from Lilat's village. Judging by her hard, accusatory stare, she recognised me too.

"How many do you command?" I asked, turning back to Roulgarth.

"None," he said. "They call me *Vahlisch*, a title which requires respect but not obedience. The Caerith have no rulers, Scribe. No kings, marshals or dukes to command them to war. They are here because the *Eithlisch* has told them their homes stand imperilled by the danger growing beyond the northern mountains. But it was their choice to come, and it will be their choice to fight. As for numbers—" he pursed his lips in consideration "—two thousand or so here with more likely to arrive by month's end."

"You'll have yet more soon enough, when the Crown Host arrives. Many are badly in need of training, and a marshal to guide them in battle."

"Your little king, or rather his mother, will be happy to place an exiled Alundian in charge of her army?" Roulgarth laughed. "I think not."

"The little king is betrothed to your niece, who will also be here soon. Does she, a queen in waiting who shares your blood, not also deserve your service?"

Roulgarth's face darkened, though not in anger this time. Here was a man resolving to bear a distasteful burden. "If such service wins Alundia back for my family, I'll suffer all the wounds to honour and pride I must. One thing these people have taught me is the power of humility."

"I've little doubt the princess regent will prove amenable to negotiation."

A shuffling among the onlooking warriors drew my eye to the sight of them parting to make way for a large, cowled figure. Even in his shrunken state, the *Eithlisch*'s appearance was enough to cause alarm to Wilhum and Juhlina. Both took a step forward as the Caerith giant advanced upon me, hands moving to their weapons, which in turn caused a ripple of aggressive agitation among the *toalisch*.

"It's all right," I said, resting a hand on my companions' shoulders.

Coming to a halt, the *Eithlisch* addressed Roulgarth in Caerith. "*Vahlisch*, are you content to wait here for the *Ishlichen* horde?"

"I am," Roulgarth replied. "Though I cannot give surety as to the outcome."

"My surety rests in you, as does that of the *toalisch*, for you have their trust. Alwyn Scribe—" the *Eithlisch* turned away, a thick arm emerging from his cloak in a beckoning gesture "—come. We have far to go."

"How far?" I called after him, but he was already striding off. Muttering a curse, I started after him, casting a string of orders over my shoulder at Wilhum and Juhlina. "I have to go with him. Stay here and prepare for the host's arrival. Lord Roulgarth has command of this outpost. If you can find some horses, scout the ground betwixt here and the northern mountains."

"How long will you be gone?" Wilhum called after me.

"I haven't the faintest notion." I paused, watching the *Eithlisch*'s cloaked form striding purposefully through the trees. Journeying alone into unknown lands with such a being, a being that detested me in truth, was not something to relish. "If I don't return," I said, turning back to address Roulgarth, "march on Albermaine come the winter. The pass at *Kain Laethil* provides a viable route. The Caerith know where to find it."

The forest seemed endless, the height and breadth of the trees marking it as distinct in nature and age from the Shavine Forest. The further we moved from the coast, the more majestic the trees became. I passed several with trunks broader than a house, ascending to a loftiness that outshone the tallest cathedral spire. A day of southward marching at the punishing pace set by my guide brought no end in sight nor notable variance in the landscape. The *Eithlisch* ignored my first flurry of questions while maintaining a long, regular stride I found hard to match. Nor did he feel the need to rest until nightfall, by which time I was both tired and hungry.

We camped in the shadow of a fallen giant of the forest, the bark of the great tree partially stripped to reveal wood a deep shade of red. The *Eithlisch* apparently felt no need of a fire, but avowed no objection to me lighting one, not that I had anything to cook over it. My companion did have food, a bundle of mushrooms and edible roots he consumed without feeling compelled to share. When I pointed out that the *Doenlisch* surely didn't wish me to starve, he drew back his cowl, revealing an expression of dour resignation.

"This one has food," he said, jutting his chin at the trees. "Though why she should strive so hard to be near you, I can't fathom."

Hearing the rustle of bracken underfoot, I rose in alarm, relaxing when Juhlina came into view. She carried two packs on her shoulders and the strain of her march showed in her stooped back and drawn features. It was clear she had run part of the way to catch up.

"Martyrs' arses, he walks fast," she said, dumping the packs beside my nascent fire. "All I could gather quickly," Juhlina said, extracting victuals from the sack. "Lucky this one's so easy to track."

"You shouldn't have come," I said, even though I knew I wouldn't order her to leave. "But I'm glad you did."

Juhlina handed me an iron skillet which I held over the fire while she cut strips of bacon. "Where are we going exactly?" she enquired, directing a cautious glance at the hulking Caerith. Shorn of his cowl, his face stood revealed in all its hairless, sculpted strangeness, a sight sure to invite stares. Seeing his visage in daylight for the first time, I was struck by the smoothness of his skin, lacking scars or stubble, despite an unfathomable span of years. I thought of the ravening, enraged creature from the night before and my conviction grew that, whatever he might be, the *Eithlisch* could not be termed fully human.

I expected him to ignore Juhlina's question as he had mine, but he responded without pause, his tone softer than before and phrased in his slightly archaic Albermaine-ish. "To council in the Mirror City, good lady. And from thence—" his gaze narrowed as his eyes slipped towards me "—to somewhere else."

"Mirror City?" Juhlina enquired.

"A clumsy translation," he told her. "The meaning of the title will become plain when you see it. Count yourself favoured, for few *Ishlischen* have ever travelled so deep into Caerith lands."

I didn't feel favoured. Instead, the weight of his gaze as he spoke of 'somewhere else' put me decidedly on edge.

"*Ishlichen*?" Juhlina asked.

"It's what they call us," I said, using my dagger to tease the bacon in the skillet while she added beans and a splash of water. "They also use it to describe things thrown on a midden heap."

"It's but one of our words for your people," the *Eithlisch* said. "Others are not so kind. Although in your case, Alwyn Scribe, I think it most fitting."

Juhlina raised an eyebrow at me. "This is the great shaman whose favour you so enjoy?"

"Well, he hasn't killed me yet." Glancing at the Caerith's features, impassive except for a very slight curving of the mouth that might have been amusement, I said, "How long until we reach this Mirror City of yours?"

"Time," the *Eithlisch* sighed, his lips forming the first smile I had seen on his face. "Why are your kind so obsessed with it? Numbers too. In your lands everything must be counted, portioned, labelled. I'd forgotten how tedious it could be."

I gritted my teeth against a retort, forcing a neutral tone. "If this is going to take weeks, we'll need to stop and hunt at some point. Since you neglected to provide sustenance for your fellow travellers."

"Do you still imagine this to be a barren wasteland, shorn of all but a handful of savages? The Caerith do not suffer their own to starve. That we leave to you. As for the journey, it will be long." I saw a small frown crease his overly smooth brow as he turned to survey the depths of the forest. "But," he added, voice fading to a whisper, "there are other dangers than hunger."

"Dangers?" I asked, but he said no more. Rising, the *Eithlisch* wandered away from the fire, his gaze still preoccupied by something I couldn't see.

"Where are you going?" I called after him, but he gave no response, his bulky form disappearing into the gathering gloom.

"What do we do if he doesn't come back?" Juhlina asked.

I forced a shrug to mask my concern and turned my attention to the simmering contents of the skillet. "Find a village and ask directions to the Mirror City, I suppose."

Chapter Twenty-Six

The *Eithlisch* failed to return that night and, after a fitful sleep in the shadow of the fallen tree, I began to harbour a half-hopeful, half-trepidatious suspicion that he might have abandoned us completely. However, upon walking a dozen paces off to relieve my nagging bladder I found him perched atop the overgrown mass of the great pine's stump. He appeared intent on paying me scant heed, so I continued my business, piss-steam billowing as I watched him standing in preoccupied concentration. His head was tilted, one ear cocked to the south as he strained to hear something. For my part, I heard only the creaking branches and birdsong typical to all forests.

"*Werleth?*" I asked him, using the Caerith word for trouble.

He ignored the question and maintained his vigil a while longer before jumping down from the stump. "Rouse her or leave her," he grunted, gesturing to a still slumbering Juhlina before striding off at an even more rapid pace than before.

"No breakfast?" Juhlina groaned at being shaken awake.

"Nor much of anything else until we get where he's taking us." I reached for her warhammer, pressing it into her hands. "Keep this ready. He's nervous about something. And anything that could make him nervous is enough to scare the shits out of me."

We spent another three days in the forest before it began to change. Gradually, gullies and ravines broke the ground while the trees lost their tallness. Oak, yew and ash became more prevalent, and the sky dwindled to an occasional flicker of blue through the canopy. The

Eithlisch never faltered in the rapidity of his stride, maintaining a southerly march through the hours of daylight. When we stopped for the night, he would disappear while Juhlina and I made camp and tried to ration our remaining supplies. I don't know if our hulking guide had need of sleep, but I never saw him at slumber throughout the entire journey. Also, his wariness increased as the days wore on. Come morning, I would see him prowling among the trees, ear cocked for the threat he refused to voice.

We came upon the settlement on the evening of the fourth day, a far larger version of the Caerith village I had wintered in the year before. The slope-roofed dwellings had the same way of blending with the landscape, and the people who clustered to greet the *Eithlisch* were similarly varied in colouring and facial markings. A group of *toalisch* were at the forefront of the crowd. They were led by a tall dark-skinned man with long, braided grey hair that belied a lean and athletic frame. Given what I knew about how Caerith age, I could only guess at his span of years, but the cautious respect with which he greeted the *Eithlisch* told of considerable experience.

"Torfaer," the *Eithlisch* said, returning the old warrior's nod before surveying the dozen or so *toalisch* at his back. "This is all? I hoped for more."

"We await those from the hill camps," Torfaer replied. "We will head north when they arrive."

"Don't tarry too long. And prevail upon your *veilisch* to join you. Every bow and blade will be needed for what lies ahead." The *Eithlisch* paused, stepping closer to speak on in a quieter voice. "Have you sighted *Paelith* recently? I smell them on the wind."

"I also, though none have been seen. We found tracks a day's march west. A large group to range so far from the plains."

The *Eithlisch* gave a soft grunt of acknowledgement before sparing a brief glance in our direction. "These *Ishlichen* need shelter for the night. And enough food for a lengthy march."

"It will be provided." Torfaer paused, his lean features tensed in reluctance. "There are some here who would welcome the touch of the *Eithlisch*. If you can spare it."

"Always."

The *Eithlisch* was duly led away among a throng of Caerith, a few lingering to gawp at Juhlina and I until a young warrior came forward. She had the copper hair common to many here, her freckled face curious rather than hostile as she spent a moment carefully looking us over.

"You . . . come," she said finally in laboured Albermaine-ish, turning away and beckoning us to follow. She led us through the winding leaf-covered lanes of the settlement to the banks of a narrow river running through its centre.

"Sleep there," the copper-haired woman said, pointing to a mill house. It was the first such structure I had seen in Caerith lands, smaller than its Albermaine equivalent, the blades of its waterwheel broader and turning at a blurringly fast rate.

"What do you mill here?" I asked her in Albermaine-ish, since I knew of no corresponding term in Caerith. "I thought your people grew no wheat."

"We grow . . . many things," she said, brow furrowed as she concentrated on the correct form of words. "As the land . . . allows."

Pushing open the mill house door, she revealed an interior bare of furniture but half-filled with barrels of corn. "I bring . . . furs," our host said. "To make sleep on."

"That would be nice," Juhlina said, grimacing as she surveyed our temporary home.

"I am Alwyn," I told the woman in Caerith before nodding to my companion. "She is Juhlina."

"I know your name," the *toalisch* said. I detected a curious shyness in her bearing and realised she felt herself to be in the presence of someone important. When she spoke again, it was in her own language, the tone tinged with a youthful eagerness for potentially forbidden knowledge.

"You have met her," she said. "The *Doenlisch*. She put her touch upon you."

"She did," I said, forcing a bland smile.

"Yes." She came closer, eyes wider now. "I sense it."

I felt Juhlina tense as the woman extended a hand, pressing her palm to my chest. "Her touch runs deep in you," she continued in a reverent murmur. "Not since my grandfather's passing have I met another who bore her mark."

"You have *vaerith*?" I ventured, discomforted by her gesture, but reluctant to cause offence by pulling away.

She smiled and nodded. "A small seed, but it may grow, so the *Eithlisch* says." Removing her hand, she straightened into brisk purposefulness, switching back to Albermaine-ish. "My name is . . . Pathera. I will bring furs now . . . and food."

"What is a *Paelith*?" I asked as she started towards the door. "I have not heard of such a beast."

"No beast," Pathera said. "*Paelith* are Caerith, those who ride the *paelah* and keep mostly to the southern plains."

I discerned a certain distaste in her bearing, even a slight hostility. "They are your enemies?"

This brought a frown of deep puzzlement to her brow, as if she couldn't fathom how one who bore the mark of the *Doenlisch* could ask such a foolish question. "Caerith do not war with each other," she told me before departing the mill house.

Feeling the weight of Juhlina's eyes on me, I spent a moment carefully inspecting the mill's workings. The gearing that drove the wheel seemed far more complex than those I had seen before, an intricate arrangement of toothed wooden wheels. The reason for such elaborate construction became apparent when I noticed a smaller stone spinning alongside the cylindrical slab of the grindstone. It spun at a faster rate and appeared to be fashioned from a dense, glittering material, whereas its larger companion was a hunk of pitted limestone. Drawing my dagger, I held the edge to the second stone, birthing an instant flurry of sparks.

"Ingenious," I said. "Never seen the like."

Juhlina, however, was not to be distracted. "She looked at you like folk looked at *her*," she said, and I didn't need to ask who she meant. Her tone bore the same demand for clarity I had heard after killing Arnabus in the Athiltor cathedral.

"The Caerith have many beliefs that seem strange to us," I replied, moving the dagger's blade along the stone.

"No." Juhlina moved to my side, her stare intent enough to command I meet it. "No more secrets, Alwyn Scribe. I left, but I came back, and I think you know why. I've followed you all this way, but I won't take another step without answers. Who is the *Doenlisch*? What is her mark? And most of all, whatever possessed you to fuck that mad bitch we were daft enough to serve?"

Fortunately, Juhlina soon found a lever that could unhook the spinning stones from the gears, sparing us the constant whirring trundle. I thought about refusing her demand, reasoning it would be a kindness of sorts. Denied answers, I had no doubt she would be true to her word, leaving me to face this journey with only the *Eithlisch* for company. But it wasn't this doleful prospect that loosened my tongue. Honesty was the very least of what I owed her.

So we sat in the increasing gloom of the mill house, only partially alleviated by the small candle Pathera brought along with the furs we huddled in, and I told the Widow my tale. I left nothing out, not even the stranger episodes that a rational mind would either scorn or decry as fanciful nonsense. Some of it flowed easily. Some was more difficult to parse from the parade of confusion and self-deceit we term as memory. But, of course, the portion of my life that defied true explanation, even to me, was the answer to her principal question.

"She killed Luminant Durehl?" Juhlina asked when I at last approached the crux of the matter, faltering over a description of the events following our escape from the Dire Keep.

"Yes," I said.

"In front of you?"

"Yes."

"And that was the first time you fucked? Right next to the corpse of a murdered Luminant?"

I could think of no better response than another muttered, "Yes."

Risking a glance at her face, I failed to find the disgusted judgement I expected. Instead, I saw only bafflement. Sighing, she gathered her furs more tightly about her, asking, "When did you know she was with child?"

"Not until the day the cathedral burned, along with most of Couravel. I tried to kill her. I *was* going to do it, but . . ." My words died in a helpless sigh, head filled with the memory of the terrible night. *Would you kill the child we made?* "Delric confirmed it when he came to my cell to tend my wounds. I don't know if she killed him for that, or for his part in her false resurrection. I doubt she needs a reason for killing any more."

"Delric was a good man, always happy to provide a sleeping draught when I asked. And the cuts he stitched left the smallest scars." She settled a steady gaze upon me. "But, he died a guilty man, Alwyn. Because we're all guilty. All of us who followed her, fought her battles and made her what she is. You're a fool, right enough, but so am I. So are Tiler and Ayin. We all have scales to be balanced."

I replied with a nod, but couldn't quite accept the fairness of her reasoning. Yes, we had all been fools, but I was the king of fools. "So, now you know why I killed Arnabus," I said. "And why she turned on me. I wonder if finding out her resurrection was nothing of the sort tipped her into madness, or the fact that it was done by Caerith hands."

Juhlina shook her head. "She was always mad. We just didn't see it. Or perhaps we were mad too and sanity dawned only when we beheld what she is." She shifted closer to me, hands emerging from her furs to clasp mine. "The child cannot be left in her hands. You know this."

"I do."

"To take it from her, you will have to kill her. You know that too."

I looked away, unsettled by the hard, unblinking purpose in her eyes.

"You know this, Alwyn!" Her grip tightened. "Love doesn't just vanish. I see it still lingers in you like a sickness you can't shake. But, love her or not, there is no end to this as long as she lives. I know you tried before, but how hard? Next time, you can't fail."

She moved closer still, pressing a kiss to my lips. I wanted to return it, pull her to me, yet I didn't. Juhlina rested her head on my chest for a second, murmuring, "Still it lingers." Turning away, she settled on to her bed of piled furs. "Like a sickness."

We departed the village with the dawn, roused by the *Eithlisch* kicking the mill house door open. No ceremony marked our leaving, which surprised me. I also noted his stride was slower this day, and he walked with a slight hunch to his broad shoulders.

"Those who require the touch of the *Eithlisch*," I commented as I enjoyed the novelty of actually walking alongside him for once. "You healed them, didn't you? As you healed me."

As was his way, he said nothing, replying with only a small, annoyed shift of his eyes.

"It tires you, doesn't it?" I went on, my curiosity stirred. I had thought him a being of perhaps inexhaustible strength, as well as arcane gifts. Now it appeared even he had limits.

"Yes," he grunted, forcing a more rapid stride in order to pull ahead. "And in your case, Alwyn Scribe, don't expect me to do it twice."

By my reckoning, we followed a south-westerly course for the next few days. The wooded hill country persisted with its occasionally steep slopes that did much to negate any enjoyment of the undeniable beauty of this land. The *Eithlisch* soon recovered his prior vitality and irksomely fast pace, though he did consent to a daily noontime rest of short duration. Pathera had provided us a sack of salted meat, flat bread and nuts, most of it consumed by the time we came upon another settlement. This was even larger than Pathera's village, a sprawl of dwellings atop a ridge overlooking a tall waterfall. Once again, the *Eithlisch* was greeted with grave respect by the gathered *toalisch*, many of whom had plainly travelled considerable distances to get here. His words to them were short but urgent. "Head north and do not linger. The *Vahlisch* awaits you. Trust his word as you trust mine."

He wouldn't permit us to rest here overnight, insisting we move on once supplies had been provided. The forest thinned considerably when we descended the ridge, broad clearings soon giving way to open fields. Juhlina and I gawped at unfamiliar herds of cattle roaming the undulating grasslands, tall beasts with huge curving horns and shaggy pelts. They bellowed warnings if we passed too close, their aggression and the absence of walls making it clear they were wild.

"The Caerith have no farmers to tend their lands or livestock?" Juhlina observed to the *Eithlisch* during one of our all too brief rest stops.

"My people keep some beasts for milk and wool," he responded. "But for the most part, we find that land and beast require no tending. When my people require meat, they hunt. Everything else can be grown, gathered and stored in accordance with the seasons. We take only what we need, not what we want." He spoke with a preoccupied air, gaze constantly roving the landscape.

"*Paelith*?" I asked, provoking an irritated tightening of the mouth, but no words. "Caerith do not war with each other, yet you fear them. Why?"

"Even the mightiest stone has cracks," he said. "And it is not me they wish to war with."

"Me, then? They object to my presence, even though I bear the *Doenlisch*'s mark?"

"Her mark is not like the metal you clad yourself in for battle. And her words are not heard by all. The *Paelith* have their own *meilah*, and those whose *vaerith* guides them along different paths."

"Will they try to kill me if they find us?"

The *Eithlisch* said nothing, which I took as a yes.

"Will you stop them?"

He resumed his rapid stride, soon disappearing into the long grass. This I took as a no.

The following weeks assumed a loose routine of sorts. Every two or three days we would arrive at a settlement, some large enough to be termed a town, others just a small hamlet nestled among the hills. Typically, a group of warriors, often joined by the local hunters, would greet the *Eithlisch*, whereupon he would urge them to begin their northward march. I soon realised that this southward trek had a dual purpose for our guide. Not only was he conveying me to his Mirror City, and the location of the as yet unexplained stone feather, he was also convincing reluctant Caerith to answer the call to war. The *toalisch* gathered along our line of march were awaiting his coming, requiring his blessing before heading north.

"This hasn't happened before," I said to him one night. It was the fifteenth day of our journey, and my voice was soured with a growing weariness. "War," I added when the observation drew a sharp glance. "Or the threat of a war on such a scale. Lilat said the *toalisch* often fight raiders on the southern coast, but never have the Caerith faced an invasion."

"Never is a stupid word," the *Eithlisch* replied. "Our history is longer than you can imagine, Alwyn Scribe. Your mad queen is not the first to cast hungry eyes upon these lands. But—" he shrugged "—it has been a very long time since so great a threat loomed. We met it then, and defeated it, though it cost us much in blood. There's a place, far from here, a cove on the southern shore where the sands turned red with it. Even today, I can feel the stain of so much slaughter."

"You talk like you were there," Juhlina observed.

To this, the *Eithlisch* said nothing. Usually, when his willingness to converse had been exhausted, he would rise and stalk off into the night. This time, for some reason, he lingered.

"He was," I said. I watched the *Eithlisch* stare into the fire, eyes distant with grim remembrance. "Do you have any notion of how old you are?"

I was unused to seeing any emotion on his face beyond disapproval, so it was jarring to see a faint smile play over his lips. "Older than you," he said. "Yet younger than the *Doenlisch*."

Abruptly, the amusement vanished from his features and he stood, eyes fixed upon the darkness beyond the firelight. At first I heard nothing, but soon it reached my ears, a steady thrum that built into the familiar drumbeat of hooves upon the earth.

"*Paelah*," I said, reaching for my sword and getting to my feet. "It means 'horse', doesn't it?"

"It means more than that," he muttered back. Seeing the sword in my hand, he added, "Keep it sheathed, for now."

The riders came into view soon after. I counted a dozen vague mounted shapes coming to a halt, keeping to the shadows. Snorts and stamping hooves filled the night air while the *Eithlisch* stood in frowning expectation. I discerned a pinched quality to his expression, as if he suffered a grave insult.

"Should've brought a crossbow," Juhlina said, shifting to my side with her warhammer in hand. A loud whinny in the dark caused her to raise the weapon to readiness.

"Easy," I told her, placing a restraining hand on her arm. "I doubt fighting will avail us much now."

Another snort sounded from the shadows and a horse stepped forward to reveal itself, drawing a muffled exclamation from Juhlina. I found the sight of the beast no less startling. It stood at least two hands taller at the shoulder than even the most impressive warhorse I had seen, its coat all black save for a flash of white in the centre of its forehead. Its neck and shoulders were a knotted mass of muscle that made the rider on its back appear almost childlike. More arresting than its size and evident power were its eyes. Blackfoot was a clever animal by horse standards, and would often exhibit his frequent scorn or occasional approval with just a glance. Looking into the bright but narrowed gaze of this creature, I knew instinctively its nature went beyond mere cleverness. Also curious was the absence of a bridle. Its head was completely unfettered, and the reins held by the rider were affixed to a harness about the animal's shoulders.

"This is him?" the rider asked. Dragging my gaze from the eyes of his mount, I saw a lean man of bronzed complexion clad in leather armour far more hardy and extensive than most *toalisch*. A lance was strapped across his back and a flat bow hung from his saddle. His words were coloured by an accent harsher than the forest and hill dwelling Caerith we had met so far.

The *Eithlisch* gave no response, merely maintaining his same frowning stance. His failure to answer appeared to act as a signal for the other *Paelith*, each one coming forward to reveal the circle they formed around us. The horses varied in colouring but were all equal in size to the black giant who continued to regard me with his too clever eyes.

"I have no patience for your pretensions, old man," the bronze-skinned *Paelith* told the *Eithlisch*. The horse brought him closer, even though I saw no signal from the rider. As he leaned forward in the saddle, I beheld a face set in stern, demanding anger. His markings were more regular than most Caerith, twin lines of pale flesh tracing from his brows and over his shaven head. "Is this him?" he asked again, jabbing a finger at me.

Still the *Eithlisch* did not consent to reply, stubborn resentment showing in his clenched jaw and bunching fists. Sensing matters were about to escalate to an uncertain outcome, I stepped forward, offering the rider the customary nod of greeting.

"My name is Alwyn Scribe," I said in Caerith. "And I bear the mark of the *Doenlisch*, if that is your meaning."

The rider stared at me with all the respect one might afford the leavings of a dog's arse. After a long interval of disdainful scrutiny, he sat back in his saddle, giving a contemptuous sniff. "Liar," he said simply, addressing his words to the circle of riders. "This *Ishlichen* filth may have learned to prattle in our tongue, but that proves nothing. I sense not the slightest hint of the *Doenlisch*'s touch upon him."

"You have no *vaerith*, Morieth!" the *Eithlisch* growled. "You are not fit to judge such things."

"And you have no say over me or mine, old man!" Morieth snapped back. "Too long have the *Paelith* suffered the weight of your decrepit creed. We will chart our own *meilah*, the path of the *paelah*, the path that tells us there is no trust or alliance to be had with the *Ishlichen*. You travel far, spreading warnings of war. Let it come and let it be the end of his kind." Moving with the swiftness of a skill learned since childhood, Morieth unslung the lance from his back, levelling the point at me. The action was repeated by his companions, the surrounding circle bristling with spearpoints. Juhlina shifted into a fighting stance, hefting her warhammer while I made ready to draw my longsword. Strangely, this display of aggression failed to rouse their mounts to more than a gentle sway of the head.

"The *Doenlisch* would never have put her mark on one such as this," Morieth continued, lance again jabbing in my direction. "You, *Eithlisch*, are either a gulled fool or a deceiver."

The *Eithlisch* let out an ominous groan, his shoulders broadening as he began to swell. It seemed he was prepared to fight for me, after all. "The only deceiver here is you," he said, the words emerging through a wall of clenched teeth. "Why?" the *Eithlisch* demanded, rounding on the other riders. "Once the *Paelith* were true to our ways. Why do you allow yourselves to be guided into folly by this spinner of lies?"

If the encircling warriors were cowed by the swollen giant's anger, none showed it. Scanning their faces, I felt a rush of recognition for the rigid, unflinching countenance of the true fanatic. This lot were every bit as committed to Morieth's creed as anyone who ever followed Evadine. Realising this confrontation would have but one ending, I took a firmer grip on my sword and began to inch the blade free of the scabbard. Morieth was still distracted by the *Eithlisch*. If I could cut him down quickly, we might have a chance, albeit a slim one.

My deadly intent, however, came to an abrupt halt, along with the increasingly voluminous argument betwixt the two Caerith, when the black horse Morieth rode raised its head to emit a sound that cannot truly be termed a whinny. It was far deeper, a low rumble lacking any shrillness. And I felt it, deep in my bones.

Morieth fell instantly silent, as did the *Eithlisch*. In an instant, the *Paelith* rider's expression lost its fanatical rictus to shift into wide-eyed fear. He started in fright as the horse came towards me, but made no move to stop it. I fought the urge to run and forced myself to lower my sword, watching the horse's mighty head loom above. As it sniffed me, I felt the hot, musty gusts of its breath, like the blasts of heated air from an open forge door. Once again, I saw the intelligence in its eyes, and knew myself to be subject to careful appraisal. I was unable to prevent my gaze slipping to the massive, shaggy hooves, my heart labouring faster with the knowledge that this animal could pound me to ruin on a whim. The great horse snorted, recapturing my attention. Was there a glint of amusement there in the slight narrowing of its gaze? I couldn't know, but, amused or not, I saw no sign of hostility.

Snorting in apparent satisfaction, the horse raised its head and retreated a few paces, whereupon it reared with such sudden violence that Morieth was cast from the saddle. He landed hard, but scrambled to his feet with lithe quickness. I expected the rage of the embarrassed braggart, but instead he appeared stricken as he gaped at his mount. The horse, however, deigned not to afford Morieth another glance. Instead, it let out another throaty rumble and the horses on either side also reared to dump their riders from the saddle. The other *paelah* drew back, much to the patent disappointment of the fanatics they carried.

"What a pitiable fool you are, Morieth," the *Eithlisch* said, his swollen bulk diminishing as he strode forward to take the reins of a russet-coloured mare with a vacant saddle. "You may be unable to discern the mark of the *Doenlisch*, but the *paelah* are not."

Morieth, all defiance and antagonism apparently leached from him, had no answer. He stumbled away like a man fleeing a scene of horror, dropping his lance to pelt into the darkness.

"A *Paelith* who will never again ride the *paelah*," the *Eithlisch* said, casting his words at the crestfallen warriors. "That is the fate of those who deny the true *meilah*. You have been fools, but no soul need be a fool forever. Atone by escorting us to the Mirror City." With that, he climbed on to the mare's back. "Mount up, Alwyn Scribe," he told me, gesturing to the black horse. "They don't like to be kept waiting."

Chapter Twenty-Seven

The *Eithlisch* told me the black *paelah*'s name was Uthren, which translated as Night Shadow. How the *Eithlisch* came to learn it was but one of the many mysteries regarding the great horses of the Caerith plains that I have never fully resolved. That first night, when they bore us away from the camp, we galloped full pelt through darkened hill country without apparent fear of stumbling. I soon understood that the reins I clung to with an occasionally desperate ferocity offered no control over the beast I rode, they were merely to prevent its rider from falling.

The *paelah* finally slowed when dawn glimmered over the eastern hilltops, by which time I had begun to sag in the saddle. I could only guess how many miles we had covered as I slipped from Uthren's back when he consented to halt. I cared little for the contempt of the *Paelith* for my weak-legged exhaustion, ignoring their muttered exchanges of derision to stumble away and sit next to an equally spent Juhlina. Naturally, the *Eithlisch* exhibited no tiredness at all, and a single glance of his glowering visage was enough to silence the murmuring scorn of our escorts.

Looking around, I saw the landscape had changed. Steep, wood-speckled hills had become rolling downs blanketed in thick grass. When the *Paelith* dismounted, Uthren and the other *paelah* wandered off to graze, tails swishing as they nickered and jostled each other.

"The *Paelith* are not their masters, are they?" I enquired of the *Eithlisch*. "They consent to be ridden."

"Such has it always been with *Paelith* and *paelah*," he replied. "In the time after the *Ealthsar*, the starved and scattered people of the plains beseeched the *paelah* for aid, and it was given, though how the compact was formed remains forever a mystery."

"*Ealthsar?*" Juhlina asked.

"It's what they call the Scourge," I explained.

"So, it really did cover all the world, as the scrolls claimed." She frowned, shaking her head. "And there I was, casting aside all Covenant lore as worthless."

"Not all." Inevitably, my mind went to Sihlda and the Pit Mines, her ever patient face flickering in the meagre candle light as she tried to impart lessons I had ultimately failed to learn. "There's wisdom there. We just chose the wrong guide."

The *paelah* allowed us until noon to rest and eat before returning. Once again, Uthren came to me, turning to offer his back with an impatient snort. He sped off just as I settled into the saddle, rearing and striking off across the grasslands at a pace even faster than the night before. I checked to ensure Juhlina and the *Eithlisch* were following, then concentrated my efforts on not falling. A tumble at this speed would surely involve more than a few broken bones. Soon, however, my trepidation gave way to exhilaration. Shorn of the terrors of a night-time ride, I began to appreciate the privilege of riding a *paelah* at full pelt. To either side, the world became a blur of green and blue while the landscape ahead unfolded in its unspoilt majesty. Once I grew accustomed to Uthren's movements, his sheer speed brought a sense of flying, one I was happy to lose myself in, for the joy of it drowned my worries, at least for a time.

Thanks to the *paelah*, our journey to the Mirror City took four more days rather than the weeks long trudge the *Eithlisch* had given me to expect. Having sped through the rolling grasslands, we entered a region characterised by increasingly tall hills that soon grew to mountains, the valleys between rich in rivers and lakes. Here, at last, the great horses slowed as they carried us along winding tracks through ridge and vale. We passed many more settlements here and saw far more people. From their rapt, often joyous stares, it was clear they were scarcely more used to the sight of the *paelah* than I was. As before, the settlements were crowded with gathered *toalisch*, but here they responded to the *Eithlisch* with deference instead of obedience.

"We await the word of the council," one grey-haired warrior said in reply to the ancient mystic's exhortations to march north. "War is not embarked upon without the consent of our elders."

I saw how the *Eithlisch* restrained himself during these meetings, clamping down on his annoyance to force out an assurance that such consent would soon be forthcoming. However, the more settlements we visited as we pushed deeper into the lake lands, the deeper his anger grew. Also, although he tried to hide it, my practised eye for duplicity detected a lack of conviction in his platitudes.

"You're not certain at all, are you?" I asked him during one of the infrequent interludes when the *paelah* consented to walk instead of the rapid trot they adopted in the mountains. "About the council's judgement. You think they might deny the *Doenlisch*'s wishes."

"I do not answer to them," he said. "Nor is any Caerith bound by their word. But the judgement of elders is never disregarded by our people. They have known strife in their time, but never the depth of danger we face now. When you stand before them, Alwyn Scribe, speak only truth. Do not attempt your wiles upon them. Do not lie, they will know."

We came upon the Mirror City shortly after dawn of our third day in the lake lands, the aptness of its name becoming instantly apparent the moment it came into view. I breathed a soft, wordless sigh of amazement as my eyes tracked over a series of tall spires rising from a group of islands in the centre of a broad lake. The spires were formed of angular walls dotted with windows and balconies ascending in a spiral over their massive flanks. Each was at least three times the height of the tallest structure in Albermaine, birds flocking and wheeling about the narrow, needle-like summits. The islands they sat upon were linked by arcing bridges, themselves adorned with smaller spires. The lake appeared possessed of an unnatural calmness, reflecting the city with only a faint shimmer to create the impression of a vast construction floating in an azure void. It all gleamed white in the sun climbing above the mountains, a blaze of untarnished marble that nevertheless conveyed a sense of considerable age. I saw echoes of the shattered city under the mountain in the way stone had been worked into something wondrous, but this was no ruin.

"This has stood since before the *Ealthsar*," I said to the *Eithlisch*, a statement rather than a question.

"Centuries before and centuries since," he said. "The only Caerith city to escape destruction."

"How many people live here?" Juhlina asked, staring at the spires in unabashed awe.

"None. It was empty at the time of the *Ealthsar*. That is what spared it. And so, to keep it preserved, it has remained empty ever since, except when council is called."

The *paelah* conveyed us down a winding track to the banks of the lake where a long-hulled boat bobbed. It sat empty, tethered to the shore with rope. Coming to a halt, Uthren shifted his shoulders, his signal to dismount. After I did so, he paused to afford me a final glance of his too knowing eyes before tossing his head and trotting away.

"Consider yourselves released from obligation," the *Eithlisch* told our *Paelith* escort as he climbed down from the russet-coated mare. "I beseech you to seek further atonement by riding north to join the *Vahlisch*."

They appeared as unmoved by his words as they had been throughout our shared journey. A fanatic's fervour doesn't simply disappear, and I knew their service had been secured solely through submission to the *paelah*'s will. Apparently disgusted by their silence, the *Eithlisch* turned his back on them and moved to the lake, wading into the water to haul himself aboard the boat.

"I hope you have some knowledge of water craft, Alwyn Scribe," he said, hefting an oar. "I've always detested boats."

Juhlina took charge of the tiller while the *Eithlisch* and I worked the oars. "Why are they still there?" I asked the *Eithlisch* as we rowed, nodding to the *Paelith* still sitting in silent watchfulness on shore. "You released them."

"Awaiting the outcome of the council, I imagine," he grunted. "Hoping their delusions will be proven correct."

"Despite the *paelahs*' judgement?"

"There are factions within all tribes. Some of the plains folk revere the *paelah* the way your kind revere the dead servants of your peculiar faith. Others, like Morieth, regard their compact as more an association of equals." His countenance darkened and he cast a glance over his shoulder at the towering city. "And Morieth's notions did not grow from nothing."

Juhlina steered for a jetty protruding from the rocky flanks of the nearest island. Climbing free of the boat, my gaze ascended the spire rising above us, birthing the dizzying sensation of being dwarfed by something almost beyond comprehension.

"How could human hands ever craft such a thing?" Juhlina wondered, echoing my thoughts.

"I've read of great tombs beyond the southern deserts said to rise to similar heights," I said. "The early scrolls talk of them being built by vast armies of slaves captured in war."

"No slave built this." She moved to the tall, pointed arch that formed the entrance to the spire, running her fingers over intricate carvings decorating the marble frame. They resembled the Caerith script I had seen in the *Doenlisch*'s book, but possessed of a flowing elegance, as if they had truly been written in the stone rather than carved. "This," Juhlina smiled as her eyes roved over the characters, "was made with love."

"She sees what you do not, Alwyn Scribe," the *Eithlisch* said, stepping past me to enter the vast structure via a tall arched opening. "This is not the product of the lash."

"How could you know?" I asked, following. The spire's base was a large, vaulted space that echoed our voices with uncanny precision. Although bare of monument or statue, its every surface, from floor to ceiling, was covered in the same flowing script. "You can't read any of this, can you?" I went on, gesturing to the mass of words. "Is that why you value ancient Caerith books so much? You hope they might provide the key to translating all of this."

The *Eithlisch* confined his answer to a brief glower before starting towards another arched opening in the opposite side of the structure. Juhlina and I followed him out and on to the bridge beyond, crossing the gentle curve of its span to the next islet. The spire here was yet taller, its hollow base once again rich in inscriptions.

"I once possessed a key to translating Caerith text," I informed the *Eithlisch* as we followed him through the spire to another bridge. Seeing his broad back tense as he resisted the impulse to reply, I found I couldn't resist an additional taunt. "It was formulated by an Ascarlian scholar of my prior acquaintance. Sadly, I was obliged to surrender it to the *Doenlisch*'s care. Surprising, don't you think, that she never felt the need to convey it into your hands?"

The *Eithlisch* kept walking, but consented to reply in a soft growl, "Be sure to tell the council that, Alwyn Scribe. There are those among the Caerith willing to torment you to death for the meaning of just one word inscribed on these stones."

After that, I felt a judicious silence to be in order. We traced our way across three more bridges to the largest of the islands, which, appropriately, also featured the tallest spire. Given the *Eithlisch*'s portentous warnings, I had expected the council of Caerith elders to be a large gathering, a parliament of strange ancients. Instead, upon entering the shadowed vastness of the spire's base, I counted only four people awaiting us at the centre of the broad swathe of inscribed stone. They remained silent as we approached, offering no greeting to our guide, and he none to them. However, the bright gleam of his eyes in the unalloyed gloom of this cavernous space told of distinct wariness.

Drawing closer to the group, I saw that it consisted of two men and two women. As seemed to be ever the case with the Caerith, they were disparate in appearance and age. I perceived a wealth of experience in their collective gaze as each of them studied me with intense scrutiny. The tallest among them exuded the least hostility. A man of peach-coloured hair and skin even more pale than the *Eithlisch*, he maintained a placid expression that bordered on a smile. Even so, his gaze was no less piercing than his companions' in the way it scoured my face and form.

The woman to his left appeared small in comparison, even though she was about Juhlina's height. Her skin was dark and flawlessly smooth, save for the reddish marks on her neck. The *tahlik* on her back and the hardiness of her leather garb marked her as a warrior, one who was either greatly skilled or very lucky, judging by the absence of scars. Her face was stripped of emotion, as if she worried what her expression would reveal.

The woman to the tall man's right appeared to be the oldest of the group, her stooped form clad in overlapping, partly ragged woollen shawls and long tendrils of untidily braided hair cascading over her face. She supported herself with a gnarled tree branch, which she clung to with both of her hands. The swollen knuckles and protruding veins made it appear as if her flesh had been welded to the branch over time. Her frailty was evident, but so too was the keen insight of the eyes that glared at me from behind her scraggly veil of hair.

The man beside her made no effort to conceal his hostility, his shaven head and deer-hide garb marking him as *Paelith*. His colouring was much like that of the fanatical Morieth, and I discerned a definite similarity of feature in his scowling face, creased with both age and, unlike the *toalisch* woman, the scars of combat. *Morieth's father?* I wondered. *Grandfather, even.* Given the span of their years, such things were always difficult to judge among the Caerith.

After we halted before them, their collective scrutiny shifted from me to Juhlina. The *Paelith* spoke first, his voice a suspicious rasp. "This *Ishlichen* was not called here," he said, pointing to Juhlina but addressing his words to the *Eithlisch*. "Why did you bring her to this most revered of places?"

"He brought her because I willed it," I said, taking some small satisfaction from the man's surprise at being addressed in his own language. "And I am here because the *Doenlisch* wills it." Reasoning that a modicum of diplomacy might serve me well, I arranged my face into bland agreeableness, spreading my hands and lowering my head. "If you have questions for me, I will answer them. Though I will not pretend to know the *Doenlisch*'s mind in all things."

The stick-clutching old woman let out a harsh, grating sound. I initially took it for a cough but, seeing the baring of yellowish-grey teeth behind her dangling hair, realised it had been a laugh. "He speaks in meaningless platitudes," she said, her voice a croaking whisper that nevertheless commanded attention. "As is always the way with his kind. Blandishments and compliments one minute, then it's all fire, blades and pillage the next."

"And yet he bears the *Doenlisch*'s mark," the tall pale-skinned man said in mild, well-modulated tones that chimed a bell of recognition in my head. *This one's a scholar*, I decided.

"You put too much stock in her," the old woman retorted. "She is not infallible. I knew her long before any of you were born, remember?"

"She never claimed infallibility," the tall man replied. "Only truth, and never did I know her to falter in that regard. He bears her mark. That cannot be denied nor ignored in our deliberations. I feel her hand upon him, and I know you do too."

"I feel it, true enough. Doesn't mean I like it." The old woman shuffled closer to me, shawls and hair swaying. "So then," she said, halting to deliver a weak jab at my foot with her stick, "what do they call you, child?"

"If you're to have my name," I replied, "I'll have yours first."

I saw the *Paelith* bridle at this, while the old woman gave another grating laugh. For their part, the scholar and the warrior displayed scant emotion.

"Names, is it?" The old woman jabbed at my foot again, harder this time. "I've got quite a few. Which do you want?"

"Whichever one pleases you most."

"Heh." She spent a moment in contemplation. "You can call me Shaelisch, then. Always liked that one. My tenth and favourite husband preferred it. That one's Turlia," she went on, flicking her stick at the *toalisch* woman, "he's Deracsh," she pointed to the scholar, before casting a sour glance in the *Paelith*'s direction. "And this whelp is Corieth."

"Kin to Morieth, perhaps?" I asked, raising an eyebrow at the plainsman. "Who we met on the way here."

This brought an abrupt silence as the other three members of this council redirected their scrutiny to the *Paelith*. He, however, kept his eyes on me. "I am proud to call Morieth my great-grandson," he said. "As fine a rider as ever to grace the back of a *paelah*."

"Strange then that the *paelah* he rode threw him off and offered his back to me."

Apparently, the *Paelith*'s wealth of years didn't ward him against a quick temper. "You lie!" he hissed, starting towards me. "Just like all your kind!"

"He speaks true," the *Eithlisch* said, a softly spoken intervention that succeeded in bringing Corieth to a halt. "Remember where you are."

My experience with the Caerith had imbued me with an impression of unity. They had always seemed to possess a cohesion and absence of discord that distinguished them from the people of Albermaine. Seeing the spasm of quivering hatred Corieth directed at the *Eithlisch* then, I wondered if such cohesion was merely a facade. Ancient and wise, they surely were, but for the first time I understood the deep divisions of belief and purpose running through the hearts of these people.

Corieth's fury, impotent though it may have been, shifted into barely concealed fear when Shaelisch addressed him. Her voice was softer now, intent rather than commanding, but it had lost the harshness of age. The voice of someone who expected all questions to be answered. "Did you set your great-grandson to prevent the *Eithlisch* bringing the *Ishlichen* here, Corieth? Did you attempt to subvert the will of this council?"

I hadn't seen a Caerith lie before. The Sack Witch could be infuriatingly vague, but never deceptive. The *Eithlisch* would simply ignore questions he didn't want to answer. Corieth, however, was the only Caerith I ever saw utter a blatant untruth. From the way his mouth twisted around the words and the rapid blinking of his eyes, he was clearly unaccustomed to deceit. So poor was his performance. In fact, I almost pitied him.

"Morieth follows his own path," he rasped, forcing himself to meet Shaelisch's eyes in the manner unique to determined, if inexpert, liars. "As all true Caerith do."

Whether Shaelisch perceived this lie or not, I couldn't tell. What appeared plain as day to me may not be so stark to a soul unused to outright dishonesty, ancient or not. Her reaction was confined to a faint sigh before she turned away from Corieth, flicking her stick at me.

"You have words for us, child," she said, voice now possessed of an impatient tetchiness. "So speak them."

I saw little point in further preamble, nor did I attempt to imbue my words with performative gestures or grandiose phrasing. Such things were beyond my command of Caerith, and I doubted they would carry much weight for this audience in any case.

"A new queen has risen in the land beyond the northern mountains," I said. "A queen I believe to be under the sway of the beings my people refer to as the Malecite. She possesses powerful *vaerith* which guides her actions. She has used this to seize power and will use it again to bring her armies against the Caerith, for she hates you and believes your destruction to be ordained by her faith. To defeat her, you must join with her enemies. To the north, exiles from my lands and *toalisch* already gather together to learn the skills of the *Vahlisch*. Only through alliance will we prevail. These are my words, and this is the will of the *Doenlisch*."

The reaction of the council was one of silent contemplation, even Corieth who had regained enough composure to mould his features into a frown of doubtful disparagement. Predictably, he was the first to speak.

"How do you know the will of the *Doenlisch*?" he demanded.

"She told me," I replied simply.

"You met her?"

"Several times."

"Where? When—?"

"Enough!" Shaelisch snapped, the tip of her stick rapping loud on the inscribed marble floor. "He has her mark. This has already been established."

"I cannot believe the *Doenlisch* would seek to embroil us in an *Ishlichen* war," Corieth stated.

"Soon it will be our war," the *Eithlisch* said. "Ever has the *Doenlisch* worked to preserve the Caerith. Her tools may be—" he spared me a brief glance "—roughly made. But always her purpose cannot be doubted."

Turlia, the *toalisch* woman, spoke for the first time then, flawless face regarding me with the same pitch of scrutiny. "Yet she is not here. If we were to hear this from her own lips, I would harbour no doubts." She turned to the *Eithlisch*. "When last we met, you agreed to send a *veilisch* to seek out the *Doenlisch*, beseech her to return to us. What became of their mission?"

The *Eithlisch*'s features tightened in sorrow and he lowered his head. I spoke up before he could answer, feeling the duty to be mine.

"Her name was Lilat," I said. "She guided me across the mountains and stayed with me when it became clear the *Doenlisch* could not be found. She saved my life." I worked my throat to banish the sudden catch before pushing the words out. "She was murdered by the queen for seeking to aid me when I lay captive."

"Lilat," Turlia repeated, her eyes still lingering on the *Eithlisch*. "The *veilisch* who would be a *toalisch*. I remember her well from the *toawild*. Her skills were great and a fine *toalisch* she would have made, yet I turned her away at your request. You told me her *mielah* would lead her to a great destiny, a great service to all Caerith. Is this what you meant? A death at the hands of an *Ishlichen* tyrant?"

I watched the *Eithlisch*'s shoulders sag, his features tensing not with anger, but guilt. I recalled his fury that first night at Castle Dreol. Had it truly been directed at me, or to himself?

"You knew?" I asked, a sudden heat building in my chest. "You knew what would happen to her and you sent her anyway?"

"Are your hands so clean, Alwyn Scribe?" he asked, a resentful gleam in his eye as he turned to address his fellow elders. "I know of no member of this council who can claim their *mielah* unsullied by a single misdeed. Lilat was precious to me, as are all Caerith. But her *mielah* could not be denied, nor would she have wished it to be."

"This does not aid our discourse," Deracsh said in his scholar's voice. "A decision lies before us, one this council has never faced before: alliance with those from beyond our borders."

"One who spends his life harvesting stories should know the folly of this," Corieth said. "Ever since the *Ealthsar* has it been proven time and again that we have no friends save ourselves. Moreover—" he jutted his chin at me "—his kind are mired in greed and violence. Allow them a foothold in our lands and they will never leave. They will stay and grow like corruption in an open wound. Our land will be spoiled, our very blood sullied, and in time we will become as they are. This is what my *vaerith* tells me. Be it known that whatever your decision this day, the *Paelith* will have no part of any alliance with the *Ishlichen*."

"It is not within your gift to speak for all *Paelith*, Corieth," Deracsh replied. "This council guides, it does not seek to instruct. Such a thing would entail the claiming of *aerleth*." This word was unfamiliar to me, but the careful, somewhat ominous emphasis with which Deracsh spoke it indicated considerable significance. "Is that your intent?" he asked, his tone far from mild now.

"You know it is not!" Self-deceit can be as obvious as any lie. In Corieth's case, it showed in the defensive pitch of his voice and the way he backed away from the council, bridling in anger and self-righteous pride. "I'll hear no more from this *Ishlichen* wretch!" he stated, affording me a disgusted glance as he continued to retreat. "You have heard my words and I'll say no more. To the plains I go. There every clan will hear my truth. Mark well that in the days to come it shall be they who stand as the true shield of the Caerith."

"If you leave now," Deracsh called after him, "you will never stand among this council again."

Corieth's echoing footsteps continued without pause. He soon dwindled to a small silhouette against the light of the tall arched exit before disappearing completely. In his absence, the remaining members of the council all took on a sorrowful aspect. I doubted any harboured particular affection for the *Paelith* elder, leading me to ascribe their darkened mood to the sundering of the council's unity.

"What does *aerleth* mean?" I asked the *Eithlisch*.

"In your tongue it would be termed 'authority' or 'governance,'" he said. "Kingship, to put it simply."

"Ah." I pursed my lips. "Among my people, a man who seeks to weaken their resolve against an enemy while accruing power to himself would be termed a traitor." There was no Caerith equivalent to this word, so I used the Albermaine-ish before going on to elaborate. "One who acts against his own people through deception. In my lands, traitors are tortured and hanged."

"And yet," the *Eithlisch* replied, "in your lands, traitors are as common as the rain. And are not you, Alwyn Scribe, called such by the very queen you seek to oppose?"

Scanning the faces before me, frowning in puzzlement but also no small measure of disdainful judgement, I realised the scale of the gulf that still existed between us. They might regret Corieth's departure, and criticise his reasoning, but the thought of acting against him was plainly anathema. *Aerleth*, I thought. *They resist it. Detest it even.* The notion made me both envious and resentful of the sudden sense of inferiority it engendered.

"I have spoken my words," I said. "A decision stands before you."

"A decision not to be taken without due consideration, Alwyn Scribe," the *Eithlisch* said. He turned and gestured to the spire's entrance. "Leave us, for what follows is not for your ears."

"There's something more," I said. "The *Doenlisch* told me to seek out the stone feather. Where is it?"

The other three elders exchanged weighty glances before Deracsh spoke, this time his scholarly tones were laden with reluctance. "Another subject for discussion."

"I'll seek it out," I told them. "With or without your leave."

"Go!" the *Eithlisch* repeated in a growl. "And wait!"

Chapter Twenty-Eight

"Six!" Juhlina said, happily triumphant as she skimmed another stone across the surface of the lake. I replied with a distracted smile, casting yet another glance at the shadowed interior of the spire.

"Didn't seem to go all that well," she commented, hunting among the islet's rocky shoreline for another stone to throw. She appeared almost childlike, her boots removed and trews drawn up to allow her to explore the water's edge. It was usually easy to forget her comparative youth given all that she had suffered, as I often forgot mine. She had allowed her hair to grow during this journey, revealed as a pleasing shade of chestnut brown. I liked seeing her like this, freed from the pall of grief and anger that had persisted ever since the ugly events that brought her into the Covenant Company. It seemed the mere act of travelling Caerith lands had a healing effect.

"That's because it didn't," I said. I had perched myself on a large boulder, my attention shifting between the spire and the tree-covered shoreline. Whatever decision the elders came to, I was resolved to seek out the stone feather on my own. Navigating these lands without a guide, however, would be no simple matter.

"So they're not going to help?" Juhlina plucked a flat piece of slate from the water and angled her arm to cast it away, letting out a laugh when it bounced across the mirror of the lake's surface no less than eight times.

"I don't know. I do know we can't go back yet. Or I can't. You're free to choose your own path, as always."

Juhlina's brief but flinty glare sufficed for me to drop that particular subject. Clearly, she wasn't going anywhere except at my side.

"So, what is it?" she asked. "This feather?"

"I haven't the slightest idea, except that it's important and I need to find it."

"Because a Caerith witch said so in a dream?"

I could only shrug. "Yes."

Juhlina sighed and resumed her rock hunting. "Makes as much sense as traipsing from one shrine to another for years because a crazed old man said so, I suppose."

The *Eithlisch* reappeared shortly after, striding from the shadowed archway, features stern with a preoccupied frown. "Come," was all he said, making for the bridge without pause.

"What of the council?" I enquired, hastening to catch up. "What was their decision?"

"They will go forth from here and proclaim their support for an alliance with the exiled *Ishlichen*." His tone was flat, lacking any sense of triumph or satisfaction.

"Isn't that a good thing?" Juhlina asked.

The *Eithlisch* gave no reply, leading me to divine another reason for his darkened mood. "Something else happened, didn't it? They made more than one decision this day."

Once again, he said nothing, but the resentful twitch of his face told me I had struck the mark. However, it was clear that he wasn't about to explain further. "What of the stone feather?" I said, moving to bar his path.

The *Eithlisch* let out a rumbling growl as he came to a halt, his form swelling a little so that he towered above me. I saw the urge to do me harm vie with his reason. Apparently, I had finally exhausted his patience. Still, I stood my ground, putting my faith in the *Doenlisch*'s mark.

"I won't leave without it," I said, impressed that I managed to keep my voice from quavering.

He growled again, more in resignation than anger, his form subsiding. "Where else do you think we're going, Alwyn Scribe?" he muttered, stepping past me and resuming his purposeful stride.

Upon reaching the boat, he took hold of the tiller and motioned for Juhlina and I to take up the oars. When we cast off, he steered not for the shore but the open waters of the lake. "Don't row so hard," he told us, "we have many miles to cover."

I thought about asking how many but knew silence would be the only response, so concentrated on working my oar at a steady rhythm. I was never an expert waterman and required guidance from Juhlina on how best to wield the paddle. The *Eithlisch* steered us wide of the Mirror City, affording a final look at its wondrous architecture. Once clear of the islands, Juhlina raised the triangular sail affixed to the boat's mast and a stiff southerly wind carried us away. Soon the great spires had faded into the distance and the lake had broadened so much the shoreline to either side shrank into misted strips of green.

For three days we sailed across the lake which I soon realised was in truth an inland sea. Occasionally, we encountered other boats, their occupants pausing in the act of casting nets into the water to call out greetings to the *Eithlisch*. The lake proved to be rich in life. Fish could be seen swarming in large shoals beneath the surface and we saw packs of otters clustered on the shores of the many islets that broke the surface. They were far larger than their northern cousins, closer to seals in size. They also displayed a sensible aversion to human kind, for they would all scatter and dive into the water if our boat came too close.

Come nightfall, Juhlina lowered the sail and we would continue to deplete our diminishing stock of supplies. I knew better than to ask our helmsman what might happen when we ran out completely, assuming he would growl an instruction to catch some fish. In the event, our voyage came to an end before such expediency became necessary.

"What is that?" Juhlina said, squinting into the haze beyond the bows on the morning of the third day. The perennial mist thickened to a near fog come the morn and I was unable to discern the object of her interest until a shadowy criss-cross pattern appeared. As it drew closer, I realised it was a timber framework rising from the lake's surface. My gaze tracked up the structure where it joined with a broad cylindrical building. Lights glowed behind the many shuttered windows in its sides from which numerous ropes and ladders descended to a complex matrix of walkways and jetties. People moved about on the walkways, some sparing a glance down at our boat, most busied with their chores. More structures loomed out of the haze as the *Eithlisch* guided us deeper into what I realised was a large settlement, all of which seemed to have been constructed atop the lake.

The *Eithlisch* was plainly no stranger here for many Caerith called greetings to him as we passed beneath their overlapping bridges and scaffolds. He returned the chorus of welcome with a raised hand, his face only marginally less stern than before. He had Juhlina and I paddle the boat towards a low-slung pier in what appeared to be the densest part of the settlement. Here numerous other watercraft were tied up or anchored. Drawing alongside the jetty, the *Eithlisch* threw the bow rope to a hefty Caerith on shore and bade us gather our things. Upon stepping free of the boat, I expected to find the usual cluster of *toalisch* and sundry local luminaries gathered to hear the *Eithlisch*'s word. Instead, the jetty was bare of anyone save the man securing the bow rope to a post.

"The Caerith of the lake have no warriors," the *Eithlisch* said in response to my query regarding the absence of a reception party. "And scant interest in anything beyond the shores of their home."

"Should she succeed in breaching the mountains," I replied, "Evadine will surely have an interest in them."

"They have been afforded ample warnings. Their choice is their choice." He paused to fix me with a hard stare. "And they won't take well to an *Ishlichen* with a contrary opinion, so guard your tongue well here."

While the *Eithlisch* continued to receive a warm reception as he led us from the jetty and up a ladder to the platform above, Juhlina and I were subjected to an unspoken but palpable suspicion bordering on outright hostility. The weight of their enmity was such that I felt only the presence of our revered guide protected us from injury. As we followed him through a maze of walkways, ladders and platforms, I heard a distant murmur above the bustle. It was like the first rumblings of thunder, but constant, and growing in volume the further we progressed. The source became clear when we finally ascended a ladder to a parapet which formed the terminus of the settlement. The waters beyond narrowed into a fast-flowing river, white with rapids for much of its length. A quarter-mile on it broadened into a lagoon fed by a vast curtain of cascading water.

"The Bright Falls," the *Eithlisch* said, the first glimmer of a smile in days appearing on his lips. "Of all the wonders to be found in Caerith lands, consider yourselves blessed to have seen this one."

The falls were certainly a spectacle, curving away to east and west where they fed other rivers all flowing into the great lake. They were so extensive, in fact, I couldn't see an obvious route around them.

"How do we proceed from here?" I asked.

The *Eithlisch*'s nascent smile broadened into a grin. "We climb, Alwyn Scribe. How else?"

We spent the night in one of the cylindrical dwellings overlooking the settlement's southern edge. It appeared to be an inn of some kind rather than a family home, although it lacked the ale and brandy barrels, or raucous clientele, that would have characterised its Albermaine-ish equivalent. The lower floor encircled a central fireplace where the elderly Caerith couple that had care of this place cooked us a supper of fish stew. We were alone for much of the evening until people began to gather on the walkway outside. I saw many with the sunken-eyed look of persistent sickness while others had arms in slings or supported themselves on crutches.

The *Eithlisch*'s features tensed at the sight of them, a momentary weariness passing across his brow before he straightened and beckoned to the first in line. A single, dismissive glare in our direction sufficed to banish Juhlina and I to a room in the upper floor.

"How does he do it?" she asked, gazing down at the hulking mystic as he grasped the leg of a crutch-bearing unfortunate. The fellow stiffened as the large hands gripped his flesh, but his face showed no pain, only a curious vacancy. I recalled my own healing at the same hands, finding the memory disturbing in a way I couldn't quite fathom.

I should have been grateful, for he had most likely saved my life when he remoulded my damaged skull. Yet, I felt only a dim resentment that arose from unwanted obligation.

"How did Evadine capture the hearts of so many?" I said. "I suspect it's just another aspect of a power we can't truly understand." I watched the *Eithlisch* remove his hands from the Caerith's leg, whereupon the fellow, after some exploratory kneading of his muscles, climbed to his feet without a flicker of discomfort. "I'm not altogether sure he knows either. Or if he does, he's not telling."

"He'll be handy to have around, in any case," Juhlina said. "After the battle."

My mind returned to that stormy first night at Castle Dreol and the monster who had surely wanted to kill me. "And during, I fancy."

We departed shortly before dawn the next day, the *Eithlisch* tracing a course along the eastern shore of the lagoon beneath the falls. The ground was all moss-covered rocks and occasional copses of stunted tree and bush. Conversation became an exercise in shouting as we drew nearer to the roar of the massive cascade. The continual noise also made sleep difficult over the course of the three days it took us to finally reach the point where the falls ended at the flank of a tall mountain. Scanning its sheer cliffs through the rainbow haze that lingered over the white deluge in daylight, I saw no clear path. The prospect of attempting to scale such an edifice appeared impossible, and our guide either ignored or failed to hear my shouted question.

Near midday, he halted at the base of the mountain where a narrow ledge ascended from the lagoon's shore to disappear into the falling water. By virtue of some curious arrangement of the landscape, the roar was lessened here to a loud but bearable thrum, enabling us to hear the sombre but determined tone of the *Eithlisch* as he turned to address us.

"What lies ahead is a path known to few among the Caerith," he said. "And never revealed to any outsider until this day. Before we proceed, I require your honest assurance that you will never speak of it, nor guide any other soul to this place."

"Then you have it," I said, starting towards the ledge. I came to an abrupt halt when the *Eithlisch* shrugged off his covering and moved to bar my path. His form swelled with frightening familiarity as he raised a plate-sized hand and, moving too swiftly to dodge, clamped it to my head.

"This is not something for which words alone will suffice, Alwyn Scribe," he said, voice reduced to a strained grunt by the enlarged muscles cording his neck. The pressure of his fingers upon my skull was acute but I knew better than to struggle. Juhlina, although plainly shocked by her first glimpse of the *Eithlisch*'s unconcealed form, hefted her warhammer and lowered herself into a fighting stance.

"Let him go," she said.

"It's all right," I said, raising a hand to hold her in place. Swallowing, I asked the *Eithlisch*, "Then what is required?"

"That I sense no lie," he replied, then extended his free hand to Juhlina. "From both of you."

"And should you sense it." I paused to wince at the unyielding grip on my skull. "You'll kill us both, I take it?"

"I will."

"This is the council's decision, I assume? Their condition for guiding us to the stone feather."

"It is." The *Eithlisch*'s tone softened a little as he spoke again to Juhlina. "You may go back. No hand will be raised against you. But if you refuse this test, your role in this journey ends here."

"All I have to do is not lie?" she asked. When he nodded, she shrugged, lowering her warhammer. "Very well—"

"Do not agree so blithely," the *Eithlisch* interrupted. "I sense there is more worth to you than this one—" he tightened his hand a fraction, drawing another wince from my lips "—but some lies are hidden. They lurk inside us, awaiting their moment to flourish when watered by greed or lust. My *vaerith* will search through your mind, stirring all you have concealed from yourself. It will hurt."

I wouldn't have blamed her for taking her leave at this juncture; the ugliness of her past surely made this trial a daunting prospect. But, although her fear showed in the sudden paleness of her face,

Juhlina didn't waver. Slowly, she lowered her weapon and came closer, bowing her head. The *Eithlisch* let out a rumbling growl of reluctance then softly placed his hand upon her head.

For the space of a full minute or so, nothing happened. The three of us stood in this strange tableau in silence, something I had always found hard to bear.

"Are we supposed to say it . . . ?" I began, only for my voice to falter when the *Eithlisch*'s hand altered its grip on my skull and the world disappeared into complete blackness.

I saw and heard nothing but felt a terrible sense of disorientation, as if I was falling from a great height in constant expectation of a bone-crushing impact that wouldn't come. Nausea contested with fear as I tumbled in the void, then both were swallowed by an upsurge of outright terror when a ball of flame blossomed around me. A vast heat seared my skin and licked at my hair, the stink of my own flesh burning assailing my nostrils. The fire snaked over my head, invading my eyes, ears, nostrils, burning its way deep into my mind. This, I knew, was the *Eithlisch*, his power, his *vaerith*, digging into my soul in search of deceit. Resisting him was, of course, impossible, and only seemed to increase my pain. Still, I fought him, outraged by the violation. I flailed and writhed in his arcane grip, my fright expressed in a stream of incoherent obscenities as bolts of agony shot through my being. Then stopped . . .

In place of fire, I now felt soft earth beneath me, the erasure of pain causing me to jerk in shock. I lay upon a patch of muddy earth, my garb stained by the damp soil. The air held the chill of late autumn and the sky above was the dark grey of wet slate. I could hear the sound of voices from not far off, mingled by a familiar grind and rattle. Rising up, I beheld a group of men labouring to service a siege engine. It was similar in construction to those Master Aurent Vassier had crafted for the siege of Highsahl, but far larger. The mightiest of Vassier's engines had required a party of ten men to work it. At least two score men toiled around the one before me. The wooden and iron basket that formed its counterweight was the size of a modest house and the great throwing arm stood close to fifty feet high. A dozen labourers strained to push a round stone as tall as they were on to the sail-sized sling. Incredibly, this impossible engine didn't stand alone. A dozen more were arrayed alongside it, each with their own small army of attendants.

As I watched, one of the more distant engines let fly with its projectile, the arm sweeping up to whip the sling and cast the massive boulder into a high arc. I tracked across the slate sky and watched it plummet on to the walls of a city. The boom and crash of its impact was smothered by the sound of another engine unleashing its deadly cargo. This one hit in much the same place, adding to the rising pall of dust. The breech they were crafting was already a deep, ragged bite mark in the wall, one of several along its length. Two more engines loosed, not stones this time but fireballs leaving an ugly black trail as they blazed their way over the wall to birth tall gouts of flame in the streets beyond.

"Did you fall, Father?"

I started at the voice, although it possessed a note of concern, albeit coloured by faint, indulgent humour. Looking up, I found a tall man in black armour standing over me, his hand extended. He was at least a decade older than I, hair greying at the temples with a face that most would call handsome, despite the creases and weathering that bespoke a far from pampered life. Surveying his features, I was beset by a rush of recognition, even though I was sure I had never seen him before.

"Come now," he said, leaning lower to grasp my hand. "Can't have you flailing in the mud in full view of the Blessed Cohort, can we?"

I allowed myself to be hauled upright, still gaping at his features, maddened by my memory's failure to tell me who he was. I *knew* him, in a fundamental way, and yet I did not. "Found someone with a stock of the good stuff, eh?" he enquired, arching an eyebrow. "Not going to finish your book that way, are you?"

Letting out a good-natured laugh, he clapped me on the shoulder and moved to the crest of the low rise we stood upon. "Not long now," he said after a short perusal of the city. As he spoke another salvo of stones and fireballs descended upon walls and streets. I didn't know this place, its architecture was unfamiliar and the empty flatness of the surrounding landscape did not correspond to anywhere I had ever been.

"Would that Mother was here to see this," the maddeningly familiar stranger said, turning to me, a sad smile on his face. It was the smile that did it. The shape of his lips as they broadened and the way his eyes narrowed in concert, transforming vague recognition into unwelcome, near sickening knowledge. Worse still was the emblem emblazoned on his breastplate, a white rose, identical in form if not colour to the motif that once adorned the banners of House Courlain.

"What . . ." I began, words scraping over a dry throat. Working my tongue about my mouth, I tasted the foulness of recent overindulgence, felt also the aching head and limbs of a man freshly woken from a binge. I was no stranger to the effects of drink, but this was far worse than any previous hangover. Also, there was a throbbing pain in my hip and back and a blurriness to my vision. Blinking, I raised my hand before my face and saw the gnarled, liver-spotted, and ink-stained claw of an aged scribe.

"Perhaps," the man said, moving to put an arm around my shoulders, "you should have a lie-down . . ."

Wrestling myself free of his grips, I tried again, fixing the now puzzled man with a demanding glare, words emerging in a rasping croak. "What is your name?"

His lips pursed in both amusement and mystification. "Father?"

"What did she call you?" My old claws slapped at his breastplate, a weak and pitiful expression of enraged despair. "Why didn't she kill me?"

"Oh." He caught my flapping hands in a strong grip, grimacing in realisation. "Had another of those dreams, did you? I had hoped they'd gone for good."

"What did she call you!?" My voice dwindled to a plaintive wail as the world around me shifted, the face of the man who would one day call me father subliming into dust that swirled away into the bottomless void . . .

Chapter Twenty-Nine

The *Eithlisch* let out a wordless exclamation of both disgust and pain as he snatched his hand from my head. I collapsed the instant his touch lifted from my skin, sinking to my hands and knees, chest heaving. The disorientation of the void vied with the lingering effects of having experienced the depredations of age. Unable to stand, I raised a wavering head to glare at the *Eithlisch*, finding him flexing his hand, lips bared in a hiss of pain.

"Why?" I grated at him. "Why did you do that?"

His frown was both wary and defensive. "I did only what I said I would do. Sometimes *vaerith* finds its own path, follows its own purpose." He paused, eyes narrowing. "What did it show you?"

I ignored the question, dragging more air into my lungs and sitting back on my haunches. After some more breaths, I recovered enough strength to stand, casting about for Juhlina. She sat at the water's edge, her expression a serene contrast to my distress.

"She suffered no pain," the *Eithlisch* grunted, noting my concern. "Nor did I sense a lie in her."

"Or in me?"

He worked the fingers of his hand some more, brow creasing in troubled contemplation. "Or in you, so far as I could tell."

I went to Juhlina's side, crouching to see tears tracing down her cheeks, although her expression lacked all sorrow. "Are you all right?" I asked her.

She nodded, saying nothing, her gaze preoccupied by the water.

"What did you see?" I prompted.

A soft smile came to her lips and she lowered a hand, playing her fingers through the rippling surface. "I saw a happy little girl who knew she was loved," Juhlina said. "That was the truth I hid from myself, Alwyn. Lyssote's death was ugly, but her life was sweet because I cherished her so."

Talk of beloved children stirred the vision of the man in black armour, the mighty engines busy in their destruction. Strangely, the worst thing was that I still didn't know his name. Was it a prophecy? A vision of a certain future, or a glimpse at what might be should I fail?

"We need to move on," the *Eithlisch* said, pulling his cloak over his muscular frame before starting towards the ledge. "This is a path not easily walked in darkness."

The ledge became higher and more treacherous as it proceeded into the shadows behind the vast curtain of falling water. I kept a close watch on where the *Eithlisch* placed his hands and feet, striving to match each movement. In this cavernous and gloomy recess, the roar of the falls became an incoherent echo. It smothered all other sound and made speech impossible, not that I felt talkative, my mind beset by the vision.

Would that Mother was here to see this, he had said. My son had said. Clearly, in this future Evadine was no longer present and the thought that I was destined to kill her was far more troubling than I expected. *You already tried*, I reminded myself. Nor did I doubt the necessity of it. And yet, the possibility that I was destined to do the deed set my guts roiling. Yet, even if I had killed her, it appeared the act had failed to secure the salvation of our child.

He didn't seem cruel, I thought. *And he loved me, that was clear.* But also he had stood and watched in satisfaction as a city was brought to destruction. Another thought occurred then, one that made my foot falter on the ledge, forcing me to clutch tighter to the handhold in the rough granite. *Evadine never appeared cruel either. He will become his mother's son. Worse, I will help him.*

An hour or more of perilous climbing brought us to a broadening of the ledge where it disappeared into a crack in the damp rock. It was a narrow opening, just wide enough to accommodate the *Eithlisch* if he stood side on. Peering into it, I saw a faint glimmer of light above.

"We must reach it before nightfall," the *Eithlisch* said. "This passage has many branches. In the dark it is easy to lose your way."

Stepping aside, he gestured for me to proceed him. I, in turn, stood back to allow Juhlina to go ahead. "If night falls before we reach the top, shout out," I said. "Or light a fire, if you can."

The confines of the passage, with its irregular footing and treacherous dampness, at least served to banish my pondering of the vision. Loss of concentration here might well prove fatal and I had no desire to find myself lost in the subterranean maze. Juhlina climbed with an enviable quickness, her bobbing silhouette occasionally obscuring the light above. It seemed to retain both an unnatural dullness and a refusal to grow by any appreciable measure regardless of how high we climbed. As we drew closer I realised why; the sky was darkening. After watching Juhlina disappear through the tunnel mouth, I fought down a rising sense of panic, for night was fully upon us now. Fortunately, the sky was cloudless and I could see the stars and the silver of moonlight edging the portal.

Climbing free of the tunnel, I beheld the oddest landscape I had yet encountered in Caerith lands. Trees surrounded us, but they were shorn of leaves. This was not the result of autumn's kiss, for these trees were strange, rendered a pale grey in the moonlight. Looking down, I saw that the soil beneath our feet was grassless.

"Dead," Juhlina said, running a hand over the trunk of the nearest tree. "Petrified, in fact," she added, twisting loose a piece of what had once been bark.

Looking around, I saw nothing but ancient, dead trees rising from barren soil. Naturally, when he emerged from the tunnel, the *Eithlisch* was not forthcoming with anything that might shed light on this peculiar landscape.

"It must have a name, at least," I pressed, Juhlina and I once again hurrying to keep up as he resumed his rapid stride.

"No," he muttered. "No name. Most Caerith do not come here. Only the elders, and then rarely."

He proved deaf to additional questions and maintained his march for another hour until calling a halt. Petrified wood doesn't burn so we lacked fuel for a fire. The night's chill compelled Juhlina and I to huddle close while the *Eithlisch* forsook his usual nightly disappearance to sit nearby, his eyes constantly roving the surrounding trees. I discerned a new wariness in his bearing, head shifting towards the slightest sound, even though all I could hear was the distant roar of the falls and the occasional creak and crack of desiccated tree limbs. There was no birdsong in this forest. No owls hooted and no small creatures skittered and scratched on the ground. This was truly a dead place, which made the *Eithlisch*'s wariness troubling.

"There can be no predators here," I said. "Yet you fear. Why?"

He spared me a short glance before resuming his nervous vigil. "Your people are fond of trade, Alwyn Scribe. So we shall trade knowledge. Tell me what my *vaerith* showed you, and I'll tell you what lurks in this forest."

Instinct warned me against telling him anything of importance. Although I couldn't term him an enemy, it would be equally absurd to call him a friend. Still, there was a distinct absence of any other soul who might be capable of shedding light on the meaning of my vision.

"It showed me something," I said. "Something yet to happen. At least, I think that's what it was. *Vaerith* can do that, yes? Put visions in the head of those who don't have your . . ." I waved vaguely in his direction ". . . power."

"It can," he said. "Though the reason is often hard to parse. What did you see in this vision?"

"Events yet to be, or that may one day be. The *Doenlisch* once told me such things are changeable. Was she right?"

"The future is her province, not mine." I glimpsed a twitch of resentment in his mouth as he continued to scan the trees. "As yet, my *vaerith* sees fit not to share such insights with me. But chose to do so for you."

I squinted at him in puzzlement. "But . . . Lilat. You knew her fate before you sent her away to seek out the *Doenlisch*."

His broad lips twitched again, this time in restrained anger. "I knew only that her *mielah* required her to go with you. And that the hunt I sent her on was important, vital in fact. I knew I was sending her into the gravest danger, for your lands are a vile place. I didn't know it would kill her." He turned to me again, face hardening. "Trade, Alwyn Scribe. I will have the full vision from you."

"My son," I said. "The son yet to be born. I saw him grown, a warrior of many battles. Perhaps even a king, of sorts. It was a vision of war, of conquest. There in that time, he had become what his mother wishes him to be. Yet I was there too, by his side. And he loved me."

The *Eithlisch* gave a soft grunt of understanding. "My *vaerith* revealed your *mielah*, or one aspect of it. Destiny is like a thread through time, twisting, coiling, sometimes breaking. And rarely, it splits. Consider the vision a warning of the consequence of failure."

"You talk about *vaerith* as if it has a mind of its own."

"A mind? No. But it does have a will, a purpose. Divining that purpose has been the work of my lifetime, and I know that I will surely pass from this earth without ever fully comprehending it."

He paused, reaching down to scoop soil into the palm of his hand. "You asked the reason for my fear," he said, large fingers working the loose earth into fine dust. "Here it lies, in the very substance of this place. You look upon it and see only death, and a great dying did once beset this land. But what dies does not always depart this plane. Sometimes it lingers. Mostly in the hidden fissures of the world we glimpse in dreams or delirium. But, in a place such as this the wretched remnants of life still cling to existence, and are not always hidden."

"Ghosts?" I said, a faint laugh escaping my lips. From the *Eithlisch*'s frown I deduced this was one Albermaine-ish word he didn't know. "The spirits of the dead," I explained. "You believe this forest haunted."

"No, I believe it cursed. And to claim the stone feather, you will have to bear that curse." He opened his hand, letting the powdered soil fall. "I have no affection for you, Alwyn Scribe. But know, at least, you have my pity."

He said nothing more after that, and I felt no urge towards further questions. Either through boredom or simple tiredness, Juhlina had fallen asleep during our conversation. I pulled the hood of her cloak over her head and settled close to her, seeking warmth and sleep I knew wouldn't come.

My prediction proved irksomely accurate, for I endured a night of twitchy agitation alleviated only a little by Juhlina's warmth. Finally, close to dawn, I fell into the senseless stupor of exhaustion only to be woken shortly after by the *Eithlisch*'s gruff command to rise. I trailed at the rear of our party for much of the day, head fogged with fatigue and only dimly aware of the gradual change in the terrain.

Around noon, I finally noticed that the trees were thinning. We now made our way across a succession of broad clearings. The ground also became dotted with large, oddly shaped boulders. They were smoothed and shaped into abstraction by centuries of wind, but where they met the ground I discerned a regularity to their form.

"This is the work of a mason," I said during our midday rest. I crouched beside one of the boulders to scrape away the soil at its base, revealing a hard edge that could only be the result of skilled hands. Digging deeper, the edge became ragged and the stone spider-webbed with cracks. "Looks like it shattered." I looked around at the numerous other boulders littering the landscape. "Something very large fell here long ago."

"It didn't fall," the *Eithlisch* said. "It was blasted apart. An entire city rendered to rubble in an instant."

"An earthquake?" Juhlina wondered. "Or the eruption of a fire mountain?"

"No." The wariness from the night before was fully evident in our guide as he turned and resumed his march, his shoulders hunched and eyes continually darting about.

Juhlina saw it too, moving alongside me to mutter, "He's scared. I don't like it."

"He says this land is haunted." I spoke with a deliberate levity which failed to assuage her fears.

"By who?" she asked, her gaze now considerably more alert.

"He didn't say. But, given we appear to be walking through the remains of an entire city, I'd hazard if any lost souls are still loitering about it would be the former residents. If they do consent to make an appearance, I hope they're more forthcoming than he is."

"It's not funny." She dug her elbow into my arm before casting a guarded glance over the sparse, dead lands surrounding us. "This place . . . feels bad. A kind of bad I've felt before. Visit enough shrines and you develop a nose for it. Most are just old buildings filled with old bones. But there are some where you can feel the Martyr's suffering lingering like a bad smell. We never stayed long in places like that."

For my own part, I felt only a persistent unease made worse by the uncertainty of our ultimate goal. It wasn't until we stopped for the night that I began to understand Juhlina's disquiet. The ground had taken on a gradual upward slant towards evening, the last of the petrified trees falling away so that we traversed an ever thicker maze of weathered rubble. The remnants of the shattered city were more recognisable here, their closeness protecting them from the constant erosion of the elements. When we camped in the lee of a particularly large chunk of stone, I found a faded but discernible relief carved into the surface. The figures were vague but still recognisably human. There was writing too, but so reduced in form it was impossible to tell how much it resembled Caerith script.

I felt it as I traced my fingers over the glyphs, the familiar itch and instinctive tension that comes from being watched. It had been my faithful guardian since my early years in the forest, and I knew to trust it. Gripping the handle of my sword, I rose, eyes tracking over the ragged stone labyrinth. Noting my alarm, Juhlina moved to my side, warhammer raised. The lack of a fire was both a hindrance and a help. The brightness of flame would have blinded us to anything beyond its reach. But the thickness of the shadows provided ample cover for any assailant, shadows that seemed unnaturally deep.

"Weapons won't help," the *Eithlisch* told us. He remained seated, staring into the gloom with a hard grimace of expectation, one that didn't quite conceal the fear in his eyes. "You can't kill the dead."

The itch came again, causing me to whirl about, gaze snapping from one shadow to another. The fearful mind will inevitably conjure form out of the formless, and so I started at the sight of a crouching assassin, complete with dagger in hand, which transformed into a cracked plinth an eye blink later. Still, even though all was utterly still, I knew we were far from alone.

"What do they want?" I asked the *Eithlisch*.

"What the dead will always want." He got to his feet, jaw clenched in decision. "To be among the living once again. To feel the warmth of a beating heart. The swell of a chest drawing in the sweet taste of air. All that is denied them. That is what they want."

Shrugging off his cloak, he stepped in front of us, spreading his arms out wide. "Stay where you are!" he snapped when Juhlina and I moved to stand at his flanks. "I cannot shield you from all of them, but I can spare you the worst."

His words grew more garbled as he spoke, the muscles of his neck bulging, shoulders and arms swelling in what I recognised as the effects of summoning his *vaerith*. He stood there for mere moments that felt like hours. Even though nothing moved around us, the feeling of presence soon grew into an oppressive weight, like a vice closing its jaws.

When it came, it was sudden, like a blast of wind even though it stirred no dust nor even twitched my hair. A chill more harsh and violent than anything wrought by the depths of winter seized me from head to toe. I could only shudder in its grip, breath misting as it gusted from my gaping mouth. The cold enveloped and invaded me, icy tendrils snaking through cloth and flesh with insistent ease. I felt the need in that touch, the desperate clutching hunger of something starved beyond reason. There were no voices to accompany this tightening, icy fist. No ethereal whispers from the needful dead, just an implacable, ravening desire for sensation.

"ENOUGH!"

The *Eithlisch*'s shout brought the invading tendrils to an abrupt halt. His form was swollen more than I had seen it before, even during his rage at Castle Dreol. Every muscle of his massive frame bulged, veins throbbing and tendons straining. I felt the heat of him then, a fast expanding bubble of warmed air. I shuddered as it enveloped me, staggering at the sudden release from the grip of the dead. Next to me, Juhlina collapsed to her knees, moaning as she hugged herself tight.

"A toll has been exacted," the *Eithlisch* grunted, teeth gritted and form shaking. Around us, frost sparkled where chilled air met his shield of warmth, a spatter of rain marking a circle around us. "You have had your due." The *Eithlisch* stiffened, back arching. "Go now! The toll has been paid!"

The heat around us intensified, beading the skin with sweat. For an instant I could see our tormentors, the collision of chilled and heated air producing a fine vapour that swirled and twisted. The shapes were mostly formless, but here and there I glimpsed the semblance of a face screaming soundlessly at the living, each one set in a rictus of both despair and rage.

"GO NOW!" The *Eithlisch*'s roar was accompanied by a blast of heat. A thunderclap rent the air, destroying the vaporous sphere and its screaming wraiths. It faded to an echo that reverberated among the rubble for a time while I stood in terror that our tormentors might return. Hearing a deep groan, I turned to see the *Eithlisch* slumping to one knee, mighty form shrinking to its former size. Steam rose from his skin and I saw a sag to his features I never expected to see. Apparently, he had displayed the limits of his power this night.

"Will . . ." Juhlina faltered, swallowing to regain command of her voice. "Will they come back?"

"No." The *Eithlisch*'s voice was a tired murmur as he got unsteadily to his feet. He stumbled to his cloak, gathering it up to slump against a stone. "They've had their fill."

"Was that it?" I asked him. Despite the sweat that bathed me and my labouring heart, I still felt the echo of the chill touch, as if invisible fingers clutched at my bones through the flesh. "The curse you spoke of? Was that it?"

The *Eithlisch* made a sound like dry wood cracking, one I took an instant to recognise as a laugh. "Merely a foretaste, Alwyn Scribe," he said, dragging his cloak over his head before settling back against the stone. "Tomorrow, you reap the full feast, if you can."

Chapter Thirty

The upward slant of the ground became more noticeable when we moved on the next day. The rubble ended abruptly after a few miles, creating a dark borderline curving away to either side. Beyond it lay a slope of dry, cracked earth leading to a crest a quarter-mile distant. Clearly, this was the centre of the event that shattered this ancient city. I felt certain that whatever we had come to find lay beyond that crest. The sense of being observed had faded now, for even the dead wouldn't linger here. In its place there was a weight to the air that put in mind the thickened atmosphere that warns of an impending storm.

The urge to stop was strong, my rational mind conjuring a parade of well-reasoned arguments for turning around and forsaking this absurd, superstitious farce. Did I not have a war to fight? An army in need of leadership? Why was I wasting my time, at no inconsiderable danger I might add, in pursuit of something no one had even seen fit to explain to me in full.

"What the fuck am I doing here?" The question emerged in a tired, bitter sigh, but my feet didn't falter. I felt as if I were being drawn on, as if what awaited me beyond the slope's crest had churned a whirling current I could never escape.

Reaching the top of the incline, I must confess that my reaction to what lay beyond was mostly one of bafflement rather than wonder or dread. Here the earth had been shaped into a large bowl, grey at the edges and deepening to shiny black in the centre. Something lay in that dark, ragged circle. From this distance it resembled a charred, twisted tree. I noted how the *Eithlisch* forced himself to look upon it, eyes narrowed and mouth set, concluding its true nature was not so mundane.

He started down the slope without further preamble while I lingered, my fear having finally overcome whatever arcane pull this place exerted.

"We can just leave," Juhlina said. Turning to her I was grateful for the absence of judgement in her expression. Instead, I saw sympathy and a pitch of fear only slightly less potent than my own. "You don't have to do this."

I reached for her hand, squeezing it hard before starting down in the *Eithlisch*'s wake. "How I wish that were true."

Close to the tree, the dry ground transformed into a dark, irregular surface that gleamed like glass and crunched underfoot as I approached. The *Eithlisch* had halted before it, staring at its twisted, blackened branches in stern and resentful contemplation.

"A blossoming of fire so hot as to render earth into glass," I said, coming to his side. "And yet it deigned to spare a lone tree."

"Look again," he said.

I did as he bid, eyes tracking over the coils and curves of the thing. Its surface was ashen rather than the gleaming sheen of the ground beneath it, petrified like the dead forest we had passed through. Parts of it were smooth and others rough, covered in marks resembling welts that put me in mind of flesh afflicted by the pox. The more I looked, the less tree-like it became. Muscle and sinew in place of bark or burr. Also, one particularly large extrusion possessed an almost wing-like appearance. Still, it took Juhlina's breathless exclamation to make me see it.

"Oh, by the Martyrs." She stared at something near the base of the structure, eyes wide and face blank with astonishment. Following her gaze, I saw two bulbous growths amid the overlapping chaos of limbs, growths that sprang into terrible clarity as I crouched to peer closer. *A face*, I realised, making out the eyes and mouth. Despite its ossified nature, it appeared smooth and unblemished, reminding me in fact of the *Eithlisch*'s sculpted features. Still, I could read an expression in it, a line in the brow and shaping to the mouth that told of a terrible anger.

The other growth also bore a face, of sorts. It was a contorted, malformed mask of spiny protrusions and blistered disfigurement, frozen in the act of a rage-filled scream. It was abruptly obvious to me that this was no tree. Nor was it any kind of monument or statue. The impression of frozen ferocity was beyond the art of human hands to craft. I beheld two inhuman creatures somehow transformed into lifeless matter that had defied the elements for incalculable years. It became even more clear as I looked again at the entwined limbs, seeing the way they grappled with each other, in places clawlike spikes dug into smooth, petrified flesh. *Not spikes*, I concluded, peering yet closer. *Talons*.

"Impossible," I said, the word emerging in a tremulous whisper as I backed away from this impossible artefact.

"What else could it be?" Juhlina asked, her voice a mirror of my own. However, instead of retreating she fell to her knees, face stricken. "It's all true, Alwyn. I so wanted it to be lies. But it's all true."

"It can't be," I said, my gaze swinging to the *Eithlisch*.

He regarded me with a grimly amused arch to his brow. "Why is it so hard to believe? Have you not spent half your life in service to a faith that avowed this truth?" He gestured to the two entwined figures, locked forever in their moment of combat. "Should you not rejoice, Alwyn Scribe? For you are privileged to behold the Seraphile and the Malecite made flesh."

"How?" I continued to back away, words faltering from my lips. "How could . . ."

"A mystery unsolved, and most likely unsolvable." The taunt faded from his voice as he returned his gaze to that terrible assemblage. "All that witnessed their coming died in the witnessing. We only know that the violence of their struggle pierced the veil between their plane and ours. All that followed, the fall, the destruction and despoilment of Caerith greatness, the collapse into chaos that covered all the world, this was the seed from which it grew."

I forced myself to a halt, heart thumping and mind fevered by a welter of competing thoughts. *Run, this is not something any human eye should see. No. Stay, and study this wonder.* I have missed Sihlda's wisdom and guidance many times during my life, but never more so than in that moment. She, I knew, would have had sage counsel for me. Instead, I was obliged to trust the *Eithlisch*'s word, and he despised me.

"What . . ." I began, finding I had to swallow to get the words out. "What do I do now?"

"Claim what you came for." He gestured to the upper portion of the dread object, the protrusion I took to be the Seraphile's wing. "The stone feather awaits you."

"Don't!" Juhlina said, scrambling to her feet to place herself in my path. "You can't touch that thing. Don't you feel it?"

I understood her meaning, although, like her, I couldn't fully articulate the sense of wrongness engendered by being in proximity to these ancient and inhuman corpses. Not then, and not now. The heaviness to the air was far more palpable here, the prickle to the skin more acute, almost like pain. It all came from them, I knew it. Old beyond comprehension and rendered into stone they may have been, but I harboured a growing certainty that neither were fully dead. So, no, I didn't want to touch them. Nor did I wish to linger here for one second longer. Yet still I gently put my hands on Juhlina's shoulders and eased her aside. She tugged at my arm as I stepped closer to the enmeshed bodies, but her fear compelled her to let go when I didn't stop.

As I eyed the Seraphile's wing, the atmosphere seemed to thicken around me, sight and sound becoming dulled. My vision dimmed at the edges, bright only in the centre where it focused on one of the feathers. I could discern them clearly now I understood the nature of this object. Most were fused into the stone substance of the wing, but a few jutted from the surface, jagged, almost thornlike. My hand shook like that of a palsied drunk as I raised it. Twice I extended my fingers towards the largest of the protruding feathers, and twice they folded involuntarily into a fist. Sometimes terror is so instinctive, it overcomes will.

Gritting my teeth, I grated out a short stream of self-flagellating profanity, a torrent of abuse in which the words "fucking coward" and "useless whoreson" featured prominently. Still, my fist refused to open. It was when my racing mind fixed upon a recent memory that a semblance of control returned.

Would that Mother was here to see this. The words of my son, yet to be born. Words he would say in a future I would craft should I fail in this moment. My self-hating diatribe faded and I felt a brief moment of calm before forcing my fingers open and reaching out to grasp the feather.

I had expected pain, agony even. Perhaps another vision forced into my mind. Instead the absence of either caused me to start in surprise as my hand closed on spiny, dry stone. I let it linger a moment, tensed for the arcane curse promised by the *Eithlisch* to descend. When nothing happened, I tightened my grip and twisted. The feather came free with surprising ease, snapping clear of the Seraphile's wing with a dry crack. Stepping back, I looked at it resting in my palm and saw small beads of blood on the tips of the spiny vanes tracing along its stem. My blood. I thought it might seep into the feather, that some arcane conjuration would arise from a taste of human essence. But still, nothing happened.

"Come," the *Eithlisch* said, casting a final grimace at the Seraphile and Malecite before turning about and starting off. His pace was even more rapid than usual, indicating a keen desire to be away from here.

"Is that all?" I called after him. "Aren't we supposed to do something more?"

"You've done all you needed to," he replied, voice a barely heard mutter. I watched him disappear over the lip of the crater then turned to exchange a baffled glance with Juhlina.

"Should any of the faithful ever hear of this place . . ." she began, voice trailing as she stooped to peer at the Seraphile's angry visage.

"They must never know," I said, consigning the feather to the inside pocket of my jerkin. "We can never speak of it. I'm doubtful there are many who would believe us, in any case, but those who did would try to come here. I doubt the Caerith would appreciate their intrusion."

I frowned as another thought occurred. "The faithful would come here," I repeated softly. "As Evadine wishes to come here."

"You think she knows about this? This is the true object of her crusade?"

"Perhaps. Her hatred of the Caerith is real, but it could be that the Malecite also sent her a vision of this. Either way, she will surely try to claim it should she succeed."

"We could destroy it." Juhlina tentatively extended her warhammer towards the Seraphile's head, the blade hovering near the dark hollows of its eyes. "It's just old stone, after all. Easily rent to powder."

The notion was tempting, but also dangerous. "I feel certain our esteemed guide would kill us for it." I reached for her hand, pulling her away. "Come on. We'd best catch up to him. I've a feeling he's in no mood to wait for us."

The journey across the blasted ruins was uneventful and our guide's pace never faltered. He wouldn't allow a moment's rest until, with night falling and his travelling companions close to exhaustion, he relented.

We had re-entered the petrified forest shortly before dusk and were now close enough to the falls to hear a muted roar. Strangely, the *Eithlisch* was more pensive than at any point in our sojourn. Instead of continually scanning the trees, his gaze mostly focused on me, dark with wary expectation. He had said little for hours but spoke up when Juhlina and I began to huddle together for warmth.

"That isn't wise," he said. "Not now."

"Why not?" Juhlina's face and voice were dull with fatigue. When he didn't answer she added, "It's cold, we have no fire, and I'm too bloody tired for your riddles."

"Do you want her to share it?" The *Eithlisch* asked me, causing me to pause in the act of putting my arm over Juhlina's shoulders.

I didn't ask what he meant. In his eyes, I now bore a curse even though the stone feather remained just an inert lump in my pocket. If anything, my mood had lightened since leaving the crater. Still, the grave certainty of his bearing was not to be taken lightly.

"Best heed him," I grunted, rising to move away from Juhlina. I settled myself at the base of a dead birch a few yards off, lying down on the hard earth and wrapping my cloak around me. Despite the chill and the discomfort, sleep was not long in coming, also blessedly free of nightmares. Those would await my waking a few short hours later.

"He fears you. You should kill him."

I came awake with a wordless gasp, jerking in the confines of my cloak as I fumbled for my sword. A few seconds of fog-minded struggle and I managed to gain my feet, sword sliding clear of the scabbard. The source of the voice that had woken me stood a few paces away, small and apparently unconcerned by the sword blade pointed at it. *A child*, I realised, eyes tracking from the figure's diminutive form before fixing on its face, a pale, hollow-eyed mask angled in curiosity atop a spindly neck. The boy was barefoot, his emaciated form clad in rags although he showed no reaction to the cold. I knew instantly what I looked upon and did not trouble myself with fear-induced denial. This child was dead.

"You really should," the boy went on. "He plans to do the same to you later." A frown creased the grey smoothness of his brow as he glanced at the *Eithlisch*. The Caerith was on his feet, staring at me rather than the boy. Noting his expression of tense but controlled alarm, I understood that it was only I who saw this talkative ghost.

I couldn't help but back away, sword still extended even though I fully appreciated its uselessness at this juncture. My retreat, however, was blocked by the petrified trunk of the birch.

"When you've killed him you should kill her." The boy skipped towards Juhlina, a smile playing over his lips as he crouched to peer at her slumbering face. "She's nice. She can be my mother. If you kill yourself too, we can all play together."

My response emerged as a strangled grunt that made the dead boy's smile broaden a good deal. "You're funny. Not like the last one. He was all grumpy, and more than happy to kill the people he came with."

"Go . . ." I forced the command from a parched throat. "Go away!"

This only seemed to puzzle the ghost, a frown appearing on his small face as he skipped towards me. "The other one didn't want me to go," he said with an aggrieved pout. "He wanted to know everything I could tell him. So I did. All the bad things his friends thought about him. When he was done killing them I could tell he wanted to kill himself too, but was a big scaredy coward and couldn't." He halted an inch short of my wavering sword point. "You're not a coward. You'll stick this—" he tapped the shuddering blade, the finger slipping through the steel as if it were mist "—all the way through your belly."

Dragging air into my lungs, I put all my strength into the shouted command: "GO AWAY!"

The boy staggered back as if slapped, his face betraying hurt and disappointment. "He really is going to kill you," he hissed at me, pointing an accusing finger at the *Eithlisch* before turning to flee into the wall of dead trees.

"What . . . ?" Juhlina said in a startled groan, roused by my shout. Using her warhammer, she levered herself upright, casting about for enemies.

"What did it tell you?" the *Eithlisch* asked me, then stiffened as I swung my sword in his direction.

"Some very interesting things," I said.

He eyed the blade carefully, though his features remained inscrutable. "It's folly to put your trust in the dead," he said. "For they lie."

I know lies, I thought. *I didn't hear one from the lips of that boy*. I also felt certain that sharing such insight with the *Eithlisch* would be a distinctly poor idea. "He spoke of another one," I said instead. "Someone else who could hear him, see him. Who did he mean?"

"Many have come here over the years. The foolish, the curious. Those hungry for power or knowledge. I know of only one who succeeded in walking away once he had touched what lies at the heart of this place. A cursed soul, one you have met, I believe."

A cursed soul. There was but one Caerith in my experience who fit that description. "The chainsman," I said. "He came here. Did he claim a feather too?"

"No. Just one touch was enough. The one you call the chainsman had powerful *vaerith*, an elder in making. Yet his many transgressions had made him a shunned, despised soul long before he came here, lusting for the power to vanquish the elders who had condemned him. Touching the Malecite was like setting a flame to a pool of oil. Cursed, maddened and wretched, he became a wandering menace until I drove him out. I expected him to perish in the mountains, but it seems he found a home in your lands, a place to which he was far more suited."

The dead would whisper to him, I remembered, mind filled with the memory of that hulking figure driving the cart taking Toria and me to the Pit Mines. Such thoughts inevitably led to the chainsman's demise at Lorine's hands, slain in the act of trying to torture answers from my bound self. *The dead told him his fate . . . He really is going to kill you.*

"Exactly what is happening?" Juhlina enquired, equal parts annoyed and baffled.

"A very bad dream," I said, lowering my sword. The movement caused the jagged lump of the feather to shift against my ribs. *I could just throw it away*, I thought, hands itching with the urge. Yet the Sack Witch had been very clear. This thing was needed, and therefore so was the curse it inflicted upon me.

"How do I stop it?" I asked the *Eithlisch* and for perhaps the only time in our entire acquaintance I saw a glimmer of sympathy in his face.

"I don't know," he told me. "I know only that you must bear it, or the *Doenlisch* would not have guided you here."

Sighing, I returned my sword to its scabbard and slumped against the dead birch, sliding to the ground. "Best sleep," I said to Juhlina, drawing my cloak tight about me. *He would sing*, I recalled huddling in faint expectation of rest, for this forest was surely filled with ghosts. *When he sang he couldn't hear them.*

* * *

Despite my fears, I saw no more ghosts in the forest. Although I was grateful for their absence, it seemed strange for a land so filled with the hungry souls of the departed.

"I have only scant ken of such things," the *Eithlisch* said when I raised the issue. "But I do know that the dead of the blasted city are incapable of much thought beyond a desire for the touch of the living. Yet the one you saw spoke, didn't it?"

"He did." I paused in realisation. "He spoke Caerith. The tongue spoken here in ages past might be similar, but I doubt I could understand it."

"Ah." The *Eithlisch* nodded. "A more recent soul then, drawn to this place as many are, only to find a deadly trap in the embrace of the long dead."

"It was a child. A boy." My gaze shifted to Juhlina. "He seemed in want of a mother."

"It's often need that shackles them to the world of the living," the *Eithlisch* said. "You should prepare yourself for more needful spectres, Alwyn Scribe."

We cleared the forest by mid-morning, beholding the distant majesty of the falls. The subsequent descent through the slanting channel and trek along the banks of the lagoon were blessedly uneventful, though I spent each night in fearful anticipation. I had begun to indulge the notion that the curse may have lifted, or at least become dormant, a hope instantly dispelled when we reached the settlement at the southern end of the lake. There I happened upon a woman standing naked atop one of the walkways, ignored by all who passed both by and through her. Her pallid skin was wet, hair twisted into coiling tendrils that dripped water with each toss of her head. And she screamed.

The sound was both beastly and human, a wordless, unending screech of rage and grief. The complete indifference of the surrounding Caerith seemed impossible, for I felt sure such a scream could pierce the veil between life and death. Yet only I heard her. One glance at her face, eyes sunken into a mask of inconsolable despair, told me this was a soul beyond reason. All I could do was shuffle past, careful to avoid catching her eye lest she realise she had finally found an audience for her wailing. I could hear it all the way to the boat and for the first mile after we cast off. When her dreadful song finally faded, I pulled the feather from my pocket, contemplating how easy it would be to let it slip from my grasp.

You must seek out the stone feather, the Sack Witch had said. *The key that unlocks all lies.*

"You didn't tell me the price," I muttered, thumb tracing over the ancient stone, once the flesh of a being Sihlda had considered little more than a metaphor. I pondered the contradiction that, even though I had now been presented with incontrovertible confirmation for the basis of Covenant belief, my faith had not been buttressed by the knowledge. In fact, the Covenant and its many Martyrs, relics, shrines and scrolls seemed absurdly infantile now. A fumbling attempt to comprehend something far beyond human understanding.

"Saw another one, didn't you?" Juhlina asked. She had charge of the tiller while the *Eithlisch* worked the sail and I lazed in morose contemplation. During the journey back, I had enlightened her about the nature of the curse and the thing I carried, reasoning that keeping it from her was pointless. When I nodded, she focused a hard glare on the feather. "Throw the bloody thing over the side," she said.

"I can't." I returned the feather to my pocket. "We need it."

"For what? How can the dead win a war?"

"They . . . know things. See things the living do not. I think that's why she sent me to fetch it."

"If it's so important, why not come get it herself?"

"The same reason he couldn't touch it." I nodded to the *Eithlisch*, recalling what he had said about the chainsman. "There's too much power in this for someone who already possesses a great deal. Only those without it can hope to carry it without going mad." I spoke with a conviction I didn't feel. Although the dead woman's screams no longer reached us, the echo of them still lingered, making me wonder how much more I could endure before this was over.

* * *

Upon arrival at the Mirror City, we were greeted by the sight of Uthren and two other *paelah* waiting on shore. There was no sign of any accompanying *Paelith*. The great horse snorted as I approached him, shuddering at the hand I touched to his flank. His eye tracked me with a wariness that had been absent during the journey south, and it wasn't hard to fathom the reason.

"Don't like what I carry, do you?" I said, smoothing a hand over his neck before climbing into the saddle. "Neither do I."

During the subsequent journey north, the *Eithlisch* eschewed visiting any Caerith settlements. Instead, we rode, fast and hard. Although more accustomed to horseback than I had been not so long ago, constant riding, with only a few hours' rest come nightfall, was a severe strain. Even so, I was grateful for it. When at the gallop there were no ghosts to plague me and they were sparse in the places we camped. Still, some would find me. Ten miles north of the lake I was woken by a *toaslisch* with an arrow embedded in his eye, insistent that I direct him to his home village. A few nights later, with Uthren slowed to a trot in the confines of the forest, I happened upon a young woman dangling by her neck from rope affixed to the branches of a tall pine. Something about her predicament must have amused her, for she laughed the whole time. After that, I resolved to try the chainsman's trick of singing whenever Uthren's pace slowed. It worked to banish the sound of their voices, but not the sight of their spectral forms. When bedding down, I became habituated to slipping into slumber while murmuring one of Ayin's songs with a strip of cloth bound over my eyes.

As the forest grew less thick we began to encounter bands of *toalisch* and *veilisch* heading north. Just a few at first, each about a dozen strong, but they grew more numerous with the passing miles. By the time the trees thinned and the heathland fringing the northern coast came into view, we rode among a veritable Caerith army. The elders' call had been heeded, at least by the warriors and the hunters. Of the *Paelith*, we still saw none.

A few miles on we were greeted by the sight of another army, this one far more familiar in character. Castle Dreol was now enclosed by a stockade of fresh-cut timber, itself surrounded by a city of tents and newly built shacks. Companies of soldiers drilled on the flat land south of the bluffs and the bay beyond was busy with craft both large and small. Flying above it all on a pole rising from the castle's tower was a banner emblazoned with the Algathinet crest. The king was in residence and the Crown Host mustered for war.

PART THREE

Why do I ask you to march to distant lands? Why must we carry the cleansing fire and purifying sword across the mountains? The answer is simple, my friends, for there evil lies. There the Malecite have laid their plans and succoured our enemies. There the malign Caerith have used their arcane sorcery to nurture the seed that will grow into the Second Scourge. But they reckon without our courage, our fortitude, our faith. Though it costs us ten thousand lives and ten thousand more, into the enemy's lands we must strike and slay the Second Scourge in its cradle. This is demanded of us by the Seraphile, for never have I heard their voice with greater clarity. Thus, they decree that all hearts must be as steel in this new Covenant, for we can no longer suffer a single foe to live.

Extract from *Martyr Evadine's Proclamation to the Ascendant Host*

Chapter Thirty-One

I expected the first council of war between the princess regent and Lord Roulgarth to be a tense affair, and I was not disappointed. Leannor and the royal household had taken over the tower, their small coterie of servants making some effort to adorn the cramped lower chamber with tapestries and curtains to create an impression of regal authority. Three chairs of suitably throne-like dimensions had been carried all the way from Tarisahl and arranged atop a hastily constructed wooden dais covered by a large gold embroidered rug. The king occupied the central position, sitting with stiff formality that must have taken his mother many hours of tutelage to instil. A less composed Princess Ducinda sat to his left and his mother on the right. Upon arrival, Wilhum had informed me that this meeting had been awaiting our return from the Caerith heartland. Leannor's emissaries to Roulgarth had been rebuffed with curt instructions for her troops to venture no more than a mile from the coast. It was only with the arrival of the *Eithlisch* that Roulgarth had consented to attend this gathering.

He and Leannor exchanged toneless greetings of clipped formality, mostly stripped of the usual effusive honorifics. Lord Merick, acting as Roulgarth's herald, introduced him simply as, "Knight Warden of Alundia and *Vahlisch* to the Caerith people".

Leannor's welcome was delivered by a stern-faced Sir Ehlbert. "The Princess Regent, on behalf of His Highness King Arthin Algathinet, Monarch of all Albermaine, bids you welcome, my lord." His tone was lacking in embellishment save for a pointed emphasis on the word "all". Seeing how Roulgarth's visage darkened, I discerned he hadn't missed the implication. Whatever accommodation might be reached here, as far as Leannor was concerned it wouldn't involve the question of Alundian sovereignty.

Consequently, when Ehlbert's voice faded, there descended what I expected to be a prolonged and uncomfortable interval of silence. Fortunately, one personage present proved heedless of the thickened atmosphere. Letting out a happy squeal, Princess Ducinda abandoned her place alongside her stiff-backed betrothed and rushed to her uncle, wrapping her arms around his neck as he knelt to welcome her. She let out a giggle as he gathered her up, extending a hand to Merick.

"You have to kiss this, Cousin," she said. "I'm a princess now, you see."

"You honour me, Cousin," the young knight said with grave solemnity before pressing his lips to the back of her hand.

I saw a shadow pass over Roulgarth's face then, his gaze taking on a distant cast as he looked closely at the smiling face of his niece. I knew he was seeing someone else, a woman whose shade, I was relieved to find, did not linger among those gathered in the castle's lower chamber. In fact, so far as I could tell, no dead had come to plague me here. I wondered if the presence of so many living souls deterred them somehow. The bustle of the lakeside settlement hadn't quelled the screams of the drowned woman, but then, she had been utterly mad. Perhaps sane ghosts were more shy.

"Ducinda!" the king snapped in a voice I assumed he thought to be commanding but instead sounded peevish. "A queen-to-be should mind her place. Don't you think, Mother?"

Judging by Leannor's clenched jaw and pained smile, I deduced that his mother's principal thought in that moment was to take a switch to the royal backside. "I think it would be ungenerous to begrudge the princess a family reunion, Majesty," she replied. Unlike her son, the note of command in her tone was very clear.

"And Uncle Scribe!" Ducinda said, artfully ignoring her future husband as she turned in Roulgarth's grasp, extending her hand to me. I could tell her true uncle was less than pleased by her addressing me in such a way, so took a small crumb of pleasure in graciously bowing to kiss her hand.

"Princess. I trust you didn't find the voyage too taxing."

"Oh, it was awful. Arthin spewed the whole way here."

"I did not!" the king interjected, to which his betrothed responded with a taunting poke of her tongue.

"You look sad, Uncle Scribe," Ducinda went on. Her small brows bunched as she peered at my face. "Why is that?"

"This is merely the face of a man who has travelled many miles, Majesty." I bowed again and stepped back. "Though, I am greatly pleased to see you again."

"The king and the princess will retire," Leannor stated, eyes narrowed as she directed a hard stare at the child in Roulgarth's arms. I wondered if her annoyance rose more from the rekindling of Ducinda's familial relationship with Roulgarth, or a sense of maternal envy. She cared for the girl deeply, I could see that. But to fulfil her ordained purpose, Ducinda's loyalties could flow in but one direction.

Arthin muttered some sullen objections but a glower from his mother was enough to quell them as he and Ducinda were duly ushered from the room.

"Now then," Leannor said, rising from her chair and clasping her hands together, brisk and businesslike. "We have much to discuss, good sirs and ladies. I believe, Lord Scribe, you have news to share regarding your meeting with the Caerith tribal chieftains."

Roulgarth gave a faintly amused grunt at this, while I felt only a welling of weary resignation. The customs of the Caerith were going to be hard for Leannor to grasp. The *Eithlisch* might have helped clarify matters, but he had stalked off into the forest shortly after our arrival that morning. Roulgarth claimed not to know where he might have gone but did intimate it would be best not to expect his swift return.

"I met with the council of Caerith elders, Majesty," I said. "I am pleased to report they recognise the danger we share and have spoken in support of war with the False Queen. Many warriors have already gathered to benefit from the guidance of the *Vahlisch*—" I inclined my head at Roulgarth "—and many more are currently marching north to muster here."

"I see. This word *Vahlisch*, may I enquire as to its exact meaning?"

"Blade master is the closest equivalent," Roulgarth said. "The Caerith rarely fight with bladed weaponry. However, they are wise enough to recognise the need to further their skills if they are to meet a northern army in open field."

"And so thousands gather to learn the way of civilised battle from you." Leannor pursed her lips. "It strikes me that 'marshal' or 'general' would be a more apt translation."

"I would have thought," Roulgarth returned, a low growl creeping into his voice, "that Your Majesty would have had enough experience of battle by now to know that it can never be described as civilised."

Instead of the expected retort, Leannor merely raised an eyebrow, mouth curving in chagrined amusement. "Quite so, my lord. Tell me, how many warriors will the Caerith commit to this war?"

"They do not bury themselves in numbers as we do. I can only estimate our strength, but it will be considerable."

"Really?" Leannor turned an inquisitive eye to Ayin, who stood just to the rear of her chair. "I think we can do better than that, don't you, Lady Ayin?"

It didn't surprise me that Leannor would have discovered Ayin's facility for numbers. Even with her mostly complete return to sanity, Ayin remained a guileless soul in many respects. I would have to warn her to be more circumspect in future.

"As of yesterday evening," she said, "there were six thousand, four hundred and seventy-two Caerith warriors encamped in the vicinity of this castle." She hesitated then bobbed her head at Leannor, adding in an awkward mutter, "If it please Your Majesty."

"It pleases me very much, my lady." The princess regent paused for a momentary rumination, the set of her brows indicating genuine calculation rather than performative artifice. "Joined to our own strength, with more being ferried here every day by Mistress Sahken's allies, it appears we will soon have a mighty host at our disposal."

"A host mighty in number will still prove weak if not properly trained and commanded," Roulgarth said. "From what I can tell, many of your soldiers are not worthy of the name."

"They will be," I said. "By the time we march for Albermaine."

"That would be the work of months," Sir Ehlbert pointed out. "Time in which the False Queen grows ever stronger."

"As will we," I returned. "A great many more Caerith warriors will come and there are veterans aplenty among our ranks who can train those carried to this shore. Besides, we have not the shipping to convey the entire host to Albermaine in one voyage. When the time comes to march, we must do so via the mountains, in winter."

The King's Champion squinted at me in patent suspicion. "The mountains are barely passable in summer. Attempting to cross in winter would invite disaster."

"There is a route, one revealed to me by the Caerith elders, a pass that only reveals itself when the snows fall. Our enemy will not expect us until the spring. Advancing into Alundia months before will throw her into disarray."

"Unless her pestilent visions warn her of our approach," Leannor pointed out.

"They won't. Not as long as I march with the army."

"So—" Leannor resumed her seat, calculating frown still in place "—you propose a delay of months while we await winter."

"Months in which to hone the Crown Host into something capable of defeating the False Queen's army, for I've no doubt she forges a formidable force as we speak, a crusade intended to bring destruction to these lands."

Leannor's head shifted in agreement. "This I'll not argue. Mistress Shilva has many agents scattered along the coast; they report that wherever the Ascendant Queen goes she gathers more recruits for her host. And everywhere she goes she talks of the arcane evil of the Caerith. Apparently, all the troubles and wars of Albermaine can be laid at the door of a people who only ever walked our lands in the smallest numbers. Sadly, such nonsense will ever find receptive ears. The False Queen inflicts a good deal of cruelty, but her lies win devotion."

"While her cruelty gathers more to us," I said, nodding in Roulgarth's direction. "Especially in Alundia where many will rise when the knight warden returns."

"It's still a long march from there to Couravel," Ehlbert pointed out. My reply faltered when I turned to him, distracted by a small movement at his back, just a slight shift in the shadows cast by the drapery. A moment of staring revealed the shadow to be a figure, a man of disconcertingly familiar bearing though his face was lost to the gloom.

"Lord Scribe?" Leannor prompted when my silence lingered.

"Forgive me," I said, averting my gaze from the watchful man, knowing I alone in this chamber could see him. Clearing my throat, I went on, "I doubt the False Queen will be content to await us in Couravel. I suspect many of her most able soldiers will be gathered at the Lady's Reach, her holdfast on the site of the old Walvern Castle. It's possible we will also find her there, if we march swiftly enough."

"Strategy is one thing," Leannor said. "But I have learned that success in war depends mostly on securing enough supplies to keep an army fed well enough to march and fight. Thanks to some profligate spending of the royal purse, not to mention provision of several loans from loyal but avaricious merchants, our fleet continues to sustain us and provide a stockpile. Yet it will be of scant use if we have no carts or horses to carry them with us to Albermaine."

"True, Majesty. But we have something our enemy does not, an entire fleet of ships which can supply us on the march, provided we keep close to the coast. Hopefully, we can secure more horses when we reach Alundia."

Leannor turned a questioning glance upon Ehlbert who consented to respond with a short nod. "Then it seems we have a stratagem," the princess regent said, settling her shrewd attention upon Roulgarth. He matched it with a gaze equally lacking in unwavering appraisal. It occurred to me that Leannor was about to commit the salient error of demanding the knight warden of Alundia swear fealty to her son. Fortunately, her wit outweighed her pride on this occasion, and she concluded the council with placid formality.

"Gentlemen, please see to the readying of your respective hosts with all the skill and energy of which I know you are capable. Lord Scribe, I also command that you form a company of masons and other suitably knowledgeable persons to see to the reshaping of this castle. Its current form is hardly befitting of the king's majesty."

The shadows behind the throne shifted again and I saw that the watchful figure was gone. I harboured only the faintest hope I wouldn't see him again.

"I'll see to it, Majesty," I said, bowing low.

The watchful ghost left me in peace for the following week, though I endured the passing days in a state of dreadful expectation. *Why him?* I asked myself continually. *And how can he be here?*

The myriad tasks of organising the ever-growing mob of recruits into something resembling an army provided a welcome distraction, as did the works on Castle Dreol. Leannor's insistence on expanding the holdfast could be interpreted as an example of wasteful pride, a diversion of labour and resources best employed elsewhere. In fact it provided a useful focus for the many souls among us unsuited to a soldier's life, not to mention the artisans who set to the task with the enthusiasm of the beggared. Driven far from home with little in the way of possessions, this new royal abode at least provided work and wages, all paid from Crown coffers buttressed by the treasure of a long dead pirate. In lieu of handing out trinkets, Leannor employed the clever device of paying her workers with promissory notes, each one signed by the king's own hand, bearing the ink stamp of the Algathinet seal. From the way the various masons, carpenters and labourers hoarded these scraps of paper you would think them spun from gold. Apparently, to people who had lost all they once owned, the word of a king still meant something. Consequently, work on the castle proceeded with far more speed than did the fashioning of the Crown Host into something battle worthy.

Years of unending war had left me with the impression that most Albermaine-ish men of fighting age, and a good portion of the women, would have some experience of soldiering. A few days attempting to impose order and discipline upon the newly arrived recruits soon disabused me of this notion. Getting more than a dozen to stand in line and march in the same direction was an achievement. Days of drill and various forms of encouragement, from the gentle to the decidedly ungentle, failed to yield much progress. We retained a core of a thousand or so reasonably disciplined troops, plus Duke Gilferd's Cordwainers, but the remainder were a dispiritingly ill-organised, and oft ill-tempered, mob that sent my recently appointed sergeants and captains into fits of angry despair.

"Take a hundred of the laziest bastards and flog 'em," was Tiler's suggestion. "Hang 'em, even. Reckon we'll have a lot less grumbling then."

"Many of them came to us in fear of the noose," I reminded him. "Start down that road and they'll be justified in asking themselves if there's any difference between us and the False Queen."

A few days later, as I watched our first attempt at a company-sized advance descend into a shambles of jostling soldiers and colliding pikes, I wondered if Tiler might have a point.

"City dwellers," a flat voice commented, a voice possessed of a strange sibilant echo. "They always made the worst soldiers. Most have never seen more blood spilled than a tavern brawl."

I closed my eyes and drew in a deep breath before turning to confront the figure at my side. The watchful ghost had returned, and this time he wanted to talk.

"Any skill can be learned," I said, forcing my eyes open. "It just requires the will to learn it. Someone told me that once."

In life, this man would have responded to having his words quoted at him with a laugh, usually. Sometimes, if his mood was sour, it would have been a cuff to the head. In death, Deckin Scarl merely blinked empty eyes at me before returning his gaze to the unfolding mess on the practice field.

"When I first marched under the banner," he said in his oddly echoing voice, "the sergeant-at-arms would take an axe stave to any man who stepped out of line. Saw him beat a fellow to death once. Freck, the lad's name was, on account of his face. Looked like a dog with the squits had shat all over it. Looked a lot worse with his brains leaking out of his skull, though."

If this delightful anecdote caused Deckin's shade any amusement, it failed to show on the flaccid grey mask of his face. As with the boy in the forest and the drowned woman, I was beset by a deep desire to be away from this spectre. If I shouted forcefully enough, he might flee like the boy had. But then all these fumbling recruits would be presented with the sight of their captain screaming at nothing. Besides, the stone feather was supposed to aid our cause and perhaps it was time I summoned the fortitude to learn how to best use it.

"How do you come to be here?" I asked Deckin after a good deal of swallowing. "You died far away and years ago."

"I died." His voice was pitched somewhere between a question and a statement, heavy brows knitting in consternation. "Yes," he muttered finally. "I remember. You were there, weren't you, Alwyn?"

"I was." The memory of Sir Althus Levalle's sword sweeping down to sever Deckin's neck was not one I was ever likely to forget. I felt a spasm of relief that at least his ghost hadn't appeared with an absent head and bloody stump.

"Althus did it," Deckin added after a moment of further reflection. "Good job he made of it too." He stared around at the practice field. "Is he here?"

"He's dead. Met a well-deserved end and I've never heard a single word of grief wasted on the bastard."

"Oh." Deckin spared the soul of his old comrade a short grimace of regret before continuing his survey of my soldiers' inexpert manoeuvres. "Won't do, Alwyn. Kindness doesn't forge an army. Give them rules and be strict in making them stick. We had rules, didn't we? Back in the forest."

"That we did." Deckin's rules had never been written down, but every member of our band could recite them by heart. Also, he had never been reluctant in making them stick, with blood if need be. "Thank you," I said, receiving a vague nod in return.

"Lorine isn't here," he said, face sagging. "I hoped she would be."

"She's Duchess of the Shavine Marches now. Everything you wanted, she took."

"Wanted?" Deckin gave a dismissive snort. "No, that wasn't it. I didn't want it, I needed it. Needed to take from him, the bastard who sired me. But no, I never wanted it. I wanted what I had. Lorine, you, the others. It was enough. Beware your needs, Alwyn, they'll bring you to your end if you're not careful."

He turned to go, then paused, noticing something on the far side of the field. A crowd of soldiers had gathered around Quintrell as he regaled them with a jaunty tune on his mandolin. It had become his habit to entertain them in between bouts of drill, earning a few tots of their grog ration by way of payment.

"I should've spotted Todman," Deckin's shade told me. "I always had a nose for the turncoats and the spillers. I missed him because of my need. Be sure you don't let yours blind you too."

"Blind me to what?" I asked, but Deckin was gone. He didn't fade like smoke in the wind or shimmer into nothing. He just slipped from whatever grasp the living world had on him, vanishing before I could even blink. I never saw him again.

Chapter Thirty-Two

The morning after Deckin's visit I posted the "Bill of Rights and Stipulations of the Crown Host", nailing it to a post erected in the centre of the practice field. Also adorning the post were a pair of leather wrist straps that would be familiar to any veterans in the ranks. I had spent much of the previous night drafting the bill, calling on Wilhum, Tiler and a few others for sage advice. Making sure to open the proclamation with a list of soldiers' rights was a deliberate ploy to sweeten the pill of the litany of rules and punishments that followed. Copies were provided to all captains and sergeants with instructions that they be read in full to their assembled companies.

"All soldiers may air grievances to the lord commander of the Crown Host without fear of reprisal or disfavour," Tiler recited to a typically untidy assemblage of recruits that morning. "Soldiers will be paid the sum of ten sheks per week. Payment will be in the form of Crown promissory notes, to be redeemed for coin following victory over the False Queen . . ."

Various other benefits were listed, mostly concerning provision of proper care if wounded and a Crown pension for veterans. Then came the rules. It was a deliberately short list, making it hard for any transgressor to claim they had forgotten it.

"For the crime of disobedience, five lashes," Tiler said, leaving a pause between each rule to ensure the words sank in. "For the crime of drunkenness without leave, ten lashes. For the crime of theft from comrades, twenty lashes. For the crime of desertion or cowardice, death by hanging. These are the rules of this host. Any unwilling to abide by them should consider themselves free of further obligation. However, you are advised not to venture far from camp, for the Caerith have made it very clear they will not take kindly to outsiders wandering their lands." Another pause as Tiler eyed his company with predatory intensity. "Any of you fuckers want out, raise your hands now. You won't get a second chance."

There were, predictably, no raised hands among any of the companies that day. Inevitably, the need to administer punishment came before the week was out. A light-fingered soldier caught pilfering brandy was brought before me and duly sentenced to the requisite twenty lashes, to be delivered before the eyes of the entire host. A slightly built fellow, the brandy thief bore the first few lashes with surprising fortitude, but screamed with increasing volume after the sixth stroke. By the time it was over he collapsed, flayed back streaked with blood.

I had none of Evadine's facility for speech making, nor did I hunger for admiration or adulation from these folk. We shared a purpose, that was all. Still, I knew this event must be marked by the words of the man who presumed to lead this nascent army into battle. I chose to mount Uthren for the occasion, the *paelah* being sure to make an impression on all present, so long as he didn't take it into his head to cast me off and gallop away. He and the *paelah* who had carried Juhlina north had lingered in the weeks since, consenting to be groomed and tended. They also allowed themselves to be ridden, but only by myself and Juhlina.

Uthren appeared to possess some understanding of his role in this performance, tossing his head and dragging his fore hoof across the ground while I sat in stern regard of the assembled ranks. They were a good deal more tidy today. I spoke without preamble or introductions; they all knew me by now. Nor did I aspire to great rhetoric. I might be able to write such doggerel, but doubted I could sway an audience into believing it. So, I resorted to the simple truth.

"I hoped this wouldn't be needed," I called out, pointing to the bloodied, sobbing man slumped against the whipping post. "I hoped that we could accomplish the task we share with the diligence it requires. For we are not children and this is no game. All who stand here have lost much. Some have lost property. Many have lost blood, their own and that of their kin. What this man did dishonours that loss. It cheapens it. We formed this army for the sole purpose of defeating a tyrant. We fight not for plunder, nor conquest, nor even faith. I offer no apology for what was done this day, nor will I hesitate to do it again. The rules of my command are simple and were communicated to you in full, and you all chose to stay. From here on in this is a true army, the Crown Host of the True King of Albermaine, a name to take pride in not to besmirch with petty thievery. You are soldiers now, so act like it."

The cheering was a surprise, causing me to pause in the act of tugging on Uthren's reins and hoping he consented to turn and gallop off at a suitably impressive speed. Led by Wilhum, Tiler and the sergeants, the cry of "Victory and freedom!" rose from the ranks with too much concordance to be spontaneous. However, I did sense a certain grim enthusiasm in it. The faces of the soldiers nearby were stern, but their voices were loud. All very different from the wild-eyed devotion of the crowds that had cheered for Evadine. Still, the anger I saw was not directed at me. These were men and women with scores to settle and they would tolerate the lash if it brought them the vengeance they craved.

Quintrell came to me a fortnight later, appearing at the tent I had chosen over a more comfortable billet in the rapidly expanding castle. There were too many shadows among those old stone walls for my liking. I had been spared further visitations since Deckin, but occasionally, in quiet moments, I caught flickers of movement where there should be none, and always seemingly crafted from the shadows.

"A foul night, my lord," Quintrell greeted me, white teeth appearing in the confines of the hood he wore against the rain. A storm had swept in from the sea at dusk, bringing a pelting deluge and thunder with it.

"That it is." I gestured for him to take a seat beneath the awning of my tent, handing him a cup of brandy.

"Not going to flog me for this, I hope," he said, drawing back his hood before accepting the cup. I searched for a barb in his tone or bearing, but found none. Just a minstrel attempting a joke.

"I'll save that for your next performance," I said.

He gave a dutiful chuckle and drank. I was impressed by the steadiness of his hand and the smoothness of his voice as he spoke on. "It is now incumbent upon me, my lord, to make unto you a confession of sorts."

"A confession?" I asked, my own voice and bearing one of interest forced through the veil of weariness from the day's toil.

"Indeed. Though I suspect what I am about to say will come as scant surprise."

"You never stopped spying." I offered a bland smile in response to his surprised frown. "You're right, that's hardly a surprise. Though, it does raise the question: who exactly are you spying for these days?"

"I am pleased to say I never, in truth, left Duchess Lorine's employ. It was to her considerable benefit that she received regular and unvarnished reports of your progress."

"Delivered by what means? The Shavine Marches are a long ways off."

"But the seas betwixt here and there are busy with Mistress Shilva's fleet, and I never met a sailor without a purse in want of filling. I'm sure your lordship wouldn't expect me to divulge any particulars. For a man in my profession, secrets are wealth, after all."

I shrugged and raised my own cup to my lips. "I shall assume that somewhere on these busy seas there sails a ship with a suitably well-paid messenger, from whom you received a recent and important communication."

"Your insight is peerless, my lord."

"Stop sticking your tongue in my arse crack and tell me what she wants."

Quintrell inclined his head with an appropriately sheepish grin. He really was quite exceptional at his craft. "As you know, my lady has, due to dire necessity, sworn fealty to the False Queen. However, having witnessed the vast cruelty of the Ascendant Host during its rampage across her lands, not to mention the emptiness of her treasury due to ever increasing Crown taxes, Duchess Lorine feels the time has come to explore other possibilities."

"She wants to turn her coat, again. It's always been something of a habit for those who govern the Shavine Marches."

"You will understand that an open declaration for the Algathinet cause will invite only bloody reprisal from the False Queen, something my lady lacks the martial strength to resist. However, she is not lacking in other resources, namely, information. You must know that she has other spies in her service. I am not privy to the exact details, but my lady has sound and credible reports concerning the future whereabouts of the False Queen. Tell me, have you ever heard of Martyr Marienne?"

"An obscure figure from the early years of the Albermaine Covenant," I said after rummaging my memory. "Killed for refusing to divulge the whereabouts of a servant of the faith to the king's heathen inquisitors. A sad tale, given that she was, by all accounts, only twelve years of age at the time."

"Tragic indeed, but often overlooked to the extent that not all are aware of the existence of a shrine to Martyr Marienne. It lies halfway up a cliff amid an inhospitable stretch of the Shavine coast, near the border with Alundia. A curious local tradition has it that, should a woman with child visit the shrine, they will be assured a safe birth. My lady has received sound intelligence that the False Queen, now heavy with child, intends to make pilgrimage to the shrine and beseech the Martyr for her blessing. Furthermore, given the remoteness and inhospitable location, she will do so with only a minimal escort."

I shifted my gaze from the minstrel's intent, serious face, contemplating the contents of my brandy cup. "And the exact date of this visit?"

"I know only that it will take place two weeks from now. Ample sailing time for a fast ship. The *Sea Crow* is more than capable of arriving in time, I'm sure."

"So, the plan would be to get there ahead of time and lie in wait for the False Queen. When she appears we could either kill her outright or orchestrate an unfortunate fall to the rocks below."

"Such details I leave to you, my lord."

"I've killed quite a lot of people, but never yet a pregnant woman, one who carries my own child, no less."

For the first time Quintrell exhibited some discomfort, swallowing a cough and tracing a finger across his brow. "Then capture would be a more fitting outcome," he said. "In either case, without their precious Risen Martyr, the Covenant Host will soon fall to disunity."

A gust of wind sent a spattering of rain under the awning, snapping canvas and straining rope. I was unable to contain a small start at the sight of something in the swirl of rain in the gloom. I had encamped away from any trees with their worrisome, abstract shadows, but still my mind, either through fear or the workings of the stone feather, conjured phantoms from the smallest details.

"Tell me, Master Quintrell," I said, "would you describe yourself as a man content with the course of his life?"

The minstrel's lips quirked before drinking more brandy. "What is contentment? I must admit I've never truly understood the word. A life on the road will do that, I suppose."

"But your conscience is untroubled?" I persisted. "Your slumber is undisturbed by memories of your misdeeds, for a spy must have many in his past."

Another swallowed cough, a red flush appearing on his cheeks as he forced a laugh. "A lesson I learned early in life: all things are subjective. A crime committed in one place is a virtuous act in another. A villainous cur becomes a hero depending on who he steals from or murders. I consider myself neither villain nor hero. I have met many of both and found little worth in either. I merely watch and report to those who pay me. If anything, I am just a spectator to the games of more earnest souls. That, I suppose, might be considered contentment."

"I am glad. You see, my recent sojourn to the Caerith heartland left me in possession of a curious gift. I can see the dead, Master Quintrell. Some of them, at least. And I've found it's the malcontents that linger. Those cursed to face the realms beyond life as unquiet, unsatisfied souls. I worried that you would be among them, but, since you profess yourself content, I shall at least be spared your future company."

I set my cup down, the contents sloshing. Quintrell was surely observant enough to note that, unlike him, I hadn't actually drunk any brandy. To my surprise there was no enjoyment in watching him squirm as terrorised realisation dawned. I have had ample experience of witnessing folk confront their end, and rarely is it done with courage or placid acceptance. By his own admission, the minstrel was no hero, as starkly demonstrated when, eyes wide and gibbering in panic he attempted to flee the tent. His legs failed him after only a few steps and he collapsed in the rain-lashed mud.

"Didn't Lorine warn you about me, Master Quintrell?" I asked him, stepping out into the deluge. I cast away the contents of my brandy cup and held it out so the rain would wash clean the dregs of its deadly contents. "I'm sure she did, for few can claim to know me as she does. So much I learned from her as a boy, a cub among wolves. You forgot her warning, didn't you? Or failed to heed it. You forgot, that at heart, I am still an outlaw and, among outlaws, betrayal has but one punishment."

I crouched at the dying minstrel's side, meeting his glaring, panic-filled eye. "It was an overplayed hand," I told him. "Even had I not been forewarned, I fancy I'd have spotted it. Too elaborate, you see? It's the simple lies that sometimes elude me."

Quintrell shuddered, mud scattering from his mouth as he attempted to plead. I heard the word 'antidote' among the babble of barely coherent promises.

"As far as I know this particular concoction has no antidote," I replied. "It was a gift from your former employer. I diluted it a good deal, for I wanted to hear your lies rather than watch you die at the first sip. I've seen the pain it inflicts at the moment of death." I drew my dagger, looking closely at Quintrell's eyes. "I'll spare you that, in return for an answer to an important question. I can guess most of it: you made an overture to Evadine during our march on Couravel, or one of her new Rhianvelan friends made an overture to you. It doesn't matter. What I do wish to know is if Lorine had any part in this. Blink once for no, twice for yes." I reached down to tug his collar aside and set the blade of my dagger against his neck. "And know that I'll see a lie."

Two blinks, and I saw the lie. "For a man who claims himself no villain," I said, withdrawing the dagger. "You do seem to have an attachment to malice."

I stood back, watching him convulse and flail in the mud until his struggles faded. Uthren appeared a short time later, trotting unbidden from the curtains of rain. I bound a rope around Quintrell's ankles and climbed on to the great horse's back. Uthren sped south, dragging the corpse to the forest where I left it in a busy, bubbling stream. Should any non-Caerith find it, they would ascribe its ragged state to the attentions of scavengers and the water. But, so far as I know, none ever did. The sudden absence of so popular a figure was noted, of course, Adlar Spinner spending a good deal of his free time searching for his vanished friend. Eventually, the Caerith grew tired of his wanderings and warned him off with some carefully placed arrows.

"Master Quintrell has a restless spirit," I told the juggler when he came running back to camp. "And, I think we both know, little appetite for battle. My guess, he's gone off to regale the people of this land with his many songs. Mayhap we'll see him again in a few years, and what stories he'll have for us then, eh?"

So, as the climate grew ever more chill and the first frost sparkled on the ground, I trained my army while Lord Roulgarth trained his. Fully aware that the coming campaign would most likely be doomed if the two contingents couldn't find a way to work in concert, I made frequent visits to the *toalisch* encampment in the forest. Each time, the number of warriors had increased, but always there was no sign of the *Eithlisch* or the *Paelith*.

"Infantry alone won't do," I commented to Roulgarth the day the first snow began to fall. "No matter how well trained."

"We'll garner horses in Alundia," he replied, though his troubled frown made it clear our lack of cavalry preoccupied him too.

"True enough," I conceded. "But we've so few riders. My scouts and Lord Wilhum's lot could hardly form a full company. There are some among Duke Gilferd's companies and the Free Host who can ride, but hardly any with the skills of a knight. While, thanks to the Duke of Rhianvel, our enemy has knights aplenty."

"There are ways to defeat a mounted charge." Roulgarth nodded to a group of warriors forming a circular pike hedge. Such weapons were unfamiliar to the Caerith and their handling of them far from expert, but my experienced eye judged the formation tight enough. However, the pikes themselves were poor things, just stripped branches, many sharpened at one end with no warhead.

"Mistress Shilva's fleet has brought us a decent supply of steel," I said. "And the castle now boasts a forge served by skilled hands. I'll set our smiths to crafting better weapons for you."

Roulgarth was never keen on expressing much emotion towards me beyond simmering resentment, but today he consented to display a glimmer of gratitude in his cautious nod. "They'll be welcome. We'll need steel arrowheads too. The *veilisch* among us rely on bone or flint."

"I'll see to it."

Roulgarth let out a sigh as his eyes tracked over the busy clearing where the assembled Caerith practised a foreign form of combat. "What absurdity is war, Scribe. I lead a host formed of people I thought savages not so long ago. While you build an army for the dynasty you strove to bring down, in order to defeat the woman you loved, no less."

There was a jibe in his voice, but considerably more muted than usual, so I didn't rise to it. Besides, he hadn't spoken a word of a lie. "History was an ever twisting path, my lord," I said.

Rouglarth replied with a vague nod before returning to the more welcome topic of our impending campaign. "It's meeting them in open field that worries me most. Each warrior here is more than a match for the best drilled, veteran man-at-arms in Albermaine, but only when faced one to one. I've little doubt they would triumph if we were to fight every battle in a forest or broken country. It's too much to hope the False Queen will be so accommodating."

"Then allow my lot to provide them with a taste of what they'll be facing. If we practise together, it stands to reason we'll have a better chance of standing together in battle."

A reluctant grimace tightened Roulgarth's face. "The Caerith show me respect, afford me the title of *Vahlisch* and heed my words closely. I may have learned their tongue to a passable standard, gleaned some insight into their customs, but I am not one of them. Nor will I ever be. Their respect is the polite regard of a host for a tolerated and useful visitor. If that's how they think of me, what do you imagine they think of you and your *Ishlichen* army?"

"I don't ask them to love us, just fight with us. In any case, I've often found that respect can arise from enmity, especially when folk spend some time beating each other bloody."

The first joint manoeuvres of the Crown Host and the assembled warriors of the Caerith dominion took place three days later. The two contingents faced each other from either side of the practice field, their ranks similarly lacking in the kind of unwavering precision expected of regular soldiery. Yet, neither was so ragged as to be ineffectual and they had both formed up with creditable speed. By mutual arrangement with Roulgarth, bladed weapons had been banned from the field, swords and halberds replaced with staves and the points removed from pikes. Still, I knew the day would not be free from injuries, some of them grievous, even fatal. I considered it an unavoidable necessity. Deckin had been right, my army needed to experience more blood and fear than that occasioned by a tavern brawl.

Knowing that any stratagem more complex than a straightforward charge was beyond the skills of my soldiers, I opted for the tactic of a staggered assault. The companies on the right were ordered to attack first, followed by the centre a short interval later. The left flank would advance last, hopefully against a line bowed or even broken by the companies assailing its right. I was fully aware that Roulgarth's generalship most likely exceeded mine and he would be sure to counter all this with some cunning device. But this day's exercise had little to do with our respective talents as commanders.

My army required blooding and his needed to learn the necessity of unified action.

I viewed the battle from atop the bluffs, eschewing the temptation to place myself in the heart of the Crown Host. I knew there was little hope of controlling events after the first clash, preferring a lofty perch from which to judge the outcome with a dispassionate eye. I was encouraged by how well the companies on the left maintained their formation all the way to the Caerith line. Less impressive was the way they instantly fragmented on contact with the enemy. As expected, Roulgarth proved a deft commander. While the struggle on the left degenerated into a general melee, he threw his own left flank and centre forward rather than await the coming blow. The Caerith advance was more rapid than the Crown Host, but also considerably less disciplined. Some knots of *toalisch* managed to clump together as they charged, but it was a mostly disorganised force that threw itself at the *Ishlichen* line. I took satisfaction from the solidity of our ranks, withstanding and repelling the first charge, then standing fast when the Caerith rallied for a second rush. The conclusion was clear: the Crown Host would be far more effective in defence than attack.

I was also heartened by the determination shown by both sides, the discordant struggle wearing on for far longer than expected. The Caerith left gave way when the warriors there grew exhausted from throwing themselves at an unyielding line and the Crown Host companies began a steady advance. On their right, the other wing of *toalisch* succeeded in pushing back the disarrayed companies before them. The result was a swirl of battle that soon lost all cohesion. By the time I signalled the trumpeters to sound the call bringing an end to the exercise, it was no more than a grand brawl in which victory could only be claimed when the last warrior or soldier remained standing.

Forcing the two sides apart proved a hazardous and protracted business, since many were eager to keep beating each other senseless with their blunted pikes and staves. Eventually, as clusters of combatants continued to thrash in unabated violence, I mounted Uthren and rode across the field calling out commands to stop. Still, some soldiers had to be dragged away by their comrades while there were many Caerith who appeared possessed of a kind of battle frenzy that only exhaustion or death would cure. These frothing warriors were eventually subdued by the intervention of Roulgarth and a select few older *toalisch*. The various bands that made up the Caerith host had no formal ranks, but there were those among them who enjoyed a great deal of authority by virtue of age and experience. Just a few words, or even a reproachful glance from one of these veteran warriors sufficed to bring even the battle crazed to heel.

"If it's a question of numbers, Scribe," Roulgarth said, striding towards me across a field littered with groaning or inert figures, "I fancy myself the victor today."

Surveying the scene, I had to concede that most of the stunned, wounded, or unconscious forms were clad in the dun-coloured garb that had become a uniform of sorts for the Free Host.

"And yet, you failed to take possession of the field, my lord," I pointed out.

Roulgarth grunted a reluctant laugh, folding his arms to cast a critical eye over the loose mass of his warriors, now returning to the forest. "Not quite ready yet," he said. "But better than we could have hoped for. It seems, Scribe, we have ourselves a true army."

Chapter Thirty-Three

The snows began in earnest a month later by which time Leannor's castle was nearly complete. She had insisted on renaming it Castle Tomas in honour of her slain brother. Apparently, the notion of a royal residence bearing the name of an ancient pirate was simply intolerable. The wall surrounding the tower had been mostly torn down and rebuilt to create a far more expansive inner courtyard. The tower itself now boasted an adjoining keep and cluster of ancillary buildings typical to castles. The forge was the largest, and busiest, the dozen or so blacksmiths in our employ labouring long hours to transform the steel Shilva brought us into weapons.

The constancy of supply across the Cronsheldt Sea had diminished with the onset of winter, so too the arrival of more recruits for the Crown Host. Throughout summer and autumn every ship to weigh anchor in the bay bore a decent number of young men and women fired with a desire to punish the False Queen for her many cruelties. Now, I counted myself lucky if we swelled our ranks by a dozen a week. This army was as large as it was likely to get, at least for as long as we remained here. My visits to the Caerith encampment also made it plain that no more warriors were coming to answer the elders' call. By Ayin's reckoning, the combined force boasted a strength surpassing thirty thousand. She also provided a calculation of the weight of supplies needed to sustain so many during the march to the mountains. It made for sobering reading.

"Can you carry all of this?" I asked Shilva during one of her infrequent visits ashore.

She spared the document a cursory glance before handing it back. "There's stores aplenty awaiting us in every port on the Albermaine coast," she said. "Hoarded by merchants and hidden from the False Queen's agents. All of it supplied free of charge, too."

"Free?" I asked with a dubious squint. "Never known a merchant deny himself a profit."

"The False Queen's taxes and petty laws make her unpopular with every subject from the meanest churl to the grandest landlord. In addition to making attendance at weekly supplications mandatory, she also decreed lending of monies an abomination before the Seraphile. The merchants' largesse is, in truth, an investment. I hope the princess regent knows just how much they'll expect by way of a return once her son's little arse is back on that throne."

The Crown Host and the assembled warriors of the Caerith dominion began their march to the mountains five weeks later. The Caerith assured Roulgarth that *Kain Laethil*, the Winter Pass, would be fully navigable by the time we reached it. Ayin bore most of the credit for the carefully calculated marching order and provision of supplies along the route. The Crown Host proceeded from one coastal inlet to another, finding stocks of supplies waiting at each camp. Armed with a fulsome inventory of the accumulated stores in Shilva's hidden warehouses, Ayin had produced tables of dates, distances, and required victuals which ensured every soldier marched with a full belly. The stockpiles were faithfully replenished by Shilva's fleet despite the harsh winter storms sweeping the Cronsheldt. Inevitably, some vessels were lost, mainly among the merchantmen rather than the smugglers who were more accustomed to sailing in foul weather.

The Caerith proceeded by a different route, sustained by the villages along their line of march. From their well-fed appearance by the time we rendezvoused in sight of the mountains, I deduced the villagers had been busy stockpiling in anticipation of this advance. The Caerith might not see much value in numbers or formal hierarchy, but they had their own brand of efficient governance.

Despite contrary counsel from myself and Ehlbert, Leannor insisted on accompanying the army, although she was wise enough to leave the king and Ducinda behind at Castle Tomas. I had left a small but doughty garrison at the bay to ensure their safety, mainly older recruits, sturdy of bearing but with a few too many years under their belt to march the many miles to Alundia. I made a muted attempt to persuade both Ayin and Juhlina to stay also, receiving a laugh from the former and a slap from the latter. In the aftermath, Juhlina maintained a decidedly frosty attitude that at times exceeded the increasingly chilled climate.

"My sole intent was to preserve your life," I offered on the tenth day of the march. The Crown Host was encamped about a small natural harbour a few miles back. As the only riders in the entire army, we had taken on the duty of scouting the route of the next day's march. It was more ritual than necessity, since we traversed a land free of foes, one Juhlina's persistent scowling silence made something of a trial.

"Meaning you expect this campaign to fail," she replied. Our mounts had come to a halt, apparently curious about the abrupt resumption of conversation. The way their ears twitched and swivelled as we spoke made me wonder just how much the *paelah* understood of human language.

"Meaning many dangers await us on the other side of the mountains," I said. "You know war as well as I. It offers no favours to either the brave or the cowardly."

"Did you try to persuade Tiler to stay behind, or Wilhum?"

They never kissed me. I didn't speak this thought, surmising it would only earn me another slap. I sighed, recognising defeat when I saw it. "I'm sorry," I said. This brought a marginal softening of her features, but it was clear she expected more. While I fumbled for more suitably worded contrition, Uthren shifted beneath me, the suddenness of the movement nearly tipping me from the saddle. Juhlina's mount was similarly alarmed, both horses wheeling about to face east.

Snow had been falling continuously for days now, rendering the landscape a perennially obscured enigma broken only occasionally by patches of forest. I squinted into the drifting swirl of wind-tossed snow, my heart stirred to a faster beat. As ever these days, when confronted with a mystery my mind instantly resorted to conjuring visions of yet more dead come to plague me. Perhaps the *paelah* were sensitive to their presence. Blinking against the icy caress of the wind, I searched for spectres, seeing nothing but smelling the familiar, musty scent of many horses. Ghosts hadn't found me, but our enemies apparently had.

"Ride back to the camp!" I ordered Juhlina, drawing my sword. "They must have crossed before the snows. Tell Wilhum to take command and make haste back to the bay."

Whether she intended to comply or argue would remain an unanswered question, for her mount consented to move not one inch. Neither did Uthren, despite my urgings. He responded to the kick of my heels with a backward glance, irritated rather than angry, before returning his gaze to the east and standing in apparently unperturbed anticipation.

"Alwyn," Juhlina said in a quiet voice as shapes began to resolve out of the snow. A dozen at first, then twice that, appearing to either side until we confronted a force several hundred-strong, and growing. I searched for a banner, expecting to see the rearing horse of Duke Viruhlis Guhlmaine. However, these riders bore no banners. Nor did I see the gleam of armour among their rapidly growing ranks. As they drew nearer, one of the riders spurred to a trot, the size of his mount becoming clear as it drew closer; a beast larger even than the mightiest warhorse to be found in all Albermaine, bearing a rider with stature to match.

"Best put that away," the *Eithlisch* advised, nodding to my sword as the *paelah* he rode came to a halt a few paces away. I had thought Uthren the most impressive horse I would ever encounter, but the stallion the *Eithlisch* rode was taller at the shoulder by at least a foot, broader too. Its coat was speckled with snow but I perceived a hide dappled in an autumnal shade of brown. The enormous *paelah* snorted as it plodded towards Uthren, both horses engaging in a bout of bobbing heads and nuzzled necks. I discerned a definite subservience in Uthren's bearing, his head swinging lower than the dappled stallion's and his snorting more muted.

"Your sword, Scribe," the *Eithlisch* persisted as I gaped at the other *paelah* appearing out of the snow, each bearing a stern-faced rider. "Confronting an ally with a weapon is considered very rude among the *Paelith*."

"How did you do it?" I asked him, sliding the sword into its scabbard. "What persuaded them to come?"

The *Eithlisch* gave no answer, though I saw an unfamiliar expression pass across his face. *Shame*, I realised. *Whatever he did, he took no pleasure in it.* Scanning the faces of the nearest *Paelith*, I recognised a few from our escort to the Mirror City, the fanatical Morieth among them. His visage today was a picture of miserable resentment rather than the ardent anger I remembered. Of his yet more ardent uncle Corieth, however, I saw no sign. I resisted the impulse to ask after the elder's fate, divining it would surely be connected to the *Eithlisch*'s guilt.

"They'll cross the mountains?" I asked instead. "They'll fight with us?"

"They will," the *Eithlisch* rumbled. "But they'll need steel to do it."

"Steel we have, and the means to shape it." Like all armies, the Crown Host travelled with a moveable forge. I raised my voice, casting it out to the onlooking *Paelith*. "Soon your lances and arrows will bear steel points! Great will our enemies across the mountains fear you!"

If this grandiloquent greeting found any credence among this mass of riders, it failed to show on their uniformly grim faces. I saw not a single warrior who appeared glad to be here, yet they had all come. The *paelah* were more appreciative of my words, at least I believe the sudden upsurge of snorts and stamping hooves bespoke an approval the folk they bore didn't share.

"The *Vahlisch* leads the *toalisch* a few miles south of here," I told the *Eithlisch*. "I'm sure he'll be glad to see you."

"We follow our own path, *Ishlichen*," Morieth snapped. "We'll fight your war for you, but don't expect us to abide your stink."

The *Eithlisch* turned a hard glance on the *Paelith*, one returned with flint-eyed defiance. It was only when the dappled stallion flicked his tail and angled his head towards Morieth that his demeanour abruptly changed. Bitter temerity became cowed discomfort, the warrior seeming to shrink in his saddle.

"Is this all the *Paelith*?" I asked the *Eithlisch*, knowing it would be pointless to enquire after the full number.

"All that can ride and fight," he replied.

"And very welcome they are." A change in the wind caused the snow to thin for a moment, affording a view of the distant grey-white peaks. The Winter Pass was still days away, but the sight of the mountains stirred a lurch in my chest. The sense of being expected had been growing during the days on the march, so too the suspicion that my invisibility to Evadine's arcane sight might not be as absolute as I imagined it to be. I wondered if the curse had brought this new pall of doubt upon me. Perhaps I had been unnerved by proximity to the dead, but I didn't think so. One thing my recently acquired curse had taught me was that truth was its only reward. In the world of the dead, lies had no dominion.

"She waits for us," the *Eithlisch* said, revealing again his uncanny facility for mirroring my thoughts. "I feel it too."

"She knows we're coming, but not where or when," I said with a confidence I didn't feel. "But battle will surely greet us when we cross those mountains, in weeks if not days. Battle the likes of which the Caerith have never seen. Roulgarth has done well in preparing the *toalisch* for what lies ahead, but the *Paelith* know nothing of what it's like to face armoured knights in combat."

"You doubt us, *Ishlichen*?" Morieth said, letting out a derisive laugh. "Worry more for your own kind, for these knights of yours have never faced the *Paelith*."

The pass of *Kain Laethil* was much as I remembered it from the shared dream with the Sack Witch, although the weather was considerably worse the day the Crown Host began to traverse it. A blizzard descended when I led the first companies into the channel betwixt the mountains, and persisted for the three days it took to complete the crossing. Since the line of march forced us away from the coast, supplies now had to be carried on our backs along with weapons and the sundries accrued by soldiers. The incline of the southern route was gentle but persistent, causing many a slip and tumble due to the frost-covered rock or packed snow we walked upon. Thanks to the unending snowfall, few fires could be successfully kindled, and nights were spent under canvas that sagged with piled snow come morning. Despite the soldiers lost to ankle-snapping falls or the depredations of the cold, I found myself thankful for the blizzard. No ambush could be laid for us amid mountains subject to such torment.

On the morning of the third day the incline levelled off and soon became a winding downward slope. By midday the snow finally began to abate, and we beheld the foothills of southern Alundia. The land was blanketed in white and most of the streams and rivers appeared frozen, but after the pass it appeared as welcoming as the lush and verdant fields of summer.

"One hundred and twenty-four," Ayin said, looking up from her neatly arranged stack of parchment.

"Is that all?" Wilhum asked. "Thought we'd have lost a thousand at least."

"One is too many," I said. We gathered atop a ridge overlooking the rolling land beyond the hills, my gaze roving the white fields for any tracks that might indicate the presence of scouts. I wouldn't have been overly surprised to have found the Covenant Host drawn up in full battle order to greet us, but so far there was no sign our passage had been detected.

"We'll camp there until the Caerith join us." I pointed to a large, flat-topped rise some miles off. "Close order and double pickets. When the *Paelith* get here they can scout the route north."

Although I chafed at the delay, I was forced to accept Roulgarth's advice to rest the army once the last few stragglers had completed their weary descent from the mountains. Striking north immediately would have pushed already tired soldiers to the brink of exhaustion. A pause was also needed to allow our smiths time to forge the steel weapons promised to the *Paelith*. The various accoutrements of our moveable workshop had been manhandled through the pass thanks to the efforts of twenty-strong teams of soldiers taking turns to drag sleds laden with anvils and steel rods across the icy route.

Morieth, who appeared to be the closest thing the *Paelith* had to a commander, agreed to my request for reconnaissance with a surprising lack of truculence. I deduced his keenness arose from a desire to spend as little time among *Ishlichen* as possible. An offer to share my carefully prepared maps of the region was met with disparaging bafflement, since the Caerith had no more use for charts than they did numbers. The *Paelith* duly divided themselves into smaller contingents according to their various clan affiliations and rode off in different directions. They returned over the course of the next few days with reports of ruined farms and villages bare of people. I knew from my previous sojourn through this region that it had suffered greatly after the fall of Duke Oberharth. Now it appeared to have become a wasteland.

With the army rested and our Caerith allies gathered, I ordered a westward march to the coast where a flotilla of Shilva's ships awaited us with much needed supplies. A week of marching brought us to a long beach where the vessels bobbed in the swell a mile offshore. Most were broad-beamed merchantmen, with one sleek exception.

"You look worse than last time," Toria said as she climbed from the *Sea Crow*'s launch, wading towards me while her crew went about unloading the barrels. Coming to a halt, she squinted at me in both mockery and concern. "Have you been sleeping at all?"

"As much as I can," I said. I didn't add that sleep had become an all too brief refuge, my waking hours being fraught with dread expectation. I had glimpsed a few wayward spectres since crossing the mountains, most fleeting and indistinct. However, once in a while I caught sight of a more solid soul, usually bearing the signs of torment on their dead flesh. These were the victims of the bannerless marauders who had ranged across southern Alundia in the aftermath of Algathinet victory. Most were set on simple plunder and cruelty, while others had claimed divine inspiration for their atrocities in the words of the Anointed Lady. In retrospect, it was a warning of things to come to which I should have paid far greater heed.

Toria's lips formed a smile that I found odd, for it was patently forced. "Well, here's another morsel of news to keep you from slumber: you're a father now, Alwyn Scribe."

I had known this was coming, but upon hearing it I found myself frozen, regarding Toria's wincing visage with mouth agape and eyes unblinking. "When?" I managed eventually, the words spoken in a hoarse mutter, "Where?"

"Seven days back, in Athiltor. The Ascendant Queen has decreed the holy city her capital, got a whole army of masons raising a wall around it." Toria paused, watching my slack-mouthed surprise shift into something far more sorrowful. "A boy," she added, as expected, but what she said next was not. "She named him Stevan, in honour of Martyr Stevanos, apparently. His official title is the Divine Prince Stevan Courlain." Toria grated out a laugh, one I might have taken as cruel if not for the sympathy I saw in her gaze. "Congratulations."

Divine Prince. The words echoed as the dream vision of my future son played out once more in my head. *Would that Mother was here to see this . . .*

"Thank you," I said, stiffening. Now was not a time to surrender to introspective despair. "Do you have any more intelligence for me?"

"Great deal of trouble in the Shavine Marches. Seems the commons aren't too keen on forking over their goods and chattels to feed the queen's taxes, regardless of what their duchess commands. Bunch of Covenant soldiers and tax collectors got themselves surrounded and massacred by a mob of churls a few miles east of Farinsahl. Story goes that they stuck the heads on pikes and posted them along the King's Road."

"Evadine will have to answer that," I mused with some satisfaction. The more soldiers she set to punitive action in the Shavine, the less the Crown Host would have to face on the march north.

"She already has," Toria said. "Word is the duchess has been presented with a royal command to appear before the queen in Athiltor and answer for this outrage."

"Lorine would never be foolish enough to go." This provoked further satisfaction, but also worry. A diversion of Evadine's attention was welcome, but the prospect of Lorine facing her might alone was not.

"How swiftly can you get a message to the duchess?" I asked.

"Eight to ten days," Toria replied after some pondering. "If the seas are kind."

"Good. I won't write it down, lest it fall into treacherous hands. Tell her to prepare Castle Ambris for siege, provision it as much as is possible and send the common folk to seek what shelter they can in the forest. All her vassal lords should be advised to do the same. And tell her the wayward cub is coming home."

Chapter Thirty-Four

Southern Alundia proved to be so bare of life that it wasn't until we marched north along the coast for two full weeks that we garnered our first batch of new recruits. *Paelith* scouts returned to complain of being assailed with arrows, fortuitously poorly aimed, amid the steep, vine-covered slopes a dozen miles to the west. Roulgarth immediately set out in company with Merick, carried on the backs of two *paelah* who appeared outside their tents that morning. They returned a few days later at the head of three score Alundian rebels, a mix of farmers and soldiers from the ducal levies. Judging by their ragged appearance, I guessed they must have been hiding in the hill country since the fall of Farinsahl. Unsurprisingly, they regarded the sudden arrival of an army under Algathinet command with a good deal of suspicion. If not for the evident, near-awed level of respect they showed to Roulgarth, I knew few if any would have consented to join our campaign.

"There's other bands north and east of here, my lord," the rebel leader told Roulgarth that night. He was a former sergeant in the Alundian ducal levies with scars too recent not to have been won in the war against the Algathinets. From the fierce glare he shot in my direction upon hearing Roulgarth's introduction, I deduced he had been at Walvern Castle. "Each a score strong or more. They'll march with you, of that I've no doubt. But they'll need to see you, hear your voice for themselves."

"And they will," Roulgarth assured him, clapping the fellow on the shoulder.

"Do you have horses?" I asked him. "Or know where any might be found?"

The sergeant's mouth formed a hard line and he only consented to speak at a nod from Roulgarth. "Most went into the pot months ago. Those that didn't were gathered up by the witch queen's bastard soldiers and taken north to that death pit of hers on the border."

"Death pit? You mean the Lady's Reach."

"That's what her murdering scum are like to call it. It's no mystery what goes on there. Folk rounded up by her soldiers are taken to the pit. Once through the gates, they never come out. You can smell the stink of death from miles away."

The sergeant spoke no word of a lie that I could detect, but doubt lingered. Clearly, Evadine had grown cruel in her delusions, but still I resisted the notion she would sink to wholesale murder. *The Scourge*, I reminded myself. *We now live amid the Second Scourge.*

"The witch queen's pit is our prime objective," Roulgarth assured the fellow with another pat to the shoulder. "Go now and rest. Tomorrow you can guide me to our brothers in the hills."

"She's not there," I told Roulgarth when the sergeant had knuckled his forehead and stomped off. "Our best intelligence puts her at Athiltor."

"While I now have intelligence that my people are being slaughtered en masse at this pit of hers."

"The Lady's Reach is well prepared against assault. Taking it will be costly."

Roulgarth's visage was implacable. "Nevertheless, that is where my Caerith and any Alundian willing to march with me will go. You can go where you will, Scribe."

"*Your* Caerith?"

Roulgarth's features twitched in repressed anger and he turned to leave.

"Of course the Crown Host will go with you," I said, making him pause. The annoyed frown faded from his brow only to return when I added, "It seems to be the only place in this ravaged land where we'll find any fucking horses."

* * *

The smell told the truth of the place before the walls even came into view, an acrid melange of rot and oil-laced smoke. Dark, wispy columns rose above the walls lining the southern hills beyond which lay the castle I had once spilled a great deal of blood to defend. The reek of death was familiar to many in this host, and we smelt it here. The *Paelith* rode ahead to reconnoitre the defences, returning near dusk to report them sparsely held.

"It could be a ruse," Wilhum warned when Roulgarth suggested an immediate assault. "Perhaps they hope to tempt us into rash action. Just the kind of thing our esteemed lord marshal would've come up with when we held the place." He inclined his head at me with a sardonic grin that quickly shifted into a sad, reflective frown. "Seems such a long time ago, now."

For this campaign, Leannor had forsaken her usual luxurious tent for a more modest arrangement of two standard size canvases stitched together. It made for an uncomfortable council as the army's captains crowded around my sketch of the Lady's Reach.

"Walls of such length would require thousands to repel a determined assault," Roulgarth said, tracing a finger along the outer defences. "My people report most of the garrison fled north weeks ago, and those that remain rarely venture forth on patrol. My guess is no more than a few hundred. In any case—" he stood back, settling a hard gaze first on me, then Leannor "—while Alundians are suffering in that pit, I will not sit idle."

"Nor would I countenance any delay, my lord," Leannor assured him. "For they are my son's subjects, to be cherished and protected by his host. My lord Scribe, be so good as to make the necessary preparations and attack as soon as is practicable."

I doubt any person present was unaware of the stark irony of an Algathinet commanding her army into battle to rescue folk her family had waged war on not so long ago. Roulgarth had it right: What absurdity is war.

Thanks to our advantage in numbers, I was able to order a multi-pronged attack on the walls. I split the Crown Host into three contingents, taking personal command of the smallest which, not coincidentally, contained the companies with the highest number of veterans. I also persuaded Roulgarth to allow me to borrow several dozen *veilisch* archers to accompany our attack. The second and marginally stronger contingent I placed in the hands of Desmena Lehville, while the largest I put under Wilhum's command. He was ordered to lead them against the most easily scaled section of wall where the hills dipped into a wide draw. While these companies, bearing a veritable forest of scaling ladders, drew most of the defenders, mine and Desmena's divisions climbed the more difficult routes to the west. With the Crown Host assault underway, Roulgarth led the Caerith and his growing band of Alundians in a wide march to the east, intending to assault the main gate with a huge ram. In the event, their attack was never delivered for it transpired that the Lady's Reach was even more poorly garrisoned than expected.

All three divisions of the Crown Host successfully scaled the walls, meeting a brief shower of arrows and sundry missiles before cresting the battlements. Clambering into the gap between crenelations, I found myself confronted by no more than a dozen Covenant soldiers. None of them were especially well armoured, clad in the hardy leather garb of the artisan rather than mail or plate. They had been driven back from the wall's edge by deadly accurate volleys from the *veilisch*'s flat bows, a few lying dead or wounded with fletched shafts jutting from their chest or neck. Still, they were undaunted in their defiance, shouting out a familiar if discordant exhortation at the sight of me: "We live for the Lady! We fight for the Lady! We die for the Lady!"

One came at me with a blacksmith's hammer in one hand and a hatchet in the other. From the pitch of hatred I saw on his screaming face, I concluded he must have recognised the great traitor. He was both brawny and fast, closing on me in a few steps with a bellowing roar that ended when my sword swept up to cleave his face from chin to brow. I kicked him aside and hacked down the markedly less impressive figure behind him, a stick-thin man wielding a billhook with more enthusiasm than expertise. Juhlina and the rest of the scouts soon scrambled to my side and the subsequent struggle was a brief one, distinguished mostly by our foe's refusal to surrender. My subsequent discoveries at the Lady's Reach would cause me no end of bitter regret for the swift end we gave them.

"Martyrs' arses, the stink of it," Tiler grunted, squinting at the smoke-hazed vale below. It rose from a dozen or so large bonfires situated in a loose circle around the once ruined Walvern Castle. The holdfast had grown in size since my last visit, the walls repaired and augmented with an outer ring of defences. The tower atop the inner mound was much the same, even featuring a bright, blazing beacon as it had during the days of the siege.

"They called for aid," Juhlina observed, nodding to the beacon. "Their queen didn't see fit to answer."

"Haul the ladders up and let's get on," I said, peering through the pall of smoke at the castle. I couldn't tell if there were any defenders atop the battlements, but it would be foolish not to expect another fight before this day was done. The odour grew even thicker when we descended the hills, forcing many among us to tie a scarf around their faces to ward off the worst of it. It was as we neared the first of the bonfires and I saw the girl that the source of the stink became horribly obvious.

She was perhaps thirteen years old, clad in a plain woollen dress with bows tied into her hair, a common custom in northern Alundia. I knew what she was from the way the smoke from the bonfire seeped through rather than around her. Even if it hadn't, the utter bafflement and despair on her small, oval face would have told the tale.

"I can't find my mother," she said. "I think that might be her." She pointed a finger at something in the base of the bonfire. "Or maybe that." The finger moved a little to the right. "But I can't tell. Will you help me find her?"

"Captain?" Tiler asked when I came to a halt.

"A moment," I said, moving to the girl's side. Following the line of her extended arm I made out a skull in the fire's smouldering fuel. Charred flesh still clung to it in places but it was unrecognisable. So too the others surrounding it amid a jagged jumble of blackened bones. The earth around the fire was greasy with rendered fat and at such close proximity the stench was enough to make me gag.

"Is it her?" the girl in the woollen dress asked, looking up at me with hopeful eyes.

"Yes," I said, swallowing bile and forcing a smile. "She's waiting for you. Go to her now."

She gave a solemn nod, features set in a serious frown that might once have made me laugh. Stepping forward, she raised her arms as if to embrace someone. I lost sight of her amid the swirling grey smoke. Whether she followed her mother to whatever awaited their souls, I would never know.

"How many, do you reckon?" Tiler wondered, voice muffled by the scarf covering his nose and mouth.

"Two . . . three hundred," Juhlina said before casting her gaze towards the other fires. "And this is just one of many."

"I want prisoners," I said, turning away from the pile of ashen skulls and starting towards the castle with a purposeful stride.

At first it seemed I would be disappointed, for our assault on Walvern Castle was met with only more corpses. They littered the courtyard we entered through an open and unguarded gate. We found more lying in storerooms and stairwells when I ordered a thorough search. Most were clad in the same artisans' garb as the defenders on the outer walls, but men and women in Supplicants' robes also lay among them. I concluded swiftly that these were cowardly fanatics, preferring death by their own hand to an assuredly more gruesome end in battle. Some had evidently drunk poison while others had opened their wrists or slashed their necks. A few among the poison drinkers hadn't yet completely succumbed, one young Supplicant blinking at me in strained detestation when I crouched at her side.

"What did you do here?" I demanded of her.

She blinked slowly, the lids sliding over orbs that retained a gleam of hatred. "We live . . . for the . . . Lady . . . traitor . . ." she murmured, her face contorting with the effort of trying to spit at me, but death claimed her before it escaped her lips. I reasoned she must have died a contented soul, for I saw no vestige of her shade in that castle, nor any of the other servants of the Ascendant Queen who had perished here. Death, I was learning, was terribly unfair in who it left to linger as a tormented spectre.

It was Tiler who found our only captive, he and another scout dragging him down the steps from the tower to dump him at my feet. "Looks like he tried to slit his wrists," Tiler reported, delivering a hard kick to the man's back. "Didn't cut deep enough did you, you worthless fuck!"

I had seen Tiler angry many times, but the scale of his rage was of a different order now. He shook with it, his features bunched as if about to weep. "Things were done in there, Captain," he rasped at me, casting a fearful look over his shoulder at the tower. "They had folk in the cells . . ." He choked off, taking a moment to master himself before adding hoarsely, "Young 'uns, some of them."

I turned my attention to the man kneeling before me, a fellow of broad stature that nevertheless appeared shrunken in his misery. The dried blood covering his forearms was a testament to his failed suicide and he hunched in bent-backed despair, weeping softly.

"Look at me," I instructed. The captive shuddered out a sob and complied, presenting me with the haggard, gaunt features of a man reduced to near madness. He was so changed in appearance it took me a moment to recognise this pitiable wretch as the former soldier and mason's son who had overseen Walvern Castle's transformation into the Lady's Reach.

"Sergeant Castellan Estrik," I said. "What have you done here?"

Estrik regarded me with empty eyes that leaked tears down a face that was as baffled as it was sorrowful. "What the Ascendant Queen commanded, my lord," he replied in a thin whisper.

I crouched before him, looking intently into his face. "She commanded you to the torture and murder of innocents?"

"Innocents?" He shook his head. "No, my lord. They were the Malecite's spawn. Every one of them. She saw it, the malignancy lurking inside them all. It must be driven out, she said. A task she entrusted to me. My holy duty—"

Juhlina's fist was a blur at the edge of my vision, descending to smash into Estrik's face. Blood erupted and teeth shattered as he reeled from the blow. "Holy duty!" Juhlina raged, hammering more punches. "You fucker!"

It required strenuous efforts from Tiler and myself to drag her off Estrik, by which time his jaw was broken. No more answers would be forthcoming, not that I expected anything he said to have even the slightest connection to sanity. Still, the castellan's failure to kill himself told me something.

"You knew," I said before the scouts dragged him away to await the princess regent's justice. Tiler had been all for hanging him from the walls there and then, but I decreed it was better for Leannor to pass judgement. Even in extremes, there should be some vestige of law.

Sagging in his bonds, Estrik failed to respond so I took hold of his hair and jerked his head up, meeting his eyes. "You knew she was mad. You knew what you were doing here was wrong. But still, you did it."

He slurred something, grinding his broken jaw in a feeble attempt at speech. I saw an entreaty in his face when they took him away, a plea for understanding. Like many who had made the sojourn to join Evadine during our days in the forest, he had come in search of a figure worthy of his faith. The Alundian war and her rise to queendom must have buttressed his belief whereas it eventually destroyed mine. If it hadn't, I might one day have found myself in command of a place like this, though I fancy I'd have found the fortitude to slit my wrists when justice came calling.

It transpired that Estrik was not the only survivor of the Lady's Reach garrison, Desmena capturing a few during her assault and Roulgarth's *toalisch* bringing in a half-dozen more. Before passing judgement on the captives, Leannor insisted on making a fulsome tour of the site, from the gruesome contents of the tower dungeons and the still smoking bonfires. In addition to the burnt bodies, we discovered several shallow mass graves near the east-facing walls. At Leannor's request, Ayin compiled an estimate of the dead, arriving at a figure close to eight thousand. Most were Alundian, though not all. Some wore the garb of churls from Alberis and the other duchies. It appeared Evadine had decided upon the Lady's Reach as the place of torment and execution for all her enemies.

The princess regent's verdict was predictable though her lack of inventiveness in the proscribed form of execution was not. "Just hang them," she said, waving a hand at our pathetic clutch of prisoners. "And get these bodies in the ground. I weary of the smell."

Her tone and bearing belied the apparent callousness of her words. Her voice had the strained quality of a suppressed sob and her posture posed in a regal bearing that didn't conceal the twitching of her hands. Burying the bodies required two days' labour from the Crown Host. I worked the companies in shifts, keen to ensure all saw the evidence of our enemy's malignancy, but also spreading the burden of such awful work. Nor did I spare myself, taking my turn hauling the stiffened cadavers from their ignominious pit to a series of orderly trenches where they were laid side by side. It was clear that most had been strangled, the marks of the cord still visible on many their necks. Although, there were many who bore the telltale mark of the heated iron or the barbed whip. The corpses from the bonfires would remain forever nameless but some from the pit were recognised by the Alundians who joined in the labour, leading to a recurrent chorus of piteous sobbing or grief-stricken wailing. Leannor ordered Ayin to make a list of those that could be identified.

Once the last body had been laid to rest and the trenches filled in, the princess regent addressed the assembled ranks of the Crown Host from atop the walls of Walvern Castle. The Alundians and a fair number of Caerith also clustered on the fringes to listen. The princess regent began by reading out a list Ayin had compiled of those victims that could be identified, ensuring a reverential hush settled upon the crowd as she spoke on.

"I'll not lay claim to the voice of a Martyr." An honest statement since she was obliged to shout to ensure her speech reached the ears of all present. Still, although lacking the effortless, commanding oratory Evadine enjoyed, the address of the princess regent that evening has been rightly celebrated. "For we have learned to our cost that to tolerate false claims of divinity is to invite upon ourselves the worst calamity. Here, in this place of horrors, we see where it leads. Here lie the fruits of our toleration, our foolish indolence. Yes, I say our, for I will not pretend to be blameless. I knew years ago that I would be doing this realm the greatest service by striking Evadine Courlain dead. But I did not. That was my crime. That was my folly. I confess it to you now, for, if we are to win this war, there must be truth and trust between us.

"I will not speak to you of glory. I will not beseech you to look to your faith or your lords for guidance, for none is needed now. Here in this place you know full well for what you fight. The False Queen speaks of the Second Scourge, and yet this is what she inflicts upon the world. She is our scourge, a blight upon all that lives. Accordingly, in the name of King Arthin, I hereby prescribe sentence of death upon the pretender Evadine Courlain and all those who follow her. We will have justice, or we will have death."

Evadine would have made a flourish of this statement, raised a fist or brandished a sword. Leannor merely spoke it in the same, anger-inflected shout, but it was enough. A low, ugly growl of agreement rippled through the ranks then built to a steady, repeated chant.

"Justice or death! Justice or death! Justice or death!"

To my surprise, even the Alundians took up the chant. There were a few at first. But soon every one of this ragged, hard-bitten group, who would have delighted in this woman's demise not so long ago, gave strident voice to the same cry.

"JUSTICE OR DEATH! JUSTICE OR DEATH!"

The hundred or so Caerith present showed no inclination to follow suit, displaying the same grim bafflement that had coloured their demeanour since arriving at this valley of horrors. They drifted away as the chanting continued, leaving one bulky figure behind, standing in immobile contemplation of the filled graves. When Leannor departed the walls and the shouting slowly died away, I dismissed the Crown Host to their encampment, instructing their captains that the usual injunction against drunkenness was lifted for the night. After an ordeal such as this, they required some form of release. The resultant brawls and general disorder were a small price to pay if it spared them a nightmare-filled slumber.

With the companies dispersed, I went to join the *Eithlisch* in his vigil. He greeted me with a wordless blink, and I was content to stand and gaze upon the recently turned earth for a time. Once again, the stone feather surprised me by conjuring no ghosts this night, something that brought a pang of guilty relief to my breast. Had every tormented soul who perished here lingered, I felt sure I would have greeted the dawn a madman.

It was the *Eithlisch* who broke the silence with a softly spoken question: "Is this how it was? The *Ealthsar*, all those many years gone?"

"I expect so," I said. "From what I've seen of it."

A twitch passed over his features, eyes dark with memory. "She told me it would come again," he said, and I didn't need to ask who he spoke of. "When we parted long ago. I didn't believe her. Even though I was old even then. Now I realise I was but a child angered by the departure of his only friend. I spoke many foolish words. Accused her of seeking to make herself a god to the superstitious savages beyond our borders. It was the only time I ever saw a tear fall from her eyes. Just one. Still, she refused to rebuke me, though I surely deserved it. She kissed my brow and said, 'When it comes, and it will, brother, neither of us shall be spared the worst of crimes.' Still, my anger lingered and I shouted after her as she walked off into the night, never again to be seen in Caerith lands, 'I will sully myself with no crime for your pestilent imaginings!'"

He paused, a hollow laugh escaping his lips. "But I have, Alwyn Scribe."

"The *Paelith*," I said. "Corieth. You killed him."

The *Eithlisch*'s head dipped lower, wide shoulders slumping under an unseen weight. "I did not, but that does not absolve me. I sought out all the *Paelith* clans, carried on the back of a *paelah* to ensure they could not deny the truth I spoke. The clan elders were divided, bitterly so. Some heard my truth and were willing to muster their warriors for a northward march, others were fully under Corieth's sway. The division grew ever more ugly, and I soon came to understand that if it were not resolved there would be war upon the plains. Caerith would spill the blood of Caerith."

The *Eithlisch* knelt, resting a hand upon the loose earth covering the grave. "Your kind kill each other with such constancy it seems a custom, a ritual almost. But it has not happened among the Caerith since even before the *Ealthsar*. Such a thing could not be borne." He scooped up a handful of earth, letting the soil run through his fingers. "A great gathering of the clans was convened, supposedly so that all could hear the words of Corieth and the *Eithlisch*, thereby deciding this matter for once and all. But I had orchestrated this gathering with another purpose in mind, for I knew as long as Corieth's words ensnared so many hearts, the *Paelith* would never ride to war. And so I invoked the only power left to me, I called upon the *paelah* themselves. I exhorted the gathered warriors that it should be for the *paelah* to judge the merits of Corieth's words. And judge him they did.

"He was so certain of his own wisdom, standing there with arms spread wide, expecting that great herd to submit to his will. But the *paelah* submit to no man. By the time the last of them had galloped across his corpse there was little left but rag and bone. After that, no *Paelith* dare speak against war, for the will of the *paelah* cannot be denied."

The *Eithlisch* opened his hand, allowing the remaining soil to cascade on to the grave. "I knew, Alwyn Scribe. I knew what the judgement of the *paelah* would mean. Corieth had the right of it, in that if nothing else. In allying with the *Ishlichen*, we sully ourselves."

Chapter Thirty-Five

We remained at the Lady's Reach for another five days, an inescapable delay to allow for rest after the arduous march through Alundia. It also enabled Roulgarth to gather more recruits from the surrounding country. Walvern Castle possessed a stable filled with well-fed and tended horses, all of which were swiftly placed in the hands of a newly minted company combining my scouts and Wilhum's riders. Intolerant of inaction, the *Paelith* had gone off ranging across the southern banks of the Crowhawl River. In need of speedy reconnaissance, I sent Wilhum east with orders to scout the ford which provided the only nearby crossing point into Alberis. Juhlina returned alone two days later, sagging atop the back of her *paelah*. I could read the nature of her report on her grave but exhausted face.

"How many?" I asked.

"We only saw the vanguard," she said, groaning as she climbed down from the saddle. "Three full companies of knights, approaching from the east."

"The east?" I had hoped Evadine would be busying herself in the Shavine Marches, but there had always been a chance she would abandon her vindictive mission to come against us here. The rapidity of her march surprised me, but so too did her line of attack. "Why bother circling around to the east?" I wondered aloud.

"The banners were unfamiliar to me," Juhlina said. "But Wilhum knew them. Apparently, the Duke of Dulsian has mustered his host for war."

* * *

By dint of some hasty organisation, I was able to get the Crown Host marching east within a day. I set a punishing pace, keeping them on the road for all the hours daylight allowed. I forbade the pitching of tents at night, forcing them to sleep clustered around fires. At the first glimmer of dawn, sergeants and captains set about their ungentle rousing and the march resumed its grim routine until the ford was reached. By then the *Paelith* had begun to return in large numbers, enabling me to send them across first to hold the northern bank while the host crossed in strength. Once Uthren bore me free of the river, I was surprised to find no sign of the Dulsian army anywhere in sight. Even the least astute commander would know that attacking us here afforded the best opportunity for victory. Yet, as the day wore on their standards failed to appear above the low hills to the east.

With the sun beginning to dip, the captains gathered atop a stretch of raised ground where I had drawn up the army. "The Duke of Dulsian is famed for his greed above all," Roulgarth commented. "A greedy man is often also a coward."

"Then why bring an army against us?" I asked.

"To bargain," Leannor replied. She was mounted on the finest horse to be found at Walvern Castle, a tall, grey mare with a long white mane that, despite its striking appearance, had a far from regal habit of constant fidgeting. Leannor didn't appear to mind, however, stroking the beast's neck as it continually bobbed its head, her own gaze fixed on the eastern horizon. "I've known Duke Lermin since girlhood, and he never comes to any meeting without something to sweeten the deal."

"You believe he intends to parley, then, Majesty?" Ehlbert enquired.

"Unless his fear of the False Queen has compelled him to risk combat for the first time in his life." Leannor turned to Ayin. "My lady, be so good as to have the larger of the treasury chests brought forth, and let's pitch the tent and standard over there." She waved a hand at the flat ground below the rise. "Where we shall await the duke's herald. I doubt he'll be long in coming."

In fact, the sky had darkened considerably by the time the duke's herald arrived, obliging me to stand the Crown Host down from full battle order. They remained in their companies but were free to light fires and cook their evening meal. On the flanks, the *Paelith* milled about in confused agitation. I had attempted to explain the concept of parley to their clan elders, but they found the notion of speaking to an enemy on the eve of battle mystifying. Still, they agreed not to launch an attack until the *Eithlisch* gave the signal. The prospect of the great horde of *Paelith* warriors hurling themselves headlong into a clash with a strong contingent of armoured knights loomed as a large and unanswered question in my mind. I had no true picture of the likely outcome, except a tall mound of corpses.

To my surprise, the Dulsian herald proved to be a pleasingly familiar figure. It wasn't that I recalled finding the company of Lord Therin Gasalle particularly edifying. Moreover, the ease with which I could read his moods spoke well for gauging his duke's intentions.

"How gratified I am to see you alive and unburnt, my lord," I greeted him as he reined his horse to a halt before the princess regent's tent. "I trust the escape from Couravel wasn't too hazardous."

Lord Therin's features betrayed only the arch dislike of the noble for the churl, sparing me the briefest glance before bowing to Leannor.

"My lady, on behalf of his grace, Lord Lermin Aspard, Duke of Dulsian, I offer greetings—"

"Majesty," Ayin cut in, the sharpness of her tone bringing Therin's flow of words to a halt. She stood to Leannor's left, straight-backed and composed in her ermine-trimmed cloak and dress of silver embroidered, pale blue cotton. Such finery seemed to sit far more comfortably on her these days.

"What?" Therin snapped with a scowl. Ayin had the appearance of a lady-in-waiting, but still retained the voice of a commoner.

"The correct form of address for the princess regent is 'Majesty,'" Ayin told him. "Mine is 'my lady'. Be so good as to correct your speech, good sir. And get your arse off that horse and pay proper obeisance while you're at it."

Receiving only a look of bland expectation from Leannor, Therin expended a moment in impotent glowering before consenting to dismount. "Majesty," he said, forcing a smile and bowing again, "it is my honour to extend to you an invitation to dine at Duke Lermin's table this night. There, it is his fervent hope, fulsome and friendly discussion will obviate any current misunderstandings that might lead to unnecessary conflict."

Leannor merely raised an eyebrow before providing a succinct response. "No. Go back and tell him to get his bloated carcass here within the hour. If he is too craven to face me in parley, he can try to summon the courage to face me in battle. And, should I ever have the misfortune to encounter you again, Lord Therin, any disrespect shown to the members of my court shall be punished by a sound flogging. Now, get you hence."

In acquiescing to the princess regent's summons, Duke Lermin prudently brought his army with him. It was fully dark by the time the torches appeared out of the gloom, spreading out to form the long, glittering line of a sizeable host. I guessed the duke had ordered many more torches lit than were strictly required, so as to create an impression of greater numbers. For my part, I commanded that half the Crown Host's campfires be doused and prevailed upon the *Eithlisch* to pull the *Paelith* back behind the rise. Should tonight's proceedings descend into a battle, it would be best not to allow our foe a clear indication of our strength.

Duke Lermin proved to be a far more robust and hardier looking fellow than his reputation supposed. He rode forth atop an impressive white charger flanked by a full company of knights. When he reined to a halt, I beheld a large, bearded man of broad stature wearing a long cloak trimmed with the yellow spotted fur from some exotic animal of far-flung origin. It was not his only display of ostentatious wealth. As he dismounted, I saw torchlight glimmer on the heavy gold chain about his neck, his wide torso clad in a dark leather tunic embellished by silver filigree and inlaid garnets.

"You'd be the Scribe then?" he asked, voice both gruff and brisk, not troubling himself to return my bow.

"Alwyn Scribe, my lord," I said, standing aside and gesturing at the open flap of Leannor's tent. "The princess regent awaits you."

"Bit small isn't it," he grunted, squinting at the tent. "Is the royal purse so light?"

"The tent may be small," I said, allowing an impatient edge to creep into my voice, "but the standard still stands tall as ever. As does our army."

The duke shifted his appraising squint to me, huffing in restrained annoyance. "Therin said you were an impudent gutter scrape," he muttered, stomping past me and ducking into the tent. Besides Ayin, Leannor had chosen to receive the duke with only myself present. Even Ehlbert had been excluded, I suspected because Leannor worried over the champion's temper, which had grown short of late. She was also the only one seated, having opted not to provide a chair for her visitor. I watched him make note of the insult as his narrow gaze roved the tent, presumably seeking threats. Apparently, he saw none in either myself or Ayin, which spoke much for his lack of observance, and he afforded much of his attention to the open chest positioned to Leannor's right. For a greedy soul, a sight such as this was irresistible.

Crammed into the chest were the choicest items from the treasure found at Castle Dreol. Jewels gleamed in silver and gold settings amid a mound of pearls and antique coinage. When Duke Lermin sank to one knee before the princess regent, I couldn't tell if he was paying homage to her or to the exposed riches.

"Majesty," he said, all gruffness gone now, "please accept my most humble apologies for not attending you sooner. And know, the king and your most honoured self have my loyalty, for now and always."

I exchanged a glance with Ayin, the amused contempt I saw in her face a mirror of my own. Here was a man who considered himself already bought. *He might have bargained a bit first*, I thought.

"I must confess, Lord Lermin," Leannor said, "I find your pledge of loyalty surprising. Lord Alwyn, did we not receive firm intelligence that the Duke of Dulsian had sworn fealty to the unholy pretender Evadine Courlain?"

"That we did, Majesty. In fact, our intelligence was that he had journeyed all the way to Athiltor for the purpose, prostrating himself before the cathedral altar and swearing his oath of undying service in the name of all the Martyrs, no less."

"Are you so quick to throw off your allegiances, my lord?" Leannor asked the still bowing duke. "If so, what surety do I have that you will not do so again the moment I slip from your sight?"

"I will swear any oath before any witness, Majesty," Lermin promised, his demeanour one of grave assurance now. "Command me and let me demonstrate my fealty. You will not find me wanting."

"I'm afraid that's a bird already flown, my lord." Leannor fell silent, extending a hand to the contents of the open chest at her side. "I see my trinkets have aroused your interest. There's a fascinating story behind it all, but I'll not trouble you with it now. Especially since you will never lay one finger upon any of this."

A loud clatter sounded as Leannor slammed the chest closed, the duke giving a visible start as the iron lock rattled.

"I do not believe," Leannor went on, "it was your famed avarice that brought you here, my lord. I believe it was fear. For you have met the False Queen when you grovelled before her. It is my belief that in doing so you understood that, should she triumph over me, she will next turn her attentions to you. She looks upon you and sees much to despise, as do I, but I have never wanted to kill you for it. Nor will your head be the only one to fall. By my best reckoning you have no less than six legitimate children and a dozen or more acknowledged bastards born to your stable of whores. Have no doubt, the False Queen will kill them all. My son, on the other hand, will not. He will, in his grace and magnanimity, allow you to keep your duchy, your lands, your castles and your whores. But you, my lord Duke, will receive not one bauble of this treasure. In fact, for the remainder of your life you will pay to the Crown one-tenth of all your personal earnings. That, my lord, is the price of abasement to a pretender, and I consider it lenient."

She stood then, stepping forward to loom over Lermin's crouched bulk. He dared to meet her eye, just a quick darting look before dipping his head even lower. "As for surety," Leannor said, "I'll take your army. Don't worry, I shan't require you to lead them. You have my leave to return to your duchy. And when this war is won, you have my leave to stay there for I find the notion of having to ever endure your presence again distinctly unappealing. Lord Scribe, escort the duke to his horse and prepare to take over leadership of his troops. Unless—" she angled her head, staring hard at the crown of Lermin's head "—you would like to voice an objection, my lord? In which case, we shall settle this on the field come the dawn."

For the most part, Duke Lermin's host were a sorry lot. A few hundred hardy veterans formed the three companies of his household guard and the four score sworn knights who rode under his banner were well armoured and mounted. The rest were a collection of pressed churls, many of whom had already begun to melt away even before their liege lord announced his second change of allegiance. Lermin's speech to his troops was brief and lacking much in the way of inspiring oratory. Before scurrying off to the safety of his own borders, he appointed a thoroughly miserable Lord Therin Gasalle to command his host in his stead. The appointment failed to raise much reaction from the ranks save a few muttered curses and disparaging whistles.

Come the following morn, Ayin counted little over a thousand Dulsians remaining and we lost more than half to desertion over the course of the succeeding week. With Lord Therin proving a predictably negligent commander, I set Duke Gilferd over what was left, forming a third cohort to the army by merging them with his Cordwainers. To my surprise, Lord Therin accepted his tacit demotion without demur. In truth, I continually expected him to follow the example of most of his soldiers and take to his heels, yet every day he would stoically, if unhappily, mount his horse to plod along with the others.

One piece of good fortune came in the form of the copious supplies the Dulsians had brought with them, a long train of carts laden with all manner of victuals. With so many of them fled, the rest could be distributed among the Crown Host to sustain them on the journey to the coast. I ordained a line of march that kept us close to the northern bank of the Crowhawl River, sending the *Paelith* and

Wilhum's riders out to screen our right flank. I harboured little hope that our presence hadn't already been noted and swiftly communicated to Evadine. The question of what she would do upon hearing the news loomed with unanswerable constancy. Had I been commanding her host, I would have counselled an immediate march south. Better to confront and eliminate this new threat before those who had suffered under the Ascendant Queen's misrule could rally to the Algathinet banner. Evadine, however, had always been unpredictable and, I fancied, would be even more so now.

I had hoped for more recruits during our march to the coast, but each day Wilhum and Juhlina returned with news of empty farmsteads and villages. Some had been burned and pillaged, the inhabitants fled or murdered and left to rot. Others were simply abandoned by churls who preferred the uncertainties of the wilderness in winter to the cruelties of the Ascendant Host. *A host I helped to build*, I reminded myself with bitter constancy. *It's as much my creation as hers.*

Of course, the dead were not absent from this march, although they came and went with irksome irregularity. One day I would see a lone, indistinct figure standing on the banks of the Crowhawl, apparently serene and silent in their ghost-hood. These were greatly preferable to the families that sometimes wandered alongside or through the ranks of the Crown Host. I had begun to recognise distinctions among the dead. The older spectres were either mad or indifferent. The more freshly killed were the least quiet, especially the families. Mothers brandished babies at me, their swaddling dark and dripping. Fathers clutched tottering infants to their side and growled warnings at the indifferent soldiers passing by.

In time, I learned to conceal my awareness of their presence, lest I invite their attentions. It was not an easy task, causing me to resume the chainsman's trick of singing to banish their voices. I had never been much of a singer and lacked Ayin's repertoire so soon switched to reciting aloud all the scholarship, poetry and scripture I could recall. Inevitably, soldiers soon took notice of the man they now referred to as the Scribe Marshal muttering to himself and I gained a wholly unearned reputation as a devout soul. Some of the more devotionally minded took heart from my recitations, seeing in me a worthy champion of a Covenant twisted into heresy by the False Queen's tyranny. My recitations did at least serve to keep the ghostly voices at bay, even if I couldn't banish them from my sight.

We reached the Crowhawl estuary twelve days after meeting the Dulsians where I ordered a shift into battle order before advancing on the port town of Yarnsahl. Reports from Shilva Sahken had indicated the place as a nest of rebellious sentiment against the Ascendant Queen, especially among the merchant class. Weeks before, Shilva had delivered to them a letter from the princess regent advising the malcontents to hold off on outright revolt until the Crown Host came within sight of their walls. It seemed they had only partially heeded the warning as the *Paelith* returned with news of fires and uproar while we were still a full day's march away.

I charged Duke Gilferd with taking all the knights and cavalry ahead to lend what aid he could to the rebels while I force marched our infantry to the town. I also sent the *Paelith* north to ward off any southern advance from Evadine's forces. Upon reaching the town, I saw columns of smoke rising above the walls but not so thick as to indicate a general conflagration as in Couravel. Gilferd met me at the main gate, his face streaked with grime and soot and a spatter of dried blood staining his gauntlets. Above him, a score or more bodies dangled by their ankles from the gatehouse battlements, all stripped naked and their bared flesh streaked red with recently inflicted torments. From beyond the gate, the streets echoed with the tumult of angry voices lost to frenzy.

"They're a vengeful lot here," Gilferd said by way of explanation. "The False Queen's garrison chose to stay and fight. Made a decent fist of it too until we arrived. They had fortified the customs house and beat back several assaults by the townsfolk. Apparently, it didn't occur to them to just set the place on fire. When we did, they all came charging out. They didn't last long." He jerked his head at the dangling bodies.

"These were tax collectors and a brace of Resurgent Supplicants. The mob's still on the rampage looking for more." Gilferd's jaw worked as he quelled his disgust and rage. "Tried to quiet them but it was no good."

"We'll see to it, my lord," I told him. "You have done fine work here today." I turned to Tiler and gestured at the dangling corpses. "Cut them down. I'll lead a company to secure the docks. Use the rest to clear the streets, and don't be too gentle about it. A ruined port is no good to us."

Fully quelling the riots required four companies of infantry and some judicious use of stave and lash before the bloodthirsty mob abandoned their vindictive amusements. Judging by the mystified wailing of the few forlorn souls revealed to me by the feather, it was clear that most of the victims had either been singled out for the settling of grudges or were simply innocents swept up in a whirlwind of unreasoning violence.

The widespread fire setting had also claimed several dockside storehouses, robbing the Crown Host of supplies and compelling a delay as we awaited the arrival of Shilva Sahken's fleet. They arrived piecemeal over the next eight days, while I eyed the horizon for the appearance of one vessel in particular. When she finally appeared with the morning tide, the *Sea Crow* approached the quay with an uncharacteristic sluggishness. As she drew closer, I saw the raggedness of her sails, untied ropes swaying and the timbers of her hull blackened in places. Welling concern made me scour the deck until, with some relief, I made out Toria's slender form.

"She's seen better days," I called to her when the ship cast her lines to the dockside.

Toria had no rejoinder for me today, however, her face as grim as I ever saw it. I made a quick count of her crew, coming up short by about half. Of those that remained, several sported bandaged heads or limbs.

"Farinsahl's gone," Toria told me upon descending the gangway. From her unsteady gait and hollowed eyes, I deduced she hadn't slept for many days.

"Gone?" I asked. "You mean fallen?"

"No," she replied with a weary impatience. "I mean gone. Torn down. Set to the torch. Pillaged and wasted." Toria closed her eyes, staggering a little until I reached out to steady her. "The people too, so far as we could tell. Those that didn't burn were being lined up on the docks to have their throats slit before being chucked into the harbour."

She swallowed, turning to run a pained gaze over the scorched flanks of her ship. "We were still loading the cargo when they came. The lord of exchange had been commanded by Lorine to fortify the city against siege, but he felt he owed his allegiance to the Ascendant Queen. So, when the Covenant Host hove into view, he threw his gates open. From what I could gather, they killed him first then started on the whole city. Apparently, the mad bitch had a vision which told her Farinsahl was so infested with Malecite influence only fire and blood could cleanse it. The harbour was crowded with Shilva's ships so getting clear before they reached the docks was impossible. They cast fire arrows at us from the quay, set fire to the rigging. Then they came at us in boats." Toria's head dipped lower. "It was an ugly fight, claimed the first and second mates too, and a load more before we scraped them off the hull and struck out for open sea. Had to navigate here myself." She ran a twitching hand through her unwashed hair. "Wasn't easy."

"Did any other ships get away?"

"A few. Saw a good deal more go up in flames. Reckon your line of supply is going to get a fair sight thinner, Alwyn."

"Shilva?"

"Wasn't there. Last I heard she was bargaining for supplies in Olversahl. It seems the Sister Queens aren't happy with the Ascendant Queen. There's rumours about a nasty letter she sent them. In any case, they might be open to trade with the Algathinet king. Expect the price to be high, though."

"Did you manage to get my message to Lorine?"

"Did that weeks ago. No reply, of course. Seems the False Queen split her army. Sent one part to ravage the ports for the crime of supporting what she called the Malecite Crusade. The other she took charge of herself, last seen making straight for Castle Ambris. Sorry, Alwyn." Toria paused to offer me a wince of sympathy. "My guess: Mother Fox is already trapped in her den."

Chapter Thirty-Six

The need to garner supplies forced a further delay at Yarnsahl, one I endured in a welter of grinding impatience. I was sorely tempted to take all the knights and cavalry, and the *Paelith*, and embark on a pell-mell ride for Castle Ambris. However, the want of food to sustain such a force in the field, and the near certainty we would find ourselves severely outnumbered by the Ascendant Host, compelled me to wait.

In strict military terms, I had to concede that our advance into the Shavine Marches had improved the fortunes of the Crown Host. Several hundred willing volunteers flocked to the Algathinet banners in Yarnsahl alone, with more arriving daily from nearby villages. Of course, a swelling of our ranks entailed a corresponding increase in our need for supplies. In addition to the basic need for more food, most of the new recruits lacked proper weapons. Our smiths took over the forges in the port and set about producing the required billhook blades with typical industry, but it would take time to fully arm every soldier and so I was consigned to yet more waiting.

To alleviate my worries, I sent Tiler and a handful of scouts to reconnoitre the approaches to Castle Ambris. "Keep to the forest," I warned him. "You know all the best hideouts, but *she* has eyes others don't, so keep moving. No lingering in any one spot for more than half a day. I need to know how many are besieging the castle. When you have a clear number, strike south and find me on the coast road."

During our stay, Leannor occupied herself by establishing her court on a more formal basis. Taking over the mansion house of an executed merchant, she appointed Ayin as Mistress of Rolls, a position that gave the lady-in-waiting authority over all aspects of the royal household. Pages and servants of various ranks were duly recruited from the townsfolk or those too old or too young for a soldier's life. Keen to convey the impression of a regal authority, Leannor also began to hear petitions from the locals, of which there were many. Evadine's tax collectors had been undiscerning in the property they seized, and the princess regent spent day after day patiently listening to variations of the same requests for restitution. Ayin diligently recorded the particulars of each petitioner, all of whom were sent on their way with a royal writ promising recompense at the close of hostilities. To those who occasionally dared voice objection to the delay, Leannor replied with a pointed observation that the day of restitution would arrive sooner if they joined the Crown Host.

At the end of our third week in Yarnsahl, Shilva Sahken's broad-beamed merchantman finally drew into the harbour. Unlike the *Sea Crow*, the vessel lacked obvious signs of damage, but the countenance of its captain was no less grave.

"All the northern ports are closed to us now, Majesty," she told Leannor upon being conveyed to the royal residence. "Some suffered the same fate as Farinsahl. Others lie abandoned, their people having fled in advance of the Covenant Host's arrival. We can expect no more support from that quarter. However—" Shilva gave a tight, wary smile as she tugged a scrolled parchment from the pocket of her heavy sailor's coat "—I do bring what may be welcome news, at least in part."

She began to drop to one knee, proffering the parchment to Leannor. "Just tell me, Mistress Shilva," the Princess Regent said. "The gist will suffice."

"I bring greetings from the Sister Queens of Ascarlia," Shilva said, unfurling the scroll. "They offer their congratulations on your recent victories and admit, in very careful language, to be desirous of an end to the Ascendant Queen's rule. Apparently, their recent diplomatic overtures to her received a decidedly unwelcome reply. Accordingly, they offer fulsome and consistent supplies of all materials needed to ensure Your Majesty's swift and just triumph. As a token of good faith, a dozen Ascarlian ships will arrive here shortly, all laden with weapons and sundry victuals. More will follow once their terms have been met as, naturally, they expect adequate compensation for their efforts."

"Naturally," Leannor echoed with a grimace. "Allow me to guess: the Algathinet dynasty will abandon all claims to the Fjord Geld and any supplies to be paid for at an exorbitant price?"

Shilva gave a stiff, apologetic nod. "I did attempt to negotiate, Majesty, but . . ."

"I'm sure you did your best." Leannor glanced at Ehlbert and, receiving a resigned shrug, straightened her back. "My lady," she said, turning to Ayin. "Please draft a response to the Sister Queens agreeing to all their terms. I shall also require a writ of ennoblement for Mistress Shilva, hereafter to be known as Lady Shilva, Duchess of the Seas and Commander of the Royal Fleet."

Like many a lifelong outlaw, Shilva Sahken was as cynical a soul as I ever met. And yet, as the full meaning of Leannor's words sank home, I saw her shudder with the strain of concealed emotion. Blinking rapidly, she knelt, head bowed low. "It shall be my honour to accept, Majesty."

Lorine and now Shilva, I mused inwardly. *Duchesses both.* I smiled a little at the curious fact that the two most important women in the life of Deckin Scarl had achieved what he had not. I like to think he would have summoned the resolve to find it amusing.

With the arrival of the Ascarlian ships, the Crown Host and its allies were at last sufficiently provisioned to begin the march north. I had raised with Leannor the prospect of appealing to the Sister Queens for warriors as well as arms and victuals, but she was quick to dismiss the notion.

"This puts me in mind of something my father used to say," she replied. "Invite an Ascarlian to a feast and they'll eat you out of house and home, then claim they were cheated. Besides, I think we have sufficient foreigners walking our lands at present, don't you, Lord Scribe?"

Once again, the army kept to the coast road, our passage eased somewhat by a change in the weather. The frosted air of winter abated to allow for recent snows to melt while still retaining enough chill to prevent the road degenerating into a muddy quagmire. During the march through Alundia the long, snaking column could expect to manage ten or twelve miles a day. Now, fifteen was the norm. I was tempted to push them even harder but feared the effects of exhaustion on our large contingent of barely trained newcomers.

Another, less desirable effect of the altered climate was the thick blanket of fog that swept in from the sea the fifth day out from Yarnsahl. I hoped it would be gone by evening, but it lingered for days, concealing much of the landscape, frustrating reconnaissance, and casting an eerie pall over the soldiers' mood. I ordered a slowing of the march and more frequent rest stops to ensure the army remained concentrated, something that was easier to enforce among the Albermaine-ish than the Caerith. The *Paelith*, always chafing at the yoke of *Ishlichen* command, were prone to taking themselves off on wide ranging sweeps of the surrounding country. The *toalisch* and *veilisch* weren't much better, groups of them disappearing for days in search of prey to hunt or driven by a simple desire to explore this strange land of hedged fields and oddly shaped houses.

"They're warriors, not soldiers," Roulgarth said in response to my complaints. "Although, feel at liberty to threaten them with flogging for disobedience. I should greatly enjoy witnessing their reaction."

Our pace slowed yet again upon entering the craggy, winding coast of the mid-Shavine. Here the sea had carved deep inlets into the shore, creating a landscape of tall cliffs and numerous streams, some too deep to be easily forded. Fortunately, this region had been Shilva's domain for many years, and the smugglers who answered to her knew every hidden cove and landing site. Consequently, the Crown Host remained well supplied, although doing so required numerous interruptions to the march.

Whist I fretted over the threat of ambush amid this difficult ground with its many ravines and gullies, the army struggled its way through without incident. Juhlina led several patrols and reported no enemies nearby, yet the persistent fog made me doubt her confidence. Consequently, I heaved a relieved sigh when I spied the rolling, partially forested hills to the north through the drifting mist. Keen to reach open country, I ordered an increase in pace, driving the Crown Host hard until midday. Duke Gilferd's mixed companies of veterans and untried volunteers straggled at the rear, losing much of their cohesion and forcing me to order a halt in order to consolidate.

"I do wish you would allow me to flog a few, Lord Scribe," Gilferd complained to me in a low mutter. I had ridden back along the column to check on his progress. The Cordwain and Dulsian infantry were arrayed in decent order while the remainder, a crowd of tired newcomers bowed under the weight of their weapons and packs, were being harangued into untidy ranks by their captains. "My grandfather was too sparing of the lash and it nearly cost him his duchy. A mistake my father never repeated."

"The lash might stiffen a few backs, my lord," I replied, "but it won't win any hearts. Docking their pay and cutting their brandy ration might have the necessary effect . . ." I trailed off as something in the fog caught my eye, a lone figure emerging out of the haze. The mist was too thick and the distance too great to make out his face, but his form and gait were chillingly familiar. *I should have known he would make an unquiet soul*, I sighed inwardly.

"Do you see something, my lord?" Gilferd enquired, puzzled by my sudden preoccupation with swirling fog.

The figure came to a halt fifty paces off, features still obscured but exuding an air of grim expectation. This meeting, apparently, could not be avoided. Should I simply ignore him and ride on, I felt a dispiriting certainty he would follow until I consented to converse.

"A moment," I said, Uthren performing his uncanny trick of reading my intentions by trotting forward without need of snapped reins or kicked heels.

"Quite a beast you have there," the spectre observed when Uthren came to a halt. "Where'd you steal it?"

"He is his own gift," I replied, surprised by the thickness of my voice for this man had never truly been a friend. I had found the dead to be an oft distracted lot, their hold upon the living world precarious and prone to confusion. The spectre of Captain Albyrn Swain, however, displayed a fierce, even implacable focus, his hard gaze rich in knowledge of who and what he was, much as it had been in life. It made me strangely nostalgic.

"Call that armour?" he went on, running a caustic eye over the mingling of Caerith and Albermaine-ish mail and plate that clad my form. "You look like a jackanapes."

"It serves well enough." I coughed, seeing an accusation on his face, one that demanded an answer. "Ofihla," I began, gaze straying to the mist beyond him, fearful of who might appear next. "She left me no choice—"

"I know," he cut in. "And worry not, Scribe, she died contented in her misjudgements."

"I should have stopped it," I said, fixing on another reason for his presence. "In Couravel. I should have saved you . . ."

"I should have saved myself, and so many others. I am not here to judge you, Scribe. I am here for my own atonement. I am here to pay for the lies I told myself, the weakness and cowardice of my inaction."

"So, you knew what she was? You knew Evadine served the Malecite, even before I did?"

"I knew that the cause we had shared was a lie. I saw the increasing cruelty of the woman in whom I had invested all my faith. I saw the nature of the queen she would become. And I did nothing."

Uthren let out a discomfited snort as Swain took a step closer. I wondered whether the *paelah* could perceive the dead or if the great horse simply sensed my mounting dread. Still, he stayed put as the spectre came to my side, looking up at me with a mingling of raw need and grim reproach.

"We both failed," he said. "I because of my faith in her, you because of your love. You may indulge the delusion your love has died, Scribe, but I see it still burning. Such things are plain to the eyes of the dead. To end this, you must slay that part of you. No matter the cost. No matter that it may mean you will never love again." He reached up to grasp my hand. His fingers slipped through my gauntlets, as insubstantial as smoke, yet I felt the icy caress of his touch. "You understand?"

I tried to draw my hand away, but his grip held me as tight as any vice. Swain, it appeared, was as strong in death as he had been in life. The numbness imbued by his touch spread up my arm and into my chest, the terrible chill of it seeping into muscle and vein, reaching for my heart.

"You understand?" Swain demanded.

"Yes!" I grated, the word shuddering from between clenched teeth.

Swain grunted and released me. Stepping back, he afforded me a final look of deep, careful appraisal before turning away. "Incidentally," he said as he faded back into the fog. "You should see to your battle lines. Duke Viruhlis approaches, and he is very desirous of impressing his queen." Then he was gone, lost to the swirling grey. Perhaps he wanders still, but, like Deckin, his business with me was forever concluded.

I strained my ears for the thud of hooves or tramp of marching feet, hearing only the faint grumbling of Gilferd's soldiers. Uthren, however, had far keener senses than I. The great horse let out a harsh, growling snort, rearing a little and tossing his head, nostrils flaring. It was enough to dispel any meagre doubts and we wheeled about, galloping back to Gilferd's still disordered companies.

"Sound battle order!" I told him. "Three ranks! Form your knights on the right flank!"

The duke's hesitation was brief, banished by the grim snap of my voice. He tugged his reins and began trotting the length of his command, barking orders that had veterans scrambling and new recruits floundering in confusion. The Dulsian and Cordwain companies were soon arrayed in their triple rank formation of pikes to the fore of the bill-men and halberdiers, with dagger men behind.

"Trooper Spinner!" I called out, spying the juggler a few dozen paces off. "Ride to Lord Wilhum. Tell him we are about to be attacked. He is to take charge of the Crown Host and form line of battle. When you've done that, carry the warning to Lord Roulgarth and the princess regent."

Adlar replied with a tense, pale-faced nod and galloped away into the fog. Following his course, I could barely glimpse the closest Crown Host companies through the haze and judged the gap as worryingly broad. "You lot!" I shouted at the nearest gaggle of milling recruits. "Get your thumbs out of your arses and form line! NOW!" I added in a furious bark that managed to get some of them moving.

"You bastards pledged to the Algathinet banner because you wanted vengeance," I raged at the rest. "Well, now's your chance!" I continued my obscenity-laden diatribe as they hurried into formation. "Stand straight, you shit-eater!" Uthren paused his trot, allowing me to growl a baleful command on a lanky youth shuffling into the first rank, his trembling hands leaving sweat stains on the haft of his pike. He gaped up at me with unblinking eyes, skin the sickly shade that indicated an imminent disgorgement of either bowels or belly. I quelled the impulse to further intimidation, instead leaning lower and placing a firm hand on his mail-covered shoulder.

"Who did you lose?" I asked.

"M-my mother and sister both, m'lord," he said, a shameful grimace passing over his jaundiced features. "The Resurgents had them locked in their house and threw torches on the thatching. They were late to daily supplications, y'see."

I tightened my grip on his shoulder. "When you kill these fuckers, think of them." The youth nodded and stood straighter. "Think on all you have lost!" I went on, raising my voice to the rest of his company. "All that has been stolen! All that has been murdered! Think on that and rejoice, for now you have the chance to extract full measure of payment, in blood!"

There was no mistaking the resolve in their subsequent cheer, but their line was still too ragged, bowed into a crescent between the veteran Cordwainer company on the right and the Crown Host on the left. But at least the gap was filled and they stood firm. I could only hope their hatred would sustain them through what was coming.

Uthren snorted again, louder than before, turning to face the fogbound emptiness to the west, his hooves digging sod from the ground. I heard them then, the steady rumble of many horses at the gallop. Apparently,

Duke Viruhlis was keen on sweeping his queen's enemies into the sea in one triumphant charge. Drawing my sword, I attempted to guide Uthren back to the line. The *paelah*, however, was not for moving. Instead, he dug more divots from the ground and tossed his head with increasing animation.

"Steady," I said, running a hand over the tense muscle of his neck. "This isn't the best place to be." I twisted my hips to urge him to the side. Instead, Uthren reared, letting out a loud challenging whinny. This had the effect of drawing another defiant cheer from the mass of novice soldiers to my rear.

"We're with you, Lord Scribe!" one called out, heralding a chorus of shouted agreement.

I responded by simultaneously raising my sword above my head while tugging fruitlessly on Uthren's reins. He, however, appeared utterly unaware of my growing distress at the prospect of facing an all-out cavalry charge single-handed. As the tumult of onrushing horseflesh and armour grew ever louder to my front, I was faced with the choice of remaining in the saddle or abandoning Uthren's back for the safety of the battle line.

It was here that I learned the essential truth of both cowardice and heroism, to wit: the line betwixt them is so thin as to be invisible. A hero's legend arises mostly by happenstance, a confluence of events that leaves no avenue for retreat. So it was that the myth of the Scribe's Charge at the Battle of the Bluffs was born, not from courage, but indecision. For, as Duke Viruhlis's force swept ever closer, unseen but near deafening in their fury, I spent a second longer than I should have debating the merits of jumping from Uthren's back for an undignified flight to comparative safety of the battle line. The short delay allowed him to make the choice for me.

The manner in which I swayed in the saddle as the great horse spurred into a gallop must have made it appear as if I was waving my sword in a command to follow. The novices cheered even louder and I turned my head to see them surging in my wake. Thanks to Uthren, I had created a hole in the Crown Host line.

"Stop, you idiot beast!" I railed as he bore me on. The great horse merely whinnied again and increased his pace. Hearing an upsurge in noise to my left, I divined Viruhlis's charge had made contact with the centre of the Crown Host line, the familiar, ugly music of battle echoing through the fog. The cacophony of clashing flesh and metal, interspersed with the shouts and screams of combat, proved an irresistible lure for Uthren. Snorting, he swerved, sod rising in a black fountain before he resumed his unrestrained gallop. I expected to slam into a wall of opposing cavalry at any second, yet for the first fifty paces or so we encountered nothing. I began to entertain the notion that we might ride through this entire struggle unmolested, but then the silhouette of a mounted knight in full armour resolved out of the haze directly to our front.

He rode a fine warhorse of impressive size, his lance straight and level as he charged. His visor was raised and I beheld the snarling face of a man primed for battle and fully intent on securing victory for the Ascendant Queen. So intent was he that he failed to notice Uthren's approach until the last instant.

The *paelah* barely paused as he leaped and brought his massive fore hoof down on the head of the knight's mount, smashing the skull and sending the beast into a spectacular tumble. Before Uthren charged on, I saw the knight fall, his neck bending at a fatal angle as it connected with the ground. Another figure loomed ahead, this one managing to turn and meet the charge before it closed. I leaned to the side to avoid the jabbing lance, making ready to slash at the wielder's head, but Uthren's bulk slammed both horse and rider aside with stunning force before I could deliver the blow.

We sped on, the *paelah* crushing more horse skulls and unseating more riders as they emerged from the mist. I exchanged blows with only one knight, a tall fellow I vaguely recalled from Duke Viruhlis's retinue in Stonebridge. A fine horseman, he managed to both halt his mount and compel it to dance aside, suffering only a glancing blow from Uthren's flank.

With a shout, the tall knight swung his mace at my head, the wrong choice of target for killing me would surely not save him from Uthren's fury. In any event, I parried the blow, my longsword flashing up to catch his gauntleted wrist with sufficient force to dislodge the mace from his grip. I drew the sword back for a slash at his face, but Uthren whirled before I could deliver it, rearing up to hammer both fore hooves into the shoulders and neck of the opposing mount. Bones cracked and bloody foam erupted from the smaller horse's mouth. The tall knight attempted to roll clear of the saddle, but Uthren's hooves were too swift. Down they came again, crushing breastplate and helm and bearing both horse and rider to the earth. Undaunted, the *paelah* kept on, rearing and pounding until what remained of our foe was no more than a mass of twisted metal and sundered flesh.

His battlelust momentarily sated, Uthren trotted away from the carnage, breath steaming from his snout in billowing clouds. I scanned the misted landscape for more enemies, seeing none while the din of combat continued to rage. Most of the noise came from the west, indicating the main weight of Viruhlis's charge had impacted the centre of the Crown Host line. I could only ascribe this to the fog, for even one so lost to fanaticism as the Duke of Rhianvel would never be so foolish as to throw cavalry at an enemy's strongest point.

A discordant tramping of many boots drew my gaze to the rear, seeing an untidy mass of my novice soldiers. Off to their right, I glimpsed the far more disciplined Cordwainers wheeling into place. Further off, the shouts and trumpets of Duke Gilferd's captains made it clear he had also brought the rest of his command forward. I could only laugh at the irony of my good fortune. Thanks to Uthren, I had succeeded in orchestrating a near perfect flank march which offered the prospect of trapping our enemy.

"Form up!" I shouted to the novices. Watching them attempt to sort themselves into formation, I knew any order to wheel to their left would be wasted breath. "Hold here," I told them instead, pointing my sword over my shoulder. "The enemy will come from there." With that, I rode off towards the Cordwainers, calling out for their captain.

"That's your anchor," I told him, pointing to the marginally neater ranks of the novices. "Wheel left and have at the enemy's rear."

As they trooped off, I felt Uthren tense beneath me. Clearly, his appetite for mayhem hadn't been fully assuaged and he sensed the possibility of more. I had intended to seek out Gilferd in order to organise cutting off the enemy's line of retreat, but surrendered to the inevitable as Uthren once again spurred to a gallop. A few crossbow bolts, presumably launched by the Crown Host, buzzed the air as we sped through the fog, the jarring dissonance of a battle in full frenzy so loud now as to pain the ears. The haze was still too thick to discern the scope of the struggle that, all too soon, resolved out of the mist, my vision filled with a writhing mass of armoured figures and horses that had bent but not yet broken the Crown Host line. But it was only a momentary glance before Uthren plunged headlong into the melee.

His hooves smashed another horse skull before he latched his teeth on to the raised arm of a knight, holding it long enough for me to hack my sword into the unprotected gap at the elbow. The knight's scream was loud but soon swallowed as he disappeared under the shifting crush of bodies. I ducked a sword blade and replied with an overhead slash, denting a helm and causing its owner to slump half out of his saddle. Uthren reared, hooves flailing to carve a path before he bore me on through the fray. What followed remains a barely comprehended jumble in my memory, dimly recalled instances of savage combat, screaming men and horses brought low by the mighty beast I rode. For all the plaudits heaped upon me for that day, I feel no shame in the admission that, but for Uthren's ferocity, I would surely have joined the ghosts that plagued me.

When it came, the absence of violence was shocking in its suddenness. I recall dragging my sword point free of a knight's visor, feeling the hot rush of his blood upon my face, then finding myself and Uthren alone with no one to fight. The *paelah* voiced another full-throated whinny as he wheeled about, while I recovered enough wit to realise that we were, in fact, surrounded. A gap of a few yards separated us from the enclosing mass of enemies. The ground was littered with fallen horses and knights, some still twitching or flailing about in vain attempts to rise despite awful wounds. Battle still raged somewhere behind. I assumed it to be the Cordwainers assaulting the stalled cavalry from the rear. Yet, in this one small corner of the field, for just a moment, silence reigned.

I dragged air into my lungs, the strain of my recent exertions instilling an acute ache from chest to feet. I saw that Uthren had suffered cuts to his flanks, staining the foam that covered them a pale shade of red. He appeared unconcerned, however, tossing his head and snorting in challenge. Many of the knights around us flinched at his gesture, some drawing back. I also saw several glowering, hate-filled faces beneath raised visors. I hadn't had the time to don my helm and many of this lot knew my face. Their combination of fear and detestation brought a perverse laugh to my lips.

"You all swore to die for her!" I taunted them, flicking my sword to spatter the closest with blood. "You mad fuckers should be thanking me!"

They shifted then, not in anger but in response to a shouted command. The sound of it drew me to the sight of a tall, armoured figure forcing his horse through the press. The rearing horse crest on his helm was unmistakable, as was the strident, hate-filled urgency of his voice.

"Make way! The traitor is mine!"

Duke Viruhlis Guhlmaine had come to administer justice on behalf of his queen.

Chapter Thirty-Seven

In consulting the various accounts of what transpired that day, I am repeatedly struck by the laziness and outright dishonesty evident in many talentless scribblers who pretend to the title of scholar. Most relate, with confident assurance and reference to supposed witnesses, the impressive clash of arms that occurred betwixt scribe and duke on those bloody bluffs. Every blow and counter-blow is described with varying degrees of absurdity. Some have it that, seeing the comparative size of our mounts, I nobly insisted on fighting Viruhlis on foot lest I enjoy too much of an advantage. Others will contest that I felled him with but a single blow. Both claims are ridiculous. I would happily have rejoiced at the sight of Uthren pounding that pestilent fanatic to ruin. Also, skilled as I was, I doubt one stroke of my sword would have sufficed to bring the bastard down. No, cherished reader, though it pains me to disappoint any unwarranted anticipation, the plain fact is that Duke Viruhlis and I did not fight at all that day. Although, I do so wish we had.

I did indeed tense in readiness as Viruhlis continued to force his way through the crush, Uthren shifting eagerly beneath me. But, before he could get within sword reach, a great tumult erupted to his rear. I had heard this signature sound before and knew instantly that the overlapping chorus of thudding flesh and clashing metal meant the Rhianvelan rear had suffered the impact of a cavalry charge.

Around us, the previously hesitant mass of knights degenerated into disorder as they struggled to reorientate their mounts. In the confusion, I lost sight of Viruhlis. A few of his banner men attempted to claim the honour of dispatching the Traitor Scribe, however, one coming at me with a raised axe only to be smashed aside when Uthren surged forward. Once again, my awareness became lost in the maelstrom of battle, the world transformed into a red-tinged nightmare of screaming, rage-filled faces and slashing blades.

The sting of a cut to my forehead brought me back to full sensibility, by which time the enemies around me had thinned considerably. Bones crunched beneath Uthren's hooves as he finished off a dismounted knight. The blade of my longsword was red from hilt to tip and my sword arm numb with strain. A sound like the ringing of a bell drew my gaze to the sight of Sir Ehlbert Bauldry hacking his sword into the helm and head of a Rhianvelan a dozen paces away. From the bodies left in his wake it was clear the King's Champion had carved an impressively deadly path to my side. Beyond him, the fray continued, a dense knot of riders thrashing about in a fury that was bound to incite Uthren's battle lust. However, before the *paelah* could charge again, the struggle abated, Rhianvelans pausing in mid-combat as if in response to some signal. Whatever it had been, it had plainly sapped the last reserves of their courage, for they all began to flee.

Uthren immediately galloped in pursuit, heedless of the score or more bleeding cuts to his flanks. As we drew close to the site of the abandoned struggle, the cause of our enemies' flight became clear. The ducal banner of Rhianvel lay in the mud, torn and spattered with muck and blood. Lying beside it was the duke himself, pierced through the belly from front to back by a shattered lance. My grim satisfaction at the sight quickly turned to utter dismay upon seeing the body that lay alongside the fallen duke.

With Uthren still intent on further slaughter, I was forced to abandon his back, landing heavily on my side but barely feeling it. Struggling to my feet, I splashed through red puddles towards the fallen figure. Viruhlis's arm lay across his chest. I shoved it away, finding the breastplate beneath streaked with blood.

"Bastard . . . got me in the armpit," Wilhum sputtered, revealing red teeth as he grinned at me. "Stuck a lance . . . all the way through him . . . and still . . . he wasn't done . . ."

A shrill, panicked voice called out for a healer, a voice I only recognised as my own when my throat began to hurt. "Lie still," I croaked as Wilhum made a vain effort to rise. A hasty inspection of his wound revealed it as deep and still gushing. Reaching for the duke's fallen banner, I ripped a strip off to staunch the flow, packing it into the wound and provoking a pained shout from Wilhum.

"I would prefer . . ." he groaned at me, "not to . . . die in the mud . . . . I find it rather . . . undignified."

"You're not fucking dying!" I snarled at him before resuming my shouted demands for a healer.

"We'll see to him," Juhlina said, appearing at Wilhum's side with Adlar in tow. At first glance, she looked to be in need of a healer herself, her face painted an unpleasant shade of reddish brown. Peering closer, I breathed in relief when it became apparent the blood wasn't hers. Adlar was not so fortunate, his neck and jerkin stained red by a deep cut along his jawline.

"Lord Scribe," a soft but insistent voice said and I turned to see Sir Ehlbert's tall form looming above. "The day is not done. Your soldiers await your orders."

He nodded to the fog-shrouded field to the north-east from where I could hear the steady tramp of marching feet. The Rhianvelan duke and his knights had been vanquished, but his infantry apparently remained undaunted. I could hear that dreadful, hated chant echoing through the haze: "We live for the Lady! We fight for the Lady . . ."

My first impulse was to snap a dismissive insult at Ehlbert, Wilhum's unfocused eyes and increasingly pale features being all that I could see in that moment. However, Juhlina had a remedy for my distraction.

"Wake up!" she snapped, shoving her palm hard into my forehead. "You take care of this—" she jerked her head over her shoulder before moving to take hold of Wilhum's arms "—we'll take care of him."

I watched her and Adlar carry Wilhum away, his wound still leaking blood across the churned, body-littered field, before Ehlbert gave a pointed cough. "Rally your riders," I told him. "Form up on the right flank. I'll see to the infantry. Do you know where Lord Roulgarth is?"

Ehlbert began to shake his head, then paused as the chants of our approaching foe abruptly shifted into discordant alarm. I could see nothing of the struggle, but the fog echoed with the sound of a great many whistling arrows shortly followed by the ugly clamour of combat.

"I think I may have a notion of his whereabouts," Ehlbert commented dryly.

It took me a good deal longer than I liked to organise the Crown Host infantry into an assault line, shortening my temper and causing me to deliver more than a few cuffs to the most laggardly soldiers. My anger was ill aimed and unjustified, for they had just stood off an armoured charge without suffering a single break in their line. Many had sold their lives in doing so, and a good deal of the folk I harried into formation bore bleeding scars in evidence of the fierceness of the fighting. Still, the sight of Wilhum's limp body loomed with terrible clarity in my mind and I was impatient to conclude this business. Fortunately, by the time I was able to order an advance, it transpired that Lord Roulgarth and the *toalisch* had done the work for us.

I would learn later that the Caerith had managed to maintain a reasonably disciplined formation when approaching the Rhianvelan line from the rear. *Veilisch* archers skirmished ahead to exact a fearful toll with their bows, apparently unhampered by the fog. When the two lines clashed, however, all order disappeared and a general melee erupted, one that suited the *toalisch* perfectly. By the time the Crown Host line reached the scene only a few clusters of diehard Rhianvelans remained, each shrinking rapidly under the steady rain of Caerith arrows. Spying one particularly large knot of hold-outs nearby, I led two Crown Host companies towards it. These Rhianvelans were a resolute lot, still calling out their chant to the Anointed Lady, ranks solid as a wall. Before we could close with them, however, the Caerith lashed them with a veritable blizzard of arrows. The *toalisch* fell upon the thinned ranks of Rhianvelans en masse, hacking them down in very short order.

I led the Crown Host on for another quarter-mile, finding only corpses and the crawling wounded. My mood was so fouled by worries over Wilhum that I raised no objection when soldiers paused to finish off these unfortunates with dagger or billhook. When at last we walked upon grassland bare of bodies, I called a halt. Victorious realisation spread through the ranks, heralding a cheer, ragged at first but soon building in volume until it echoed through the befogged landscape. As if in response, the mist finally began to thin, the occluded golden flare of the sun shimmering above. Those soldiers of devout leanings began to proclaim this as a sign of the Seraphiles' favour. *If so,* I reflected sourly, *we could have done with their assistance a good deal sooner.*

As the cheers wore on, Uthren came plodding out of the diminishing haze. His pelt was matted with blood but he held his head as high as ever. When I climbed on to his back, the acclaim of the Crown Host rose to yet greater volume. Pikes and billhooks stabbed the air and I heard my name chanted much as the Ascendant Host chanted Evadine's. I almost hated them for it.

Wilhum Dornmahl lay on a bed of furs beneath an awning raised atop the bluffs. The canvas snapped in the stiff wind and waves pounded the rocks below to spectacular effect. Wilhum had refused the various pain-banishing concoctions offered by the healer, irritably waving the fellow away and avowing a desire to meet his end with faculties undimmed. The tired, blood-spattered healer, a former Supplicant of the orthodox Covenant with many years' service in wars uncounted, bore my raging invective with the stoicism common to his trade.

"It's a simple stabbing!" I hissed at him in a desperate whisper. "I've seen men rise from worse."

"A simple stabbing that severed two of his most vital vessels, my lord," the healer replied, tone low and careful. "They lie deep in the body, beyond our reach and so cannot be stitched. I'm sorry." He bowed, taking a backward step. "If you will excuse me, there are many souls in need of my care this night."

"Supplicant Delric could have saved him," I said, anger mounting. "If you had a fraction of his skill—"

"Leave the poor fellow alone . . . Alwyn," Wilhum interrupted, his voice a thin rasp. "He's needed . . . elsewhere."

The healer bowed again and pressed a small bottle into my hand. "Should the pain get worse," he said, voice lowered to a whisper. "This will ease his passing."

I consigned the bottle to my pocket and slumped down at Wilhum's side, watching Juhlina press a cloth to his forehead. I wasn't sure what good it did but she appeared to be in need of something to do. Ayin apparently could find no such refuge in distraction and so wandered back and forth continually, sometimes folding her arms, sometimes not. The scouts and Wilhum's riders, those who had survived the charge against the Rhianvelan knights, sat together a short way off, passing a bottle among them. By the looks of him, Adlar Spinner was already drunk, which at least spared him the pain of the long, stitched cut tracing along his jawline from ear to chin.

"We won . . . I take it?" Wilhum said, the third time he had asked this question.

"We did," Juhlina told him. "A great victory. Thanks to you."

"The duke . . ." Wilhum's gaze lost focus for a second before he blinked and spoke on. "I trust . . . they buried him with . . . all due honours?"

Another question he had already asked. I couldn't fathom why this concerned him so. "Yes," I said, patting his forearm. "All due honours." In fact, Leannor had ordered the traitorous duke's head removed from his body and stuck on a pike before decreeing his lands, riches and titles forfeit to the Crown. Under the law, at least, the duchy of Rhianvel was now a possession of the Algathinet dynasty. Whether the folk who lived there would accept this was another question entirely, and not one I felt inclined to ponder. One war was enough, at present.

"You remember . . . that day at Walvern Castle, Alwyn?" Wilhum asked, blinking his dulled eyes at me. "The day they brought the ram . . . against the walls?"

"I remember," I said.

"I was . . . on the verge of running . . . you know." He licked his lips as they formed a wry smile. "Had my horse saddled . . . and everything. If the walls had fallen—"

"They didn't," I cut in. "And you would never have run."

He frowned, apparently about to argue the point, but I saw his grasp on the moment slip and he sank deeper into his furs. For a time, he drifted between torpor and wakefulness, his words become more slurred as he talked of shared times.

"That mysterious Ascarlian brute . . . what did he called himself?"

"Margnus Gruinskard," I supplied. "The Tielwald."

"That's him. Had a sense of something . . . not right about him . . . something arcane."

"More than just a sense. I'd say he was steeped in it. It's how he seized Olversahl."

"Olversahl . . ." Wilhum huffed a humourless laugh. "That was quite a night . . . We saved her, may the Martyrs curse us for it."

"We didn't know."

"Didn't we?" For a second, clarity shone in the gaze he settled on me. "Or was it just . . . that we didn't want to?"

I could only return his stare, helpless in a barely contained welter of anger and guilt.

"Well," he said, blinking and turning away, "at least I'll die . . . in some way redeemed. I hope the Seraphile noticed . . ." He trailed off, his attention drawn to a new arrival at this wake for the not yet dead. Desmena Lehville approached the clifftop with a stiff, hesitant gait, cloak wrapped tight against the wind. Her face, marred by the bruises and scratches of recent combat, was set in an inexpressive mask that bespoke rigid control.

"You came," Wilhum said, managing to raise a hand in greeting. "Thank you."

Desmena halted a few paces away, meeting Wilhum's gaze with much the same fierce dislike she had always shown him. "My brother . . ." she began, pausing to cough before forcing the words out. "My brother would have wished me to be here."

"I suppose." Wilhum beckoned her closer. "Come. I have . . . words for you."

Juhlina stepped back as Desmena moved to Wilhum's side, her features betraying a distinct wariness now. I rose to depart, recognising this as a private conversation, but Wilhum gestured for me to stay. "I should like . . . a witness for this dying man's . . . testament."

Turning back to Desmena, Wilhum took a long, shuddering breath. "I, Wilhum Dornmahl, disgraced and disinherited son of Lord Arther Dornmahl, do hereby make final testament. I wish it known that, as a boy, I did relate unto my father the whereabouts of one Wildar Redmaine, famed master of the arts martial, father to Aldric Redmaine and Desmena Lehville, and a former servant to my father's household wanted for treason. By surreptitious means, I did follow Aldric and his sister to the house where their father, wounded in a recent skirmish, had concealed himself. Upon relating this information to my father, Master Redmaine was seized . . ." Wilhum paused, coughing again and staining his lips red. I began to proffer a flask of water, but he waved me away, continuing in a halting wet rasp. "And . . . under Crown law, he was put to death. I hoped . . ." a sob coloured Wilhum's voice as he spoke on, blood trickling from the corner of his mouth ". . . by this act, I would win my father's acclaim. In this . . . I was, as ever, disappointed. I know . . . both brother and sister suspected each other of . . . this act, so, by this testament . . . I set the truth before all."

He subsided into a gasping repose while Desmena stared in silence. "I never," she said eventually, "once suspected my brother. But I always suspected you."

Wilhum's lips shifted into a weak smile. "You were right . . ."

Desmena let out an ominous growl, stepping towards the bed then halting when my sword scraped free of its sheath. "I'll thank you to step back, my lady," I said, levelling the blade at her throat.

She glowered at me before fixing her blazing countenance upon Wilhum. "You utterly worthless, vile wretch of a man," she grated. "How many times I pleaded with my brother to cut you away like the diseased limb you are. I shall rejoice at your death." With that, she turned and strode away.

"Actually," Wilhum murmured, "she took it better . . . than I expected. You will . . . write it all down. Won't you, Alwyn?"

"If that's your wish." I reached out to grasp his hand, finding it cold, and soon to be colder still. "Though, my scholarly tendencies chafe at the prospect of recording a lie." I smiled at the faint creasing of his brow. "It was Aldric, wasn't it? He told your father where to find Redmaine. One beating too many, I suppose."

"Not just the beatings. Aldric . . . had grown old enough . . . to recognise that Redmaine's interest in his daughter . . . was far from . . . natural. Strange, that so brave a soul, could be so . . . monstrous. But then—" he coughed out another laugh, blood speckling the blanket that covered him "—that's a lesson . . . we both took too long . . . in learning, eh?"

His body began to shake then, face flushing with what reserves of blood his body could summon. "I think," he grunted, "I'll take a taste . . . of that healer's bottle . . . if I may."

I held it to his lips and he gulped it down to the last drop before subsiding, all but the last mite of strength seeping away. He lingered only for a short time, the light fading from his eyes until one final blossoming of life. The words that accompanied it were so faint I had to put my ear to his lips to catch them.

"You know . . . you'll have to kill her, don't you? Even if . . . it costs . . . the life of your . . . son."

Chapter Thirty-Eight

We laid Wilhum to rest in a mass grave alongside the riders who had fallen in the charge. There were twelve in all. Orthodox Supplicants said words I barely heard after which we shovelled the earth to cover them. This was but one of several such graves dug that evening, although most were filled with Rhianvelan corpses. Ayin reckoned the Crown Host losses as near four hundred. Our enemies she put at near three thousand. The Caerith dead could not be counted as the *toalisch* had swiftly carried them away to the nearest woodland to lay them to rest among the trees. They, and much of the army, spent the succeeding night in muted repose. I had noted before that victorious armies tend to subside into morbid reflection once the initial rush of triumph fades. This quietude was not shared by the *Paelith*, however, who spent the evening clustered around large bonfires, voices raised in furious, shouted exhortations.

"What are they celebrating?" I asked the *Eithlisch*. "I don't remember seeing any of them on the field." Drawn by curiosity, I had wandered close to the *Paelith* encampment, finding him standing alone at the edge of the firelight.

"They're not celebrating," he said. "What you see here is a rite of shame."

Looking again at the many figures encircling the nearest bonfire, I saw that most had stripped either partially or fully naked. Also, all seemed to holding knives. As I watched, a *Paelith* warrior, teeth bared in an angry grimace, called out something in a dialect I didn't fully comprehend. However, as the fellow ranted on I did catch words similar to the Caerith for "obligation" and "disgrace". When his diatribe ended, the warrior promptly slashed a diagonal cut across his chest and fell to his knees.

"He makes an oath to seek death in battle," the *Eithlisch* explained. "They all do. To have arrived late to this field of slaughter is a great stain to their honour, one they may spend the rest of their lives seeking to wash clean." From the grimness of his sculpted features, I divined he bore his own weight of guilt. The Caerith of the plains were still Caerith, after all.

"Then," I said, finding myself indifferent to his distress, "in future I trust they'll deign to stay with the army."

His eyes narrowed at the rebuke evident in my tone but the expected caustic rejoinder failed to rise to his lips. Instead, he shifted to cast his gaze north. "Do you feel it, Alwyn Scribe?" he asked, voice soft and possessed of a worrying note of uncertainty. Whatever his faults, I hadn't yet known the *Eithlisch* to lack surety.

"Feel what?" I said, my own focus on the surrounding fields. As ever, the curse of the stone feather was inconstant and hadn't yet to reveal any wandering dead, but I had no confidence I would escape this night without a visitation of some kind. *Please*, I implored the feather. *Don't let it be Wilhum . . .*

"It's hard to describe," the *Eithlisch* said. He paused, brows creasing in consternation that bordered on fear. "Something is happening north of here. An accumulation of *vaerith*."

"Evadine has power, you know that. The Malecite's power, and she awaits our coming. Within days this army will meet the Ascendant Host." I let out a long, weary sigh. "And a bloody day it will be."

"I feel your dread woman, Alwyn Scribe, and it is a wonder to me that you failed to perceive the depths of her malice. But now I sense something more. An alignment of paths, a junction where fate meets fate and all futures are decided. And I know not how it will end."

Fear ruled his features now, his eyes wide and staring. It was so utterly unlike all I knew of him that I found myself backing away.

"There has never been a war with a certain outcome," I told him.

"But we are strong, in number and in resolve. I wondered if this army would stand when battle dawned and today I had my answer. We will march to Castle Ambris, defeat our enemy, and there I will claim my son." I inclined my head and turned to go. "As for now, I have a somewhat pressing need to get drunk . . ."

"I note you make no mention of killing her," the *Eithlisch* observed. I refused to pause, striding off into the dark, hoping the journey to my tent and the brandy within would be made without spectral interruption.

Towards the evening of the next day's march the long, green swathe of the Shavine Forest crested the northern horizon. Tiler and the two scouts duly appeared on the road shortly after with a fulsome account of the Ascendant Queen's dispositions at Castle Ambris.

"Somewhere between fifteen to twenty thousand in all," he said. "Encamped about the castle. Mostly infantry, so far as we could tell. A real jumbled bag too. There's a big mob of barely trained churls with pitchforks, axes and such, as well as Covenant Host veterans."

"The state of the siege?" I asked.

"No engines, but they're busy digging trenches. Judging by the bodies around the walls, it looks like they tried to storm the place early on and suffered for it." Tiler's narrow features tightened into a grim frown. "Then there's the gallows."

"Gallows?"

"A dozen of them lined up on a platform out of arrow reach of the main gate, a body dangling from each one. Seems the False Queen captured a bunch of churls loyal to Duchess Lorine. She's been hanging twelve a day since the siege began."

Our mission is greater than us, she had said once. Did she still believe that or had her mind now slipped fully into vindictive insanity? "All right," I told Tiler. "Get some rest . . ."

"There's, uh," Tiler cast a meaningful glance over his shoulder at the forest, "something else, Captain. We found an emissary waiting where the road joins the forest. That Rhianvelan Supplicant bitch. All alone, if you can believe it. She's carrying a parley flag, otherwise I'd've killed her on the spot."

"Her message?" I asked.

"Says she'll speak only to the Scribe."

"Very well." I started towards Uthren. "May as well see what she has to say."

"It won't be good, whatever it is," Juhlina advised. "Best if you just let me go and kill her."

"Such is not the act of a lord commanding an army engaged in a crusade of righteous justice." Mounting Uthren, I trotted to her side as she climbed on to the back of her *paelah*. "But," I added, leaning closer, "should I scratch my chin at any point, feel at liberty to split her skull open."

Supplicant Ildette's demeanour of rigid, glaring defiance would have been more impressive but for the way her horse, unnerved by the *paelah*, fidgeted in constant agitation. I felt no inclination towards civility nor the usual ritualised exchanges common to such occasions. Nor did she. Hatred for the man who had killed her brother was writ large upon the woman's features. Although, given the depth of her fanatical attachment to Evadine, I doubted her expression would have been any less fierce if I'd let the bastard live.

"State your business," I said, resting my hands on the pommel of Uthren's saddle.

"My queen sends a gift," she replied, mouth twisting with enjoyment of the moment as she reached for something in her lap. Her hands moved with too much rapidity for Juhlina's liking. Her *paelah* lurched forward, Juhlina raising her warhammer for a killing stroke. Ildette's mount, already fearful, reared before the blow could land, tipping its rider from its back before wheeling about and galloping off into the forest.

"Hold!" I barked at Juhlina as she drew her arm back for a swipe at the dismounted Ildette. I saw that her hands held no weapon. Instead, she clutched a small canvas bundle. "Bring that to me."

Ildette and Juhlina exchanged glares of mutual loathing as the Widow used the spike of her warhammer to snag the bundle and lift it from the Supplicant's grasp. Even before I unravelled it, I felt a sickening certainty at what I would find. *An accumulation of vaerith*, the *Eithlisch* had said, and, as ever, he hadn't been wrong. The canvas fell away to reveal a sack of rough, homespun cloth into which two holes had been cut to create a crude mask.

"If the Scribe does not present himself alone at Castle Ambris within ten days," Ildette said, getting to her feet, "the witch dies. If his army enters the Shavine Forest, she dies."

"How . . ." My voice failed me before I summoned the will to force the words from my lips. "How did you capture her?"

"Ask nothing of me, traitor," Ildette said. "You have my queen's summons. Answer it or no. For my part, I should greatly enjoy watching the witch burn." She afforded me a final, mocking bow then strode back along the King's Road into the gloomy refuge of the woods. I remain proud of the fact that I didn't tell Juhlina to go and retrieve her head.

"I would forbid this," Leannor mused, "if I thought you would heed me."

I had intended to slip away in the small hours of the morning, but, following Ildette's departure, Juhlina had gone straight to the princess regent with a fulsome account of our parley. Ehlbert and Roulgarth duly appeared at my tent shortly after with a summons to the royal presence.

"Forbid it anyway," Ayin said, her distress causing her to forget formality. She stepped from her place at Leannor's side, regarding me with a face so stricken by concern I found it hard to look upon.

"I have to go," I told her, voice pitched in gentle solicitation that utterly failed to allay her fears.

"She'll kill you!" Ayin's frantic gaze swung from one face to another, seeking support. "You all know this."

"I find it hard to argue the point, Scribe," Roulgarth said. "And this army puts much stock in its commander."

"They'll put just as much stock in you, I'm sure, my lord."

Roulgarth's demeanour was a good deal more grim at the prospect of my demise than I would have expected. "I doubt it. After your unwise antics at the bluffs, it's hard to contest with a legend. Nor do I think much of our prospects of holding them in check while you ride off to certain execution."

"The Caerith won't linger here either," the *Eithlisch* rumbled. His bulk occupied a good portion of the royal tent, and even then he was obliged to stoop so as not to disturb the overhead canvas. This was the first council he had attended and it was strange, even comical to see him so ill at ease. "Once they learn the *Doenlisch* is in the dread woman's clutches, they *will* march to her aid."

"Then don't tell them," I said.

He spared me a withering glance. "I am not the only soul with *vaerith* here. Others have already sensed what I sense. It won't be long before they understand the cause. Besides, I do not lie to my people. That I leave to your kind."

"If you can't halt them, at least delay them," I said, turning back to Leannor. "The Crown Host too, for as long as you can. That is all I ask, Majesty. As for the certitude of my death, I do not believe that to be the False Queen's object."

"If she's not going to kill you," Juhlina said, fixing me with a hard accusing stare, "what is she going to do?"

"Attempt to win me to her cause. When she fails—" I shrugged "—then, in truth, I know not what she'll do. I do know she will kill the *Doenlisch* if I am not there to stop it, and that I will not allow."

"This *Doenlisch*, you speak of," Leannor said. "Our people know her as the Sack Witch, do they not?"

"They do, Majesty. We thought her a pedlar of charms and remedies, but to the Caerith she is far more than that." I glanced at the *Eithlisch*. "Their reaction should any harm befall her will be . . . extreme in nature."

"And you will trade your life for hers? You owe her so much?"

"It is not a question of debt or obligation." I hesitated. The bond that existed between myself and the Sack Witch was hard to explain, even to myself. "It is my belief that she does good in this world. Such a soul must be preserved."

Leannor sighed and settled back on her throne-like chair. It was a plain, solidly made thing fashioned by one of the more skilled carpenters to march with the Crown Host, lacking the grandeur and finery of the throne where Leannor's brother had once sat. Still, I fancied she conveyed a far more regal presence in this small tent perched on that chair than King Tomas ever had in his most impressive chamber and gilded finery. It was not an inherent quality either, rather an accumulation of authority and experience earned through calamity and twisting fortunes. Up until this point, my service to this woman had been a convenience, something forged through common purpose. Now, I felt for the first time that she might actually be equal to the task of bringing peaceful governance to this ever troubled land. Her truculent son was another matter, but one best set aside for later.

"Very well," the princess regent said. "Lord Alwyn Scribe, I hereby commission you to carry a royal missive to the False Queen Evadine Courlain. She is commanded to disband her army and surrender her person for judgement under Crown law on charges of high treason and mass murder. News of your mission will be announced to the Crown Host one day after your departure. After that, I make you no promises as to how long it will take them to march upon Castle Ambris, with or without my leave."

I nodded and turned to the *Eithlisch*. "Can you hold back the Caerith for a day?"

"What surety do I have that you will preserve the *Doenlisch* if I do?"

"None, save the promise that I will do all I can to save her."

The muscles of his broad features tensed and a vein pulsed in his temple, evidence of a fierce internal struggle. "One day," he said, fixing me with a glower. "But know, when that day is done, they will follow you with all the speed they can muster. The *toalisch* are swift but the *Paelith* are swifter, even through a forest. And I will ride with them."

I departed that night, keen to make use of all the time allowed me. Juhlina, Ayin and the scouts insisted on providing an escort into the forest. Uthren set a steady but not excessive pace until the sky grew fully dark whereupon we made camp. The mood around the fire was understandably sombre, made worse by the frequency with which Ayin succumbed to tears. I found it both unnerving and aggravating.

"Can't you sing, instead?" I asked as she crouched in miserable contemplation of the campfire.

"No!" she snapped back, her recently acquired ladylike poise replaced by juvenile peevishness. Wiping angrily at her eyes, she got up and stalked off into the gloom-shrouded trees.

"She doesn't understand why you're doing this," Juhlina said. "But then, neither do I."

"I'm doing it for the same reason you once kicked a line of men from a battlement to have their necks snapped." I regretted both my tone and my words the instant they escaped my lips, wincing at the hurt I saw on her face. "Sorry," I sighed, moving closer. "In truth, I think I knew it was going to come to this. This is a road I have no choice but to travel."

"Like what the Caerith call *Cairh*." I heard a reluctant, bitter concession in her voice, a knowledge that there was no turning me from this path. "You go to meet your fate."

"If you like." I reached into my jerkin, extracting the leather-bound bundle secreted there. "I must ask you to do something for me, something that will be very hard."

I thought she might recoil from it, but the sight of the stone feather as I undid the bundle's ties stirred only puzzlement in her brow. "I thought you needed to take it to her," she said. "Perhaps kill her with it."

"I'd never get close enough. Her guards are sure to search me. I think it would be best if it didn't fall into her hands. Besides—" I touched a tentative finger to the spiked vanes, wondering why so powerful a thing should feel so very ordinary "—I think it served its purpose at the bluffs."

Juhlina nodded and reached for the feather, pausing when I spoke on.

"Carrying this is no easy thing. It may not afflict you the way it does me. I don't know. But if it does . . ."

"Then it does," she muttered, taking the feather and its coverings.

She regarded it with a brief, wary scrutiny before binding it up and consigning it to her pack.

"If . . . I don't return to reclaim it," I said, meeting her eyes to ensure she saw the seriousness of my intent, "have Toria sail you to the deepest portion of ocean she knows, and throw it in."

I leaned closer, planting a kiss on her lips. She accepted it but didn't return it. Nor did she say anything when I rose and went to mount Uthren.

"Still hours till dawn, Captain," Tiler said.

"Time I need to make full use of," I replied. It was strange to watch this man, one I despised not so long ago, fidget and fumble for words of parting to someone he fully expected never to see again, at least not alive.

"The *Paelith* will be along soon enough," I told him, tone brisk to spare him the trial of concocting a farewell. Unbuckling my sword, I tossed it to him. "Ride with them, and bring this to me at Castle Ambris."

"We will, Captain." He and the other scouts all went to one knee, each bowing low.

"Whatever happens from here on," I said, "consider yourselves washed clean of the crimes we shared, or as clean as you're ever going to get."

I spared them a brief smile and Uthren started towards the road. As he did so, Ayin came rushing from the dark, pressing herself against my leg. "I wrote you a song," she said, staring up at me with bright, moist eyes. "So you have to come back. Otherwise, you'll never hear it."

I reached down to cup her face, thumbing the tears from her cheek. "Sing it even if I don't," I said. "It's likely to be the only testament I'll get."

Uthren spurred to a gallop then, pulling me from her and thundering off along the darkened track of the King's Road.

Chapter Thirty-Nine

I had known Uthren to be a creature of immense power but the speed with which he bore me towards Castle Ambris was something far beyond my experience. Miles of darkened forest passed in a black blur that shifted to grey as dawn light caressed the trees. I could only speculate as to how much this beast knew or understood of our mission. However, as he galloped for hours with no sign of tiring, I felt a growing sensation of being pulled rather than carried. Something was drawing Uthren towards our goal. I recalled what the *Eithlisch* had said about the *paelahs*' connection to the Caerith, how the origin of the bond remained a mystery. Now, I suspected the *Doenlisch* might have had a hand in it. Her true age was incalculable, and might even reach all the way back to the aftermath of the Scourge. If so, her *vaerith* apparently carried enough power to seep into the blood of successive generations of these great horses.

Thanks to Uthren's preternatural swiftness, a journey that should have taken three full days of hard riding took little more than one. When the moon had risen to a bright disc, I saw the flicker of the Covenant Host's campfires through the trees. While my mount appeared tireless, I was not. Several times I had snapped awake after succumbing to exhaustion. On each occasion, however, Uthren had managed to keep me in the saddle. Now, with our destination so close, I began to haul on his reins and, this time at least, he consented to halt.

Once I climbed down from his back, Uthren reared, letting out a disgruntled snort. Reaching out to pat a calming hand to his flank I felt his muscles twitch, looking up to see a confused glint in his eye. I stood back as he started forward then retreated several steps, tossing his head in annoyance, as if repelled by an unseen barrier.

"She doesn't want you getting any closer, eh?" I asked, inclining my head at the campfires.

Uthren gave another snort and scraped the earth with his hooves then, with a final glance in my direction, he wheeled about and galloped off into the gloom.

The siege lines surrounding Castle Ambris were easily discerned even at night, being illuminated by the many torches that blazed atop the battlements. As I drew closer, I made out the telltale marks of a recent assault; black streaks on the walls with the ground betwixt trenches and wall rich in the detritus of battle. Ladders lay broken upon a field littered by corpses and speckled with the fletchings of arrows and bolts. The massive iron and oak gate appeared undamaged and the banner of the Blousset family rose high above the walls, signals that the mighty seat of the Shavine duchy was not even close to falling. The gallows Tiler had spoken of were also easily identified, the bodies they held swaying in the night air. Most were full grown, but two were smaller and so swayed more.

However, the most curious aspect of the scene, one that became more potent as I approached the outer picket of the Covenant Host, was the smell. All battlefields stink to varying degrees. Those that take place in open field tend to reek of disturbed earth and the shit of both people and horses, taking on the sickly tang of corruption in the aftermath. Sieges produce a melange of smoke, dung, and the mingled aromas of many cook-fires. This one was different, for it reminded me more of the slums of Couravel, a musty, unpleasant amalgam of unwashed bodies and uncovered latrines. It told of a slovenliness that would have had Swain reaching for his whip.

The source of the stink became apparent upon encountering the first pickets, a pair of Ascendant Host halberdiers who exuded the kind of odour that arises only from weeks spent in the same heavy, part-armoured garb. They also sported unruly beards and tendrils of unwashed hair coiled from beneath the rim of their helms. Still, they weren't lacking in soldierly awareness. Both were quick to level their weapons at me as I appeared in the circle of light cast by their torch. From the instant snarl that came to their lips, it appeared I required no introduction.

"Traitorous filth!" the larger of the two greeted me, stepping forward to deliver a threatening jab with his halberd. His companion moved to the side, wary but equally hostile.

"Alwyn Scribe," I said, affording them a courteous bow. "Come in accordance with the Ascendant Queen's summons. I believe I'm expected."

They bound my hands behind my back, tighter than was comfortable, but were otherwise assiduous in not doing me any injury. More soldiers were summoned to provide an escort, all just as foul smelling and unkempt as the two pickets.

"Don't you bother with inspections nowadays?" I enquired in disgust, earning a growling response from their sergeant.

"The traitor will shut his vile mouth or I'll shut it for him."

He was a powerfully built fellow I vaguely recalled from the assault on Athiltor, an event that now seemed a very long time ago. I wrinkled my nose at his breath as he loomed closer, all baleful eyes and bared yellow teeth, then drove my forehead into his nose. As he jerked back, I cast an inquisitive gaze across the faces of the other soldiers. They all had their halberds poised for a killing thrust, but none seemed about to deliver it. They could have used the staves of their weapons to beat me down, but they didn't do that either. Even the sergeant, when he was done snorting and spitting blood, responded with only yet more baleful glaring rather than the expected flurry of punches.

"No harm shall be done to the Traitor Scribe, eh?" I asked, forcing a grin to mask my concern. That they were so bound by Evadine's word was not a good sign. For all their hatred, I saw a strange light in the eyes of these men. It was much the same gleam I noted even during the early sermons of the Anointed Lady, the cast of those lost in devotion. But then it had been momentary, subsiding into some semblance of rationality when the sermon ended. Now it seemed to have permanent possession of the soldiers of the Ascendant Host. Was this why they stank so? Even the basic ablutions of military life were a distraction from devotion to their Martyr queen.

"Enough dawdling," I said, putting an authoritative snap in my voice. "Let's get where we're going, shall we?"

The camp they led me through was a malodorous mire of rutted, muddy tracks winding between tents arrayed in irregular order. Dirty, unshaven men and straggle-haired women lined the route, voices raised in a chorus of condemnatory abuse. However, like the soldiers who flanked me, their rage didn't erupt into violence, so complete was their adherence to the word of the Risen Martyr.

"You will burn, traitor!" one woman screeched at me. I could see her breasts through the ragged blouse she wore, not that she seemed to care. Others were even more ill-attired, bare-chested men and half-naked women crowding in to add their voices to the rising tumult.

"Heretic! Oathbreaker! Burn him!"

Their frenzied detestation rose to such a pitch that I started to fear it would overcome their obedience to Evadine's will. Several times, my escort was obliged to push away the more enthusiastic tormentor, the cordon of soldiers tightening around me as the crowd thickened and their discordant hate inevitably coalesced into a chant.

"Burn him! Burn him! BURN HIM!"

Then, with a jarring suddenness, it all stopped. The chant choked off in mid-word and those around me, soldiers and mob alike, sank to their knees. We had progressed to a point near the centre of the camp where a large tent sat atop a low rise. A single figure stood there, cloaked and cowled, but all present felt the weight of her regard. She said nothing and made no gesture, merely turning and disappearing into the tent, but after that, the mob remained on their knees and the guards escorted me on in the wordless silence of the utterly cowed.

Upon reaching the tent, the sergeant, blood still trickling from his busted nose, pulled aside the flap and jerked his head for me to enter. I noted the care he took not to look inside. Once again, I grimaced at the stench of him as I passed by. Inside, Evadine had removed her cloak and stood rocking a large, ornately carved cot. Her attention was fixed on the cot's occupant and she didn't look up as I entered. Unlike her soldiers, she was clean, the light cotton shift she wore beneath her cloak unstained. Still, I saw lines in her face that hadn't been there at our parting, small but perceptible hardening around her mouth and eyes. As was ever the case with her, I found they made her more attractive. Even steeped in countless sins, Evadine Courlain was incapable of not being beautiful.

"Your soldiers are a disgrace," I informed her.

Evadine didn't answer at first, continuing to rock the cot, the gaze she directed at what lay within one of studious fascination rather than love. "Don't you wish to see your son, Alwyn?" she enquired. I found her voice a distinct contrast to the grating, agonised mix of rage and betrayal from our last meeting in Couravel. Now she spoke with calm reflection, tinged with a note of weariness that bordered on cynicism.

"Careful," I warned, staying put. "Your deranged congregation might overhear." I did indeed wish to look upon the child in that cot, but knew in this moment he was but another tool in this woman's armoury. In him, I knew she saw the key to restoring my loyalty. "Wouldn't want them knowing the fruit of your womb is but an outlaw's bastard, would you?"

"They know what I wish them to know and question it not." She turned her gaze to me for the first time and I saw with surprise that she had a smile for me. It was a sad smile, full of regret I thought genuine. "I find it . . . trying, Alwyn, not to be questioned, something you never shied from. So here you have your last chance to do so. Ask of me any question and I shall endeavour to answer. But first, please, look at your son."

I approached the cot on unsteady legs, though it wasn't from hours on Uthren's heaving back. I didn't know what I expected to find when I beheld the child we had made. Something monstrous, perhaps? A vile creature twisted by the malice of its mother's soul. Instead, I saw only an infant at slumber, one tiny hand clutching his coverings while the other pushed a minuscule thumb into his mouth. Just a babe, like countless others, yet in that moment the most perfect and beautiful thing I had ever seen.

"He sleeps well," Evadine said. "Fusses little, though when the mood takes him he can scream loud enough to wake the dead. And he's clever, even at so young an age, I see it in him. The way he looks at everything, so bright, so curious. We made something wonderful, did we not, Alwyn?"

I strained against my bonds, wanting badly to reach into the cot, touch a finger to the child's hand on the covers, feel him grasp it. Evadine, I knew, saw my need but made no move to cut the binding from my wrists. Regretful she was, but cruelty was not beyond her either. So, I could only gaze upon the child, lost in the wonder of something so perfect arising from a union as imperfect as ours. "Yes," I breathed. "Yes, we did."

"Which compels me to ask, why did you turn from us? Why have you allied with our enemies?"

Looking up, I saw her face bore the same sadness, but it had hardened somewhat, the first gleam of recrimination showing in her eyes. "You promised I would be the one to ask questions," I said.

She stiffened, features hardening further. "Then ask?"

"Where is the Sack Witch?"

She raised an eyebrow in caustic surprise. "So you truly did place yourself in my hands just for the sake of a Caerith charm spinner?"

"She's more than that, as I think you know. And I ask again, where is she?"

"Securely bound, well guarded, and unharmed. For her to remain in such condition depends largely on you."

"How did you capture her?"

Both eyebrows rose now, a small laugh escaping her lips. "Capture her? You imagine I have spent all these many months scouring the realm for one heretic? I didn't capture her, Alwyn. She walked into this camp two weeks ago and requested an audience with the Ascendant Queen."

"One you didn't grant, I'd wager."

Her humour faded and I saw a small twitch of discomfort on her brow. "I have more pressing matters at hand than to be gabbled at by a Caerith mystic—"

"No," I cut in. "That wasn't it. You were afraid, or rather something inside you was afraid to face her. I fancy you haven't even spent one moment in her presence."

Her face twitched again, more violently this time.

"You feel it now, don't you?" I persisted, stepping closer to her. "The thing that commands you. You've probably always felt it but told yourself it was the Seraphile, despite how ugly it feels, despite how it grew with every crime you committed, every bloody step on the journey that brought you here . . ."

She had always been a strong woman, and skilled in the use of violence, but the blow she struck me in that instant told of a woman changed, altered. Her hand slammed into the centre of my chest with the force of a battering ram. Fortunately, she chose not to make a fist otherwise I doubt I would have survived it. I felt my feet lose contact with the carpet, all the air in my lungs expelled in an instant before I landed on my back several feet away, retching for breath, my vision dimming. Of all the many times I had been hit, only Sir Althus ever came closer to killing me with one blow.

I regained my senses with an infant's cries loud in my ears and a hard flare of pain in my chest. Spitting bile, I sat up, finding Evadine holding our son, a scowl of admonition on her brow.

"You've upset him," she said, every bit the chiding wife to a foolish husband. Had I entertained any doubts as to the fulsomeness of her madness, they dissolved in that instant. The Evadine Courlain I had known was gone now, replaced by a deranged soul who imagined herself a righteous queen in service to the divine. I knew the wall of delusion she had raised around herself was too strong a barrier to be broken by mere words, but still I felt compelled to try.

"Don't . . ." I began in a croaking rasp. Spitting, I tried again. "Don't you ever pause to think on all the deaths you have caused? All the corpses in your wake? Couravel and Farinsahl burned, along with Martyrs know how many villages. Did you see the carnage you ordained at the Lady's Reach or were you content to simply orchestrate the slaughter from afar? You have murdered children, Evadine . . ."

"I have done what the Seraphile required of me!" she snapped, loud enough to cause the child in her arms to redouble his wailing. Sighing in annoyance, she held him closer, swaying gently from side to side as she whispered calming words. "Shhh now, Stevan. Mother and Father are only playing."

Suddenly, I found the sight of her holding him repulsive, a disgusting parody of motherhood. "What will you tell him?" I demanded, groaning as I struggled to my feet. "In years to come? How his mother began the Second Scourge she swore to avert?"

"No," she replied, voice clipped but calm. "I will tell him the truth. His father was once a good man seduced into evil ways by the heathen Caerith. And so, I punished them with fire and sword, for the crimes of taking the man I loved from me and their malign service to the Malecite. And I'll start with that witch you're so fond of."

I sagged in weary despair, shaking my head. "You ensure only your destruction. You don't know what she is, what the Caerith will do should you harm her. Wilhum died killing Viruhlis, did you know that? Do you even care? You create vengeful enemies with every step you take on this road of chaos. It's over, Evadine, you just haven't realised it yet."

She afforded me a look that mixed pity and resignation, still rocking the child in her arms as his cries subsided. "You forget, Alwyn, I have seen what will come. I have seen the witch burn. I have seen armies that dwarf the Ascendant Host carry my banner across a thousand miles of righteous conquest. Ascarlia, the eastern kingdoms, the lands across the southern seas, all shall be united in the Covenant. It will be his mission, in time." She raised Stevan up, the coverings falling away to reveal a happy face, his wails from seconds before abruptly forgotten. His cheeks bulged as he giggled and waved his arms in my direction. "And I saw you at his side. So, I won't kill you, Alwyn. Nor do I think I could, for my love does not die so easily as yours."

Would that Mother was here to see this . . . "Never," I hissed at her as the vision ached in my head. It occurred to me that the glimpse of the future I had been gifted may well be a mirror of her own. But where she saw wondrous triumph, I saw a destiny I was determined to avoid. "I'll have no part of any crusade. I've walked that road before and this is where it's led us."

"To the precipice of glory." Evadine gave a grim smile and, pressing a kiss to Stevan's head, settled him in his cot. "Glory that will be his in time."

Straightening, she turned and barked an order which had the broken-nosed sergeant hurriedly pulling aside the tent flap. "Take Lord Scribe to his witch. Even one such as her should have the comfort of friends before just execution. And when you stack the fire, build it high. We burn her come the dawn."

Chapter Forty

The Sack Witch had been imprisoned in the blackened and part roofless inn that comprised the only building still standing in the ruin of Ambriside village. The cluster of cottages and workshops were all either burned or torn down to their foundations, the lanes littered with broken crockery and furnishings. I saw no bodies, meaning Lorine had wisely commanded the inhabitants take shelter in the castle. To my surprise, upon being shoved into the gloomy disordered mess of the inn, I saw light gleaming on a row of bottles behind the bar. Any other army would have looted and drunk the lot, but not the Ascendant Host.

"We've orders not to spill your blood, traitor," the broken-nosed sergeant growled at me, the intended intimidation diluted somewhat by the nasal burr with which he spoke. "But that doesn't mean I won't smash your feet with a hammer if you take one step outside these walls."

"You're most likely going to die tomorrow," I told him, wincing at the ache in my chest. "Think on that when you're building the fire."

He growled again, glaring in baleful impotence as he retreated to slam the inn door closed. Looking around at the varied shadows, I saw no movement that might signify another occupant and felt a moment of panic. *If she's already dead . . .* But then I heard the soft rustle of cloth and my eyes detected a shift in the shadows near the cold and empty hearth. Moving closer, I found her perched on a chair in calm repose. Unlike me, she hadn't been bound, her hands resting in her lap, uncovered face regarding me in warm welcome.

"Alwyn," she said. As she smiled, I saw the mottled bruises that discoloured her features.

"She had them beat you," I said, moving to crouch at her side.

"Actually no," she said. "Her followers got somewhat excited when I appeared. Her captains were obliged to rescue me. What use is a dead hostage, after all?" She smiled again and gestured to the shadows at her back. "You'll find another chair back there somewhere, if you would care to join me."

"I would. But first—" I rose and went to the bar "—I think I would like a drink."

After several attempts, I managed to dislodge one of the bottles behind the bar, sinking to my haunches to retrieve one of the glass shards with my bound hands. "It occurs to me," I grunted as I worked the fragment's edge along the cord about my wrist, "that I have never learned your name. Seems a trifle insulting to call you Sack Witch, and I would find addressing you as *Doenlisch* overly formal."

"I had a name once," she replied. "But it means nothing now. Feel at ease to call me what you wish."

"No." I hissed in relief as the glass completed its cut and the cord fell away. "That won't do." I stood to inspect the bottles, removing the stoppers to sniff the contents until I found the least acrid brandy. Retrieving two goblets from the floor, I returned to the fireplace.

"Do you indulge perchance?" I asked, setting the goblets down on the hearth and pouring a measure into both.

"It has been . . ." she paused, brow wrinkling in calculation ". . . at least two centuries since I partook of liquor. I wonder if the taste has improved."

"I doubt it." I handed her a goblet and went in search of the chair she mentioned. It was a poorly made, rickety thing that creaked under my weight. Still, after the day's exertions I was grateful for any relief. We drank in silence for a time, the Sack Witch grimacing at her first sip, but choosing not to put the brandy aside. I soon drained my goblet and reached for the bottle.

"I had thought," she said, "you would have many questions for me."

"I do, but I've become tired of meaningless answers." My chair squeaked as I settled back into it. "I found out where that book came from, but I suppose you know that. Do you still have it?"

"It's in safe hands far from here. I thought it best kept from the mother of your child."

Was there a slightly acidic edge to her voice then? A hint of reproach? "You knew this would all come to pass," I pointed out. "It's there in the book, is it not?"

"Much of it. But not all. Some things are different. I told you before about the vagaries of fate."

"Is this in those pages?" I waved a hand at our surroundings. "You, me, her, all here at this moment? Your impending death, I mean to say."

"Yes." She sipped more brandy, her grimace less pronounced this time.

"And yet you came anyway."

"Some fates can never be avoided. Some tangles in the unseen skein of the world will always snare you, regardless of how hard you struggle."

"There is much I could have avoided if I had been permitted to read that book. A great many people now dead would still be alive."

"Are you still so naive, Alwyn? Her rise was always inevitable, but the birth of your son was not."

There was a weight to her words now, an emphatic note that caused me to lean forward, brow furrowed in realisation. "Stevan. He was the reason you kept it from me. You wanted him to be born."

She met my gaze, her expression that of a woman forcing herself to confront deserved censure. "It has never been a question of wants, Alwyn. Just necessities. Speaking of which, your son will need your guidance for what lies ahead."

"And what is that?"

"I know you won't believe me when I say this, but I simply don't know. All I can say is that the world will turn upon his fate, as it turned so long ago when the veil between the worlds was pierced."

"You expect me to watch you burn and stay at Evadine's side?"

"We both know you won't stay with her, whatever the outcome

tomorrow. But yes, I do expect you to watch me burn. So, please forget any daring plans or schemes of escape you may be hatching." She drank again, and to my astonishment I saw the goblet tremble in her hand.

"You're afraid," I said. "Why would one who can't die be afraid?"

"Why would you imagine I can't die? You placed yourself in this peril to save me, did you not? Or was there another reason you came?"

"I came for you!" My vehemence had me shifting in my chair, causing its weakened limbs to give way. I stood before it could deposit me on my arse, kicking the treacherous bundle of sticks away. I tossed my now empty goblet aside and reached for the bottle, resting an arm on the lintel above the fireplace and drinking deep. The Sack Witch allowed me a short interval of indulgence before speaking again.

"Do you hate me, Alwyn?"

I looked at the bottle in my hand, finding it half empty even though I felt not the slightest bit drunk. Muttering a curse, I threw it into the shadowed recess of the inn, hearing it shatter. "Would there be any point to it, if I did?" I asked her. "For I fancy hating you would be like hating the rain or the wind. You simply are."

She rose to her feet and came to my side, voice softer now, coloured by a need for understanding. "I searched for you for such a long time, always wondering who you would be. A king? A prince? A mighty warrior famed for both mercy and fury? I'll admit I never expected you to be an outlaw, one I first saw running from men intent on hanging him from the nearest tree, no less."

"Then it pains me to have been such a disappointment."

"No, Alwyn." She reached for my hand, squeezing it hard. "Never that."

Looking at her open, pleading face, I was struck once more by her beauty, ageless and undimmed by her bruises. "I have an inkling of what the *Eithlisch* is," I said. "For he is but a child next to you. But I have no notion whatsoever of what you truly are."

She squeezed my hand again before sinking back into her chair. "A question that will be answered on the morrow." Lifting her goblet to her lips, she frowned at finding it empty. "I find this doesn't irk me so much as it once did. Do you think you could find me some more?"

So, we sat together as she drank and talked of many things. I asked her no more questions, even though I had many. Demanding answers now felt out of place, almost insulting. Instead, she talked of the lands she had walked in her vast span of years. Some were peaceful and rich in wonders, others even more riven by strife and misery than Albermaine, yet no matter how far she travelled, she found one trait common to all cultures.

"The Fall," she said. "The *Ealthsar* to the Caerith. The Scourge to you. In the Satrapy of Uhlmesh they call it the Shattering. In Ishtakar the Saluhtan's archive has an entire vault wherein lie the preserved accounts of what their scholars call the Dawn of the Shadow Age. A singular lesson I've learned is that, if there is one thing that unites humanity, it's catastrophe."

Although I had resisted asking more questions, there was one I found I couldn't contain. "Were you there? Did you witness the Scourge?"

"Even I am not so old. No, I was born in the years that followed, when the Caerith were still a broken, scattered people. We were degraded, reduced in spirit and number. Yet, I could see the vestiges of what we once were, what we could become again. Guiding them was the work of decades, for they had fallen so deeply into the mire of ignorance. In time, as I found others who shared my peculiar abilities, the Caerith changed, they grew. And so, I reasoned, if such a thing could be done for the Caerith, why could it not be done for the world? But I was not fully prepared for what I would find when I ventured forth. I thought myself wise, for was I not ancient and steeped in lore? But I was an innocent lost amid a vast and confusing ocean. I came to understand that my mission was absurd, an infantile and arrogant conceit, but in coming to that understanding I uncovered a deeper truth. As I laboured to remake the world, something else laboured to bring it once again to ruin."

"The Malecite." I shifted on my perch atop a footstool found among the wreckage, recalling the entwined, inhuman corpses in the crater beyond the petrified forest. "How can it have lived? I've seen its corpse."

"The smoke of a candle flame will linger after it's snuffed."

"So, it's a spectre, like so many I've seen recently. Incidentally, it would have been courteous of you to warn me what carrying the stone feather entailed."

"Would you have carried it if I had? And, if you hadn't, would you be standing before me now?"

I said nothing, seeing no sign of contrition in her bearing. I understood then that her compassion was matched, or perhaps even exceeded, by her ruthlessness. She cared for me, I knew that. But I also knew, should her design require it, she would forfeit my life in an instant.

"So, the Malecite lingers," I said, turning my gaze from her. "Formless yet potent enough to twist Evadine to its purpose."

The Sack Witch nodded. "For generations I hunted it, finding only traces. It has journeyed as far as I, yet always insubstantial, denied a vessel for its ambitions, until, two decades ago, it found one, in her."

My mind returned to the sight of Evadine gazing upon Stevan in his cot, the intensity of both love and need I saw in her. "My son, does he carry it too? The Malecite's . . . essence. Its soul."

"His blood is hers, but also yours, Alwyn. That is why, after tomorrow, you must remain at his side. Only you can keep him on the path he must follow."

"The path to where? To what?"

She shook her head, a sad smile of apology on her lips. "I have been given only glimpses. It's like looking at a mountain in the far distance, one you know must be climbed but the route and the goal are hidden."

"And if he can't climb it? If he strays from the path?"

The smile faded from her lips and she looked away. It was all the answer I required.

"I would let the whole world fall to ruin before I did such a thing," I told her, my words hard and precise. "You chose your mission. I chose none of this."

"You chose to ignore the evidence of what she was becoming. You chose to march at her side through one needless war after another. You chose to love her. Your son is the result of those choices. Some responsibilities cannot be shirked, Alwyn."

"When did I ever shirk anything? I came here for you, fully expecting death as a reward."

"You stood and watched as Deckin Scarl tortured captives, did you not? Sometimes to the death. You stole from the beggared and the destitute so that your band might have full bellies for the winter. And you did murder at his behest."

"I was an orphaned, unwanted bastard cast into a forest. A child who knew no better."

"Did he? Being so clever, so insightful. A clever boy could have found another way, could he not?"

I glared at her, heat building in my chest, even though I couldn't deny a word she had said. "If I am guilty then so are you. We saved her, remember? I didn't know what she would become, but you did. So why?"

"Because your son needed to be born. His presence in this world is worth all the blood that flowed from our act. In time, you will understand. But I will not shy from your anger, for I deserve it."

Suddenly she seemed weary, slumping in her chair, the goblet dangling from a listless hand. She blinked tired eyes at me as I took the vessel from her and set it aside. For a second I caught a glimpse of her true age in those eyes, the depth of experience and knowledge behind them shining bright.

"Is that why you came?" I asked her. "To face the punishment you feel you deserve?"

"As you came for me." She reached out to stroke a hand across my face. "So I came for you." She huddled into her chair, concealing her hands in the sleeves of her robe. "I think I will sleep for a while. Something I haven't done for such a long time."

A rush of panic gripped me then, a desperate realisation that I couldn't allow any harm to come to her. "I can get us clear of here," I said, gripping her arm. "That idiot sergeant won't be hard to take down. We can light a fire in here, the smoke will shroud our escape . . ."

"No." Her ancient eyes stared into me, halting my scheming with inarguable resolve. My distress must have shown in my face for her gaze softened and she smiled again. "Just let me sleep, Alwyn." She settled back and closed her eyes, voice dwindling to a soft murmur. "I'm curious to see if I'll dream . . ."

It was Supplicant Ildette who appeared some hours after dawnlight glimmered through the shattered windows of the inn. The door slammed open from the weight of her kick before she strode into view, flanked by a pair of impressively tall Covenant soldiers. The Supplicant and her escorts were notably cleaner than the unwashed mob I had been led through the night before, their polished breastplates emblazoned with an unfamiliar crest: a white shield flanked by columns of flame. *The Lady's Shield*, I recalled Evadine saying when this fanatic and her brother had turned up in Athiltor. *The Ascendant Queen has her own personal guard.* From the hungry anticipation on the Rhianvelan woman's face, I concluded that they also had another role in this army: the queen's executioners.

"Bind the traitor!" she snapped, quick to notice my unfettered hands. "And the witch!"

My companion had remained asleep until roused by the slamming door, while I had spent the intervening hours veering from hopeless, infuriated despair to yet more panicked scheming. Many times I went to rouse her, intent upon forcing her to follow as I orchestrated our escape. Yet each time I reached for her, my hand shook with such violence I quickly abandoned the attempt. I couldn't tell if it was the result of some arcane agency on her part, or if I was simply unable to act against her will. She was determined upon submitting to the fire this day, and nothing I could do would prevent it.

I stood and allowed my wrists to be bound once again, to the front this time, watching one of Ildette's guardsmen loop rope around the Sack Witch's slender frame. His forcefulness in drawing it tight to fasten the knots provoked a pained gasp from her, causing me to lurch towards him, snarling insults only to be brought low when his comrade delivered a kick to my legs.

"No trouble from you now, Scribe," Ildette said, crouching to purr into my ear. "The queen decrees no harm to you, but that doesn't stop me fixing a gag in that shithole mouth of yours." She stood back, snapping brisk instructions at the guards. "Get them up and let's be about the day's business. You have leave to use your blades if that lot outside gets too bothersome."

A twenty-strong contingent of the Lady's Shield awaited us outside, their swords drawn. Beyond the ruins of Ambriside I saw the ground before the siege works was thick with people, all faces turned in our direction and the air pregnant with hushed expectation. Rising above the multitude stood a tall conical stack of timber, a pole rising from its centre. I could see workmen busily dousing the timber with oil and shoving wooden kindling into the cracks.

Turning to the Sack Witch I saw neither the serene calm I expected or the terror I feared. Instead, her demeanour was one of concentrated interest, her gaze surveying the scene as if intent on recalling every detail. Had my hands been free I know I would have snatched a dagger from one of the guards and plunged it into her chest in that moment. Better that the death that awaited her atop the bonfire.

"You can still stop this," I said, uncaring of the thin, pleading desperation in my voice. "I know you can. Please!"

"Got a spell up your sleeve, have you, witch?" Ildette enquired with a harsh chuckle. "Do you imagine those of us bathed in the light of the Risen Martyr have anything to fear from your tricks?"

The Sack Witch spared her only a brief, irritated glance, before nodding at the waiting crowd. "Best not keep them waiting," she said.

I watched the humour on Ildette's face stiffen into anger before she reached out to grab the ropes about the Sack Witch's midriff, dragging her forward then shoving her so she stumbled to her knees. "No," she hissed, "let's not!" Hauling the prisoner upright she pushed her on, calling out a loud command, "Make way for the heretic!"

In contrast to the vocal hatred of the night before, this time the assembled mass of the Covenant Host was silent. They parted before the procession without complaint, or any shouted insults or hail of spit. Still, I could taste their bloodlust, it hung over them just as thick and potent as the stench of their unwashed bodies. I fancied that the siege lines must have been abandoned for the day, so numerous was this unspeaking mob. The reason for their quietude was obvious in the person of the Ascendant Queen herself. Evadine sat mounted atop Ulstan, viewing the proceedings from the elevated position of a rise where her banner fluttered from a tall pole. She was clad in full armour, a gleaming contrast to the besmirched throng of her soldier congregants. Clutched to her breastplate was a small bundle swaddled in white coverings.

It is often opined by the lazy of mind that love and hate are but two edges of the same blade. I tend to think of them as the same sea but with an ever-changing coastline. In the good days the waves wash gently on sun-kissed beaches beneath cloudless azure skies. When strife inevitably arrives, they pound and roil against rocky inlets and sheer, rain-lashed cliffs. Sometimes, calm will be restored, sometimes not. The sight of my son in the arms of a woman about to do gruesome murder forever changed what had existed between myself and Evadine Courlain. Only a soul transformed beyond all human conscience would have brought a child, no matter how young, to this atrocity. The shreds of reluctance that had dogged my intent since the destruction of Couravel vanished in that moment. From here on, there would only be storms between us.

A cordon of more guards from the Lady's Shield had been established around the stacked timber, creating a circle of bare ground between crowd and bonfire. Ildette gave the Sack Witch a final shove upon reaching the cordon, sending her to her knees once more and drawing a hungry murmur from the crowd.

"Tie her to the pole," Ildette instructed a pair of guards who dutifully reached down to haul the captive to her feet. However, as their hands touched her woollen robe, they both froze. For a second they remained in the same stooped position, faces turning a sickly shade of white. Then, unbidden, they retreated several steps, limbs trembling. My heart gave a hopeful lurch at the sight. Finally, the *Doenlisch* was about to unleash her power. Instead, she merely got to her feet and began to climb the piled timber.

"What are you doing?" I demanded of her, suffering a punch to the gut from Ildette. Plainly enraged and unnerved by the odd behaviour of her subordinates, the Supplicant drew her gauntleted fist back for a strike at my face, then stopped as the voice of the Ascendant Queen was heard for the first time.

"Abide by your faith, Supplicant." As ever, Evadine's voice carried to all ears present even though she appeared not to shout. Also, her tone was mild, chiding rather than critical. Still, it sufficed to cause Ildette's raised arm to fall to her side, her own features now a similar shade to the pair of trembling guards.

Something is at work here, I knew, barely feeling the ache in my belly, my attention now fixed upon the Sack Witch. Her progress to the bonfire's crest was swift, despite her bound arms. Upon reaching the pole, she turned and rested her back against it, casting her gaze over the rapt, staring multitude before her. I thought she might say something, assail them with either castigation or sage insight. She did neither, merely frowning in sorrow before shifting her gaze to the mounted woman on the rise, her expression becoming one of stern, almost insistent expectation.

If Evadine was disturbed by her victim's absence of terror, she failed to show it, although I noted how Ulstan tossed his head and snorted. The Ascendant Queen returned the Sack Witch's regard with a signal absence of emotion, her visage more glacial and statue-like than I had seen before. Then, expression unchanging, she turned to address her congregation.

"Look upon this woman, friends," she said, casting a hand towards the Sack Witch. "What do you see? A heretic? Certainly, for she is of the Caerith breed and therefore forever deaf to the Martyrs' example and the Seraphiles' grace. Do you also see, I wonder, a witch? If so, then you are correct once more, for this is yet another spinner of baubles and meaningless cants. Is it for these transgressions that I have ordered her just execution? No, friends. It is not. You look upon her and see something merely human. Vile and heathen, to be sure, but still a mortal body fashioned as we are. In this, you are wrong. So *very* wrong."

The child in her arms began to cry then, unleashing a loud wailing that said much for the strength of his tiny lungs. Evadine drew him closer to her breastplate, rocking him until his cries diminished. Her audience surely missed it, but I saw the brief tightening to her features as she quieted Stevan, the resentment and irritation of a performer irked by an unwanted interruption. Still, even in her more rational days, she had never been one to forsake an opportunity.

"See how my son is distressed by this creature's proximity," she went on. "For creature she is, friends. This is no mere woman. No mere witch. This, make no mistake, is a Malecite made flesh. My son, born from the divine light of the Seraphile, senses this creature's malice, her desire to do him harm. For that is her mission here, friends. That was why, with carnal lust and whispered deceit, did she lure my most trusted captain to her side."

Another hungry murmur swept through the throng as all eyes turned upon me. Surprisingly, I saw more hatred in their collective gaze than that shown to the Sack Witch. Perhaps, as a merely human agent of the Malecite's evil, I was easier to hate. But I felt it owed more to my status as traitor. Many of these folk had drilled at my direction; some had followed me into battle. I had been the architect of the Anointed Lady's victories, at her side throughout all the tribulations that marked her ascendancy. A betrayal is always worse when delivered by a trusted soul.

"Yes, this man is degraded in the eyes of the Seraphile," Evadine continued. "And I know many would see it as simple justice were I to place him atop the fire along with his seducer. But, as both queen and Risen Martyr, I must be above the pettiness of revenge. It has been revealed unto me that this man can be saved, turned from the darkness to the light. It will be the work of years, a labour of tears, pain and sweat, but I will not shirk it. And the road to his redemption begins here and now. Supplicant Ildette, to your duty."

Ildette bowed to her queen then extended a hand to one of the guards who passed her an unlit torch. She held it under one arm as she struck a flint, the oil-soaked rags covering one end sparking to fiery life at the first strike. Without thinking, I lunged towards her, intending to dislodge the torch from her grip. But the guards to my rear were quick to grab my arms, holding me in place. I expected Ildette to cast the torch on to the bonfire, but she turned to me instead, moving to push it into my confined grip.

"You're out of your fucking mind," I told her, immediately dropping the flaming implement.

At a barked order from Ildette, the guards holding my arms forced me to my knees. "Our queen, in her mercy, offers you a chance at absolution, traitor," the Supplicant said, voice pitched low so that the crowd couldn't hear. "I suggest you take it."

Raising my head, I glared into her smiling face. She was certainly enjoying the moment. "Your brother died easy," I told her. "Like sticking a pig. How easy will you die, I wonder?"

Her smile dissolved, replaced by the livid features of one desperate to do me harm but constrained by her queen's word. "Pick it up," she commanded, voice hoarse with repressed violence. "Light the fire."

"You pick it up," I replied, putting as much volume into the words as I could. I doubted the crowd would be moved by my defiance, but I was determined not to allow this grotesque performance to play out as intended. "And fuck yourself with it."

Ildette shook with the effort of keeping her hand from the handle of her sword while an angry growl rose from the Ascendant Queen's congregants.

"And fuck all of you too!" I railed at them, summoning the strength to lurch to my feet. "You pitiful idiots! Can't you see the madness of this? That woman is no queen." I jerked my bound hands in Evadine's direction before the guards managed to reassert their grip. "She was not raised from death by the Seraphile! Nor was her child born of union with their divinity . . ."

This was too much for my guards. With wordless, enraged grunts they forced me to the ground, strong hands pressing my head into the dry mud with crushing weight. It was then that I felt it: a tremor in the earth, dim and distant, but undeniable and growing. I wasn't enough of a tracker to gauge the distance but knew the source of this disturbance couldn't be far off.

"Alwyn!" I thought it would be Evadine's voice that cut through the burgeoning discord among the Covenant Host, but this was far less strident, if no less commanding.

The pressure on my head eased, allowing me to look up and see the Sack Witch regarding me from atop the bonfire. Her face was not lacking in fear, and I saw the glimmer of tears in her eyes, but neither did I see the slightest flicker of uncertainty.

"Pick up the torch," she told me. "Light the fire."

The guards dragged me to my feet and Ildette once again thrust the torch into my hands. I gripped it hard, feeling sorely tempted to swing its flaming end into her face. I could still feel the tremor under my feet and hoped these mindless fanatics couldn't. I moved to the bonfire in a hesitant stumble, hoping the tumult would erupt before I reached it, but it didn't. Looking again at the Sack Witch I found her face tense, but still absent of any doubt. When I raised my brows in hopeless entreaty she nodded.

So, with trembling hands, I lowered the torch to the timber and touched its flame to the kindling.

CHAPTER FORTY-ONE

The fire caught quickly, the oil-soaked kindling flaring bright and birthing an instant pall of smoke. Timbers crackled and tongues of flame licked over the untidy mound of the bonfire. The conflagration swept from base to summit in the space of the few choking breaths I gasped amid the burgeoning, acrid miasma. A sudden blast of heat had me reeling back, along with Ildette and the soldiers of the Lady's Shield. I peered through the fumes with desperate eyes, hoping to find that the Sack Witch had vanished amid the swirling confusion. But, I saw, with dismay, there she stood, a dim but unmoving silhouette, her straight-backed, resolute stance unchanging even as the flames licked around her feet. If she had screamed, I doubt I would have heard it above the increasing roar of the flames, but I knew she hadn't.

"Witness this, traitor! Witness the end of your Caerith whore!"

I turned at the sound of the gleeful screech, finding Ildette advancing towards me through the billowing grey-black clouds. The smoke was so thick it concealed much of the congregation and completely obscured Evadine from my sight, meaning we were also hidden from hers. Glancing back at Ildette, I saw that she had her sword drawn and moved with hunched, predatory intent.

"Your queen's commands mean so little, then?" I asked as she came closer, sword drawn back in readiness.

"Her compassion blinds her." Ildette let out a guttural gasp that was almost carnal in its need. "She must be protected from it. I will do what she cannot."

The vibration in the earth was unmistakable now, heralding an eruption of alarm among the assembled soldiery. Above the sudden chorus of cries and panicked orders I could hear the thunder of a great many hooves. I was familiar with the sound of cavalry at the charge, but this was of a different order, more discordant but also more ominous in the sheer weight of horseflesh it portended.

"Then you'd best be quick about it," I advised Ildette. "For I fancy your queen is about to fall."

The Supplicant was too fixated on her vengeance to be distracted by the thunder, letting out an ugly yell of triumph, she lunged at me. I knew this woman had some skill with arms, but her experience of real combat must have been minimal. Her thrust was clumsy and overextended, easily evaded and countered even by a man with bound hands. I arced my body to avoid the blade, allowing Ildette's sword to lance into the gap between my bound arms. Clamping my wrists together, I snared her sword arm and spun, pushing my hip into her midriff. We spun together in an untidy pirouette before I bore her to the ground beneath me. She thrashed under my weight, trying to buck me off. My attention, however, was fixed on dislodging the sword from her grip. I jabbed an elbow into her face, stunning her, then slammed my bulk on to her sword arm, once, then twice. The sword came free and I rolled off her, scooping up the weapon and whirling in time to parry an overhead slash from one of the guards. He was even less expert than Ildette, overreacting to the thrust I feinted at his face and then failing to block the slash I delivered to his left leg. His armour was thick enough to prevent a dismembering injury but not smashed bones. Screaming, he fell to one knee and I finished him with a skull-opening blow to the crown of his bare head.

Casting around, I saw that all was chaos now. The congregation a roiling mass of bodies in the smoke while less distinct figures appeared beyond them. A brief change in the wind banished the pall long enough to reveal the expected but still impressive sight of a long wall of *Paelith* charging headlong at the Covenant Host. Looking to either side, I saw more streaming from the forest, the sound of *paelah* hooves now a roaring storm.

A snarl from my left sent me into a crouch, avoiding the dagger that jabbed the air above my head. Undaunted, Ildette came at me again, slashing at my face in a hissing frenzy. Incoherent hate gibbered from her lips in a cloud of spittle, eyes wide and unblinking, a soul lost to the madness of all-consuming vengeance. When my sword point pierced her throat, splitting her through the neck much as I had her brother, I felt it to be a mercy, for her if not the world.

I kicked Ildette's still twitching body off the blade and turned back to the bonfire, finding it now a fiery mound. The flames reached high, wreathing the summit in smoke. Compelled beyond reason to seek some way of saving the Sack Witch, I started towards it, managing only a few paces before being forced back. Somewhere inside the bonfire, an as yet untouched portion of fuel caught a spark and erupted, sending forth a yellow-red blossom that sent me sprawling in a mass of cinders.

Hearing a concordance of angry voices not far off, I rose to my knees, planting the sword in the earth and working my bonds along the blade. The remaining soldiers of the Lady's Shield came for me just as the cord fell away. Dragging the sword from the ground, I ducked a swinging halberd, parried a sword, and slashed open the face of its wielder. The guardsmen drew back a little, forming a circle around me, weapons levelled and faces alive with hate. I would have laughed at them but for a fresh outpouring of flame from the bonfire. Glancing at the still obscured summit, I knew with a plummeting heart that nothing could have survived such a maelstrom of heat.

I do expect you to watch me burn, she had said. "Why?" I asked aloud, my sword arm wilting as despair claimed me. If she had intended to ignite some form of battle rage in me, she had failed. In that moment I felt only the utter weariness of grief and guilt.

A collective shout came from the encircling guards as they braced for the killing thrusts that would end my traitorous life. But before they could drive their blades home a fresh gust of wind swept a blizzard of embers across the field, causing them to retreat a pace or two, arms thrown over their faces. Another, stronger gust descended, sending a hot rush of air across the field and dispelling much of the smoke. I crouched low, hissing at the pinprick sting of sparks upon my skin as a loud, high-pitched scream sounded nearby. Lowering my arm from my face, I saw that the sound came from one of the guards. A broad, stocky man with the grizzled, scarred features of a veteran, he stared upwards with a face rendered childlike by unreasoning, quivering terror. His halberd dropped from his grip and he fell to his knees, screams continuing and tears streaming down his face. To either side, his comrades were backing away, some displaying a similar pitch of fear, others in white-faced shock.

Another gust swept us, chunky pieces of half-burnt timber joining the hail of embers, which was enough to send these previously murderous soldiers of the Lady's Shield into flight, apart from the screamer. He was disinclined to halt his wailing, still staring upwards with unblinking eyes. When I turned to follow his gaze and beheld the object of his terrorised fascination, I didn't join in his screaming, but nor did I fault him for it.

"Wings," I recall myself saying, mostly for want of anything else that came to mind in that moment of utter astonishment. "She has wings."

They blossomed from her in twin arcs of flame, rising twenty or more feet into the air before sweeping down to banish yet more smoke and reveal her in full. The ropes that bound her had been burned away, along with her robe and her hair, but otherwise the Sack Witch appeared utterly unharmed. Another beat of her wings bore her higher, so that she hovered over the scene. I saw twin beads of white light where her eyes should have been, the gaze that she cast over the panicking multitude below that of a hawk seeking prey. For a second, the glowing orbs alighted on me, and I felt the warmth of her regard, like a soft touch upon my heart, one that brought understanding. The shape of those wings was familiar, for I had seen it before, in ancient, twisted bone rather than flame.

"The Malecite's spirit found a vessel," I murmured, transfixed by the being hovering above. "So did the Seraphile."

The fiery gleam of her gaze dimmed once, then shifted, the pitch of her wings altering so that she angled her body towards the disordered mass of the Covenant Host. Many were screaming, others stood frozen in shock while yet more fled. Some, apparently ignorant of the profound shift in their fortunes, found the resolve to try and form themselves into companies to resist the fast-approaching charge of the *Paelith.* It was when the wall of onrushing horses and warriors met the outer edge of the host that the being above folded its wings and plummeted down.

The ugly, wrenching sound of the *Paelith* charge striking home was instantly swallowed by the roar of newborn fire as the Sack Witch's wings flared. She swept low over the writhing throng of Covenant soldiery, a river of flame erupting in her wake. Faced with the fury of the *Paelith* to their front and an inferno to their rear, the nascent battle line of the Ascendant Queen's army disintegrated. *Paelith* warriors hacked and stabbed as their mounts reared to pound their hooves into the mass of soldiers before them, cutting deep channels through what remained of their enemies' ranks.

Soldiers fled past me as I strove to discern Evadine among the chaos of it all, hurrying towards the rise where she had perched herself. Soon, however, the tide of fleeing or maddened folk became too thick and I was obliged to hack my way through. Still, there were too many and I found myself enveloped in a dense mob, some burnt, some patently driven beyond reason, all screaming and thrashing at each other and at me. I slashed down at the hand that dug fingers into my thigh, severing it at the wrist, punched a leering, gibbering face repeatedly until it disappeared from view. The crush closed in as I stabbed at a blistered, smoking chest, finding myself jammed in a heaving swirl, the air being forced from my lungs as my feet lost purchase on the ground.

Release came with shocking suddenness, the press of bodies forced apart amid a flurry of choked screams and wet thuds. Gasping, I went to my knees, convulsing until the red mist clouding my vision faded. Something both hard and wet landed close by, spattering me with warm liquid, some of which invaded my mouth with a familiar, iron sting. Spitting the blood out, I raised my gaze to behold a monster.

A red, flesh-speckled slick covered the *Eithlisch*'s bared torso from head to waist. He had swollen to a far greater size than I had seen before, obscenely enlarged muscles laced with corded veins I thought would surely burst at any second. Looking at his face, I expected to see the snarling rictus of battle-born madness. Instead, I beheld narrow, dark calculation. *He's going to kill you*, the spectral boy had warned me in the petrified forest. Now, once again, I was confronted with stark evidence of the truthfulness inherent in the dead.

"Is it just jealousy?" I asked him. "Or something more worthy?" Turning, I cast a pointed glance at the fire-winged creature once again hovering above. "Whatever love you think she owes you, she does not. If you've always known what she is, then you know that too."

His eyes narrowed further, and I knew that if he were to kill me now it would forever be a secret crime witnessed only by the mad, for the eyes of the *Doenlisch* were elsewhere. Then, with a growl, he reached down to clamp a massive hand on my shoulder and haul me to my feet.

"Your dread woman, Alwyn Scribe," he demanded. "Where is she?"

Finding to my surprise that I still held my stolen sword, I pointed it in the direction of the rise. The crowd was thinned around us, the ground littered by bodies in varied states of fractured disorder or dismemberment. However, the Covenant Host appeared to be attempting to rally around Evadine. I could just glimpse her tall armoured form above the thicket of halberds and pikes, my stomach clenching in nauseous distress at the sight of the babe still clutched in her arms.

"Follow close," the *Eithlisch* grunted, his voice now possessed of a bestial, inhuman quality. Lowering his massive shoulders, he hurled himself into the stiffening ranks before us. Understandably, those soldiers who had begun to recover some vestige of courage quickly lost it again when faced with such a creature. The wise and the terror-stricken scattered before him, while the foolishly brave attempted to stand, and died for it. The monster swatted a dozen aside in as many paces, armour buckling and bones cracking as he forged a path. I kept as close to his back as I dared, wary of catching a skull-crushing backswing from one of his arms. A few cunning souls, smart enough to make way for the murderous giant but still keen on spilling a traitor's blood, came at me in his wake and I was obliged to do some killing of my own.

By the time we began to ascend the slope, I could see Evadine clearly. She had her sword raised high, calling out exhortations to those deluded souls still willing to cleave to her.

"Steel your hearts against the witch's illusions! Know that the Seraphile's blessing resides only in me!"

Her words still retained much of their power, for the *Eithlisch*'s progress slowed then, the number of assailants to either side swelling. I found myself fending off a thicket of jabbing halberds and pikes. Others were so enthused by their queen's invective that they threw themselves at the monster. Their blades made little impression on his skin, leaving shallow scratches rather than cuts while he responded with blurring swipes of his arms. Soldiers tumbled like skittles or were cast into the air by the strength of his blows, yet, undaunted, still they sought to bar his path. Screaming, wild-eyed congregants swarmed at him, and at me as I pressed myself against his wall-like back, hacking wildly with my sword.

I slashed at one leering, yelling face after another while the *Eithlisch* crushed skulls and pounded bodies, our progress now halted. Possessed of the strength of the desperate, my sword arm kept up its bloody work until frenzied hands grabbed hold of the blade, heedless of the fingers it cost them. Vainly, I tried to tug the weapon free, kicking and punching the howling mob. One wiry figure consented to loosen his grip on the blade, but only so he could launch himself at me. He bore no weapon but clawed at my face with his bloodied hands, jaw snapping as he lunged closer, trying to fix his teeth upon my flesh. I clamped a hand to his neck, forcing him back and up, then felt him shudder as the steel head of a crossbow bolt erupted from the bridge of his nose.

The familiar overlapping whistle and thud of a crossbow volley striking home caused me to duck, keeping hold of the wiry man as I did so. Another bolt found his side as I crouched beneath him, the soldiers around us withering under the deadly hail. When it faded, I heaved the corpse away, standing to witness the sight of three companies of infantry advancing towards the rise in close order behind a skirmish line of crossbowmen. Above their ranks fluttered the banner of the Blousset family. Beyond them I could see the gates of Castle Ambris standing open and more ducal soldiers marching forth. Lorine had never been one to miss an opportunity. Looking to my left, I saw that the flank of the Ascendant Host had been utterly routed, the *Paelith* wheeling among the carnage as they massed for another charge. From the din to my rear, it seemed fierce fighting still raged beyond the rise.

I chanced a glance around the *Eithlisch*'s stalled bulk, seeing the ground before him piled with pulverised bodies but the route to the crest now free of defenders. Evadine remained in place, however, as implacable as ever. She wheeled Ulstan to and fro, calling out exhortations to her troops and, just for an instant, our gazes met. I thought I would see hatred, instead I saw the stern resolve of a divinely ordained warrior queen shift into something far more human. In the brief span of seconds before she looked away, I beheld a woman bereft, broken of heart and despairing in the betrayal she had suffered. Then, as another blast of heat swept from above, she turned her face skywards and all vestige of humanity fled, replaced by depthless, snarling hatred.

Looking up, I saw the winged figure streaking down, birthing a wake of fire that flared into a bright arc as she swept low over the remaining ranks of the Ascendant Host. Evadine's scream was swallowed by the roar of the inferno engulfing her soldier congregants. It rose in an ugly yellow and orange wall that quickly morphed into a thick pall of black smoke. I lost sight of Evadine as the acrid cloud swept over the battlefield and, seizing the chance, I stepped from the *Eithlisch*'s shadow and sprinted for the crest.

I stumbled over smashed or burnt corpses, my eyes stinging from the smoke, hacking away a hand that emerged from the carpet of bodies to latch on to my ankle. The smoke faded as I reached the top, letting out a feral shout of anger at the sight of Ulstan bearing Evadine away, my son still clutched to her breast. The charger galloped and leaped across the blasted field of horrors, making for the forest while, above, I saw the Sack Witch angle her wings and fly in pursuit.

Chapter Forty-Two

Shuddering with a jarring mix of exhaustion and fear, I could only manage a stumbling run in pursuit of Evadine, sprawling to the ground when my feet caught on a charred corpse. Forcing myself to my knees, I let out a howl of impotent rage at the sight of her disappearing into the dark welcome of the forest. Above, the Sack Witch drew in her wings to sweep low over the trees, a river of flame blossoming in her wake. *Does she intend to kill them both?* I wondered, finding it hard to credit. *He will need your guidance*, she had told me, so why seek to destroy him now? Unless the hatred of a Seraphile for a Malecite was so powerful it banished all other concerns.

Hearing the drum of hooves upon sod, I found I lacked the fortitude to turn. It was the hot breath of a *paelah* on my neck that summoned a sudden flowering of strength. Looking up, I saw Uthren tossing his head with impatient insistence. He wore no saddle and his flanks were streaked with the stains of battle, a few minor cuts darkening the grime with blood. Snorting, he went to his knees, head lowered. I reached to grasp his mane and hauled myself on to his back.

I clung to Uthren's neck as he rose to his full height, glancing at the gore-covered bulk of the *Eithlisch*. He regarded me with such resentment, eyes narrowed beneath the granite slab of his brows, I wondered if he had already begun to regret not killing me.

"She has to die, Alwyn Scribe," he told me, his voice still possessed of its animalistic growl.

I said nothing, gripping Uthren's mane tighter as he reared then spurred towards the forest at full gallop. Any horse other than a *paelah* would surely have shied from burning woodland but Uthren sped across the charred ground and plunged into the wall of blazing trees without even a tremor of fear. Embers swirled like hornets and the air thickened with choking fumes, but the great horse bore me on through this avenue of blackened trunks with the same speed he had shown the day before. For a time, the forest became an orange-green blur as I clung to Uthren's mane, my sword held low and to the side until, finally, I glimpsed the vague silhouette of a galloping horse and rider.

Ulstan was as finely bred and fleet a warhorse to ever ride the battlefields of Albermaine, but he was little more than a weakling foal next to Uthren. Whinnying in triumph, the *paelah* lengthened his stride to close the distance to his prey. Before he reared to lunge, fore hooves flashing, I saw Evadine look back at me, pale face set in the same aggrieved, accusatory mask.

Ulstan's rear legs snapped like twigs under Uthren's hooves, the warhorse collapsing on to his belly. My heart lurched in panic at the sight of Evadine being thrown from his back, my son still clutched in her arms. Seeing the small bundle slipping from her grasp as she impacted the forest floor, I leaped clear of Uthren. The child's wailing cry of distress cut through me like a knife as he rolled across the ground, coming to rest at the base of a blazing birch. I charged towards him the instant my feet touched the earth, then came to a halt as Evadine's sword slashed across my jerkin, cutting through the leather but sparing the flesh beneath.

"Back, Alwyn," she told me, stepping into my path, sword levelled. To her rear, the child continued to wail as the burning tree scattered flaming debris all around. "He is not for you."

"He'll burn!" I snarled at her, hurling myself forward, sword slashing at her head. It was a clumsy stroke, intended to force her aside, but she parried it with ease.

"Back!" she said again, moving with impossible speed to plant an open hand in the centre of my chest. The air fled my lungs as I flew from my feet, coming to earth at least a dozen feet away. "He is mine!" Evadine stated, advancing towards me. The hurt I had seen on her face moments before had shifted into the dark, hardened visage of a wronged woman. Before she closed on me I had the perverse thought that, in her madness, she might perceive all of this as a lovers' quarrel.

A loud, angry snort sounded to my left and Uthren, having pounded Ulstan to a broken ruin, came charging through the smoke. Evadine swung to face him but the cracking of thick timber and the whoosh of shifting fire heralded the sight of a tall pine toppling into Uthren's path. Flames erupted as it crashed down, too tall and too thick even for the great horse to leap.

Keen to take advantage of the distraction, I fortified myself with a deep breath of scratchy air before scrambling upright and once again sprinting towards Stevan.

"NO!" Evadine's sword flashed at the edge of my vision and I dived forward, rolling clear of the blade. "You forfeited all rights to him when you allied with that Caerith filth!" She loomed closer, forcing me to face her. "Liar!" she railed as our blades clashed. "Traitor!"

I sidestepped a thrust and attempted a counter by flicking my sword point at her eyes, one of Roulgarth's favourite tricks. She batted my blade aside with inhuman speed and replied with an arcing overhead swing of her sword. Earth and ash erupted in a cloud as I sidestepped the blow, fast enough to spare myself a certain death but not to avoid the backhanded cuff she delivered to my head.

The world spun and I along with it, the blow sending me into an untidy pirouette. For what most likely lasted mere seconds but may have been hours, I knew only a numbing, black void. When sensation returned it was with the taste of ash upon my tongue and a throbbing pain on the side of my head. My fingers twitched, scraping soil but not the hard wood of a sword hilt.

Groaning, I rolled on to my back, eyes tracking along the length of Evadine's sword to her stricken, anguished face. "Why?" she asked me, tears trickling from her eyes and over her lips. "Why did you do it, Alwyn?"

"You know why," I told her, looking deep into those grieving eyes and wondering what truly looked back. "You must know by now. What you are. What you're becoming."

"This . . ." She shook her head, stifling a sob. "This is the witch's doing. Her Malecite's curse upon you."

"You are the Malecite!" I lurched at her, uncaring of the tip of her sword pressing into my throat. "That's where your visions come from! That's what lives inside you!"

She could have killed me so easily in that moment, just an inch more pressure upon her sword and the tale of Alwyn Scribe, outlaw, murderer, sometime knight and, I like to think, scholar of some renown, would have been told. Yet, she didn't. Instead, she frowned, blinking in confusion, the sword point slipping from my neck.

"How could she have twisted you so?" she asked in bleak wonder. "You who were once so true?"

"Twisted me?" I barked a laugh. "You killed your own father! You have murdered or driven away every friend you ever had! You have led thousands to their deaths and slaughtered thousands more! You are the Scourge you foretold, Evadine!"

A calm settled upon her then, the conflict I saw in her eyes fading away into sorrow. "I had hoped you could be reached, that Stevan would know his father as a good man. But," her sword arm stiffened and once again its point began to dig into my flesh, "I see now that cannot be. The path I walk, must be walked alone. I have seen this, though I tried to blind myself to it. From the fire will a new blade be forged . . ."

I tensed, ready to grab the sword and roll away, but a sudden flare from above sent a blinding white light into my eyes. It was accompanied by a sound, a voice, but not one that could ever be called human. It was both a shriek and a song. Wordless and unknowable but also rich in meaning. I heard a terrible sadness in that sound, but also I heard condemnation. The light flickered as the sound continued and I blinked tears to behold a figure suspended in the sky above.

The Sack Witch's wings were white now, flared wide and blazing like diamonds. She shone brighter still, exuding streams of light in concert with her song. They bathed Evadine in their glow as she staggered back from me, all thought of murder apparently forgotten. At first she stared up at the being above in blank astonishment, then her face changed with a shocking suddenness. In an instant the statuesque beauty of Evadine Courlain became something so riven with rage and defiance words such as ugly or hideous barely come close to describing how it felt to behold it.

Her mouth gaped open, creating a black maw from which its answering cry emerged. It was at that sound, so cutting in its vileness, so alien in the scale of its hatred, that I understood myself to be witnessing a confrontation between two absolute opposites. The shadows beneath Evadine began to coil as her shriek continued, stretching and winding like vines, reaching up to lash at the incandescent streams that bathed her. The Sack Witch, the Seraphile, was a creature of light. Evadine, the Malecite, was a creature of shadow.

Dark, coiling tendrils thrashed at shimmering shafts as I felt the air thrum with accumulated power. My skin prickled and hair bristled as the contest continued, both creatures still crying out their impossible songs. Then, with a thunderclap of unleashed energy, the struggling concordance of light and shadow exploded. Blasted by hot air and debris, I huddled on the ground, arms covering my head.

In the absence of the Seraphile's song and the Malecite's shriek, the silence was vast, causing me to wonder if it might in fact be the silence of death. However, when I recovered enough wit to lower my arms from my face, I saw Evadine collapsed to her knees, head bowed and unmoving. Standing, I cast about for the Sack Witch, seeing a naked and very human form lying atop a blanket of ash a short distance away. I couldn't tell if she still drew breath but, returning my gaze to Evadine, I saw the slow but present bob of her head. Spying the gleam of my sword nearby, I snatched it up, approaching Evadine on stumbling legs.

Her head rose slowly when I staggered to a halt before her. My task would have been easier had I looked upon that inhuman, hateful visage from moments before. But, to my eternal regret, Evadine was once again herself. The hurt of betrayal still shone in eyes lacking all but a small vestige of sanity. But still, it was her.

"You desire to end me, Alwyn?" she enquired, her eyes slipping to regard the sword in my hand. "You would kill all that we shared?" Her voice was mostly flat, save for a faint note of mystified despair, truly a woman wronged by the worst of men.

Suffering the plea in her gaze was the hardest blow I took that day, for in it I saw a terrible truth: *She doesn't know*.

The realisation brought a sob to my lips, but didn't prevent me raising the sword. To this day, I know not if I would truly have struck the blow that ended her life. Even though I accepted the necessity of her death, the depth of my attachment to this woman went far deeper than I ever imagined. I could so easily have struck down a Malecite, but not her.

It was as I tightened my grip on the sword hilt, arms trembling with both fatigue and the pain of indecision, that my son chose to spare me the agony by letting out a cry of such plaintive need that I couldn't help but pause and turn to him. He still lay at the base of the flaming birch, the ground about him smoking from the constant rain of fiery debris. Before I could stumble towards him, however, Evadine lunged. Fingers unyielding as steel clamped hard on my wrists, not with the uncanny strength from before, but still fierce enough to force me to my knees.

"I told you," Evadine grated into my face as she loomed above. "He is not for y—"

A sudden thunder of hooves, a sound like wet leather being torn by a blunt knife and Evadine Courlain shuddered and stiffened. I tore my wrists from her suddenly flaccid grip as she tottered back, turning slowly to reveal the spiny object protruding from the base of her skull. Beyond her, Juhlina swayed atop the back of her *paelah* as the great horse reared, her gaze lacking all mercy as she looked upon the woman she had impaled with the stone feather. I loved Evadine, but Juhlina never had and I knew this to be a blow struck without hesitation.

Evadine tried to speak then, but the words emerged as bloody spittle, turning to face me, staring in terrorised realisation. I wondered if the feather's invasion of her flesh had brought understanding, or at least a last semblance of sanity, for I saw an appeal in her eyes. Whether she sought forgiveness, or it was a desperate expression of hope from a dying soul, I never knew. It faded quickly, however, and Evadine could only gabble out more blood-flecked gibberish before she fell face down to the charred earth and lay still.

I might have continued to stand in shocked regard of her corpse if not for another cry from Stevan. The fires were closer now, building in ferocity, the cascade of debris around the child growing thicker. Stumbling towards the screaming infant, I covered no more than a few steps before collapsing. I began to crawl towards him, but Juhlina was faster, leaping down from her *paelah* to rush past me and gather the infant into her arms.

"Can you walk?" she asked, kneeling at my side.

I shook my head, pushing her away. "Go! Get him out from here!"

"I can't . . ."

"GO!"

"Not without you! Now, get up!" Juhlina put her shoulder under mine and managed to lever me upright. Once on my feet, I staggered back from her. I might well have fallen again if I hadn't stiffened at the sound of Uthren's hooves pounding a passage through the burnt wreckage of the pine that barred his path. He trotted to my side and went to his knees, allowing me to clamber on to his back. Reaching down, I took Stevan from Juhlina before she rushed to her own mount, quickly leaping into the saddle.

"Come on!" she shouted, voice almost swamped by the surging roar of the flames. Yet, I lingered, first to afford Evadine's corpse one final look. Despite the current-day rantings of those who still cleave to the creed of the Risen Martyr, I can assure you, dearest reader, that I saw no sign of animation in her slumped form. Evadine Courlain died that day and, if she rose, it was only as ash spiralling on the wind.

I lingered just one moment longer, searching the thicket of flame to my rear for any sign of the Sack Witch, but her naked, unmoving form was nowhere to be seen.

"Alwyn!" Juhlina called again, her *paelah* spurring into a gallop as yet more trees began to tumble around us. Uthren surged in pursuit, and I once again took firm hold of his mane, holding my son close as the mighty horse bore us clear of the inferno.

Chapter Forty-Three

I have scant experience of weddings, such occasions being signally absent from my childhood and much of the years since. So, being asked to take on the role of guardian of Ayin's virtue during her nuptials was an experience made doubly uncomfortable by unfamiliarity, as well as my sense of absurdity at the entire ritual.

"I trust I'm not expected to provide a dowry into the bargain," I grumbled, causing Ayin to deliver a chastising brush to the face with her bouquet.

"Propriety demands someone fill the role," she said. "My own poor dear papa having fallen in battle under the king's banner when I was but a babe."

"I didn't know that."

"Neither do I. Mama was ever sparing with details when it came to my father. However, a duchess requires a little colour to her story, don't you think? Especially when her veins carry not a drop of noble blood."

"That sounds like something the princess regent would say."

Ayin grinned in response, her smile slowly fading as her eyes lingered upon my face. "I'm sorry . . ." she began, the words faltering in her mouth. She had learned a good deal of eloquence at Leannor's side, but some circumstances still stumped her. "For all you have lost," she managed after a short cough. "I wouldn't have asked this of you, but . . ." She shrugged, letting out a discomfited laugh. "Well, there wasn't anyone else."

"Such honour you do me, my lady." I bowed and gestured to the cathedral steps. "Shall we?"

The edifice of the great building was a good deal cleaner now, such things having been neglected during the Ascendant Queen's residence in Athiltor. It was still a city of grim aspect, for Evadine had not been sparing with her wrath even here. The extensive gallows had been dismantled and the rubble of the many destroyed houses cleared away. I took some comfort from finding the library intact along with most of its books, save the most valuable which had been stolen when Evadine's appointed librarians fled in advance of the Crown Host.

King Arthin's victory over the False Queen had been marked by a good deal of celebration throughout the realm, but also an eastward migration of undaunted adherents to the creed of the Risen Martyr. Little remained of the Ascendant Host itself save a few maddened souls who continued to haunt the woods near Castle Ambris, raving or muttering about the Seraphile visitation they had witnessed. But the crusading army of the Ascendant Queen had mostly been reduced to ash or corpses that required weeks of labour by Lorine's servants to clear away or consign to the earth.

Others who still proclaimed Evadine a Risen Martyr and clung to her example began their eastward trek although a few had been foolish enough to try and preach in Evadine's name, proclaiming reports of her death as Algathinet lies and promising her imminent return and righteous vengeance. The reward for such oratory was usually a hail of stones if they were lucky or a lynching if they were not. However, most of these Risen-ites, as they came to be known, wisely chose to flee for safer climes, hopefully never to trouble these lands again.

"It's part of your role to make sure I don't trip," Ayin reminded me, placing a dainty hand in mine as we started up the steps. "This dress is not made for such simple tasks as walking from one place to another."

The dress, with its long train, ivory-hued lace and gold-embroidered bodice, had been insisted upon by the princess regent with the words, "A duchess cannot marry in rags." To our rear, Princess Ducinda dutifully raised the hem of the silken train in her small hands as we ascended the steps.

The ceremony itself was mercifully brief, conducted by an unfamiliar senior cleric of Aspirant rank who had escaped Evadine's purges via the good fortune of having been on pilgrimage far to the east throughout the crisis. Duke Gilferd cut a reasonably handsome dash in a suit of silver gilded armour and was unabashedly delighted in his bride. For her part, Ayin maintained a serene, dignified aspect throughout the proceedings, apparently unconcerned by the presence of a large proportion of Albermaine nobility, those who had survived what had become known as the Martyr's War. Duke Lermin of Dulsian was, of course, absent as he remained under royal stricture not to venture beyond his duchy's borders. Duchess Lorine had sent impressively expensive gifts but begged forgiveness for her absence due to many pressing duties in the Shavine Marches, repairing the damage to Castle Ambris being chief among them. Also, only a handful of Rhianvelan nobles had complied with the princess regent's summons, former ambassador Jacquel Ebrin principal among them in his newly appointed role as lord governor. From his strained demeanour I could tell he would much rather be playing dice in a tavern somewhere, and the sparsity of his retinue boded ill for the future unity of the realm. I chose not to dwell upon it, for such concerns were no longer my province.

When the time came and the Aspirant asked "Who passes guardianship of this woman into her husband's care?" I duly placed Ayin's hand in Gilferd's outstretched palm whereupon the cleric bound them together with a silk ribbon. "And so," he intoned, "these two souls are joined in the sight of the Seraphile and in accordance with the Martyrs' example, for now and ever more."

When they kissed and I saw the fierceness with which Ayin embraced her husband, any doubts I harboured regarding the wisdom of her choice slipped away. This was a healed soul, one for whom killing would, I hoped, be a dim and ugly memory. In her, at least, I felt I had done something right.

The formal ceremony was followed by a gathering in the cathedral gardens, where once I had watched Evadine strike a bargain with Leannor's kingly brother. It all seemed so long ago now, an event already consigned to history rather than relatively recent memory. I drank wine from a crystal goblet and watched Ayin and Gilferd, arms entwined, make a tour of the guests. I felt the young duke to be a stiff and awkward contrast to his bride's gregarious charm.

"I flatter myself," Leannor said, coming to my side and inclining her head at the happy couple, "that I've taught her rather well, don't you think?"

"She'll govern the duchy, with your kind guidance, and he'll fight any battles that need fighting." I raised my glass to her. "A fine match, Majesty."

"Entirely their own choice, I assure you. In truth, I asked her to forgo marriage for a while, finding her quite the most useful lady-in-waiting ever to grace the court. But love, especially young love, cannot be so easily denied." She paused, sipping her wine, eyes cautious above the rim of the glass. "I wonder, my lord, have you given any more thought to my offer?"

"I have, and I find my opinion unchanged. Though, of course, I thank you for your consideration."

"To become Lord Marshal of the Crown Host is perhaps the pinnacle of knightly ambition, and yet you shun it."

"I have never entertained any knightly ambitions, Majesty, and I feel I've seen enough battles in this life. I shall consider myself the most fortunate of souls if I never witness another. Besides—" I gestured to the small contingent of Alundian nobles present, Roulgarth standing tallest among them "—I feel there is a far more suitable candidate at hand."

"An Alundian lord marshal." Leannor gave a short laugh. "I think not. Besides, Lord Roulgarth has graciously accepted the role of Lord Governor of Alundia, until such time as his niece comes of age. When that day comes, he has avowed a desire to return to Caerith lands. Apparently, he feels more at home there."

My gaze shifted to Ducinda at play with a clutch of other children. Young King Arthin stood apart from the group as they ran and giggled, a peevish scowl upon his face. "So," I said, "Ducinda will be both Duchess of Alundia and Queen of Albermaine. A good deal of power to invest in one so young."

"My future daughter-in-law is precious to me."

More precious than the spoilt, humourless whelp that is your son? I thought, fighting down the terrible temptation to ask the question aloud.

"So, my lord," Leannor went on, "if I can't tempt you with matters military, what role would you accept?"

"Extreme as your kindness is, Majesty, I am minded to spend some time travelling, alone. I feel my spirits would be enlivened by solitude and a change of surroundings."

Leannor's humour faded and she gave a tight smile. "You have much to grieve over, I know. Your son . . ." It wasn't like her to be lacking in the correct form of words, but expressing due commiseration with a man who watched his infant child burn to death would defeat even the most verbose soul.

"With your leave, Majesty," I said with a bow, deciding to spare her the trial. "I have preparations to make for my journey."

"Of course, my lord." She returned the bow then, as I turned to go, reached out to clasp my hand. "Should you ever weary of the journey, and the solitude, know that there is always a place for you in this court."

Bowing lower, I backed away, and my last ever view of the Princess Regent Leannor Algathinet-Keville was of her approaching the newly married bride and groom, laughing as she clasped hands with her favourite lady-in-waiting. In a life of storms, I hazard this may have been Leannor's happiest moment. Although never afforded the title of monarch, she remains the greatest ruler ever to govern Albermaine, though if you are of historical inclinations, you will know she paid a very high price for the many years of peace that were her legacy.

I found Desmena lurking among the columns at the top of the cathedral steps. Twilight had settled upon the sky and the shadows were long and apt for concealment. Had she wished me harm she might have succeeded where so many others failed. Yet, I saw no knife in her hand, just a question writ large upon her face.

"Not joining the celebrations, my lady?" I asked.

She gave a dismissive grunt. "Wasn't invited. Not all rebels are truly welcome in the court of the princess regent, regardless of what pardons she issues."

"So, you won't be joining the Crown Host, I assume?"

Her features bunched in affronted disgust. "Serve an Algathinet? Never."

"Holding fast to the True King's cause, even now?"

"A cause so just can never be forsaken. I shall go east, find others exiled for their part in the Lochlain's crusade. Mark you well, Scribe, his banner will fly again."

I swallowed a weary sigh and nodded in farewell. "Then, I bid you safe travels. Although you will, I'm sure, forgive me for not also wishing you success. This land has seen enough of war."

"Wait," she said as I started down the steps. Pausing, I saw a rare uncertainty on her face, a plea in her eyes that told me the nature of her question before she asked it. "He lied, didn't he? Wilhum. It wasn't him who betrayed my father."

This time I didn't conceal my sigh, coloured now by anger rather than tiredness. "Your father was a sadistic bully of vile inclinations who fully earned the ugliness of his end, and more. Whoever set him on the path to the gallows deserves your gratitude." Seeing the sudden paleness of her face as the words struck home, my anger dissipated. "As Wilhum deserved a better death," I added. "For he was worthy of your brother, even though I don't think he agreed. Mourn them both, my lady."

I turned and descended the steps without waiting for an answer.

The Caerith had mostly disappeared from the Shavine Marches within days of the battle's end. A few lingered, I assumed due to curiosity or an adventurous spirit, but within a few weeks the bulk of the great host of *toalisch*, *veilisch* and *Paelith* had made its way back beyond the mountains. Uthren, however, chose to stay and it was upon his back that I departed Athiltor that night. I made no farewells and was careful to check I wasn't followed as I made my way through the disused earthworks at the edge of town to discover the *paelah* waiting for me.

"Thought you'd gone home," I said, raising a hand to his muzzle. He responded with a brief nibble at my palm before tossing his head, apparently keen to be off.

It took two days for him to carry me to the heart of the Shavine Forest. The inferno birthed at Castle Ambris had wreaked considerable destruction before the skies consented to unleash a welcome torrent of rain. We rode through several charred swathes of ground and it was a relief to find the familiar overgrown stone oval of Leffold Glade undamaged and concealed amid a thick band of trees.

"Started to think you weren't coming, Captain," Tiler greeted me as Uthren came to a halt in the lee of the ancient amphitheatre.

"Leaving before the wedding would've aroused suspicion," I said, getting down from the *paelah*'s back. "Besides, it felt right that Ayin should have one of us there. Any trouble?"

"Quiet as a whorehouse during supplications, though I reckon his cries could be heard miles off. Seems the forest's empty, of people at least."

"Get them saddled," I said, nodding to where Adlar and the other scouts were tending to the horses. "We set off before nightfall."

"We've a visitor, by the way," he told me as I started towards the gap in the amphitheatre's vine-covered wall. "Turned up this morn with gifts for the young 'un."

Lorine's face was a picture of maternal joy as she cradled Stevan in her arms, cooing softly and teasing his lips with a finger. Her only escort was a familiar figure in armour who greeted me with a stiff bow. Dervan Pressman had been elevated to the rank of knight after leading the foray from Castle Ambris, an act that also earned him a livid burn scar to his forehead.

"Alwyn!" Lorine said, adjusting her hold on the infant in her arms, provoking a shrill cry of protest. "Aww." Lorine hugged him closer. "Aren't you happy to see your papa?"

Stevan, in truth, appeared more intent on fulsomely proclaiming his displeasure than affording any notice to his father's arrival. "Here," Juhlina said, gently taking the child from Lorine. "Once he starts, he tends to keep on for a while."

She gave me a tired smile of greeting and wandered off, rocking Stevan and humming a calming song.

"How went the wedding?" Lorine asked me.

"Well," I said. "Your gifts were much appreciated."

"And the princess regent? Not too miffed, I hope."

"Apparently not, but it's hard to tell."

Lorine's lips formed a rueful grin. "From the number of spies she's been seeding in my duchy, I'm forced to conclude I don't fully have that woman's trust, as yet."

"You turned your coat, more than once. Such things don't breed trust. Sir Dervan's heroics at Castle Ambris served to redress the balance somewhat. However, I wouldn't press your luck in future. She's learned a good deal of toleration, but she does have her limits."

Lorine accepted my judgement with a raised eyebrow, before inclining her head at Juhlina and a still screaming Stevan. "And your story. Did she believe it?"

"As far she knows, Stevan Courlain died in the conflagration at Castle Ambris."

"He'll need a new name, in time. The child of the Risen Martyr will have enough burdens to bear, her name should not be one of them. And, tolerant as the princess regent may be, she could never suffer him to live. Nor could the Covenant."

"I know."

Our eyes met, grave with mutual understanding, not just of my son's vulnerability, but also the fact that this might well be the last time we ever met.

"I . . ." Lorine said, swallowing and pointing to a small chest at Dervan's feet. "I brought presents. Toys and such. Coin too. Best if you leave it in Juhlina's hands, eh? You were never very good at holding on to it, as I recall."

"True enough."

Lorine clasped her hands together, brisk and ladylike. "As per your request, Captain Toria awaits you in Farinsahl. The port is mostly empty these days so there'll be few eyes to witness your departure."

"My thanks, Duchess."

She nodded again, entwined fingers twitching. I had rarely seen Lorine so flustered. "I have every confidence," I said, moving to take her hands in mine, "that our association is far from over, my lady." Leaning closer, I placed a kiss on her cheek, whispering, "Deckin's dead, and you've mourned long enough." Stepping back, I cast a short but meaningful glance at Dervan.

Duchess Lorine Blousset of the Shavine Marches, formerly Lorine D'Ambrile, queen to the Outlaw King Deckin Scarl, then did something I never saw her do before. She blushed.

"Fare you well, Alwyn Scribe," she told me, blinking tears and turning to her knightly escort. "Sir Dervan, the hour grows late and the road is long."

It required another three days to reach Farinsahl, the journey prolonged by the need to keep to the forest, avoiding the curious eyes of folk we might encounter on the roads. It was when we encamped on the last night that I felt able to ask Juhlina a question that had nagged at me for weeks. I watched her settle Stevan into his makeshift bed, positioned just close enough to the fire for warmth. Seeing the way she smiled as she tucked in his blanket, I debated the wisdom of asking my question, for it seemed wrong to spoil such a picture. However, she was ever perceptive of my moods and glanced up with a faint scowl.

"What is it?"

"The feather," I said. "Why that and not a blade?"

Sighing, she sat back from Stevan's crib, eyes hooded with reluctance. I thought she might not answer, that this would be an eternal mystery between us, but then she spoke in a soft murmur, "I had a visitor who told me it had to be done that way."

The weight in her voice made the nature of this visitor clear. "Someone we knew?"

"No." Juhlina shifted, pulling her cloak more tightly about her. "An old man I'd never seen before, with a very strange accent, as if he had learned Albermaine-ish from a poor teacher. And his clothing was odd. He came to me the night before we rode with the *Paelith* to Castle Ambris. Until then, I hadn't seen any of the . . . things you warned me of. He was the only spirit the feather saw fit to summon." She paused, hands twitching in discomfort. "He knew things, events only you and I had shared. That night in the mill, for instance. And other things, such as the truth about the Risen Martyr's healing. He said they were surety for the truth of his word. And he told me this: 'Truth is the only means to loose the Malecite's grip on a living soul,' he said. 'The feather's gift is truth.'"

"Was he tall?" I asked. "Dark of skin with a grey beard?"

"He was stooped, as old folk often are, but I'd guess he'd been tall once. And his beard was white, and long. But yes. His skin was dark."

The historian. I found myself suppressing a shudder. *Could his soul really have lingered so long just to impart this warning?*

"Did he tell you anything else?" I asked. "His name? Anything?"

Juhlina shook her head and reached for my hand. "He did seem greatly tired, though, and greatly relieved. Like a man ready to depart this world. I think he was done, Alwyn. I think, once he had delivered his message, he could go. To where, I know not."

We sat together for a time while Stevan gurgled and fidgeted until sleep took him. It was as I watched his small mouth draw breath, wondering if the shape of his lips favoured me or Evadine, that I heard Uthren's loud snort of warning.

"Up!" I snapped to the scouts, disentangling myself from Juhlina and reaching for my sword.

"Where?" Tiler asked, busily winding his crossbow while the scouts armed themselves. "Who?"

Looking to Uthren, I saw the great horse standing in tense regard of a dense patch of forest on the edge of the clearing. He snorted again and trotted forward, breath steaming in the cool night air.

"Adlar," I called to the juggler as I led the others in the *paelah*'s wake, "stay with Juhlina."

The scouts fanned out to either side as we followed Uthren into the trees. He drew up short after only a few paces, letting out a low rumbling whinny, the muscles of his massive body tensing. "No bugger here," Tiler muttered, squinting as he peered into the confusion of shadows, primed crossbow at his shoulder.

For a creature that had once carved a bloody swathe through an entire army, the *Eithlisch* was indeed hard to spot that night. When I made out the shape of his cowled form, slumped and still atop a fallen pine trunk, my heart took on a far more rapid beat. Tiler noticed him a moment later, jerking in surprise and finger tightening on the crossbow's lock until I clapped a hand to his arm, sternly shaking my head.

"I thought you'd gone home," I said to the *Eithlisch*, forcing my voice to an even temper I didn't feel.

His cowl swayed a little, a soft sound emerging from its shadow. "Home," he repeated. "A word with scant meaning for me now."

"What do you want?"

He gave no immediate answer, instead getting slowly to his feet. Uthren emitted more rumbling as the cowled giant came closer. Sensing the tension, the scouts began to draw their steel, halting when I barked out an order to stop.

"You know what I want, Alwyn Scribe," the *Eithlisch* said, coming to a halt. He was not the size he had been on the field at Castle Ambris, but even now he cut an impressive powerful figure. "The child. Give him to me."

The fear that had been building in my breast abruptly shifted to fierce, unflinching anger. "No," I stated, hand moving to my sword.

"You know he cannot stay in your care." The *Eithlisch* took another step forward and I saw his fists clench. "The *vaerith* in his blood is too potent."

"My son stays with me." Slowly, purposefully, I drew my sword, provoking the other scouts to follow suit. "That was the *Doenlisch*'s wish, as it is mine."

"So you claim. But I hear her voice not." Another step, a definite swelling in his shoulders accompanied by the sibilant grind of muscle and sinew expanding. "Did she perish in the fire? Did you watch her burn?"

"I know not where she is, or if she still lives. A creature such as her may not even be capable of death. But I do know her heart, and it rests with my son in my hands."

"You are not worthy." His words had a strangled quality now, mangled by the swelling of his neck and jaw. "Of her heart, or the child. Give him to me!"

He lurched forward then, massive hands outstretched as I raised my sword and Tiler unleashed his bolt. It tore the fabric of the *Eithlisch*'s cloak but careened harmlessly off the flesh beneath. Before I could deliver what I knew would be a similarly useless thrust at the fast-approaching monster, Uthren let out a vast, ear-straining whinny then leaped into the *Eithlisch*'s path. The great horse reared, hooves flashing close to the monster's head. The *Eithlisch* snarled in return, his cowl drawn back to reveal features even more bestial than the feral mask displayed in the thick of battle. I understood then that this creature had never been fully human, that he existed in a state between nature and man. His true face was this teeth-baring, roaring thing of the wilds.

The mingled cries of the two beasts faded as they faced each other, Uthren tensed and ready for combat while the *Eithlisch* slowly lost his snarl. His features subsided into a dark, resentful version of the previous sculpted smoothness. Turning to me, he straightened, his form losing its swell until once again he appeared almost the man he pretended to be. Uthren gave another snort then, shifting his massive head to meet my eye, blinking once before turning and trotting to the *Eithlisch*'s side, swishing his tail in impatience.

Uthren's actions made one thing very clear, at least. "She lives," I told the *Eithlisch*. "Somewhere. Though I know not whether you and I will ever see her again."

"She was always a mystery to me," the *Eithlisch* said. "But nothing so mystified me more than why, with all the world to choose from, she chose you."

Fixing his cowl in place once more, he climbed on to Uthren's back, the great horse immediately spurring forward, bracken cracking and earth rising as he carried his prisoner away, lost to the gloom of the forest in a few heartbeats.

"Din Faud owns the entire island?" I asked, peering ahead at the towering city looming out of the morning haze. The sea was placid, the *Sea Crow*'s sails stirred by a gentle breeze that carried us towards harbour. The reflection of the great metropolis shimmered in the swell, adding to a palpable sense of majesty. Houses, shops, temples and towers appeared to cover every foot of the island's conical, mountainous form, save for the summit which consisted of bare rock. As the ship drew closer, I saw the mountain was crowned by a tall statue, a womanly form with the head of an eagle, her arms outstretched as if delivering a blessing to the city below.

"In spirit if not in fact," Toria replied. "He ran the streets of Lesturia as an unloved orphan until he grew old enough to get himself on a ship. He doesn't talk about his boyhood much, lot of dark memories I think. In truth, I'm not sure if he hates or loves the place, but it was always his passion to rule it. And so, thanks to the riches brought to him by his beloved, if adopted daughter, he does. They have an official ruler, the Satrapine of something or other, but it's just ceremonial. As with most places, it's the hand that wields the fattest purse that holds power here."

"And you're sure he'll welcome us?"

Toria glanced over her shoulder at her passengers crowding the foredeck. Juhlina bounced Stevan in her arms, his eyes agog at the spectacle of Adlar juggling no fewer than seven daggers at once. Tiler and the scouts sat close by, sharpening their blades and casting narrow glances at Toria's crew. The weeks at sea had done little to assuage the former outlaw's ingrained suspicion of those who once shared his proclivities. I didn't fault him for it, in fact I welcomed his suspicion. He and the rest of my much diminished company had taken on the charge of protecting my son. It would be the work of years, yet none had shirked it.

"My word carries a good deal of weight with him," Toria said. "But he'll need to know the truth. About the boy. About all of it. He's a bit like you, y'see? Got an irksomely keen ear for untruth." Noting the doubt lining my brow, she jostled my shoulder. "Don't fret. You'll find a home here."

I saw how her eyes lingered on Stevan, as if she were looking for some sign of his mother. I knew the look well, for I had seen it on Juhlina's face too.

"I'd best be about it," Toria said. "Got some orders to shout, mostly for appearances' sake. You can't take a ship into harbour without a lot of shouting. It's expected." She strode away across the deck, casting a series of commands into the rigging which appeared to occasion little change in the tasks of the sailors labouring among the masts.

Moving to Juhlina, I took Stevan from her and turned his face towards the approaching island and its remarkable city. He appeared to find it less fascinating than Adlar's tricks, however, sticking his fingers in his mouth with a gurgle. I also often looked for a resemblance when gazing upon this face, and, on occasion, found it in the shade of his eyes. Dark like hers, sometimes baffled too, as she had been before the feather took her life. *She didn't know. Even at the end, she didn't know.*

I pushed the memory away with a habitual grimace, something I suspected I would be doing for the rest of my life.

"This is home," I told Stevan, pressing a kiss to his head. "Here, you will grow of age, with a mother and a father. Here, no one will beat you, or cast you out into the cold woods, or force you to steal and murder. And, should anyone in this world ever try to do you harm, I'll kill them."

Stevan gurgled again, squirming in my arms and slapping a small, wet hand to my face while I laughed and wondered how it could be that I could ever deserve to feel such joy.

But, I hear you ask, what of his name? What name did you choose for your son, Alwyn Scribe? Is it a name I have heard? To which I answer, yes, I fancy that it is. But this portion of my testament is now at an end, and my son's name and all that goes with it, is, dearest, most gentle and beloved reader, a tale for another time.

Acknowledgements

Many thanks to all those who helped bring the testament of Alwyn Scribe to a conclusion. Special thanks to my agent Paul Lucas, my editors James Long and Bradley Englert, and my most enthusiastic critic Paul Field.

extras

meet the author

Ellie Grace Photography

Anthony Ryan lives in London and is the *New York Times* bestselling author of the Raven's Shadow and Draconis Memoria series. He previously worked in a variety of roles for the UK government, but now writes full time. His interests include art, science and the unending quest for the perfect pint of real ale.

Find out more about Anthony Ryan and other Orbit authors by registering for the Orbit newsletter at orbitbooks.net.

if you enjoyed
THE TRAITOR
look out for
THE LOST WAR
Book One of The Eidyn Saga
by
Justin Lee Anderson

Justin Lee Anderson's sensational epic fantasy debut follows an emissary for the king as he gathers a group of strangers and embarks on a dangerous quest across a war-torn land.

The war is over, but the beginnings of peace are delicate.

Demons continue to burn farmlands, violent mercenaries roam the wilds, and a plague is spreading. The country of Eidyn is on its knees.

In a society that fears and shuns him, Aranok is the first mage to be named king's envoy. And his latest task is to restore an exiled foreign queen to her throne.

The band of allies he assembles each have their own unique skills. But they are strangers to one another, and at every step across the ravaged land, a new threat emerges, lies are revealed, and distrust threatens to destroy everything they are working for. Somehow, Aranok must bring his companions together and uncover the conspiracy that threatens the kingdom—before war returns to the realms again.

"An eclectic cast of characters traverse a war-ravaged kingdom as Anderson's cleverly constructed plot winds its way toward a truly unexpected denouement. Rich in action and intrigue, this fantasy adventure with a Scottish flavor is sure to please fans of David Gemmell." —Anthony Ryan

Chapter 1

Fuck.

The boy was going to get himself killed.

"Back off!"

Aranok put down his drink, leaned back and rubbed his dusty, mottled brown hands across his face and behind his neck. He was tired and sore. He wanted to sit here with Allandria, drink beer, take a hot bath, collapse into a soft, clean bed and feel her skin against his. The last thing he wanted was a fight. Not here.

They'd made it back to Haven. This was their territory, the new capital of Eidyn, the safest place in the kingdom—for what that was worth. He'd done enough fighting, enough killing. His shoulders ached and his back was stiff. He looked up at the darkening sky, spectacularly lit with pinks and oranges.

The wooden balcony of the Chain Pier Tavern jutted out over the main door along the front length of the building. Aranok had thought it an optimistic idea by the landlord, considering Eidyn's usual weather, but there were about thirty patrons overlooking the main square with their beers, wines and whiskies.

Allandria looked at him from across the table, chin resting on her hand. He met her deep brown eyes, pleading with her to give him another option. She looked down at the boy arguing with the two thugs in front of the blacksmith's forge, then back at him. She shrugged, resigned, and tied back her hair.

Bollocks.

Aranok knocked back the last of his beer and clunked the empty tankard back on the table. As Allandria reached for her bow, he signalled to the serving girl.

"Two more." He gestured to their drinks. "I'll be back in a minute."

The girl furrowed her brow, confused.

He stood abruptly to overcome the stiffness of his muscles. The chair clattered against the wooden deck, drawing some attention. Aranok was used to being eyed with suspicion, but it still rankled. If they knew what they owed him—owed both of them...

He leaned on the rail, feeling the splintered, weather-beaten wood under his palms; breathing in the smoky, sweaty smell of the bar. Funny how welcome those odours were; he'd been away for so long. With a sigh, Aranok twisted and turned his hands, making the necessary gestures, vaulted over the banister and said, "*Gaoth.*" Air burst from his palms, kicking up a cloud of dirt and cushioning his landing. Drinkers who had spilled out the front of the inn coughed, spluttered and raised hands in defence. A chorus of gasps and grumbles, but nobody dared complain. Instead, they watched.

Anticipating.

Fearing.

Aranok breathed deeply, stretching his arms, steeling himself as he passed the newly constructed stone well—one of many, he assumed, since the population had probably doubled recently. A lot of eyes were on him now. Maybe that was a good thing. Maybe they needed to see this.

As he approached the forge, Aranok sized up his task. One of the men was big, carrying a large, well-used sword. A club hung from his belt, but he looked slow and cumbersome, more a butcher than a soldier. The other was sleek, though—wiry. There was something ratlike about him. He stood well-balanced on the balls of his feet, dagger twitching eagerly. A thief most likely. Released from prison and pressed into the king's service? Surely not. Hells. Were they really this short of men? Was this what they'd bought with their blood?

"You've got the count of three to drop your weapons and move," the fat one wheezed. "King's orders."

"Go to Hell!" The boy's voice cracked. He backed a few steps toward the door. He couldn't be more than fifteen, defending his father's business with a pair of swords he'd probably made himself. His stance was clumsy, but he knew how to hold them. He'd had some training, if not any actual experience. Enough to make him think he could fight, not enough to win.

The rat rocked on his feet, the fingertips of his right hand frantically rubbing together. Any town guard could resolve this without blood. If it was just the fat one, he might manage it. But this man was dangerous.

Now or never.

"Can I help?" Aranok asked loudly enough for the whole square to hear.

All three swung to look at him. The thief's eyes ran him up and down. Aranok watched him instinctively look for pockets, coin purses, weapons—assess how quickly Aranok would move. He trusted the rat would underestimate him.

"Back away, *draoidh*!" snarled the butcher. The runes inscribed in Aranok's leather armour made it clear to anyone with even a passing awareness of magic what he was. *Draoidh* was generally spat as an insult, rarely welcoming. He understood the fear. People weren't comfortable with someone who could do things they couldn't. He only wore the armour when he knew it might be necessary. He couldn't remember the last day he'd gone without it.

"This is king's business. We've got a warrant," grunted the big man.

"May I see it?" Aranok asked calmly.

"I said piss off." He was getting tetchy now. Aranok began to wonder if he might have made things worse. It wouldn't be the first time.

He took a gentle step toward the man, palms open in a gesture of peace.

The rat smiled a confident grin, showing him the curved blade as if it were a jewel for sale. Aranok smiled pleasantly back at him and gestured to the balcony. The thief's face confirmed he was looking at the point of Allandria's arrow.

"Shit," the rat hissed. "Cargill. Cargill!"

"What?" Cargill barked grumpily back at him. The thief mimicked Aranok's gesture and the fat man also looked up. He spun around to face Aranok, raising his sword—half in threat, half in defence. Nobody likes an arrow trained on them. The boy took another step back—probably unsure who was on his side, if anyone.

"You'll swing for this," Cargill growled. "We've got orders from the king. Confiscate the stock of any business that can't pay taxes. The boy owes!"

"Surely his father owes?" Aranok asked.

"No, sir," the boy said quietly. "Father's dead. The war."

Aranok felt the words in his chest. "Your mother?"

The boy shook his head. His lips trembled until he pressed them together.

Damn it.

Aranok had seen a lot of death. He'd held friends as they bled out, watching their eyes turn dark; he'd stumbled over their mangled bodies, fighting for his life. Sometimes they cried out, or whimpered as he passed—clinging desperately to the notion they could still see tomorrow.

Bile rose in his gullet. He turned back to Cargill. Now it was a fight.

"If you close his business, how do you propose he pays his taxes?" Aranok struggled to maintain an even tone.

"I don't know," the thug answered. "Ask the king."

Aranok looked up the rocky crag toward Greytoun Castle.

Rising out of the middle of Haven, it cast a shadow over half the town. "I will."

There was a hiss of air and a thud to Aranok's right. He turned to see an arrow embedded in the ground at the thief's feet. He must have crept a little closer than Allandria liked. The rat was lucky she'd given him a warning shot. Many didn't know she was there until they were dead. Eyes wide, he sidled back under the small canopy at the front of the forge.

Cargill fired into life, brandishing his sword high. "I'll cut your fucking head off right now if you don't walk away!" His bravado was fragile, though. He didn't know what Aranok could do—what his *draoidh* skill was. Aranok enjoyed the thought that, if he did, he'd only be more scared.

"Allandria!" he called over his shoulder.

"Aranok?"

"This gentleman says he's going to cut my head off."

"Already?" She laughed. "We just got here."

All eyes were on them now. The tavern was silent, the crowd an audience. People were flooding out into the square, drinks still in hand. Others stood in shop doors, careful not to stray too far from safety. Windows filled with shadows.

Cargill's bravado disappeared in the half-light. "You... you're... we're on the same side!"

"Can't say I'm on the side of stealing from orphans." Aranok stared hard into his eyes. Fear had taken the man.

"We've got a warrant." Cargill pulled a crumpled mess from his belt and waved it like a flag of surrender. Now he was keen to do the paperwork.

Perhaps they'd get out of this without a fight after all. Unusually, he was grateful for the embellishments of legend. He'd once heard a story about himself, in a Leet tavern, in which he killed three demons on his own. The downside was that every braggart and mercenary in the kingdom fancied a shot at him, which was why he tended to travel quietly—and anonymously. But now and again...

"How much does he owe?" Aranok asked.

"Eight crowns." Cargill proffered the warrant in evidence. Aranok took it, glancing up to see where the rat had got to. He was too near the wall for Aranok's liking. The boy was vulnerable.

"Out here," Aranok ordered. "Now."

"With that crazy bitch shooting at me?" he whined.

"Thül!" Cargill snapped.

Thül slunk back out into the open, watching the balcony. Sensible boy. Though if this went on much longer, Allandria might struggle to see clearly across the square. He needed to wrap it up.

The warrant was clear. The business owed eight crowns in unpaid taxes and was to be closed unless payment was made in full. Eight bloody crowns. Hardly a king's ransom—except it was.

Aranok looked up at the boy. "What can you pay?"

"I've got three…" he answered.

"You've got three or you can pay three?"

"I've got three, sir."

"And food?"

The boy shrugged.

"A bit."

"Why do you care?" Thül sneered. "Is he yours?"

Aranok closed the ground between them in two steps, grabbed the thief by the throat and squeezed—enough to hurt, not enough to suffocate him. He pulled the angular, dirty face toward his own. Rank breath escaping yellow teeth made Aranok recoil momentarily.

"Why do I care?" he growled.

The thief trembled. He'd definitely underestimated Aranok's speed.

"I care because I've spent a year fighting to protect him. I care because I've watched others die to protect him." He stabbed a finger toward the young blacksmith. "And his parents died protecting you, you piece of shit!"

There were smatterings of applause from somewhere. He released the rat, who dropped to his knees, dramatically gasping for air. Digging some coins out of his purse, Aranok turned to the boy.

"Here. Ten crowns as a deposit against future work for me. Deal?"

The boy looked at the gold coins, up at Aranok's face and back down again. "Really?"

"You any good?"

"Yes, sir." The boy nodded. "Did a lot of Father's work. Ran the business since he went away."

"How is business?"

"Slow," the boy answered quietly.

Aranok nodded. "So do we have a deal?" He thrust his hand toward the blacksmith again.

Nervously, the boy put down one sword and took the coins from Aranok's hand, tentatively, as though they might burn. He put the other sword down to take two coins from the pile in his left hand, looking to Aranok for reassurance. He clearly didn't like being defenceless. Aranok nodded. The boy turned to Cargill and slowly offered the hand with the bulk of the coins. Pleasingly, the thug looked to Aranok for approval. He nodded permission gravely. Cargill took the coins and gestured to Thül. They walked quickly back toward the castle, the thief looking up at Allandria as they passed underneath. She smiled and waved him off like an old friend.

Aranok clapped the boy on the shoulder and walked back toward the tavern, now very aware of being watched. It had cost him ten crowns to avoid a fight... and probably a lecture from the king. It was worth it. He really was tired. The crowd returned to life—most likely chattering in hushed tones about what they'd just seen. One man even offered a hand to shake as Aranok walked past; quite a gesture—to a *draoidh*. Aranok smiled and nodded politely but didn't take the hand. He shouldn't have to perform a grand, charitable act before people engaged with him.

The man looked surprised, smiled nervously and ran his hand through his hair, as if that had always been his intention.

Aranok felt a hand on his elbow. He turned to find the boy looking up at him, eyes glistening. "Thank you," he said. "I... thank you."

"What's your name?" Aranok asked. He tried to look comforting, but he could feel the heavy dark bags under his eyes.

"Vastin," the boy answered.

Aranok shook his hand.

"Congratulations, Vastin. You're the official blacksmith to the king's envoy."

Aranok righted his chair and dramatically slumped down opposite Allandria. The idiot was playing up the grumpy misanthrope because every eye on the top floor was watching him. He looked uncomfortable. Secretly, she was certain he enjoyed it.

Allandria raised an eyebrow. "Was that our drinking money, by any chance?"

"Some of it..." he answered, more wearily than necessary.

Despite his reluctance, Allandria knew part of him had enjoyed the confrontation—especially since it had ended bloodless. The man loved a good argument, if not a good fight—particularly one where he outsmarted his opponent. Not that she'd had any desire to kill the two thugs, but she would have, to save the boy. It was better that Aranok had been able to talk them down and pay them off.

"You could have brought my arrow back," she teased.

He looked down to where the arrow still stood, proudly embedded in the dirt. It was a powerful little memento of what had happened. Interesting that the boy had left it there too... maybe to remind people he had a new patron.

"Sorry." He smiled. "Forgot."

She returned the smile. "No, you didn't."

"You missed, by the way."

Allandria stuck out her tongue. "I couldn't decide who I wanted to shoot more, the greasy little one or the big head in the fancy armour." The infuriating bugger had an answer to everything. But for all his arrogance, she loved him. He'd looked better, certainly. The war had been kind to no one. His unkempt brown hair was flecked with grey now—even more so the straggly beard he'd grown in the wild. Leathery skin hid under a layer of road dust;

green eyes were hooded and dark. But they still glinted with devilment when the two sparred.

"Excuse me..." The serving girl arrived with their drinks. She was a slight, blonde thing, hardly in her teens if Allandria guessed right. Were there any adults left? Aranok reached for his coin purse.

"No, sir." The girl stopped him, nervously putting the drinks on the table. "Pa says your money's no good here."

Aranok looked up at Allandria, incredulous. When they'd come in, he wasn't even certain they'd be served. *Draoidhs* sometimes weren't. Innkeepers worried they would put off other customers. She'd seen it more than once.

Aranok tossed down two coppers on the table. "Thank you, but tell your pa he'll get no special treatment from the king on my say-so, or anyone else's."

It was harsh to assume they were trying to curry favour with the king now they knew who he was. Allandria hoped that wasn't it. She still had faith in people, in human kindness. She'd seen enough of it in the last year. Still, she understood his bitterness.

"No, sir," the girl said. "Vastin's my friend. His folks were good people. We need more people like you. Pa says so."

"Doesn't seem many places want people like me..."

"Hey..." Allandria frowned at him. He was punishing the girl for other people's sins now. He looked back at her, his eyes tired, resentful. But he knew he was wrong.

"Way I see it"—the girl shifted from foot to foot, holding one elbow protectively in her other hand—"you've no need of a blacksmith. A fletcher, maybe"—she glanced at Allandria—"but not a blacksmith. So I want more people like you."

Good for you, girl.

Allandria smiled at her. Aranok finally succumbed too.

"Thank you." He picked up the coins and held them out to her. "What's your name?"

"Amollari," she said quietly.

"Take them for yourself, Amollari, if not for your pa. Take them as an apology from a grumpy old man."

Grumpy was fair; *old* was harsh. He was barely forty—two years younger than Allandria.

Amollari lowered her head. "Pa'll be angry."

"I won't tell him if you don't," said Aranok.

Tentatively, the girl took the coins, slipping them into an apron pocket. She gave a rough little curtsy with a low "thank you" and turned to clear the empty mugs from a table back inside the tavern.

The girl was right. Aranok carried no weapons and his armour was well beyond the abilities of any common blacksmith to replicate or repair. He probably had no idea what he'd use the boy for.

Allandria raised the mug to her lips and felt beer wash over her tongue. It tasted of home and comfort, of warm fires and restful sleep. It really was good to be here.

"Balls." A crack resonated from Aranok's neck as he tilted his head first one way, then the other.

"What?" Allandria leaned back in her chair.

"I really wanted a night off."

"Isn't that what we're having?" She brandished her drink as evidence. "With our free beer?" She hoped the smile would cheer him. He was being pointlessly miserable.

Aranok rubbed his neck. "We have to see the king. He's being an arsehole."

A few ears pricked up at the nearest tables, but he hadn't said it loudly.

"It can't wait until tomorrow?" Allandria might have phrased it as a question, but she knew he'd be up all night thinking about it if they waited. "Of course it can't," she answered when he didn't. "Shall we go, then?"

"Let's finish these first," Aranok said, lifting his own mug.

"Well, rude not to, really."

Her warm bed seemed a lot further away than it had a few minutes ago.

if you enjoyed

THE TRAITOR

look out for

GODS OF THE WYRDWOOD

Book One of The Forsaken Trilogy

by

RJ Barker

Ours is a land of many gods, and we are a people with the ability to pick the worst of them.

Cahan Du-Nahere is known as the forester—a man who can navigate the dangerous Woodedge like no one else. But once he was more. Once he belonged to the god of fire.

Udinny serves the goddess of the lost, a keeper of the small and helpless. When Udinny needs to venture into Woodedge to find a lost child, she asks Cahan to be her guide.

But in a land where territory is won and lost for uncaring gods, where the woods are teeming with monsters—Cahan will need to choose the forest or the fire... and his choice will have consequences for his entire world.

1

The forester watched himself die. Not many can say that.

He did not die well.

The farm in Woodedge was the one rock in his life, the thing he had come to believe would always be there. Life had taken him from it, then returned him to it many years later – though all those he had once loved were corpses by then. The farm was mostly a ruin when he returned. He had built it back up. Earned himself scars and cuts, broken a couple of fingers but in an honest way. They were wounds and pains worth having, earned doing something worthwhile and true. He liked it here in the farthest reaches of Northern Crua, far from the city of Harnspire where the Rai rule without thought for those who served them, where the people lived among refuse, blaming it on the war and not those who caused it.

His farm was not large, three triangular fields of good black earth kissed with frost and free of bluevein that ruined crops and poisoned those foolish enough to eat them. It was surrounded by the wall of trees that marked Woodedge, the start of the great slow forest. If he looked to the south past the forest he knew the plains of Crua stretched out brown, cold and featureless to the horizon. To the west, hidden by a great finger of trees that reached out as if to cradle his farm, was the village of Harn, where he did not go unless pressed and was never welcome.

When he was young he remembered how, on Ventday, his family would gather to watch the colourful processions of the Skua-Rai and their servants, each one serving a different god. There had been no processions since he had reclaimed the farm. The new Cowl-Rai had risen and brought with them a new god, Tarl-an-Gig. Tarl-an-Gig was a jealous god who saw only threat in the hundreds of old gods that had once littered the land with lonely monasteries or slept in secret, wooded groves. Now only a fool advertised they held onto the older ways. Even he had painted the balancing man of Tarl-an-Gig on the building, though there was another, more private and personal shrine hidden away in Woodedge. More to a memory of someone he had cared about than to any belief in gods. In his experience they had little power but that given to them by the people.

The villagers of Harn were wont to say trouble came from the trees, but he would have disagreed; the forest would not harm you if you did not harm the forest.

He did not believe the same could be said of the village.

Trouble came to him as the light of the first eight rose. A brightness reaching through Woodedge, broken up into spears by the black boughs of leafless trees. A family; a man, his wife, his daughter and young son who was only just walking. They were not a big family, no secondmothers or fathers, and no trion who stood between. Trion marriages were a rare thing to see nowadays, as were the multi-part families Cahan was once part of. The war of the Cowl-Rai took many lives, and the new Cowl-Rai had trion taken to the spire cities. None knew why and the forester did not care. The business of the powerful was of no interest to him; the further he was from it the better.

He was not big, this man who brought trouble along with his family, to the farm on the forest edge. He stood before the forester in many ways his opposite. Small and ill-fed, skin pockmarked beneath the make-up and clanpaint. He clasped thin arms about himself as he shivered in ragged and holed clothes. To him the forester must have seemed a giant, well fed during childhood, worked hard in his youth. His muscles built up in training to bear arms and fight battles, and for many years he had fought against the land of his farm which gave up its treasures even more grudgingly than warriors gave up their lives. The forester was bearded, his clothes of good-quality crownhead wool. He could have been handsome, maybe he was, but he did not think about it as he was clanless, and none but another clanless would look at him. Even those who sold their companionship would balk at selling it to him.

Few clanless remained in Crua. Another legacy of Tarl-an-Gig and those that followed the new god.

The man before Cahan wore a powder of off-white make-up, black lines painted around his mouth. They had spears, the weapon the people of Crua were most familiar with. The woman stood back with the children, and she hefted her weapon, ready to throw, while her husband approached. He held a spear of gleaming bladewood in his hand like a threat.

Cahan carried no weapon, only the long staff he used to herd his crownheads. As the man approached he slowed in response to the growling of the garaur at the forester's feet.

"Segur," said Cahan, "go into the house." Then he pointed and let out a sharp whistle and the long, thin, furred creature turned and fled inside, where it continued to growl from the darkness.

"This is your farm?" said the man. The clanpaint marked him of a lineage Cahan did not recognise. The scars that ran in tracks beneath the paint meant he had most likely been a warrior once. He probably thought himself strong. But the warriors who served the Rai of Crua were used to fighting grouped together, shields locked and spears out. One-on-one fighting took a different kind of skill and Cahan doubted he had it. Such things, like cowls and good food, belonged to the Rai, the special.

"It is my farm, yes," said Cahan. If you had asked the people of Harn to describe the forester they would have said "gruff", "rude" or "monosyllabic" and it was not unfair. Though the forester would have told you he did not waste words on those with no wish to hear them, and that was not unfair either.

"A big farm for one clanless man," said the soldier. "I have a family and you have nothing, you are nothing."

"What makes you think I do not have a family?" The man licked his lips. He was frightened. No doubt he had heard stories from the people of Harn of the forester who lived on a Woodedge farm and was not afraid to travel even as far as Wyrdwood. But, like those villagers, he thought himself better than the forester. Cahan had met many like this man.

"The Leoric of Harn says you are clanless and she gifts me this land with a deed." He held up a sheet of parchment that Cahan doubted he could read. "You do not pay taxes to Harn, you do not support Tarl-an-Gig or the war against the red so your farm is forfeit. It is countersigned by Tussnig, monk of Harn, and as such is the will of the Cowl-Rai." He looked uncomfortable; the wind lifted the coloured flags on the farm and made the porcelain chains chime against the darker stone of the building's walls. "They have provided you with some recompense," said the man, and he held out his hand showing an amount of coin that was more insult than farm price.

"That is not enough to buy this farm and I care nothing for gods," said Cahan. The man looked shocked at such casual blasphemy. "Tell me, are you friends with the Leoric?"

"I am honoured by her..."

"I thought not." The forester took a step around the man, casually putting him between Cahan and the woman's spear. The man stood poised somewhere between violence and fear. The forester knew it would not be hard to end this. The woman had not noticed her line of attack was blocked by her husband. Even if she had, Cahan doubted she could have moved quickly enough to help with her children hanging onto her legs in fear. A single knuckle strike to the man's throat would end him. Use the body as a shield to get to the woman before she threw her spear.

But there were children, and the forester was no Rai to kill children without thought. They would carry back the news of their parents' death to Harn, no doubt to the great pleasure of Leoric Furin as she could offer these new orphans up to be trained as soldiers instead of the village's children.

If he did those things, killed this man and this woman, then tomorrow Cahan knew he would face a mob from the village. They only tolerated him as it was; to kill someone above his station would be too much. Then the Leoric would have what she wanted anyway, his farm. Maybe that was her hope.

The man watched the forester, his body full of twitches. Uncertainty on his face.

"So, will you take the money?" he said. "Give up your farm?"

"It is that or kill you, right?" said Cahan, and the truth was he pitied this frightened man. Caught up in a grim game Cahan had been playing with the Leoric of Harn ever since he had made the farm viable.

"Yes, that or we kill you," he replied, a little confidence returning. "I have fought in the blue armies of the Cowl-Rai, to bring back the warmth. I have faced the southern Rai. I do not fear clanless such as you." Such unearned confidence could end a man swiftly in Crua.

But not today.

"Keep the money, you will need it," said the forester and he let out a long breath, making a plume in the air. "Farming is a skill that must be learned, like anything else, and it is hard here when it is cold. You will struggle before you prosper." Cahan let out a whistle and Segur, the garaur, came from the house. Its coat blue-white and its body long, sinuous and vicious as it sped across the hard ground and spiralled up his leg and chest to sit around his neck. Bright eyes considered the forester, sharp teeth gleamed in its half-open mouth as it panted. Cahan scratched beneath the garaur's chin to calm it. "The far field," he told the man, pointing towards the field between the rear of the house and Woodedge. "The ground there is infested with rootworm, so grow something like cholk. If you grow root vegetables they will die before they are born and that attracts bluevein to the fields. The other two fields, well, grow what you like. They have been well dug over with manure. There are nine crownheads, they stay mostly at the edges of the forest. They will give you milk, shed their skin for fur once a year, and allow you to shear them once a year also."

"What will you do?" said the man, and if Cahan had not been

giving up his livelihood such sudden interest would have been comical.

"That does not concern you," he told him, and began to walk away.

"Wait," he shouted and Cahan stopped. Took a deep breath and turned. "The garaur around your neck, it is mine. I will need it to herd the crownheads." The forester smiled; at least he could take one small victory away from this place. Well, until this new tenant ran into the reality of farming and left, as others had before. The man took a step back when he saw the expression on Cahan's face, perhaps aware he had pushed his luck a little further than was good for him. Wary of the forester's size, of his confidence even though he was walking away from his home.

"Garaur bond with their owners. Call Segur by all means. If you can make it come it is yours, but if you knew anything about farming you would know it is wasted breath." With that he turned and walked away. The man did not call out for Segur, only watched. Cahan found himself tensing his shoulders, half expecting a thrown spear.

They were not bad people, not really, the forester thought. They were not ruthless enough for this land either. Crua was not the sort of place where you leave an enemy at your back. Maybe the man and his family did not know that, or maybe they were shocked by how easy it had been to steal the farm.

"And stay away," shouted the man after him, "or I'll send you to the Osere down below!"

Nothing easy turns out well was a favoured saying of the monks who trained Cahan in his youth. In that there was a truth these people would eventually discover.

He made camp in the forest. In Harnwood, where it was dangerous, and definitely not in Wyrdwood among the cloudtrees that touched the sky, where strange things lived, but also not so shallow in Woodedge that the new owner of the farm would notice him.

Further in than most would go, but not far enough to be foolish. Good words to live by. There he sat to watch. He thought a sixth of a season would be enough, maybe less, before the family realised it was not an easy thing to scratch a living from ground that had been cold for generations. No one had stayed yet. War had taken so many lives that little expertise was left in the land and Cahan, barely halfway through his third decade, was considered an old man. The farmers would not last, and in the end the fact that Cahan could reliably bring spare crops to market, and knew how to traverse the forest safely, would be more important than the small amount of sacrifice he refused to give.

Though it was a lesson the Leoric struggled to learn. But the people of Harn had never liked outsiders, and they liked clanless outsiders even less. He pitied them, in a way. The war had been hard on them. The village was smaller than it had ever been and was still expected to pay its way to Harnspire. Lately, more hardship had been visited on Harn as the outlaws of the forest, the Forestals, were preying upon their trade caravans. As it became poorer the village had become increasingly suspicious. Cahan had become their outsider, an easy target for a frightened people.

No doubt the monks of Tarl-an-Gig believed the struggle was good for Harn; they were ever hungry for those who would give of themselves and feed their armies or their Rai.

Cahan had no time for Tarl-an-Gig. Crua used to be a land of many gods, its people had an unerring ability to pick the worst of them.

It was cold in the forest. The season of Least, when the plants gave up their meagre prizes to the hungry, had passed and Harsh's bite was beginning to pinch the skin and turn the ground to stone. Soon the circle winds would slow and the ice air would come. In the south they called the season of Least, Bud, and the season the north called Harsh they called Plenty. It had not always been so, but for generations the southerners had enjoyed prosperity while the north withered. And the southern people wondered why war came from the north.

Each day throughout Harsh, Cahan woke beneath skeletal trees, feeling as if the silver rime that crunched and snapped beneath his feet had worked its way into his bones. He ate better than he had on the farm, and did less. Segur delighted in catching burrowers and histi and bringing them to him; brought him more than he could eat, so he set up a smoker. Sitting by the large dome of earth and wood as it gently leaked smoke. Letting its warmth seep into him while he watched the family on the farm struggle and go hungry and shout at each other in frustration. They were colder than he was despite the shelter of the earth-house. Their fire had run out of wood and they were too frightened to go into the forest to collect more. Cahan watched them break down a small shrine he had made to a forgotten god named Ranya for firewood. They did not recognise it as a shrine – few would – or get much wood from the ruin of the shrine tent, covered with small flags. Of all the gods, Ranya was the only one he had time for, and the one least able to help him – if gods even cared about the people.

He had learned of Ranya from the gardener at the monastery of Zorir, a man named Nasim who was the only gentleness in the whole place. He did not think Nasim would begrudge the family the wood of the shrine. Cahan tried not to begrudge them the wood either, though he found it hard as grudging was one of his greatest strengths.

He did his best to ignore the people on his farm and live his own life in Woodedge. It was true that much in the forest would kill you, but largely it left you alone if you left it alone. Especially in Woodedge, where, if you ran into anything more dangerous than a gasmaw grazing on the vines in the treetops, you were truly unlucky. "Take only what you need, and do not be greedy, and none of the wood shall take a price from you." They were vaguely remembered words and he did not know where from, though they carried a warmth with them, and he liked to imagine it was the ghosts of the family he had left when he was young.

The death of the forester – the death of Cahan Du-Nahere – happened towards the end of Harsh, when the circle winds were beginning to pick up once more and the ice in the earth was starting to slip away. Frosts had kissed the morning grass and the spines of the trees, making the edges of the forest a delicate filigree of ice. He heard the drone of flight as a marant approached. The sky it cut through was clear and blue enough to please even a hard god like Tarl-an-Gig. Far in the distance he could see a tiny dot in the sky, one of the skycarts that rode the circle winds, bringing food to trade for skins and wood.

The marant was not big for its kind: long body, furred in blues and greens. The wide, flat head with its hundreds of eyes looking down, and there would be hundreds more looking up. Body and wings the shape of a diamond, the wings slowly beating as it filled the air with the strange hiss of a flying beast. From its belly hung the brightly coloured blue pennants of Tarl-an-Gig and the Cowl-Rai in rising. In among the blue were the green flags of Harnspire, the Spire City that was the capital of Harn county, and on its back was a riding cage, though he could not see those within.

It had been long years since Cahan had seen a marant. When he had been young and angry and striking out at the world they had been a common sight, ferrying troops and goods to battles. But marants were slow and easy targets so most of the adults died early in the war. It was good to see one; it made him smile as they were friendly beasts and he had always liked animals. For a moment it felt as if the world was returning to how it had been before the rising of the Cowl-Rai, and the great changes of Tarl-an-Gig had come to pass.

Those changes had been hard for everyone.

He was less pleased to see the beast when it did not pass over. Instead it turned and began to slow before floating gently down to land on eight stubby, thick tentacles before his farm.

From the cage on its back came a small branch of troops, eight, and their branch commander. The soldiers wore cheap bark armour, the wood gnarled and rough. Their officer's armour was better, but not by much. After them came one of the Rai who wore darkwood armour, polished to a high sheen and beautiful to look at. They all wore short cloaks of blue. Four of the troops carried a large domed box, as big as a man, on long poles and their branch commander was pointing, showing them where to put it. That struck Cahan as strange, worrying. He had seen the new Cowl-Rai's army use such things before. It was a duller, to stop cowl users performing their feats. But the man who had taken his farm was no cowl user, Cahan was sure of that. If the creature which let the Rai manipulate the elements had lived under the man's skin Cahan was sure he would have known it, just as he knew it lived within the Rai who led the troops, even if their armour had not been painted with glowing mushroom juice sigils, proclaiming power and lineage.

The Rai was larger than the soldiers, better fed, better treated, better lived. Cowlbound, like all Rai, and with that came cruelty.

"Why hobble their Rai's power, Segur?" asked Cahan as he scratched the garaur's head. It looked at him but gave no answer. It probably thought people foolish and useful only for their clever hands. Who could blame it?

The woman, not the man, left Cahan's house and walked out to meet the troops. She stayed meek, head down because she knew what was expected of her. The Rai said something. The woman shook her head and pointed towards Woodedge. A brief exchange between them and then the Rai motioned to the branch commander, who sent their troops towards the house. The farmer shouted and she was casually backhanded for it, falling to the floor before the Rai, clutching her cheek. He heard more shouting from within the house but could not make it out. Cahan crept nearer, using all the stealth of a man raised in the forests of Crua, staying low among the dead vegetation of Harsh, right up to the edge of the treeline where young trees fought with scrub brush for light. From here he could hear what was being said at the farm. The beauty of living in such a quiet place was that sound carried, and the arrival had quietened the usually boisterous creatures of Woodedge.

The man who had taken the farm was dragged from the house. "Leave me be!" his voice hoarse with panic. "I have done nothing! The Leoric gave me this place! Leave me alone!" As he was dragged out the troops followed, spreading out around him, spears at the ready. No obscured sightlines here.

"Please, please," the woman on her knees, entreating the Rai. She grabbed hold of their leg, hands wrapping around polished greaves. "We have done nothing wrong, my husband fought on the right side, he was of the blue, we have done nothing wrong."

"Do not touch the Rai!" shouted the branch commander, and he drew his sword, but the Rai lifted a hand, stopping him.

"Quiet, woman," said the Rai, and then they spoke again, more softly, dangerously. "I did not give you leave to touch me." The woman let go, went down on her face, sobbing and apologising as the Rai walked over to her husband.

"I come here on the authority of the Skua-Rai of Crua and the High Leoric of Harnspire, carrying the black marks of Tarl-an-Gig, who grinds the darkness of the old ways beneath their hand, to pronounce sentence on you." The Rai grabbed his hair, pushed his head back. "Clan marks that you are not entitled to. Punishable by death."

At that, Cahan went cold. He had wanted to believe this Rai and their soldiers were here for the man. A nonsense, a lie, but he had ever been good at lying to himself.

"I am of the clans," shouted the man. "My firstmother and firstfather and secondfather were all of the clans! And all that came before them!" The Rai paused in their pronouncement, looking down at the man.

"The first action of the condemned is always to deny," they said. "Your sentence is death, you can no longer hide." They raised their sword. It was old, carved of the finest heartwood from the giant cloudtrees that pierced the sky. Sharp as ice.

"It is not my farm!" shouted the man. The sword stayed up.

"Really?"

"Please," weeping, tears running down his face, "please, Rai. I was given this farm by the Leoric of Harn and the priest there."

"And where is the previous owner?"

"Gone, into the forest."

A brief pause, the Rai shrugged.

"Convenient," they said, "too convenient." The man began to beg again but for naught, the sword fell. He died.

Silence. Only the chime of flags and the hiss of the marant. Then his woman screamed, she remained prostrate and was too frightened to look up, but her grief was too great to be contained.

"Rai," said the branch commander, paying no attention to the screams or the corpse spilling blood into the soil, "there are children in the house. What shall we do?"

"This well is poisoned," said the Rai. "No good will come of it." The woman screamed again, scrambled to her feet and turned to run for her house. Never got the chance. The Rai cut her down with a double-handed stroke, more violence than was needed. From his place Cahan saw the Rai lift their visor and smile as they bent and cleaned their bloody blade on the woman's clothes. Two of the Rai's soldiers moved into the house and Cahan almost stood, almost ran forward to try and stop them as he knew what they intended. But he was one man with nothing but a staff. What would one more death serve?

They were quick in their task at least. No one suffered. Once the farm was silent they tore down his colourful flags and strung the building with small blue and green flags, so all would know this was done on the authority of the Cowl-Rai.

Cahan watched them load the duller and board the marant, heard one of the troops say to another, "That was a lot easier than I thought," and the creature lifted off, turning a great circle overhead. The forester stayed where he was, utterly still, knowing how hard it was to see one man amid the brush if he did not move. Once the shadow of the marant had passed over he watched it glide away into the blue sky towards Harn-Larger and Harnspire beyond. Then he looked back at his house, now strewn with dark flags, as if spattered by old, dry blood.

He heard a voice, one meant only for him, one audible only to him.

You need me.

He did not reply.

By Anthony Ryan

THE RAVEN'S SHADOW

Blood Song

Tower Lord

Queen of Fire

THE DRACONIS MEMORIA

The Waking Fire

The Legion of Flame

The Empire of Ashes

THE RAVEN'S BLADE

The Wolf's Call

The Black Song

THE COVENANT OF STEEL

The Pariah

The Martyr

The Traitor

Praise for Anthony Ryan and the Covenant of Steel Trilogy

"A master storyteller."

—Mark Lawrence, author of *Prince of Thorns*, on *The Pariah*

"Gritty and well-drawn, this makes a rich treat for George R. R. Martin fans."

—*Publishers Weekly* (starred review) on *The Pariah*

"A gritty, heart-pounding tale of betrayal and bloody vengeance. I loved every single word."

—John Gwynne, author of *The Shadow of the Gods*, on *The Pariah*

"Ryan's evocative prose enhances the suspenseful, intricate story, and the cliffhanger ending will have fans counting the days until the next volume. This fires on all cylinders."

—*Publishers Weekly* (starred review) on *The Martyr*

"*The Martyr* continues the brilliance of *The Pariah* with more grit and adventure that Anthony Ryan fans and newcomers will devour."

—*Grimdark Magazine*

I rose, offering Evadine an apologetic frown.

"I know you wanted to avoid this, but the Covenant of Martyrs will fracture. A schism of the faithful is upon us."

"The Anointed Lady enjoys the love and devotion of the commons and the faithful," Wilhum said.

"Not all. The Covenant has stood in its present form for centuries. Folk have spent generations comforted by its permanency. That won't just vanish overnight." I shifted my gaze to Evadine, speaking with complete honesty now. "Make no mistake, my lady. We have another war to fight."